D0582045

Great Historical Romances

Great Historical Romances

The Talisman Ring
Georgette Heyer

The Gambling Man
Catherine Cookson

The King's Pleasure
Norah Lofts

Sundial

The Talisman Ring
first published in Great Britain in 1936 by William Heinemann Ltd
The Gambling Man
first published in Great Britain in 1975 by William Heinemann Ltd
The King's Pleasure
first published in Great Britain in 1970 by Hodder & Stoughton Ltd

This edition first published in 1978 and reprinted in 1979 by

Sundial Publications Limited, 59 Grosvenor Street, London W.1.

in collaboration with

William Heinemann Limited, 15–16 Queen Street, London W.1.

and

Martin Secker & Warburg Limited, 14 Carlisle Street, London W.1.

The Gambling Man © Copyright – Catherine Cookson 1975
The King's Pleasure © 1969 by Norah Lofts

ISBN 0 904230 73 2

Printed and bound in Great Britain at
William Clowes & Sons Limited
Beccles and London

Contents

The Talisman Ring

Georgette Heyer

CHAPTER 1

Sir Tristram Shield, arriving at Lavenham Court in the wintry dusk, was informed at the door that his great-uncle was very weak, not expected to live many more days out. He received these tidings without comment, but as the butler helped him to take off his heavy-caped driving-coat, he inquired in an unemotional voice: 'Is Mr. Lavenham here?'

'At the Dower House, sir,' replied the butler, handing the coat and the high-crowned beaver hat to a footman. He nodded austere dismissal to this underling, and added with a slight cough: 'His lordship has been a little difficult, sir. So far his lordship has not received Mr. Lavenham.'

He paused, waiting for Sir Tristram to inquire after Mademoiselle de Vauban. Sir Tristram, however, merely asked to be conducted to his bedchamber, that he might change his dress before being admitted to his great-uncle's presence.

The butler, as well aware as everyone else at the Court of the reason of Sir Tristram's sudden arrival, was disappointed at this lack of interest, but reflected that Sir Tristram, after all, had never been one to show what he was thinking. He led the way in person across the hall to the oak stairway and went with Sir Tristram up to the Long Gallery. Here, on one side, portraits of dead Lavenhams hung, and, on the other, tall, square-headed mullioned windows looked south over a well-timbered park to the Downs. The silence of the house was disturbed by the rustle of a skirt and the hasty closing of a door at one end of the Gallery. The butler had a shrewd suspicion that Mademoiselle de Vauban, more curious than Sir Tristram, had been waiting in the Gallery to obtain a glimpse of him. As he opened the door into one of the bedchambers he cast a glance at Shield, and said: 'His lordship has seen no one but the doctor, sir – once, and Mamzelle Eustacie, of course.'

That dark, harsh face told him nothing. 'Yes?' said Shield.

It occurred to the butler that perhaps Sir Tristram might not know why he had been summoned into Sussex. If that were so there was no saying how he might take it. He was not an easy man to drive, as his great-uncle had found more than once in the past. Ten to one there might be trouble.

Sir Tristram's voice interrupted these reflections. 'Send my man up to me, Porson, and inform his lordship of my arrival,' he said.

The butler bowed and withdrew. Sir Tristram walked over to the window, and stood looking out over the formal gardens to the woods beyond, still dimly visible through the gathering twilight. There was a sombre frown in his eyes, and his mouth was compressed in a way that made it appear more grim than usual. He did not turn when the door opened to admit his valet, accompanied by one footman carrying his cloak-bag, and another bearing two gilded candelabra, which he set down on the dressing-table. The sudden candlelight darkened the prospect outside. After a moment Shield came away from the window to the fireplace and stood leaning his arm along the high mantelshelf, and looking down at the smouldering logs. The footman drew the curtains across the windows and went softly away. Jupp, the valet, began to unpack the contents of the cloak-bag, and to lay out upon the bed an evening coat and breeches of mulberry velvet, and a Florentine waistcoat. Sir Tristram stirred the logs in the grate with one top-booted foot. Jupp glanced at him sideways, wondering what was in the wind to make him look so forbidding. 'You'll wear powder, sir?' he suggested, setting the pounce-box and the pomatum down on the dressing-table.

'No.'

Jupp sighed. He had already learned of Mr. Lavenham's presence at the Dower House. It seemed probable that the Beau might come up to the Court to visit his cousin, and Jupp, knowing how skilled was Mr. Lavenham's gentleman in the arrangement of his master's locks, would have liked for his pride's sake to have sent his own master down to dinner properly curled and powdered. He said nothing, however, but knelt down to pull off Sir Tristram's boots.

Half an hour later Shield, summoned by Lord Lavenham's valet, walked down the Gallery to the Great Chamber, and went in unannounced.

The room, wainscoted with oak and hung with crimson curtains, was warmed by a leaping fire and lit by as many as fifty candles in branching candelabra. At the far end a vast four-poster bed was set upon a slight dais. In it, banked up with pillows, covered with a quilt of flaming brocade, wearing an exotic bedgown and the powdered wig without which no one but his valet could ever remember to have seen him, was old Sylvester, ninth Baron Lavenham.

Sir Tristram paused on the threshold, dazzled momentarily by the blaze of unexpected light. The grimness of his face was lessened by a slight sardonic smile as his eyes took in the magnificence and the colour about him. 'Your death-bed, sir?' he inquired.

A thin chuckle came from the four-poster. 'My death-bed,' corroborated Sylvester with a twinkle.

Sir Tristram walked across the floor to the dais. A wasted hand on which a great ruby ring glowed was held out to him. He took it, and stood holding it, looking down into his great-uncle's parchment-coloured face, with its hawk-nose, and bloodless lips, and its deep-sunk brilliant eyes. Sylvester was eighty, and dying, but he still wore his wig and his patches, and clasped in his left hand his snuff-box and laced handkerchief.

Sylvester returned his great-nephew's steady look with one of malicious satisfaction. 'I knew you'd come,' he remarked. He withdrew his hand from the light clasp about it, and waved it towards a chair which had been set on the dais. 'Sit down.' He opened his snuff-box and dipped in his finger and thumb. 'When did I see you last?' he inquired, shaking away the residue of the snuff and holding an infinitesimal pinch to one nostril.

Sir Tristram sat down, full in the glare of a cluster of candles on a torchère pedestal. The golden light cast his profile into strong relief against the crimson velvet bed-curtains. 'It must have been about two years ago, I believe,' he answered.

Sylvester gave another chuckle. 'A loving family, ain't we?' He shut his snuff-box and dusted his fingers with his handkerchief. 'That other great-nephew of mine is here,' he remarked abruptly.

'So I've heard.'

'Seen him?'

'No.'

'You will,' said Sylvester. 'I shan't.'

'Why not?' asked Shield, looking at him under his black brows.

'Because I don't want to,' replied Sylvester frankly. 'Beau Lavenham! *I* was Beau Lavenham in my day, but d'ye suppose that I decked myself out in a green coat and yellow pantaloons?'

'Probably not,' said Shield.

'Damned smooth-spoken fellow!' said Sylvester. 'Never liked him. Never liked his father either. His mother used to suffer from the vapours. She suffered from them – whole series of 'em! – when she wanted me to let her have the Dower House.'

'Well, she got the Dower House,' said Shield dryly.

'Of course she did!' said Sylvester snappishly, and relapsed into one of the forgetful silences of old age. A log falling out on to the hearth recalled him. He opened his eyes again and said: 'Did I tell you why I wanted you?'

Sir Tristram had risen and gone over to the fire to replace the smoking log. He did not answer until he had done so, and then he said in his cool, disinterested voice: 'You wrote that you had arranged a marriage for me with your granddaughter.'

The piercing eyes gleamed. 'It don't please you much, eh?'

'Not much,' admitted Shield, coming back to the dais.

'It's a good match,' offered Sylvester, 'I've settled most of the un-entailed property on her, and she's half French, you know – understands these arrangements. You can go your own road. She's not at all like her mother.'

'I never knew her mother,' said Sylvester discouragingly.

'She was a fool!' said Sylvester. 'Never think she could be a daughter of mine. She eloped with a frippery Frenchman: that shows you. What was his damned name?'

'De Vauban.'

'So it was. The Vidame de Vauban. I forgot when he died. Marie died three years ago, and I went over to Paris – a year later, I think, but my memory's not what it was.'

'A little more than a year later, sir.'

'I dare say. It was after—' He paused for a moment, and then added harshly: '—after Ludovic's affair. I thought France was growing too hot for any grandchild of mine, and by God I was right! How long is it now since they sent the King to the guillotine? Over a month, eh? Mark me, Tristram, the Queen will go the same road before the year is out. I'm happy to think I shan't be here to see it. Charming she was, charming! But you wouldn't remember. Twenty years ago we used to wear her colour. Everything was Queen's Hair: satins, ribbons, shoes. Now' – his lip curled into a smear – 'now I've a great-nephew who wears a green coat and yellow pantaloons, and a damned absurd sugar-loaf on his head!' He raised his heavy eyelids suddenly, and added: 'But the boy is still my heir!'

Sir Tristram said nothing in answer to this remark, which had been flung at him almost like a challenge. Sylvester took snuff again, and when he next spoke it was once more in his faintly mocking drawl. 'He'd marry Eustacie if he could, but she don't like him.' He fobbed his snuff-box with a flick of his finger. 'The long and the short of it is, I've a fancy to see her married to you before I die, Tristram.'

'Why?' asked Shield.

'There's no one else,' replied Sylvester bluntly. 'My fault, of course. I should have provided for her – taken her up to London. But I'm old, and I've never pleased anyone but myself. I haven't been to London above twice in the last three years. Too late to think of that now. I'm dying, and damme, the chit's my grandchild! I'll leave her safely bestowed. Time you was thinking of marriage.'

'I have thought of it.'

Sylvester looked sharply at him. 'Not in love, are you?'

Shield's face hardened. 'No.'

'If you're still letting a cursed silly calf affair rankle with you, you're a fool!' said Sylvester. 'I've forgotten the rights of it, if ever I knew them, but they don't interest me. Most women will play you false, and I never met one yet that wasn't a fool at heart. I'm offering you a marriage of convenience.'

'Does she understand that?' asked Shield.

'Wouldn't understand anything else,' replied Sylvester, 'She's a Frenchwoman.

Sir Tristram stepped down from the dais, and went over to the fireplace. Sylvester watched him in silence, and after a moment he said: 'It might answer.'

'You're the last of your name,' Sylvester reminded him.

'I know it. I've every intention of marrying.'

'No one in your eye?'

'No.'

'Then you'll marry Eustacie,' said Sylvester. 'Pull the bell!'

Sir Tristram obeyed, but said with a look of amusement: 'Your dying wish, Sylvester?'

'I shan't live the week out,' replied Sylvester cheerfully. 'Heart and hard living, Tristram. Don't pull a long face at my funeral! Eighty years is enough for any man, and I've had the gout for twenty of them.' He saw his valet come into the room, and said: 'Send Mademoiselle to me.'

'You take a great deal for granted, Sylvester,' remarked Sir Tristram, as the valet went out again.

Sylvester had leaned his head back against the pillows, and closed his eyes. There was a suggestion of exhaustion in his attitude, but when he opened his eyes they were very much alive, and impishly intelligent. 'You would not have come here, my dear Tristram, had you not already made up your mind.'

Sir Tristam smiled a little reluctantly, and transferred his attention to the fire.

It was not long before the door opened again. Sir Tristram turned as Madamoiselle de Vauban came into the room, and stood looking at her under bent brows.

His first thought was that she was unmistakably a Frenchwoman, and not in the least the type of female he admired. She had glossy black hair, dressed in the newest fashion, and her eyes were so dark that it was hard to know whether they were brown or black. Her inches were few, but her figure was extremely good, and she bore herself with an air. She paused just inside the door, and, at once perceiving Sir Tristram, gave back his stare with one every whit as searching and a good deal more speculative.

Sylvester allowed them to weigh one another for several moments before he spoke, but presently he said: 'Come here, my child. And you, Tristram.'

The promptness with which his granddaughter obeyed this summons augured a docility wholly belied by the resolute, not to say wilful, set of her pretty mouth. She trod gracefully across the room, and curtseyed to Sylvester before stepping up on to the dais. Sir Tristram came more slowly to the bedside, nor did it escape Eustacie's notice that he had apparently looked his fill at her. His eyes, still sombre and slightly frowning, now rested on Sylvester.

Sylvester stretched out his left hand to Eustacie. 'Let me present to you, my child, your cousin Tristram.'

'Your very obedient cousin,' said Shield, bowing.

'It is to me a great happiness to meet my cousin,' enunciated Eustacie with prim civility and a slight, not unpleasing French accent.

'I am a little tired,' said Sylvester. 'If I were not I might allow you time to become better acquainted. And yet I don't know: I dare say it's as well as it is,' he added cynically. 'If you want a formal offer, Eustacie, no doubt Tristram will make you one – after dinner.'

'I do not want a formal offer,' replied Mademoiselle de Vauban. 'It is to me a matter quite immaterial, but my name is Eustacie, which is, *enfin*, a very good name, and it is *not* Eu-sta-ci-a, which I cannot at all pronounce, and which I find excessively ugly.

This speech, which was delivered in a firm and perfectly self-possessed voice, had the effect of making Sir Tristram cast another of his searching glances at the lady. He said with a faint smile: 'I hope I may be permitted to call you Eustacie, cousin?'

'Certainly; it will be quite *convenable*,' replied Eustacie, bestowing a brilliant smile upon him.

'She's eighteen,' said Sylvester abruptly. 'How old are you?'

'Thirty-one,' answered Sir Tristram uncompromisingly.

'H'm!' said Sylvester. 'A very excellent age.'

'For what?' asked Eustacie.

'For marriage, miss!'

Eustacie gave him a thoughtful look, but volunteered no further remark.

'You may go down to dinner now,' said Sylvester. 'I regret that I am unable to bear you company, but I trust that the Nuits I have instructed Porson to give you will help you to overcome any feeling of *gêne* which might conceivably attack you.'

'You are all consideration, sir,' said Shield. 'Shall we go, cousin?'

Eustacie, who did not appear to suffer from *gêne*, assented, curtseyed again to her grandfather, and accompanied Sir Tristram downstairs to the dining-room.

The butler had set their places at opposite ends of the great table, an arrangement in which both tacitly acquiesced, though it made conversation a trifle remote. Dinner, which was served in the grand manner, was well chosen, well cooked, and very long. Sir Tristram noticed that his prospective bride enjoyed a hearty appetite, and discovered after five minutes that she possessed a flow of artless conversation, quite unlike any he had been used to listen to in London drawing-rooms. He was prepared to find her embarrassed by a situation which struck him as being fantastic, and was somewhat startled when she remarked: 'It is a pity that you are so dark, because I do not like dark men in general. However, one must accustom oneself.'

'Thank you,' said Shield.

'If my grandpapa had left me in France it is probable that I should have married a Duke,' said Eustacie. 'My uncle – the present Vidame, you understand – certainly intended it.'

'You would more probably have gone to the guillotine,' replied Sir Tristram, depressingly matter of fact.

'Yes, that is quite true,' agreed Eustacie. 'We used to talk of it, my cousin Henriette and I. We made up our minds we should be entirely brave, not crying, of course, but perhaps a little pale, in a proud way. Henriette wished to go to the guillotine *en grande tenue*, but that was only because she had a court dress of yellow satin which she thought became her much better than it did really. For me, I think one should wear white to the guillotine if one is quite young, and not carry anything except perhaps a handkerchief. Do you not agree?'

'I don't think it signifies what you wear if you are on your way to the scaffold,' replied Sir Tristram, quite unappreciative of the picture his cousin was dwelling on with such evident admiration.

She looked at him in surprise. 'Don't you? But consider! You would be very sorry for a young girl in a tumbril, dressed all in white, pale, but *quite* unafraid, and not attending to the *canaille* at all, but——'

'I should be very sorry for anyone in a tumbril, whatever their age or sex or apparel,' interrupted Sir Tristram.

'You would be more sorry for a young girl – all alone, and perhaps bound,' said Eustacie positively.

'You wouldn't be all alone. There would be a great many other people in the tumbril with you,' said Sir Tristram.

Eustacie eyed him with considerable displeasure. 'In my tumbril there would *not* have been a great many other people,' she said.

Perceiving that argument on this point would be fruitless, Sir Tristram merely looked sceptical and refrained from speech.

'A Frenchman,' said Eustacie, 'would understand at once.'

'I am not a Frenchman,' replied Sir Tristram.

'*Ca se voit!*' retorted Eustacie.

Sir Tristram served himself from a dish of mutton steaks and cucumber.

'The people whom I have met in England,' said Eustacie after a short silence, 'consider it very romantic that I was rescued from the Terror.'

Her tone suggested strongly that he also ought to consider it romantic, but as he was fully aware that Sylvester had travelled to Paris some time before the start of the Terror, and had removed his granddaughter from France in the most unexciting way possible, he only replied: 'I dare say.'

'I know a family who escaped from Paris in a cart full of turnips,' said Eustacie. 'The soldiers stuck their bayonets into the turnips, too.'

'I trust they did not also stick them into the family?'

'No, but they might easily have done so. You do not at all realize what it is like in Paris now. One lives in constant anxiety. It is even dangerous to step out of doors.'

'It must be a great relief for you to find yourself in Sussex.'

She fixed her large eyes on his face, and said: 'Yes, but – do you not like exciting things, *mon cousin*?'

'I do not like revolutions, if that is what you mean.'

She shook her head. 'Ah no, but romance, and – and adventure!'

He smiled. 'When I was eighteen I expect I did.'

A depressed silence fell. 'Grandpère says that you will make me a very good husband,' said Eustacie presently.

Taken by surprise, Shield replied stiffly: 'I shall endeavour to do so, cousin.'

'And I expect,' said Eustacie, despondently inspecting a dish of damson tartlets, 'that he is quite right. You look to me like a good husband.'

'Indeed?' said Sir Tristram, unreasonably annoyed by this remark. 'I am sorry that I cannot return the compliment by telling you that you look like a good wife.'

The gentle melancholy which had descended on Eustacie vanished. She dimpled delightfully, and said: 'No, I don't, do I? But do you think that I am pretty?'

'Very,' answered Shield in a damping tone.

'Yes, so do I,' agreed Eustacie. 'In London I think I might have a great success, because I do not look like an Englishwoman, and I have noticed that the English think that foreigners are very *épatantes*.'

'Unfortunately,' said Sir Tristram, 'London is becoming so full of French *émigrés* that I doubt whether you would find yourself in any way remarkable.'

'I remember now,' said Eustacie. 'You do not like women.'

Sir Tristram, uncomfortably aware of the footman behind his chair, cast a glance at his cousin's empty plate, and got up. 'Let us go into the drawing-room,' he said. 'This is hardly the place to discuss such – er – intimate matters!'

Eustacie, who seemed to regard the servants as so many pieces of furniture, looked round in a puzzled way, but made no objection to leaving the dining-table. She accompanied Sir Tristram to the drawing-room, and said, almost before he had shut the door: 'Tell me, do you mind' very much that you are to marry me?'

He answered in an annoyed voice: 'My dear cousin, I do not know who told you that I dislike women, but it is a gross exaggeration.'

'Yes, but do you mind?'

'I should not be here if I minded.'

'Truly? But everybody has to do what Grandpère tells them.'

'Not quite everybody,' said Shield. 'Sylvester knows, however, that——'

'You should not call your great-uncle Sylvester!' interrupted Eustacie. 'It is not at all respectful.'

'My good child, the whole world has called him Sylvester for the past forty years!'

'Oh!' said Eustacie doubtfully. She sat down on a sofa upholstered in blue-and-gold-striped satin, folded her hands, and looked expectantly at her suitor.

He found this wide, innocent gaze a trifle disconcerting, but after a moment he said with a gleam of amusement: 'There is an awkwardness in this situation, cousin which I, alas, do not seem to be the man to overcome. You must forgive me if I appear to you to be lacking in sensibility. Sylvester has arranged a marriage of convenience for us, and allowed neither of us time to become in the least degree acquainted before we go to the altar.'

'In France,' replied Eustacie, 'one is not acquainted with one's betrothed, because it is not permitted that one should converse with him alone until one is married.'

This remark certainly seemed to bear out Sylvester's assurance that his granddaughter understood the nature of his arrangements. Sir Tristram said: 'It would be absurd to pretend that either of us can feel for the other any of those passions which are ordinarily to be looked for in betrothed couples, but——'

'Oh yes, it *would*!' agreed Eustacie heartily.

'Nevertheless,' pursued Sir Tristram, 'I believe such marriages as ours often prosper. You have accused me of disliking females, but believe me——'

'I can see very well that you dislike females,' interrupted Eustacie. 'I ask myself why it is that you wish to be married.'

He hesitated, and then answered bluntly: 'Perhaps if I had a brother I should not wish it, but I am the last of my name, and I must not let it die with me. I shall count myself fortunate if you will consent to be my wife, and so far as it may lie in my power I will promise that you shall not have cause to regret it. May I tell Sylvester that we have agreed to join hands?'

'*Qu'importe*? It is his command, and naturally he knows we shall be married. Do you think we shall be happy?'

'I hope so, cousin.'

'Yes, but I must tell you that you are not at all the sort of man I thought I should marry. It is very disheartening. I thought that in England one was permitted to fall in love and marry of one's own choice. Now I see that it is just the same as it is in France.'

He said with a touch of compassion: 'You are certainly very young to be married, but when Sylvester dies you will be alone, and your situation would be awkward indeed.'

'That is quite true,' nodded Eustacie. 'I have considered it well. And I dare say it will not be so very bad, our marriage, if I can have a house in town, and perhaps a lover.'

'Perhaps a *what?*' demanded Shield, in a voice that made her jump.

'Well, in France it is quite *comme il faut* – in fact, quite *à la mode* – to have a lover when one is married,' she explained, not in the least abashed.

'In England,' said Sir Tristram, 'it is neither *comme il faut* nor *à la mode.*'

'*Vraiment?* I do not yet know what is the fashion in England, but naturally if you assure me it is not *à la mode*, I won't have any lover. Can I have a house in town?'

'I don't think you know what you are talking about,' said Sir Tristram, on a note of relief. 'My home is in Berkshire, and I hope you will grow to like it as I do, but I can hire a house in town for the season if your heart is set on it.'

Eustacie was just about to inform him that her heart was irrevocably set on it when the butler opened the door and announced the arrival of Mr. Lavenham. Eustacie broke off in mid-sentence, and said under her breath: 'Well, I would much rather be married to you than to him, at all events!'

Her expression did not lead Sir Tristram to set undue store by this handsome admission. He frowned reprovingly at her, and went forward to greet his cousin.

Beau Lavenham, who was two years younger than Shield, did not resemble him in the least. Sir Tristram was a large, lean man, very dark, harsh-featured, and with few airs or graces; the Beau was of medium height only, slim rather than lean, of a medium complexion and delicately-moulded features, and his graces were many. Nothing could have been more exquisite than the arrangement of his powdered curls, or the cut of his brown-spotted silk coat and breeches. He wore a waistcoat embroidered with gold and silver, and stockings of palest pink, a jewel in the snowy folds of his cravat, knots of ribbons at his knees, and rings on his slender white fingers. In one hand he carried his snuff-box and scented handkerchief; in the other he held up an ornate quizzing-glass that hung on a riband round his neck. Through this he surveyed his two cousins, blandly smiling and quite at his ease. 'Ah, Tristram!' he said in a soft, languid voice, and, letting fall his quizzing-glass, held out his hand. 'How do you do, my dear fellow?'

Sir Tristram shook hands with him. 'How do you do, Basil? It's some time since we met.'

The Beau made a gesture of deprecation. 'But, my dear Tristram, if you *will* bury yourself in Berkshire what is one to do? Eustacie——!' He went to her, and bowed over her hand with incomparable grace. 'So you have been making Tristram's acquaintance?'

'Yes,' said Eustacie. 'We are betrothed.'

The Beau raised his brows, smiling. 'Oh la, la! so soon? Did Sylvester call this tune? Well, you are, both of you, very obedient, but are you quite, quite sure that you will deal well together?'

'Oh, I hope so!' replied Sir Tristram bracingly.

'If you are determined – and I must warn you, Eustacie, that he is the most determined fellow imaginable – I must hope so too. But I do not think I expected either of you to be so *very* obedient. Sylvester is prodigious – quite prodigious! One cannot believe that he is really dying. A world without Sylvester! Surely it must be impossible!'

'It will seem odd, indeed,' Shield said calmly.

Eustacie looked disparagingly at the Beau. 'And it will seem odd to me when you are Lord Lavenham – very odd!'

There was a moment's silence. The Beau glanced at Sir Tristram, and then said: 'Ah yes, but, you see, I shall not be Lord Lavenham. My dear Tristram, do I beg of you, try some of this snuff of mine, and let me have your opinion of it. I have added the veriest dash of Macouba to my old blend. Now, was I right?'

'I'm not a judge,' said Shield, helping himself to a pinch. 'It seems well enough.'

Eustacie was frowning. 'But I don't understand! Why will you not be Lord Lavenham?'

The Beau turned courteously towards her. 'Well, Eustacie, I am not Sylvester's grandson, but only his great-nephew.'

'But when there is no grandson it must surely be you who are the heir?'

'Precisely, but there is a grandson, dear cousin. Did you not know that?'

'Certainly I know that there was Ludovic, but he is dead after all!'

'Who told you Ludovic was dead?' asked Shield, looking at her under knit brows.

She spread out her hands. 'But Grandpère, naturally! And I have often wanted to know what it was that he did that was so entirely wicked that no one must speak of him. It is a mystery, and, I think, very romantic.'

'There is no mystery,' said Shield, 'nor is it in the least romantic. Ludovic was a wild young man who crowned a series of follies with murder, and had in consequence to fly the country.'

'Murder!' exclaimed Eustacie. '*Voyons*, do you mean he killed someone in a duel?'

'No. Not in a duel.'

'But, Tristram,' said the Beau gently, 'you must not forget that it was never proved that Ludovic was the man who shot Matthew Plunkett. For my part I did not believe it possible then, and I still do not.'

'Very handsome of you, but the circumstances were too damning,' replied Shield. 'Remember that I myself heard the shot that must have killed Plunkett not ten minutes after I had parted from Ludovic.'

'But I,' said the Beau, languidly polishing his quizzing-glass, 'prefer to believe Ludovic's own story, that it was an owl he shot at.'

'Shot – but missed!' said Shield. 'Yet I have watched Ludovic shoot the pips out of a playing-card at twenty yards.'

'Oh', admitted, Tristram, 'but on that particular night I think Ludovic was not entirely sober, was he?'

Eustacie struck her hands together impatiently. 'But tell me, one of you! What did he do, my cousin Ludovic?'

The Beau tossed back the ruffles from his hand, and dipped his finger and thumb in his snuff-box. 'Well, Tristram,' he said with his glinting smile. 'You know more about it than I do. Are you going to tell her?'

'It is not an edifying story,' Shield said. 'Why do you want to hear it?'

'Because I think perhaps my cousin Ludovic is of this family the most romantic person!' replied Eustacie.

'Oh, romantic!' said Sir Tristram, turning away with a shrug of the shoulders.

The Beau fobbed his snuff-box. 'Romantic?' he said meditatively. 'No, I do not think Ludovic was romantic. A little rash, perhaps. He was a gamester – hence the disasters which befell him. He lost a very large sum of money one night at the Cocoa-Tree to a man who lived at Furze House, not two miles from here.'

'No one lives at Furze House,' interrupted Eustacie.

'Not now,' agreed the Beau. 'Three years ago Sir Matthew Plunkett lived there. But Sir Matthew – three years ago – was shot in the Longshaw Spinney, and his widow removed from the neighbourhood.'

'Did my cousin Ludovic shoot him?'

'That, my dear Eustacie, is a matter of opinion. You will get one answer from Tristram, and another from me.'

'But why?' she demanded. 'Not just because he had lost money to him! That, after all, is not such a great matter – unless perhaps he was quite ruined?'

'Oh, by no means! He did lose a large sum to him, however, and Sir Matthew, being a person of – let us say indifferent breeding – was ill-mannered enough to demand a pledge in security before he would continue playing. Of course, one should never play with Cits, but poor dear Ludovic was always so headstrong. The game was piquet, and both were in their cups. Ludovic took from his finger a certain ring, and gave it to Sir Matthew as a pledge – to be redeemed, naturally. It was a talisman ring of great antiquity which had come to Ludovic through his mother, who was the last of a much older house than ours.'

Eustacie stopped him. 'Please, I do not know what is a talisman ring.'

'Just a golden ring with figures engraved upon it. This of Ludovic's was, as I have said, very old. The characters on it were supposed to be magical. It should, according to ancient belief, have protected him from any harm. More important, it was an heirloom. I don't know its precise value. Tristram, you are a judge of such things – you must make him show you his collection, Eustacie – what was the value of the ring?'

'I don't know,' answered Shield curtly. 'It was very old – perhaps priceless.'

'Such a rash creature, poor Ludovic!' sighed the Beau. 'I believe there was no stopping him – was there, Tristram?'

'No.'

Eustacie turned towards Shield. 'But were you there, then?'

'Yes, I was there.'

'But no one, not even Tristram, could manage Ludovic in his wilder moods,' explained the Beau. 'He pledged the ring, and continued to lose. Sir Matthew, with what one cannot but feel to have been a lamentable want of taste, left the Cocoa-Tree with the ring upon his finger. To redeem it Ludovic was forced to go to the Jews – ah, that means moneylenders, my dear!'

'There was nothing new in that,' said Shield. 'Ludovic had been in the Jews' hands since he came down from Oxford – and before.'

'Like so many of us,' murmured the Beau.

'And did he get the money from the Jews?' asked Eustacie.

'Oh yes,' replied the Beau, 'but the matter was not so easily settled. When Ludovic called upon Plunkett to redeem the ring our ingenious friend pretended that the bargain had been quite misunderstood, that he had in fact staked his guineas against the ring, and won it outright. He would not give it up, nor could anyone but Tristram be found who had been sober enough to vouch for the truth of Ludovic's version of the affair.'

Eustacie's eyes flashed. 'I am not at all surprised that Ludovic killed this *canaille*! He was without honour!'

The Beau played with his quizzing-glass. 'People who collect objects of rarity, my dear Eustacie, will often, so I believe, go to quite unheard-of lengths to acquire the prize they covet.'

'But you!' said Eustacie, looking fiercely at Sir Tristram. 'You knew the truth!'

'Unfortunately,' replied Sir Tristram, 'Plunkett did not wait for my ruling. He retired into the country – to Furze House, in fact – and somewhat unwisely refused to see Ludovic.'

'Did Grandpère know of this?' Eustacie asked.

'Dear me, no!' said the Beau. 'Sylvester and Ludovic were so rarely on amicable terms. And then there was that little matter of Ludovic's indebtedness to the Jews. One can hardly blame Ludovic for not taking Sylvester into his confidence. However, Ludovic came home to this house, bringing Tristram, with the intention of confronting Plunkett with the one – er – reliable witness to the affair. But Plunkett was singularly elusive – not unnaturally, of course. When Ludovic called at Furze House he was never at home. One must admit that Ludovic was not precisely the man to accept such treatment patiently. And he was drinking rather heavily at that time, too. Discovering that Plunkett was to dine at a house in Slaugham upon the very day that he had been refused admittance to Furze House for the third time, he conceived the plan of waylaying him upon his return home, and forcing him to accept bills in exchange for the ring. Only Tristram, finding him gone from here, guessed what he would be at, and followed him.'

'The boy was three parts drunk!' said Sir Tristram over his shoulder.

'I have no doubt he was in a very dangerous humour,' agreed the Beau. 'It has always been a source of wonderment to me how you persuaded him to relinquish his purpose and return home.'

'I promised to see Plunkett in his stead,' replied Shield. 'Like a fool I let him take the path through the spinney.'

'My dear fellow, no one could have expected you to have foreseen that Plunkett would return by that path,' said the Beau gently.

'On the contrary, if he came from Slaugham it was the most natural way for him to take,' retorted Shield. 'And we knew he was riding, not driving.'

'So what happened?' breathed Eustacie.

It was Shield who answered her. 'Ludovic rode back through the Longshaw Spinney, while I went on towards Furze House. Not ten minutes after we had parted I heard a shot fired in the distance. At the time I made nothing of it: it might have been a poacher. Next morning Plunkett's body was discovered in the spinney with a shot through the heart and a crumpled handkerchief of Ludovic's lying beside it.'

'And the ring?' Eustacie said quickly.

'The ring was gone,' said Shield. 'There was money in Plunkett's pockets, and a diamond pin in his cravat, but of the talisman ring no sign.'

'And it has never been seen since,' added the Beau.

'By us, no!' said Sir Tristram.

'Yes, yes, I know that you think Ludovic has it', said the Beau, 'but Ludovic swore he did not meet Plunkett that night, and I for one do not think that Ludovic was a liar. He admitted freely that he carried a pistol in his pocket, he even admitted that he had fired it – at an owl.'

'Why should he not shoot this Plunkett?' demanded Eustacie. 'He deserved to be shot! I am very glad that he was shot!'

'Possibly,' said Sir Tristram in his driest tone, 'but in England, whatever it may be in France, murder is a capital offence.'

'But they did not hang him for just killing such a one as this Plunkett?' said Eustacie, shocked.

'No, because we got him out of the country before he could be arrested,' Shield answered.

The Beau lifted his hand. 'Sylvester and you got him out of the country,' he corrected. 'I had no hand in that, if you please.'

'Had he stayed to face a trial nothing could have saved his neck.'

'There I beg to differ from you, my dear Tristram,' said the Beau calmly. 'Had he been permitted to face his trail the truth might have been found out. When you – and Sylvester, of course – smuggled him out of the country you made him appear a murderer confessed.'

Sir Tristram was spared the necessity of answering by the entrance of Sylvester's valet, who came to summon him to his great-uncle's presence again. He went at once, a circumstance which provoked the Beau to murmur as the door closed behind him: 'It is really most gratifying to see Tristram so complaisant.'

Eustacie paid no heed to this, but said: 'Where is my cousin Ludovic now?'

'No one knows, my dear. He has vanished.'

'And you do not do anything to help him, any of you!' she said indignantly.

'Well, dear cousin, it is a little difficult, is it not?' replied the Beau. 'After that well-meaning but fatal piece of meddling, what could one do?'

'I think,' said Eustacie with a darkling brow, 'that Tristram did not like my cousin Ludovic.'

The Beau laughed. 'How clever of you, my dear!'

She looked at him. 'What did you mean when you said he must show me his collection?' she asked directly.

He raised his brows in exaggerated surprise. 'Why, what should I mean? Merely that he has quite a notable collection. I am not a judge, but

I have sometimes felt that I should like to see that collection myself.'

'Will he not let you, then?'

'Oh, but with the greatest goodwill in the world!' said the Beau, smiling. 'But one has to remember that collectors do not always show one quite *all* their treasures, you know!'

CHAPTER 2

Sir Tristram, standing once more beside Sylvester's bed, was a little shocked to perceive already a change in him. Sylvester was still propped up by a number of pillows, and he still wore his wig, but he seemed suddenly to have grown frailer and more withdrawn. Only his eyes were very much alive, startlingly dark in his waxen face.

Sir Tristram said in his deep voice: 'I'm sorry, sir: I believe my visit has too much exhausted you.'

'Thank you, I am the best judge of what exhausts me,' replied Sylvester. 'I shan't last much longer, I admit, but by God, I'll last long enough to settle my affairs! Are you going to marry that chit?'

'Yes, I'll marry her,' said Shield. 'Will that content you?'

'I've a fancy to see the knot well tied,' said Sylvester. 'Fortunately, she's not a Papist. What do you make of her?'

Sir Tristram hesitated. 'I hardly know. She's very young.'

'All the better, as long as her husband has the moulding of her.'

'You may be right, but I wish you had broached this matter earlier.'

'I'm always right. What did you want to do? Come a-courting her?' jibed Sylvester. 'Poor girl!'

'You are forcing her to a marriage she may easily regret. She is romantic.'

'Fiddlededee!' said Sylvester. 'Most women are, but they get the better of it in time. Is that damned mincing puppy-dog downstairs?'

'Yes,' said Shield.

'He'll put you in the shade if he can,' said Sylvester warningly.

Sir Tristram looked contemptuous. 'Well, if you expect me to vie with his graces you'll be disappointed, sir.'

'I expect nothing but folly from any of my family!' snapped Sylvester.

Sir Tristram picked up a vinaigrette from the table by the bed and held it under his great-uncle's nose. 'You're tiring yourself, sir.'

'Damn you!' said Sylvester faintly. He lifted his hand with a perceptible effort and took the bottle, and lay in silence for a time, breathing its aromatic fumes. After a minute or two his lips twitched in a wry smile, and he murmured: 'I would give much to have been able to see the three of you together. What did you talk of?'

'Ludovic,' replied Shield with a certain cool deliberation.

Sylvester's hand clenched suddenly; the smile left his face. He said scarcely above a whisper: 'I thought you knew his name is never to be mentioned in this house! Do you count me dead already that you should dare?'

'You're not a greater object of awe to me on your death-bed, Sylvester, than you have ever been,' said Shield.

Sylvester's eyes flashed momentarily, but his sudden wrath vanished in a chuckle. 'You're an impudent dog, Tristram. Did you ever care for what I said?'

'Very rarely,' said Shield.

'Quite right,' approved Sylvester. 'Damme, I always liked you for it! What have you been saying about the boy?'

'Eustacie wanted to hear the story. Apparently you told her he was dead.'

'He is dead to me,' said Sylvester harshly. 'Of what use to let her make a hero of him? You may depend upon it she would. Did you tell her?'

'Basil told her.'

'You should have stopped him.' Sylvester lay frowning, his fingers plucking a little at the gorgeous coverlet. 'Basil believed the boy's story,' he said abruptly.

'I have never known why, sir.'

Sylvester flashed a glance at him. 'You didn't believe it, did you?'

'Did any of us, save only Basil?'

'He said we should have let him stand his trial. I wonder. I wonder.'

'He was wrong. We did what we could for Ludovic when we shipped him to France. Why tease yourself now?'

'You never liked him, did you?'

'You have only to add that I am something of a collector of antique jewellery, Sylvester, and you will have said very much what Basil has been saying, far more delicately, below stairs.'

'Don't be a fool!' said Sylvester irritably. 'I told you he'd do what he could to spoil your chances. Send him about his business!'

'You will have to excuse me, sir. This is not my house.'

'No, by God, and nor is it his!' said Sylvester, shaken by a gust of anger. 'The estate will be in ward when I die, and I have not made him a trustee!'

'Then you are doing him an injustice, sir. Who are your trustees?'

'My lawyer, Pickering, and yourself,' answered Sylvester.

'Good God, what induced you to name me?' said Shield. 'I have not the smallest desire to manage your affairs!'

'I trust you, and I don't trust him,' said Sylvester. 'Moreover,' he added with a spark of malice, 'I've a fancy to make you run in my harness even if I can only do it by dying. Pour me out a little of that cordial.'

Sir Tristram obeyed his behest, and held the glass to Sylvester's lips. Perversely, Sylvester chose to hold it himself, but it was apparent that even this slight effort was almost too great a tax on his strength.

'Weak as a cat!' he complained, letting Shield take the glass again. 'You'd better go downstairs before that fellow has time to poison Eustacie's mind. I'll have you married in this very room just as soon as I can get the parson here. Send Jarvis to me; I'm tired.'

When Sir Tristram reached the drawing-room again the tea-table had been brought in. Beau Lavenham inquired after his great-uncle, and upon Sir Tristram's saying that he found him very much weaker, shrugged slightly, and said: 'I shall believe Sylvester is dead when I see him in his coffin. I hope you did not forget to tell him that I am dutifully in attendance?'

'He knows you are here,' said Shield, taking a cup and saucer from Eustacie, 'but I doubt whether he has strength enough to see any more visitors to-night.'

'My dear Tristram, are you trying to be tactful?' inquired the Beau, amused. 'I am quite sure Sylvester said that he would be damned if he would see that frippery fellow Basil.'

Shield smiled. 'Something of the sort. You should not wear a sugar-loaf hat.'

'No, no; it cannot be my taste in dress which makes him dislike me so much, for that is almost impeccable,' said the Beau, lovingly smoothing a wrinkle from his satin sleeve. 'I can only think that it is because I stand next in the succession to poor Ludovic, and that is really no fault of mine.'

'For all we know you may be further removed than that,' said Tristram. 'Ludovic may be married by now.'

'Very true,' agreed the Beau, sipping his tea. 'And in some ways a son of Ludovic's might best solve the vexed question of who is to reign in Sylvester's stead.'

'The estate is left in trust.'

'From your gloomy expression, Tristram, I infer that you are one of the trustees, remarked the Beau. 'Am I right?'

'Oh yes, you're right. Pickering is joined with me. I told Sylvester he should have named you.'

'You are too modest, my dear fellow. He could not have made a better choice.'

'I am not modest,' replied Shield. 'I don't want the charge of another man's estate; that is all.'

The Beau laughed, and setting down his tea-cup turned to Eustacie. 'It has occurred to me that I am here merely in the rôle of chaperon to a betrothed couple,' he said. 'I do not feel that I am cut out for such a rôle, so I shall go away now. Dear cousin!——' He raised her hand to his lips. 'Tristram, my felicitations. If we do not meet before we shall certainly meet at Sylvester's funeral.'

There was a short silence after he had gone. Sir Tristram snuffed a candle which was guttering, and glanced down at Eustacie, sitting still and apparently pensive by the fire. As though aware of his look, she raised her eyes and gazed at him in the intent, considering way which was so peculiarly her own.

'Sylvester wants to see us married before he dies,' Shield said.

'Basil does not think he will die.'

'I believe he is nearer to it than we know. What did the doctor say?'

'He said he was very irreligious, and altogether insupportable,' replied Eustacie literally.

Sir Tristram laughed, surprising his cousin, who had not imagined that his countenance could lighten so suddenly. 'I dare say he might, but was that all he said?'

'No, he said also that it was useless for him to come any more to see Grandpère, because when he said he should have gruel Grandpère at once sent for a green goose and a bottle of Burgundy. The doctor said that it would kill him, and *du vrai*, I think he is piqued because it did not kill Grandpère at all. So perhaps Grandpère will not die, but on the contrary get quite well again.'

'I am afraid it is only his will which keeps him alive.' Shield moved towards the fire and said, looking curiously down at Eustacie: 'Are you fond of him? Will it make you unhappy if he dies?'

'No,' she replied frankly. 'I am a little fond of him, but not very much, because he is not fond of anybody, he. It is not his wish that one should be fond of him.'

'He brought you out of France,' Shield reminded her.

'Yes, but I did not want to be brought out of France,' said Eustacie bitterly.

'Perhaps you did not then, but you are surely glad to be in England now?'

'I am not at all glad, but, on the contrary, very sorry,' said Eustacie. 'If he had left me with my uncle I should have gone to Vienna, which would have been not only very gay, but also romantic, because my uncle fled from France with all his family, in a berline, just like the King and Queen.'

'Not quite like the King and Queen if he succeeded in crossing the frontier,' said Shield.

'I will tell you something,' said Eustacie, incensed. 'Whenever I recount to you an interesting story you make me an answer which is like – which is like those snuffers——*enfin!*'

'I'm sorry,' said Shield, rather startled.

'Well, I am sorry too,' said Eustacie, getting up from the sofa, 'because it makes it very difficult to converse. I shall wish you good night, *mon cousin.*'

If she expected him to try to detain her she was disappointed. He merely bowed formally and opened the door for her to pass out of the room.

Five minutes later her maid, hurrying to her bedchamber in answer to a somewhat vehement tug at the bell-rope, found her seated before her mirror, stormily regarding her own reflection.

'I will undress, and I will go to bed,' announced Eustacie.

'Yes, miss.'

'And I wish, moreover, that I had gone to Madame Guillotine *in* a tumbril, *alone!*'

Country-bred Lucy, a far more appreciative audience than Sir Tristram, gave a shudder, and said: 'Oh, miss, don't speak of such a thing! To think of you having your head cut off, and you so young and beautiful!'

Eustacie stepped out of her muslin gown, and pushed her arms into the wrapper Lucy was holding. 'And I should have worn a white dress, and even the *sans-culottes* would have been sorry to have seen me in a tumbril!'

Lucy had no very clear idea who the *sans-culottes* might be, but she assented readily, and added, in all sincerity, that her mistress would have looked lovely.

'Well, I think I should have looked nice,' said Eustacie candidly. 'Only it is no use thinking of that, because instead I am going to be married.'

Lucy passed in her task of taking the pins out of her mistress's hair to clasp her hands, and breathe ecstatically: 'Yes, miss, and if I may make so bold as I do wish you so happy!'

'When one is forced into a marriage infinitely distasteful one does not hope for happiness,' said Eustacie in a hollow voice.

'Good gracious, miss, his lordship surely isn't a-going to force you?' gasped Lucy. 'I never heard such a thing!'

'Oh!' said Eustacie. 'Then it *is* true what I have heard in France, that English ladies are permitted to choose for themselves whom they will marry!' She added despondently: 'But I have not seen anyone whom I should like to have for my husband, so it does not signify in the least.'

'No, miss but – but don't you like Sir Tristram, miss? I'm sure he's a very nice gentleman, and would make anyone a good husband.'

'I do not want a good husband who is thirty-one years old and who has no conversation!' said Eustacie, her lip trembling.

Lucy put down the hair-brush. 'There, miss, you're feeling vapourish, and no wonder, with everything coming upon you sudden, like it has! No, one can't force you to marry against your true wishes – not in England, they can't, whatever they may do in France, which everyone knows is a nasty murdering place!'

Eustacie dried her eyes and said: 'No, but if I do not marry my cousin I shall have to live with a horrid chaperon when my grandpapa dies, and that would be much, much worse. One must resign oneself.'

Downstairs Sir Tristram had just reached the same conclusion. Since, sooner or later, he would have to marry someone, and since he had determined never again to commit the folly of falling in love, his bride might as well be Eustacie as another. She seemed to be tiresomely volatile, but no sillier than any other young woman of his acquaintance. She was of good birth (though he thought her French blood to be deplored), and in spite of the fact that if he had a preference it was for fair women, he was bound to admit that she was very pretty. He could have wished she were older, but it was possible that Sylvester, whose experience was undoubtedly wide, knew what he was talking about when he said that her extreme youth was in her favour. In fact, one must resign oneself.

Upon the following morning the betrothed couple met at the breakfast-table and took fresh stock of each other. Sir Tristram, whose mulberry evening-dress had not met with Eustacie's approval, had had the unwitting tact to put on a riding-suit, in which severe garb he looked his best; and Eustacie, who had decided that, if she must marry her cousin, it was only proper that he should be stimulated to admiration of her charms, had arrayed herself in a *bergère* gown of charming colour and design. Each at first glance felt moderately pleased with the other, a complacent mood which lasted for perhaps ten minutes, at the end of which time Sir Tristram was contemplating with grim misgiving the prospect of encountering vivacity at the breakfast-table for the rest of his life, and Eustacie was wondering whether her betrothed was capable of uttering anything but the most damping of monosyllables.

During the course of the morning, Sir Tristram was sent for to Sylvester's bedroom. He found his great-uncle propped up very high in bed, and alarmingly brisk, and learned from him that his nuptials would be celebrated upon the following day. When he reminded Sylvester that marriages could not be performed thus out of hand, Sylvester flourished a special licence before his eyes, and said that he was not so moribund that he could not still manage his affairs. Sir Tristram, who liked being driven as little as most men, found this instance of his great-uncle's forethought so annoying that he left him somewhat abruptly, and went away to cool his temper with a gallop over the Downs. When he returned it was some time later, and he found the doctor's horse being walked up and down before the Court, and the household in a state of hushed expectancy. Sylvester, having managed his affairs to his own satisfaction, drunk two glasses of Madeira, and thrown his snuff-box at his valet for daring to remonstrate with him, had seemed suddenly to collapse. He had sunk into a deep swoon from which he had been with difficulty brought round, and the doctor, summoned post-haste, had announced that the end could not now be distant more than a few hours.

Regaining consciousness, Sylvester had, in a painful but determined whisper, declined the offices of a clergyman, recommended the doctor to go to hell, forbidden the servants to open his doors to his nephew Basil, announced his intention of dying without a pack of women weeping over him, and demanded the instant attendance of his nephew Tristram.

Sir Tristram, hearing these details from the butler, stayed only to cast his hat and coat on a chair, and went quickly up the stairs to the Great Chamber.

Both the valet and the doctor were in the room, the valet looking genuinely grieved and the doctor very sour. Sylvester was lying flat in the huge bed with his eyes shut, but when Tristram stepped softly on to the dais, he opened them at once, and whispered: 'Damn you, you have kept me waiting!'

'I beg your pardon, sir.'

'I did not mean to die until to-morrow,' said Sylvester, labouring for breath. 'Damme, I've a mind to make a push to last the night if only to spite that snivelling leech! . . . Tristram!'

'Sir?'

Sylvester grasped his wrist with thin, enfeebled fingers. 'You'll marry that child?'

'I will, Sylvester: don't tease yourself!'

'Always meant Ludovic to have her . . . damned young scoundrel! Often wondered. Do you think he was telling the truth – after all?'

Shield was silent. Sylvester's pale lips twisted. 'Oh, you don't, eh? Well, you can give him my ring if ever you see him again – and tell him not to pledge it! Take it: I've done with it.' He slid the great ruby from his finger as he spoke, and dropped it into Shield's hand. 'That Madeira was a mistake. I ought to have kept to the Burgundy. You can go now. Don't let there be any mawkish sentiment over my death!'

'Very well, sir,' said Shield. He bent, kissed Sylvester's hand, and without more ado turned and went out of the room.

Sylvester died an hour later. The doctor who brought the news to Shield, and to Beau Lavenham, both waiting in the library, said that he had only spoken once more before the end.

'Indeed, and what did he say?' inquired the Beau.

'He made a remark, sir – I may say, a gross remark! – derogatory to my calling!' said the doctor. 'I shall not repeat it!'

Both cousins burst out laughing. The doctor cast a look of shocked dislike at them and went away, disgusted but not surprised by their behaviour. A wild, godless family, he thought. They were not even profitable patients, these Lavenhams: he was glad to be rid of them.

'I suppose we shall never know what it was that he said,' remarked the Beau. 'I am afraid it may have been a trifle lewd.'

'I should think probably very lewd,' agreed Shield.

'But how right, how fitting that Sylvester should die with a lewd jest on his lips!' said the Beau. He patted his ruffles. 'Do you still mean to be married to-morrow?'

'No, that must be postponed,' Shield answered.

'I expect you are wise. Yet one cannot help suspecting that Sylvester would enjoy the slightly macabre flavour of a bridal presided over by his mortal remains.'

'Possibly, but I never shared Sylvester's tastes,' said Shield.

The Beau laughed gently, and bent to pick up his hat and cane from the chair on which he had laid them. 'Well, I do not think I envy you the next few days, Tristram,' he said. 'If I can be of assistance to you, do by all means call upon me! I shall remain at the Dower House for some little time yet.'

'Thank you, but I don't anticipate the need. I rely on Pickering. The charge of the estate would be better borne by him than by me. God knows what is to be done, with the succession in this accursed muddle!'

'There is one thing which ought to be done,' said the Beau. 'Some effort should be made to find Ludovic.'

'A good deal easier said than done!' replied Sir Tristram. 'He could not set foot in England if he were found, either. If he stayed in France he may have lost his head for all we know. It would be extremely like him to embroil himself in a revolution which was no concern of his.'

'Well,' said the Beau softly, 'I do not want to appear unfeeling, but if Ludovic has lost his head, it would be of some slight interest to me to hear of it.'

'Naturally. Your position is most uncertain.'

'Oh, I am not repining,' smiled the Beau. 'But I still think you ought – as trustee – to find Ludovic.'

During the next few days, however, Sir Tristram had enough to occupy him without adding a search for the heir to his duties. Upon the arrival of the lawyer, Sylvester's will was read, a document complicated enough to

try the temper of a more patient man than Shield. A thousand and one
things had to be done, and in addition to the duties attendant upon the
death of Sylvester there was the problem of Eustacie to worry her betrothed.

She accepted both her bereavement and the postponement of her
wedding-day with perfect fortitude, but when Sir Tristram asked her to
name some lady living in the neighbourhood in whose charge she could for
the present remain, she declared herself quite unable to do so. She had no
acquaintance in Sussex, Sylvester having quarrelled with one half of the
county and ignored the other half. 'Besides,' she said, 'I do not wish to be
put in charge of a chaperon. I shall stay here.'

Sir Tristram, feeling that Sylvester had in his time created enough
scandal in Sussex, was strongly averse from giving the gossips anything
further to wag their tongues over. Betrothed or not, his and Eustacie's
sojourn under the same roof was an irregularity which every virtuous
dame who thought the Lavenhams a godless family would be swift to
pounce upon. He said: 'Well, it is confoundedly awkward, but I don't see
what I can do about it. I suppose I shall have to let you stay.'

'I shall stay because I wish to,' said Eustacie, bristling. 'I do not have to
do what you say yet!'

'Don't be silly!' said Sir Tristram, harassed, and therefore irritable.

'I am not silly. It is you who have a habit which I find much more silly of
telling me what I must do and what I must not do. I am quite tired of
being *bien élevée*, and I think I will now arrange my own affairs.'

'You are a great deal too young to manage your own affairs, I am
afraid.'

'That we shall see.'

'We shall, indeed. Have you thought to order your mourning clothes?
That must be done, you know.'

'I do not know it,' said Eustacie. 'Grandpère said I was not to mourn
for him, and I shall not.'

'That may be, but this is a censorious world, my child, and it will be
thought very odd if you don't accord Sylvester's memory that mark of
respect.'

'Well, I shan't,' said Eustacie simply.

Sir Tristram looked her over in frowning silence.

'You look very cross,' said Eustacie.

'I am not cross,' said Sir Tristram in a somewhat brittle voice, 'but I
think you should know that while I am prepared to allow you all the
freedom possible, I shall expect my wife to pay some slight heed to my
wishes.'

Eustacie considered this dispassionately. 'Well, I do not think I shall,' she said. 'You seem to me to have very stupid wishes – quite absurd, in fact.'

'This argument is singularly pointless,' said Sir Tristram, quelling a strong desire to box her ears. 'Perhaps my mother will know better how to persuade you.'

Eustacie pricked up her ears at that. 'I did not know you had a mother! Where is she?'

'She is in Bath. When the funeral is over I am going to take you to her, and put you in her care until we can be married.'

'As to that, it is not yet decided. Describe to me your mother! Is she like you?'

'No, not at all.'

'*Tant mieux*! What, then, is she like?'

'Well,' said Sir Tristram lamely, 'I don't think I know how to describe her. She will be very kind to you, I know.'

'But what does she do?' demanded Eustacie. 'Does she amuse herself at Bath? Is she gay?'

'Hardly. She does not enjoy good health, you see.'

'Oh!' Eustacie digested this. 'No parties?'

'I believe she enjoys card-parties.'

Eustacie grimaced expressively. 'Me, I know those card-parties. I think she plays Whist, and perhaps Commerce.'

'I dare say she does. I know of no reason why she should not,' said Shield rather stiffly.

'There is not any reason, but I do not play Whist or Commerce, and I find such parties quite abominable.'

'That need not concern you, for whatever Sylvester's views may have been, I feel sure that my mother will agree that it would be improper for you to go out in public immediately after his death.

'But if I am not to go to any parties, what then am I to do in Bath?'

'Well, I suppose you will have to reconcile yourself to a period of quiet.'

'Quiet?' gasped Eustacie. '*More* quiet? No, and no, and no!'

He could not help laughing, but said: 'Is it so terrible?'

'Yes, it is!' said Eustacie. 'First I have to live in Sussex, and now I am to go to Bath – to play backgammon! And after that you will take me to Berkshire, where I expect I shall die.'

'I hope not!' said Shield.

'Yes, but I think I shall,' said Eustacie, propping her chin in her hands and gazing mournfully into the fire. 'After all, I have had a very unhappy life without any adventures, and it would not be wonderful if I went into a decline. Only nothing that is interesting ever happens to me,' she added bitterly, 'so I dare say I shall just die in child-bed, which is a thing anyone can do.'

Sir Tristram flushed uncomfortably. 'Really, Eustacie!' he protested.

Eustacie was too much absorbed in the contemplation of her dark destiny to pay any heed to him. 'I shall present to you an heir,' she said, 'and then I shall die.' The picture suddenly appealed to her; she continued in a more cheerful tone: 'Everyone will say that I was very young to die, and they will fetch you from the gaming-hell where you——'

'Fetch me from where?' interrupted Sir Tristram, momentarily led away by this flight of imagination.

'From a gaming-hell,' repeated Eustacie impatiently. 'Or perhaps the Cock-Pit. It does not signify; it is quite unimportant! But I think you will feel great remorse when it is told you that I am dying, and you will spring up and fling yourself on your horse, and ride *ventre à terre* to come to my death-bed. And *then* I shall forgive you, and——'

'What in heaven's name are you talking about?' demanded Sir Tristram. 'Why should you forgive me? Why should— What *is* this nonsense?'

Eustacie, thus rudely awakened from her pleasant dream, sighed and abandoned it. 'It is just what I thought might happen,' she explained.

Sir Tristram said severely: 'It seems to me that you indulge your fancy a deal too freely. Let me assure you that I don't frequent gaming-hells or cock-pits! Nor,' he added, with a flicker of humour, 'am I very much in the habit of flinging myself upon my horses.'

'No, and you do not ride *ventre à terre*. It does not need that you should tell me so. *I* know!'

'Well, only on the hunting-field,' said Sir Tristram.

'Do you think you might if I were on my death-bed?' asked Eustacie hopefully.

'Certainly not. If you were on your death-bed it is hardly likely that I should be from home. I wish you would put this notion of dying out of your head. Why should you die?'

'But I have told you!' said Eustacie, brightening at this sign of interest. 'I shall——'

'Yes, I know,' said Sir Tristram hastily. 'You need not tell me again. There will be time enough to discuss such matters when we are married.'

'But I thought it was because you must have an heir that you want to marry me?' said Eustacie practically. 'Grandpère explained it to me, and you yourself said——'

'Eustacie,' interposed Sir Tristram, 'if you must talk in this extremely frank vein, I'll listen, but I do beg of you not to say such things to anyone but me! It will give people a very odd idea of you.'

'Grandpère,' said Eustacie, with the air of one quoting a major prophet, 'told me not to mind what I said, but on no account to be a simpering little *innocente.*'

'It sounds to me exactly the kind of advice Sylvester would give you,' said Shield.

'And you sound to me exactly the kind of person I do not at all wish to have for my husband!' retorted Eustacie. 'It will be better, I think, if we do not marry!'

'Possibly!' said Sir Tristram, nettled. 'But I gave my word to Sylvester that I would marry you, and marry you I will!'

'You will not, because I shall instantly run away!'

'Don't be a little fool!' said Sir Tristram unwisely, and walked out of the room, leaving her simmering with indignation.

Her wrath did not last long, for by the time she had taken a vow to put her threat into execution, all the adventurous possibilities of such a resolve struck her so forcibly that Sir Tristram's iniquities were quite ousted from her mind. She spent a pleasurable hour, thinking out a number of plans for her future. These were varied, but all of them impracticable, a circumstance which her common sense regretfully acknowledged. She was forced in the end to take her handmaiden into her confidence, having abandoned such attractive schemes as masquerading in male attire, or taking London by storm by enacting an unspecified tragic rôle at Drury Lane. It was a pity, but if one had the misfortune to be a person of Quality one could not become an actress; and although the notion of masquerading as a man appealed strongly to her, she was quite unable to carry her imagination farther than the first chapter of this exciting story. One would naturally leap into the saddle and ride off somewhere, but she could not decide where, or what to do.

Lucy, at first scandalized by the idea of a young lady setting out into the world alone, was not a difficult person to inspire. The portrait drawn for her edification of a shrinking damsel condemned to espouse a tyrant of callous instincts and brutal manners profoundly affected her mind, and by the time Eustacie had graphically described her almost inevitable demise in child-bed, she was ready to lend her support to any plan her mistress might see fit to adopt. Her own brain, though appreciative, was not fertile, but upon being adjured to think of some means whereby a lady could evade a distasteful marriage and arrange her own life, she had the happy notion of suggesting a perusal of the advertisements in the *Morning Post*.

Together mistress and maid pored over the columns of this useful periodical. It was not, at first glance, very helpful, for most of its advertisements appeared to be of Well-matched Carriage Horses, or Superb Residences to be Hired for a Short Term. Further study, however, enlarged the horizon. A lady domiciled in Brook Street required a Governess with a knowledge of Astrology, Botany, Water-Colour Painting, and the French Tongue to instruct her daughters. Dismissing the first three requirements as irrelevancies, Eustacie triumphantly pointed to the last, and said that here was the very thing.

That a governess's career was unlikely to prove adventurous was a consideration that did not weigh with her for more than two minutes, for it did not take her longer than this to realize that her young charges would possess a handsome brother, who would naturally fall in love with his sisters' governess. Persecution from his Mama was to be expected, but after various vicissitudes it would be discovered that the humble governess was an aristocrat and an heiress, and all would end happily. Lucy, in spite of never having read any of the romances which formed her mistress's chief study, saw nothing improbable in this picture, but doubted whether Sir Tristram would permit his betrothed to leave the Court.

'He will know nothing about it,' said Eustacie, 'because I shall escape very late at night when he thinks I am in bed, and ride to Hand Cross to catch the mail-coach to London.'

'Oh, miss you couldn't do that, not all by yourself!' said Lucy. 'It wouldn't be seemly!'

Paying no heed to this poor-spirited criticism, Eustacie clasped her hands round her knees, and began to ponder the details of her flight. The scheme itself might be fantastical, but there was a streak of French rationality in her nature which could be trusted to cope with the intricacies of the wildest escape. She said: 'We shall need the stable keys.'

'*We*, miss?' faltered Lucy.

Eustacie nodded. 'But yes, because I have never saddled a horse, and though I think it would be a better adventure if I did everything quite by myself, one must be practical, after all. Can you saddle a horse?'

'Oh yes, miss!' replied Lucy, a farmer's daughter, 'but——'

'Very well, then, that is arranged. And it is you, moreover, who must steal the stable keys. That will not be a great matter. And you will pack for me two bandboxes, but not any more, because I cannot carry much on horseback. And when I reach Hand Cross I shall let Rufus go, and it is certain that he will find his way home, and that will put my cousin Tristram in a terrible fright when he sees my horse quite riderless. I dare say he will think I am dead.'

'Miss, you don't really mean it?' said Lucy, who had been listening open-mouthed.

'But of course I mean it,' replied Eustacie calmly. 'When does the night mail reach Hand Cross?'

'Just before midnight, miss, but they do say we shall be having snow, and that would make the mail late as like as not. But, miss, it's all of five miles to Hand Cross, and the road that lonely, and running through the

Forest – oh, I'd be afeard!'

'I am not afraid of anything,' said Eustacie loftily.

Lucy sank her voice impressively. 'Perhaps you haven't ever heard tell of the Headless Horseman, miss?'

'No!' Eustacie's eyes sparkled. 'Tell me at once all about him!'

'They say he rides the Forest, miss, but never on a horse of his own,' said Lucy throbbingly. 'You'll find him up behind you on the crupper with his arms round your waist.'

Even in the comfortable daylight this story was hideous enough to daunt the most fearless. Eustacie shuddered, but said stoutly: 'I do not believe it. It is just a tale!'

'Ask anyone, miss, if it's not true!' said Lucy.

Eustacie, thinking this advice good, asked Sir Tristram at the first opportunity.

'The Headless Horseman?' he said. 'Yes, I believe there is some such legend.'

'But is it true?' asked Eustacie breathlessly.

'Why, no, of course not!'

'You would not then be afraid to ride through the Forest at night?'

'Not in the least. I've often done so, and never encountered a headless horseman, I assure you!'

'Thank you,' said Eustacie. 'Thank you very much!'

He looked a little surprised, but as she said nothing more very soon forgot the episode.

'My cousin Tristram,' Eustacie told Lucy, 'says that it is nothing but a legend. I shall not regard it.'

CHAPTER 3

Had Sir Tristram been less preoccupied he might have found something to wonder at in his cousin's sudden docility. As it was, he was much too busy unravelling the intricacies of Sylvester's affairs with Mr. Pickering to pay any heed to Eustacie's change of front. If he thought about it at all he supposed merely that she had recovered from a fit of tantrums, and was heartily glad of it. He had half expected her to raise objections to his plan to convey her to Bath on the day after her grandfather's burial, but when he broached the matter to her she listened to him with folded hands and downcast eyes, and answered never a word. A man more learned in female wiles might have found this circumstance suspicious; Sir Tristram was only grateful. He himself would be returning to Lavenham

Court, but he told Eustacie that he did not expect to be obliged to remain for more than a week or two, after which time he would join the household in Bath, and set forward the marriage arrangements. Eustacie curtseyed politely.

She did not attend Sylvester's funeral, which took place on the third day after his death, but busied herself instead with choosing from her wardrobe the garments she considered most suited to her new calling, and directing Lucy how to bestow them in the two bandboxes. Lucy, too devoted to her glamorous young mistress to think of betraying her, but very much alarmed at the idea of all the dangers she might encounter on her solitary journey, sniffed dolefully as she folded caracos and fichus and said that she would almost prefer to accompany Miss, braving the terror of the Headless Horseman, than be left behind to face Sir Tristram's wrath. Eustacie, feeling that to take her maid with her would be to destroy at a blow all the romance of the adventure, told her to pretend the most complete ignorance of the affair, and promised that she would send for her to London at the first opportunity.

The forlorn sight of snowflakes drifting down from a leaden sky affected Lucy with a sense of even deeper foreboding, but only inspired her mistress to say she would wear her fur-lined cloak after all, and the beaver hat with the crimson plume.

Her actual escape from the Court was accomplished without the least difficulty, the servants having gone to bed, and Sir Tristram being shut up in the library with Beau Lavenham, who had come over from the Dower House to dine with his cousins. Eustacie had excused herself from their company soon after dinner, and gone up to her bedchamber. At eleven o'clock, looking quite enchanting in her riding-dress and crimson cloak and wide-brimmed beaver, with its red feather curling over to mingle with her dark, silky curls, she tiptoed down the back stairs, holding up her skirts in one hand and in the other grasping her whip and gloves. Behind her tottered the shrinking Lucy, carrying the two bandboxes and a lantern.

Half-way down the stairs Eustacie stopped. 'I ought to have a pistol!'

'Good gracious sakes alive, miss!' whispered Lucy. 'Whatever would you do with one of them nasty, dangerous things?'

'But, of course, I must have a pistol!' said Eustacie. 'And I know where there is a pistol, too!' She turned, ignoring her abigail's tearful protests, and ran lightly up the stairs again, and disappeared in the direction of the Long Gallery.

When she returned she was flushed and rather out of breath and carried in her right hand a peculiarly deadly-looking duelling pistol with a ten-inch barrel and silver sights. Lucy nearly dropped the bandboxes when she saw it, and implored her mistress in an agitated whisper to put it down.

'It is my cousin Ludovic's,' said Eustacie triumphantly. 'There were two of them in a case in the bedchamber that was his. How fortunate that I should have remembered! I saw them – oh, a long time ago! – when they put the new curtains in that room. Do you think it is loaded?'

'Oh, mercy, miss, I hope not!'

'I must be careful,' decided Eustacie, handling the weapon somewhat gingerly. 'I think it has a hair-trigger, but I do not properly understand guns. Hurry, now!'

The snow had stopped falling some time before, but a light covering of it lay upon the ground, and there was a sharp, frosty nip in the air. The two females, one of them in high fettle and the other shivering with mingled cold and fright, trod softly down the drive that led from the house to the stables. No light showed in the coachman's cottage, nor in the grooms' quarters, and no one appeared to offer the least hindrance to Eustacie's escape. She unlocked the door of the harness-room, pulled Lucy in after her, and setting the lantern down on the table, selected a bridle from the wall, and pointed out her saddle to the abigail. The next thing was to unlock the stable door, and to saddle and bridle Rufus, who seemed sleepy but not displeased to see his mistress. Lucy, dreading the consequences of this exploit, had begun to weep softly, but was told in a fierce whisper to saddle Rufus and to stop being a fool. She was an obedient girl, so she gulped down her tears, and heaved the saddle up on to Rufus's back. The girths having been pulled tight, the head-stall removed and the bridle put on, it only remained to attach the two bandboxes to the saddle. This called for a further search in the harness-room for a pair of suitable straps, and by the time these had been found and the bandboxes suspended from them, Eustacie had decided that the only possible way to carry a pistol was in a holster. A lady's saddle not being equipped with this necessary adjunct, one had to be removed from a saddle of Sylvester's, and buckled rather precariously on to the strap that held one of the bandboxes. It seemed to be far too large a holster for the slender pistol that was pushed into it, but that could not be helped. Eustacie remarked that it was fortunate there was snow upon the ground, since it would muffle the sound of Rufus's hooves on the cobble-stones, and led him out to the mounting-block. Once safely in the saddle, she reminded Lucy to lock all the doors again and to replace the keys, gave her her hand to kiss, and set off, not by way of the avenue leading to the closed lodge gates, but across the park to a farm-track with an unguarded gate at the end of it which could be opened without dismounting.

This feat presently accomplished, Eustacie urged Rufus to a trot, and set off down the lane towards the rough road that ran north through Warninglid to join the turnpike road from London to Brighton at Hand Cross.

She knew the way well, but to one wholly unaccustomed to being abroad after nightfall, the countryside looked oddly unfamiliar in the moonlight. Everything was very silent, and the trees, grown suddenly to preposterous heights, cast black, distorted shadows that might, to those of nervous disposition, seem almost to hold a menace. Eustacie was glad to think that she was a de Vauban, and therefore afraid of nothing, and wondered why a stillness unbroken by so much as the crackle of a twig should, instead of convincing her that she was alone, have the quite opposite effect of making her imagine hidden dangers behind every bush or thicket. She was enjoying herself hugely, of course – that went without saying – but perhaps she would not be entirely sorry to reach Hand Cross and the protection of the mail-coach. Moreover, the bandboxes bobbed up and down in a tiresome way, and one of them showed signs of working loose from its strap. She tried to rectify this, but only succeeded in making things worse.

The lane presently met the road to Hand Cross, and here the country began to be more thickly wooded, and consequently darker, for there were a good many pines and hollies which had not shed their foliage and so obscured the moonlight. It was very cold, and the carpet of snow made it sometimes difficult to keep to the road. Once Rufus stumbled almost into the ditch, and once some creature (only a fox, Eustacie assured herself) slipped across the road ahead of her. It began to seem a very long way to Hand Cross. A thorn-bush beside the road cast a shadow that was unpleasantly like that of a misshapen man. Eustacie's heart gave a sickening bump, and all at once she remembered the Headless Horseman, and for one dreadful moment felt positive that he was close behind her. Every horrid story she had heard of St. Leonard's Forest now came unbidden to her mind, and she discovered that she could even recall with painful accuracy the details of *A Discourse relating a strange and monstrous Serpent (or Dragon) lately discovered and yet living*, which she had found in a musty old volume in Sylvester's library.

Past Warninglid the country grew more open, but although it was a relief to get away from the trees Eustacie knew, because Sylvester had told her, that the Forest had once covered all this tract of ground, and she was therefore unable to place any reliance on the Headless Horseman keeping to the existing bounds. She began to imagine moving forms in the hedges, and when, about a mile beyond the Slaugham turning, her horse suddenly put forward his ears at a flutter of white seen fleetingly in the gloom of a thicket and shied violently across the road, she gave a sob of pure fright, and was nearly unseated. She pulled Rufus up, but his plunge had done all that was necessary to set the troublesome bandbox free. It slipped from the strap and went rolling away over the snow, and came to rest finally quite close to the thicket at the side of the road.

Eustacie, patting Rufus's neck with a hand which, though meant to convey reassurance, was actually trembling more than he was, looked after her property with dismay. She did not feel that she could abandon it (which she would have liked to have done), for in spite of being afraid of nothing, she was extremely loth to dismount and pick it up. She sat still for a few minutes, intently staring at the thicket. Rufus stared, too, with his head up and ears forward. Nothing seemed to be stirring, however, and Eustacie, telling herself that the Headless Horseman was only a legend, and that the monstrous Serpent (or Dragon) had flourished nearly two hundred years ago and must surely be dead by now, gritted her teeth, and dismounted. She was disgusted to find that her knees were shaking, so to give herself more courage she pulled the duelling pistol out of the holster and grasped it firmly in her right hand.

Rufus, though suspicious of the thicket, allowed her to lead him up to the bandbox. She had just stooped to pick it up when the shrill neigh of a pony not five yards distant startled her almost out of her wits. She gave a scream of terror, saw something move in the shadow, and the next minute was struggling dementedly in the hold of a man who had seemed to pounce upon her from nowhere. She could not scream again because a hand was clamped over her mouth, and when she pulled the trigger of her pistol nothing happened. A sinewy arm was round her; she was half lifted, half dragged into the cover of the thicket; and heard a rough voice behind her growl: 'Hit her over the head, blast the wench!'

Her terrified eyes, piercing the gloom, saw the dim outline of a face above her. Her captor said: 'I'll be damned if I do!' in the unmistakable accents of a gentleman, and bent over her, and added softly: 'I'm sorry, but you mustn't screech. If I take my hand away, will you be quiet – quite quiet?'

She nodded. At the first sound of his voice, which was oddly attractive, a large measure of her fright had left her. Now, as her eyes grew accustomed to the darkness, she saw that he was quite a young man, and, judging from the outline of his profile against the moonlit sky, a very personable young man.

The voice of the man behind her spoke again. 'Adone do! She'll be the ruin o' we! Let me shut her mouth for her!'

Eustacie made a strangled sound in her throat and tried to bring her hands up to clutch at the young man's arm. The barrel of her pistol, which she was still clutching, gleamed in the moonlight, and caught the attention of her captor, who said under his breath: 'If you let that pistol off I'll murder you! Ned, take the gun away from her!'

A heavy hand wrenched it out of her grasp; the rough voice said: 'It ain't loaded. If you won't do more, tie her up with a gag in her mouth!'

'No, no, she's much too pretty,' said the young man, taking the pistol and slipping it into the pocket of his frieze coat. 'You won't squeak, will you, darling?'

As well as she could Eustacie shook her head. The hand left her mouth and patted her cheek. 'Good girl! Don't be frightened: I swear I won't hurt you!'

Eustacie, who had been almost suffocated, gasped thankfully: 'I thought you were the Headless Horseman!'

'You thought I was what?'

'The Headless Horseman.'

He laughed. 'Well, I'm not.'

'No, I can see you are not. But why did you seize me like that? What are you doing here?'

'If it comes to that, what are *you* doing here?'

'I am going to London,' replied Eustacie.

'Oh!' said the young man, rather doubtfully. 'It's no concern of mine, of course, but it's a plaguey queer time to be going to London, isn't it?'

'No, because I am going to catch the night mail at Hand Cross. You must instantly let me go, or I shall be too late.'

The other man, who had been listening in scowling silence, muttered: 'She'll have the pack of them down on us!'

'Be damned to you, don't croak so!' said the young man. 'Tether that nag of hers!'

'If you let her go——'

'I'm not going to let her go. You keep a look-out for Abel, and stop spoiling sport!'

'But certainly you are going to let me go!' interposed Eustacie in an urgent undertone. 'I must go!'

The young man said apologetically: 'The devil's in it that I can't let you go. I would if I could, but to tell you the truth——'

'There's no call to do that!' growled his companion. 'Dang me, master, if I don't think you're unaccountable crazed!'

Eustacie, who had had time by now to take stock of her surroundings, discovered that the darker shadows a little way off were not shadows at all, but ponies. There seemed to be about a dozen of them, and as she peered at them she was gradually able to descry what they were carrying. She had been living in Sussex for two years, and she was perfectly familiar with the appearance of a keg of brandy. She exclaimed: 'You are smugglers, then!'

'Free-traders, my dear, free-traders!' replied the young man cheerfully.
'At least, I am. Ned here is only what we call a land smuggler. You need
not heed him.'

Eustacie was so intrigued that for the moment she forgot all about the
mail-coach. She had heard a great deal about smugglers, but although she
knew that they were in general a desperate, cut-throat set of outlaws, she
was so accustomed to her grandfather and most of his neighbours having
dealings with them that she did not think their illicit trade in the least
shocking. She said: 'Well, you need not be afraid of me, I assure you. I do
not at all mind that you are smug— free-traders.'

'Are you French?' asked the young man.

'Yes. But tell me, why are you hiding here?'

'Excisemen,' he replied. 'They're on the watch. You know, the more I
think of it the more it seems a very odd thing to me that you should be
riding about by yourself in the middle of the night.'

'I have told you: I am going to London.'

'Well, it still seems very odd to me.'

'Yes, but, you see, I am running away,' explained Eustacie. 'That is
why I have to catch the night mail. I am going to London to be a
governess.'

She had the impression that he was laughing, but he said quite gravely:
'You'll never do for a governess. You don't look like one. Besides, you're
not old enough.'

'Yes, I am, and I shall look just like a governess.'

'You can't know anything about governesses if that's what you think.'

'Well, I don't, but I thought it would be a very good thing to become.'

'I dare say you know best, but to my mind you're making a mistake.
From all I've heard, they have a devilish poor time of it.'

'I wish I could be a smuggler,' said Eustacie wistfully. 'I think I should
like that.'

'You wouldn't do for a smuggler,' he replied, shaking his head. 'We
don't encourage females in the trade. It's too dangerous.'

'Well, I do not think it is fair that just because one is a female one should
never be allowed to have any adventures!'

'You seem to me to be having a deal of adventure,' he pointed out. 'I
might easily have choked the life out of you – in fact, I may still if you don't
behave yourself. You're in a mighty tight corner.'

'Yes, I know I am having an adventure now,' agreed Eustacie, 'and, of
course, I am enjoying it, but I should like to continue having adventures,
which is a thing not at all easy to arrange.'

'No, I suppose it's not,' said the free-trader thoughtfully.

'You see, if I were a man I could be a highwayman, or a smuggler like you. I expect you have had many, many adventures.'

'I have,' said the young man rather ruefully. 'So many that I'm devilish tired of 'em.'

'But I have had only this one small adventure, and I am not yet tired. That is why I am going to London.'

'If you take my advice,' said the young man, 'you'll give up this notion of being a governess. Try something else!'

'Well, perhaps I will be a milliner,' said Eustacie. 'When I get to London I shall consider carefully what is best for me to do.'

'Yes, but you aren't going to London to-night,' he said.

'I am going to-night! You do not understand! If I do not go to-night I shall be found, and then I shall have to go to Bath to play backgammon, and be married to a person without sensibility!'

He seemed to be much struck by this, and said seriously: 'No, that would be too bad. We must think of something. You'll have to stay with me, at least till Abel reports all clear, of course, but there's bound to be a London coach through Hand Cross in the morning.'

'And I tell you that in the morning it will be too late!' said Eustacie crossly. 'I find that you are quite abominable! You spoil everything, and, what is more, I think you are excessively impertinent, because you have taken my horse away and stolen my pistol!'

'No, I haven't,' he replied. 'I've only had your horse tethered so that he can't stray. As for your pistol, you can have that back now if you wish,' he added, diving his hand into his pocket and pulling out the weapon. 'Though what in the world you want with an unloaded duelling pistol——' He stopped suddenly, feeling the balance of the gun, and stepped into the moonlight to examine it more closely. Eustacie saw that he was very tall and fair, dressed in a common frieze coat and breeches, with a coloured handkerchief round his neck, and his pale gold hair loosely tied back from his face. He looked up from the pistol in his hand, and said sharply: 'How did you come by this?'

'Well, it is not precisely my own,' said Eustacie. 'It——'

'I know that. Who gave it to you?'

'Nobody gave it to me!'

'Do you mean you stole it?'

'Of course I did not steal it! I have just borrowed it because I thought it would be a good thing to take a pistol with me. *Du vrai*, it belongs to my cousin Ludovic, but I feel very certain that he would not mind lending it to me, because he is of all my family the most romantic.'

The free-trader came back to her side in two quick strides. 'Who the devil are you?' he demanded.

'I do not see what concern it is——'

He put his hands on her shoulders and shook her. 'Never mind that! Who are you?'

'I am Eustacie de Vauban,' she answered, with dignity.

'Eustacie de Vauban. . . . Oh yes, I have it! But how do you come to be in England?'

'Well, my grandpapa thought that they would send me to the guillotine if I stayed in France, so he fetched me away. But if I had known that he would make me marry my cousin Tristram, who is not amusing, I should have preferred infinitely to have gone to the guillotine.'

'I don't blame you,' he said. 'Is he at the Court? If you're running away from him I'll do what I can to help you!'

'Do you know him, then?' asked Eustacie, surprised.

'Do I know him! I'm your romantic cousin Ludovic!'

She gave a small shriek, which had the effect of making him clap his hand over her mouth again. 'Fiend seize you, don't make that noise! Do you want to bring the Excisemen down on me?'

She pulled his hand down and stood clasping it between both her own. 'No, no I promise I will be entirely quiet! I am so enchanted to meet you! I thought I never should, because Tristram said you could not set foot in England any more.'

'I dare say he did,' replied Ludovic. 'But here I am for all that. You've only to breathe one word and I shall have Bow Street Runners as well as Excisemen on my trail.'

She said fiercely: 'I shall not breathe any word at all, and I think you are quite insulting to say that!'

He put his other hand over hers. 'Did they tell you why I can't set foot in England?'

'Yes, but I do not care. Did you kill that person whose name I have forgotten?'

'No, I did not.'

'*Bon*! Then we must at once discover who did do it,' said Eustacie briskly. 'I see now that this is a much better adventure than I thought.'

'Do you believe me, then?' he asked.

'But certainly I believe you!'

He laughed, and pulling her to him, kissed her cheek. 'Well, save for Basil, you're the only person who does.'

'Yes,' said Eustacie. 'But me, I do not like Basil.'

He was about to answer her when Ned Bundy loomed up through the darkness and twitched his sleeve. 'Abel,' he said laconically.

Eustacie heard the crunch of a pony's hooves on the snow and the next moment saw the pony, with a short, thickset man sitting astride the pack-saddle. Ludovic took her hand and led her up to the newcomer.

'Well?' he said.

'There's a dunnamany Excisemen out. We'll have to make back to Cowfold – if we can,' said Mr. Bundy, dismounting. He became aware of Eustacie, and favoured her with a long, dispassionate look. 'Where did that dentical wench come from?' he inquired.

'She's my cousin. Can't we win through to Hand Cross?'

Mr. Bundy accepted Eustacie's identity without comment and apparently without interest. 'We'm not likely to win to Cowfold,' he replied. 'They're on to us.'

At this gloomy pronouncement his brother Ned, pulling him a little apart, broke into urgent, low-voiced speech. Ludovic strode over to join in the discussion, and returned in a few minutes to Eustacie's side, saying briskly: 'Well, I'm sorry for it, but I can't let you go to London to-night. You'll have to come with us.'

'Oh, I would much rather come with you,' Eustacie assured him. 'Where are we going?'

'South,' he replied briefly. 'Those damned riding officers must have got wind of this convoy. There may be some rough work done before the night's out, I warn you. Come along!'

He seized her by the wrist again and strode off with her to where her horse had been tethered, and without ceremony tossed her up into the saddle. Eustacie, seeing the two Bundys busy with the laden ponies, said emulatively: 'Can I help to lead them, please?'

'No. Keep quiet.'

'But what *can* I do?'

'Nothing.'

'Ned Bundy said something under his breath.

'I dare say, but I'm not going to have a cousin of mine hit over the head,' said Ludovic. 'Ready, Abel?'

A grunt answered him; the train began to move southward, Abel at its head. Ludovic mounted a rough pony and brought up the rear, still holding Eustacie's bridle. She took instant exception to this, and after a short but pungent argument he let her go free, much against the advice of Ned Bundy, who was ranging alongside the convoy, whipping up the stragglers.

Eustacie interrupted Mr. Bundy's muttered suggestions for the disposal of her person by announcing calmly that she was quite tired of him, a remark which surprised that ferocious gentleman so much that he could think of nothing to say, and retired towards the head of the train. 'Why does he want to hit me on the head?' asked Eustacie, looking critically after him. 'He seems to me entirely stupid.'

'Well, he don't hold with women being mixed up in these affairs,' explained Ludovic. 'You're devilish in the way, you know.'

'But you do not mind having me with you, do you?' asked Eustacie anxiously.

'Lord, no, I like it!' replied Ludovic light-heartedly. 'Only you won't care for it if there's any shooting done.'

'Yes, I shall,' said Eustacie. 'In fact, I wish very much that you will load my pistol for me and give it back to me, because if there is to be shooting I should like to shoot, too.'

'It's not your pistol,' retorted Ludovic. 'It's mine, and let me tell you that I don't lend my duelling-pistols to anyone. Where is the other?'

'I left it in the case. I think you should be glad to lend it to me.'

'Well, I'm not. Where did you get this notion I was romantic?'

'But you have had a very romantic life; of course, I knew you were romantic!'

'I've had a damned uncomfortable life. Tell me more about this marriage of yours. Why must you marry Tristram if you don't want to? Is it Sylvester's doing?'

'Yes, he made for me a *mariage de convenance*, but he is dead now, and I am going to arrange my own affairs.'

'What! is Sylvester dead?' exclaimed Ludovic.

'Yes, since three days. So now it is you who are Lord Lavenham.'

'Much good will that do me!' said Ludovic. 'Where's Basil?'

'He is at the Dower House, of course, and Tristram is at the Court.'

'I must try to see Basil. Something will have to be done about the succession. *I* can't wear Sylvester's shoes.'

'Well, I do not want him to wear them, and I think it would be better if you did not see him,' said Eustacie.

'Oh, there's no harm in the Beau!' He broke off suddenly as the convoy halted, and grasped Rufus's bridle above the bit, pulling him to a standstill. 'Quiet, now!' He sat still, intently listening. Eustacie, straining her ears, caught faintly the sound of horses' hooves in the distance. 'Stay where you are!' ordered Ludovic, and went forward to the head of the train.

Eustacie, though she would have liked to have taken part in the council which was being held between the three men, thought it as well to obey. Her cousin Ludovic seemed to be of an autocratic disposition, reminding her strongly of his grandfather.

He came back to her side after a short colloquy with the Bundys and said in his quick, authoritative way: 'We shall have to try and lead these damned Excisemen off the trail. I don't know what the devil to do with you, so you'd better come with me. After all, you wanted an adventure, and I can't let you jaunt about the countryside alone at this hour of night.'

That a solitary journey to London might conceivably be attended by fewer dangers than a night spent hand-in-glove with a party of smugglers apparently did not occur to him. He dismounted from his pony, adding: 'Besides, I want your horse.'

'Am I to ride the pony, then?' asked Eustacie, willing but dubious.

'No, I'm going to take you up before me,' he replied. 'I can look after you better that way. Moreover, the pony couldn't keep up.' He gave the animal into the elder Bundy's care as he spoke, and said: 'Good luck to you, Abel. Don't trouble your head on my account!'

'You'd best be careful,' said Mr. Bundy gloomily. 'You never had no sense and never will have.'

Ludovic had got up behind Eustacie by this time, and settled her in the crook of his arm. 'It beats me how you can ride with a saddle like this,' he remarked, wheeling Rufus about. 'And what in thunder is this thing?'

'It is a bandbox, of course!'

'Well, it's devilishly in the way,' said Ludovic. 'Do you mind if I cut it loose?'

'No, certainly I do not mind. I, too, am quite tired of it,' replied Eustacie blithely. 'Besides, I have already lost the other one.

The bandbox was soon got rid of. Eustacie watched it bounce to the ground, and remarked with a giggle that if Tristram found it he would be sure to think she had been murdered.

Ludovic had urged Rufus to a canter. He seemed to Eustacie to be heading straight in the direction of the pursuing Excisemen. She pointed this out to him, and he replied: 'Of course I am. I told you I was going to lead them off the trail. If I can get them to chase me Abel will have time to reach a hiding-place he knows of. We'll lead them into the Forest.'

'And when we have done that what shall we do?'

'Oh, give 'em the slip!' said Ludovic carelessly. 'I shall have to think what's to be done with you after that, but there's no time to waste on that now.' He reined in as he spoke, and Eustacie saw that they had retraced their steps almost to the thicket where she had first encountered the train. She could hear movement somewhere near at hand, and the faint sound of voices. Ludovic rode softly forward, off the road into the shelter of the trees. 'I thought as much,' he said. 'They're searching the thicket. Mustn't give 'em time to find the pony-tracks. Now keep quite, and hold on to that pommel.'

His gyrations after that were bewildering, but apparently purposeful. It seemed to Eustacie, dutifully grasping the pommel, that they were circling round the thicket to the north. She could now hear plainly the sound of trampling hooves and snapping twigs.

'We must give the poor devils something to think about,' said Ludovic in her ear. 'Don't screech now!'

It was as well that he uttered this warning, for the immediate explosion of his pistol made Eustacie jump nearly out of her skin. She managed by the exercise of heroic self-control not to scream, but when a shot almost at once answered Ludovic's she could not forbear a gasp of fright.

'I thought that would tickle them up,' said Ludovic. 'Now for it!'

He wheeled the snorting, trembling Rufus, and let him have his head. Rufus plunged forward, crashing through the undergrowth with the maximum amount of noise and alarm; a shout sounded somewhere in the rear; another shot was fired; and Eustacie had the satisfaction of knowing that she was now fairly embroiled with His Majesty's Excise Office. She removed one hand from the pommel and took a firm grasp of Ludovic's coat, which seemed to her to afford a safer hold. He glanced down at her, smiling. 'Frightened?'

'No!'

'Well, we're going to have a trifle of a gallop now, so cling tight!'

They came out from the cover of the trees as he spoke on to a tract of more open ground. The moon was momentarily obscured by a drifting cloud, but there was light enough for the flying horse to be seen by its pursuers. Two shots cracked almost simultaneously, and Eustacie felt the arm that cradled her give a queer jerk, and heard her cousin catch his breath sharply. 'Winged, by Gad!' he said. 'Now, who'd have thought an Exciseman could shoot as straight as that?'

'Are you hurt?' Eustacie cried.

'Devil a bit!' was the cheerful response. He looked fleetingly back over his shoulder. 'Four of 'em, I think. Riding hard, too. You can always trust an Exciseman to follow his nose. . . . That's better.'

They were under cover again, and he let Rufus slacken his pace to a trot, bending him easily this way and that through the outskirts of the Forest. Eustacie, after a very little of this erratic progress, began to feel quite lost, but it was evident that her cousin knew the Forest like the palm of his hand, for they steadily penetrated further into its darkness. Behind them the pursuit sounded as though it were in difficulties, but they had not yet outstripped it, and once Ludovic reined in altogether to give it time to come nearer, and, since it showed signs of abandoning the chase, fired his second pistol invitingly. This had the required effect; the Forest reverberated with shots, and they moved forward again, heading northward.

It was fully half an hour later before they finally lost the Excisemen, and Ludovic was swaying in the saddle.

'You *are* hurt!' Eustacie said, alarmed.

'Oh no, only a scratch!' he murmured. 'Anyway, we've led them in such circles they'll be hunting one another till daylight.'

Eustacie put her hands over his, and pulled Rufus up. 'Where are you hurt?' she demanded.

'Left shoulder. I think we'd better take the risk and make Hand Cross.'

'Yes, but first I will bind up your shoulder. Are you bleeding very much?'

'Like a pig,' said Ludovic.

She slid to the ground, stiff and somewhat bruised, and said imperatively: 'Get down! If you bleed like a pig you will die, and I do not at all want you to die.'

He laughed, but dismounted, and found himself steadied by two small but capable hands. He reeled and sank on his knees, saying: 'Damme, I must be worse hit than I knew! You'd best take the horse and leave me.'

'I shall not leave you,' replied Eustacie, busily ripping the flounce off her petticoat. 'I shall take you to Hand Cross.'

Receiving no answer, she looked closely at him and found to her dismay that he had fainted. For a moment she was at a loss to know what to do, but when she touched him and brought her hand away wet with blood, she decided that the most urgent need was to bind up his wound, and promptly set about the task of extricating him from his coat. It was by no means easy, but she accomplished it at last, and managed as well as she could for the lack of light to twist the strips of her petticoat round his shoulder. He regained consciousness while she was straining her bandage as tight as possible, and lay for a moment blinking at her.

'What in – oh, I remember!' he said faintly. 'Give me some brandy. Flask in my coat.'

She tied a firm knot, found the brandy, and, raising his head, held the flask to his lips. He recovered sufficiently to struggle up and to put on his coat again. 'You know, you'd be wasted on Tristram,' he told her. 'Help me into the saddle, and we'll make Hand Cross yet.'

'Yes, but this time it is I who will take the reins,' said Eustacie.

'Just as you say, my dear,' he replied meekly.

'And you will put your arms round me and not fall off.'

'Don't worry. I shan't fall off.'

'Eustacie, finding a conveniently fallen tree-trunk, led her weary horse to it, and by using it as a mounting-block contrived to get into the saddle. She then rode back to Ludovic, and adjured him to mount behind her. He managed to do this, but the effort very nearly brought on another swooning fit. He had recourse to the brandy again, which cleared his head sufficiently to enable him to say: 'Follow this track; it'll bring us out on to the pike-road, north of Hand Cross. If you can wake old Nye at the Red Lion he'll take me in.'

'What shall I do if I see an Exciseman?' inquired Eustacie.

'Say your prayers,' he replied irrepressibly.

No Exciseman, however, was encountered on the track that led through the Forest, and by the time they came out on to the turnpike road, a mile from Hand Cross, Eustacie was far too anxious about her cousin to have much thought to spare for a questing Excise-officer. Ludovic seemed to stay in the saddle more by instinct than by any conscious effort. Eustacie dared not urge Rufus even to a trot. She had drawn Ludovic's sound arm round her waist, and held it there, clasping his slack hand. It seemed an interminable way to Hand Cross, but at last the lonely inn came into sight, a dark huddle against the sky. It was by now long after midnight, and no light shone behind the shuttered windows. Eustacie pulled Rufus up before the door and let go of Ludovic's hand. It fell nervelessly to his side; she realized that he must have swooned again; he was certainly sagging against her very heavily; she hoped he would not fall out of the saddle when she dismounted. She slid down, and was relieved to find that he only fell forward across Rufus's neck. The next moment she had grasped the bell-pull and sent an agitated peal ringing through the silent inn.

It was answered so speedily that Eustacie, who had heard rumours that Joseph Nye, of the Red Lion, knew more about the free-traders than he would admit, instantly suspected that he had been waiting up for the very convoy she had met. He opened the door in person, fully dressed, and holding a lantern, and looking a good deal startled. When he saw Eustacie he stared as though he could not believe his eyes, and gasped: 'Miss! Why, *miss!*'

Eustacie grasped his arm urgently. 'Please help me at once! I have brought my cousin Ludovic, and he said you would take him in, but he is wounded, and I think dying!' With which, because she had been through a great deal of excitement and was quite worn out by it, she burst into tears.

CHAPTER 4

The landlord took an involuntary step backward.

'Miss, have you gone mad?'

'No!' sobbed Eustacie.

He looked incredulously out into the moonlight, but when he saw the sagging figure on Rufus's back he gave an exclamation of horror, thrust his lantern into Eustacie's hand, and strode out. He was a big man, with mighty muscles, and he lifted Ludovic down from the saddle with surprising ease, and carried him into the inn, and lowered him on to a wooden settle by the fireplace. 'My God, what's come to him? What's he doing here?' he demanded under his breath.

'An Exciseman shot him. Oh, do you think he will die?'

'Die! No! But if he's found here——!' He broke off. 'I must get that horse stabled and out of sight. Stay you here, miss, and don't touch him! Lordy, lordy, this is a pretty kettle of fish!' He took a taper from the high mantelpiece, kindled it at the lantern's flame, and gave it to Eustacie. 'Do you light them candles, miss, and keep as quiet as you can! I've people putting up in the house.' He took up the lantern as he spoke and went out of the inn, softly closing the door behind him.

A branch of half-burned candles was standing on the table. Eustacie lit them, and turned to look fearfully down at her cousin.

He was lying with one arm hanging over the edge of the settle, and his face alarmingly pale. Not knowing what to do for him, she sank down on her knees beside him and lifted his dangling hand, and held it between her own. For the first time she was able to see him clearly; she thought that had she met him in daylight she must have known him for a Lavenham, for here was Sylvester's hawk-nose and humorous mouth, softened indeed by youth but unmistakable. He was lean and long-limbed, taller than Sylvester had been, but with the same slender hands and arched feet, and the same cleft in his wilful chin.

He seemed to Eustacie scarcely to breathe; she laid his arm across his chest and loosened the handkerchief about his neck. 'Oh, please, Cousin Ludovic, don't die!' she begged.

She heard a slight movement on the stairs behind her, and, turning her head, beheld a tall woman in a dressing-gown standing on the top step with a candle in her hand, looking down at her. She sprang up and stood as though defending the unconscious Ludovic, staring up at the newcomer in a challenging way.

The lady with the candle said with a twinkle in her grey eyes: 'Don't be alarmed! I'm no ghost, I assure you. You woke me with your ring at the bell, and because I'm of a prying disposition, I got up to see what in the world was going forward.' She came down the stairs as she spoke, and saw Ludovic. Her eyebrows went up, but she said placidly: 'I see I've thrust myself into an adventure. Is he badly hurt?'

'I think he's dying,' answered Eustacie tragically. 'He has bled, and bled, and bled!'

The lady put down her candle and came to the settle. 'That sounds very bad, certainly, but perhaps it is not desperate after all,' she said. 'Shall we see where he is hurt?'

'Nye said I was not to touch him,' replied Eustacie doubtfully.

'Oh, he's a friend of Nye's, is he?' said the lady.

'No – at least, yes, in a way he is. He is my cousin, but you must not ask me anything about him, and you must not tell anyone that you have ever seen him!'

'Very well, I won't,' said the lady imperturbably.

At that moment the landlord came into the coffee-room from the back of the house, followed by a little man with a wizened, leathery face and thin legs. When he saw the tall woman, Nye looked very much discomfited, and said in his deep, rough voice: 'I beg your pardon, ma'am: you've been disturbed. It's nothing – naught but a lad I know who's been getting into trouble through a bit of poaching.'

'Of course, he would be poaching in the middle of February,' agreed the lady. 'You had better get him to bed and take a look at his hurt.'

'It's what I'm going to do, ma'am,' returned Nye in a grim voice. 'Take his legs, Clem!'

Eustacie watched the two men carefully lift her cousin from the settle and begin to carry him upstairs, and turned her attention to the tall woman, who was regarding her with a kind of amused interest. 'I dare say it seems very odd to you,' she said austerely, 'but you should not have come downstairs.'

'I know,' apologized the lady, 'but pray don't tell me to go to bed again, for I couldn't sleep a wink with an adventure going on under my very nose! Let me present myself to you: I'm one Sarah Thane, a creature of no importance at all, travelling to London with my brother, whom you may hear snoring upstairs.'

'Oh!' said Eustacie. 'Of course, if you quite understand that this is a very secret affair——'

'Oh, I do!' said Miss Thane earnestly.

'But I must warn you that there is a great deal of danger.'

'Nothing could be better!' declared Miss Thane. 'You must know that I have hitherto led the most humdrum existence.'

'Do you, too, like adventure?' asked Eustacie, looking her over with a more lenient eye.

'My dear ma'am, I have been looking for adventure all my life!'

'Well,' said Eustacie darkly, 'this is an adventure of the most romantic, and it is certain that my cousin Tris—— that people will come to search for me. You must promise not to betray me, and in particular not my cousin Ludovic, who is not permitted to set foot in England, you understand.'

'No power on earth shall ring a syllable from me,' Miss Thane assured her.

'Then perhaps I will let you help me to conceal my cousin Ludovic,' said Eustacie handsomely. 'Only I think it will be better if I do not tell you anything at all until I have spoken with him, because I do not know him very well, and perhaps he would prefer that you should know nothing.'

'Oh no, don't tell me anything!' said Miss Thane. 'I feel it would almost spoil it for me if you explained it. You're not eloping with your cousin, by any chance?'

'But, of course, I am not eloping with him! *Voyons*, how could I elope with him when I have only just met him? It would be quite absurd!'

'Oh, if you have only just met him, I suppose it would,' agreed Miss Thane regretfully. 'It is a pity, for I have often thought that I should like to assist an elopement. However, one can't have everything. You know, I feel very strongly that we ought to see what can be done for that wound of his. Not that I wish to interfere, of course.'

'You are entirely right,' said Eustacie. 'I shall immediately go up to him. You may come with me if you like.'

'Thank you,' said Miss Thane meekly.

Joseph Nye had carried Ludovic to a little bedchamber at the back of the house and laid him upon his side on the chintz-hung bed. The tapster was kindling a fire in the grate, and Nye had just taken off Ludovic's coat and laid bare his shoulder when the two women came into the room.

Eustacie shuddered at the sight of the ugly wound, still sluggishly bleeding, but Miss Thane went up to the bed and watched what Nye was about. In spite of their size, his hands were deft enough. Miss Thane nodded, as though satisfied, and said: 'Can you get the bullet out, do you think?'

'Ay, but I'll want water and bandages. Clem! leave that and fetch me a bowl and all the linen you can find!'

'You had better bring some brandy as well,' added Miss Thane, taking the bellows out of the tapster's hands and beginning to ply them.

Eustacie, standing at the foot of the bed, watched Nye draw from his pocket a clasp-knife and open it, and somewhat hastily quitted her post. 'I think,' she said in a rather faint voice, 'that it will be better if it is I who attend to the fire, mademoiselle, and you who assist Nye. It is not that I do not like blood,' she explained, 'but I find that I do not wish to watch him dig bullets out of my cousin Ludovic.'

Miss Thane at once surrendered the bellows into her charge, saying that such scruples were readily understandable. Clem came back in a few minutes with a bowl and a quantity of old linen, and for quite some time Eustacie kept her attention strictly confined to the fire.

Miss Thane, finding that the landlord knew what he was about, silently did what he told her, offering no criticism. Only when he had extracted the bullet and was bathing the wound did she venture to inquire in a low voice whether he thought any vital spot had been touched. Nye shook his head.

'I'll get some Basilicum Powder,' said Miss Thane, and went softly away to her own room.

By the time the powder had been applied and the shoulder bandaged, Ludovic was showing signs of recovering consciousness. Miss Thane's hartshorn held under his nose made his eyelids flutter, and a little neat brandy administered by Nye brought him fully to his senses. He opened a pair of dazed blue eyes, and blinked uncomprehendingly at the landlord.

'Eh, Mr. Ludovic, that's better!' Nye said.

Ludovic's gaze wandered past him to Miss Thane, dwelt on her for a frowning moment, and returned to the contemplation of Nye's square countenance. A look of recognition dawned. 'Joe?' said Ludovic in a faint, puzzled voice.

'Ay, it's Joe, sir. Do you take it easy, now!'

Remembrance came back to Ludovic. He struggled up on his sound elbow. 'Damn that Exciseman! The child – a cousin of mine – where is she?'

Eustacie at the first sound of his voice had dropped the bellows and flown to the bedside. 'I'm here, *mon cousin!*' she said, dropping on her knees beside him.

He put out his sound hand and took her chin in it, turning her face up that he might scrutinize it. 'I've been wanting to look at you, my little cousin,' he said. A smile hovered round his mouth. 'I thought as much! You're as pretty as any picture.' He saw a tear sparkling on her cheek, and said at once: 'What are you crying for? Don't you like your romantic cousin Ludovic?'

'Oh yes, but I thought you were going to die!'

'Lord, no!' he said cheerfully. He let Nye put him back on to the pillows, and drew Eustacie's hand to his lips, and kissed it. 'You must promise me you'll not go further with this trip of yours to London. It won't do.'

'Oh no, of course I shall not! I shall stay with you.'

'Egad, I wish you could!' he said.

'But certainly I can. Why should I not?'

'*Les convenances*,' murmured Ludovic.

'Ah bah, I do not regard them! When one is engaged upon an adventure it is not the time to be thinking of such things. Besides, if I do not stay with you, I shall have to marry Tristram, because I have lost both my band-boxes, which makes it impossible that I should any longer go to London.'

'Oh well, you can't marry Tristram, that's certain!' said Ludovic, apparently impressed by this reasoning.

Nye interposed at this point. 'Mr. Ludovic, what be you doing here?' he demanded. 'Have you gone crazy to come into the Weald? Who shot you?'

'Some damned Exciseman. We landed a cargo of brandy and rum two nights ago, and I'd fancy to learn what's been going forward here. I came up with Abel.'

Nye laid a quick hand across his lips and glanced warningly in Miss Thane's direction.

'You needn't regard me,' she said encouragingly. 'I am pledged to secrecy.'

Ludovic turned his head to look at her. 'I beg pardon, but who in thunder are you?' he said.

'It's Miss Thane, sir, who's putting up in the house.'

'Yes,' interrupted Eustacie, 'and I think she is truly very sensible, *mon cousin*, and she would like infinitely to help us.'

'But we don't want any help!'

'Certainly we want help, because Tristram will search for me, and perhaps the Excisemen for you, and you must be hidden.'

'And that's true, too,' muttered Nye. 'You'll stay where you are to-night, sir, but it ain't safe for longer. I'll have you where you can slip into the cellar if the alarm's raised.'

'I'll be damned if I'll be put in any cellar!' said Ludovic. 'I'll be off as soon as I can stand on my feet.'

'No, you will not,' said Eustacie. 'I have quite decided that you must stop being a free-trader and become instead Lord Lavenham.'

'That seems to me a most excellent idea,' remarked Miss Thane. 'I suppose it will be quite easy?'

'If Sylvester's dead, I am Lord Lavenham, but it don't help me. I can't stay in England.'

'But we are going to discover who it was who killed that man whose name I cannot remember,' explained Eustacie.

'Oh, are we?' said Ludovic. 'I'm agreeable, but how are we going to set about it?'

'Well, I do not know yet, but we shall arrange a plan, and I think perhaps Miss Thane might be very useful, because she seems to me to be a person of large ideas, and when it is shown to her that she holds your life in her hands, she will be interested, and wish to assist us.'

'Do I really hold his life in my hands?' inquired Miss Thane. 'If that's so, of course I'm interested. I will certainly assist you. In fact, I wouldn't be left out of this for the world.'

Ludovic moved on his pillows, and said with a grimace of pain: 'You seem to know so much, ma'am, that you may as well know also that I am wanted by the Law for murder!'

'Are you?' said Miss Thane, gently removing one of the pillows. 'How shocking! Do you think you could get a little sleep if we left you?'

He looked up into her face and gave a weak laugh. 'Ma'am, take care of my cousin for me till morning, and I shall be very much in your debt.'

'Why, certainly!' said Miss Thane in her placid way.

Ten minutes later Eustacie was ensconced in a chair by the fire in Miss Thane's bedchamber, gratefully sipping a cup of hot milk. Miss Thane sat down beside her, and said with her friendly smile: 'I hope you mean to tell me all about it, for I'm dying of curiosity, and I don't even know your name.'

Eustacie considered her for a moment. 'Well, I think I will tell you,' she decided. 'I am Eustacie de Vauban, and my cousin Ludovic is Lord Lavenham of Lavenham Court. He is the tenth Baron.'

Miss Thane shook her head. 'It just shows how easily one may be mistaken,' she said. 'I thought he was a smuggler.'

'He prefers,' said Eustacie, with dignity, 'that one should call him a free-trader.'

'I'm sorry,' apologized Miss Thane. 'Of course, it is a much better title. I should have known. What made him take to s—— free-trading? It seems a trifle unusual.'

'I see that I must explain to you the talisman ring,' said Eustacie, and drew a deep breath.

Miss Thane, a sympathetic listener, followed the story of the talisman ring with keen interest, only interpolating a question when the tale became too involved to be intelligible. She accepted Ludovic's innocence without the smallest hesitation, and said at the end of the recital that nothing would give her greater pleasure than to assist in unmasking the real culprit.

'Yes,' said Eustacie, 'and me, I think it was perhaps my cousin Tristram, for he has a collection of jewellery, and, besides, he is a person who might murder people – except that he is not at all romantic,' she added.

'He sounds very disagreeable,' said Miss Thane.

'He is – very! And, do you know, I have suddenly thought that perhaps I had better marry him, because then he would have to show me his collection, and if I found the talisman ring it would make everything right for Ludovic.'

Miss Thane bent down to poke the fire. She said with a slight tremor in her voice: 'But then if you did not find the ring it would be tiresome to have married him all to no purpose. And one has to consider that he might not wish to marry you.'

'Oh, but he does!' said Eustacie. 'In fact, we are betrothed. That is why I have run away. He has no conversation. Moreover, he said that if I went to London, I should not find myself in any way remarkable.'

'He was wrong,' said Miss Thane with conviction.

'Yes, I think he was wrong, but you see he is not *sympathique*, and he does not like women.'

Miss Thane blinked at her. 'Are you sure?' she said. 'I mean, if he wants to marry you——'

'But he does not *want* to marry me! It is just that he must have an heir, and because Grandpère made for us a *mariage de convenance*. Only Grand-père is dead now, and I am not going to marry a person who says that he would not care if I went to the guillotine in a tumbril!'

'Did he really say that?' inquired Miss Thane. 'He must be a positive Monster!'

'Well, no, he did not say exactly that,' admitted Eustacie. 'But when I asked him if he would not be sorry to see me, a *jeune fille*, in a tumbril, and dressed all in white, he said he would be sorry for anyone in a tumbril, "whatever their age or sex or – or apparel"!'

'You need say no more; I can see that he is a person of no sensibility,' said Miss Thane. 'I am not surprised that you ran away from him to join your cousin Ludovic.'

'Oh, I didn't!' replied Eustacie. 'I mean, I never knew I was going to meet Ludovic. I ran away to become a governess.'

'Forgive me,' said Miss Thane, 'but have you then just met your cousin Ludovic by chance, and for the first time?'

'But yes, I have told you! And he said I should not do for a governess.' She sighed. 'I wish I could think of something to be which is exciting! If only I were a man!'

'Yes,' agreed Miss Thane. 'I feel very strongly that you should have been a man and gone smuggling with your cousin.'

Eustacie threw her a glowing look. 'That is just what I should have liked! But Ludovic says they never take females with them.'

'How wretchedly selfish!' said Miss Thane in accents of disgust.

'Yes, but I think it is not perhaps entirely Ludovic's fault, for he said he liked to have me with him. But the others did not like it at all, in particular Ned, who wanted to hit me on the head.'

'Is Ned a s—— free-trader too?'

'Yes, and Abel. But they are not precisely free-traders, but only land-smugglers, which is, I think, a thing inferior.'

'It sounds quite inferior,' said Miss Thane. 'Did you meet your cousin Ludovic, and Ned, and Abel on your way here?'

'Yes, and when he seized me of course I thought Ludovic was the Headless Horseman!'

Miss Thane was regarding her as one entranced. 'Of course!' she echoed. 'I suppose you were expecting to meet a headless horseman?'

'Well,' replied Eustacie judicially, 'my maid told me that he rides the Forest, and that one finds him up on the crupper behind one, but my cousin Tristram said that it was only a legend.'

'The more I hear about your cousin Tristram,' said Miss Thane, 'the more I am convinced he is not at all the husband for you.'

'No, and what is more he is thirty-one years old, and he does not frequent gaming-hells or cock-pits, and when I asked him if he would ride *ventre à terre* to come to my death-bed, he said "Certainly not!"'

'This is more shocking than all the rest!' declared Miss Thane. 'He must be quite heartless!'

'Yes,' said Eustacie bitterly. 'He says I am not in the least likely to die.'

'A man like that,' pronounced Miss Thane, 'would be bound to say the Headless Horseman was only a legend.'

'That is what I thought, but my cousin Ludovic was not after all the Headless Horseman, and I must admit that I have not yet seen him – or the Dragon which was once in the Forest.'

'Really, you have had a very dull ride when one comes to think of it.'

'Yes, until I met my cousin Ludovic, and after that it was not dull, because when he discovered who I was Ludovic said I must go with him, and I helped to lead the Excisemen into the Forest. He mounted behind me on Rufus, you see. That was when I lost the other bandbox.'

'Oh, you had a bandbox?'

'But yes, I had two, for one must be practical, you understand. But one I dropped just before I met Ludovic, and I forgot about that one. We threw the other away.'

Miss Thane bent over the fire again rather hastily. 'I expect it was the right thing to do,' she said in an unsteady voice.

'Well, it was in the way,' explained Eustacie. 'But I must say it now becomes awkward a little because all my things were in it.'

'Don't let a miserable circumstance like that worry you!' said Miss Thane. 'I will lend you a nightdress, and to-morrow we will decide whether to go and look for the bandboxes (though I feel that would be a spiritless thing to do) or whether to break into your home at dead of night and steal some more clothes for you.'

This suggestion appealed instantly to Eustacie. While she got ready for bed she discussed with Miss Thane the various ways in which it might be possible to break into the Court. Miss Thane entered into every plan with an enthusiasm which made Eustacie say as she blew out the candle: 'I am *very* glad I have met you. I shall tell my cousin Ludovic that he must permit you to share the adventure.'

The excitements of the night had quite worn her out, and it was not long before she fell asleep, curled up beside Miss Thane in the big four-poster.

Sarah Thane lay awake for some little time. It seemed to her that she had undertaken a responsibility that would keep her well occupied during the immediate future. What would be the outcome of it all she had not the smallest idea, but she was fully determined, being entered into the adventure, to remain in it to the finish.

She was twenty-eight years old, an orphan, and for the past ten years had been living with her brother, an easy-going baronet some six or seven years her senior. Having been left in his ward, she considered, upon leaving school, that her proper place was at his side. Sir Hugh had not the least objection, so in defiance of several female relatives who one and all expressed the most complete disapproval she assumed control of the old manor-house in Gloucestershire, and when Sir Hugh took it into his head to travel (which was often) packed her trunks and went with him. For the past few years she had consented to take an elderly cousin with her as chaperon; the elderly cousin was indeed still nominally her chaperon, but she had long since ceased to accompany Sir Hugh and his sister upon their erratic journeys. For no one could deny that Sarah Thane was very well able to take care of herself, and the elderly cousin had not in the least enjoyed wandering about Europe in the wake of Sir Hugh's vague fancy. Sarah, on the other hand, enjoyed it so much that she had never yet been tempted to exchange the companionship of a brother for that of a husband.

She and Sir Hugh were, at the moment, on their way to town, having been visiting friends in the neighbourhood of Brighton. They had spent a dull fortnight, and were now intending to spend two or three months in London. Their presence at the Red Lion was attributable to two causes, the first being an incipient cold in Sir Hugh's head, and the second the excellence of Mr. Nye's brandy. Their original intention had been to stop only for a change of horses, but by the time they had arrived at Hand Cross it had begun to snow, and Sir Hugh had sneezed twice. While the horses were being taken out of the shafts, Sir Hugh, regarding the weather with a jaundiced eye, had let down the chaise-window to call for some brandy. It had been brought to him; he had taken one sip, and announced his intention of putting up at the Red Lion for the night.

'Just as you wish,' had said Miss Thane, most admirable of sisters. 'But I don't fancy the snow will amount to much.'

'Snow?' said Sir Hugh. 'Oh, the *snow*! I believe I'm going to have a demmed bad cold, Sally.'

'Then we had better push on to London,' said Miss Thane.

'This brandy,' said Sir Hugh earnestly, 'is some of the best I've tasted.'

'Oh!' said Miss Thane, instantly comprehending the situation, 'I see!'

That the excellence of the brandy was not a matter of interest to her was an objection she did not dream of putting forward. She was far too well used to Sir Hugh's vagaries not to accept them with equanimity, and she had followed him into the inn, resigning herself to a spell of inaction.

From this she seemed to have been miraculously saved. Sir Hugh might not know it, but there was now small chance of his journey being resumed upon the morrow. His sister had stumbled upon an adventure which appealed forcibly to her ever-lively sense of humour, and she had no intention of abandoning it.

In the morning she awoke before Eustacie, and got up out of bed without disturbing her. As soon as she was dressed she went along the passage to her brother's room, and found him sitting up in bed, with his night-cap still on, being waited on by the tapster, who seemed to combine his calling with the duties of a general factotum. A tray piled high with dishes was placed on a table by the bed: Sir Hugh was breakfasting.

He gave his sister a sleepy smile as she entered the room, and, of habit rather than of necessity, picked up his quizzing-glass, and through it inspected a plate of grilled ham and eggs from which Clem had lifted the cover. He nodded, and Clem heaved a sigh of relief.

Miss Thane, taking in at a glance the proportions of this breakfast, shook her head, and said: 'My dear, you must be very unwell indeed! Only one plate of ham, and those few wretched slices of beef to follow! How paltry!'

Sir Hugh, accustomed like so many large men to being a butt, received this sally with unruffled placidity, and waved Clem away. The tapster went out, and Miss Thane thoughtfully handed her brother the mustard. 'What are your engagements in town, Hugo?'

Sir Hugh reflected while masticating a mouthful of ham. 'Have I any?' he asked after a pause.

'I don't know. Should you mind remaining here for a time?'

'Not while the Chambertin lasts,' replied Sir Hugh simply. He consumed another mouthful, and added: 'It's my belief the liquor in this place never paid duty at any port.'

'No, I think it was probably all smuggled,' agreed Miss Thane. 'I met a smuggler last night, when you had gone to bed.'

'Oh, did you?' Sir Hugh washed down the ham with a draught of ale, and emerged from the tankard to say, as a thought occurred to him: 'You ought to more careful. Where did you meet him?'

'He arrived at the inn, very late, and wounded. He's here now.'

A faint interest gleamed in Sir Hugh's eye. He lowered his fork. 'Did he bring anything with him?'

'Yes, a lady,' said Miss Thane.

'No sense in that,' said Sir Hugh, his interest fading. He went on eating, but added in a moment: 'Couldn't have been a smuggler.'

'He is a smuggler, a nobleman, and one of the most handsome young men I have ever clapped eyes on,' said Miss Thane. 'Tell me now, did you ever hear of one Ludovic Lavenham?'

'No,' said Sir Hugh, exchanging his empty plate for one covered with slices of cold beef.

'Are you sure, Hugo? He was used to play cards at the Cocoa-Tree – rather a wild youth, I apprehend.'

'They fuzz the cards at the Cocoa-Tree,' said Sir Hugh. 'It's full of Greeks. Foulest play in town.'

'This boy lost a valuable ring at play there, and was afterwards accused of having shot the man he played against,' persisted Miss Thane.

'I was very nearly done-up myself there once,' said Sir Hugh reminiscently. 'Found a regular Captain Sharp at the table, thought the dice ran devilish queerly——'

'Yes, dear, but do you remember?'

'Of course I remember. Sent for a hammer, split the dice, and found they were up-hills, just as I'd expected.'

'No, not that,' said Miss Thane patiently. 'Do you recall this other affair?'

'What other affair?'

Miss Thane sighed, and began painstakingly to recount all that Eustacie had told her. Sir Hugh listened to her with an expression of considerable bewilderment, and at the end shook his head. 'It sounds a demmed silly story to me,' he said. 'You shouldn't talk to strangers.'

When it was conveyed to him that his sister had pledged herself to assist these strangers in whatever perilous course they might decide to adopt he at first protested as forcibly as a man of his natural indolence could be expected to, and finally begged her not to embroil him in any crazy adventure.

'I won't,' promised Miss Thane. 'But you must swear an oath of secrecy, Hugh!'

Sir Hugh laid down his knife and fork. 'Sally, what the deuce is all this about?' he demanded.

She laughed. 'My dear, I've scarcely any more notion than you have. But I am sure of my clear duty, which is to chaperon the little heroine. Moreover, I admit to a slight feeling of curiosity to see the wicked cousin. I am at present at a loss to decide whether Sir Tristram Shield is the villain of the piece or merely a plain man goaded to madness.'

'Shield?' repeated Sir Hugh. 'Member of Brooks's?'

'I don't know. Do you?'

'If he's the man I'm thinking of he hunts with the Quorn. Bruising rider to hounds. Good man in a turn-up, too.'

'This sounds very promising,' said Miss Thane.

'Spars with Mendoza,' pursued Sir Hugh. 'If he's the man, I've met him at Mendoza's place. But I dare say I'm thinking of someone else.'

'What is he like?' inquired Miss Thane.

'I've told you,' said Sir Hugh, buttering a slice of bread. 'He's got a right,' he added helpfully.

Miss Thane gave it up, and went back to her own bedchamber to see how her protégée did.

Eustacie, not a whit the worse for her adventure, was trying to arrange her hair before the mirror. As she had never attempted anything of the kind before the result was not entirely successful. Miss Thane laughed at her, and took the brush and the pins out of her hand. 'Let me do it for you,' she said. 'How do you feel this morning?'

Eustacie announced buoyantly that she had never felt better. Her first and most pressing desire was to see how her cousin did, so as soon as Miss Thane had finished dressing her hair they went off to the little back bedchamber.

Nye was with Ludovic, apparently trying to induce him to descend into the cellar. Ludovic, whose eyes were a trifle too bright and whose cheeks were rather flushed, was sitting up in bed with a bowl of thin gruel. As the two ladies came into the room he was saying carelessly: 'Don't croak so, Joe! I tell you I have it all fixed.' He looked up and greeted his visitors with a smile of pure mischief. 'Good morning, my cousin! Ma'am, your very obedient! Have you seen any Excisemen below-stairs yet?'

'Mr. Ludovic, I tell you your tracks lead right to my door, and there's blood on the snow!'

'You've told me that twice already,' said Ludovic, quite unmoved.

'Why don't you send Clem to clear the snow away?'

'I have sent him to clear it away, sir, but don't you realize they'll be able to trace you all the way from the Forest?'

'Of course I realize it! Haven't I made my plans? Eustacie, my sweet cousin, will you have me for your groom?'

'But yes, I will have you for anything you wish!' said Eustacie instantly.

His eyes danced. 'Will you so? Begad, if I can settle my affairs creditably I'll remind you of that!'

'Sir, will you listen to reason?' implored Nye.

An imperious finger admonished him. 'Quiet, you! I'll thank you to remember I'm in the saddle now, Joe.'

'Are you indeed, Mr. Ludovic? Well, I'll do no pillion-riding behind you, for well I know what will come of it!'

'Take away this gruel!' commanded Ludovic. 'And get it into your head that I'm not Mr. Ludovic! I'm mademoiselle's groom, whom the wicked smugglers fired at.' He cocked his head considering. 'I think I'll be called Jem,' he decided. 'Jem Brown.'

'No!' said Eustacie, revolted. 'It is a name of the most undistinguished.'

'Well, grooms aren't distinguished. I think it's a good name.'

'It is not. It will be better if you are Humphrey.'

'No, I'll be damned if I'll be called Humphrey! If there's one name I dislike that's it.'

Miss Thane interposed placably. 'Don't argue with him, Eustacie. It's my belief he's in a high fever.'

He grinned at her. 'I am,' he agreed. 'But my head's remarkably clear for all that.'

'Well, if it's clear enough to grapple with the details of this story of yours, tell us what became of the groom's horse,' said Miss Thane.

'The smugglers killed it,' offered Eustacie.

Ludovic shook his head. 'No, that won't do. No corpse. Damn the horse, it's a nuisance! Oh, I have it. When I was shot the brute threw me, and made off home.'

'Maddened by fright,' nodded Miss Thane. 'Well, I'm glad to have that point settled. I feel I can now face any number of Excisemen.'

'*Mon cousin*,' interrupted Eustacie suddenly, 'do you think it is Tristram who has your ring?'

The laugh vanished from Ludovic's eyes. 'I'd give something to know!'

'Well, but I must tell you that I thought of a very good plan last night,' said Eustacie. 'I will marry Tristram, and then I can search in his collection for the ring.'

'You'll do no such thing!' snapped Ludovic.

Nye said roughly: 'For shame, Mr. Ludovic! What's this unaccountable nonsense? Sir Tristram's no enemy of yours!'

'Is he not?' retorted Ludovic. 'Will you tell me who, besides myself, was in the Longshaw Spinney that accursed night?'

Nye's face darkened. 'Are you saying it was Sir Tristram as did a foul murder all for the sake of a trumpery ring, my lord? Eh, you're crazed!'

'I'm saying it was he who met me in the spinney, he who would have given his whole collection for that same trumpery ring! Didn't he always dislike me? Can you say he did not?'

'What I wish to say,' interrupted Miss Thane in a calm voice, 'is that I want my breakfast.'

Ludovic sank back on to his pillows with a short laugh. Nye, reminded of his duty, at once led both ladies down to the parlour, apologizing as he went for there being no one but himself and Clem to wait upon them. 'I've only my sister besides, who does the cooking,' he told them, 'and a couple of ostlers, of course. We don't get folk stopping here in the winter in the general way. Maybe it's as well, seeing who's under my roof, but I doubt it's not what you're accustomed to, ma'am.'

Miss Thane reassured him. He set a coffee-pot down on the table before her, and said gloomily: It's in my mind that no one in his senses would take Mr. Ludovic for a groom, ma'am. If you could get him only to see reason——! But there, he never did, and I doubt he never will! As to this notion he's taken into his head that 'tis Sir Tristram who has his ring, I never heard the like of it! It was Sir Tristram as got him out of England – ay, and in the very nick!'

'Yes, and my cousin Basil says that it was to make him a murderer confessed!' said Eustacie.

Nye looked at her from under his rugged brows. 'Ay, does he so? Well, I've not had the gloves on with Mr. Lavenham, miss, but I've sparred with Sir Tristram a-many times, and I say he's a clean-hitting gentleman! With your leave, ma'am, I'll go back to Mr. Ludovic now.'

He went out, and Miss Thane, pouring out two cups of coffee, said cheerfully: 'At all events there seems to be some doubt about Sir Tristram's guilt. I think, if I were you, I would not marry him until we can be positive he is the murderer.'

Upon reflection Eustacie agreed to the wisdom of this course. She ate a hearty breakfast, and returned to Ludovic's room, leaving Miss Thane in sole possession of the parlour. Miss Thane finished her meal in a leisurely fashion, and had gone out into the coffee-room, on her way to the stairs, when the sound of an arrival made her pause. An authoritative, not to say peremptory voice outside called the landlord by name, and the next moment the door was flung open and a tall gentleman in riding-dress strode in, carrying a somewhat battered bandbox in either hand. He checked at sight of Miss Thane, favouring her with a hard stare, and putting down the bandboxes, took off his hat, and bowed slightly. 'I beg your pardon: do you know where I may find the landlord?' he asked.

Miss Thane, one hand on the banisters, one foot on the bottom stair, looked at him keenly. A pair of stern, rather frowning grey eyes met hers with an expression of the most complete indifference. Miss Thane let go of the banisters, and came forward. 'Do tell me!' she said invitingly. 'Are you "my cousin Tristram"?'

CHAPTER 5

Sir Tristram's worried frown lightened. He stared at Miss Thane with an arrested look in his eyes, and his stern mouth relaxed a little. 'Oh!' he said slowly, and seemed for the first time to take stock of Sarah Thane. He saw before him a tall, graceful woman, with a quantity of light, curling brown hair, a generous mouth, and a pair of steady grey eyes which held a distinct twinkle. He noticed that she was dressed fashionably but without furbelows in a caraco jacket over a plain blue gown, a habit as nearly resembling a man's riding-dress as was seemly. She looked to be a sensible woman, and she was obviously gently born. Sir Tristram was thankful to think that his betrothed had (apparently) fallen into such unexceptionable hands, and said with a slight smile: 'Yes, I am Tristram Shield, ma'am. I am afraid you have the advantage of me?'

Miss Thane saw her duty clear before her, and answered at once: 'Let me beg of you to come into the parlour, Sir Tristram, and I will explain to you who I am.'

He looked rather surprised. 'Thank you, but as you have no doubt guessed, I am come in search of my cousin, Mademoiselle de Vauban.'

'Of course,' agreed Miss Thane, 'and if you will step into the parlour——'

'Is my cousin in the house?' interrupted Sir Tristram.

'Well, yes,' admitted Miss Thane, 'but I am not at all sure that you can see her. Come into the parlour, and I will see what can be done.'

Sir Tristram cast a glance up the stairs, and said in a voice edged with annoyance: 'Very well, ma'am, but why there should be any doubt about my seeing my cousin I am at a loss to understand.'

'I can tell you that too,' said Miss Thane, leading the way to the private parlour. She shut the door, and said cheerfully: 'One cannot after all be surprised. You have behaved with a shocking lack of sensibility, have you not?'

'I was not aware of it, ma'am. Nor do I know why my cousin should leave her home at dead of night and undertake a solitary journey to London.'

'She was wishful to become a governess,' explained Sarah.

He stared at her in the blankest surprise. 'Wishful to become a governess? Nonsense! Why should she wish anything of the kind?'

'Just for the sake of adventure,' said Miss Thane.

'I have yet to learn that a governess's life is adventurous!' he said. 'I should be grateful to you if you would tell me the truth!'

'Come, come, sir!' said Miss Thane pityingly, 'it must surely be within your knowledge that the eldest son of the house always falls in love with the governess, and elopes with her in the teeth of all opposition?'

Sir Tristram drew a breath. '*Does* he?' he said.

'Yes, but not, of course, until he has rescued her from an oubliette, and a band of masked ruffians set on to her by his mother,' said Miss Thane matter-of-factly. 'She has to suffer a good deal of persecution before she elopes.'

'I am of the opinion,' said Sir Tristram with asperity, 'that a little persecution would do my cousin a world of good! Her thirst for romance is likely to lead her into trouble. In fact, I was very much afraid that she had already run into trouble when I found her bandboxes upon the road. Perhaps, since she appears to have told you so much, she has also told you how she came to lose them?'

Miss Thane, perceiving that this question would lead her on to dangerous ground, mendaciously denied all knowledge of the bandboxes. She then made this discovery that Sir Tristram Shield's eyes were uncomfortably penetrating. She met their sceptical gaze with all the blandness she could summon to her aid.

'Indeed!' he said, politely incredulous. 'But perhaps you can tell me why, if she was bound for London by the night-mail, as her maid informed me, she is still in this inn?'

'Certainly!' said Sarah, rising to the occasion. 'She arrived too late for the mail, and was forced to put up for the night.'

'What did she do for night-gear?' inquired Shield.

'Oh, I lent her what she needed!'

'I suppose she did not think the loss of her baggage of sufficient interest to call for explanation?'

'To tell you the truth——' began Sarah confidingly.

'Thank you! I *should* like to hear the truth.'

'To tell you the truth,' repeated Sarah coldly, 'she had a fright, and the bandboxes broke loose.'

'What frightened her?'

'A Headless Horseman,' said Sarah.

He was frowning again. 'Headless Horseman? Fiddlesticks!'

'Very well,' said Sarah, as one making a concession, 'then it was a dragon.'

'I think,' said Sir Tristram in a very level voice, 'that it will be better if I see my cousin and hear her story from her own lips.'

'Not if you are going to approach it in this deplorable spirit,' replied Miss Thane. 'I dare say you would tell her there are no such things as dragons or headless horsemen!'

'Well?'

Miss Thane cast down her eyes to hide the laughter in them, and replied in a saddened tone: 'When she told me the whole I thought it impossible that anyone could be so devoid of all sensibility, but now that I have seen you I realize that she spoke no less than the melancholy truth. A man who could remain unaffected by the thought of a young girl, dressed in white, all alone, and in a tumbril——'

His brow cleared; he gave a short laugh. 'Does that rankle? But really I am past the age of being impressed by such absurdities.'

Miss Thane sighed. 'Perhaps *that* might be forgiven, but your heartlessness in refusing to ride *ventre à terre* to her death-bed——'

'Good God, surely she cannot have fled the house for such a ridiculous reason?' exclaimed Shield, considerably exasperated. 'Why she should continually be harping on the notion of her own death passes my comprehension! She seems to me a perfectly healthy young woman.'

Miss Thane looked at him in horror. 'You did not tell her *that*, I trust?'

'I don't know what I told her. I might very easily.'

'If I were you,' said Miss Thane, 'I would give up this idea you have of marrying your cousin. You would not suit.'

'I'm fast coming to that conclusion myself,' he said. 'Moreover, Miss—— What *is* your name?'

'Thane,' replied Sarah.

'Thane?' he repeated. 'I fancy I have met someone of that name, but I do not immediately recall——'

'At Mendoza's Saloon,' interpolated Sarah helpfully.

He looked a little amused. 'Yes, possibly. But do you——'

'Or even at Brooks's.'

'*I* am certainly a member.'

'My brother,' said Sarah. 'He is at present in bed, nursing a severe cold, but I dare say he will like to receive you.'

'It is extremely obliging of him, but my sole desire is to see my cousin, Miss Thane.'

Sarah, whose attention had been caught by the sound of an arrival, paid no heed to this hint, but peeped over the short window-blind. What she saw made her feel uneasy; she turned her head and requested Sir Tristram to come at once. 'Tell me,' she commanded, 'who are these two men in uniform?'

He came to the window. 'Only a couple of Excisemen,' he answered, after a casual glance.

'Oh, is *that* all?' said Miss Thane in rather a hollow voice. 'I expect they have come to see what Nye keeps in his cellars. My brother fancies it is all smuggled liquor.'

He looked at her in some perplexity. 'They won't find anything. May I remind you, ma'am, that I wish to see my cousin?'

Miss Thane, having watched one of the Excisemen dismount and go into the inn, was straining her ears to catch what was being said in the coffee-room. She heard the landlord's deep voice, and wondered whether he had succeeded in persuading Ludovic to descend into the cellar. She looked at Sir Tristram, reflecting that he could not have chosen a more inopportune moment for his arrival. She ought to get rid of him, she supposed, but he did not seem to be the sort of man to be easily fobbed off. She said confidentially: 'Do you know, I think it would be wisest if you were to leave your cousin with me for the present?'

'You are extremely good, ma'am, but I mean to carry her to my mother in Bath.'

'Backgammon?' said Miss Thane knowledgeably. 'She won't go. In fact, I hardly think it is worth your while to remain here, for she is set against seeing you.'

'Miss Thane', said Sir Tristram dangerously, 'it is quite evident to me that you are trying to prevent my seeing my cousin. I have not the smallest notion why she does not wish to see me. But I am going to see her. I trust I have made myself quite plain?'

'Yes, quite,' said Miss Thane, catching an echo of Eustacie's voice joined with Nye's in the coffee-room.

It seemed as though Shield had heard it too, for he turned his head towards the door, listening. Then he looked back at Sarah and said: 'You had better tell me at once, ma'am: what scrape is she in?'

'Oh, none at all!', Miss Thane assured him, and added sharply: 'Where are you going?'

'To find out for myself!' said Shield, opening the door, and striding off to the coffee-room.

Miss Thane, feeling that as an accomplice she had not been a success, followed him helplessly.

In the coffee-room were gathered the landlord, Mademoiselle de Vauban, an Excise officer, and the tapster. The Excise officer was looking suspiciously from Eustacie to Nye, and Eustacie was talking volubly and with a great deal of gesticulation. When she saw her cousin on the threshold she broke off, and stared at him in consternation. The landlord shot a look at Sir Tristram under his jutting brows, but said nothing.

'I'm sorry,' said Miss Thane, in answer to a reproachful glance from Eustacie. 'I could not stop him.'

'You should have stopped him!' said Eustacie. 'Now what are we going to do?'

Miss Thane turned to Sir Tristram. 'The truth is, my dear sir, that your cousin fell in with a band of smugglers last night upon the road here, and had a sad fright.'

'Smugglers?' repeated Shield.

'Yes,' averred Eustacie. 'And I am just telling this stupid person that it was I who came here last night, and not a smuggler.'

'Begging your pardon, sir,' said the riding-officer, 'but the young lady's telling me that she rid here last night to catch the mail-coach.' His tone inferred that he found the story incredible, as well he might.

'I'll have you know,' growled Nye, 'that the Red Lion's a respectable house! You'll find no smugglers here.'

'And it's my belief I'd find a deal you'd like to hide if I knew just where those cellars of yours are, Mr. Nye!' retorted the Exciseman. 'It's a fine tale you've hatched, and Miss knowing no better than to back you up in it, but you don't gammon me so easily! Ay, you've been careful to sweep the snow from your doorstep, but I've followed the trail down the road, and seen the blood on it!'

'Certainly you have seen the blood,' said Eustacie. 'There was a great deal of blood.'

'Miss, do you ask me to believe that you went galivanting about on horseback in the middle of the night? Come now, that won't do!'

'Yes, but you do not understand. I was making my escape,' said Eustacie.

'Making your *escape*, miss?'

'Yes, and my cousin here will tell you that what I say is true. I am Mademoiselle de Vauban, and I am the granddaughter of Lord Lavenham, and he is Sir Tristram Shield.'

The Exciseman seemed to be a little impressed by this. He touched his hat to Sir Tristram, but still looked unconvinced. 'Well, miss, and supposing you are, what call have you to go riding off in the night? I never heard of the Quality doing such!'

'I was running away from Sir Tristram,' said Eustacie.

'Oh!' said the Exciseman, looking more dubious than ever.

Sir Tristram stood like a rock. Miss Thane, taking one look at his outraged profile, was shaken by inward laughter, and said unsteadily: 'This is a – a matter of no little delicacy, you understand?'

'I'm bound to say I don't, ma'am,' said the Exciseman bluntly. 'What for would the young lady want to run away from her cousin?'

'Because he would have forced me to marry him!' said Eustacie recklessly.

The Exciseman cast a glance of considerable respect at Sir Tristram, and said: 'Well, but surely to goodness, miss——'

'My grandfather is dead, and I am quite in my cousin's power,' announced Eustacie. 'And when I was on my way here I met the smugglers. And I was naturally very much afraid, and they were too, because they fired at my groom, and wounded him, and he fell off his horse with *both* my bandboxes.'

Sir Tristram continued to preserve a grim silence, but at mention of the groom a slight frown knit his brows, and he looked intently at Eustacie.

'Indeed, miss?' said the Exciseman. 'Then it queers me how there come to be only the tracks of one horse down the road!'

'The other horse bolted, of course,' said Eustacie. 'It went back to its stable.'

'Maddened by fright,' murmured Miss Thane, and encountered a glance from Shield which spoke volumes.

'And may I inquire, miss, how you come to know that the horse went back to its stable?'

Miss Thane held Sir Tristram's eye with her own. 'Why, Sir Tristram here has just been telling us!' she said with calm audacity. 'When the riderless horse arrived at the Court he at once feared some mishap had overtaken his cousin, and set out to ride – *ventre à terre* – to the rescue. Is that not so, dear sir?'

Aware of one compelling pair of humorous grey eyes upon him, and one imploring pair of black ones, Sir Tristram said: 'Just so, ma'am.'

The look he received from his cousin should have rewarded him. Eustacie said: 'And then I must tell you that I took my poor groom up behind me on my own horse, but I did not know the way very well, and he was too faint to direct me, and so I was lost a long time in the Forest.'

The Exciseman scratched his chin. 'I'll take a look at this groom of yours, miss, if it's all the same to you. I'm not saying I don't believe your story, but what I do say is that ladies take queer notions into their heads when it comes to wounded men, and the late lord – begging your pardon, sir, and miss – was never one to help us officers against them pesky smugglers, any more than what most of the gentry hereabout are!'

'Help a smuggler?' said Miss Thane in shocked accents. 'My good man, do you know that you are addressing the sister of a Justice of the Peace?

Let me tell you that my brother, who is in the house at this moment, holds the strongest views on smugglers and smuggled goods!' This, after all, she reflected, was quite true, and ought to impress the Exciseman – provided, of course, that Sir Hugh did not take it into his head to appear suddenly and explain the nature of his views.

The Exciseman certainly seemed rather shaken. He looked uncertainly from Miss Thane to Eustacie, and said in a sulky voice that his orders were to search the house.

'Oh, they are, are they?' said Nye. 'P'raps you'd like to go and tell Sir Hugh Thane yourself that you're wishful to search his bedchamber? And him a Justice, like miss has told you! You get out of this before I lose my temper, that's my advice to you!'

'You lay a hand on me and you'll suffer for it, Mr. Nye!' said the Exciseman, keeping a wary eye on the landlord's massive form.

'Just a moment!' said Sir Tristram. 'There is no need for all this to-do. If you suspect my cousin's groom of being a smuggler——'

'Well, sir, we fired on one last night, and I'm ready to swear we hit him. And it can't be denied that females is notably soft-hearted when it comes to a wounded man!'

'Possibly,' said Shield, 'but I am not soft-hearted, nor am I in the habit of assisting smugglers, or any other kind of law-breaker.'

'No, sir,' said the Exciseman, abashed by Sir Tristram's blighting tone. 'I'm sure I didn't mean——'

'If the wounded man is indeed a groom from the Court I shall recognize him,' continued Shield. 'The affair can quite easily be settled by taking me to his room.'

There was one moment's frozen silence. Sir Tristram was looking not at the Exciseman, but at Eustacie, who had turned as white as her fichu, and was staring at him in patent horror.

Nye's voice broke the silence. 'And that's a mighty sound notion, sir!' he said deliberately. 'I'll lay your honour knows the lad as well as I do myself.'

Sir Tristram's eyes narrowed. 'Do I?' he said.

Eustacie said breathlessly: 'You cannot see him! He is in a fever!'

'Never you fret, miss,' said Nye. 'Sir Tristram's not one to go blaming the lad for doing what you ordered him to, nor he won't do anything to upset him. If you'll come upstairs, sir, I'll take you to him right away.'

'Begging your pardon, but I'd as lief come too,' said the Exciseman firmly.

'That's it, Nosy, you come!' replied Nye. 'No one ain't stopping you.'

Eustacie moved swiftly to the foot of the stairs, as though she would bar the way, but before she could speak Miss Thane was at her side, and had swept her forward, up the stairs, with an arm round her waist. 'Yes, my love, by all means let us go too, in case the lad should be alarmed at having to face Sir Tristram.'

'He must not see him! He must not!' whispered Eustacie, anguished.

'In my back bedchamber, sir,' said Nye loudly. 'I always house smugglers there to be handy for the riding-officers.'

This withering piece of sarcasm made the Exciseman say, defensively, that he was only trying to do his duty. Nye ignored him, and threw open the door of the back bedchamber, saying: 'Step in, Sir Tristram: I know I needn't warn you not to go for to startle a sick lad.'

A small, insistent had grasped Sir Tristram's coat-sleeve. He glanced down into Eustacie's white face, saw in it entreaty and alarm, and shaking off her hand strode into the room.

Ludovic had raised himself on his elbow. Across the room his strained blue eyes met Shield's hard grey ones. Shield checked for an instant on the threshold, while Miss Thane gave Eustacie's hand a reassuring squeeze, and the Exciseman said hopefully: 'Do you know him, sir?'

'Very well indeed,' replied Shield coolly. He went forward to the bed, and laid a hand on Ludovic's shoulder. 'Well, my lad, you have got yourself into trouble through this piece of folly. Lie down now: I'll talk to you later.' He turned, addressing the Exciseman: 'I can vouch for this fellow. He does not look very like a smuggler, do you think?'

'No, sir, I'm bound to say he don't,' said the Exciseman slowly, staring at Ludovic. 'I'd say he looked uncommon like the old lord – from what I remember. It's the nose. It ain't a nose one forgets, somehow.'

'It's a nose often seen in these parts,' said Sir Tristram with dry significance.

The Exciseman blinked at him for a moment, and then, as light broke in on him, said hurriedly: 'Oh, that's the way it is! I beg pardon, I'm sure! No offence meant! If you can vouch for the young fellow of course I ain't got no more to say, sir.'

'Then if you ain't got no more to say you can take yourself off!' said Nye, thrusting him out of the room. 'It don't do the house any good having your kind in it. Next you'll be telling me I've got smuggled liquor in my cellar!'

'And so you have!' rejoined the Exciseman immediately.

The door closed behind them; those in the little chamber could hear the altercation gradually growing fainter as Nye shepherded his unwelcome guest down the stairs.

No one moved or spoke until the voices had died away. Then Eustacie caught Sir Tristram's hand, and pressed it to her cheek, saying simply: 'I will do anything you wish. I will even marry you!'

'Oh no, you will not!' exploded Ludovic, struggling to sit up. 'If this last don't beat all! What the devil did you mean by telling that long-nosed tidesman that I'm one of Sylvester's by-blows?'

'But no, Ludovic, no! I find that was very clever of him!' protested Eustacie. 'Did you not think so, Sarah?'

Miss Thane said gravely: 'I'm lost in admiration of so quick a wit. You never told me he was such an excellent conspirator.'

'Well, truly I did not think that he would be,' confessed Eustacie.

Sir Tristram, ignoring the interchange, said: 'In God's name, Ludovic, what are you doing here?'

'Free-trading,' replied Ludovic, with complete sang-froid.

Shield's face darkened. 'Are you jesting?'

'No, no, he really is a smuggler, Cousin Tristram!' said Eustacie earnestly. 'It is very romantic, I think. Do not you?'

'No, I do not!' said Shield. 'Hasn't your name been smirched enough, you young fool? Smuggling! And you can lie there and blandly tell me of it!'

'You see!' Eustacie made a disgusted face at Miss Thane.

'Yes, he seems to have no feeling for romance at all,' agreed Sarah.

Ludovic said savagely: 'You may be thankful I can do nothing but lie here! Do you think I care whether I'm hanged for a free-trader or a murderer? I'm ruined, aren't I? Then, damn it, I'll go to the devil my own way!'

'I don't want to interrupt you,' said Miss Thane, 'but you'll find yourself with the devil sooner than you think for if that wound of yours starts bleeding again.'

'Ah, let be!' Ludovic said, his right hand clenching on the coverlet.

Sir Tristram was looking at that hand. He bent, and grasped Ludovic's wrist, and lifted it, staring at the bare fingers. 'Show me your other hand!' he said harshly.

Ludovic's lips twisted into a bitter smile. He wrenched his wrist out of Shield's hold, and put back the bedclothes to show his left arm in a sling. The fingers were as bare as those of his right hand.

Sir Tristram raised his eyes to that haggard young face. 'If you had it it would never leave your finger!' he said. 'Ludovic, where is the ring?'

'Famous!' mocked Ludovic. 'Brazen it out, Tristram! Where is the ring indeed? *You* do not know, of course!'

'What the devil do you mean by that?' demanded Shield, in a voice that made Eustacie jump.

Ludovic flung off Miss Thane's restraining hand, and sat up as though moved by a spring. 'You know what I mean!' he said, quick and panting. 'You laid your plans very skilfully, my clever cousin, and you took care to ship me out of England before I'd time to think who, besides myself, could want the ring more than anything on earth! Does it grace your collection now? Tell me, does it give you satisfaction when you look at it?'

'If you were not a wounded man I'd give you the thrashing of your life, Ludovic!' said Shield, very white about the mouth. 'I have stood veiled hints from Basil, but not even he dare say to my face what you have said!'

'Basil – Basil believed in me!' Ludovic gasped. 'It was you – you!'

Miss Thane caught him as he fell back, and lowered him on to his pillows. 'Now see what you have done!' she said severely. 'Hartshorn, Eustacie!'

'I would like very much to kill you!' Eustacie told her cousin fiercely, and bent over the bed, holding the hartshorn under Ludovic's nose.

He came round in a minute or two, and opened his eyes. 'Tristram!' he muttered. 'My ring, Tristram!'

Shield brought a glass of water to the bed, and, raising Ludovic, held it to his lips. 'Drink this, and don't be a fool!'

'Damn you, take your hands off me!' Ludovic whispered.

Sir Tristram paid no heed to this, but obliged him to drink some of the water. He laid him down again, and handed the glass to Miss Thane. 'Listen to me!' he said, standing over Ludovic. 'I never had your ring in my hands in my life. Until this moment I would have sworn it was in your possession.'

Ludovic had averted his face, but he turned his head at that. 'If you have not got it who has?' he said wearily.

'I don't know, but I'll do my best to find out,' replied Shield.

Eustacie drew a deep breath. I see that I have misjudged you, Cousin Tristram,' she said handsomely. 'One must make reparation, *enfin*. I will marry you.'

'Thank you,' said Sir Tristram, 'but the matter does not call for such a sacrifice as that, I assure you.' He saw a certain raptness steal into her eyes, and added: 'Don't waste time picturing yourself in the rôle of a martyred bride, I beg of you! I haven't the smallest desire to marry you.'

Eustacie frowned. 'But you must have an——'

'Yes, we won't go into that again,' he said hastily.

'And I think,' continued Eustacie, visibly attracted by the vision of herself as a martyred bride, 'that perhaps it is my duty to marry you.'

Ludovic raised his head from the pillows. 'Well, you can't marry him. I'm the head of the family now, and I forbid it.'

'Oh, very well!' submitted Eustacie. 'I dare say I should not like always to be a sacrifice, after all.'

'Am I to understand,' inquired Miss Thane, 'that Sir Tristram is to become one of us? If you are satisfied he is not the villain it is not for me to raise objections, of course, but I must say I am disappointed. We shall have to remake all our plans.'

'Yes, we shall,' agreed Eustacie. 'And that reminds me that if Tristram truly did not steal Ludovic's ring, there is not any need for me to marry him. I had forgotten.'

Sir Tristram looked rather startled, observing which, Miss Thane said kindly: 'You must know that we had it all fixed that Eustacie was to marry you so as to be able to search in your collection for the missing ring.'

'What a splendid notion, to be sure!' said Sir Tristram sardonically.

'Yes, it was, wasn't it?' said Eustacie. 'But now we do not know who is the villain, so it is of no use.'

Ludovic was watching Shield intently. 'Tristram, you know something!'

Shield glanced down at him. 'No. But Plunkett was shot by someone who wanted the talisman ring and only that. If you were not the man I know of only one other who could have done it.'

Ludovic raised himself slightly, staring at his cousin with knit brows. 'My God, but he believed me! He was the only one who believed me!'

'So implicitly,' said Shield, 'that he advised you to face your trial – with evidence enough against you to hang you twice over! Have *you* never wondered why he did that?'

Ludovic made a gesture as though brushing it aside. 'Oh, I guessed he would be glad to step into my shoes, but damme, he would not run the risk of committing murder – he of all men!'

Eustacie gave a joyful shriek. 'Basil!' she exclaimed, clapping her hands together. 'Yes, yes, of a certainty it was he! Why did I not think of that before? Miss Thane, it is my cousin Basil who is the villain, and although you do not know him I assure you it is much, much better, because he wears a silly hat, and I do not at all like him!'

'Oh well, in that case I am perfectly willing to have him for the villain in Sir Tristram's place,' said Sarah. 'I did not like to seem to criticize your choice, but to tell you the truth, Sir Tristram is not sinister enough for my taste.'

Sir Tristram looked a little amused. Ludovic said: 'Wait, Eustacie, wait! This is not certain! Let me think!'

'But there is not any need to think, *mon cousin*. It is clear to me that Basil is the man, because he wants very much to be Lord Lavenham, and besides, there is no one else.'

'I can't believe he'd put his neck in such jeopardy!' Ludovic said. 'When did the Beau ever court a risk?'

'Whoever did it, Ludovic, was able to obtain a handkerchief of yours to leave beside the body,' Shield reminded him. 'He must also have known that Plunkett was dining at Slaugham that evening, and guessed at least that he would return by the path through the Longshaw Spinney.'

'Yes, but to plan a cold-blooded murder just to dispose of me, and then pretend belief in my story—— No, surely he could not do it!'

'Hush!' said Miss Thane impressively. 'The whole affair is becoming as clear as daylight to me. He did not plan it; I dare say he never went beyond wishing that some accident would befall Ludovic – oh, I beg your pardon! – befall Lord Lavenham——'

'"Ludovic" will do,' interposed his lordship, grinning up at her. 'I count you as quite one of the family.'

'I wish you may, for I assure you I regard myself as irrevocably bound to this adventure. Do not interrupt me! Let us say that he thought quite idly how fortunate it would be if Ludovic met with an accident. He would not dare to contrive one, for being the next in succession suspicion might fall on him. Well then, Ludovic lost his talisman ring, and Basil saw—— No, I am wrong! At first he saw nothing. But Ludovic began to play into his hands – really, Ludovic, I believe it was all your fault: you tempted Basil beyond what he could resist.'

'I did not!' said Ludovic indignantly.

'You know nothing of the matter, my dear boy. You and Chance between you showed Basil how he could be rid of you. You became enraged with the man whose name Eustacie cannot remember (or I, for that matter), and I dare say you were drinking heavily, and——'

'He was,' said Sir Tristram.

'Of course. He was in a mood for violence. I've no doubt he talked very wildly, and swore he would be avenged. Now you must think, Ludovic, if you please! Did not Basil know that you meant to waylay that man upon – upon the fatal night?'

'I don't know. I think I made no secret of it. Basil knew the whole story.'

'I am quite sure he did,' said Miss Thane. 'Now you see, do you not, how easy it was for him? It needed no planning at all. He had only to lie in wait for that man in the spinney, to leave a handkerchief of yours beside the body, and to steal the ring. Afterwards he had nothing to do but enact the rôle of champion. I perceive that he must have a very subtle brain.' She closed her eyes, and said in a seer-like voice: 'He is, I am sure, a sinister person.'

'The Beau?' said Ludovic. 'No, he isn't!'

Miss Thane frowned. 'Nonsense, he must be!'

'Yes,' said Eustacie regretfully, 'but truly he is not.'

Miss Thane opened her eyes again. 'You put me out. What then is he like?'

'He is very civil,' said Eustacie. 'He has manners of the most polished.'

Miss Thane readjusted her ideas. 'I will allow him to be smooth-spoken. I think he smiles.'

'Yes, he does,' admitted Eustacie.

Miss Thane gave a shudder. 'His smile hides a wolfish soul!' she announced.

Ludovic burst out laughing. 'Devil a bit! There's nothing wolfish about him. He's a mighty pleasant fellow, and I'd have sworn not one to wish anybody harm.'

'Alas, it is true!' said Eustacie sadly. 'He is just nothing.'

Sir Tristram's eyebrows went up a shade. Miss Thane pointed a triumphant finger at him, and said: 'Sir Tristram knows better! A wolf, sir?'

He shook his head. 'No, I don't think I should put it quite like that, Miss Thane. He is pleasant enough – a little too pleasant. He purrs like a cat.'

'He does,' agreed Ludovic. 'But do you know any ill of him? I don't.'

'One thing,' replied Shield. 'I know that Sylvester mistrusted him.'

'Sylvester!' said Ludovic scornfully.

'Oh, Sylvester was no fool,' answered Shield.

'Good God, he mistrusted scores of people, me amongst them!'

'So little did he mistrust you,' said Shield, putting his hand into his waistcoat-pocket, 'that he bade me give you that if ever I should see you again, and tell you not to pledge it.'

Ludovic stared at the great ruby. 'Thunder and Turf, did he leave me *that?*'

'As you see. He asked me just before he died whether I thought your story had been true after all.'

'I dare swear you told him No,' remarked Ludovic, slipping the ring on to his finger.

'I did,' said Shield calmly. 'You must remember that I heard that shot not ten minutes after I had parted from you, and I knew what sort of a humour you were in.'

Ludovic shot a fiery glance. 'You thought me capable of murder, in fact!'

'I thought you three-parts drunk,' said Shield. 'I also thought you a rash young fool. I still think that. What possessed you to turn smuggler? Have you been sailing off the coast of Sussex all this time?'

' "Hovering" is the word,' said Ludovic, with a gleam of mischief. 'Free-trading seemed to me an occupation eminently suited to an outlaw. Besides, I always liked the sea.'

Sir Tristram said scathingly: 'I suppose that was reason enough.'

'Why not? I knew some of the Gentlemen, too, from old days. But I was never off these shores till now. Don't like 'em: there's too much creeping done, and the tidesmen are too cursed sharp. I've been helping to run cargoes of brandy and rum – under Bergen papers, you know –into Lincolnshire. That's the place, I can tell you. I've been dodging revenue cruisers for the past fifteen months. It's not a bad life, but the fact of the matter is I wasn't reared to it. I only came into Sussex to glean what news there might be from Nye.'

'But you will stay, *mon cousin*, won't you?' asked Eustacie anxiously.

'He can't stay,' Shield said. 'It was madness to come at all.'

Ludovic lifted his head, and regarded Sylvester's ring through half-closed eyes. 'I shall stay,' he said nonchalantly, 'and I shall find out who holds the talisman ring.'

'Ludovic, you may trust me to do all I can to discover it, but you must not be found here!'

'I'm not going to be found here,' replied Ludovic. 'You don't know Joe's cellars. I do.'

'Go over to Holland, and wait there,' Shield said. 'You can do no good here.'

'Oh yes, I can!' said Ludovic, turning his hand so that the jewel caught the light. 'Moreover, I'll be damned if I'll be elbowed out of my own business!'

'What can you hope to do in hiding that I cannot do openly?' asked Shield. 'Why add to your folly by running the risk of being arrested?'

'Because,' said Ludovic, at last raising his eyes from the ruby, 'if the Beau has the ring I know where to look for it.'

CHAPTER 6

This announcement produced all the effect upon the ladies which Ludovic could have desired. They gazed at him in surprise and admiration, breathlessly waiting for him to tell them more. Shield, not so easily impressed, said: 'If you really know where to look for it you had better tell me, and I'll do it for you.'

'That's just the trouble,' replied Ludovic shamelessly. 'I'm not at all sure of the place.' He saw Eustacie's face fall, and added: 'Oh, I should know it again if I saw it! The thing is that I'd be mighty hard put to it to direct anyone how to find it. I shall have to go myself.'

'Go where?' demanded Sir Tristram.

'Oh, to the Dower House!' replied Ludovic airily. 'There's a secret panel. You wouldn't know it.'

'A secret panel?' repeated Miss Thane in an awed voice. 'You mean actually a secret panel?'

Ludovic regarded her in some slight concern. 'Yes, why not?'

'I thought it too good to be true,' said Miss Thane. 'If there is one thing above all others I have wanted all my life to do it is to search for a secret panel! I suppose,' she added hopefully, 'it would be too much to expect to find an underground passage leading from the secret panel?'

Eustacie clasped her hands ecstatically. 'But yes, of course! An underground passage——'

'With bats and dead men's bones,' shuddered Miss Thane.

French common sense asserted itself. Eustacie frowned. 'Not bats, no. That is not reasonable. But certainly some bones, chained to the wall.'

'And damp – it must be damp!'

'Not damp; cobwebs,' put in Ludovic. 'Huge ones, which cling to you like——'

'Ghostly fingers!' supplied Miss Thane.

'Oh, Ludovic, there is a passage?' breathed Eustacie.

He laughed. 'Lord, no! It's just a priest's hole, that's all.'

'How wretched!' said Miss Thane, quite disgusted. 'It makes me lose all heart.'

'If there is not a passage we must do without one,' decreed Eustacie stoutly. 'One must be practical. *Tout même*, it is a pity there is not a passage. I thought it would lead from the Court to the Dower House. It would have been *magnifique*! We might have found treasure!'

'That is precisely what I was thinking,' agreed Miss Thane. 'An old iron chest, full of jewels.'

Sir Tristram broke in on these fancies with a somewhat withering comment. 'Since we are not searching for treasure, and no passage exists save in your imaginations, this discussion is singularly unprofitable,' he said. 'Where is the panel, Ludovic?'

'There you have the matter in a nutshell,' confessed Ludovic. 'I know my uncle used to use it as a strong-room, and I remember Sylvester showing it to me when I was a lad, but what I can't for the life of me recall is which room it's in.'

'That,' said Tristram, 'is, to say the least of it, unfortunate, since the Dower House is panelled almost throughout.'

'I think it's either in the library or the dining-room,' said Ludovic. 'There are two tiers of pillars with a lot of fluted pilasters and carvings. I dare say I shall recognize it when I see it. You twist one of the bosses on the frieze between the tiers, and one of the square panels below slides back.'

'How do you propose to see it?' asked Shield. 'The Beau is at the Dower House now, and means to stay there.'

'Well, I shall have to break in at night,' replied Ludovic.

'A very proper resolve,' approved Miss Thane, before Sir Tristram could condemn it. 'But something a trifle disturbing has occurred to me: are you sure that your cousin would have kept the ring?'

'Yes, for he would not dare sell it,' replied Ludovic at once.

'He would not perhaps have thrown it away?'

Ludovic shook his head. 'Not he. He knows its worth,' he answered simply.

'Oh well, in that case, all we have to do is to find the panel!' said Miss Thane.

Sir Tristram looked at her across Ludovic's bed. 'We?' he said.

'Certainly,' replied Sarah. 'Eustacie told me I might share the adventure.'

'You are surely not proposing to remain here!'

'Sir,' said Miss Thane. 'I shall remain here until we have cleared Ludovic's fair name.'

'But, of course!' said Eustacie, opening her eyes very wide. 'What else?'

Sir Tristram told her in a few brief words. When it was made plain to him that both ladies meant to play important parts in Ludovic's affair, and that neither of them would so much as listen to the notion of retiring, the one to London, the other to Bath, he said roundly that he would have nothing to do with so crazy an escapade. Eustacie at once replied with the utmost cordiality that he might retire from it with her good-will, but Ludovic objected that since his left arm would be useless for some little time, he would need Tristram to help him with his housebreaking.

'Do you imagine that I am going to break into Basil's house?' demanded Sir Tristram.

'Why not?' said Ludovic.

'Not only that,' said Miss Thane thoughtfully, 'but we might need you if there is to be any fighting. My brother tells me you have a Right.'

'If,' said Sir Tristram forcibly, 'you would all of you rid yourselves of the notion that you are living within the pages of one of Mrs. Radcliffe's romances, I should be grateful! Do you realize that tongues are already wagging up at the Court over Eustacie's ill-judged, unnecessary, and foolish flight? I dare swear the news of it has even now reached Basil's ears. If she remains here, what am I to tell him?'

'Let me think,' said Miss Thane.

'Don't put yourself to that trouble!' said Sir Tristram, with asperity. 'Eustacie must go to my mother in Bath.'

'I have it!' said Miss Thane, paying no heed to him. 'I knew Eustacie in Paris some years ago. Finding myself in the vicinity of her home, I sent to inform her of my arrival, whereupon the dear creature, misliking the Bath

scheme, formed the idea of putting herself under my protection. Unfortunately, you, Sir Tristram, knowing nothing of me, and being possessed of
a tyrannical disposition – I beg your pardon?'

'I did not speak,' replied Sir Tristram, eyeing her frostily.

Miss Thane met his look with one of limpid innocence. 'Oh, I quite
thought you did!'

'I choked,' explained Sir Tristram. 'Pray continue! You had reached
my tyrannical disposition.'

'Precisely,' nodded Sarah. 'You refused to accede to Eustacie's request,
thus leaving her no alternative to instant flight. But now that you have
seen me, you realize that I am a respectable female, altogether a proper
person to have the charge of a young lady, and you relent.'

The corners of his mouth twitched slightly. 'Do I?' he said.

'Certainly. We arrange that Eustacie will stay with me in London on a
visit. All is in train for our departure when my brother, finding his cold to
be no better, declares himself to be unable to risk the dangers of travel in
this inclement weather. Which reminds me,' she added, rising from her
chair, 'that I had better go and inform Hugh that his cold is worse.'

A little while later, coming down from Sir Hugh's bedchamber, she
found Sir Tristram waiting in the coffee-room. He looked up as she
rounded the bend in the stairs, and said sardonically: 'I trust you were
able to convince your brother, ma'am?'

'It was unnecessary,' she returned. 'Nye has taken him up a bottle of
Old Constantia. He thinks it would be foolhardy to brave the journey to
London until he is perfectly recovered.'

'I thought he held strong views on the subject of smuggled liquor?'
remarked Sir Tristram.

'He does,' replied Miss Thane, not in the least abashed. 'Very strong
views.' She went to the fire and seated herself on one of the high-backed
settles placed on either side of it. A gesture invited Sir Tristram to occupy
the other. 'I think those two children will make a match of it, do not you?'

'Ludovic cannot ask any woman to be his wife as matters now stand,' he
responded, frowning into the fire.

'Then we must certainly establish his innocence,' said Miss Thane.

He glanced up. 'Believe me, I should be glad to do anything in my
power to help the boy, but this coming into Sussex is madness!'

'Well,' said Miss Thane reasonably, 'he cannot be moved until his
wound is in some sort healed, so we must make the best of it. Tell me, do
you think his cousin Basil is indeed the real culprit?'

He was silent for a moment. At last he said: 'I may be prejudiced
against him. Its sounds fantastic, but I would not for the world have him
know of Ludovic's whereabouts now.' He looked at her searchingly.

'What is your part in this, Miss Thane?'

She laughed. 'My dear sir, my part is that of Eustacie's chaperon, of course. To tell you the truth, I have taken a liking to your romantic cousins, and I mean to see this adventure to a close.'

'You are very good, ma'am, but——'

'But you would do very much better without any females,' nodded Miss Thane.

'Yes,' said Sir Tristram bluntly. 'I should!'

'I expect you would,' said Miss Thane, quite without rancour. 'But if you imagine you can induce Eustacie to leave this place now that she has found her cousin Ludovic, you have a remarkably sanguine nature. And if you are bound to have Eustacie, you may just as well have me as well.'

'Certainly,' said Shield, 'but do you – does your brother realize that this is an adventure that is likely to lead us all to Newgate?'

'I do,' she replied placidly. 'I doubt whether my brother realizes anything beyond the facts of a cold in the head and a well-stocked cellar. If we do reach Newgate, perhaps you will be able to get us out again.'

'You are very intrepid!' he said, with a look of amusement.

'Sir,' said Miss Thane, 'during the course of the past twelve hours my life seems to have become so full of smugglers, Excisemen, and wicked cousins that I now feel I can face anything. What in the world possessed the boy to take to smuggling, by-the-by?'

'God knows! You might as well ask what possessed Eustacie to leave the Court at midnight to become a governess. They should deal extremely well together if ever they can be married.' He rose. 'I must go back and do what I can to avert suspicion. Somehow or other we must find this panel Ludovic speaks of before he can thrust his head into a noose.'

Miss Thane gave a discreet cough. 'Do you – er – place much dependence on the panel, Sir Tristram?'

'No, very little, but I place every dependence upon Ludovic's breaking into the Dower House in search of it,' he replied frankly. 'For the moment we have him tied by the heels, but that won't be for long, if I know him. They are tough stock, the Lavenhams.' He walked to the table and picked up his hat and riding-whip. 'I'll take my leave now. I fancy we have fobbed off the riding-officer, but there may be others. If you should want me, send Clem over to the Court with a message, and I'll come.'

She nodded. 'Meanwhile, is Ludovic in danger, do you think?'

'Not at Nye's hands, but if information were lodged against him at Bow Street by anyone suspecting his presence here, yes, in great danger.'

'And at his cousin's hands?'

He met her questioning look thoughtfully, and after a moment said:

'I may be wrong, but I believe so. There is a good deal at stake.' He tapped his riding-whip against his top-boot. 'It all turns on the talisman ring,' he said seriously. 'Whoever has that is the man who shot Plunkett. I must cultivate a more intimate acquaintance with the Beau.'

He took his leave of her and went out, calling for his horse to be brought round. Miss Thane saw him riding away, and went slowly back to her patient.

Had it been possible to have sent for a surgeon to attend Ludovic, cupping would certainly have been prescribed. Miss Thane was a little anxious lest serious fever should set in, but both Shield and the landlord maintained that Ludovic had a strong enough constitution to weather worse things than a mere wound in his shoulder, and after a couple of days she was bound to acknowledge that they were right. The wound began to heal just as it should, and the patient announced his intention of leaving his sick-bed. This perilous resolve was frustrated by Shield, who, though he visited the Red Lion every day, omitted to bring with him the raiment he had promised to procure from Ludovic's abandoned wardrobe at the Court.

While Ludovic lay in the back bedchamber, either playing picquet with his cousin or evolving plans for the recovery of his ring, Sir Hugh Thane continued to occupy one of the front rooms. His cold really had been a great deal worse on the morning of Shield's first visit, and once having gained a hold on the unfortunate baronet, it ran the whole gamut of sore throat, thick head, watering eyes, loss of taste, and ended up with a cough on the chest which Sarah, with unwonted solicitude, declared to be bad enough to lead (if great care were not taken) to an inflammation of the lungs.

It was not, therefore, in the least difficult to persuade Sir Hugh to keep to his room. His only complaint was that he was without his valet, this indispensable person having gone to London in advance of his master with the major part of the baggage and Sarah's abigail. It took all Sarah's ingenuity to think out enough plausible reasons for not summoning Satchell to his master's sick-bed. Satchell had been in Sir Hugh's employment for some years, but Miss Thane did not feel that he could be trusted with the secret of Ludovic's presence at the Red Lion. Luckily Clem proved himself a deft attendant, and beyond remarking two or three times a day that he wished he had Satchell with him, Sir Hugh made no complaint. He accepted Sarah's story of the heiress fleeing from a distasteful marriage. It was doubtful whether the original tale of Ludovic's misfortunes occupied any place in his erratic memory, but he did once ask his sister whether she had not mentioned having met a smuggler. She admitted it, but said that he had left the inn.

'Oh!' said Sir Hugh. A pity. If you should see him again, you might let me know.'

What Sir Tristram Shield told Beau Lavenham the ladies did not know, but it brought him over to Hand Cross within two days. He came in his elegant chaise, a graceful affair slung on swan-neck perches, and upholstered with squabs of pale blue. He was ushered into the parlour, where Miss Thane and Eustacie were sitting, early one afternoon, and was greeted by his cousin with a baleful stare.

He had discarded his fur-lined cloak in the coffee-room, so that all the glory of his primrose pantaloons and lilac-striped coat burst upon Miss Thane without warning. He wore the fashionable short boot, and bunches of ribbons at the ends of his pantaloons; his cravat was monstrous, his coat collar very high at the back, and he carried a tall sugar-loaf hat in his hand. He paused in the doorway and lifted his ornate quizzing-glass, smiling. 'So here we have the little runaway!' he said. 'My dear cousin, all my felicitations! Poor, poor Tristram!'

'I do not know why you have come here,' responded Eustacie, 'but I do not at all wish to see you. It is my cousin, Sarah. This is my friend, Miss Thane, Basil.'

He bowed, a hand on his heart. 'Ah yes, the – er – acquaintance of Paris days, I believe. What a singularly happy chance it was that brought you to this unlikely spot, ma'am!'

'Yes, was it not?' agreed Miss Thane cordially. 'Though until my brother was took ill, I had really no notion of remaining here. But the opportunity of seeing my dear Eustacie again quite reconciled me to the necessity of putting up at this inn. Pray, will you not be seated?'

He thanked her, and took the chair she indicated, carefully setting his hat down upon the table. Looking at Eustacie with an amused glint in his eyes, he said: 'So you have decided not to marry Tristram after all! I liked the notion of your spirited flight to the arms of your friend. But how dark you kept her, my dear cousin! Now if only you had confided with me, I would have conveyed you to her in my carriage, and you would have been spared a singularly uncomfortable ride through the night.'

'I preferred to go myself,' said Eustacie. 'It was an adventure.'

He said: 'It is a pity you dislike me so much, and trust me so little, for I am very much your servant.'

To Miss Thane's surprise Eustacie smiled quite graciously, and answered: 'I do not dislike you: that is quite absurd. It is merely that I think you wear a silly hat, and, besides, I wanted to have an adventure all by myself.'

He gave his soft laugh. 'I wish you did not dislike my hat, but that can be remedied. Shall I wear an old-fashioned tricorne like Tristram, or do you favour the *chapeau-bras?*'

'You would look very odd in a *chapeau-bras*,' she commented.

'Yes, I am afraid you are right. Tell me, what do you mean to do with your life, Eustacie, now that you have given Tristram his *congé?*'

'I am going to stay in town with Miss Thane.'

He looked thoughtfully at Miss Thane. 'Yes? Have I Miss Thane's permission to call upon her in London?'

'Oh, but certainly! She will be delighted,' said Eustacie. '*Du vrai*, she would like very much to call upon you at the Dower House, because it is such a very old house, and that is with her a veritable passion. But I said, No, it would not be *convenable*.'

Miss Thane cast a look of considerable respect, and tried to assume the expression of an eager archaeologist.

The Beau said politely: 'I should be honoured by a visit from Miss Thane, but surely the Court would be better worth her study?'

'Yes, but you must know that I will not go to the Court with her,' said Eustacie glibly. 'Tristram is very angry, and I do not wish that there should be any awkwardness.'

The Beau raised his brows. 'Is Tristram importuning you to marry him?' he inquired.

Not having any exact knowledge of what Tristram had told him, Eustacie thought it prudent to return an evasive answer. She spread out her hands, and said darkly: 'It is that he gave his word to Grandpère, you know. I do not understand him.'

'Ah!' sighed the Beau, running his hand gently up and down the riband of his quizzing-glass. 'You are, of course, an heiress.' He let that shaft sink in, and continued smoothly: 'I have never been able to feel that you and Tristram were quite made for each other, but I confess your sudden flight took me by surprise. They tell me that your ride was fraught with adventure, too. Some tale of smugglers – but I dare say much exaggerated.'

'I suppose,' said Miss Thane opportunely, 'that there is a great deal of smuggling done in these parts?'

'I believe so,' he responded. 'I have always understood that my great-uncle encouraged the Trade.'

'Basil,' interrupted Eustacie, 'is it permitted that I bring Miss Thane to the Dower House one morning, perhaps? I thought that you would be like Tristram, and try to make me go to Bath, but now I see that you are truly *sympathique*, and I do not at all mind coming with Sarah to call on you.'

He looked at her for a moment. 'But, pray do!' he said. 'Have I not said that I shall count myself honoured?'

Miss Thane, summoning up every recollection of historical houses she had visited during the course of her travels, at once engaged him in conversation. Luckily she had her foreign journeys to draw upon. This she did with great enthusiasm, and no lack of imagination. The Beau was diverted from the topic of smugglers, and although his knowledge of antiques was slight and his interest in them almost non-existent, he was too well-bred to attempt to change the subject. Miss Thane kept his attention engaged for the remaining twenty minutes of his visit, and when he got up to go, thanked him profusely for his permission to visit the Dower House, and promised herself the treat of exploring his premises on the first day that offered. Eustacie thoughtfully reminded her that she would like to bring her sketching-book, to which she assented, as one in honour bound.

The Beau bowed himself out, was shepherded to his chaise by the mistrustful Nye, and drove off, watched from behind the parlour blinds by his gleeful cousin.

Miss Thane sank into a chair, and said: 'Eustacie, you are a wretch!'

'But no, but no!' Eustacie cried, dancing in triumph. 'You did so very well!'

'I am not at all sure that I convinced him. My dear, I know nothing of pictures, or wood-panelling! If he had not taken his leave of us when he did, my tongue must have run dry. I am convinced he thought me a chattering fool.'

'It does not matter in the least. We shall go to the Dower House, and while I talk to Basil you will find the secret panel and steal the ring!'

'Oh,' said Miss Thane blinking. 'Just – just find the panel and steal the ring. Yes, I see. I dare say it will be quite easy.'

'Certainly it will be easy, because I have thought of a very good plan, which is to pretend to Basil that I do not at all know what to do. I shall say to him that I have no one to advise me, and I am afraid of Tristram, and you will go away to draw a picture and you will see that he will be very glad to let you. Come, we must immediately tell Ludovic what we have done!'

Ludovic, when the scheme was breathlessly divulged to him, at first objected to it on the score that he had thought of a better plan. Once the coast was clear, he said, Abel Bundy would be bound to work his way up to the Red Lion to deliver his kegs of brandy, and to try to get news of him. If Tristram misliked the notion of breaking into the Dower House Abel, not so nice, would make a very good substitute.

'Yes, but it is altogether dangerous for you, and for us not at all,' Eustacie pointed out. 'Besides, I do *not* see that it is fair that you should keep the whole adventure to yourself.'

'Damme, it's my adventure, isn't it?'

'It is not your adventure. It is mine too, and also it is Sarah's and she will not help us any more if you do not share it with her.'

'Oh, very well!' said Ludovic. 'Not that I believe in this precious scheme of yours, mind you! Ten to one the Beau will suspect something. You can't hunt for the catch to the panel under his very nose.'

'*Entendu*, but I have provided. I shall desire to speak with Basil alone, and he will like that, and permit it.'

Ludovic eyed her somewhat narrowly. 'He will, will he?'

'Yes, because he has said that he would like to marry me.'

Ludovic sat up. 'I won't have you going up to the Dower House to let that fellow make love to you, so don't think it!'

'Not that, stupid! I shall ask for his advice, and he will not make love to me, because Sarah will be there.'

'She won't. She'll be hunting for the panel.'

'But I could scream if he tried to make love to me!'

'Ay, so you could. You've a mighty shrill scream, what's more. All the same, it's my belief the scheme will fail. It's a pity I can't recall which room the curst panel is in.'

'Yes, I have been feeling that, too,' agreed Miss Thane. 'I mean – it would be easier, wouldn't it?'

'In an adventure,' said Eustacie severely, 'it is not proper to have everything quite easy.'

Miss Thane was about to beg pardon when the sound of a quick, firm footstep on the stairs made them all look towards the door. It opened, but it was only Sir Tristram who came in, so that both ladies were able to relax their suddenly strained attitudes.

'Oh, it's you, is it?' said Ludovic, withdrawing his hand from under his pillows, where it had been grasping the butt of a serviceable pistol. 'Come in, and shut the door. Eustacie has thought of a plan. I don't say it's a good one, but it might answer.'

'Has the Beau been here?' Sir Tristram demanded.

'Yes, that's what put this scheme of hers into Eustacie's head. I wish I might have seen him. She tells me he has taken to wearing a lilac-striped coat.'

'I thought I could not be mistaken in his chaise. Why did he come?'

'He came to see me, and you must at once listen to me, *mon cousin*, because I have made a plot. I am going to take Sarah to the Dower House, because she has an *envie* to see it. I have told Basil that she likes old houses, and he was very content that she should see his. And when we are there I shall pretend that I wish to consult Basil, and while I am explaining to him how it is that I do not wish to marry you, Sarah will ask leave to make a drawing of the woodwork in the library. In that way she will be able to search for the secret panel, and when she has found it, she must steal the ring, and make just one little drawing to show Basil. Is it not a very good plot?'

'Yes,' said Shield, somewhat to her surprise, 'it is a good plot, but if you do find the ring you must on no account remove it, Miss Thane. Make a sketch of that particular portion of the frieze so that we may easily find it again, and leave the rest to me.'

'Certainly,' said Miss Thane. 'But there is just one thing——'

'Where's the sense in leaving it there?' interrupted Ludovic. 'I want my ring. I haven't had a day's good luck since I lost it.'

'There is just one thing,' began Miss Thane again, 'which perhaps I ought to——'

'Of course, he must have the ring at once!' declared Eustacie. 'Why should she leave it?'

'Because we must be able to prove that the ring is in the Beau's possession. Steal it, and it is merely a matter of your word against his. Once we can prove that the Beau has it, Ludovic is cleared. Until then Ludovic is the last person in the world to hold the ring. If Miss Thane can find the panel, and sketch the frieze for us——'

'Yes,' said Miss Thane. 'But I have been trying to tell you for quite some time now that there is a – a trifling hitch. I cannot draw.'

They stared at her in incredulity. 'Can't *draw*?' repeated Ludovic. 'Nonsense, of course you can! All females can draw!'

'I can't.'

'I thought,' said Sir Tristram, with a touch of scorn, 'that drawing and water-colour painting were taught in every young ladies' seminary?'

'They may be,' retorted Sarah, 'but I still cannot draw.'

'Well, why the devil can't you, if you were taught?' demanded Ludovic reasonably.

'I had no aptitude,' explained Sarah.

'But consider, Sarah!' said Eustacie. 'It is most important that you should be able to make just a *little* drawing!'

'I know,' said Sarah. 'I am very sorry, and I quite see that a person who is unable to draw is unfit to take part in any adventure.'

'It seems to me,' said Ludovic, 'that girls merely waste their time at school.'

'Yes, and what is worse, I have told Basil that she will bring her sketching-book,' added Eustacie. 'Now it appears that she has not got one, and we are quite undone.'

'If she can't draw, she can't,' said Sir Tristram. 'I shall have to join your party.'

Eustacie shook her head. 'No, because I have told Basil that I do not care to see you, and he would think it very odd if you were to be of my party.'

Sir Tristram gave a resigned sigh. 'You had better let me know at once just what lie it is you have told the Beau. What am I now held to have done?'

Eustacie's eyes twinkled wickedly. 'Well, you see, I had to make up a reason why I could not take Sarah to the Court, so I said that you were very angry with me.'

'Oh, is that all?' Sir Tristram sounded relieved.

Miss Thane, feeling that she had something to avenge, said meditatively: 'Yes, it was the Beau himself who suggested the rest. No one could really blame Eustacie.'

'The rest?'

'Oh, it was nothing to signify!' said Sarah, with an airy gesture. 'Mr. Lavenham just asked if you were still importuning Eustacie to marry you.'

'Why should I be doing anything of the sort?'

'On account of her being an heiress,' explained Sarah.

Sir Tristram said dryly: 'Of course. I should have thought of that. I trust neither of you will hesitate to vilify my character whenever it seems expedient to you to do so.'

'No, of course we shall not,' Miss Thane assured him.

'But you do not mind, *mon cousin*, do you?'

'On the contrary, I am becoming quite accustomed to it. But I'm afraid even your imagination must fail soon. I have been in swift succession a tyrant, a thief and a murderer, and now a fortune-hunter. There is really nothing left.'

'Oh!' said Ludovic gaily, 'we have acquitted you of theft and murder, you know.'

'True,' Shield retorted. 'But as your acquittals are invariably accompanied by fresh and more outrageous slanders, I almost dread the moment when you acquit me of fortune-hunting.'

Eustacie looked a little distressed. 'But, Tristram, you do not understand! We do not really think you are a fortune-hunter!'

Ludovic gave a delighted crack of laughter, and caught her hand to his lips, 'I lied, I lied! I have had one day's good luck at least, when I met my cousin Eustacie!'

'Yes, but——'

Sir Tristram said gravely: 'Of course, if you do not really think it——'

'No, I do not. In fact, I am beginning quite to like you,' Eustacie assured him.

'Thank you,' said Sir Tristram, much moved.

'But I thought it would be a very good thing to pretend to Basil that you still wished to marry me, and so, you see, you cannot come to his house with us. I perceive now that it is a pity that I said it, perhaps, but one cannot always look far enough ahead.'

'On the whole,' said Shield, 'I am inclined to think that you did right. I must, after all, have some excuse for visiting this inn so often. I will join your party at the Dower House, and you may counterfeit all the disgust you please.'

Miss Thane nodded approvingly. '*I* see! You will arrive upon some Pretext, just in time to rescue Mr. Lavenham from my importunities. Eustacie having signified her desire to hold private speech with him, he will hail your arrival with joy. I shall have to be a very stupid sort of a woman, and ask a great many questions. Tell me something to say about his house.'

'Comment enthusiastically upon the silver-figured oak wainscoting in the dining-room,' said Sir Tristram.

'Also the strap-and-jewel work overmantel in the drawing-room,' struck in Ludovic. 'Sylvester used to say it was devilish fine; that I *do* remember.'

'Strap-and-jewel work,' repeated Miss Thane, committing it to memory.

'Dutch influence,' said Sir Tristram. 'Detect the school of Torrigiano in the library.'

'Is it there?' inquired Ludovic, vaguely interested.

'Heaven knows. Basil won't, at any rate. Say that it is a pity the muntins are not covered by pilasters. Talk of cartouches, and caryatids, and scratch-mouldings. Ask for the history of every picture, and discover that the staircase reminds you of one you have seen somewhere else, though you cannot immediately recall where.'

'Say no more! I see it all!' declared Miss Thane. 'Heaven send he does not fob me off on to the housekeeper!'

Fortunately for the success of her plot the Beau's manners were far too polished to permit of his resorting to this expedient. According to a carefully-laid plan, the two ladies set out upon the following morning in Sir Hugh's chaise, and drove at a sedate pace to the Dower House, which was situated on the northern side of Lavenham Court, about five miles from Hand Cross. It was a sixteenth-century house of respectable size, approached by a short carriage sweep. Its gardens, which were separated from the Park by a kind of ha-ha, were laid out with great propriety of taste, and some very fine clipped yews, flanking the oaken front door, at once met with Miss Thane's approbation.

They were admitted into the house by a town-bred and somewhat supercilious butler, and led through the hall to the drawing-room. This was an elegant apartment, furnished in the first style of fashion, but Miss Thane had no time to waste in admiring what were obviously quite up-to-date chairs and tables. Her attention was fixed anxiously upon the overmantel.

The Beau joined his guests in a very few minutes. If he felt any surprise at a somewhat vague engagement having been kept with such promptness, no trace of it appeared in his countenance. He greeted both ladies with his usual grace, feared they must have been chilled during their drive in such hard weather, and begged them to draw near the fire. Eustacie, whose cheeks were rosy where a nipping east wind had caught them, promptly complied with the suggestion, but Miss Thane was unable to tear herself away from the contemplation of the overmantel. She stood well back from it, assuming a devout expression, and breathed: 'Such exquisite strap-and-jewel work! You did not tell me you had anything so fine, Mr. Lavenham! I declare, I do not know how to take my eyes from it!'

'I believe it is considered to be a very good example, ma'am,' the Beau acknowledged. 'The late Lord Lavenham was used to say it was finer than the one up at the Court, but I am afraid I am not a judge of such things.'

But this Miss Thane would not allow to be true. No protestations that he could make succeeded in shaking her belief that it was his modesty which spoke. She launched forth into a sea of talk, in which Dutch influence, the style of the Renaissance, the inferiority of Flemish craftsmanship, and a singular beauty of the Gothic jostled one another like rudderless boats adrift in a whirlpool. From the overmantel she passed with scarcely a check to the pictures on the walls. She detected a De Hooge with unerring judgment, and was at once reminded of a few weeks spent in the Netherlands some years ago. Her reminiscences, recounted with a vivacious artlessness which made Eustacie stare at her in rapt admiration, were only put an end to by the Beau's seizing the opportunity afforded by her pausing to take breath to propose that they should step into the dining-parlour for some refreshment.

The Beau opened the door for the ladies to pass out into the hall. Miss Thane went first, still chattering, leaving Eustacie to hang back for a moment, and to say in an urgent undertone to her cousin: 'We came to-day because I have suddenly thought that perhaps you, who are very much of the world, could advise me. Only, you understand, I do not like to say anything before Sarah, because although she is extremely amiable, she is not, after all, of my family.'

He bowed. 'I am always at your service, my dear cousin, even though I may be – surprised.'

'Surprised?' said Eustacie, with a look of child-like innocence.

'Well,' said the Beau softly, 'you have not been precisely in the habit of seeking either my company or my advice, have you, *ma chère*?'

'Oh!' said Eustacie, brushing that aside with a flutter of her expressive little hands, '*quant à ça*, when Grandpapa was alive I did not wish for anyone's advice but his. But I find myself now in a situation of the most awkward.'

He looked at her with narrowed eyes, as though appraising her. 'Yes, your situation is awkward, he said. 'I could show you how to end that.'

Miss Thane's voice, requesting him to tell her whether the staircase was original, put an end to all private conversation. He followed Eustacie out into the hall, saying that he believed it was quite original.

Wine and sandwiches had been set out on the table in the dining-parlour. While she ate, and sipped her glass of ratafie, Miss Thane took the opportunity of scrutinizing the wainscoting as closely as she dared. It was in two tiers, as Ludovic had described, the upper being composed of circular cartouches, carved with heads and devices, and separated from the lower by a broad frieze. The lower tier was divided vertically at every third panel by fluted pilasters with carved capitals. The whole was extremely beautiful, but the predominant thought in Miss Thane's mind was that to find one particular boss, or carved fruit, amongst the wealth on the wall would be an arduous labour.

Her meaningless prattle flowed on; she could not help being diverted by her own idiocies; nor, though she did not like him, could she fail to give the Beau credit for unwearied civility. By the time she had exhibited her commonplace book (in which Sir Tristram had had the forethought to sketch a few rough pictures of totally imaginary houses), and hoped that her host would grant her the indulgence of drawing just a tiny corner of his lovely panelled dining-parlour, her tongue was beginning to cleave to the roof of her mouth, and she heard with feelings of profound relief the ringing of a bell. It was at this moment that the Beau proposed escorting her to the library, in which room the wainscoting, though similar to that in the dining-parlour, was generally held, he believed, to be superior. They passed out into the hall, just as the butler opened the front door to admit Sir Tristram. The first sound that met his ears as he stepped over the threshold was Miss Thane's voice extolling the style of Torrigiano. A quiver of emotion for an instant disturbed the severity of his expression, but he controlled it immediately, and taking a hasty step forward, addressed Eustacie in outraged tones. 'I have been to the Red Lion, and was told I should find you here! I do not understand what your purpose can have been in coming, for I particularly requested the favour of an interview with you this morning!'

Eustacie drew back with a gesture conveying both alarm and repugnance. 'I told you I would not have any interview with you. I do not see why you must follow me, for it is not at all your affair that I choose to bring mademoiselle on a visit to my own cousin!'

'It is very much my affair, since I am held responsible for you!'

The Beau intervened in his sweetest voice. 'My dear Tristram, do pray come in! You are the very man of all others we need. I believe you are acquainted with Miss Thane?'

Sir Tristram bowed stiffly. 'Miss Thane and I have met, but——'

'Nothing could be better!' declared the Beau. 'Miss Thane has done me the honour of coming to see my house, and, alas, you know how lamentably ignorant I am on questions of antiquity! But you, my dear fellow, know so much——'

'Oh!' exclaimed Miss Thane, clasping her hands together. 'If it would not be troubling Sir Tristram——!'

Sir Tristram assumed the expression of a man forced against his will to be complaisant, and said somewhat ungraciously that he would, of course, be pleased to tell Miss Thane anything in his power. The Beau at once reminded him that the wainscoting in the library was held to be worthy of close study, and begged him to take Miss Thane there. He added that if she cared to make a sketch of the room, he was sure his cousin's taste and knowledge would be of assistance to her.

'Eustacie and I will wait for you in the drawing-room,' he said.

It seemed as though Sir Tristram would have demurred, but Miss Thane frustrated this by breaking into profuse expressions of gratitude. He made the best of it, and the instant the library door was closed on them, said: 'Have you been talking like that all the time?'

Miss Thane sank into a chair in an exhausted attitude. 'But without pause!' she said faintly. 'My dear sir, I have been inspired! The mantle of my own cousin fell upon my shoulders, and I spoke like her, tittered like her, even thought like her! She is the silliest woman I know. It worked like a charm! He was itching to be rid of me!'

'I should imagine he might well!' said Sir Tristram. 'The wonder is that he did not strangle you.'

She chuckled. 'He is too well-bred. Did I sound really feather-headed? I tried to.'

'Yes,' he said. He looked at her with a hint of a smile. 'You are an extremely accomplished woman, Miss Thane.'

'I have a natural talent for acting,' she replied modestly. 'But your own efforts were by no means contemptible, I assure you,' She got up. 'We have no time to waste if we are to find this panel. Do you take this side of the room and I will take that.'

'Oh – the panel!' said Sir Tristram. 'Yes, of course.'

Having got rid of his cousin and of Miss Thane, the Beau turned to Eustacie, and murmured: 'Could anything be better? Shall we go into the drawing-room?'

Eustacie assented, wondering how long she would be able to hold him in conversation. She did not feel that she possessed quite Miss Thane's talent for discursive chatter, and she was far too ingenuous to realize that her enchanting little face was enough to keep the Beau by her side until she herself should be pleased to declare the interview at an end. It did occur to her that he was looking at her with an expression of unusual warmth in his eyes, but beyond deciding that she did not like it, she paid very little heed to it. She sat down by the fire, her soft, dove-coloured skirts billowing about her, and remarked that if her dearest Sarah had a fault it was that she was a trifle too talkative.

'Just a trifle,' agreed the Beau. 'Do you really propose to accompany her to town?'

'Oh yes, certainly!' she replied. 'But I cannot remain with her for ever, and it is that which makes everything very awkward. I meant to become a governess, but Sarah does not advise it. What do you think I should do?'

'Well,' said the Beau slowly, 'you could, of course, engage a lady of birth and propriety to live with you and be your chaperon. Sylvester had left you well provided for, you know.'

'But I do not want a chaperon!' said Eustacie.

'No? There is an alternative.'

'Tell me, then!'

'Marriage,' he said.

She shook her head. 'I will *not* marry Tristram. He is not amusing, and, besides, I do not like him.'

'I am aware,' said the Beau, 'but Tristram is not the only man in the world, my little cousin.'

Foreseeing what was coming, Eustacie at once agreed with this pronouncement, and launched out into a euology of the Duke she would have married had her grandfather not brought her to England. The fact that she had never laid eyes on this gentleman did not deter her from describing him in detail, and it was fully fifteen minutes before her invention gave out and her cousin was able to interpolate a remark. He observed that since the Duke had gone to the guillotine, her fate, had she married him, would have been a melancholy one.

In his opinion, however, Eustacie could not concur. To have become a widow at the age of eighteen would, she held, have been *épatant*, and of all things the most romantic. 'Moreover,' she added, 'it was a very good match. I should have been a duchess, and although Grandpapa says – said – that it is vulgar to care for such things, I do think that I should have liked to have been a duchess.'

'Oh, I agree with you, *ma chère!*' he said cordially. 'You would have made a charming duchess. But in these revolutionary times one must moderate one's ideas, you know. Consider, instead, the advantages of becoming a baroness.'

'A baroness?' she faltered, fixing her eyes on his face with an expression of painful intensity. 'What do you mean?'

He met her eyes with slightly raised brows, and for a moment stood looking down at her as though he were trying to read her thoughts. 'My dear cousin, what in the world have I said to alarm you?' he asked.

Recollecting herself, she answered quickly: 'I am not at all alarmed, but I do not understand what you mean. Why should I think about being a baroness?'

He pulled up a chair and sat down on it, rather nearer to her than she liked, and stretching out his hand laid it on one of hers. 'I might make you one,' he said.

She sat as straight and as stiff as a wooden puppet, but her cheeks glowed with the indignation that welled up in her. The glance she bent on him was a very fiery one, and she said bluntly: 'You are not a baron, you!'

'We don't know that,' he replied, 'but we might find out. In fact, I have already recommended Tristram to do so.'

'You mean that you would like very much to know that Ludovic is dead?'

He smiled. 'Let us say rather that I should like very much to know *whether* he is dead, my dear,'

She repressed the impulse to throw off his hand, and said in a thoughtful voice: 'Yes, I suppose you want to be Lord Lavenham. It is very natural.'

He shrugged. 'I do not set great store by it, but I should be glad of the title if it could win me the one thing I want.'

This was too much for Eustacie, and she did pull her hand away, exclaiming: '*Voyons*, do you think I marry just for a title, me?'

'Oh no, no, no!' he said, smiling. 'You would undoubtedly marry for love were it possible, but you have said yourself that your situation is awkward, and, alas, I know that you are not in love with me. I am offering a marriage of expediency, and when one is debarred from a love-match, dear cousin, it is time to give weight to material considerations.'

'True, very true!' she said. 'And you have given weight to them, *n'est-ce pas*? I am an heiress, as you reminded me yesterday.'

'You are also enchanting,' he said, with unwonted feeling.

'*Merci du compliment*! I regret infinitely that I do not find you enchanting, too,'

'Ah, you are in love with romance!' he replied. 'You imagine to yourself some hero of adventure, but it is a sad truth that in these humdrum days such people no longer exist.'

'You know nothing of the matter: they do exist!' said Eustacie hotly.

'They would make undesirable husbands,' he remarked. 'Take poor Ludovic, for instance, whose story has, I believe, a little caught your fancy. You think him a very figure of romance, but you would be disappointed in him if ever you met him, I dare say.'

She blushed, and turned her face away. 'I do not wish to talk of Ludovic. I do not think of him at all.'

He looked amused. 'My dear, it is as bad as that? I should not – I really should not waste a moment's thought on him. One is sorry for him, one even liked him, but he was nothing but a rather stupid young man, after all.'

She compressed her lips tightly, as though afraid some unguarded words might escape her. He watched her for a moment, and presently said: 'Do you know, you look quite cross, cousin? Now, why?'

She replied, keeping her gaze fixed on a blazing log of wood in the grate: 'It does not please me that you should suppose I am in love with someone I have never seen. It is a *bêtise*.'

'It would be,' he agreed. 'Let us by all means banish Ludovic from our minds, and talk, instead, of ourselves. You want certain things, Eustacie, which I could give you.'

'I do not think it.'

'It is nevertheless true. You would like a house in town, and to lead precisely the life I lead. You could not support the thought of becoming Tristram's wife, because he would expect you to be happy in Berkshire, rearing his children. Now, I should not expect anything so dull of you. Indeed, I should deprecate it. I do not think the domestic virtues are very strong in me. I should require only of my wife that her taste in dress should do me justice.'

'You propose to me a *mariage de convenance*,' said Eustacie, 'and I have made up my mind that that is just what I do not want.'

'I propose to you what I thought might be acceptable. Forget it! I love you.'

She got up quickly, a vague idea of flight in her mind. He, too, rose, and before she could stop him, put his arms round her. 'Eustacie!' he said. 'From the moment of first laying eyes on you I have loved you!'

An uncontrollable shudder ran through her. She wrenched herself out of his embrace, and cast him such a glance of repulsion that he stepped back, the smile wiped suddenly from his face.

He looked at her with narrowed eyes, but after a slight pause the ugly gleam vanished, and he was smiling again. He moved away to the other side of the fireplace, and drawled: 'It seems that you do not find me so sympathetic as you would have had me believe, cousin. Now, I wonder why you wanted to come here to-day?'

'I thought you would advise me. I did not suppose that you would try to make love to me. That is quite another thing!'

He lifted an eyebrow at her. 'Is it? But I think – yes, I think I have once or twice before informed you of my very earnest desire to marry you.'

'Yes, but I have said already that I will not. It is finished.'

'Perfectly,' he bowed. 'Let us talk of something else. There *was* something I had in mind to ask you, as I remember. What can it have been? Something that intrigued me.' He half closed his eyes as though in an effort of memory. 'Something to do with your flight from the Court . . . ah yes, I have it! The mysterious groom! Who was the mysterious groom, Eustacie?'

This question came as a shock to her; her heart seemed to leap in her chest. To gain time she repeated: 'The mysterious groom?'

'Yes,' he smiled. 'The groom who did not exist. Do tell me!'

'Oh!' she said, with a rather artificial laugh, 'that is my very own adventure, and quite a romantic history! I assure you. How did you know of it?'

'In the simplest way imaginable, my dear cousin. My man Gregg fell in with a certain riding-officer at Cowfold yesterday, and from him gleaned this most interesting tale. I am consumed by curiosity. A groom whom you vouched for, and whom Tristram vouched for, and who yet did not exist.'

'Well, truly, I think it was wrong of me to save him from the riding-officer,' confessed Eustacie, with a great air of candour, 'but you must understand that I was under an obligation to him. One pays one's debts, after all!'

'Such a sentiment does you credit,' said the Beau affably. 'What was the debt?'

'Oh, the most exciting thing!' she replied. 'I did not tell you the whole yesterday, because Sarah's brother is a Justice of the Peace, and one must be careful, but I was captured by smugglers that night, and but for the man I saved I should have been killed. Murdered, you know. Conceive of it!'

'How very, very alarming for you!' said the Beau.

'Yes, it was. There were a great many of them, and they were afraid I should betray them, and they said I must at once be killed. Only this one – the one I said was my groom – took my part, and he would not permit that I should be killed. I think he was the leader, because they listened to him.'

'I never till now heard that chivalry existed amongst smugglers,' remarked the Beau.

'No, but he was not a *preux chevalier*, you know. He was quite rough, and not at all civil, but he had compassion upon me, and that led to a great quarrel between him and the other men. Then the riding-officers came, and my smuggler threw me up on to my horse and mounted behind me, because he said that the Excisemen must not find me, which, I see, was quite reasonable. Only the Excisemen fired at him, and he was wounded, and Rufus bolted into the Forest. And I did not know what to do, so I went to the Red Lion and asked Nye to help the smuggler, because it seemed to me that I could not give him up after he had saved me from being killed.'

The Beau was listening with his usual air of courteous interest. He said: 'What strange, what incredible things do happen, to be sure! Now if I had heard this tale at second-hand, or perhaps read it in a romance, I should have said it was far too improbable to bear the least resemblance to the truth. It shows how easily one may be mistaken. I, for instance, on what I conceived to be my knowledge of Nye's character, can even now scarcely credit him with so much noble disregard for his own good name. You must possess great influence over him, dear cousin.'

Eustacie felt a little uneasy, but replied carelessly: 'Yes, perhaps I have some influence, but I am bound to confess he did not at all like it, and he would not by any means keep the smuggler in his house.'

'Oh, the smuggler has departed has he?'

'But yes, the very next day! What else?'

'I am sure I do not know. I expect I am very stupid,' he added apologetically, 'but there do seem to me to be one or two unexplained points to this adventure. I find myself quite at a loss to understand Tristram's part in it. How were you able to persuade so stern a pattern of rectitude to support your story, my dear?'

Eustacie began to wish very much that Tristram and Sarah would finish their search and come to her rescue. 'Oh, but, you see, when it was explained to him Tristram was grateful to my smuggler for saving me!'

'Oh!' said the Beau, blinking. 'Tristram was grateful. Yes, I see. How little one knows of people, after all! It must have gone sadly against the grain with him, I feel. He has not breathed a word of it to me.'

'No, and I think it is very foolish of him,' returned Eustacie. 'Tristram does not wish anyone to know of my adventure, because he says I have behaved with impropriety, and it had better immediately be forgotten.'

'Ah, that is much better!' said the Beau approvingly. 'I feel that he may well have said that.'

This rejoinder, which seemed to convey a disturbing disbelief in the rest of her story, left Eustacie without a word to say. The Beau, seeing her discomfiture, smiled more broadly, and said: 'You know, you have quite forgotten to tell me that your smuggler was one of Sylvester's bastards.'

Eustacie felt the colour rise in her cheeks, and at once turned it to account, exclaiming in shocked tones: 'Cousin!'

'I beg your pardon!' he said, with exaggerated concern. 'I should have said love-children.'

She threw him a reproachful, outraged look, and replied: 'Certainly I have not forgotten, but I do not speak of indelicate things, and I am very much *émue* to think that you could mention it to me.'

He apologized profusely, but with an ironical air which made her feel rather uncomfortable. Luckily an interruption occurred before he could ask any more awkward questions. Miss Thane and Sir Tristram came into the room. Sir Tristram wore an expression of long-suffering, but in Miss Thane's eyes there peeped an irrepressible twinkle.

The quick, anguished glance thrown at him by Eustacie was enough to warn Shield that all was not well. He gave no sign of having noticed it, however, but waited for Miss Thane to come to the end of her eulogies and thanks. The Beau received these with smiling civility, and when they ceased, turned to his cousin, and said in a languid voice that he had been hearing more of her adventure from Eustacie. Sir Tristram quite unwittingly bore out the character bestowed on him by Eustacie by saying curtly that the sooner the adventure was forgotten the better it would be.

'You are too harsh, my dear Tristram,' said the Beau. 'But we know how kind-hearted you are under your – er – severity.'

'Indeed!' said Shield, looking most forbidding.

'Yes, yes, I have heard all about Eustacie's smuggler, and how you helped to protect him from the riding-officers. I have been much moved. A – a connection of Sylvester, I believe?'

Sir Tristram replied coolly: 'Just so. I thought there would be less noise made over the affair if he were allowed to escape.'

'I expect you were right, my dear fellow. How quick of you to recognize one of Sylvester's – ah, I must not offend Eustacie's sensibilities again! – one of Sylvester's relations.'

Sir Tristram was not in the least put out by this. He said: 'Oh, I knew him at once! So would you have done. You remember Jem Sunning, don't you?'

'Jem Sunning!' There was just the faintest suggestion of chagrin in the

Beau's voice. 'Is that who it was? I thought he went to America.'

'So did I. Apparently he found free-trading more to his taste, however. Eustacie, if you are ready to return to Hand Cross, I shall do myself the honour of escorting your carriage.'

Bearing in mind her avowed dislike of him, Eustacie thought it proper to demur at this suggestion, and some time was wasted in argument. Miss Thane enacted the rôle of peacemaker, and finally the whole party took their leave of the Beau, and set off for Hand Cross.

When he had handed the ladies into their chaise, and seen it drive off with Sir Tristram riding beside it, the Beau walked slowly back to the house, and made his way to the library. His face wore an expression of pensive abstraction, and he did not immediately occupy himself in any way. He wandered instead to the window and looked out over the neat beds of his formal garden. His gaze seemed to question the clipped hedges; his eyebrows were a little raised; his hand went as though unconsciously to his quizzing-glass, and began to play with it, sliding it up and down the silk ribbon that was knotted through the chased ring at the end of the shaft. At this idle employment he was found a few minutes later by his valet, a discreet, colourless person of self-effacing manners and unequalled skill in all details concerning a gentleman's toilet. He came into the room with his usual hushed tread, and laid a folded journal on the table with a finicking care that seemed to indicate the handling of some precious and brittle object.

The Beau, recognizing these stealthy sounds, spoke without turning his head. 'Ah, Gregg! That riding-officer.'

The valet folded his hands meekly and stood with slightly bowed head. 'Yes, sir?'

'He described mademoiselle's groom to you, I think?'

'Imperfectly, sir. He was struck by a resemblance to the late lord, but I could not discover that this lay in anything but the nose.' He coughed, and added apologetically: 'That may be seen in Sussex – occasionally, sir.'

The Beau made no response. Gregg waited, his eyes lowered. After a short interval the Beau said slowly: 'A young man, I think?'

'I was informed so, sir.'

The Beau bit the rim of his quizzing-glass meditatively. 'How old by your reckoning would Jem Sunning be at this present?'

The valet's eyes lifted, and for a moment stared in surprise at the back of his master's powdered head. He replied after a moment's reflection: 'I regret, sir, I am unable to answer with any degree of certainty. I should suppose him to be somewhere in the region of one- or two-and-thirty.'

'My memory is very imperfect,' sighed the Beau, 'but I think he always used to be dark, was he not?'

'Yes, sir.' The valet gave another of his deprecating coughs. 'It is generally said amongst the country people, sir, that my lord gave his own colouring to his descendants.'

'Yes,' agreed the Beau. 'Yes, I have heard that. In fact, I think I can call only one exception to mind.' He turned, and came away from the window to stand in front of the fire. 'I cannot but feel that it would be interesting to know whether mademoiselle's groom conformed to the rule – or not.'

'The riding-officer, sir,' said Gregg, in an expressionless voice, 'spoke of a fair young man.'

'Ah!' said the Beau gently. 'A fair young man! Well, that is very odd, to be sure.'

'Yes, sir. A trifle unusual, I believe.'

The Beau's gaze dwelled thoughtfully upon a portrait hanging on the opposite wall. 'I think, Gregg that we sometimes purchase our brandy from Joseph Nye?'

'We have very often done so, sir.'

'We will purchase some more,' said the Beau, polishing his eye-glass on his sleeve. 'Attend to it, Gregg.'

'Yes, sir.'

'That is all,' said the Beau.

The valet bowed and walked towards the door. As he reached it the Beau said softly: 'I should not like you to display any vulgar curiosity at the Red Lion, Gregg.'

'No, sir. You may rely on me.'

'Oh, I do, Gregg, I do!' said the Beau, and picking up the journal from the table, sat down with it in a winged armchair by the fire.

The valet lingered for a moment. 'If I may venture to say something, sir?' he suggested meekly.

'By all means, Gregg.'

'The lady who accompanied Sir Tristram into this room, sir. I understand she was desirous of inspecting the panelling?'

The Beau raised his eyes from the journal. 'Well?'

'Just so, sir. It would, of course, explain conduct which seemed to Thomson and myself a trifle odd. I beg pardon, I'm sure.'

'In what way odd?'

'Well, sir, it appeared to Thomson and myself that Sir Tristram and the lady were inspecting the woodwork very closely,' said the valet. 'The lady went so far as to stand upon a chair to inspect the frieze, and Sir Tristram, when I entered the room, seemed to me (but I might be mistaken) to be sounding the lower panels.'

The Beau lowered the journal. 'Did he?' he said slowly. 'Did he, indeed? Well, well!'

Gregg bowed himself out. It was a few minutes before the Beau picked up his journal again. His eyes stared across the room at a certain portion of the wainscoting; and there was for once no trace of a smile upon his thin lips.

Meanwhile Miss Thane, seated beside Eustacie in the chaise, had nothing to report but failure. She said that her fingers were sore from pulling and pressing wooden bosses, and that her nervous system was shattered for ever. No fewer than three interruptions had occurred during the short time she and Sir Tristram had had at their disposal. First had come the housekeeper with a bowl of flowers to set upon the table, and a tongue only too ready to wag. She had hardly been got rid of when the door opened again, this time to admit the butler, who had come in to make up the fire. 'And what he must have thought, I dare not imagine!' said Miss Thane. 'I was standing upon a chair at that precise moment, trying to move a wooden pear well above my reach.'

Eustacie gave a giggle. 'What did you do?'

'Most unfortunately,' said Miss Thane, 'my back was turned to the door, and I had not heard it open. I am bound to confess, however, that your cousin Tristram showed great presence of mind, for he immediately told me to look closely at the carving, and to observe most particularly the top chamfer of the cross-rail.'

'One must admit that Tristram is not stupid,' said Eustacie fair-mindedly.

'No,' agreed Miss Thane, casting a glance out of the window at the straight figure riding beside the chaise, 'not stupid, but (I am sorry to say) both autocratic and dictatorial. His remarks to me once the butler had left the room were quite unappreciative and not a little unfeeling, while his way of handing me down from the chair left much to be desired.'

'He does not like females,' explained Eustacie.

Miss Thane's eyes returned to the contemplation of Sir Tristram's stern profile. 'Ah!' she said. 'That would account for it, of course. Well, we did what we could to make my standing upon a chair seem a natural proceeding – but I doubt the butler thinks us a pair of lunatics – and being once more alone, and Sir Tristram having spoken his mind to me on the subject of female folly, we returned to our search. It affords me some satisfaction to reflect that it was Sir Tristram, and not I, who was engaged in sounding the panels when a most odiously soft-footed individual stole in to place a snuff-jar upon the desk. At least, it afforded me the opportunity to show that I, too, have some presence of mind. I begged your cousin to admire the spear-head finish.'

'I think that you are very clever!' said Eustacie approvingly. 'I should not have known that there was a – a spear-head finish.'

'There wasn't,' said Miss Thane. 'In fact, the mere mention of a spear-head finish in connection with those panels was a solecism which caused a spasm to cross Sir Tristram's features. When the snuff-bearer had taken himself off he was obliging enough to inform me that before he accompanied me on another such search he would give me a few simple lessons in what to look for in wood-panelling of that particular kind. By that time I had undergone so many frights that my spirit was quite in abeyance, and I not only thanked him meekly, but I even acquiesced in his decision to abandon the quest. Yes, I know it was wretchedly weak of me,' she added, in answer to a look of reproach from Eustacie, 'but to tell you the truth, I think the task is well-nigh hopeless. Ludovic must remember more precisely where the panel is.'

'But you know very well that he cannot!'

'Then he must go and look for it himself,' said Miss Thane firmly.

Eustacie was inclined to be indignant, but the chaise had by this time drawn up outside the Red Lion, and she was forced to postpone her recriminations until a more convenient occasion. Shield, dismounting lightly from his horse, himself opened the door and let down the steps for the ladies to descend. Having handed them out of the chaise, he gave his horse into the charge of one of the ostlers and followed them into the inn. Here they were met by Nye, who informed them in the voice of one who had done his best to avert disaster but failed, that they would find Ludovic in Sir Hugh Thane's room.

'In my brother's room?' exclaimed Miss Thane. 'What in the world is he doing there?'

'He's playing cards, ma'am,' replied Nye grimly.

'But how came he to go into my brother's room at all?' demanded Miss Thane. 'We left him in bed!'

'You did, ma'am, but you hadn't been gone above five minutes before his lordship started ringing the bell for Clem. Nothing else would do for him but to get up and dress, and me not being by Clem helped him. That's how it always was: what Mr. Ludovic took it into his head to do, Clem would help him to, no matter what.'

Eustacie turned to her cousin. 'You should not have brought his clothes!'

'Nonsense!' said Shield. 'Ludovic must leave his bed sooner or later. He'll take no hurt.'

'That is all very well,' said Miss Thane, 'but even though he might get up, I can see no reason for him to go into Hugh's room. I have a great value for Hugh, but I cannot feel that he is the man to keep a momentous secret. Nye, you should have intervened.'

Nye smiled somewhat wryly. 'It's plain you don't know his lordship, ma'am. No sooner was he dressed than what must he do but walk out of his room just to see how his legs would carry him. While he was showing Clem how well he could manage, Sir Hugh (who'd been pulling his bell fit to break it, according to what he told me) put his head out of his room to shout for Clem. By what I can make out from Clem, Sir Hugh and Mr. Ludovic got into conversation right away, Sir Hugh not seeming to be surprised at finding another gentleman in the house, and Mr. Ludovic, of course, as friendly as you please. "Oh, are you Sir Hugh Thane?" he says. "My name's Lavenham——" Oh yes, ma'am, he came out with that quite brazen! That's Mr. Ludovic all over. "Well," says Sir Hugh, "I can't say I call your face to mind at the moment, but if you know me I'm devilish glad of it, for I've had more than enough of my own company. Do you play piquet?" Well, that was quite sufficient for Mr. Ludovic, and before Clem rightly knew what was happening, he'd been sent off downstairs to fetch a couple of packs of cards and a bottle of wine. By the time I was back in the house there was no doing anything, ma'am, for they was both in Sir Hugh's room, as thick as thieves, as the saying is.'

The ladies looked at one another in consternation. 'I had better go upstairs and see what is happening,' said Miss Thane resignedly.

It was, however, just as Nye had described. Lord Lavenham and Sir Hugh Thane, both attired in dressing-gowns, were seated on opposite sides of a small table drawn close to the fire in Sir Hugh's bedchamber playing piquet. A glass of wine was at each gentleman's elbow, and so absorbed were they in the game that neither paid the least heed to the opening of the door, or, in fact, became aware of Miss Thane's presence until she stepped right up to the table. Sir Hugh glanced up then, and said in an abstracted voice: 'Oh, there you are, Sally!' and turned his attention to the cards again.

Miss Thane laid her hand on Ludovic's shoulder to prevent his rising, but remarked significantly: 'What if I had been the Beau, or an Exciseman?'

'Oh, I'm well prepared!' Ludovic assured her, and in the twinkling of an eye had whisked a small, silver-mounted pistol from his pocket.

'Good God, I hope you don't mean to fire on sight!' said Miss Thane.

Sir Hugh put up his glass to look at the pistol. 'That's a nice little gun,' he observed.

Ludovic handed it to him. 'Yes, it's one of Manton's. I've a pair of his duelling-pistols, too – beautiful pieces of work!'

Sir Hugh subjected the pistol to a careful inspection. 'Myself I don't care for silver sights. Apt to dazzle the eye.' He sighted along the pistol. 'Nice balance, but too short in the barrel. No accuracy over twelve yards.'

Ludovic's eye gleamed. 'Do you think so? I'll engage to culp a wafer at twenty!'

'With this gun?' said Sir Hugh incredulously.

'With that gun.'

'I'll lay you a pony you don't.'

'Done!' said Ludovic promptly.

'And where,' inquired Miss Thane, 'do you propose to hold this contest?'

'Oh, in the yard!' said Ludovic, receiving the pistol back from Sir Hugh.

'That, of course, will be very nice,' said Miss Thane politely. 'The ostlers will thus be able to see you. I forbid you to encourage him, Hugh. Let us admit that he is a crack shot, and be done with it.'

'Well, I am a crack shot,' said Ludovic, smiling most disarmingly up at her.

'Talking of crack shots,' said Sir Hugh, 'what was the name of the fellow who put out all the candles in the big chandelier at Mrs. Archer's once? There were fifteen of them, and he never missed one!'

'Fifteen?' said Ludovic. 'Sixteen!'

'Fifteen was what I was told. He did it for a wager.'

'That's true enough, but I tell you there were sixteen candles!'

Sir Hugh shook his head. 'You've got that wrong. Fifteen.'

'Damn it, I ought to know!' said Ludovic. 'I did it!'

'You did it?' Sir Hugh regarded him with renewed interest. 'You mean to tell me you are the man who shot the wicks off fifteen candles at Mrs. Archer's?'

'I shot the wicks off *sixteen* candles!' said Ludovic.

'Well, all I can say is that it was devilish fine shooting,' said Sir Hugh. 'But are you sure you have the figure right? I rather fancy fifteen was the number.'

'Where's Tristram?' demanded Ludovic of Miss Thane. 'He was there! Sixteen candles I shot. I used my Mantons, and Jerry Matthews loaded for me.'

'I don't know him,' remarked Sir Hugh. 'Would he be a son of old Frederick Matthews?'

Miss Thane at this point withdrew to summon Sir Tristram. When she returned with him she found that the question of Mr. Jerry Matthew's parentage had led inexplicably to an argument on the precise nature of a certain bet entered in the book at White's three years before. The argument was broken off as soon as Sir Tristram entered the room, for Ludovic at once commanded him to say whether he had put out fifteen or sixteen candles at Mrs. Archer's house.

'I don't remember,' replied Sir Tristram. 'All I remember is that you shattered a big mirror to smithereens and brought the Watch in on us.'

Sir Hugh, who was looking fixedly at Sir Tristram, said suddenly, and with a pleased air: 'Shield! That's who you are! Recognized you at once. What's more, I know where I saw you last.'

Sir Tristram shook hands with him. 'At Mendoza's fight with Warr last year,' he said, without hesitation. 'I recall that you were on the roof of the coach next to my curricle.'

'That's it!' said Thane. 'A grand turn-up! Did you see Dan's last fight with Humphries? A couple of years ago that would be, or maybe three.'

'I saw him beat Humphries twice, and I was at the Fitzgerald turn-up in '91.'

'You were? Then tell me this – Was Fitzgerald shy, or was he not?'

'Not shy, no. Rather glaringly abroad once or twice, I thought.'

'He was, was he? I'm glad to know that, because——'

'If you are going to talk about prize-fights, I'll leave you,' interposed Miss Thane.

'No, don't do that,' said Ludovic. 'I'm not interested in prize-fights. By-the-by, did you find that panel?'

This casual reference to her morning's labour made Miss Thane reply tartly: 'No, Ludovic, we did *not* find that panel.'

'I didn't think you would,' he said.

Miss Thane appeared to struggle with her emotions. Her brother, showing a faint interest in what he had caught of the conversation, said sympathetically: 'Lost something?'

'No, dear,' replied Sarah, with awful calm. 'It is Lord Lavenham who has lost a talisman ring. I told you all about it three days ago. He lost it at play one night at the Cocoa-Tree.'

'I do remember you telling me some rigmarole or another,' admitted Thane. 'If you want my advice, Lavenham, you won't play at the Cocoa-Tree. I met a Captain Sharp there myself once. Hazard it was, and the dice kept running devilish high. I'd my suspicions of them from the start, and sure enough they were up-hills.'

'Oh, the play was fair enough,' said Ludovic indifferently.

'What I'm telling you is that it wasn't,' said Sir Hugh, patient but obstinate. 'I split the dice myself, and found 'em loaded.'

'I wasn't talking about that. *My* game was piquet. Never played hazard at the Cocoa-Tree in my life. I used to play at Almack's, and Brooks's, of course.'

'Very high-going at Brooks's,' said Thane, with a reflective shake of the head.

Sarah, seeing that a discussion of the play at the various gaming clubs in London was in a fair way to being begun, intervened before Ludovic could say anything more. She reminded him severely that they had more important things to discuss than gaming, and added with a good deal of feeling that her efforts on his behalf had not only been fruitless, but quite possibly disastrous as well. 'Your cousin,' she said, 'has heard about Eustacie's groom, and there is no doubt that he feels suspicious. Luckily, Sir Tristram had the presence of mind to tell him that the groom was—— Whom did you say he was, Sir Tristram?'

'Jem Sunning,' replied Shield. 'You remember him, Ludovic?'

'Yes, but I thought he went to America.'

'He did,' said Shield. 'That was why I chose him. But I'm not sure that the Beau believed me. It is more imperative than ever that you should get to some place of safety. If you won't go to Holland——'

'Well, I won't,' said Ludovic flatly.

Sir Hugh came unexpectedly to his support. 'Holland?' he said. 'I shouldn't go to Holland if I were you. I didn't like it at all. Rome, now! That's the place – though they have a demmed sight too many pictures there, too,' he added gloomily.

'I am going to stay here,' said Ludovic. 'If the worst comes to the worst, there's always the cellar.'

'Just what I was thinking myself!' said Thane approvingly. 'I've a strong notion there's more in that cellar than we've discovered. Why, I didn't get hold of this Canary till yesterday!'

No one paid the slightest heed to this interruption. Sir Tristram said: 'Very well, if you are determined, Ludovic, I don't propose to waste time in trying to persuade you. Are you serious in thinking that the ring may be behind that panel?'

'Of course I'm serious! It's the very place for it. Where else would he be likely to put it?'

'If I help you to get into the house, can you find the panel?'

'I can try,' said Ludovic hopefully.

'Yes, no doubt,' returned Shield, 'but I have assisted in one aimless search for it, and I've no desire to repeat the experience.'

'Once I'm in the house you can leave it to me,' said Ludovic. 'I'm bound to recognize the panelling when I see it.'

'I hope you may,' replied Shield. 'The Beau spoke of going to town one day this week, and that should be our opportunity.'

Miss Thane coughed. 'And how – the question just occurs to me, you know – shall you get into the Dower House, sir?'

'We can break in through a window,' answered Ludovic. 'There's no difficulty about that.'

She cast a demur glance up at Shield. 'I am afraid you will never get Sir Tristram to agree to do anything so rash,' she said.

He returned her glance with one of his measuring looks. 'I must seem to you a very spiritless creature, Miss Thane.'

She smiled, and shook her head, but would not answer. Her brother, who had been following the conversation with a puzzled frown, suddenly observed that all sounded very odd to him. 'You can't break into someone's house!' he objected.

'Yes, I can,' returned Ludovic. 'I'm not such a cripple as that!'

'But it's a criminal offence!' Sir Hugh pointed out.

'If it comes to that it's a criminal offence to smuggle liquor into the country,' replied Ludovic. 'I can tell you, I'm in so deep that it don't much signify what I do now.'

Sir Hugh sat up. 'You're never the smuggler my sister spoke to me about?'

'I'm a free-trader,' said Ludovic, grinning.

'Then just tell me this!' said Thane, his interest in housebreaking vanishing before a more important topic. 'Can you get me a pipe of the same Chambertin Nye has in his cellar?'

CHAPTER 8

It was agreed finally that Ludovic should attempt nothing in the way of housebreaking until his cousin had discovered which day the Beau proposed to go to London. Ludovic, incurably optimistic, considered his ring as good as found already, but Shield, taking a more sober view of the situation, saw pitfalls ahead. If the Beau, like his father before him, were indeed in the habit of using the priests's hole as a hiding-place for his strong-box, nothing was more likely than his keeping the ring there as well. Almost the only point on which Shield found himself at one with his volatile young cousin was the belief, firmly held by Ludovic, that the Beau, if he ever had the ring, would neither have sold it nor have thrown it away. To sell it would be too dangerous a procedure; to throw away an antique of great value would require more resolution than Sir Tristram believed the Beau possessed. But Sir Tristram could not share Ludovic's easy-going contempt of the Beau. Ludovic persisted in laughing at his affectations, and thinking him a mere fop of no particular courage or enterprise. Sir Tristram, though he had no opinion of the Beau's courage, profoundly mistrusted his suavity, and considered him to be a great deal more astute than he seemed.

The circumstance of the Beau's butler and valet having seen part at least of the search for the secret panel Sir Tristram found disturbing. That the Beau was already suspicious of Eustacie's supposed groom was apparent; Sir Tristram believed that if he got wind of his cousins' odd behaviour in his library he would be quite capable of putting two and two together and not only connecting Ludovic with the episode but realizing that he himself had at last fallen under suspicion. And if the Beau suspected that Ludovic, who knew the position of the priest's hole, had come into Sussex to find his ring he would surely be very unlikely to leave it where it would certainly be looked for.

Some part of these forebodings Shield confided to Miss Thane, enjoining her to do all that lay in her power to keep Ludovic hidden from all eyes but their own.

'Well, I will do my best,' replied Sarah, 'but it is not an easy task, Sir Tristram.'

'I know it is not an easy task,' he said impatiently, 'but it is the only way in which you can assist us – which I understand you to be desirous of doing.'

She could not forbear giving him a look of reproach. 'You must be forgetting what assistance I rendered you at the Dower House,' she said.

'No,' replied Sir Tristram, at his dryest. 'I was not forgetting that.'

Miss Thane rested her chin in her hand, pensively surveying him. 'Will you tell me something, Sir Tristram?'

'Perhaps. What is it?'

'What induced you ever to contemplate marriage with your cousin?'

He looked startled, and not too well pleased. 'I can hardly suppose, ma'am, that my private affairs can be of interest to you,' he said.

'Some people,' remarked Miss Thane wisely, 'would take that for a set-down.'

Their eyes met; Sir Tristram smiled reluctantly. 'You do not seem to be of their number, ma'am.'

'I am very thick-skinned,' explained Sarah. 'You see, I have not had the benefit of a correct upbringing.'

'Have you always lived with your brother?' he inquired.

'Since I left school, sir.'

'I suppose that accounts for it,' he said, half to himself.

'Accounts for what?' asked Miss Thane suspiciously.

'Your – unusual quality, ma'am.'

'I hope that is a compliment,' said Miss Thane, not without misgiving.

'I am not very apt at compliments!' he retorted.

Her eyes twinkled appreciatively. 'Yes, I deserved that. Very well, Sir Tristram, but you have not answered my question. Why did you take it into your head to marry your cousin?'

'You have been misinformed, ma'am. The idea was taken into my great-uncle's head, not mine.'

She raised her brows. 'Had you no voice in the matter then? Now, from what I have seen of you, I find that very hard to believe.'

'Do you imagine that I wanted to marry Eustacie for the sake of her money?' he demanded.

'No,' replied Miss Thane calmly. 'I do not imagine anything of the kind.'

His momentary flash of anger died down; he said, less harshly: 'Being the last of my name, ma'am, I conceive it to be my duty to marry. The alliance proposed to me by my great-uncle was one of convenience, and as such agreeable to me. Owing to the precarious circumstances to which the upheaval in France has reduced her paternal relatives, her grandfather's death leaves Eustacie alone in the world, a contingency he sought to provide against by this match. I promised Sylvester upon his death-bed that I would marry Eustacie. That is all the story.'

'How do you propose to salve your conscience?' asked Miss Thane.

'My conscience is not likely to trouble me in this instance,' he answered. 'Eustacie does not wish to marry me, and it would take more than a promise made to Sylvester to make me pursue a suit which she has declared to be distasteful to her: Moreover, had events turned out otherwise, Sylvester would have given her to Ludovic, not to me.'

'Oh, that is famous!' said Miss Thane. 'We can now promote her betrothal to him with clear consciences. But it is vexing for you to be obliged to look about you for another lady eligible for the post you require her to fill. Are you set on marrying a young female?'

'I am not set on marrying anyone, and I beg that you——'

'Well, that should make it easier,' said Miss Thane. 'Very young ladies are apt to be romantic, and that would never do,'

'I certainly do not look for romance in marriage, but pray do not let my affairs——'

'It must be someone past the age of being hopeful of getting a husband,' pursued Miss Thane, sinking her chin in her hand again.

'Thank you!' said Sir Tristram.

'Not handsome – I do not think we can expect her to be more than passable,' decided Miss Thane. 'Good birth would of course be an essential?'

'Really, Miss Thane, this conversation——'

'Luckily,' she said, 'there are any number of plain females of good birth but small fortune to be found in town. You may meet a few at the subscription balls at Almack's, but I dare say I could find you a dozen to choose from whose Mamas have long since ceased to take them to the "Marriage Market". After a certain number of seasons they have to yield place to younger sisters, you know.'

'You are too kind, ma'am!'

'Not at all; I shall be delighted to help you,' Miss Thane assured him. 'I have just the sort of female that would suit you in my mind's eye. A good, affectionate girl, with no pretensions to beauty, and a grateful disposition. She must be past the age of wanting to go to parties, and she must not expect you to make pretty speeches to her. I wonder—— Would you object to her having a slight – a *very* slight squint in one eye?'

'Yes, I should,' said Sir Tristram. 'Nor have I the smallest desire to——'

Miss Thane sighed. 'Well, that is a pity. I had thought of the very person for you.'

'Let me beg you not to waste your time thinking of another! The matter is not urgent.'

She shook her head. 'I cannot agree with you. After all, when one approaches middle age——'

'Middle—— Has anyone ever boxed your ears, Miss Thane?'

'No, never,' said Miss Thane, looking blandly up at him.

'You have been undeservedly fortunate,' said Sir Tristram grimly. 'We will, if you please, leave the subject of my marriage. I do not anticipate an immediate entry into wedlock.'

'Do you know,' said Miss Thane, with an air of candour, 'I believe you are wise. You are not cut out for matrimony. Your faith in females was shattered by an unfortunate affair in your youth; your eyes were opened to the defects of the female character; you are——'

Sir Tristram looked thunderous. 'Who told you this?' he snapped.

'Why, you did!'

'*I?*' he repeated.

'Most certainly.'

'You are mistaken. I am ready to allow that there may be many excellent women in the world. I do not know by what sign you knew that there had been an affair in my past about which I do not care to think. I can assure you that it has not prejudiced me against your sex.'

Miss Thane listened to this with her usual placidity, and, far from showing discomfiture, merely said: 'It seems to me very inexplicable that you can have met your cousin with so open a mind and yet failed to fall instantly in love with her.'

He gave a short laugh. 'There is no fear of my falling in love, ma'am. I learned my lesson early in life, but believe me, I have not forgotten it!'

'How melancholy it is to reflect that so few people have the good sense to profit by their experience as you have done!' said Miss Thane soulfully. 'I wonder if we should warn your cousins of the disillusionment in store for them?'

'I do not think it will be necessary, Miss Thane. Moreover, there is no immediate likelihood of their being married. Ludovic's affairs seem to me to be in as bad a way as they well might be.'

She became serious at once. 'Do you think them hopeless?'

'No, not hopeless,' he replied. 'But we have no certainty of the talisman ring being in Basil Lavenham's possession, and to be frank with you, I don't place much dependence upon its being in the priest's hole, even if he has got it. Assuming that he has, I think he would remove it from a hiding-place known to Ludovic the instant he suspected his presence in the neighbourhood.'

'But does he suspect his presence?'

'There is no saying what the Beau suspects, Miss Thane. Don't allow Ludovic to convince you that we have to deal with a fool! He is no such thing, I assure you.'

'You need not tell me that: I have met him. Will you think me fanciful if I say that I have a strong feeling that he is truly at the bottom of all Ludovic's troubles?'

'No, I think it myself. The difficulty will be to prove it.'

'If you cannot find the ring what is to be done?'

She saw his mouth harden. He had evidently considered this question, for he replied at once: 'If the worst come to the worst, the truth will have to be got out of him by other methods.'

Miss Thane, looking at Sir Tristram's powerful frame, and observing the grimness in his face, could not help feeling sorry for the Beau if the worst should come to the worst. She replied lightly: 'Would – er – other methods answer, do you suppose?'

'Probably,' said Sir Tristram. 'He has very little physical courage. But until we have more to go upon than conjecture, we need not consider that.'

She sat thinking for a few moments, and presently said: 'In one way it might not be so bad a thing if he did suspect Ludovic's presence here. If he suspected it he must, I imagine, realize that you have been convinced of Ludovic's innocence. I have frequently observed that when people are a little alarmed they are apt to behave with less than common sense. Your cousin has been so secure until now that it has been easy to act with coolness and presence of mind.'

'Very true,' he conceded. 'I have thought of that, but the risks outweigh the advantages. If it were not for one circumstance I should seriously consider removing Ludovic from this country.'

'He seems very determined. I don't think that he would consent to go,' said Miss Thane.

'I shouldn't ask his consent,' replied Shield.

'Dear me, you seem to be in a very ruthless mood!' she remarked. 'What makes you hesitate to kidnap poor Ludovic?'

'His marksmanship,' he answered. 'A man would have to be in desperate straits before he engaged in a shooting-match with Ludovic. The Beau won't risk it.'

'Well,' said Miss Thane, getting up from her chair, 'I am far from wishing you to ship Ludovic out of the country (besides, it's my belief he would come back), but I've a notion we are going to see some stirring adventures before we leave this place.'

'It's very possible,' he agreed. 'Are you afraid?'

She raised her eyes to his face. There was a hint of amusement in them. 'My dear sir, can you not see that I am positively trembling with fright?' she said.

He smiled. 'I beg your pardon. But to have a finger in a pie of Ludovic's making is enough to cause the bravest to quail! What I chiefly dread is his taking it into his head to break into the Dower House without waiting for word from me. Do you think you can prevent him?'

'I don't know,' said Sarah candidly. 'But I can at least get word to you if he becomes unmanageable.'.

For the time being, however, even Ludovic himself was forced to admit that his strength was not sufficiently recovered to permit of his riding five miles to the Dower House. He had lost a good deal of blood, and had been feverish for long enough to make him tiresomely weak upon first getting up out of his sick-bed. He was not one to submit patiently to being an invalid, nor did it seem to be possible to impress him with a sense of the dangerous nature of his situation. Once he was possessed of his clothes, nothing short of turning the key on him could keep him in his room. He strolled about the inn in the most careless way imaginable, his left arm disposed in a sling and Sylvester's great ruby on his finger. When begged to conceal this too well-known ring somewhere about his person, or to give it back to Tristram for safe-keeping, he said No, he had a fancy to wear Sylvester's ruby. Twice he nearly walked into the arms of local visitors to the Red Lion, who had come in for a tankard of ale and a chat over the coffee-room fire, and only Miss Thane's timely intervention prevented him sallying forth into the yard with Sir Hugh to win his bet with a little marksmanship. Miss Thane, accustomed to handling the male, did not attempt to dissuade him from shooting. She merely suggested that if he wished to fire a noisy pistol the cellar would be the best place for such a pastime. Ludovic was just about to argue the point when Sir Hugh providentially pooh-poohed his sister's suggestion, on the score that no one could be expected to culp a wafer in the wretched light afforded by a branch of candles. This was quite enough to make Ludovic instantly engage to win his wager under these or any other conditions, and down they both went, with Clem in attendance. There being no wafers available a playing-card had to suffice. When Ludovic tossed the ace of hearts to Clem, and said carelessly: 'Hold it for me, Clem!' Sir Hugh was shocked almost out of his sleepy placidity, and indeed went so far as to adjure the tapster not to be fool enough to obey. Clem, who, besides possessing boundless faith in Ludovic, would never have dreamed of disobeying his orders, merely grinned at this piece of advice, and held up the card by one corner. Ludovic, lounging on a barrel, inspected the priming of his pistol, requested Thane to move the candles a little to one side, levelled the pistol, and fired. The card fluttered to the ground. Clem, grinning more than ever, picked it up and showed it to Sir Hugh with the pip blown clean out of it.

This feat seemed to call for celebration, and Miss Thane, descending into the cellar in search of them some time later, found that they had broached a keg of Nantes brandy, and had no immediate intention of returning to upper ground. Invigorated by the brandy, Sir Hugh was seized by a desire to emulate Ludovic's skill – but without Clem's assistance. His efforts, unattended by success, brought Nye down to put a stop to a sport which was not only riddling the walls of the cellar, but creating enough noise to lead anyone above-stairs to suppose that the inn was being besieged.

Since he was not allowed to step outside the Red Lion, and dissuaded from wandering about at large in it, it was a fortunate circumstance that Eustacie was staying under the same roof with Ludovic. Her presence beguiled the most tedious hour, and her vehement way of saying: 'But no, Ludovic, you shall not!' had the power of restraining him where Miss Thane's reasoned arguments might have failed. He taught Eustacie how to throw dice and how to play piquet; he told her hair-raising and entirely apocryphal tales of adventures to be met with at sea; he teased her, and laughed at her, and ended inevitably by catching her in his sound arm and kissing her.

No sooner had he done it than he recollected the impropriety of such conduct. He released her at once, and said, rather pale, and with the laugh quite vanished from his eyes: 'I'm sorry! Forgive me!'

Eustacie said earnestly: 'Oh, I do not mind at all! Besides, you kissed me before, do you not remember?'

'Oh, that!' he said. 'That was a mere cousinly kiss!'

'And this one, not?' she said simply. 'I am glad.'

He ran his hand through his fair locks. 'I'm a villain to have kissed you at all! Forget that I did! I had no right – I ought to be shot for doing such a thing!'

Eustacie stared at him in the blankest surprise. '*Voyons*, I find that you are excessively rude! I thought you wanted to kiss me!'

'Of course I wanted to! Oh, devil take it, this won't do! Eustacie, if everything were different: if I were not a smuggler and an exile I should beg you to marry me. But I am these things, and——'

'I do not mind about that,' she interrupted. 'It is not at all *convenable* that you should kiss me and then refuse to marry me. I am quite mortified.'

'I wish to God I could ask you to marry me!'

'It doesn't signify,' said Eustacie, handsomely waiving this formality. 'If it is against your honour you need not make me an offer. We will just be betrothed without it.'

'No, we won't. Not until I have cleared my name.'

'Yes, but if you cannot clear your name, what then are we to do?' she demanded.

'Forget we ever met!' said Ludovic with a groan.

This Spartan resolve did not commend itself to Eustacie at all. Two large tears sparkled on the ends of her eyelashes, and she said in a forlorn voice: 'But me, I have a memory of the very longest!'

Ludovic, seeing the tears, could not help putting his arm round her again. 'Sweetheart, don't cry! I can't possibly let you marry me if I'm to remain an exile all my life.'

Eustacie stood on tiptoe, and kissed his chin. 'Yes, you can. It is quite my own affair. If I want to marry an exile I shall.'

'You won't.'

'But yes, I have thought of a very good plan. We will go and live in Austria, where my uncle the Vidame is.'

'Nothing would induce me to live in Austria!'

'*Bien*, then we will live in Italy, at Rome.'

'Not Rome,' objected Ludovic. 'Too many English there.'

'Oh! Then you will choose for us some place where there are not any English people, and Tristram who is a – is a trustee will arrange that you can have some money there.'

'Tristram is more likely to send you to Bath and kick me out of the country,' said Ludovic. 'What's more, I don't blame him.'

But Sir Tristram, when the news of the betrothal was broken to him, did not evince any desire to resort to such violent methods. He did not even show much surprise, and when Ludovic, half defiant, half contrite, said: 'I ought never to have done it, I know,' he merely replied: 'I don't suppose you did do it.'

Eustacie, taking this as a compliment, said cordially: 'You are quite right, *mon cousin*; it was I who did it, which was not perhaps *comme il faut*, but entirely necessary, on account of Ludovic's honour. And if we do not find that ring we shall go away to Italy, and you will arrange for Ludovic to have his money there, will you not?'

'I expect so,' said Shield. 'But if you are determined to marry Ludovic I think we had better find the ring.'

Miss Thane, who had come into the parlour in the middle of this speech, thought it proper to assume an expression of astonishment and to say incredulously: 'Do I understand, Sir Tristram, that this betrothal has your blessing?'

He turned. 'Oh, you are there, are you? No, it has *not* my blessing, though I have no doubt it has yours?'

'Of course it has,' said Miss Thane. 'I think it is delightful. Have you discovered when the Beau means to go to London?'

But this he had been unable to do, the Beau having apparently decided to postpone the date. Shield had come to inform Ludovic of it, and to warn him that this change of plan might well mean that the Beau's suspicions had been aroused. When he heard from Nye that Gregg had visited the inn on the previous day for the ostensible purpose of purchasing a keg of brandy for his master, he felt more uneasy than ever, and said that if only Ludovic had not entered upon an ill-timed engagement he would have had no hesitation in forcibly removing him to Holland.

Miss Thane, to whom, in the coffee-room, this remark was addressed, said that the betrothal, though perhaps a complication, had been inevitable from the start.

'Quite so, ma'am. But if you had not encouraged Eustacie to remain here it need not have been inevitable.'

'I might have known you would lay it at my door!' said Miss Thane in a voice of pious resignation.

'I imagine you might, since you are very well aware of having fostered the engagement!' retorted Shield. 'I had thought you a woman of too much sense to encourage such an insane affair.'

'Oh!' said Miss Thane idiotically, 'but I think it is so romantic!'

'Don't be so foolish!' said Sir Tristram, refusing to smile at this sally.

'How cross you are!' marvelled Miss Thane. 'I suppose when one reaches middle age it is difficult to sympathize with the follies of youth.'

Sir Tristram had walked over to the other side of the room to pick up his coat and hat, but this was too much for him, and he turned and said with undue emphasis: 'It may interest you to know, ma'am, that I am one-and-thirty years old, and not yet in my dotage!'

'Why, of course not!' said Miss Thane soothingly. 'You have only entered upon what one may call the sober time of life. Let me help you to put on your coat!'

'Thank you,' said Sir Tristram. 'Perhaps you would also like to give me the support of your arm as far as to the door?'

She laughed. 'Can I not persuade you to remain a little while? This has been a very fleeting visit. Do you not find it dull alone at the Court?'

'Very, but I am not going to the Court. I am on my way to Brighton, to talk to the Beau's late butler.'

She said approvingly: 'You may be shockingly cross but you are certainly not idle. Tell me about this butler!'

'There is nothing to tell as yet. He was in the Beau's employment at the time of Plunkett's murder, and it occurred to me some days ago that it might be interesting to trace him, and discover what he can remember of the Beau's movements upon that night.'

This scheme, though it would not have appealed to Eustacie, who preferred her plans to be attended by excitement, seemed eminently practical to Miss Thane. She parted from Sir Tristram very cordially, and went back into the parlour to tell Ludovic that although he might still be unable to do anything towards his reinstatement, his cousin had the matter well in hand.

As she expected, Eustacie did not regard Sir Tristram's errand with much favour. She said that it was very well for Tristram, but for herself she preferred that there should be adventure.

But upon the following morning, when Miss Thane had gone out with her brother for a sedate walk, adventure took Eustacie unawares and in a guise that frightened her a good deal more than she liked.

She was seated in the parlour, waiting for Ludovic, who was dressing, to come downstairs, when the mail-coach from London arrived. She heard it draw up outside the inn, but paid no attention to it, for it was a daily occurrence, and the coach only stopped at the Red Lion to change horses. But a minute or two later Clem put his head into the room, and said, his face as white as his shirt: 'It's the Runners, miss!'

Eustacie's embroidery-frame slipped out of her hands. She gazed at Clem in horror, and stammered: 'The B-Bow Street Runners?'

'Yes, miss, I'm telling you! And there's Mr. Ludovic trapped upstairs, and Mr. Nye not in!' said Clem, wringing his hands.

Eustacie pulled herself together. 'He must instantly go into the cellar. I will talk to the Runners while you take him there.'

'It's too late, miss! Whoever it was sent them knew about the cellars, for there's one of them standing over the backstairs at this very moment! I never knew they was even on the coach till they come walking into the place, as bold as brass!'

'They may be searching the house now!' exclaimed Eustacie in sudden alarm. 'You should not have left them! Oh dear, do you think my cousin will shoot them? If he does we must bury them quickly, before anyone knows!'

'No, no, miss, it ain't as bad as that yet! What they wants is to see Mr. Nye. They daresn't go searching the place afore ever they tell him what they're here for. They think I've gone to look for him, but what I've got to do is to hide the young master, and lordy, lordy, how can I get upstairs without them knowing when one of 'em's lounging round the backstairs, and t'other sitting in the coffee-room?'

'Go immediately, and find Nye!' ordered Eustacie. 'He must think of a way. I will talk to these Runners, and if I can I will coax the one in the coffee-room to come into the parlour.'

With this praiseworthy resolve in mind, and an uncomfortable feeling of panic in her breast, she sallied forth from the parlour and made her way to the coffee-room. Here, at a table in the middle of the room which commanded a view of the staircase and the front door, was seated a stockily-built individual in a blue coat and a wide-brimmed hat, casually glancing over the contents of a folded journal, which he had extricated from one capacious pocket. Eustacie, surveying him from the open doorway, noticed that his figure was on the portly side, a circumstance which afforded her a certain amount of satisfaction, since it seemed improbable that a stout, middle-aged man would have much hope of catching Ludovic if that young gentleman were forced to take to his heels.

Summoning up a smile, and a look of inquiry, Eustacie said, as though startled: 'Oh! Why, who are you?'

The Bow Street officer looked up, and finding that he was being addressed by a young and enchantingly pretty female, laid the journal down upon the table and rose to his feet. He touched his hat, and said that he was wishful to see the landlord.

'But yes, of course!' said Eustacie. 'You have come on the mail-coach, *sans doute*, and you want a drink! I understand!'

By this time the Runner had assimilated the fact that she was not English. He did not care for foreigners, but her instant grasp of his most pressing need inclined him to regard her with less disapproval than he might otherwise have done. He did not precisely admit that he wanted a drink, but he said that it was a very cold, raw day to be sure, and waited hopefully to see what she would do about it.

'Yes,' she said, 'and it is, moreover, very draughty in a coach. I think you ought to have some cognac.'

The Runner thought so to. He had not wanted to come down to Sussex on what would probably turn out to be a wild-goose chase. He felt gloomily that he would not have been chosen for the task if the authorities over him had set much store by the information lodged with them, for he was not at the moment in very good odour at Bow Street. Such epithets as Blockhead and Blunderer had been used in connection with his last case, since when he had not been employed upon any very important business. In his more optimistic moments he dreamed rosily of the glory attaching to the capture of so desperate a character as Ludovic Lavenham, but when his throat was dry and his fingers chilled he did not feel optimistic.

'When Nye comes he must at once give you some cognac,' announced Eustacie. 'But I do not understand what you are doing here and you have not told me who you are.'

The Runner was not much acquainted with the Quality, but it did occur to him that it was a little unusual for young ladies to address strange men in public coffee-rooms. He bent a penetrating and severe eye upon her, and replied, awe-inspiringly, that he was an Officer of the Law.

Eustacie at once clasped her hands together, and cried: 'I *thought* you were! Are you perhaps a Bow Street Runner?'

The Runner was accustomed to having his identity discovered with fear, or even loathing, but he had not till now encountered anyone who became ecstatic upon learning his dread profession. He admitted that he was a Runner, but looked so suspiciously at Eustacie that she made haste to explain that in France they had no such people, which was the reason why she was so particulary anxious to meet one.

When she mentioned France the Runner's brow cleared. The French, what with their guillotines and one thing and another, were the worst kinds of foreigners, and it was no use being surprised at them behaving queerly. They were born that way; there wasn't any sense in them; and the silly habit they had of holding that everyone was equal accounted for this young lady speaking so friendly to a mere Bow Street Runner.

'You are one of the so famous Runners!' said Eustacie, regarding him with rapt admiration. 'You must be very brave and clever!'

The Runner coughed rather self-consciously, and murmured something inarticulate. He had not previously given the matter much thought, but now the lady came to mention it he realized that he was rather a brave man.

'What is your name?' inquired Eustacie. 'And why have you come here?'

'Jeremiah Stubbs, miss,' said the Runner. 'I am here in the execution of my dooty.'

Eustacie opened her eyes to their widest extent, and asked breathlessly whether he had come to make an arrest. '*How* I should like to see you make an arrest!' she said.

Mr. Stubbs was not impervious to flattery. He threw out his chest a little, and replied with an indulgent smile that he couldn't say for certain whether he was going to make an arrest or not.

'But who?' demanded Eustacie. 'Not someone in this inn?'

'A desprit criminal, missy, that's the cove I'm after,' said Mr. Stubbs.

Eustacie's straining ears caught the sound of an opening door upstairs and a light footfall. She said as loudly as she dared: 'I suppose you, who are a *Bow Street Runner*, have to capture a great many desperate criminals?' As she spoke she moved towards the fire, so that to address her Mr. Stubbs had to turn slightly, presenting his profile, and no longer his full face to the staircase.

'Oh well, miss,' he said carelessly, 'we don't take much account of that!'

Eustacie caught a glimpse of Ludovic at the top of the stairs, and said quickly: 'Bow Street Runners! It must be very exciting to be a Bow Street Runner, I think!' She glanced up as she spoke, and saw that Ludovic had vanished. Feeling almost sick with relief, she pressed her handkerchief to her lips, and said mechanically: 'Who is this criminal, I wonder? A thief, perhaps?'

'Not a thief, miss,' said Mr. Stubbs. 'A murderer!'

The effect of this announcement was all he had hoped for. Eustacie gave a shriek and faltered: 'Here? A m-murderer? Arrest him at once, if you please! But at once!'

'Ah!' said Mr. Stubbs, 'if I could do that everything would be easy, wouldn't it? But this here murdering cove has been evading of the law for two years and more.'

'But how could he evade you, who must, I know, be a clever man, for two years?'

Mr. Stubbs began to think rather well of Eustacie, French though she might be. 'That's it,' he said. 'You've put your finger on it, missy, as the saying is. If they'd had me on to him at the start p'raps he wouldn't have done no evading.'

'No, I think not, indeed. You look very cold, which is not at all a thing to wonder at when one considers that there is a great *courant d'air* here. I will take you into the parlour, where it is altogether cosy, and procure for you a glass of cognac.'

Mr. Stubbs's eye glistened a little, but he shook his head. 'It's very kind of you, miss, but I've a fancy to stay right where I am, d'ye see? You don't happen to be staying in this here inn, do you?'

'But certainly I am staying here!' responded Eustacie. 'I am staying with Sir Hugh Thane, who is a Justice of the Peace, and with Miss Thane.'

'You are?' said Mr. Stubbs. 'Well now, that's a very fortunate circumstance, that is. You don't happen to have seen anything of a young cove – a mighty flash young cove – Lurking?'

Eustacie looked rather bewildered, and said: '*Plaît-il?* Lurking?'

'Or skulking?' suggested Mr. Stubbs. He drew forth from his pocket a well-worn notebook, and, licking his thumb, began to turn over its pages.

'What is that?' asked Eustacie, eyeing the book with misgiving.

'This is my Occurrence Book, missy. There are plenty of coves would like to get their dabblers on it, I can tell you. There's things in this book as'll send a good few to the Nubbing Cheat one day,' said Mr. Stubbs darkly.

'Oh,' said Eustacie, wishing that Nye would come, and wondering how to lure Mr. Stubbs away from the stairs. If only Ludovic had not injured his shoulder he might have climbed out of the window, she thought, but with one arm in a sling that was out of the question.

Mr. Stubbs, finding his place in his Occurrence Book, said: 'Here we are, now. Has there been a young cove here, missy, with blue eyes, light hair, features aquiline, height about five feet ten inches——'

Eustacie interrupted this recital. 'But yes, you describe to me Sir Hugh Thane, only he is taller, I think, and me, I should say that he has grey eyes.'

'The cove this here description fits is a cove by the name of Loodervic Lavenham,' said Mr. Stubbs.

Eustacie at once executed a start. 'But are you mad? Ludovic Lavenham is my cousin, *enfin!*'

Mr. Stubbs stared at her fixedly. 'You say this Loodervic Lavenham's your cousin, miss?' he said, his voice pregnant with suspicion.

'Of course he is!' replied Eustacie. 'He is a very wicked creature who has brought disgrace to us, and we do not speak of him even. Why have you come to look for him? He went away from England two years ago!'

Mr. Stubbs caressed his chin, still keeping his eyes on Eustacie's face. 'Oh!' he said slowly. 'He wouldn't happen to be staying in this inn right now, I suppose?'

'Staying here?' gasped Eustacie. 'In the same place with *me*? No! I tell you, he is in disgrace – quite cast-off!'

'Ah!' said Mr. Stubbs. 'What would you say if I was to tell you that this very Loodervic Lavenham is lurking somewhere in these parts?'

'I do not think so,' said Eustacie, with a shake of her head. 'And I hope very much that it is not true, because there has been enough disgrace for us, and we do not desire that there should be any more.' An idea occurred to her. She added 'I see now that you are a *very* brave man, and I will tell you that if my cousin is truly in Sussex you must be excessively careful.'

Mr. Stubbs looked at her rather more fixedly than before. 'Oh, I must, must I?' he said.

'You have not been warned then?' cried Eustacie, shocked.

'No,' said Mr. Stubbs. 'I ain't been warned particular.'

'But it is infamous that they have not told you!' declared Eustacie. '*Je n'en reviendrai jamais!*'

'If it's all the same to you, miss, I'd just as soon you'd talk in a Christian language,' said Mr. Stubbs. 'What was it they had ought to have warned me about?'

Eustacie spread out her hands. 'His pistols!' she said dramatically. 'Do you not know that my cousin is the man who put out sixteen candles by shooting them, and did not miss one?'

Mr. Stubbs cast an involuntary glance behind him. 'He put out sixteen candles?' he demanded.

'But yes, have I not said so?'

'And he didn't miss one of them?'

'He never misses,' said Eustacie.

Mr. Stubbs drew in his breath. 'They *had* ought to have warned me!' he said feelingly.

'Certainly they——' Eustacie broke off, startled by a crash in the room above their heads, and the muffled sound of a shriek. Who could possibly be upstairs save Ludovic, she could not imagine, but Ludovic would hardly shriek, even if he had knocked something over in one of the bedchambers.

Then, to her amazement, she heard a door open, and hurrying footsteps approach the head of the stairs. A high-pitched voice wailed: 'Oh, oh, what shall I do? Oh, Mr. Nye, look what I've done!' And down the stairs came a gawky female in a large mob-cap and a stuff gown which Eustacie transfixed by astonishment, instantly recognized as Miss Thane's. A shawl enveloped the apparition's shoulders, and she held one corner of it up to her eyes with her left hand. In her right she carried the fragments of a flagon that had once contained Miss Thane's French perfume. 'Oh, Mr. Nye!' she whimpered. 'Mistress will kill me if she finds out – oh!' The last word took the form of a scream as the newcomer caught sight of Eustacie. 'Oh, miss, I beg pardon!' she gasped. 'I thought you was gone out! I've – I've had an accident, miss! Oh, I'm that sorry, miss, I'm sure.'

Eustacie made a strangled sound in her throat, and rose nobly to the occasion. Running forward, she seized the gawky female's right wrist, and cried in a quivering voice: 'Wretched, wicked creature! You have broken my scent bottle! Ah, it is too much, *enfin!*'

The jagged fragments of glass were relinquished into her keeping, and with them, slid into the palm of her hand, a great ruby ring.

CHAPTER 9

A torrent of impassioned French smote the Runner's bemused ears. He stared, quite aghast, at Eustacie, who had changed in a flash from a pleasant-spoken young female into a raging virago. She snatched the jagged fragments of glass from the abigail's hand, broke into English for one moment to implore Mr. Stubbs to look at what the wicked, clumsy creature had done, threw the fragments into the grate, shook the abigail, and in French said rapidly: 'He means to search the house. Have you taken your clothes out of your room? Answer yes, or no!'

'Oh yes, miss, indeed I took them to Sir Hugh's room, like you told me!'

Mr. Stubbs began to feel sorry for the hapless abigail, whose sobs grew more and more shattering. This suddenly terrible little Frenchwoman seemed to have what he would call a real spiteful temper. Nothing appeased her; he was not at all surprised to see the abigail so frightened; he wouldn't put it beyond the young lady to box the poor girl's ears at any moment.

In the middle of this spirited scene Nye came into the coffee-room with Clem at his heels, and stopped upon the threshold, transfixed by astonishment. For a moment he did not connect Ludovic with the great gawky girl, noisily weeping into her shawl, but before he had time to speak, Eustacie whirled round to face him, and poured forth a string of complaints about her supposed abigail. She desired him to tell her whether she had not sufficient cause to hand the girl over to the Law, and indicated with a sweep of her hand the presence of a Bow Street Runner.

Nye, who had caught the glint of pale-gold hair peeping from under the gawky female's mob-cap, now observed that her left arm seemed in some odd fashion to be wound up in the voluminous shawl. The puzzled look vanished from his face; he came farther into the room, and joined with Eustacie in reproaching 'Lucy' for her carelessness. Mr. Stubbs, quite overwhelmed by so much loud and confused talk, withdrew to the other end of the room, and mopped his brow. He gazed at Eustacie in growing consternation, and took a hasty step backward, when she suddenly rounded on him and demanded why he stood there doing nothing, instead of instantly arresting 'Lucy'.

'Oh come, miss! Come, now!' said Nye soothingly. 'It's not as bad as that! The wench meant no harm. I'll have Clem take up a pail of water and a scrubbing-brush, or we'll have the whole house reeking of scent.'

'And in my room!' exclaimed Eustacie. 'It is an outrage! It must be at once scrubbed, and I will tell you that it is Lucy herself who shall scrub it, for it is not at all Clem's fault. Up, you!'

The Runner, seeing 'Lucy' driven towards the staircase, heaved a sigh of relief. Mistress and maid vanished from sight; Clem, at a nod from Nye, went away to draw a pail of water; and Nye turned to his unwelcome visitor, and said with a wry smile, and a jerk of his thumb over his shoulder: 'Them Frenchies!'

'Unchristian, that's what I call 'em,' responded Mr. Stubbs severely. 'I fair compassionate that wench.'

'She'll be turned off,' said Nye with a resigned shrug. 'That will make the third in as many weeks. Miss has the temper of the fiend, *as* I know. What can I do for you?'

Above, in Miss Thane's bedchamber, Eustacie, from whom stifled giggles had escaped all the way up the stairs, sank down upon the bed, and with her handkerchief pressed to her mouth, gave way to inextinguishable laughter. Ludovic, twisting the shawl more securely round his arm, said: 'Of all the spitfires! I wouldn't be a maid of yours for any money. Now what's the matter?'

'You l-look so rid-ridiculous!' gasped Eustacie, rocking herself to and fro.

Ludovic looked critically at his reflection in the mirror. 'A fine, strapping girl,' he said. 'But what beats me is how you females ever contrive to dress at all. *I* couldn't do up the plaguey hooks and eyes on this gown. That's why I took the shawl. I don't care for Sarah's scent, do you?'

Indeed, the room reeked of heavy scent. Eustacie raised her head to say unsteadily: 'But of course not, a whole bottle of it! It is *affreux*! Open the window! Those Runners have come for you, Ludovic. What are we to do?'

He had thrust open one of the casements, and was leaning out to breathe the unscented air, but he turned his head at that. 'How many of them are there?'

'Two. There is one on guard over the backstairs. I think it is Basil who must have told them to look for you here.'

'I saw the one on the backstairs. If there are no more than two, and Nye can't fob them off, we'd better lock them up in the cellar, I think. Just until I've found my ring,' he added reassuringly, seeing Eustacie's face of disapproval.

'But no, for if we lock them up we shall be put in prison for it!'

'There is that, of course,' agreed Ludovic. 'Still, if only I could clear myself of this murder charge I shouldn't mind taking the risk. Ten to one we'd get off with a fine.'

They were still arguing the point when Clem appeared with a pail and a scrubbing-brush. They pounced upon him for news, and he was able to tell them that Nye had the situation well in hand, and had already gone far towards convincing the Runners that they had been sent to look for a mare's nest. At the moment he was regaling them with brandy, after which he had promised to conduct them personally all over the inn. Hearing this, Eustacie was at once struck by the notion of spreading a few pieces of female apparel about Ludovic's room. She went off to do this, leaving Ludovic with instructions to start scrubbing the floor the instant he heard the Runners ascending the stairs.

By the time Mr. Stubbs, fortified by brandy, did come up, Eustacie had returned to Miss Thane's room, and no sooner did Nye tap on the door, asking whether the officer might come in, than she broke forth again into indignant repinings. Both the Runner and Nye were adjured to come in and judge for themselves whether the smell of the perfume would ever be got rid of. When Nye asked permission for the Runner to search her room, she first stared at him with an expression of outrage on her face, and then flung open the door of the cupboard and said tragically that it needed only this, that a great rough man should pry into her wardrobe. She begged Mr. Stubbs not to consider her feelings in the least degree, but to pull all her dresses out, and throw them on the floor if he pleased. Mr. Stubbs, acutely uncomfortable, assured her that he had no desire to do anything of the kind. She said that she wished she were back in France, where ladies were treated with civility, and, covering her face with her handkerchief, burst into tears. Ludovic, inexpertly scrubbing the damp patch on the floor, sniffed dolefully over the pail of water, and the Runner, casting a perfunctory glance into the wardrobe and another under the bed, beat a somewhat hasty retreat.

It was not long before Nye returned, this time alone. He found Eustacie peeping out of the window at the receding forms of the two officers, and Ludovic, the mob-cap and shawl already discarded, trying to extricate himself from Miss Thane's gown. Characteristically, the first words he addressed to Ludovic were of decided reproof. 'And who might those clothes belong to, my lord, if I may make so bold as to ask?'

'To Miss Thane, of course. Help me to come out of this curst dress!'

'And that's a nice thing!' said Nye. 'Couldn't you find nothing else to break but a flask of scent that don't belong to you? For shame, Mr. Ludovic!'

Eustacie came away from the window. '*Enfin*, they are gone. Do they believe that my cousin is not here, Nye?'

'That's more than I can tell you, miss,' replied Nye, picking up Miss Thane's dress from the floor. 'Nor I don't think they've gone far. They would have put up here for the night if I hadn't shown them I haven't a bed to spare. It's my belief they're off no farther than to the ale-house down the road.'

'Do you mean to tell me those fellows are going to hang around this place?' said Ludovic, himself again in shirt and breeches. 'Who set them on?'

Nye shook his head. 'They wouldn't say. The fat one don't seem to me to set much store by the information. But for all that, I'll have the cellar made ready for you, sir.'

'Make it ready for the Runners,' said Ludovic briskly. 'We'll have to kidnap them.'

'There'll be no such foolishness in this house, Mr. Ludovic, and so I'll have you know!'

Some twenty minutes later Miss Thane, accompanied by her brother, came back to the Red Lion, and was at once met by Eustacie, who drew her upstairs to her room, her story tripping off her tongue.

'Runners in the house, and I not here to see them?' exclaimed Miss Thane, suitably impressed. 'I declare I am the most ill-used creature alive! How I should have liked to have helped to hoodwink them!'

'Yes, it was sad for you to be out, but you did help us, Sarah, because Ludovic put on one of your dresses, and pretended to be my maid.'

They had by this time reached Miss Thane's bedchamber. Eustacie opened the door and Miss Thane took one step into the room and recoiled.

'It's only the scent,' said Eustacie kindly. 'And indeed it is already much fainter than it was. Ludovic thought that it would be a good thing to break the bottle, pretending that it was mine. In that way, you understand, he was able to hide his face, because he made believe to cry, and to be frightened. And I scolded him – oh, àfaire croire!'

'I'm glad,' said Miss Thane. 'I suppose it had to be my French perfume?'

Ludovic, hearing their voices, strolled across the passage from his own room, and said with a grin: 'Sarah, are you savage with me for having spilled your scent? I will buy you some more one day.'

'Thank you, Ludovic!' said Miss Thane with feeling. 'And this is the gown you chose to wear, is it? Yes, I see. After all, I never cared for it above the ordinary.'

'It got split a trifle across the shoulders,' explained Ludovic.

'Yes, I noticed that,' agreed Miss Thane. 'But what is a mere gown compared with a man's life?'

Eustacie greeted this sentiment with great approval, and said that she knew Sarah would feel like that.

'Of course,' said Miss Thane. 'And I have been thinking, moreover, that we do not consider Ludovic enough. Look at this large, airy apartment of mine, for instance, and only consider the stuffy little back chamber he is obliged to sleep in! I will change with you, my dear Ludovic.'

Ludovic declined this handsome offer without the least hesitation. 'I don't like the smell of the scent,' he said frankly.

Miss Thane, overcome by her emotions, tottered to a chair and covered her eyes with her hand. In a voice of considerable feeling she gave Ludovic to understand that since he had saturated the carpet in her room with scent, he and not she should sleep in that exotic atmosphere.

The rest of the day was enlivened by alarms and discussions. The Runners had, as Nye suspected, withdrawn merely to the ale-house a mile down the road, and both of them revisited the Red Lion at separate times, entering it in the most unobtrusive, not to say stealthy, manner possible, and explaining their presence in unexpected corners of the house by saying that they were looking for the landlord. The excuses they put forward for these visits, though not convincing, were accepted by Nye with obliging complaisance. Secure in the knowledge that Ludovic was hidden in his secret cellar, he gave the Runners all the facilities they could desire to prowl unaccompanied about the house. The only person to be dissatisfied with this arrangement was the quarry himself who, in spite of the amenities afforded by a brazier and a couple of candles, complained that the cellar was cold, dark, and devilish uncomfortable. His plan of remaining above-stairs in readiness to retreat to the cellar upon the arrival of a Runner was frustrated by the tiresome conduct of these gentlemen, who seemed to spend the entire afternoon prowling around the house. Twice Eustacie was startled by an inquiring face at the parlour-window, and three times did Clem report that one of the officers was round the back of the house by the stables, hobnobbing with the ostler and the post-boys. Even Sir Hugh became aware of an alien presence in the inn, and complained when he came down to dinner that a strange fellow had poked his head into his bedchamber while he was pulling off his boots.

'A demmed, rascally-looking fellow with a red nose,' he said. 'Nye ought to be more careful whom he lets into the place. Came creeping up the passage and peered into my room without so much as a "by your leave."'

'Did he say anything to you?' asked Miss Thane anxiously.

'No,' replied Sir Hugh. He added fair-mindedly: 'I don't say he wouldn't have, but I threw a boot at him.'

'Threw a boot at him?' cried Eustacie, her eyes sparkling.

'Yes, why not? I don't like people prowling about, and I won't have them poking their red noses into my room,' said Sir Hugh.

'Hugh, you will have to know, so that you may be on your guard,' said Miss Thane. 'That was a Bow Street Runner.'

'Well, he's got no right to come prying into my room,' replied Sir Hugh, helping himself from a dish of beans. 'Where's young Lavenham?'

'In the cellar. He——'

Sir Hugh laid down his knife and fork. 'What's he found there? Is he bringing it up?'

'No. He is in the cellar because the Runners are looking for him.'

Sir Hugh frowned. 'It seems to me,' he remarked somewhat austerely, 'that there's something queer going on in this place. I won't have anything to do with it.'

'Very proper, my dear,' approved his sister. 'But do contrive to remember that you know nothing of Ludovic Lavenham! I fear that these Runners may try to get information from you.'

'Oh, they may, may they?' said Sir Hugh, his eye kindling a little. 'Well, if that red-nosed fellow is a Runner, which I doubt, I'll have some information to give him on the extent of his duty. They're getting mighty out of hand, those Runners. I shall speak to old Sampson Wright about 'em.'

'Certainly, Hugh; I hope you will, but do, pray, promise me that you won't divulge Ludovic's presence here to them!'

'I'm a Justice of the Peace,' said Sir Hugh, 'and I won't have any hand in cheating the Law. If they were to ask me I should tell them the truth.'

Eustacie, pale with alarm, gripped the edge of the table, and said: 'But you must not! you shall not!'

Sir Hugh cast an indulgent glance towards her. 'They won't ask me,' he said simply.

It seemed improbable that the Runners' zeal would lead them to haunt the vicinity of the Red Lion after dark, so as soon as the windows were bolted and the blinds drawn, Ludovic emerged from his underground retreat and joined the rest of the party in the parlour. Some expectation was felt of receiving a visit from Sir Tristram, and at a little after eight o'clock he walked into the inn, having taken advantage of the moonlight to drive over from the Court.

He was met by demands to know whether he had met any men lurking outside the house. He had not, but the anxious question at once aroused his suspicions, and he asked what had been going forward during his absence. When he heard that information had been laid against Ludovic in Bow Street, he did not say anything at all for some moments, thus disappointing Eustacie, who had hoped to startle him into an expression at least of surprise. When he did speak, it was not in admiration of the stratagem which had hoodwinked the Runners, but in a serious voice, and with his eyes on his cousin. 'If you won't go to Holland, will you at least leave Sussex, Ludovic?'

'Devil a bit! There's no danger. The Runners think they're on a wild-goose chase.' He observed a tightening of Shield's lips, a certain considering look in the eyes which rested on himself, and sat up with a jerk. 'Tristram, if you try to kidnap me, I swear I'll shoot you!'

Sir Tristram laughed at that, but shook his head. 'I won't promise not to kidnap you, but I will promise to get your gun first.'

'It never leaves me,' grinned Ludovic.

'That's what I'm afraid of,' retorted Shield. 'If there's an attempt made on you, you'll shoot, and there'll be a charge of real murder to fight.'

Eustacie said sharply: 'An attempt on him? Do you mean on his life?'

'Yes, I do,' replied Shield. 'We may not be certain that the Beau killed Plunkett, but we can have no doubt that it is he who brought the Runners down on Ludovic now. He would like the Law to remove Ludovic from his path, but if the Runners fail, I think he may make the attempt himself. Have you ever considered how easy of access this place is?'

Eustacie cast an involuntary glance over her shoulder. 'N-no,' she faltered. 'Is—is it easy? Perhaps you had better go after all, Ludovic. I do not want you to be killed!'

'Ah, fiddlesticks,' Ludovic said impatiently. 'The Beau don't even know I'm here. He may suspect it, but there's not a soul has seen me outside ourselves, and Nye, and Clem.'

'You are forgetting the Excise officer,' interpolated his cousin.

'What odds? I'll admit it was he who put the notion into Basil's head, but it's no more than a notion, and when Basil hears the Runners found no trace of me, he'll think himself mistaken, after all. Nye's of the opinion they don't set much store by the information laid.'

'It's plain they set very little store by it, since they didn't send their best men down to investigate it, but they are likely to take a more serious view of the matter when they discover that Eustacie has no abigail with her.'

'Ludovic,' said Miss Thane in a meditative voice, 'thinks it would be a good thing to capture the Runners and bestow them in the cellar.'

'A famous plan!' said Sir Tristram sardonically.

'Yes, but me, I do not agree,' said Eustacie, frowning.

'You surprise me.'

'Just a moment!' interposed Thane, who all this time had been sitting at a small table by the fire, casting his dice, right hand against left. 'You can't imprison law officers in the cellar. For one thing, it's a criminal offence, and for another there's a deal of precious liquor in the cellar. I don't like that red-nosed fellow; I think he ought to be got rid of. What's more, I've had a score against Sampson Wright for a long time, and I don't mind putting a spoke in his wheel. But I won't have his Runners kidnapped.'

'Well!' said his sister. 'I think you are most unreasonable, Hugh, I must say. After all, it was you who threw a boot at the Runner.'

'That's a very different thing,' replied Thane. 'There's nothing to be said against throwing a boot at a fellow who comes nosing into one's room. But kidnapping's another matter.'

'Oh well!' said Ludovic airily. 'Ten to one we shan't see any more of them. I dare say they will go back to London on to-morrow's coach.'

Had Mr. Stubbs followed his own inclination, he would not have waited for the morrow's coach but would have boarded the night mail, deeming a night on the road preferable to one spent at the ale-house. But his companion, a grave person with a painstaking sense of duty and an earnest desire to prove himself worthy of his office, held the opinion that their search had not been sufficiently thorough.

'What we've done is, we've Lulled them,' he said, slowly nodding his head. 'Properly Lulled them, that's what we've done. We didn't find no trace of any desperate criminal, and they know we didn't find no trace. So what happens?'

'Well, what does happen?' said Mr. Stubbs, lowering his tankard.

'They're Lulled, that's what happens.'

'You said that before,' remarked Mr. Stubbs, with slight asperity.

'Ah, but what do we do now we've got them Lulled?' demanded his companion. 'We makes a Pounce, and takes this Ludovic Lavenham unawares.'

Mr. Stubbs turned it over in his mind. 'I won't say you're wrong, William,' he pronounced cautiously. 'Nor I've no objection, provided we *do* take him unawares. It's a queer thing, but I can't get out of my mind what that French hussy told me about this Loodervic being so handy with his pops. It makes things awkward. I won't say no more than that. Awkward.'

'I've been thinking about that,' said the zealous Mr. Peabody, 'and the conclusion I've come to, Jerry, is that she made it up out of her head just for to scare you.'

For a moment Mr. Stubbs pondered this. Then he said somewhat severely: 'She should ha' known better.' He took a pull at his ale, and wiping his mouth on the back of his hand, added: 'Mind you, I've had my doubts about it all along. Sixteen candles is what she said. Now, I put it to you, William, is that a likely story?'

Mr. Peabody gave it as his opinion that it was a most unlikely story. They discussed the question for a little while, Mr. Stubbs contending that had Eustacie spoken of six candles, he might have believed her, and Mr. Peabody, a more practical man, distrusting the entire story on the grounds that there was no sense in firing at candles at all.

They had, by these divergent paths, arrived at the same comfortable conclusion when their privacy was disturbed by the arrival of a visitor, who turned out to be none other than Gregg, Beau Lavenham's discreet valet. He came into the tap-room with a prim little bow and a tight-lipped smile, and ordered a brandy with hot water and lemon. Until this had been procured for him, he stayed by the bar, only glancing once out of the corners of his eyes at the two Runners snugly ensconced in the ingle-nook by the fire. When his glass had been handed to him, however, he walked over to the fireplace, drew up a chair close to the high-backed settle, and bade the Runners good evening.

They returned this civil greeting without showing any marked degree of cordiality. They were aware that he was the man to whom they were indebted for what information they had, but although they would be grateful for any further information that he might be able to give them, they had a prejudice against informers as a race, and saw no reason to make an exception in this one's favour. Accordingly, when Gregg leaned forward in his chair, and said in a keen but subdued voice: 'Well?' it was in chilly accents that Mr. Stubbs replied: 'It ain't well. We've been fetched down for nothing, that's what.'

'So you didn't find him!' said Gregg, frowning.

'Nor him, nor any sign of him. Which I will say didn't surprise me.'

'But he was there, for all that,' said Gregg, tapping his front teeth with one finger-nail. 'I am sure he was there. You looked everywhere?'

'There now!' said Mr. Stubbs, with scathing irony. 'If you haven't put me in mind of it! Dang me, if I didn't forget to look inside of one of the coal-boxes!'

Gregg, perceived that he had offended, smiled and made a deprecating movement with his hand. 'It is an old house, and full of nooks and hidden cupboards. You are sure – I expect you are sure – that he had no opportunity to seek safety in the cellars?'

'Yes,' replied Mr. Stubbs. 'I am sure. By the time I was in by the front door, Mr. Peabody here was in the back. And not so much of a sniff of any criminal did we get. What's more, we had very nice treatment from the landlord, very nice indeed we had. There are plenty as would have behaved different, but Mr. Nye, he made no bones at all. "It's not what I like," he says, "but I don't blame you, nor I'm not one to stand in the way of an officer what is only executing his dooty."'

The valet's light eyes flickered from one stolid face to the other. 'He had him hidden. When I went he was not hidden. The tapster would not let me set foot outside the tap-room. They did not wish me to go anywhere inside the house. It was most marked.'

'That don't surprise me,' said Mr. Stubbs. He put his empty tankard down and regarded the valet narrowly. 'What's your interest in this Loodervic Lavenham? What makes you so unaccountable anxious to have him laid by the heels?'

The valet folded his lips closely, but after a moment replied: 'Well, you see, Mr. Stubbs, that is my business. I have my reasons.'

The Runner eyed him with growing disfavour. 'Lookee!' he pronounced. 'When I go ferreting for news of a desprit criminal, that's dooty. When you does the same thing, Mr. Gregg, it looks to me uncommon like Spitefulness, and Spitefulness is what I don't hold with, and never shall.'

'That's right,' agreed Mr. Peabody.

The valet smiled again, but unpleasantly, and said in his silky way: 'Why, you may say so if you choose, Mr. Stubbs. And I hope I may ask whom you saw at the Red Lion?'

'I didn't see no desprit criminal,' answered Mr. Stubbs. 'It's my belief there ain't no desprit criminal. Is it likely the place would house such with a Justice of the Peace putting up there?'

'You went into the little back bedchamber? They let you go there?'

'I went into two back bedchambers, one which is the landlord's and the other which the young French lady's maid has.'

The valet's eyelids were quickly raised. 'Her maid? Did you see her maid?'

'Ay, poor wench, I saw her right enough, and I heard Miss a-scolding of her all for breaking a bottle.'

'What was she like?' demanded Gregg, leaning forward again.

Mr. Stubbs looked at him with a shade of uneasiness in his eyes. 'Why, I didn't get much sight of her face, she being crying into her shawl fit to break her heart.'

'Ah, so you didn't see her face!' said Gregg. 'Perhaps she was a tall girl – a very tall girl?'

Mr. Stubbs had been engaged in filling a long clay pipe, but he laid it down, and said slowly: 'Ay, she was a rare, strapping wench. She had yaller hair, by what I could see of it.'

Gregg sat back in his chair and set his finger-tips together, and over them surveyed the Runners with a peculiar glint in his eyes. 'So that was it!' he said. 'Well, well!'

'What do you mean, "that was it"?' said Mr. Stubbs.

'Only that you have seen Ludovic Lavenham; yes, and let him slip through your fingers too, I dare say.'

Mr. Peabody, observing his colleague's evident discomfiture, came gallantly to the rescue. 'That's where you're wrong,' he said. 'What we've done is, we've Lulled him – if so be it is him, which we ain't proved yet. What we have to do now is to make a Pounce, and that, Mr. Gregg, is what we decided to do without any help of yourn.'

'You had better have made your pounce when you had him under your hand,' said the valet dryly. 'It is said in these parts that there are cellars below the ones you may see at the Red Lion; cellars which only Nye and Clem know the way into.'

'If that's true, we shall find them,' said Mr. Stubbs, with resolution.

'I hope you may,' responded Gregg. 'But take my advice, and go armed! The man you are after is indeed desperate, and I fancy he will not be without his pistols.'

The Runners exchanged glances. 'I did hear tell of him being handy with his pops,' remarked Mr. Stubbs in a casual voice.

'They say he never misses,' said Gregg, lowering his eyes demurely. 'If I were in your shoes, I should think it as well to shoot him before he could shoot me.'

'Yes, I dare say,' said Mr. Stubbs bitterly, 'but we ain't allowed to go a-shooting of coves.'

'But if you told – both of you – how he shot first, and would have escaped, it would surely be overlooked?' suggested Gregg gently.

It was left to Mr. Peabody to sum up the situation, but this he did not do until the valet had gone. Then he said to his troubled companion: 'You know what this looks like to me, Jerry? It looks to me like as if there's someone unaccountable anxious to have this Ludovic Lavenham put away quick – ah, and quiet, too!'

Mr. Stubbs shook his head gloomily, and after a long silence, said: 'We got to do our dooty, William.'

Their duty took them up the road to the Red Lion very early next morning. Their plan of surprising the household was frustrated by Nye, who had taken the precaution of setting Clem on the watch. By the time the Runners had reached the inn Ludovic had been roused, and haled, protesting, to the cellar, and his room swept bare of all trace of him. The Runners were not gratified by the least sign of surprise in Nye, who greeted them with no more than the natural annoyance of a landlord knocked up at an unreasonable hour. In the tap-room Clem was prosaically engaged in scrubbing the floor; he turned a blank, inquiring face towards the Runners, and with the stolid air of one who has work to do, returned to his task.

'Well, and what might you be wanting at this hour of the morning?' asked Nye testily.

'What we want is a word with that abigail we saw yesterday,' said Mr. Stubbs.

'Do you mean Mamzelle's Lucy?' said Nye.

'Ah, that's the one I mean,' nodded Mr. Stubbs.

'Well, if you want a word with her, you'd best get on the Brighton stage. She ain't here any longer.'

Mr. Stubbs gave him a very penetrating look, and said deeply: 'You're quite sure of that, are you, Mr. Nye?'

'Of course I'm sure! I told you yesterday how it would be. Miss turned her off. What do you want with her? She was a rare silly wench, and not so well-favoured neither.'

'You know what I want with her,' said Mr. Stubbs. 'You're harbouring a dangerous criminal, Mr. Nye, and that wench was him!'

This pronouncement, so far from striking terror into the landlord, seemed to afford him the maximum amount of amusement. After staring at the Runners in a bemused way for several minutes, he allowed a smile to spread slowly over his face. The smile led to a chuckle, the chuckle to a veritable paroxysm of laughter. The landlord, wiping his eyes with the corner of his apron, bade Clem share the joke, and as soon as it had been explained to him, Clem did share it. In fact, he continued to snigger behind his hand for much longer than the Runners thought necessary.

When Nye was able to stop laughing he begged Mr. Stubbs to tell him what had put such a notion into his head, and when Mr. Stubbs, hoping that this card at least might prove to be a trump, said that he had received information, he at first looked at him very hard, and then said: 'Information, eh? Then I'll be bound I know who gave you that same information! It was a scrawny fellow with a white face and the nastiest pair of daylights you ever saw! A fellow of the name of Gregg: that's who it was!'

Mr. Stubbs was a trifle disconcerted, and said guardedly: 'I don't say it was, and I don't say it wasn't.'

'Lord love you, you needn't tell me!' said Nye, satisfied that his shot had gone home. 'He's had a spite against me since I don't know when, while as for his master, if a stranger was to stop for half a day in this place, he'd go mad thinking it was Mr. Ludovic come home to stop him taking what don't belong to him. You've been properly roasted, that's what you've been.'

'I don't know about that,' replied Mr. Stubbs. 'All I know is it's very highly suspicious that that abigail ain't here no more, and what I want to see, Mr. Nye, is those cellars of yourn.'

'Well, I've got something better to do than to take you down to my cellars,' said Nye. 'If you want to see 'em, you go and see 'em. I don't mind.'

An hour later, when Sir Hugh came down to breakfast, a pleasing idea dawned in Nye's brain, and as he set a dish of ham and eggs before his patron, he told him that the Runners were in the house again. Sir Hugh, more interested in his breakfast than in the processes of the Law, merely replied that as long as they kept from poking their noses into his room, he had no objection to their presence.

'Oh, they won't do that, sir!' said Nye, pouring him out a cup of coffee. 'They're down in the cellar.'

Sir Hugh was inspecting a red sirloin, and said in a preoccupied voice: 'In the cellar, are they?' Suddenly he let his eyeglass fall, and swung round in his chair to look at the landlord. 'What's that you say? In the cellar?'

'Yes, sir. They've been there the best part of an hour now – off and on.'

Sir Hugh was a man not easily moved, but this piece of intelligence roused him most effectively from his habitual placidity. 'Are you telling me you've let that red-nosed scoundrel loose in the cellars?' he demanded.

'Well, sir, seeing as he's an officer of the Law, and with a warrant, I didn't hardly like to gainsay him,' said Nye apologetically.

'Warrant be damned!' said Sir Hugh. 'There's a pipe of Chambertin down there which I bought from you! What the devil are you about, man?'

'I thought you wouldn't be pleased, sir, but there! what can I do? They've got it into their heads there's a secret cellar. They're hunting for it. Clem tells me it's something shocking the way they're pulling the kegs about.'

'Pulling the——' Words failed Sir Hugh. He rose, flinging down his napkin, and strolled from the parlour towards the tap-room and the cellar stairs.

Fifteen minutes later Miss Thane, entering the room, was mildly surprised to find her brother's chair empty, and inquired of Nye what had become of him.

'It was on account of them Runners, ma'am,' said Nye.

'What! are they here again?' exclaimed Miss Thane.

'Ay, they're here, ma'am, a-hunting for the way into my hidden cellar. Oh, Mr. Ludovic's safe enough! But on account of my mentioning to Sir Hugh how them Runners was disturbing the wine downstairs, he got up, leaving his breakfast like you see, and went off in a rare taking to see what was happening.'

Miss Thane cast one glance at Nye's wooden countenance, and said: 'You were certainly born to be hanged, Nye. What *was* happening?'

'Well, ma'am, by what I heard in the tap-room they had pulled my kegs about a thought roughly, and what with that and Sir Hugh getting it into his head they was wishful to tap the Nantes brandy, there was a trifle of a to-do. Clem tells me it was rare to hear Sir Hugh handle them. By what I understand, he's laid it on them not to move my kegs by so much as an inch, and what he told them about wilful damage frightened them fair silly – that and the high tone he took with them.'

'They didn't ask him what he knew of Lord Lavenham, did they?' said Miss Thane anxiously.

'They didn't have no chance to ask him, ma'am. He told them they might look for all the criminals they chose, so long as they didn't tamper with the liquor, nor go nosing round his bedchamber.'

'But, Nye, what if they find your hidden cellar?' said Miss Thane.

He smiled dourly. 'They won't do that – not while they keep to the open cellars. In fact, while Sir Hugh was telling them what their duty was, and what it wasn't, I was able to take Mr. Ludovic his breakfast.'

'Where is your secret cellar, Nye?'

He looked at her for a moment, and then replied: 'You'll be the ruin of me yet, ma'am. It's under the floor of my store-room.'

Sir Hugh came back into the room presently. He gave it as his opinion that the Runners were either drunk or half-witted, and said that he fancied they would have no more trouble with them. Upon his sister's inquiring hopefully whether he had contrived to get rid of them, he replied somewhat severely that he had made no such attempt. He had merely defined their duties to them and warned them of the consequences of overstepping the limits of the law.

Both Nye and Miss Thane were dissatisfied, but there was no doubt that the irruption of Sir Hugh into the cellars had done much to damp the Runners' ardour. His air of unquestionable authority, his knowledge of the law, and the fact of his being acquainted, with the magistrate in charge at Bow Street made them conscious of a great disinclination to fall foul of him again. Nor could they feel, when they had discussed the point between themselves, that a house which held so rigid a legal precisian was the place in which to look for a hardened criminal. They had failed on two occasions to find the least trace of Ludovic Lavenham; the landlord, who should be most nearly concerned, seemed to look upon their search with indifference; and had it not been for the suspicious circumstance of the abigail's disappearance, they would have been much inclined to have returned to London. The valet's words, however, had been explicit. They decided to prosecute a further search for a hidden cellar, and to keep the inn under observation in the hope of surprising Ludovic in an attempt to escape.

While this search, which entailed a patient tapping of the walls and floor of the other cellars, was in progress, Nye seized the opportunity to visit Ludovic. He returned presently and reported that his lordship wouldn't stay patient for long; in fact, was already threatening to come out of hiding and deal with the Runners in his own fashion.

'Really, one cannot blame him,' said Miss Thane judicially. 'It is most tiresome of these people to continue to haunt us. It quite puts an end to our adventures.'

'Yes, it does,' agreed Eustacie. 'Besides, I am afraid that Ludovic will catch cold in the cellar.'

'Very true,' said Miss Thane. 'There is nothing for it: since Hugh has been so useless in the matter, we must get rid of the Runners ourselves.'

'*You* have not seen them,' said Eustacie bitterly. 'They are the kind of men who stay, and stay, and stay.'

'Yes, they seem to be a dogged couple, I must say. I am afraid it is your abigail who is at the root of their obstinacy.' She broke off, and suddenly stood up. 'My love, I believe I have hit upon a notion! Would you – now, would you say I was a strapping wench?'

'Of a certainty I should not say anything of the kind!' replied Eustacie, indignant at the implication that she could be capable of such discourtesy. 'You are very tall, *bien entendu*, but——'

'Say no more!' commanded Miss Thane. 'I have a Plan!'

CHAPTER 10

In pursuance of her plan, Miss Thane took care to remain out of sight of the two Runners for the rest of the day. She repaired to her own room, and sat there with an agreeable and blood-curdling romance, and from time to time Eustacie came up to report on the proceedings below-stairs.

Mr. Stubbs took an early opportunity of subjecting Eustacie to a searching cross-examination, but from this she emerged triumphant. Having established a reputation for excitability, it was easy for her when in difficulties to become incoherent, and consequently (since she at once took refuge in the French tongue) unintelligible. At the end of half an hour's questioning, Mr. Stubbs, and not his victim, felt quite battered.

He and his companion spent a wearing and an unsatisfactory day. The cellar, besides being extremely cold, revealed no secrets, and a locked cupboard which Mr. Peabody discovered in a dark corner of the passage leading to the kitchen was responsible for an unpleasant interlude with the landlord. As soon as Mr. Peabody discovered the cupboard, which was partly hidden behind a pile of empty cases and baskets, he demanded the key of Nye. When the landlord, after a prolonged search in which Clem joined, announced that he had lost it, the hopes of both Runners rose high, and Mr. Stubbs warned Nye that if he did not immediately produce the key, they would break the door. Nye retorted that if damage were done to his property, he would lodge a complaint in Bow Street. He said so many times, and with such unwonted emphasis, that there was nothing in the cupboard but some spare crockery that both Runners became agog with suspicion, and resembled nothing so much as a couple of terriers at a rat-hole. They pulled all the empty cases away from the cupboard door, so that Miss Nye, coming out of the kitchen with a loaded tray, fell over them, smashing three plates and scattering a dish of cheese-cakes all down the narrow passage. Miss Nye, too deaf to hear Mr. Peabody's profuse apologies, spoke bitterly and at length on the subject of Men in general, and Bow Street Runners in particular, and when Mr. Peabody, with an unlucky idea of repairing the damage, collected all the dusty cheese-cakes together on the larger portion of the broken dish and handed them to her, she so far forgot herself as to box his ears.

The next thing to do, Miss Nye having retired, seething, to the kitchen, was to break down the door of the cupboard. Mr. Stubbs thought that Mr. Peabody should perform this office, and Mr. Peabody considered Mr. Stubbs, who was of bulkier build, the man for the task. It was not until the argument had been settled that they discovered that the door opened outwards. When Mr. Stubbs demanded of Nye why he had not divulged this fact at the outset, Nye replied that he did not wish them to break into that cupboard. He added that they would regret it if they did, a hint that made Mr. Stubbs draw an unwieldy pistol from his pocket, and warn the supposed occupant of the cupboard that if he did not instantly give himself up, the lock would be blown out of the door. No answer being forthcoming, Mr. Stubbs told his assistant to stand ready to Pounce, and, setting the muzzle of his pistol to the lock, pulled the trigger.

The noise made by the shot was quite deafening, and an ominous sound of breaking glass was heard faintly through its reverberations. Commanding Mr. Peabody to cover the cupboard with his own pistol, Mr. Stubbs seized the handle of the door and pulled it open, carefully keeping in the lee of it as he did so.

Mr. Peabody lowered his gun. The cupboard was quite a shallow one, and contained nothing but shelves bearing glass and crockery. Such specimens as had come within the range of the shot had fared badly, a circumstance which roused Nye to immediate and loud-voiced wrath.

The explosion had been heard in other parts of the house, and even a dim echo of it by Miss Nye. She erupted once more from the kitchen, this time armed with the rolling-pin, at precisely the same moment as Sir Hugh Thane, eyeglass raised, loomed up at the other end of the passage.

'What the devil's toward?' demanded Sir Hugh, with all the irritability of a man rudely awakened from his afternoon sleep.

Mr. Stubbs tried to say that it was only a matter of his duty, but as Miss Nye, who had the peculiarly resonant voice of most deaf persons, chose at the same time to announce that if she were given her choice, she would sooner have a pair of wild bulls in the house than two Runners, his explanation was not heard. Before he could repeat it, Nye had given Sir Hugh a brief and faithful account of the affair, particularly stressing his own part in it. 'Over and over again I told them there was only some spare crockery in the cupboard, sir, but they wouldn't listen to me. I hope I'm a patient man, but when it comes to them smashing four of my best glasses, not to mention spoiling a whole dish of cheese-cakes that was meant for your honour's dinner, it's more than what I can stand!'

'It's my belief,' said Sir Hugh, looking fixedly at the unfortunate Runners, 'that they're drunk. Both of them.'

Mr. Stubbs, who had not been offered any liquid refreshment at all, protested almost tearfully.

'If you're not drunk,' said Sir Hugh, with finality, 'you're mad. I had my suspicions of it from the start.'

After this painful affair the Runners withdrew to watch the inn from the outside. While one kept an eye on the back door from the post-boy's room, the other walked up and down in front of the inn. From time to time they met and exchanged places. They were occasionally rewarded by the sight either of Nye or of Clem peeping out of one or other of the doors as though to see whether the coast were clear. These signs of activity were sufficiently heartening to keep them at their posts. But it was miserable work for a raw February day, and had the house under observation been other than an inn, it was unlikely that a sense of duty would have triumphed. However, although Nye, according no more nice treatment to the Runners, might withhold all offers of brandy, he could not refuse to serve them as customers. The only pleasant moments they spent during the remainder of the afternoon were in the cosy tap-room, and even these were somewhat marred by the black looks cast at them by the landlord and the caustic comments he made on the drinking proclivities of law officers.

But when dusk fell they had their reward. It was Mr. Stubbs's turn to sit at the window of the stable-room, and it was consequently he who saw the back door open very gradually, and Eustacie look cautiously out into the yard. He knew it was she, because the candles had been lit inside the house, and she stood full in a beam of light.

Mr. Stubbs drew back from the window and watched from behind the curtain. Behind him one post-boy sprawled in a chair by the fire, snoring rhythmically, and two others sat at the table playing cards.

Eustacie, having peered all round through the twilight, turned and beckoned to someone inside the house. Mr. Stubbs, breathing heavily, reached for his stout ash-plant, and grasped it in his right hand. With his eyes starting almost out of his head, he saw a tall female figure, muffled from head to foot in a dark cloak, slip out of the house and glide round it towards the front, keeping well in the shadow of the wall. Eustacie softly closed the door; but Mr. Stubbs did not wait to see this. In two bounds he had reached the yard, and was creeping after his quarry, taking care, however, to stay well behind until he could summon Mr. Peabody to his assistance.

The cloaked figure was moving swiftly, yet in a cautious fashion, pausing at the corner of the house to look up and down the road before venturing further. Mr. Stubbs stopped too, effacing himself in the shadows, and realized, when the quarry made a dart across the road, that Mr. Peabody must be enjoying a session in the tap-room, saw dimly that the unknown female (or male) was hurrying down the road under cover of the hedge, and bounced into the inn, loudly calling on Mr. Peabody for support.

Mr. Peabody, ever-zealous, hastened to his side, wiping his mouth on the back of his hand. When he heard the glorious news, he stayed only to pick up his cudgel, and ran out with Mr. Stubbs in pursuit of the fugitive.

'It were that self-same abigail, William,' panted Mr. Stubbs. 'All along I thought – too big for a female! There he goes!'

Hearing the sounds of heavy-footed pursuit, the figure ahead looked once over its shoulder, and then broke into a run. Mr. Stubbs had no more breath to spare for speech, but Mr. Peabody, a leaner man, managed to shout: 'Halt!'

The figure ahead showed signs of flagging; the Runners, getting their second wind, began to gain upon it, and in a few moments had reached it, and grabbed at the enveloping cloak, gasping: 'In the name of the Law!'

The figure spun round, and landed Mr. Stubbs a facer that made his nose bleed.

'Mind his pops, Jerry!' cried Mr. Peabody, grappling with the foe. 'Lordy, what a wild cat! Ah, would you, then!'

Mr. Stubbs caught the figure's left arm in a crushing grip, and panted: 'I arrest you in the name of the Law!'

The captive said in a low, breathless voice: 'Let me go! Let me go at once!'

'You're coming along with us, that's what you're going to do,' replied Mr. Stubbs.

The sound of a horse trotting towards them made the Runners drag their captive to the side of the road. The horse and rider came into sight, and the prisoner, recognizing the rider, cried: 'Sir Tristram, help! Help!'

The horse seemed to bound forward as under a sudden spur. The prisoner, struggling madly, shrieked again for help, and the next instant Sir Tristram was abreast of the group, and had swung himself out of the saddle. Before the Runners could explain matters, he had taken the management of the affair into his own swift and capable hands. Mr. Stubbs, starting to proclaim his calling, encountered a smashing right and left which dropped him like a log, and Mr. Peabody, releasing his captive and aiming a blow at Sir Tristram with his cudgel, quite failed to find his mark, and the next moment was sprawled on the road, having been neatly thrown on Sir Tristram's hip.

Sir Tristram paid no further heed to either of them, but took a quick stride towards the cloaked figure, saying sharply: 'Are you hurt? What in heaven's name is the meaning of this, Miss Thane?'

'Oh, I am bruised from head to foot!' shuddered Miss Thane. 'These dreadful creatures set upon me with cudgels! I shall die of the shock!'

This dramatic announcement, instead of arousing Sir Tristram's chivalrous instincts anew, made him look penetratingly at her for one moment, and say in a voice torn between amusement and exasperation: 'You must be out of your mind! How dare you do such a crazy thing?'

The Runners had by this time begun to pick themselves up. Mr. Stubbs, cherishing his nose, seemed a little dazed, but Mr. Peabody advanced heroically, and said: 'I arrest you, Ludovic Lavenham, in the name of the Law, and it will go hard with them as seeks to interfere!'

Sir Tristram released Miss Thane's hands, which he had been holding in a sustaining manner, and replied: 'You fool, this is not Ludovic Lavenham! This is a lady!'

Mr. Stubbs said thickly: 'It's the abigail. It ain't no female.'

'Oh, don't let them touch me!' implored Miss Thane, shrieking artistically towards Sir Tristram.

'I've no intention of letting them touch you, but don't get in my way,' said Sir Tristram unromantically. 'Now then, my man, perhaps you will tell me what the devil you mean by arresting this lady?'

'It ain't a lady!' said Mr. Peabody urgently. 'He's a desperate criminal dressed up for an abigail! No lady couldn't fight like him!'

'I tell you she is Sir Hugh Thane's sister!' said Sir Tristram. 'Look, is this a man's face?' He turned as he spoke, and put back the hood from Miss Thane's head.

The Runners peered at her doubtfully. 'When my brother hears of this, you will be sorry!' said Miss Thane in a tearful voice.

A look of deep foreboding stole into Mr. Stubbs's watering eyes. 'If we've made a mistake——' he began uncertainly.

'It's my belief it's a plot, and they're both in it!' declared Mr. Peabody.

'Take me to my brother!' begged Miss Thane, clinging to Sir Tristram's arm. 'I fear I may be going to swoon!'

Mr. Stubbs looked at her over the handkerchief which he was holding to his nose. Also he looked at Sir Tristram, and rather unwisely accused him of having assaulted an officer of the Law.

'Oh, you're law officers, are you?' said Sir Tristram grimly. 'Then you may come and explain yourselves to Sir Hugh Thane. Can you walk, ma'am, or shall I carry you?'

Miss Thane declined this offer, though in a failing voice, and accepted instead the support of his arm. The whole party began to walk slowly towards the Red Lion, Sir Tristram solicitously guiding Miss Thane's tottering steps, and Mr. Peabody leading Sir Tristram's horse.

They entered the inn by the door into the coffee-room, and here they were met by Eustacie, who, upon sight of Miss Thane, gave a dramatic start, and cried: '*Bon Dieu!* What has happened? Sarah, you are ill!'

Miss Thane said faintly: 'I scarce know.... Two men attacked me....'

'Ah, she is swooning!' exclaimed Eustacie. 'What an outrage! What villainy!'

Miss Thane, having assured herself that Sir Tristram was close enough to catch her, closed her eyes, and sank gracefully back into his arms.

'Hartshorn! vinegar!' shrieked Eustacie. 'Lay her on the settle, *mon cousin!*'

Nye, who had come in from the tap-room, said: 'What! Miss Thane in a swoon? I'll call Sir Hugh this instant!' and strode away to the parlour.

Sir Tristram carried his fair burden to the settle, and laid her down upon it. A glance at her charming complexion was sufficient to allay any alarm he might otherwise have felt, and with his fingers over her steady pulse, he said: 'I think we should throw water over her, my dear cousin. Cold water.'

Miss Thane's lips parted a little. A very soft whisper reached Sir Tristram's ears. 'You dare!' breathed Miss Thane.

'Wait! I will instantly fetch the hartshorn!' said Eustacie, and turning sharp on her heel, collided with Mr. Peabody, who was anxiously peeping over her shoulder at Miss Thane's inanimate form. 'Brute! Bully! *Imbecile!*' she stormed.

Mr. Peabody stepped aside in a hurry. Having seen Miss Thane's shapely figure in the candlelight, he was now quite sure that a mistake had been made, and the look he cast at Mr. Stubbs, standing glumly by the door, was one of deep reproach.

Eustacie came running down the stairs again just as Sir Hugh walked into the coffee-room with the landlord at his heels.

'What's all this?' demanded Sir Hugh. 'Here's Nye telling me some story about Sally fainting. She never faints!'

Sir Tristram, looking down at Miss Thane, saw a shade of annoyance in her face. His lips twitched slightly, but he answered in a grave voice: 'I fear it is too true. You may see for yourself.'

'Well, of all the odd things!' said Sir Hugh, surveying her through his eyeglass with vague surprise. 'I've never known her do that before.'

'She has sustained a great shock to her nerves,' said Shield solemnly. 'We can only trust that she has received no serious injury.'

'Ah, *la pauvre!*' exclaimed Eustacie, enjoying herself hugely. 'I wonder she is not dead with fright!' She thrust her cousin out of the way as she spoke, and sank upon her knees by the settle, holding the hartshorn under Miss Thane's nose. 'Behold, she is recovering! *C'est cela, ma chère! Douce-ment, alors, doucement!*' Over her shoulder she addressed Sir Hugh. 'Those wicked men attacked her – with sticks!' she added, observing the Runners' cudgels.

It took a moment for Sir Hugh to assimilate this. He turned and stared at the two Runners, incredulous wrath slowly gathering in his eyes. 'What!' he said. 'They attacked my sister? These gin-swilling, cross-eyed numskulls? This pair of brandy-faced, cork-brained——'

Miss Thane interrupted this swelling diatribe with a faint moan, and opened her eyes. 'Where am I?' she said in a weak voice.

'*Dieu soit béni!*' said Eustacie devoutly. 'She is better!'

Miss Thane sat up, her hand to her brow. 'Two men with sticks,' she said gropingly. 'They ran after me and caught me. . . . Oh, am I safe indeed?'

'A little brandy, ma'am?' suggested Nye. 'You are all shook up, and no wonder! It's a crying scandal, that's what it is! I never heard the like of it!'

'Sally,' said Sir Hugh, 'do you tell me that these blundering jackasses set upon you?'

She followed the direction of his pointing finger, and gave a small shriek, and clutched his arm. 'Do not let them touch me!'

'Let them touch you?' said Sir Hugh, a martial light in his eye. 'They had better try!'

'It was all a mistake, ma'am! No one don't want to touch you!' said Mr. Peabody. 'I am sure we never meant no harm! It was the poor light, and us not knowing you.'

'All a matter of Dooty,' said Mr. Stubbs, still holding his handkerchief to his nose.

'You hold your tongue!' said Sir Hugh. 'Sally, what happened?'

'I scarce know,' replied his sister. 'I went out for a breath of air, and before I had gone above a dozen steps I heard someone running behind me, and turning, saw these two men coming for me, and waving their sticks. I tried to escape, but they caught me, and handled me so roughly that I was near to swooning away on the spot. Then, by the mercy of Providence, who should come riding by but Sir Tristram! I screamed to him for help – indeed, I thought I was to be murdered or beaten into insensibility – and he flung himself from his horse and rescued me! He knocked the fat man down, and when the other one made for him with his cudgel threw him sprawling in the road!'

'Tristram did that?' exclaimed Eustacie. '*Voyons, mon cousin*, I begin to like you very much indeed!'

Sir Hugh, his wrath giving place momentarily to professional interest, said: 'Threw him a cross-buttock, did you?'

'On my hip,' said Shield. 'You know the trick.'

Sir Hugh put up his glass and surveyed Mr. Stubbs's afflicted nose. 'Drew his cork, too,' he observed, with satisfaction.

'No,' replied Sir Tristram. 'I fancy Miss Thane deserves the credit for that.'

'I did hit him,' admitted Sarah.

'Good girl!' approved her brother. 'A nice, flush hit it must have been. But what were they chasing you for? That's what beats me.'

'They said I was Ludovic Lavenham, and they arrested me,' said Miss Thane.

Sir Hugh repeated blankly: 'Said you were Ludovic Lavenham?' He looked at the Runners again. 'They *are* mad,' he said.

'Drunk more like, sir,' put in the landlord unkindly. 'they've spent the better part of the afternoon in my tap-room, drinking Blue Ruin till you'd wonder they could walk straight.'

A protesting sound came from behind Mr. Stubbs's handkerchief.

'So that's it, is it? said Sir Hugh. 'You're right: they reek of gin!'

'It ain't true, your Honour!' said Mr. Peabody, much agitated. 'If we had a drop just to keep the cold out——'

'Drop!' ejaculated the landlord. 'Why, you've pretty near had all there is in the house!'

Mr. Stubbs ventured to emerge from behind his handkerchief. 'I take my solemn oath it ain't true,' he said. 'We suspicioned the lady was this Loodervic Lavenham – that's how it come about.'

Sir Tristram looked him over critically. 'That settles it: they must be badly foxed,' he remarked.

'Of course they are,' agreed Thane. 'Thought my sister was a man? I never heard anything to equal it! They're so foxed they can't see straight.'

Mr. Peabody hastened to explain. 'No, your Honour, no! It were all on account of that abigail we saw here, and which was turned off so sudden, and which we thought was the lady.'

'You are making matters worse for yourselves,' said Sir Tristram. 'First you say you thought Miss Thane was Ludovic Lavenham, and now you say you thought she was my cousin's abigail. Pray, what were you about to chase an abigail?'

'It's as plain as a pikestaff what they were about,' said Thane severely.

'I knew she was a low, vulgar wretch!' cried Eustacie, swift to improve on this point.

The maligned Runners could only gape at her in dismay.

'Well, Wright shall know how his precious Runners conduct them-selves once they are out of his reach!' promised Sir Hugh.

'But, your Honour – but, sir – it weren't like that at all! It was the abigail we thought was Loodervic Lavenham, on account of her being such a great, strapping wench, and when Miss here came so cautious out of the back door, like as if she was scared someone might see her, it was natural we should be mistook in her. What would the lady go out walking for when it was almost dark?'

Sir Hugh turned to look at his sister, his judicial instincts roused. 'I must say, it seems demmed odd to me,' he conceded. 'What were you doing, Sally?'

Miss Thane, prompted partly by a spirit of pure mischief, and partly by a desire to be revenged on Sir Tristram for his inhuman suggestion of throwing cold water over her, turned her face away and implored her brother not to ask her that question.

'That's all very well,' objected Thane, 'but did you go out by the back door?'

'Yes,' said Miss Thane, covering her face with her hands.

'Why?' asked Sir Hugh, faintly puzzled.

'Oh,' said Miss Thane, the very picture of maidenly confusion, 'must I tell you, indeed? I went to meet Sir Tristram.'

'Eh?' said Thane, taken aback.

Miss Thane found that she had underrated her opponent. Not a muscle quivered in Shield's face. He said immediately: 'This news should have been broken to you at a more suitable time, Thane. Spare your sister's blushes, I beg of you!'

Miss Thane, for once put out of countenance, intervened in a hurry. 'We cannot discuss such matters now! Do, pray, send those creatures away! I will believe they meant me no harm, but I vow and declare the very sight of them gives me a Spasm!'

This request was so much in accordance with the Runners' own wishes that they both looked hopefully at Sir Hugh, and gave him to understand that if he cared to order them back to London, they would be very glad to obey him. The day's disasters had succeeded in convincing them that their errand was futile; and their main concern now was not to arrest a fugitive from the Law but to induce Sir Hugh to refrain from complaining of them to his friend, Sampson Wright. They were not drunk, and their motives had been of the purest, but against the testimony of Sir Hugh and his sister, and Sir Tristram, and the landlord, they did not feel that they had any hope of being attended to in Bow Street.

Somewhat to their surprise, Miss Thane came to their support, saying magnanimously that for her part she was ready to let the matter rest.

'Wright ought to know of it,' said Sir Hugh, shaking his head.

'Very true, but you forget that they have been punished already for their stupidity. Sir Tristram was very rough with them, you know.'

Sir Hugh was slightly mollified by this reflection. After telling the Runners that he hoped it would be a lesson to them, and warning them that if he ever caught sight of their faces again within the portals of the Red Lion it would be the worse for them, he waved them away. They assured him they would go back to London by the night mail, and with renewed apologies to Miss Thane, bowed themselves out of the inn as fast as they could.

'Well, now that they've taken themselves off,' said Nye, 'I'll go and let Mr. Ludovic out of the cellar.'

Sir Hugh was not at the moment interested in Ludovic's release. He was regarding Shield in a puzzled way, and as soon as the landlord had left the room, accompanied by Eustacie, said: 'I dare say Sally knows what she's about, but I don't think you should appoint her to meet you like that. It's not at all the thing. Besides, there's no sense in it. If you want to see her, you can do it here, can't you? *I've* no objection.'

'I fear you can have no romantic leanings,' said Shield, before Miss Thane could speak. 'A star-lit sky, the balmy night breezes——'

'But this is February! The breeze isn't balmy at all – in fact, there's been a demmed north wind blowing all day,' pointed out Sir Hugh.

'To persons deep in love,' said Sir Tristram soulfully, 'any breeze is balmy.'

'Hateful wretch!' said Miss Thane, with deep feeling. 'Pay no heed to him, Hugh! Of course, I did not go to meet him!'

Sir Tristram appeared to be overcome. 'You play fast and loose with me,' he said reproachfully. 'You have dashed my hopes to the ground, shattered my self-esteem——'

'If you say another word, I'll box your ears!' threatened Miss Thane.

Sir Hugh shook his head at her in mild disapproval. 'I see what it is: you've been flirting again,' he said.

'Don't be so vulgar!' implored Miss Thane. 'There's not a word of truth in it! I went out merely to trick the Runners. Sir Tristram's arrival was quite by chance.'

'But you told me——'

'The truth is that you have stumbled upon a secret romance, Thane,' said Sir Tristram, with a great air of candour.

Thane looked from Sir Tristram's imperturbable countenance to his sister's indignant one, and gave it up. I suppose it's all a hum,' he remarked. 'Are you coming into the parlour? There's a devilish draught here.'

'Presently,' replied Sir Tristram, detaining Miss Thane by the simple expedient of stretching out his hand and grasping her wrist.

She submitted to this, and when her brother had gone back to the parlour, said: 'I suppose I deserved that.'

'Certainly you did,' agreed Sir Tristram, releasing her. 'You would have been well served had I really thrown cold water over you. Are you at all hurt?'

'Oh no, merely a bruise or two! Your intervention was most timely.'

'And if I had not happened to have been there?'

'I should have allowed them to drag me back here, of course, and fainted in Hugh's arms instead of yours.'

He smiled a little, but only said: 'You shouldn't have done it.'

'Oh, perhaps it was not, as Eustacie would say, quite *convenable*,' she replied, 'but you will admit that it has rid us of a grave danger.'

'You might have been badly hurt,' he answered.

'Well, I was not badly hurt, so we shall not consider that.'

At this moment Ludovic strolled into the room, and slid his sound arm round Miss Thane's waist, and kissed her cheek. 'Sally, I swear you're an angel!' he declared.

'Anything less angelic than her conduct during the past half-hour I have yet to see,' observed Sir Tristram. 'An accomplished liar would be nearer the mark.'

'*Quant à ça*, you also told lies,' said Eustacie. 'You pretended to be in love with her: you know you did!'

'Did he?' said Ludovic. 'Perhaps he is in love with her. I vow I am!'

'Cream-pot love, my child,' interposed Miss Thane composedly. 'You are pleased with me for having rid you of those Runners. And now that they have gone, when shall we break into the Dower House?'

'Rid your mind of the notion that you are to make one of that party,' said Shield. 'Neither you nor Eustacie will come with us – if we go at all.'

'Hey, what's this?' demanded Ludovic. 'Of course we shall go!'

Miss Thane looked at Shield with a humorous gleam in her eyes. 'Now pray do not tell me that after all the trouble I have been put to to remove the bars of our adventure we are not to have any adventure!'

'I think you are likely to have all the adventure you could desire without going to the Dower House to look for it,' replied Shield. 'I fancy the Beau's suspicions will not be as easily allayed as the Runners' were.'

'Well, if Basil comes spying after me himself, we shall see some sport,' said Ludovic cheerfully. 'I wish you will discover when he means to go to town, Tristram.'

This was not a difficult task to accomplish, for the Beau, paying a friendly call upon his cousin that evening after dinner, volunteered the information quite unprompted. He wandered into the library at the Court, a vision of pearl-grey and salmon-pink, and smiled sweetly at Shield, lounging on the sofa by the fire.

Shield greeted him unemotionally, and nodded towards a chair. 'Sit down, Basil: I'm glad to see you.'

The Beau raised his brows rather quizzically. 'My dear Tristram, how unexpected!'

'Yes,' said Shield, 'I've no doubt it is. I feel you should be told of an excessively odd circumstance. Are you aware that there have been a couple of Bow Street Runners in the neighbourhood, searching for Ludovic?'

For a moment the Beau made no reply. The smile still lingered on his lips, but an arrested expression stole into his eyes, as though he found such direct methods of warfare disconcerting. He drew up a chair to the fire and sat down in it, and said: 'For Ludovic? Surely you must be mistaken? Ludovic is not in Sussex, is he?'

'Not that I am aware of,' replied Sir Tristram coolly, 'but from what I could make out from the Runners someone has started a rumour that Eustacie's smuggler was he.'

The Beau opened his snuff-box. 'Absurd!' he murmured. 'If Ludovic were in Sussex, he must have sent me word.'

'That is what I thought,' agreed Shield. 'You are quite sure he has not sent you word?'

The Beau was in the act of raising a pinch of snuff to his nostrils, but he paused and looked across at his cousin with a slight frown. 'Certainly not,' he answered.

'Oh, you need not be afraid to tell me if you have heard from him,' said Sir Tristram. 'I wish the boy no harm. But if the rumour *should* be true, after all, you would be wise to get him out of the country again.'

The Beau did not say anything for several moments, nor did he inhale his snuff. His eyes remained fixed on Shield's face. He shut his snuff-box again, and at last replied: 'Perhaps. Yes, perhaps. But I do not anticipate that I shall hear from him.' He leaned back in his chair and crossed one leg over the other. 'I am amazed that such a rumour should have arisen – quite amazed. It had not reached my ears. In fact, my errand to you had nothing to do with poor Ludovic, wherever he may be.'

'I am happy to hear you say so. What is your errand to me?'

'Oh, quite a trifling one, my dear fellow! It is merely that I find myself obliged to go to London on a matter of stern necessity to-morrow – my new coat, you know: it sags across the shoulders: the most lamentable business! – and it occurred to me that you might wish to charge me with a commission.'

'Why, that is very good of you, Basil, but I believe I need not trouble you. I expect to leave this place almost any day now.'

'Oh?' The Beau regarded him thoughtfully. 'I infer then that Eustacie is also leaving this place?'

Sir Tristram replied curtly: 'I believe so. Shall you be in London for many days? Do you mean to return here?'

'Why, yes, I think so. I shall remain in town for a night only, I trust. I have given the servants leave to absent themselves for no longer. Ah, and that reminds me, Tristram! I wish you will desire that fellow – now, what is the name of Sylvester's carpenter? Oh, Johnson! – yes, I wish you will desire him to call at the Dower House some time. My man tells me the bolt is off one of the library windows. He might attend to it, perhaps.'

'Certainly,' said Shield impassively. But when his cousin presently went away, he looked after him with a faint smile on his lips, and said: 'How very clumsy, to be sure!'

Ludovic, however, when the encounter was described to him on the following morning, exclaimed, with characteristic impetuosity: 'Then to-night is our opportunity! We have gammoned the Beau!'

'He seems to have been equally fortunate,' said Shield dryly.

Ludovic cocked an intelligent eyebrow. 'Now what might you mean by that?' he inquired.

'Not quite equally,' said Miss Thane, with a smile.

'No,' admitted Shield. 'He did underrate me a trifle.'

Ludovic perched on the edge of the table, swinging one leg. 'Oh, so you think it's a trap, do you? Nonsense! Why should you? He can never have had more than a suspicion of my being here, and you may depend upon it we have convinced him that he was mistaken.'

'I do not depend upon anything of the kind,' replied Shield. 'In fact, I am astonished of the crudity of this trap. Consider a moment, Ludovic! He has told me that he will be in London to-night, that he has given his servants leave of absence, and that the bolt is off one of the library windows. If you are fool enough to swallow that, at least give me credit for having more common sense!'

'Oh well!' said Ludovic airily. 'One must take a risk now and again, after all. Basil daren't lay a trap for me in his own house. Damn it, man, he can't take me prisoner and hand me over to the Law! It wouldn't look well at all.'

'Certainly not,' answered Sir Tristram. 'I have no fear of Basil himself coming into the open, but you are forgetting that he has a very able deputy in the shape of that valet of his. If his servants were to catch you in the

Dower House, and hand you over to the Law as a common thief, you would be identified, and beyond any man's help while Basil was still discreetly in London. He would dispose of you without incurring the least censure from anyone.'

'Well, they may try and take me prisoner if they like,' said Ludovic. 'It'll go hard with them if they do.'

Miss Thane regarded him in some amusement. 'Yes, Ludovic, but it will make everything very awkward if you are to leave a trail of corpses in your wake,' she pointed out. 'I cannot help feeling that Sir Tristram is right. He is one of those disagreeable people who nearly always are.'

Ludovic thrust out his chin a little. 'I'm going to take a look in that priest's hole if I die for it!' he said.

'If you go, you'll go alone, Ludovic,' said Sir Tristram.

Ludovic's eyes flashed. 'Ratting, eh? I'll get Clem in your stead.'

'You may take it from me that Clem won't go with you on this venture,' replied Sir Tristram.

'Oh, you've been working on him, have you? Damn you, Tristram, I must find the ring!'

'You won't do it that way. It's to run your head into a noose. You've a better hope than this slender chance of finding the ring in a priest's hole.'

'What is it?' Ludovic said impatiently.

'Basil's valet,' replied Shield. 'He lodged the information against you. I judge him to be fairly deep in Basil's confidence. How deep I don't know, but I'm doing what I can to find out.'

'I dare say he is, but what's the odds? Depend upon it, he's paid to keep the Beau's secrets. Slimy rogue,' Ludovic added gloomily.

'No doubt,' agreed Shield. 'So I have set Kettering to work on him. If he knows anything, you may outbid Basil.'

'Who is Kettering?' interrupted Miss Thane. 'I must have everything made clear.'

'Kettering is the head groom at the Court, and one of Ludovic's adherents. His son works for the Beau, and he is on good terms with the servants at the Dower House. If he can put it into Gregg's head that I am collecting evidence that will make things look ugly for Basil, we may find it quite an easy matter to induce the fellow to talk. Have patience, Ludovic!'

'Oh, you're as cautious as any old woman!' said Ludovic. 'Only let me set foot in the Dower House——'

'You may believe that I am too much your friend to let you do anything of the kind,' said Sir Tristram, with finality.

CHAPTER 11

Ludovic, knowing his cousin too well to attempt to argue with him once his mind was made up, said no more in support of his own plan, but left Miss Thane to entertain Shield while he went off to try his powers of persuasion upon the hapless Clem. Quite forgetting that he must not run the risk of being seen by any stranger, he walked into the tap-room, saying: 'Clem, are you here? I want you!'

Clem was nowhere to be seen, but just as Ludovic was about to go away again, the door on to the road opened, and a thick-set man in a suit of fustian walked into the inn. Ludovic took one look at him, and ejaculated: 'Abel!'

Mr. Bundy shut the door behind him, and nodded. 'I had word you was here,' he remarked.

Ludovic cast a quick glance towards the door leading to the kitchen quarters, where he judged Clem to be, and grasped Bundy by one wrist. 'Does Nye know you're here?' he asked softly.

'No,' replied Bundy. 'Not yet he don't, but I'm wishful to have a word with him.'

'You're going to have a word with me,' said Ludovic. 'I don't want Nye to know you're here. Come up to my bedchamber!'

'Adone-do, sir!' expostulated Bundy, standing fast. 'You know, surelye, what I've come for. I've a dunnamany kegs of brandy waiting to be delivered here so soon as Nye gives the word.'

'He won't dare give it yet; the house is full. I've other work for you to do.'

Bundy looked him over. 'Are you joining Dickson on board the *Saucy Annie* again?' he inquired.

'No; my grandfather's dead,' said Ludovic.

'He'll be a loss,' remarked Mr. Bundy thoughtfully. 'Howsoever, if you're giving up the smuggling lay, I'm tedious glad. What might you be wanting me to do?'

'Come upstairs, and I'll tell you,' said Ludovic.

As good luck would have it, there was no one in the coffee-room. Ludovic led Bundy through it and up the stairs to the front bedchamber which had once been Miss Thane's. It still smelled faintly exotic, a circumstance which did not escape Mr. Bundy. 'I thought there was a wench in it,' he observed.

Ludovic paid no heed to this sapient remark, but having locked the door, just in case Sir Tristram should take it into his head to come up to see him again before he left the inn, thrust Bundy towards a chair, and told him to sit down. 'Abel, you know why I took to smuggling, don't you?' he asked abruptly.

Mr. Bundy laid his hat on the floor beside him, and nodded.

'Well, understand this!' said Ludovic. 'I didn't commit that murder.'

'Oh?' said Bundy, not particularly interested. He added after a moment's reflection: 'Happen you'll have to prove that if you'm wishful to take the old lord's place.'

'That's what I mean to do,' replied Ludovic. 'And you are going to help me.'

'I'm agreeable,' said Bundy. 'They do tell me we shall have that cousin of yourn up at the Court, him they call the Beau. It would be unaccountable bad for the Trade if that come about. He'll give no aid to the Gentleman.'

'You won't have the Beau at the Court if you help me to prove it was he committed the murder I was charged with,' said Ludovic.

Mr. Bundy looked rather pleased. 'That's a rare good notion,' he approved. 'Have him put away quiet same like he'd be glad to do to you. How will we set about it?'

'I believe him to have in his possession a ring which belongs to me,' Ludovic answered. 'I haven't time to explain it all to you now, but if I can find that ring, I can prove I was innocent of Plunkett's death. I want a man to help me break into my cousin's house to-night. You see how it is with me: that damned riding-officer winged me.'

'Ay, I heard he had,' said Bundy. 'I told you you shouldn't ought to have come.' He looked ruminatingly at Ludovic. 'I don't know as I rightly understand what you'm about. Milling kens ain't me lay. Seems to me you'd have taken Clem along o' you – if he'd have gone.'

'I might be able to make him, but I've a cousin here – a cursed, cautious, interfering cousin, who don't mean me to make the attempt. He thinks it's too dangerous, and it's odds he's persuaded Clem into seeing eye to eye with him.'

Mr. Bundy scratched his nose reflectively. 'One way and another, you've been in a lamentable deal of danger since you growed up,' he remarked.

Ludovic grinned. 'I shall be in some more yet.'

'Happen you will,' agreed Bundy. 'There's some as seem to be born to it, and others as takes uncommon care of their skins. It queers me how folks manage to keep out of trouble. I never did, but I know them as has.'

'Devilish dull dogs, I'll be bound. There may be trouble at the Dower House to-night, and for all I know there's been a trap laid for me. Will you take the risk?'

'How I look at it is this way,' said Bundy painstakingly. 'It ain't no manner of use trying to keep out of trouble if so be you'm born to it. For why? Because if you don't look for trouble, trouble will come a-looking for you – ah, come sneaking up behind to take you unawares, what's more. Does Joe Nye know what's in the wind?'

'No. He's hand-in-glove with my cousin.'

Mr. Bundy looked rather shocked. 'What, with that dentical, fine gentleman?'

'Lord, no! Not with him! My cousin Shield – my cautious cousin.'

Mr. Bundy stroked his chin. 'I never knew Joe to be mistook in a man,' he said. 'I doubt I'm doing wrong to go against his judgment. Howsoever, if you've a fancy to go, I'd best come with you, for you'll go anyway, unless you've changed your nature, which don't seem to me likely. What's the orders?'

'I want a horse to be saddled and bridled ready for me at midnight,' answered Ludovic promptly. 'Everyone should be asleep here by then, and I can slip out. Have a couple of nags waiting down the Warninglid road, as close to this place as you can come without rousing anyone. I'll join you there. We'll ride to the Dower House – it's only a matter of five miles – and once inside the place, the rest should be easy. You may want your pistols, though I'd as soon not make it a shooting affair, and we shall certainly need a lantern.'

'Well, that's easy enough,' said Bundy. 'There's only one thing as puts me into a bit of a quirk, and that's how to keep Joe from suspicioning what we'm going to do. Joe's not one of them as has more hair than wit: there's a deal of sense in his cockloft.'

'He must not know you've been here to-day,' said Ludovic. 'You can get away without him seeing you if I make sure all's clear.'

'Oh ay, I can do that,' agreed Bundy, 'but it's odds they'll tell him in the stables I've been around. I've left my nag there.'

'The devil you have! Well, you'd best see Joe if that's so, but take care you don't let him guess you've had speech with me. You might ask for me. He won't let you see me, and it'll look well.'

In accordance with this plan, Bundy, having been smuggled out of the inn by the back way, ten minutes later entered through the front door a second time. He found Clem in the tap-room, and Clem no sooner laid eyes on him than he said that upon no account must Mr. Ludovic know of his presence. He thrust him into Nye's stuffy little private room and went off to summon the landlord. Mr. Bundy sat down by the table and chewed a straw.

His interview with Nye did not take long, nor, since both men were taciturn by nature, was there much conversation. 'Where's young master?' inquired Bundy over his tankard.

Nye jerked a thumb upward. 'Safe enough.'

'I reckoned you'd hide him up,' nodded Bundy, dismissing the subject.

'Ay.' The landlord regarded him thoughtfully. 'He's ripe for mischief, I can tell you. Maybe you'd best keep out of his way. You're as bad as Clem for letting him twist you round his finger.'

'Happen you'm right,' conceded Bundy, retiring into his tankard.

Sir Tristram did not wait for Ludovic to reappear, and for obvious reasons Nye did not tell him of Bundy's presence in the inn. He had a great value for Sir Tristram, but he preferred to keep his dealings with free-traders as secret as possible. So Sir Tristram, having extracted a promise from Clem not to assist Ludovic to leave the inn that night, departed, secure in the conviction that without support his reckless young cousin could achieve nothing in the way of house-breaking.

'I am afraid we shall have Ludovic like a bear with a sore head,' prophesied Miss Thane pessimistically.

But when Ludovic came downstairs to the parlour again, he seemed to be in unimpaired spirits, a circumstance which at first relieved Miss Thane's mind, and presently filled it with misgiving. She fancied that the sparkle in Ludovic's angelic blue eyes was more pronounced than usual, and after enduring it for some little while, was impelled to comment upon it, though in an indiscreet fashion. She said that she feared that Sir Tristram's decision must be unwelcome to him. She was embroidering a length of silk at the time, but as she spoke she raised her eyes from her task and looked steadily at him.

'Oh well!' said Ludovic. 'I've been thinking it over, and I dare say he may be in the right of it.'

Voice and countenance were both quite grave, but Miss Thane was unable to rid herself of the suspicion that he was secretly amused. He met her searching look with the utmost limpidity, and after a moment smiled, and reminded her that it was uncivil to stare.

She was quite unable to resist his smile, which was indeed a very charming one, but she said in a serious tone: 'It would be useless if you were to make the attempt alone, you know. You would not do anything so foolish, would you?'

'Oh, I'm not as mad as that!' he assured her.

She lowered her embroidery. 'And you would not – no, of course you would not! – take Eustacie upon such a venture?'

'Good God, no I'll swear it. if you wish.'

She resumed her stitchery, and as her brother came into the room at that moment said no more. When, later, Ludovic discussed exhaustively the various means by which the Beau's valet might be induced to disclose what he knew, she concluded that her suspicions had been unfounded;

and when, midway through the evening, he sat down to play piquet with Sir Hugh she felt herself able to retire to bed with a quiet mind. She had seen him play piquet before, and she knew that once a green baize cloth was before him, and a pack of cards in his hand, all other considerations were likely to be forgotten. Neither he nor Sir Hugh, she judged, would seek their beds until the small hours, by which time he would be too sleepy, and not sufficiently clear-headed (for it was safe to assume that a good deal of wine would flow during the course of the play) to attempt anything in the way of a solitary adventure. He bade her a preoccupied good night, and she went away without the least misgiving. She was not, however, privileged to see the swift, sidelong look he shot at her as she went through the doorway.

That was at half-past nine. At ten o'clock Ludovic undertook to mix a bowl of rum punch for Sir Hugh's delectation. He promised him something quite above the ordinary, and Sir Hugh, after one sip of the hot, potent brew, admitted that it certainly was above the ordinary. Ludovic drank one glass, and thereafter sat in admiration of Sir Hugh's capacity. When Sir Hugh commented upon his abstinence, he said frankly that a very little of the mixture would suffice to put him under the table. Sir Hugh, rather pleased, said that he fancied he had a harder head than most men. During the next half-hour he proceeded to demonstrate the justice of this claim. The only effect Ludovic's punch had upon him was to make him unusually sleepy, and when Ludovic, as the clock struck eleven, yawned, and said that he was for bed, he was able to rise from the table with scarcely a stagger, and to pick up his candle without spilling any more wax on to the floor than was perfectly seemly. Ludovic, relieved to discover that at least the brew had made him feel ready for bed at an unaccustomed hour, conducted him upstairs to his room and saw him safely into it before tiptoeing along the corridor to his own apartment.

Nye had locked up the inn and gone to bed some time before. Ludovic stirred the logs in his fireplace to a blaze, and sat down to while away half an hour.

His preparations for the venture took him some time, since his left arm was still almost useless, but he contrived, though painfully, to pull on a pair of top-boots, and to struggle into his great-coat. Having assured himself that his pistols were properly primed, he stowed one into the top of his right boot, and the other into the right-hand pocket of his coat, and putting on a tricorne of the fashion of three years before, stole softly out on to the corridor, candle in hand.

The stairs creaked under his feet as he crept down them, but it was not this noise which awoke Miss Thane. She was aroused, ironically enough, by the rhythmic and resonant snores proceeding from her brother's room across the passage. She lay for a few minutes between waking and sleeping, listening to these repulsive sounds, and wondering whether it would be worth while to get up and rouse Sir Hugh, or whether the snoring would recommence the instant he fell asleep again. Just as she decided that the best thing to do was to draw the bedclothes over her ears, and try to ignore the snoring, a faint sound, as of a bolt being drawn downstairs, jerked her fully awake. She sat up in bed, thought that she could hear the click of a latch, and the next instant was standing on the floor, groping for her dressing-gown.

An oil lamp burned low on the table by the bed. She turned up the wick, and picking up the lamp, went softly out on to the passage.

The house was in pitch darkness, and only Sir Hugh's snores broke the silence, but Miss Thane was convinced that there had been other and very stealthy sounds. Her first thought was that someone had entered the house, presumably in search of Ludovic, and she was about to steal along the passage to rouse Nye, when another explanation of the faint sounds occurred to her. She went quickly to Ludovic's room and scratched on the door-panel. There was no answer, and without the slightest hesitation she turned the handle and looked in.

One glance at the unruffled bed was enough to send her flying along the passage to wake Nye. This was easily done, and within two minutes of an urgent, low-voiced call to him through the keyhole, he was beside her on the passage, with a pair of breeches dragged on over his night-shirt, and his night-cap still on his head. When he heard that Ludovic was not in his room he stared at Miss Thane with a pucker between his brows, and said slowly: 'He wouldn't do it – not alone!'

'Where's Clem?' demanded Miss Thane under her breath.

He shook his head. 'No, no, Clem was of my own mind over this. You must have been mistook, ma'am. He wouldn't set out to walk that distance, and he can't saddle a horse with his arm in a sling.' He broke off suddenly, and his eyes narrowed. 'By God, you're right, ma'am!' he said. 'He must have seen Abel! That accounts for him being so uncommon cheerful, drat the boy! Get you back to your room if you please, ma'am. I'll have Clem saddle me a horse while I get some clothes on, and be off after them.'

Miss Thane had been thinking. 'Wait, Nye, I've a better notion. Send Clem to inform Sir Tristram. You'll not catch that wretched boy in time to stop him entering the Dower House, and once he has stepped into whatever trap may have been set for him, Sir Tristram's perhaps the one person who might be able to get him out of it.'

Nye paused. After a moment's reflection he said reluctantly: 'Ay, that's true enough. And Clem's a smaller man than what I am, and will ride faster. It's you who have the head, ma'am.'

While Clem was flinging on his clothes, and Nye was in the stable
saddling a horse, and Miss Thane was sitting on the edge of her bed
wondering whether there was anything more she could do to avert disaster from Ludovic, the object of all this confusion was striding down the
lane leading to Warninglid, quite oblivious of the possibility of pursuit.
The moon, hidden from time to time behind drifting clouds, gave enough
light to enable him to see his way, and in a little while showed him two
horses, drawn up in the lee of a hedge of hornbeam.

Abel greeted him with a grunt, and offered him a flask produced from
the depths of his pocket. 'Play off your dust afore we start,' he recommended.

'No, I must keep a clear head,' replied Ludovic. 'So must you, what's
more. I don't want you disguised.'

'You've never seen me with the malt above the water – not to notice,'
said Mr. Bundy, refreshing himself with a nip.

'I've seen you as drunk as a wheelbarrow,' retorted Ludovic, taking the
flask away from him and putting it in his own pocket. 'It makes you
devilish quick on the pull, and taking the fat with the lean, I think we
won't do any shooting unless we're forced. My cautious cousin's against
it, and I admit there's a deal in what he says. I don't want to be saddled
with any more corpses. Give me a leg-up, will you?'

Bundy complied with this request, and asked what he was to do if it
came to a fight.

'Use your fists,' answered Ludovic. 'Mind you, I dare say there'll be no
fighting.'

'Just as well if there ain't,' said Bundy, hoisting himself into the saddle.
'A hem set-out it will be if you get yourself into a mill with only one arm! I
doubt I done wrong to come with you.'

This was said not in any complaining spirit but as a mere statement of
fact. Ludovic, accustomed to Mr. Bundy's processes of thought, agreed,
and said that there was a strong likelihood of them ending the night's
adventure in the County Gaol.

They set off down the lane at an easy trot, and since Clem had chosen
the shorter but rougher way to the Court that led through the Forest, they
were not disturbed by any sound of pursuit. As they rode, Ludovic
favoured his companion with a brief explanation of what they were to do
at the Dower House. Bundy listened in silence, and at the end merely
expressed his regret that he was not to be given an opportunity of
darkening Beau Lavenham's daylights for him. His animosity towards
the Beau seemed to be groundless but profound, his main grudge against
him being that he stood a good chance of stepping into Sylvester's shoes.

When he spoke of Sylvester he betrayed something as nearly approaching enthusiasm as it was possible for a man of his phlegmatic temperament to feel. 'His was a rare one, the old lord,' he said simply.

When they arrived within sight of the Dower House they reined in their horses and dismounted. The house stood a little way back from the lane, in a piece of ground cut like a wedge out of the park belonging to the Court. After a brief consultation they led their horses through a gap in the straggling hedge, and tethered them inside the park. Bundy set about the task of lighting the lantern he had brought while Ludovic went off to reconnoitre.

When he had circumnavigated the house he returned to Bundy's side to find that that worthy, having covered his lantern with a muffler, was seated placidly beside it on a tree-stump.

'There's no light showing in any window that I can see,' reported Ludovic. 'Now, the Beau told my cautious cousin that the bolt was off one of the library casements, and as that's the room I fancy I want, we'll risk a trap and try to get in by that window.' He drew the pistol from his boot as he spoke, and said: 'If there is a trap this is our best safeguard. In these parts they believe I can't miss, and it makes 'em wary of tackling me. If they mean to capture me they'll try to take me unawares.'

'Well,' said Bundy judicially, 'I'm bound to say I disremember when I've seen you miss your target.'

Ludovic gave a short laugh. 'I missed an owl once, the fool that I was!'

Bundy looked at him with disapproval. 'What would you want to go shooting owls for, anyways?'

'Drunk,' said Ludovic briefly. 'Now, get this into your head, Abel! If we walk into a trap it's one laid for me, not for you, and I'll save myself. Get yourself out of it, and don't trouble your head over me. All I want you to do is to help me to get into the house.

Mr. Bundy arose from the tree-stump and picked up the lantern, vouchsafing no reply.

'Understand?' said Ludovic, a ring of authority in his voice.

'Oh ay!' said Bundy. 'But there! When I see trouble I'm tedious likely to get to in-fighting with it. If you take my advice, which I never known you do yet, you'll turn up that coat-collar of yourn, and pull your hat over your face. You don't want no one to reckernize you.'

Ludovic followed this sage counsel, but remarked that he had little expectation of being known. 'The valet would know me, if he's there, but the butler is since my time.'

'Maybe,' said Bundy. 'But I'll tell you to your head what I've said a-many times behind your back, Master Ludovic, which is that you've got a bowsprit that's the spit and image of the old lord's.'

'Damn this curst family nose!' said Ludovic. 'It'll ruin me yet.'

'That's what I'm thinking,' agreed Bundy. 'However, there's no sense in dwelling on what can't be helped. If you're ready to start milling this ken we'd best start without wasting any more time. And if you keep in mind that though maybe there ain't enough light for anyone to know you by, there's enough and to spare to make you a hem easy target for any cove as might be sitting inside the house with a gun, I dare say you'll come off safe yet.'

'It's odds there's no one there at all,' returned Ludovic. 'But you needn't fear me: I'm taking no risks to-night.'

This remark seemed to tickle Bundy's sense of humour. He went off without warning into a paroxysm of silent laughter, which made his eyes water and his whole frame shake like a jelly. Ludovic paid not the least heed to this seizure, but led the way to a wicket-gate at the back of the house, which gave on to the park from the shrubbery.

Traversing the shrubbery they made their way round to the front of the house, taking care not to tread upon the gravel path. Under the tall casement windows there were flowerbeds, in which a few snowdrops thrust up their heads. Ludovic counted the windows, made up his mind which room must be the library, and indicated it to Bundy with a jerk of his head. Bundy stepped across the path on to the flowerbed, and laid his ear to the glass. He could detect no sound within the room, nor any light behind the drawn curtains, and after a few moments of intent listening he put down his muffled lantern and produced a serviceable knife from his pocket. While he worked on the window Ludovic stood beside him, on the look-out for a possible ambush in the garden. His hat cast a deep shadow over his face, but the moonlight caught the silver mountings on his pistol, and made them gleam. The garden was planted with too many trees and shrubs to make it possible for him to be sure that no one was in hiding there, but he could discover no movement in any of the shadows, and was more than ever inclined to discount his cousin Tristram's forebodings.

A click behind him made him turn his head. Bundy jerked his thumb expressively at one of the windows, and shut his knife. Having forced back the latch he gently prised the window open with his finger-nails. It swung outwards with a slight groan of its hinges. Bundy picked up his lantern in his left hand, unveiled it, and with his right grasped a fold of the velvet curtain, and drew it aside. The muzzle of Ludovic's gun almost rested on his shoulder, but there was no need for it. The lantern's golden beam, travelling round the room, revealed no lurking danger. The room was empty, its chairs primly arranged, its grate laid with sticks ready to be kindled when the master should return.

Bundy took a second look round, and then whispered: 'Will you go in?'

Ludovic nodded, slid the pistol back into his boot and swung a leg over the window-sill.

'Easy now!' Bundy muttered, helping him to hoist himself into the room. 'Wait till I'm with you!'

Ludovic, alighting in the room, said under his breath: 'Stay where you are: I'm not sure whether it's this room I want, or another. Give me the lantern!'

Bundy handed it to him, and he directed its beam on to the wainscoting covering the west wall. Bundy waited in untroubled silence while the golden light travelled backwards and forwards over carved capitals, and fluted pilasters, and the rich intricacies of a frieze composed of cartouches and devices.

It came to rest on one section of the frieze, shifted to another, lingered a moment, and returned again to the first. Ludovic moved forward, counting the divisions between the pilasters. At the third from the window-end of the room he stopped, and held the lantern up close to the wall. He drew his left arm painfully from its sling, and raised it, wincing, to fumble with the carving on the frieze. His tongue clicked impatiently at his own helplessness; he returned his arm to the sling, and stepped back to the window. 'You'll have to hold the lantern, Abel.'

Bundy climbed into the room and took the lantern, directing its beam not on to the wainscoting but on to the lock of the door. He looked thoughtfully at it, and said: 'No key.'

Ludovic frowned a little, but replied: 'It may be lost. Wait!' He trod softly over the carpet to the door, and stood listening with his ear to the crack. He could hear nothing, and moved away again. 'If I don't find what I want in the priest's hole we'll open that door, and take a look round the rest of the house,' he said. 'Hold the light so that I may see the frieze. No, more to the right.' He put up his hand, and grasped one of the carved devices. 'I think – no, I'm wrong! It's not the fourth, but the third! Now watch!'

Bundy saw his long fingers twist the device, and simultaneously heard the scroop of a door sliding back. The sudden noise, slight though it was, sounded abnormally loud in the stillness. He swung the lantern round, and saw that between two of the pilasters on the lower tier the panelling had vanished, disclosing a dark cavity.

'The lantern, man, give me the lantern!' Ludovic said, and almost snatched it from him.

He reached the priest's hole in two strides, and as he bent peering into it, Bundy heard a faint sound, and wheeling about saw a thin line of light appear at one end of the room, gradually widening. Someone was stealthily opening the door.

'Out, sir! Save yourself!' he hissed, and pulling his pistol out of his pocket prepared to hold all comers at bay until Ludovic was through the window.

Ludovic heard the warning, and quick as a flash, thrust the lantern into the priest's hole, and swung round. He said clearly: 'The window, man! Be off!' and bending till he was nearly double, slipped backwards into the priest's hole, and pulled the panel to upon himself.

Wavering candlelight illuminated the room, a voice shouted: 'Stand! Stand!' and Bundy, hidden behind the window-curtains, saw a thin man with a pistol in his hand rush into the room towards the priest's hole, and claw fruitlessly at the panel, saying: 'He's here, he's here! I saw him!'

The butler, who was standing on the threshold with a branch of candles in his hand, stared at the wainscoting and said: 'Where?'

'Here, behind the panel! I saw it close, I tell you! There's a priest's hole; we have him trapped!'

The butler looked a good deal astonished, and advancing further into the room said: 'Since you know so much about this house, Mr. Gregg, perhaps you know how to get into this priest's hole you talk of?'

The valet shook his head, biting his nails. 'No, we were too late. Only the master knows the catch to it. We must keep it covered.'

'It seems to me that there's someone else as knows,' remarked the butler austerely. 'I'm bound to say that I don't understand what it is you're playing at, Mr. Gregg, with all this mysterious talk about house-breakers, and setting everyone on to keep watch like you have. Who's behind the panel!'

Gregg answered evasively: 'How should I know? But I saw a man disappear into the wall. We must get the Parish Constable up here to take him the instant the master gets back and opens the panel.'

'I presoom you know what you're about, Mr. Gregg,' said the butler in frigid tones. 'If I were to pass an opinion I should say that it was more my place than yours to give orders here in the master's absence. These goings-on are not at all what I have been accustomed to.'

'Never mind that!' said Gregg impatiently. 'Send one of the stable-hands to fetch the Constable!'

'Stand where you be!' growled a voice from the window. 'Drop that gun! I have you covered, and my pop's liable to go off unaccountable sudden-like.'

The valet wheeled round, saw Mr. Bundy, and jerked up his pistol-hand. The two guns cracked almost as one, but in the uncertain light neither bullet found its mark. The butler gave a startled gasp, and nearly let the candles fall, and through the window scrambled a third man, who flung himself upon Bundy from the rear, panting: 'Ah, *would* you, then!'

Abel Bundy was not, however, an easy man to overpower. He wrenched himself out of the groom's hold, and jabbed him scientifically in the face. The groom, a young an enthusiastic man, went staggering back, but recovered, and bored in again.

The butler, seeing that a mill was in progress, set down the branch of candles on the table, and hurried, portly but powerful, to join in the fray. Gregg called out: 'That's not the man! The other's here, behind the panelling! This one makes no odds!'

'This one's good enough for me!' said the groom between his teeth.

It was at this moment that Sir Tristram, mounted on Clem's horse, reached the wicket-gate at the back of the garden. He had heard the pistol-shots as he rode across the park, and had spurred his horse to a gallop. He pulled it up, snorting and trembling, flung himself out of the saddle, and setting his hand on the wicket-gate, vaulted over, and went swiftly round the house to the library window.

An amazing sight met his eyes. Of Ludovic there was no sign, but three other men, apparently inextricably entangled, swayed and struggled over the floor, while Beau Lavenham's prim valet hovered about the group, saying: 'Not that one! I want the other!'

Sir Tristram stood for a moment, considering. Then he drew a long-barrelled pistol from his pocket, and with deliberation cocked it and took careful aim. There was a flash, and a deafening report, and the branch of candles on the table crashed to the ground, plunging the room into darkness.

Sir Tristram, entering the library through the window, heard the valet shriek: 'My God, he must have got out! No one else could have fired that shot!'

'Oh, could they not?' murmured Sir Tristram, with a certain grim satisfaction.

Half in and half out of the window, his form was silhouetted for a moment against the moonlit sky. The valet gave a shout of warning, and Sir Tristram, coolly taking note of his position from the sound of his voice, strode forward. The valet met him bravely enough, launching himself upon the dimly-seen figure, but he was no match for Sir Tristram, who evaded his clutch, and threw in a body-hit which almost doubled him up. Before he could recover from it Sir Tristram found him again, and dropped him from a terrific right to the jaw. He crashed to the ground and lay still, and Sir Tristram, his eyes growing accustomed to the darkness, turned his attention to Bundy's captors. For a few seconds there was some wild fighting. The groom, leaving Bundy to the butler, tried to grapple with Shield, was thrown off, and rattled in again as game as a pebble. There was no room for science; hits went glaringly abroad, furniture was sent flying, and the confused bout ended in Shield throwing his opponent in a swinging fall.

Bundy, who had very soon accounted for the butler, turned to assist his unknown supporter, but found it unnecessary. He was thrust towards the window, and scrambled through it just as the groom struggled to his feet again. Sir Tristram followed him fast, and two minutes later they confronted one another on the park side of the wicket-gate, both of them panting for breath, the knuckles of Shield's right hand bleeding slightly and Bundy's left eye rapidly turning from red to purple.

'Dang me if I know who you may be!' said Bundy, breathing heavily. 'But I'm tedious glad to meet a cove so uncommon ready to sport his canvas, that I will say!'

'You may not know me,' said Shield wrathfully, 'but I know you, you muddling, addle-pated jackass! Where's Mr. Ludovic?'

Bundy, rather pleased than otherwise by this form of address, said mildly: 'What might you be up in the bows for, master? I misdoubt I don't know what you'm talking about.'

'You damned fool, I'm his cousin! Where is he?'

Bundy stared at him, a slow smile dawning on his swollen countenance. 'His cautious cousin!' he said. 'If he hadn't misled me I should have guessed it, surelye, for by the way you talk you might be the lord himself! Lamentable cautious you be! Oh, l-a-amentable!'

'For two pins I'd give you into custody for a dangerous law-breaker!' said Shield savagely. 'Will you answer me, or do I choke it out of you? Where's my cousin?'

'Now don't go wasting time having a set-to with me!' begged Mr. Bundy 'I don't say I wouldn't like a bout with you, but it ain't the time for it. Mr. Ludovic's got himself into that priest's hole he was so just about crazy to find.'

'In the priest's hole? Then why the devil didn't he come out when I shot the candles over?'

'Happen it ain't so easy to get out as what it is to get in,' suggested Bundy. 'What's more, the cat's properly in the cream-pot now, for that screeching valet knows where he is, ay, and who he is! He means to watch till his precious master gets home.'

'He'll do no watching yet awhile,' said Sir Tristram. 'I took very good care to put him to sleep. He's the only one we have to fear. The butler has never seen my cousin, and I doubt is not in his master's confidence.'

'You'm right there,' corroborated Bundy, 'he ain't. But he know's there's a man in the priest's hole, because t'other cove told him so.'

'I can handle him,' said Shield briefly, and catching his horse's bridle, set his foot in the stirrup. 'Stay here, and if I whistle come to the window. I may need you to show me where to find the catch that opens the panel.' He swung himself into the saddle as he spoke, wheeled the horse, and cantered off towards the gap in the hedge through which Ludovic and Bundy had entered the park.

Mr. Bundy, tenderly feeling his contused eye, was shaken by inward mirth for the second time that evening. 'Lamentable cautious!' he repeated. 'Oh ay, l-a-amentable!'

Sir Tristram, breaking through on to the road, turned towards the Dower House, and rode up the neat drive at a canter. Dismounting, he not only pulled the iron bell violently, but also hammered an imperative summons with the knocker on the front door.

In a few minutes the door was cautiously opened on the chain, and the butler, looking pale and shaken, and with a black eye almost equal to Bundy's, peered out.

'What the devil's amiss?' demanded Sir Tristram. 'Don't keep me standing here! Open the door!'

'Oh, it's you, sir!' gasped the butler, much relieved, and making haste to unfasten the chain.

'Of course it's I!' said Sir Tristram, pushing his way past him into the hall. 'I was on my way home from Hand Cross when I heard unmistakable pistol-shots coming from here. What's the meaning of it? What are you doing up at this hour?'

'I'm – I'm very glad you've come, sir,' said the butler, wiping his face. 'Very glad indeed, sir. I'm so shook up I scarce know what I'm about. It was Gregg's doing, sir. No, not precisely that neither, but it was Gregg as had his suspicions there was a robbery planned for to-night. He was quite right, sir: we've had house-breakers in, and one of them's hidden in some priest's hole I never heard of till now. I've never been so used in all my life, sir, never!'

'Priest's hole! What priest's hole?' said Shield. 'How many house-breakers were there? Have you caught any of them?'

'No, sir, and there's Gregg laying like one dead. There was a great many of them. We did what we could, but the candlestick was shot over, and in the dark they got away. It was the one in the panelling Gregg set such store by catching, so I've left one of the stable-lads there to keep watch. In the library, sir.'

'It seems to me you have conducted yourselves like a set of idiots!' said Sir Tristram angrily, and walked into the library.

The candelabra had been picked up from the wreckage on the floor, and the candles, most of them broken off short by their fall, had been relit. The valet's inanimate form was stretched on the couch, but the young groom, looking bruised and dishevelled but still remarkably pugnacious, was standing in the middle of the room, his serious grey eyes fixed on the wainscoting. He touched his forelock to Sir Tristram, but did not move from his commanding position.

Shield went over to look at the valet, who was breathing stertorously. 'Knocked out,' he said. 'You'd better carry him up to his bed. Where's this precious panel you talk of?'

'It's here, sir,' answered the groom. 'I'm a-watching of it. Only let the cove come out, that's all I ask!'

'I'll keep an eye on that,' replied Sir Tristram. 'You take this fellow's legs, and help Jenkyns carry him up to his room. Get water and vinegar, and see what you can do to bring him round. Gently, now!'

Under his authoritative instructions the groom and the butler lifted Gregg from the couch, and bore him tenderly from the room. No sooner had they started to mount the stairs than Sir Tristram closed the library door and called softly: 'Ludovic! All's clear: come out!'

'Happen he's suffocated inside that hole,' remarked Mr. Bundy's fatalistic voice from the window.

'Nonsense, there must be enough air! Where's the catch that opens the panel?'

Bundy, leaning his head and shoulders in at the window, indicated the portion of the frieze where it might be found. Shield ran his hand over the carving, presently found the device Ludovic had twisted, and turned it. The panel slid back once more, and Shield, picking up the candelabra, went to it, saying sharply: 'Ludovic! Are you hurt?'

There was no answer. Sir Tristram bent, so that the candles illumined the cavity, and looked in. It was quite empty.

CHAPTER 12

Sir Tristram put the candelabra down, and once more twisted the device, closing the panel. 'He's not there,' he said.

Mr. Bundy betrayed no surprise. 'Ah!' he remarked, preparing to climb into the room. 'I'd a notion we shouldn't get out of this so hem easy. As good be nibbled to death by ducks as set out on one of Master Ludovic's ventures! Where's he got to, by your reckoning?'

'God knows! He must have slipped out after the candles were knocked over. Don't come in!'

Bundy obediently stayed where he was. 'Just as you say, master. But it ain't like him to keep out of a fight.'

'He'd be no use in a mill with one arm in a sling,' replied Sir Tristram.

'Go and see if he has gone back to where you left your horses. If he's not there he must be somewhere in the house.'

'Well, I'll do it,' said Bundy, 'but I reckon it's no manner of use. 'Twouldn't be natural if young master were to start behaving sensible all on a sudden. You'd be surprised the number of cork-brained scrapes he's got himself into these two years and more.'

'You're wrong; I shouldn't,' retorted Sir Tristram.

'Ah well, he's a valiant lad, surelye!' said Bundy, indulgently, and withdrew.

Sir Tristram stayed where he was, and in a very few minutes Mr. Bundy once more appeared at the window and said simply: 'He ain't there.'

'Damn the boy!' said Sir Tristram. 'Get away from that window! There's someone coming!'

Bundy promptly ducked beneath the level of the window-sill just as the door opened, and Gregg staggered in, supported by the butler.

His jaw was much swollen and two front teeth were broken. Sir Tristram put his grazed right hand into his pocket. It was evident that although his head might be swimming, the valet still had some of his wits about him, for no sooner did his bleared gaze fall upon Shield than he turned an even more sickly colour, and catching at a chair-back to steady himself, said in a thick voice: 'It's like that, is it? But I'll watch. I have the keys of the doors. If he's there still he won't get away!'

The groom came into the room and said in his serious young voice: 'I'd get him a drop of brandy if I were you, Mr. Jenkyns. Regular shook to pieces he is. Now, don't you fret, Mr. Gregg! No one can't get out while you've got them keys.'

The butler, who thought that a drop of brandy would do him good also, said graciously that he believed the lad was right, and went away to fetch the decanter. The groom, coming up behind the valet, said solicitously: 'You shouldn't ought to have come down, Mr. Gregg,' and knocked him out with one nicely-delivered blow under the ear. The unfortunate valet collapsed on to the floor, and the groom, looking down at him with a smouldering expression of wrath in his pleasant grey eyes, said grimly: 'Maybe that'll be a lesson to you, you cribbage-faced tooth-drawer, you!'

Before Sir Tristram, considerably astonished by this unexpected turn of events had taken, had time to speak, the butler, hearing the sound of Gregg's fall, came hurrying back into the room. The groom at once turned to meet him, saying: 'Blessed if he ain't swooned off again, Mr. Jenkyns! Done to a cow's thumb, he is!'

'Carry the poor fellow up to his room again, and this time keep him there!' commanded Sir Tristram, recovering from his surprise.

'Just what I was a-going to do, sir,' said the groom. 'Now, Mr. Jenkyns, if you'll take his legs we'll soon have him in his bed!'

'Ah, I warned him not to get up!' said the butler, shaking his head.

The groom thrust a hand into Gregg's pocket and extracted the keys from it. 'I'm thinking your Honour had best keep these,' he said, and held them out to Sir Tristram.

The butler, puffing as he bent to raise Gregg, agreed that Sir Tristram was certainly the man to take charge of the keys. For a second time the valet was borne off upstairs. Mr. Bundy, reappearing at the window, like a jack-in-the-box, remarked phlegmatically: 'It looks to me like young master's met a friend. Who's that young cove?'

'I fancy he must be Jim Kettering's boy,' replied Sir Tristram.

'Well, he's caused us a peck of trouble this night,' said Bundy, 'but I'm bound to say he seems an unaccountable nice lad! Handy with his fives he is.'

At this moment Ludovic strolled into the room. 'Well, of all the shambles!' he remarked, glancing around. 'I'd give a monkey to see the Beau's face when he comes home! What brought you here, Tristram?'

'Clem fetched me,' replied Shield. 'How did you get out of the priest's hole, and what the devil have you been doing all this while?'

'There's another way out of the hole,' explained Ludovic. 'I thought there might be. It leads up to Basil's bedchamber. It seemed to me I might as well hunt for the ring since you had the affair so well in hand down here. Then I heard Bob Kettering's voice, and gave him a whistle——'

'Gave him a whistle?' echoed Sir Tristram. 'With the whole household looking for you, you *whistled*?'

'Yes, why not? I knew he'd recognize it. It's a signal we used when we were boys. Bob hadn't a notion he'd been set on to hunt for me. Lord, we used to go bird's-nesting together!'

'I thought you'd met a friend,' nodded Bundy. 'Did you happen to find that ring o' yourn?'

Ludovic's face clouded over. 'No. Bob helped me to ransack Basil's room, but it's not there, and it wasn't in the priest's hole.'

'Did young Kettering chance to remember that he is in Basil's service?' inquired Sir Tristram.

Ludovic looked at him. 'Yes, but this was for *me*, my dear fellow!'

Sir Tristram smiled faintly. 'I suppose he is as shameless as you are. Do you feel that you have done enough damage for one night, or is there anything else you'd care to set your hand to before you go?'

'Damage!' said Ludovic. 'If that don't beat everything! Who smashed all this furniture, I should like to know? *I* didn't!'

The groom came back into the library as he spoke, and said urgently: 'Mr. Ludo, you'd best go while you may. We'll have Jenkyns down again afore we know where we are!'

'Have you ever thought to go into the prize-ring, young fellow,' inter-rupted Bundy, who was leaning in at the window with his arms folded on the sill, after the fashion of one who was prepared to remain there indefinitely. 'You've a sizeable bunch of fives, and you display none so bad.'

Kettering grinned rather deprecatingly, and said in an apologetic tone to Sir Tristram: 'I didn't know it was Mr. Ludo, sir. Nor I didn't know it was you neither. I'm proud, surelye, to have had a turn-up with you, even if it were in the dark.'

'Well, it's more than I'd care to do,' remarked Ludovic. 'To hell with you, Bob! Don't keep on pushing me to the window! I'll go all in good time, but I've mislaid that damn lantern.'

Sir Tristram grasped him by his sound shoulder, and propelled him to the window. 'Take him away, Bundy. Kettering can find the lantern when you've gone. If you don't go you'll find yourself in difficulties again, and I warn you I won't get you out of any more tight corners.'

Ludovic, astride the window-sill, said: 'You don't call this a tight corner, do you? I was as safe be damned!'

'Just about, you were,' growled Bundy, trying to haul him through the window, 'playing your silly rat-in-the-wall tricks, with a whole pack of gurt fools fighting who was to find you first! And you saying you wasn't going to take no risks! Now, come out of it, master!'

'I can't help it if you disobey my orders!' said Ludovic indignantly. 'Didn't I tell you to save yourself? Instead of doing anything of the kind you blazed off your pistol (and a damned bad shot it must have been) and started a mill, so that my cousin had to make a wreck of the place to bring you off! What's more, that's not the sort of thing he likes. He's a cautious man – aren't you, Tristram?'

'I am,' replied Sir Tristram, thrusting him through the window into Bundy's arms, 'but my love of caution isn't going to stop me knocking you on the head and carrying you away if you don't go immediately. Wait for me by your horses. I shan't be many moments.'

He saw Ludovic go off under Bundy's escort, and turned back to Kettering. His level gaze seemed to measure the younger man. He said: 'I take it you can keep your mouth shut?'

The groom nodded. 'Ay, sir, I can that. Me to help trap Mr. Ludo! Begging your pardon, sir, but it do fair rile me to think of it!'

'Well, if you get turned off for this night's work come to me,' said Sir Tristram. 'Now where's that butler?' He went out into the hall, and called to Jenkyns, who presently came hurrying down the stairs. 'Here are your keys,' said Sir Tristram, holding them out to him. 'Now let me out!'

The butler took the keys, but said in a blank voice: 'Are—are you going now, sir?'

'Certainly, I am going,' replied Shield, with one of his coldest glances. 'Do you imagine that I propose to remain here all night to keep watch for a house-breaker who, if he ever entered the priest's hole (which I take leave to doubt), must have escaped half an hour ago?'

'No, sir. Oh no, sir!' said the butler very chap-fallen.

'You are, for once, quite right,' said Shield.

Five minutes later he joined Ludovic in the park and dismounted from Clem's horse. Clem had by this time reached the scene of activity, having walked from the Court, and Ludovic was already in the saddle, looking rather haggard and spent. Sir Tristram gave his bridle into Clem's hand, and looked shrewdly up at his cousin. 'Yes, you are feeling your wound a trifle,' he remarked. 'I am not in the least surprised, and not particularly sorry. If you had your desserts for this night's folly you would be in gaol.'

'Oh, my wound's well enough!' replied Ludovic. 'Do you want me to say that you were in the right, and there was a trap? Well, then, you were damnably right, even to saying that I'd not find my ring. I haven't found it. What else?'

'Nothing else. Go back to Hand Cross, and for God's sake stay there!'

Ludovic let the reins go, and stretched down his hand. 'Oh curse you, Tristram, I am sorry, and you're a devilish good fellow to embroil yourself in my crazy affairs! Thank you for coming to-night!'

Shield gripped his hand for a moment, and said in a softer voice: 'Don't be a fool! We will find your ring, Ludovic. I'll see you to-morrow.'

'I'll try and keep out of trouble till then,' promised Ludovic. He gathered the reins up again, and the irrepressible twinkle crept back into his eyes. 'By the way, my compliments: a nice shot!'

Shield laughed at that. 'Was it not? Gregg thought you must have fired it.'

'Extravagant praise, Tristram: you shouldn't listen to flattery,' retorted Ludovic, grinning.

When the adventurers got back to the Red Lion they found both Nye and Miss Thane awaiting them by the coffee-room fire. Relief at seeing Ludovic safe and sound had its natural effect on Nye, and instead of greeting his graceless charge with solicitude he rated him with such severity that Bundy was moved to expostulate. 'Adone-do, Joe!' he said. 'There's no harm done, and we've had a nice little mill. Just you take a look at my eye.'

'I am looking at it,' replied Nye. 'If I ever meet the man as gave it you I'll shake him by the hand! I wish he'd blacked t'other as well.'

'You'd have kissed him if he had,' remarked Ludovic. 'It was Bob Kettering.'

'Bob Kettering!' ejaculated the landlord. 'Now, what have you been about, sir? If I ever met such a plaguey—— where's Sir Tristram?'

'Gone home to bed,' yawned Ludovic. 'I dare say he'll be glad to get there; he's had a full evening, thanks to you, Sally.'

Mr. Bundy nodded slowly at Nye. 'It would do your heart good to see that cove in a turn-up, Joe. Displays to remarkable advantage, he does. Up to all the tricks.'

'Many's the time I've sparred with Sir Tristram,' replied Nye crushingly. 'I don't doubt he'd be a match for the lot of you, but what I do say, and hold to, is that he hit the wrong man.'

'I don't know when I've took such a fancy to a cove,' said Bundy, disregarding this significant remark. 'He gave the valet one in the bone-box, and a tedious wisty castor to the jaw. What he done to young Kettering I don't know, but from the sounds of it he threw him a rare cross-buttock.'

At this point Miss Thane interrupted him, demanding to be told the full story of the night's adventure. It seemed to amuse her, and when Sir Tristram arrived at the Red Lion midway through the following morning, she met him with a pronounced twinkle in her eyes.

He saw it, and a rueful smile stole into his own eyes. He took the hand she held out to him, saying: 'How do you do? This should be a day of triumph for you.'

She put up her brows. 'I believe you are quizzing me. Why should it be a day of triumph for me?'

'My dear ma'am, did you not guess that at last you have succeeded in making me feel grateful towards you?'

'Odious creature!' said Miss Thane, without heat. 'I had a mind to go myself to rescue Ludovic.'

'You would have been very much in the way, I assure you. How is the boy this morning?'

'I fancy he has taken no harm. He is a little in the dumps. Tell me, have you any real hope of finding his ring?'

'I have every hope of clearing his name,' he replied. 'His adventure last night will at least serve to convince the Beau that we mean to bring him to book. While no danger threatened, Basil was easily able to behave with calmness and good sense, but I do not think he is of the stuff to remain cool in the face of a very pressing danger.'

'You think he may betray himself. But one must not forget that last night's affair must surely have betrayed *you*.'

'All the better,' said Shield. 'The Beau is a little afraid of me.'

'I imagine he might well be. But he cannot be so stupid that he will not realize what your true purpose in his house must have been.'

'Certainly,' he agreed, 'but his situation is awkward. He will hardly admit to having laid a trap for the man whose heir he is. He will be obliged to pretend to accept my story. Where is Ludovic, by the way?'

'Eustacie has persuaded him to stay in bed this morning. Five miles to the Dower House, and five miles back again, with an adventure between, was a trifle too much for one little better than an invalid. Do you care to go up? You will find Hugh with him, I think.'

He nodded, and waited for her by the door, and when she seemed not to be coming, said: 'You do not mean to secede from our councils, I hope?'

She smiled. 'You are not used to being so civil. Fighting must have a mellowing effect upon you, I think.'

'Have I been uncivil?' he asked, looking at her with disconcerting seriousness.

'Well, perhaps not uncivil,' she conceded. 'Just disapproving.'

He followed her out of the room, and as they mounted the stairs, said: 'I wish you will rid yourself of this nonsensical notion that I disapprove of you.'

'But do you not?' inquired Miss Thane, turning her head.

He stopped two stairs below her, and stood looking up at her, something not quite a smile at the back of his eyes. 'Sometimes,' he said.

They found Ludovic drinking Constantia wine, and arguing with Sir Hugh about the propriety of breaking into other people's houses to recover one's own property. Eustacie, seated by the window, upheld the justice of his views, but strongly condemned the insensibility of persons who allowed others to sleep while such adventures were in train. She was rash enough to appeal to her cousin Tristram for support, but as he only replied that he had not till now thought that he had anything to be thankful for with regard to last night's affair, he joined Miss Thane in her ill-graces.

Ludovic's immediate desire was to learn from his cousin by what means he now proposed to find the talisman ring, but they had not been discussing the matter for more than five minutes when a chaise was heard approaching at a smart pace down the road. It drew up outside the inn, and Eustacie, peeping over the blind, announced in a shocked voice that its occupant was none other than Beau Lavenham.

'What audacity!' exclaimed Miss Thane.

'Yes, and he is wearing a waistcoat with coquelicot stripes,' said Eustacie.

'What!' ejaculated Ludovic. 'Here, where's my dressing-gown? I must take a look at him!'

'Oh no, you must not!' said Sir Tristram, preventing his attempt to leap out of bed.

'It's too late: he has entered the house. What can he want?'

'Probably to convince us that he was really in London last night,' said Shield. 'We'll go down to him, Eustacie.'

'*Je le veux bien!* What shall I say to him?'

'Whatever you please, as long as it does not concern Ludovic,' He looked across the room at Miss Thane. 'Do you think you can contrive to be as stupid and talkative as you were when he last saw you?'

'Oh, am I to be allowed to take part?' asked Miss Thane. 'Certainly I can be as stupid. To what purpose?'

'Well, I think it is time we frightened Basil a little,' said Sir Tristram. 'Since he must now be very sure that Ludovic is in Sussex, we will further inform him that we suspect him of being Plunkett's real murderer.'

'That's all very well,' objected Ludovic, 'but what do you expect him to do?'

'I haven't a notion,' said Shield calmly, 'but I am reasonably certain that he will do something.'

'Tell me what you wish me to say!' begged Miss Thane.

Beau Lavenham was not kept waiting long in the parlour. In a very few minutes his cousins joined him there. He shot a quick, searching look at them under his lashes, and advanced, all smiles and civility. 'My dear Eustacie – Tristram, too! You behold me on my way home from a most tedious disagreeable sojourn in town. I could not resist the opportunity of paying a morning call upon you. I trust I do not come at an awkward time?'

'But no!' said Eustacie, opening her eyes at him. 'Why should it be?'

Sir Tristram came over to the fire in a leisurely fashion, and stirred it with his foot. 'Oh, so you've not yet been home, Basil?' he inquired.

'No, not yet,' replied the Beau. He put up his ornate quizzing-glass, and through it looked at Shield. 'Why do you ask me so oddly, my dear fellow? Is anything amiss at the Dower House?'

'Something very much amiss, I am afraid,' said Shield. He waited for a moment, saw a flash of eagerness in the Beau's eyes, and added: 'One of your Jacobean chairs has been broken.'

There was a moment's silence. The Beau let his glass fall, and replied in rather a mechanical voice: 'A chair broken? Why, how is that?'

The door opened to admit Miss Thane. Until she had exclaimed at finding the Beau present, greeted him, inquired after his health, the condition of the roads, and the state of the weather in London, there was no opportunity of reverting to the original subject of conversation. But as soon as she paused for breath the Beau turned back to Shield, and said: 'You were telling me something about one of my chairs being broken. I fear I don't——'

'Oh!' exclaimed Miss Thane, 'have you not heard, then? Has Sir Tristram not told you of the shocking attempt to rob you last night? I declare I shall not know how to go to bed this evening!'

'No,' said the Beau slowly. 'No. He has not told me. Is it possible that my house was broken into?'

'Exactly,' nodded Sir Tristram. 'If your servants are to be believed a band of desperate ruffians entered through the library window.'

'Yes,' chimed in Miss Thane, 'and only fancy, Mr. Lavenham! Sir Tristram had been dining with us here, and was riding back to the Court when he heard shots coming from the Dower House. You may imagine his amazement! I am sure you should be grateful to him, for he instantly rode up to the house. You may depend upon it it was the noise of his arrival which frightened the wretches into running away.'

The glance the Beau cast at his cousin was scarcely one of gratitude. He had turned rather pale, but he said in quite level tones: 'I am indeed grateful. What a fortunate chance that you should have been passing the house just at that moment, Tristram! I suppose none of these rogues was apprehended?'

'I fear not,' replied Shield. 'By the time I entered the house there was no sign of them. There had been (as you will see for yourself presently) a prodigious struggle in the library – quite a mill, I understand. I am afraid your fellows were much knocked about. In fact, your butler,' he pursued, stooping to put another log on the fire, 'welcomed my advent with profound relief.'

'No doubt!' said the Beau, breathing rather quickly. 'I do not doubt it!'

'The poor butler!' said Miss Thane, with a tinkling laugh. 'I am sure I do not wonder he should be alarmed! He must feel you to be his preserver, Sir Tristram. He will be doubly glad to exchange his masters!'

The Beau looked at her. 'I beg your pardon, ma'am?'

Miss Thane said: 'I only meant, since he was about to enter Sir Tristram's service——'

'You are mistaken, Miss Thane,' Sir Tristram interrupted, frowning at her. 'There is no question of my cousin's butler leaving his service that I know of.'

'Oh, how stupid of me! Only you were saying to Eustacie that you had found Mr. Lavenham's butler, and she asked, do you not remember, whether his memory——'

Eustacie said in a hurry: 'I hope so much that nothing has been stolen from your house, Basil. To have——'

'So do I hope it, my dear cousin. But pray let Miss Thane continue!'

Miss Thane, encountering a frown from Eustacie, stammered: 'Oh, indeed it was nothing! I would not for the world – I mean, I was mistaken!

I confused one thing with another. My brother tells me I am a sad shatterbrain.'

Sir Tristram intervened, saying in his cool way: 'I am making no attempt to steal your butler from you, I assure you, Basil.'

'Of course not! The stupidest mistake!' said Miss Thane, all eagerness to atone. 'It is not your present butler, Mr. Lavenham, but one you were used to employ. I remember perfectly now!' She looked from Sir Tristram to Eustacie and faltered: 'Have I said something I ought not? But you *did* tell Eustacie.'

The Beau was gripping his snuff-box tightly. 'Yes? A butler I once employed? Are you thinking of taking him into your service, Tristram?'

'Why, yes, I confess I had some such notion,' admitted Shield. 'You have no objection, I trust?'

'Why should I?' said the Beau, with a singularly mirthless smile. 'I doubt, though, whether you will find him so useful as you expect.'

'Oh, I dare say I shall not engage him after all,' replied Shield, and made haste to change the subject.

The Beau did not linger. Excusing himself on the score of being obliged to go home to ascertain what losses, if any, he had sustained, he very soon took his leave of the party, and drove away in the direction of Warninglid.

No sooner had he left the inn than Eustacie cast herself upon Miss Thane's bosom, announcing that she forgave her for her unfeeling conduct of the night before. 'You did it so *very* well, Sarah! He was *bouleversé*, and I think frightened.'

'He was certainly frightened,' agreed Miss Thane. 'He forgot to smile. What do you suppose he will do, Sir Tristram?'

'I hope he may make an attempt to find Cleghorn and buy his silence. If he does he will have delivered himself into our hands. But don't let Ludovic stir from the house! I'll warn Nye to be careful whom he lets into the inn.'

'I can feel my flesh creeping already,' said Miss Thane, with a shudder. 'It has suddenly occurred to me that that very unpleasant person thinks Ludovic is occupying the back bedchamber.'

Eustacie gave a gasp. 'Oh, Sarah, you do not think he will come to murder Ludovic, do you?'

'I shouldn't be at all surprised,' said Miss Thane. 'And *I* am occupying the back bedchamber! I just mention it, you know.'

'So you are!' Eustacie's face cleared. 'But it is of all things the most fortunate! It could not be better, *enfin*!'

'That,' said Miss Thane, with strong feeling, 'is a matter of opinion. *I* can see where it could be much better.'

'But no, Sarah! If Basil comes to murder Ludovic in the night he will find not Ludovic, but you!'

'Yes, that was what I was thinking,' said Miss Thane.

'Well, but it would be a good thing, Sarah!'

'A good thing for whom?' demanded Miss Thane with asperity.

'For Ludovic, of course! You do not *mind* doing just that little thing to help him, do you? You said that you wanted to have an adventure!'

'I may have said that I wanted to have an adventure,' replied Miss Thane, 'but I never said that I wanted to be murdered in my bed!'

'But I find that you are absurd, Sarah! Of course he would not murder you!'

'Unless, of course, he regarded it as a good opportunity to rid the world of a chattering female,' said Sir Tristram, with a gravity wholly belied by the twinkle in his eyes. 'That is a risk, however, which we shall have to run.'

Miss Thane looked at him. 'You did say "we," didn't you?' she said in a failing voice.

He laughed. 'Yes, I said it. But in all seriousness, Miss Thane, I do not think there will be any risk. If you are afraid, share Eustacie's bed.'

'No,' said Miss Thane, with the air of one going to the stake. 'I prefer that my blood should be upon your heads.'

She spoke in jest, and certainly did not give the matter another thought, but the exchange had made an impression on Eustacie's mind, and for the rest of the day she could scarcely bear to let Ludovic out of her sight. When Sir Tristram had gone, and Miss Thane proposed they should take their usual morning walk, she refused with such resolution that Miss Thane forebore to press the matter, but went out with her brother, leaving Eustacie keeping guard over Ludovic like a cat with one kitten.

As the day drew towards evening Eustacie's fears became more pronounced. When the candles were lit and the blinds drawn, she persisted in hearing footsteps, and fancying some stranger to have got into the inn. She confided in Miss Thane that she was sure there was someone in the house, hiding, and insisted, in spite of his protestations that no one could have entered without his knowledge, upon Nye's searching every nook and cranny. The house was an old and rambling one, and the boards creaked a good deal. Miss Thane, when Eustacie held up her finger for the fifth time, enjoining silence that she might listen for a fancied noise, said roundly: 'A little more, and I shall be quite unable to sleep a wink all night. *Now* what's amiss?'

Eustacie, drawing the curtains more closely across the window, said: 'There was just a crack. Someone might look in and see Ludovic. I think it will be better if I pin the curtains together.'

Sir Hugh, who was engaged upon his nightly game of piquet with

Ludovic, became aware of her restlessness, and turned to look at her. 'Ah!' he said. 'So you don't like the moonshine either! It's a queer thing, but if ever I have a bad dream you may depend upon it the moon's up. There's another thing, too: if ever it gets into my room it wakes me. I'm glad to meet someone else who feels the same.'

No one thought it worth while to explain Eustacie's real motive to him, so after recounting various incidents illustrative of the baneful effect of the moon upon human beings, he returned to his game, and speedily became oblivious of Eustacie's fidgets.

Since Eustacie could not bring herself to go up to bed leaving Ludovic, quite heedless of danger, below-stairs, the piquet came to an early end, and the whole party went up to bed soon after ten o'clock. Having assured herself that the windows in Ludovic's room were securely fastened and his pistols loaded and under his pillow, Eustacie at last consented, though reluctantly, to seek her own couch. Ludovic took her in his sound arm, and kissed her, and laughed at her fears. She said seriously: 'But I am afraid. I love you so much that it seems to me very probable that you will be taken away from me. Promise me that you will lock your door and draw the bolts!'

He laid his cheek against her hair. 'I'll promise anything, sweetheart. Don't trouble your pretty head over me! I'm not worth it.'

'To me, you are.'

'I wish I had two arms!' he sighed. 'Do you know that you are marrying a ne'er-do-well?'

'Certainly I know it. It is just what I always wanted,' she replied.

Miss Thane came along the passage at this moment and put an end to their *tête-à-tête*. She quite agreed with Eustacie that Ludovic must lock his door. She had every intention, she said, of locking her own. She bore Eustacie off to her room, stayed with her till she was safely tucked up in bed, turned the lamp down, made up the fire, and went away wondering whether there really might be something to fear, or whether they had allowed their fancy to run riot. This problem kept her awake for some time, but after a couple of hours spent in straining her ears to catch the sound of a footfall she did at last fall asleep, lulled by the monotonous rise and fall of her brother's snores, drifting to her ears from across the passage.

At one o'clock these ceased abruptly. The moon had reached a point in the heavens from which its rays were able to find out a chink between the blinds over Sir Hugh's window. A sliver of silver light stole across his face. Its baleful influence was instantly felt. Sir Hugh awoke.

He knew at once what had aroused him, and with a muttered curse, got up out of bed and stalked over to the window. A tug at the blind failed to put matters right, and Sir Hugh, blinking with sleep, perceived that a fold of the chintz had been caught in the hinge when the casement was shut. 'Damned carelessness!' he said severely, and opened the window to release the blind.

There was a smart wind blowing; a sudden gust tore the casement out of his slack hold, and flung it wide. He leaned out to pull it to again, and as he did so noticed that one of the windows in the coffee-room directly beneath his bedchamber was also standing wide. It seemed to him unusual and undesirable that windows should be left open all night, and after regarding it for a moment or two with slightly somnolent disapproval, he drew in his head, turned up the wick of the lamp that stood by his bed, and lit a candle at its flame. Yawning, he groped his way into his dressing-gown, and then, picking up the candlestick and treading softly for fear of waking the rest of the household, sallied forth to rectify Nye's omission.

He went carefully down the steep stairs, shading the flame of the candle from the draught. As he reached the bend in the staircase, and rounded it, he caught the glow of a light, suddenly extinguished, and knew there was someone in the coffee-room.

Sir Hugh might be of a natural indolent disposition, but he had rooted objection to fellows nefariously creeping about the house. He reached the bottom of the stairs with most surprising celerity, and, holding up the candle, looked keenly round the room.

A figure loomed up for an instant out of the darkness; he had a glimpse of a man with a mask over his face, and a dagger in his hand, and the next moment the candle was struck from his hold.

Sir Hugh launched himself forward, grappling with the unknown marauder. His right hand encountered something that felt like a neck-cloth, and grasped it, just as the hilt of the dagger crashed down upon his shoulder, missing his head by a hair's breadth. Before the unknown could strike again he had grabbed at the dagger-hand, and found it, twisting it unmercifully. The dagger fell; and Sir Hugh's grip slackened a little. The masked man, putting forth every ounce of strength, tore himself free, and made a dart for the window. Sir Hugh plunged after him, tripped over a stool, and came down on his hands and knees with a crash. The intruder was visible for a brief moment in the shaft of moonlight; before Sir Hugh could pick himself up he had vanished through the window.

CHAPTER 13

Sir Hugh swore, and got up. The noise of his fall seemed to have penetrated to the rooms above, for a door was opened, footsteps were heard
flying along the passage towards his bedchamber, and Eustacie's voice
sounded, begging the landlord to wake up and come at once.

'It's only I!' called Sir Hugh, tenderly massaging his grazed shin-bone.
'Don't start screeching, for the lord's sake! Bring me a light!'

Another door opened; Miss Thane's voice said: 'What was that? I
thought I heard a crash!'

'I dare say you did,' returned her brother. 'I fell over a demmed stool.
Send that scoundrel Nye down here. I've a bone to pick with him.'

'Good gracious, Hugh!' exclaimed Miss Thane venturing half-way
down the stairs, and holding up a candle. 'What in the world are you
doing there? You do not know what a fright you put me into!'

'Never mind that,' said Sir Hugh testily. 'What I want is a light.'

'My dear, you sound very cross,' said Miss Thane, coming down the
remainder of the stairs, and setting her candlestick on the table. 'Why are
you here? She caught sight of the curtain half-drawn back from the
windows, and the casement swinging wide, and said quickly: 'Who
opened that window?'

'Just what I want to ask Nye,' replied Sir Hugh. 'The moon woke me,
and I chanced to look out of my own window and saw this one open. I
came down, and I'd no sooner got to the bottom of the stairs than a
demmed fellow in a loo-mask knocked the candle out of my hand and tried
to hit me on the head. No, it's no use looking round for him: he's gone,
thanks to Nye leaving stools strewn about all over the floor.'

Eustacie, who had come downstairs with Nye, gave a sob of fright, and
stared at Miss Thane. 'He did come!' she said. 'Ludovic!' She turned on
the word, and fled upstairs, calling: 'Ludovic, Ludovic, are you safe?'

Sir Hugh looked after her in somewhat irritated surprise. 'French!' he
said. 'All alike! What the devil does she want to fly into a pucker for?'

Nye had gone over to the window and was leaning out. He turned and
said: 'The shutter's been wrenched off its hinge, and a pane of glass cut out
clean as a whistle. That's where he must have put his hand in to open the
window. You didn't get a sight of his face, sir?'

'No, I didn't,' replied Sir Hugh, stooping to pick up the dagger at his
feet. 'I keep telling you he wore a mask. A loo-mask! If there's one thing
above others that I hate it's a lot of demmed theatrical nonsense! What
was the fellow playing at? Highwaymen?'

'Perhaps,' suggested Miss Thane tactfully, 'he did not wish to run the risk of being recognized.'

'I dare say he didn't, and it's my belief,' said Sir Hugh, bending a severe frown upon her, 'that you know who he was, Sally. It has seemed to me all along that there's a deal going on here which is devilish unusual.'

'Yes, dear,' said Miss Thane, with becoming meekness. 'I think your masked man was Ludovic's wicked cousin come to murder him with that horrid-looking knife you have in your hand.'

'There ain't a doubt of it!' growled Nye. 'Look what's here, ma'am!' He went down on his knees as he spoke and picked from under the table a scrap of lace, such as might have been ripped from a cravat, and an ornate gold quizzing-glass on a length of torn ribbon. 'Have you ever seen that before?'

Sir Hugh took the glass from him, and inspected it disparagingly. 'No, I haven't,' he said, 'and what's more, I don't like it. It's too heavily chased.'

Miss Thane nodded. 'Of course I've seen it. But I was sure without that evidence. He must be feeling desperate indeed to have taken this risk!'

At this moment Eustacie came downstairs again, with Ludovic behind her. Ludovic, in a dressing-gown as exotic as Thane's, looked amused, and rather sleepy, and dangled a pistol in his right hand. His eyes alighted first on the dagger, which Thane had laid down on the table, and he put up his brows with a rueful expression of incredulity, and said: 'What was that pretty thing meant to be plunged into my heart? Well, well! What have you got there, Thane?'

'Do you recognize it?' said Miss Thane. 'It is your cousin's quizzing-glass.'

Ludovic glanced at it casually, but picked up the dagger. 'Oh, is it? No, I can't say I recognize it, but I dare say you're right. To think of the Beau daring to come and tackle me with nothing better than this mediæval weapon! It's a damned impertinence, upon my soul it is!'

'Depend upon it, he hoped to murder you while you slept, and so make no noise about it,' said Miss Thane. 'And, do you know, for all I jested with Sir Tristram over it, I never really thought that he would come!'

Sir Hugh looked at Ludovic and said: 'I wish you would be serious. Do you tell me it was really your cousin here to-night?'

'Oh, devil a doubt!' answered Ludovic, testing the dagger's sharpness with one slender forefinger.

'A cousin of yours masquerading about in a loo-mask?'

'Was he?' said Ludovic, interested. 'Lord yes, that's Basil all over! He'd run no risk of being recognized.'

'And you think he came here to murder you in bed?' demanded Sir Hugh.

For answer, Ludovic held up the dagger.

Sir Hugh looked at it in profound silence, and then said weightily, 'I'll tell you what it is, Lavenham, he's a demmed scoundrel. I never heard of such a thing!'

Eustacie, who had sunk into a chair, raised a very white face from her hands, and said in a low fierce voice: 'Yes, and if he does not go to the scaffold I myself will kill him! I will make a sacred vow to kill him!'

'No, don't do that!' said Sir Hugh, regarding her with misgiving. 'You can't go about England killing people, whatever you may do in your own country.'

'Yes, I can, and I will,' retorted Eustacie. 'To fight a duel, that is one thing! Even to try to take what belongs to Ludovic I can pardon! But to try to stab Ludovic in the dark, while he sleeps, *voyons*, that is an infamy of the most vile!'

'There's a great deal in what you say,' acknowledged Sir Hugh, 'but to my mind what you need is a sip of brandy. You'll feel the better for it.'

'I do not need a sip of brandy!' snapped Eustacie.

'Well, if you don't, I do,' said Sir Hugh frankly. 'I've been getting steadily colder ever since I came down to this demmed draughty coffee-room.'

Miss Thane, taking Eustacie's hand, patted it reassuringly, and suggested that they should go back to bed. Eustacie, who felt that at any moment the Beau might return to make a second attempt, at first refused to listen to such a notion, but upon Nye's saying grimly that she need have no fears for Ludovic's safety, since he proposed to spend the rest of the night in the coffee-room, she consented to go upstairs with Miss Thane, having first adjured Nye and Sir Hugh on no account to let Ludovic out of their sight until they saw him securely bolted into his bedchamber.

Sir Hugh was quite ready to promise anything, but his rational mind had little expectation of further adventures that night, and as soon as the two women had disappeared round the bend in the staircase, he reached up a long arm, and placing the Beau's quizzing-glass on the mantelshelf above his head, said: 'Well, now that they've gone, we can make ourselves comfortable. Go and get the brandy, Nye, and bring a glass for yourself.'

There were no more alarms during the rest of the night, but next morning Nye, and Miss Thane, and Eustacie met in consultation, and agreed that, however distasteful to him it might be, Ludovic must at least during the day be confined to the cellar. Nye, uncomfortably aware that there were no less than three doors into the Red Lion which must of necessity be kept unlocked and any number of windows through which a man might enter unobserved, flatly refused the responsibility of housing Ludovic if he persisted in roaming at large about the inn. The boldness of the attempt made in the night convinced him that the Beau would not easily relinquish his purpose of disposing of Ludovic, and he could not but realize that for such a purpose no place could be more convenient than a public inn. The month being February, there were very few private chaises on the Brighton road, but from time to time one would pass, and very likely pull up at the Red Lion for its occupants to refresh themselves in the coffee-room. In addition to this genteel custom there was a fairly constant, if then, flow of country people drifting in and out of the tap-room, so that it would be quite an easy matter for a stranger to step into the inn while the landlord and Clem were busy with their customers.

As might have been expected, Ludovic, when this decision was made known to him, objected with the utmost violence to his proposed incarcer-ation. Not all Nye's promises of every arrangement for his comfort being made could reconcile him to the scheme. Comfort, he said roundly, could not exist in a dark cellar smelling of every kind of liquor and crowded with pipes, barrels, spiders, and very likely rats.

Sir Hugh, wandering into the parlour in the middle of this speech, and imperfectly understanding its significance, said that, for his part, he had no objection to the smell of good liquor; in fact, quite liked it, a remark which made Ludovic retort: 'You may like the smell of liquor, but how would you like to be shut up in a wine-cellar the whole day long?'

'It depends on the wine,' said Sir Hugh, after giving this question due consideration.

In the end the combined arguments and entreaties of the two ladies prevailed with Ludovic, and he consented to repair to his underground retreat, Eustacie offering to share his imprisonment, and Sir Hugh, appealed to by his sister, promising to visit him for a game of piquet during the afternoon. 'Though why you should want to go and sit in the cellar if you don't like the smell of liquor I can't make out,' he said.

This unfortunate remark, pounced on immediately by Ludovic to support his own view of the matter, called forth a severe rebuke from Miss Thane. She tried to explain the exigencies of Ludovic's situation to Sir Hugh, but after listening incredulously to her for a few minutes, he said with a resigned shake of his head that it all sounded like a lot of nonsense to him, and that if any more people came poking and prying into the inn they would have him to deal with.

'Very likely,' said Miss Thane, displaying admirable patience, 'but if you did not happen to see Beau Lavenham enter the house he might well kill Ludovic before you knew anything about it.'

'If that fellow calls here to-day I want a word with him,' said Sir Hugh, his brow darkening. 'I've a strong notion I've caught another demmed cold, thanks to him getting me up out of my bed in the small hours.'

'I may have only one sound arm,' interrupted Ludovic, 'but if you think

I can't defend myself, you much mistake the matter, Sally.'

'I am quite sure you can defend yourself, my dear boy, but I want your cousin's corpse on my hands as little as I want yours.'

Sir Hugh was never at his best in the early morning, nor did a disturbed night, crowned by liberal potations, help to dispel a certain sleepy vagueness that clung to him, but these significant words roused him sufficiently to make him say with decision that he had borne with a great deal of irregularity at the Red Lion, what with Bow Street Runners bobbing in and out of the house, people living in cellars, and scoundrels breaking in through the windows, but that his tolerance would on no account extend to corpses littering the premises.

'Mind, Sally!' he said. 'The first corpse I find means that we go back to London, wine or no wine!'

'In that case,' said Miss Thane, 'Ludovic must certainly go down to the cellar. The man we want now, of course, is Sir Tristram. I wonder if he means to visit us to-day, or whether we should send for him?'

'Send for him?' repeated Sir Hugh. 'Why, he practically lives here!'

Ludovic, descending into the cellar, announced that he proposed to spend the morning making up his loss of sleep, and taking Miss Thane aside, told her to take Eustacie upstairs, and, if possible, for a walk. 'It's not fit for her down here,' he said. 'Don't let her worry about me! She's a trifle done up by all this romance.'

She laughed, promised to do what she could to keep Eustacie from fretting, and departed to suggest to her that they should presently go for a walk in the direction of Warninglid, in the hopes of encountering Sir Tristram.

At about eleven o'clock the weather, which had been inclement, began to improve, and by midday a hint of sunshine behind the clouds tempted Eustacie to put on her hat and cloak and go with Sir Hugh and his sister upon their usual constitutional. While Ludovic was in the cellar she could feel her mind at rest, and since he would not permit her to join him there, even a staid walk down the lane was preferable to sitting in the inn parlour with nothing to do and no one to talk to.

The sun came through the clouds in good earnest shortly after they left the Red Lion and made walking pleasant. They stepped out briskly, the two ladies discussing the night's adventure and trying to decide what were best to be done next, and Sir Hugh interpolating remarks which were occassionally apt and were more often inappropriate. Half-way to Warninglid they were compelled to abandon their scheme of meeting Sir Tristram and to turn back to retrace their footsteps, but they had not gone very far when he overtook them, hacking a fine bay hunter which instantly attracted and held Sir Hugh's attention.

He dismounted as soon as he drew abreast of the walking party, and looked pleased at the encounter. Eustacie, barely allowing him to exchange greetings with the Thanes, poured into his ears the full history of the night's adventure, while Sir Hugh commented upon the hunter's points. The account of masked men, daggers, and broken shutters was punctuated by such irrelevant phrases as a sweet-goer, a beautiful-stepper, and Sir Tristram had to exert all his powers of concentration to prevent himself from becoming hopelessly confused. Miss Thane took no part in the recital, but derived considerable amusement from watching Shield's face while he tried to resolve two conversations into their component parts.

'——like his knee-action – came to murder Ludovic – had a thorough-bred hack like him once – he had a dagger – kept on throwing out a splint – tried to stun Sir Hugh – took his fences as well standing as flying – wore a mask – had a slight curve in his crest!' announced Eustacie and Thane in chorus.

Sir Tristram drew a deep breath, and desired Miss Thane to give him a plain account of the affair.

She did so; he listened in silence, and at the end observed that he had hardly expected so prompt or so desperate a response to his veiled challenge. 'I am afraid you have had an alarming night of it,' he said, 'but I must confess I am delighted to hear that we succeeded so well in frightening the Beau. He must feel his position to be more dangerous than we suspect.'

'It seems to me that it is Ludovic who is in a dangerous position,' Eustacie pointed out.

'Not if you have had the sense to hide him in the cellar,' replied Sir Tristram.

'We have done so, but he went under protest, and I think won't remain there long,' said Miss Thane.

'He can take his choice of remaining there or being shipped out of the country,' said Sir Tristram briefly. 'That Basil went actually to the length of attempting to kill Ludovic with his own hand convinces me that that one-time butler of his knows something.'

'You have not found him yet?'

'No. He seems quite to have disappeared. If Basil knows his where-abouts and seeks him out I shall hear of it, however. I have been at pains to see young Kettering and have instructed him to keep me posted in the Beau's movements. Depend upon it, if Basil sees that butler, so shall I.'

They walked on up the lane, quickening their steps as the sky became once more overcast, with a threat of rain to come. Sir Hugh discovered that they had been out more than an hour, promised Shield a glass of very tolerable Madeira at the Red Lion, and, with another appraising look over the hunter's points, inquired whether he had any notion of selling the horse.

'None,' replied Shield. 'It is not in my power.'

'How is that?' demanded Sir Hugh.

'He is not mine,' said Shield. 'He belonged to my great-uncle, and – provided we can reinstate the boy – is now Ludovic's property.'

'Well, I've taken a strong liking to him,' said Sir Hugh. 'He looks to be well up to my weight. It seems to me that the sooner young Lavenham takes possession of his inheritance the better. I'll speak to him about it as soon as I get back to the inn.'

Upon arrival at the Red Lion, however, Sir Hugh's first thought was to call to Nye to bring up a bottle of Madeira. Receiving no response he walked into the tap-room to look for him. There was no sign either of Clem or Nye, and a gentleman in a moleskin waistcoat, who was waiting patiently by the bar, volunteered the information that he himself had been hollering for the landlord till he was fair parched. He added that if the Red Lion wanted no customers there were other inns which did, and upon this bitter remark, stumped out to go in search of one.

Sir Hugh went back to the coffee-room, and had just begun to say that Nye seemed to have gone out when a cry from above made him break off and look inquiringly towards the staircase. Miss Thane, who had gone up to take off her hat and coat, came quickly down, looking perturbed and startled. 'Sir Tristram, something has happened while we have been out! Someone has been here: my room has been ransacked, all our rooms! Where is Nye?'

'That,' said Sir Tristram grimly, 'is what we shall have to find out. A more pressing question is, where is Ludovic?'

Ludovic was found to be sleeping peacefully in his underground retreat. He had heard nothing, and when he learned that every room in the house had been turned upside down by unknown hands, he showed a marked inclination to laugh, and said that he supposed Basil had been searching for him again.

'Well, if he expected to find you amongst my clothing I can only say that he must have a very indelicate idea of me,' said Miss Thane. 'Sir Tristram, do you suppose him to have kidnapped Nye and Clem?'

'Hardly,' Shield answered, shutting the cellar door upon Ludovic, and replacing the chest that stood upon the trap. He walked across the passage to the tap-room, noticed that the trap leading down to the main cellar was shut, and pulled it up, calling: 'Nye! Are you there, man?'

No one answered him; Sir Hugh strolled in to report that he had found no trace of Nye, and observing that Shield had opened the trap-door said that the particular Madeira he had in mind was not in that cellar.

Shield had found a taper by this time, and kindled it at the fire. 'What I want to find is Nye, not Madeira!' he said, and went down the stairs into the gloom of the cellar. A moment later his voice sounded, summoning Sir Hugh to his assistance. 'Thane! Bring a lamp down here, I've found them!'

Sir Hugh selected a lamp from several standing on a shelf, and lit it in a leisurely fashion. Armed with this he descended into the cellar, where he found Shield calmly waiting for him, with the taper in his hand, and at his feet two neatly-trussed, gagged men. 'Well, I'll be damned!' said Sir Hugh, blinking. 'First it's one thing and then it's another! This is the queerest inn I've ever stayed at in my life.'

Shield blew out his taper, directed Sir Hugh to put the lamp down and ungag Clem, and set to work to free the landlord. This was very soon done, and no sooner was Nye able to speak than he said: 'Is Mr. Ludovic safe still?'

'He's safe enough,' replied Shield. 'What the devil happened? Who set upon you?'

'I never seen them before to my knowledge,' Nye said, rubbing his cramped limbs. 'Lord, to think of them taking me unawares! *Me*! They come in, as I thought, off the Brighton stage. There was no one in the tap-room but myself at the time, and I hadn't no more than turned my back to get a couple of mugs down from the shelf when something hit me on the head, and when I woke up, here I was like you saw with Clem beside me! I've got a lump on the back of my head like a hen's egg.'

'Good God, Nye, the oldest trick in the world, and you must needs fall a victim to it!' said Sir Tristram scornfully.

'I know it, sir: there ain't no call for you to tell me. Fair bamboozled I was.'

'This sort of thing,' said Sir Hugh, cutting the cord that bound Clem's arms, 'is past a jest! Were you knocked on the head too?'

Clem, however, had escaped this particular violence. He was a good deal shaken and bruised, but his assailants had overpowered him without being obliged to stun him. He recounted that he had heard someone calling for the drawer, and had gone at once to the tap-room. He had seen only one man, standing in quite an innocent-seeming fashion by the bar, but no sooner had he entered the room than a heavy coat had been thrown over his head by someone hidden behind the door, and before he could disentangle himself from its folds both men were upon him and he was speedily gagged and trussed up like the landlord.

Having released the captives Sir Tristram's next concern was to discover what the intruders had done in the inn. This was soon seen. They had visited every bedchamber, wrenched drawers out of the chests, and turned their contents on to the floor, ripped the clothes out of the wardrobes, burst open the locks of Sir Hugh's cloak-bags, and tossed out their contents higgledy-piggledy.

Sir Hugh, when he beheld the havoc amongst his possessions, was rendered quite speechless. His sister, staring about her said: 'But it is mad! This can have been no search for Ludovic! One would imagine they must have been common house-breakers, but there is my trinket-box broken open and my trinkets in a heap on my dressing-table. Have you lost anything, Hugh? I think I have not.'

'Have I——' Sir Hugh choked. 'How the devil can I know whether I've lost anything in this confusion?'

'Shield was looking frowningly round the disordered room. 'No, they were not searching for Ludovic,' he said. 'But what were they searching for? What can you have that the Beau wants so desperately?'

Sir Hugh caught the name and said: 'Do you mean to tell me that this outrage was committed by this cousin of Lavenham's who broke in last night?'

'I am afraid so,' replied Shield, smiling a little at Sir Hugh's face of Jovean wrath.

'Then understand this, Sally!' said Sir Hugh. 'Not a yard from this place do I stir until I have that fellow laid by the heels! It's bad enough when he comes creeping into the house to try to stick a knife into young Lavenham, but when he has the infernal impudence to turn my room into a pig-sty, then I say he's gone a step too far!'

'The knife!' exclaimed Eustacie. 'He came for the knife, of course! Sir Hugh seized it last night, Tristram!'

'Where was it put?' asked Shield. 'Has it been taken?' Nye said: 'We'll soon see that, sir. Sir Hugh left it on the coffee-room table, and thinking we might need to produce it as evidence I put it away this morning in my china-cupboard – the same them Runners blew the lock out of, sir.'

'Go and see if it's there,' commanded Sir Tristram. 'It may have been that – I suppose it must have been that, yet somehow——' He broke off, obviously puzzled.

'But yes, Tristram, he does not wish to be known to have come here last night, *naturellement*, therefore he must recover his dagger for fear we might recognize it!'

'It seems to me a most unnecessary risk to run,' said Sir Tristram. 'As matters now stand we cannot bring him to book for breaking in here any more than he can bring us to book for breaking into the Dower House. He must know that! He's not a fool.'

'I believe him to be too much alarmed to think calmly,' said Miss Thane.

Nye came back into the room. 'Well, they didn't think to look in the back premises, your Honour, that's certain. Here's the dagger.'

Sir Tristram took it in his hand and looked at it, more puzzled than ever. 'I dare say it is his,' he said, 'but I for one could not swear to it. It is in no way remarkable.'

Miss Thane said suddenly: 'Oh, how stupid of us! Of course he did not come to look for that! He came for his quizzing-glass. There could be no mistaking *that*! It is quite an unusual one: I knew it immediately for his and so did Nye. Now what became of it? Hugh, you had it! Where did you put it?'

'Put what?' said Sir Hugh, who was wandering about the room, attempting in a singularly helpless fashion to restore order.

'The Beau's quizzing-glass, my dear. I am sure you had it in your hand when Eustacie and I went up to bed last night.'

'I don't know where I put it,' said Sir Hugh, stooping to pick up a crumpled cravat. 'I laid it down somewhere.'

'Where?' insisted Miss Thane.

'I forget. Sally, this is my new riding-coat, I'll have you know! Just look at it! It's ruined!'

'No, dear, Clem will iron out the creases for you. You must know where you put that quizzing-glass. Do think!'

'I've something more important to think about than a quizzing-glass that don't belong to me, and which I don't like. Ugly, cumbersome thing, it was. I dare say I left it on the table in the coffee-room.'

Nye shook his head. 'It wasn't there this morning, sir.'

'Well, I may have brought it upstairs. I tell you I don't know, and I don't care.'

'I suppose it doesn't signify,' said Miss Thane reflectively. 'Depend upon it, that was what the Beau wanted. I must say, I hope he found it, for the prospect of any more ransacking I find quite appalling.'

Eustacie, helping Sir Hugh to smooth and fold several crumpled neck-cloths, said carefully: 'This is a very good adventure, and of course I am enjoying it – *cela va sans dire*! – but – but do you think that Basil will again try to come and kill Ludovic?'

'I should think it unlikely,' answered Shield, 'but I am going to ride back to the Court for my night-gear, and spend the night in Ludovic's room.'

'Famous!' said Miss Thane. 'I declare I never dreamed of such a romantic adventure as this turns out to be. In a little while we shall be barricading ourselves into the inn in a state of siege. Nothing would be more delightful!'

'I've no objection to Shield's putting up here, if he wants to,' stated Sir Hugh, 'but if I am to be roused out of my bed by fellows in loo-masks I won't be answerable for the consequences!'

Miss Thane, perceiving that his placidity was seriously impaired, set herself to coax him back into good humour. Nye promised to send Clem up immediately to put away all the scattered belongings, and he presently allowed himself to be escorted down to the parlour and installed in an easy chair by the fire, with a bottle of Madeira at his elbow. All he asked, he said, was a little peace and quiet, so his sister tactfully withdrew, leaving him to the mellowing influence of his wine.

Sir Tristram did not remain long at the Red Lion, but soon called for his horse, promising to return in time for dinner. No more startling events occurred during the course of the afternoon, and no suspicious strangers entered the tap-room. Sir Tristram came back shortly after six o'clock, and Nye, bolting the door into the coffee-room, released Ludovic, who had reached the point of announcing with considerable acrimony that if coming into possession of his inheritance entailed many more days spent underground, he would prefer to return to his free-trading.

After dinner Miss Thane had the tact to suggest that they should sit down to a game of loo, and in this way the evening passed swiftly, Ludovic's problem being for the time forgotten, and the game proving so engrossing that it was not until after eleven o'clock that Miss Thane thought to look at the timepiece on the mantelshelf. The party then broke up, and the ladies had just picked up their candles when Nye's voice was suddenly heard somewhat above-stairs, raised in ferocious surprise.

Sir Tristram, signing to the others to remain where they were, went quickly out into the coffee-room, just as Nye came down the stairs, dragging by the collar a scared-looking stable-boy. When he saw Shield he said: 'I've just found this young varmint in Sir Hugh's bedchamber, your Honour. Down you come, you! Now then, what were you doing up there?'

The stable-boy whimpered that he meant no harm, and tried to squirm out of the landlord's hold. Nye shook him, almost lifting him from the ground, and Sir Tristram said: 'Is he one of your lads, Nye?'

'Ay, sir, he's one of my lads right enough, but he'll belong to the Parish Constable in the morning,' said Nye with awful meaning. 'A thief, that's what he is, and will likely be transported. That or hanged.'

'I ain't a thief! I never meant no harm, Mr. Nye, I swear I didn't! I ain't took a thing that belongs to the big gentleman, nor wouldn't!'

'What were you doing in his bedchamber?' demanded Nye. 'You've no business inside the house, and well you know it! Came creeping in through a window, that's what you did, and don't you dare to deny it! There's the ladder you used for anyone to see. Feeling in the pockets of Sir Hugh's coats he was, sir, the young vagabond! What's that you've got in your hand? Give it up this instant!'

The boy made a futile attempt to break away, but Nye seized his right arm and gave it a twist that made him cry out and relinquish the object he had been trying to conceal. It was a quizzing-glass belonging to Sir Hugh Thane.

Nye stared at it for a moment, his countenance slowly reddening with wrath. His grip tightened on the stable-boy's collar. So that's it, is it?' he said. 'You'll be sorry for this, Sam Barker!'

Sir Tristram, taking the glass from him, interposed in his quiet way: 'Let him go, Nye. Now, my lad, if you speak the truth no harm shall come to you. Who told you to steal this?'

The boy cowered as far from Nye as he was able, and said: 'It were Mr. Lavenham's gentleman, your Honour, and 'deed I didn't know there was any harm! He come asking me if I'd like to earn twenty guineas for myself, all for finding an eyeglass Mr. Lavenham mislaid here. It was the big gentleman as had got it, he said, and if I found it, and no one the wiser, there'd be twenty golden guineas for me. It weren't like stealing, sir! I ain't a thief!'

'Oh, you ain't, eh?' said Nye. 'And if Mr. Lavenham mislaid his glass what should stop him coming to ask for it open? Don't tell me you didn't think there was any harm in it!'

'It was Mr. Lavenham's eyeglass. Mr. Gregg said if I didn't ask no questions there'd be no trouble for anyone.'

'There will be a great deal of trouble for you at least if you do not do precisely what I tell you now,' said Sir Tristram sternly. 'If you had your desserts you would be handed over to the Constable. But if you keep your mouth shut I will engage for it that Nye will overlook this fault. Understand me, I want no word of what has occurred to-night to come to Gregg's ears, or to Mr. Lavenham's. If you are questioned you will tell them that you have had no opportunity to search Sir Hugh's room. Is that clear?'

The stable-boy, thankful to have escaped the retribution he had thought inevitable, assured him that it was quite clear. He stammered out his gratitude, promised eternal good behaviour, and fled.

Nye drew a long breath. 'Begging your pardon, sir, but I'd a deal rather be rid of the young good-for-nothing. My own lads bribed! What next will we have, I'd like to know?'

Sir Tristram was looking at the quizzing-glass in his hand. He said slowly: 'So they didn't find it! I wonder . . .' He broke off, and strode suddenly towards the parlour. He was met by demands to know what had happened, and replied briefly: 'One of Nye's stable-hands had been bribed to find the Beau's quizzing-glass. He found this instead.'

'But that's mine!' said Sir Hugh, regarding it fixedly.

'I know it.'

'Do you mean to tell me I've had my room ransacked again?' demanded Sir Hugh.

'No, I think you've merely had your pockets turned out. That's not important.'

'Not important!' ejaculated Sir Hugh, considerably incensed. 'And what if I've been robbed? I suppose that's not important either! Burn it, I never was in such a house in my life! It's for ever full of a set of rascals broken out of Newgate, and what with masked assassins, and Bow Street Runners, and young Lavenham here taking it into his head to live in a cellar, I don't know where I am from one minute to the next. What's more, you're as bad as the rest of them, Sally!'

'You haven't been robbed,' said Sir Tristram. 'What I want to discover is why it is so vital to Basil to regain possession of that glass. Thane, where did you put it? For God's sake try to remember! I suspect it may be of the utmost importance!'

'It is still in the inn, then!' Miss Thane said. 'Hugh, think, I implore you!'

'Are you talking about the quizzing-glass you all said was Basil's?' inquired Ludovic.

Shield turned. 'What do you mean, Ludovic? Did you not recognize it?'

'No, I can't say that I did,' answered Ludovic. 'Not that I'm disputing that it's his, mind you. I dare say he bought it since my time.'

'That,' said Sir Tristram, 'is precisely what I think he did do. It must be found if we have to turn this whole place upside down to do it!'

'You needn't do that,' said Ludovic calmly. 'Thane put it on the mantelshelf in the coffee-room. I saw him do it.'

Sir Tristram wheeled about, and went quickly back to the coffee-room, and stretching up his arm ran his hand along the high mantelpiece. The quizzing-glass was just where Sir Hugh had left it. Shield held it in his hand, looking at it so oddly that Nye, who was standing beside him, ventured to ask if anything were amiss.

Sir Tristram shook his head, and carried the prize back into the parlour.

'You have found it!' exclaimed Eustacie. 'But why is it important?'

He put her aside, and sitting down at the table, subjected the quizzing-glass to a minute inspection. The others gathered round him, even Sir Hugh betraying a mild interest.

'Myself I like 'em made slimmer,' remarked Ludovic. 'The shaft's too thick. Clumsy.'

Sir Tristram said dryly: 'I think there is a reason.' He had picked up Sir Hugh's eyeglass, and through its magnifying lens was looking at the heavily-encrusted circlet at the end of the shaft, through which a ribbon was meant to pass. He put Sir Hugh's glass down and inserted his thumb-nail into a groove on the circlet.

There was a tiny click; the circle parted, and something fell out of it on to the table, rolled a little way, and lay still.

'The talisman ring!' said Sir Tristram.

CHAPTER 14

A sound almost like a sob broke from Ludovic. His hand shot out across the table and snatched up the ring. 'My ring!' he whispered. 'My ring!'

'Well, upon my soul, that's a devilish cunning device!' said Sir Hugh, taking the quizzing-glass out of Shield's hand. 'You see, Sally? The ring fitted into the circlet at the end of the shaft.'

'Yes, dear,' said Miss Thane. 'I see it did. When I think how it has been lying where anyone might have found it I feel quite faint with horror.'

Eustacie was looking critically at it. 'Is that a talisman ring?' she inquired. 'I thought it would be quite different! It is nothing but a gold ring with some figures on it!'

'Careful, Eustacie!' said Sir Tristram, with a slight smile. 'You will find that Ludovic regards it as sacrosanct.'

Ludovic raised his eyes from adoration of the ring. 'By God, I do! There is nothing I can say to you Tristram, except that I could kiss your feet for what you have done for me!'

'I beg you won't, however. I have done very little.'

Miss Thane said: 'It had been under our very noses. The audacity of it! How could he dare?'

'Why not?' said Sir Tristram. 'Would any of us have suspected it had it not been lost, and then searched for in such a desperate fashion?'

An idea occurred to Miss Thane. She turned her eyes towards her brother, and said in moved tones: 'So we owe it all to Hugh! My dear, this becomes too much for me. I shall not easily recover from the shock.'

'And everything – but everything! – we did was quite useless!' said Eustacie, quite disgusted.

'I know,' said Miss Thane, sadly shaking her head. 'It does not bear thinking of.'

'I do not know why you should complain,' remarked Sir Tristram. 'You have had a great deal of adventure, which is what I understood you both to want.'

'Yes, that is true,' acknowledged Eustacie, 'but some of it was not very comfortable. And I must say that I am not at all pleased that it is you who have found the ring, because you did not want to have an adventure, or to do anything romantic. It seems to me very unfair.'

'So it is!' said Miss Thane, much struck by this point of view. 'It is quite odious, my love, for who could have been more disagreeable, or more discouraging? Really, it would have been better in some ways had we insisted upon his remaining the villain.'

Sir Tristram smiled a little at this, but in rather an abstracted way, and said: 'It's very well, but we are not yet out of our difficulties. Let me have the ring, Ludovic. It is true that we have found it, but we did not find it in the Beau's possession. Oh, don't look so dubious, my dear boy! I shan't lose it.'

'Ah!' said Miss Thane, nodding wisely. 'One has to remember, after all, that you are a collector of such things. I don't blame him, I dare say it is all a Plot.'

'Sarah, you're outrageous!' said Ludovic, handing the ring across the table to his cousin. 'For God's sake be careful with it, won't you, Tristram? What do you mean to do?'

Sir Tristram fitted the ring back into its hiding-place, and closed the circlet with a snap. 'For the present I'll keep this. I think our best course——' He stopped, frowning.

They waited in anxious silence for him to continue, but before he spoke again Nye caught the sound of a coach pulling up in the yard and said apologetically: 'Beg pardon, sir, but I'll have to go. That'll be the night-mail.'

Sir Tristram's voice arrested him as he reached the door. 'Do you mean it's the London mail, Joe?'

'Ay, that's the one, sir. I want a word with the guard, if you'll excuse me.'

Sir Tristram's chair rasped on the oaken floor as he sprang up. 'Then that's my best course!' he said. 'I'll board it!'

Nye stared at him. 'If that's what you mean to do, you'd best make haste, sir. It don't take them more than two minutes to change the horses, and they'll be off the moment that's done.'

'Go and tell them to wait!' ordered Sir Tristram. 'I have but to get my hat and coat.'

'They won't wait, sir!' expostulated Nye. 'They've got their time to keep, and you've no ticket!'

'Never mind that! Hurry, man!' said Sir Tristram, thrusting him before him out of the room.

'But what are you going to do?' cried Eustacie, running after them.

'I've no time to waste in explaining that now!' replied Sir Tristram, already half-way up the stairs.

Miss Thane, following in a more leisurely fashion with Ludovic, said darkly: 'I said it was a Plot. It's my belief he is absconding.' She discovered that her butt was already out of hearing, and added: 'There! How provoking! That remark was quite wasted. Who would have supposed that the wretched creature would be taken with such a frenzy?'

Sir Tristram reappeared again at this moment, his coat over his arm, his hat in his hand. As he ran down the stairs, he said: 'I hope to return to-morrow if all goes well. For God's sake take care of yourself, Ludovic!'

He was across the coffee-room and out of the door almost before they could fetch their breath. Miss Thane, blinking, said: 'If only we had a horse ready saddled!'

'Why? Isn't the mail enough for him?' inquired Ludovic.

'If there had been a horse, I am persuaded we should have seen him ride off *ventre à terre*!' mourned Miss Thane.

'But where is he going?' stammered Eustacie. 'He seems to me suddenly to have become entirely mad!'

'He's going to London,' replied Ludovic. 'Don't ask me why, for I haven't a notion!'

'Well!' Eustacie turned quite pink with indignation. 'It is too bad! This is *our* adventure, and he has left us without a word, and, in fact, is trying to take it away from us!'

'Men!' said Miss Thane, with a strong shudder.

Sir Hugh came wandering into the coffee-room at this moment, and asked what had become of Shield. When he heard that he had departed suddenly for London, he looked vaguely surprised, and complained that he seemed to be another of these people who spent their time popping in and out of the inn like jack-in-the-boxes. 'It's very unrestful,' he said severely. 'No sooner do we get comfortably settled than either someone breaks into the house or one of you flies off the Lord knows where! There's no peace at all. I shall go to bed.'

Nye came back just then and announced with a reluctant smile that Sir Tristram had succeeded in boarding the coach, in spite of all the guard's representations to him that such high-handed proceedings were quite out of order. When asked by Ludovic if he knew what Sir Tristram meant to do, he replied in his stolid way: 'I do not, sir, but you may depend upon it he'll do what's best. All he said to me was, I was to see you safe into your room. Myself, I'm having a truckle-bed set up here, and it'll be a mighty queer thing if anyone gets into the house without I'll hear them. Not but what it don't seem to me likely that anyone will try that game to-night. They'll be waiting up at the Dower House till to-morrow in the hopes that Sam Barker will have found that plaguey ring of yours, sir.'

Miss Thane sighed. 'How abominably flat it will seem to have no one breaking in any more! Really, I do not know how I am to support life once all these exciting happenings are at an end.'

Nye favoured her with a grim little smile. 'By what I can make out, they ain't ended yet, ma'am. We'll do well to keep an eye lifted for trouble as soon as that Beau learns Barker ain't found his quizzing-glass. I'll be glad when I see Sir Tristram back, and that's a fact. Now, Mr. Ludovic, if you're ready, I'll help you get to bed. You'll have to go down to the cellar again to-morrow, and the orders are I'm to see you into it before I unbar the doors in the morning. And what's more, sir,' he added, forestalling Ludovic's imminent expostulation, 'I've orders to knock you out if you don't go willing.'

This ferocious threat was not, however, put into execution. Ludovic descended into the cellar at an early hour on the following morning, and the rest of the party, with the exception of Sir Hugh, who was only interested in his breakfast, prepared themselves to meet whatever peril should lie in store for them. Eustacie, who thought that she had taken far too small a part in the adventure, was feeling somewhat aggrieved, Ludovic having refused without the least hesitation to lend her one of his pistols. 'I never lend my pistols,' he said. 'Besides, what do you want it for?'

'But to fire, of course!' replied Eustacie impatiently.

'Good God! What at?'

'Why, at anybody who tries to come into the house!' she said, opening her eyes in surprise at his stupidity. 'And if you would let Sarah have one too, she could help me. After all, we may find ourselves in great danger, you know.'

'You won't find yourselves in half such danger as you would if I let you have my pistols,' said Ludovic, with brutal candour.

This unfeeling response sent Eustacie off in a dudgeon to Miss Thane. Here at least she was sure of finding a sympathetic listener. Nor did Miss Thane disappoint her. She professed herself to be quite at a loss to understand the selfishness of men, and when she learned what Eustacie had planned for her also to fire upon possible desperadoes, she said that she could almost wish that she had not been told of the scheme, since it made her feel quite disheartened to think of it falling to the ground.

'Well, I do think we ought to be armed,' said Eustacie wistfully. 'It is true that I do not know much about guns, but one has only to point them and pull the trigger, after all.'

'Exactly,' agreed Miss Thane. 'I dare say we should have accounted for any number of desperate ruffians. It is wretched indeed! We shall be forced to rely upon our wits.'

But the morning passed quietly, the only excitement being provided by Gregg, who came to the inn with the ostensible object of inquiring whether Nye could let his master have a pipe of Burgundy. He left his horse in the yard, and was thus able to exchange a word with Barker, who, with the fear of transportation before him, faithfully obeyed Sir Tristram's instructions, and said that he had no chance yet to search for the quizzing-glass.

In the afternoon Sir Hugh, following his usual custom, went upstairs to enjoy a peaceful sleep. Miss Thane and Eustacie watched the Brighton mail arrive, but since it did not set Sir Tristram down at the Red Lion, their interest in it swiftly waned. They had begun to question whether they were to experience any adventures whatsoever when, to their amazement, Beau Lavenham's chaise passed the parlour window, drew up outside the coffee-room door, and set down the Beau himself.

He alighted unhurriedly, took care to remove a speck of dust from his sleeve, and in the calmest way imaginable walked into the inn.

'Well,' said Miss Thane, 'I think this passes the bounds of reasonable effrontery! Do you suppose that he has come to pay us a ceremonious visit?'

Apparently this was his purpose, for in a few minutes Nye ushered him into the parlour. He came in with his usual smile, and bowed with all his usual flourish. 'Such a happiness to find you still here!' he said. 'Your very obedient, ma'am!'

'If you should be needing aught, ma'am, you have only to call,' said Nye, with slow deliberation.

'Oh yes, indeed! Pray do not wait!' said Miss Thane, slipping into her rôle of empty-headed femininity. 'I will certainly call you if I need anything. How delightful it is to see you, Mr. Lavenham! Here you find us yawning over our stitchery, quite enchanted to be receiving company. You must know that we have made all our plans for departure, and mean to set forward for London almost immediately. I am so glad to have the opportunity of taking leave of you! So very obliging you were in permitting me to visit your beautiful house! I am for ever talking of it!'

'My house was honoured, ma'am. Do I understand that your brother has at last recovered from his sad indisposition? It must have been an unconsciously bad cold to have kept him in this dull inn for so many days.'

'Yes, indeed, quite the worst he has ever had,' agreed Miss Thane. 'But he has not found it dull, I assure you.'

'No?' said the Beau gently.

'Indeed, no! You must understand that he is a great judge of wine. A well-stocked cellar will reconcile him to the hardest lot. It is quite absurd!'

'Ah, yes!' said the Beau. 'Nye has a great deal in his cellars, I apprehend – more perhaps than he will admit.'

'That is true,' remarked Eustacie, with considerable relish. 'Granpère was used to say that he would defy anyone to find what Nye preferred to keep hidden.'

'I fear he must have been speaking with a little exaggeration,' said the Beau. 'I trust Nye will never find himself compelled to submit to a search being made for his secret cellar. Such things are very well while no one knows of their existence, but once the news of them gets about it becomes a simple matter to discover them.'

Miss Thane listening to this speech with an air of the most guileless interest, exclaimed: 'How odd that you should say that! I must tell you that my brother said at the very outset that he was convinced Nye must possess some hidden store!'

'I felicitate you, ma'am, upon being blessed with a brother of such remarkable perspicacity,' said the Beau in a mellifluous voice. He turned towards his cousin. 'My dear Eustacie, I wonder if I may crave the indulgence of a few moments' private speech with you? Miss Thane will readily understand that between cousins——'

Miss Thane interrupted him at this point, with an affected little cry. 'Oh, Mr. Lavenham, no, indeed! It is not to be thought of! You must know that I am this dear child's chaperon – is it not ridiculous? – and such a thing would not do at all!'

He looked at her with narrowed eyes, and after a moment, said: 'I do not recollect, ma'am, that these scruples weighed with you so heavily when you visited my house not so long since.'

Miss Thane looked distressed, and replied: 'It is very true. Your reproach is just, sir. I'm such a sad shatterbrain that I forgot my duties in admiration of your library.'

He raised his brows in polite scepticism. Eustacie said: 'I do not have secrets from mademoiselle. Why do you wish to see me alone? *Je n'en vois pas la nécessité!*'

'Well,' said the Beau, 'if I may speak without reserve, my dear cousin, I desire to drop a word of warning in your ear.'

She looked him over dispassionately. 'Yes? I do not know why I must be warned, but if you wish to warn me, I am perfectly agreeable.'

'Let us say,' amended the Beau, 'that I desire you to convey a warning to the person most nearly concerned. You must know that I am aware – have been aware from the oustset – that you are concealing – a certain person in this house. I do not need to mention names, I am sure. Now, I wish this person no harm; in the past I think I may say that I have been very much his friend, but it will not be in my power to assist him if once his presence in this inn becomes known. And I fear – I very much fear – that it is known. You have already been a trifle discommoded, I collect, by two Runners from Bow Street. They seem, by all accounts, to have been a singularly stupid couple. But you must remember that all the Runners are not so easily – shall we say, duped?' He paused, but Eustacie, contenting herself with gazing at him blankly, said nothing. He smiled slightly, and continued: 'You should consider, dear cousin, what would happen if someone who knows this person well were to go to Bow Street and say: "I have proof that this man is even now lying in a hidden cellar at the Red Lion at Hand Cross."'

'You recount to me a history of the most entertaining,' said Eustacie, with painstaking civility. 'I expect you would be very glad to know that Ludovic – I name names, me – had gone abroad.'

'Very glad,' replied the Beau sweetly. 'I should be much distressed if he brought any more disgrace on the family by ending his career on the scaffold. And that, my dear Eustacie, is what he will do if ever he falls into the hands of the Law.'

'But I find you inexplicable!' said Eustacie. 'I thought you at least believed him to be innocent.'

He shrugged. 'Certainly, but his unfortunate flight, coupled with the disappearance of the talisman ring which was at the root of the trouble, will always make it impossible for him to prove his innocence.' He put the tips of his fingers together, and over them surveyed Eustacie. 'It is very disagreeable to be a hunted man, you know. It would be much better to have it given out that one had died – abroad. I am anxious to be of what assistance I can. If I had proof that my cousin Ludovic was no more, I would gladly engage to provide – well, let us say a man who looked like my cousin Ludovic but bore another name – to provide this man, then, with an allowance I believe he would not consider ungenerous.' He stopped and took a pinch of snuff.

'I ask myself,' said Eustacie meditatively, 'why you should wish to overwhelm Ludovic with your generosity. It is to me not at all easy to understand.'

'Ah, that is not clever of you, dear cousin,' he replied. 'Surely you must perceive the disadvantages of my situation?'

'But yes, very clearly,' said Eustacie, with disconcerting alacrity.

'Precisely,' smiled the Beau. 'Of course, were there but the slimmest chance of Ludovic's being able to prove his innocence, it would be another matter. But there is no such chance, Eustacie, and I should be a very odd sort of creature if I did not look forward with misgiving to an indefinite number of years spent in waiting beside a vacant throne.'

'A vacant throne?' suddenly said Miss Thane, raising her head from the book she had taken up. 'Oh, are you speaking of the murder of the French King? I was never more shocked in my life than when I heard the news of it!'

The Beau paid no heed to her. His eyes still rested on Eustacie; he said pensively: 'One may live very comfortably on the Continent, I believe. *You*, for instance, would like it excessively, I dare say.'

'I? But we do not speak of me!'

'Do we not? Well, I shall not pretend that I am not glad to hear you say so,' he answered. He got up from his chair. 'You will think over what I have said, will you not? You might even tell Ludovic.'

Eustacie assumed an expression of doubt. 'Yes, but perhaps if he did what you suggest you would not give him any money after all,' she said.

'In that case,' replied the Beau calmly, 'he would only have to come to life again to deprive me of title, land, and wealth. One might almost say that he would hold me quite in his power.'

'True, yes, that is very true,' nodded Eustacie. 'But I do not know – it is not possible for me to say——'

'My dear cousin, I do not wish you to say anything. No doubt you will discuss the matter with Ludovic and inform me later of your decision. I will take my leave of you now.' He turned and bowed to Miss Thane. 'Your servant, ma'am. Do not trouble to accompany me to the door, my dear cousin; I know the way. I have been here before, you know.' He broke off and said: 'Ah, that reminds me! I believe that upon the occasion of my last visit I lost my quizzing-glass here. I wonder if it has been found?'

'Your quizzing-glass?' repeated Eustacie. 'How came you to lose that, pray?'

'The ribbon was a trifle worn,' he explained. 'The glass is of sentimental value to me. May I have it, if you please?'

She shook her head. 'You are mistaken. It is certainly not here.'

He sighed. 'No? Tax your memory again, cousin. It would be wiser to remember, I think.'

'It is impossible. I do not know where your glass may be,' said Eustacie, with perfect truth.

Miss Thane, quite unable to resist the temptation of taking part in this scene, said: 'A quizzing-glass? Oh yes, I know!'

'Indeed, ma'am?' The Beau turned rather quickly. 'Enlighten me, I beg of you!'

Miss Thane nodded at Eustacie. 'Do you not remember, my love, how Nye found one half hidden beneath a chair only yesterday? Oh no, I believe you were not by at the time! He laid it on the mantelshelf in the coffee-room. I will fetch it for you directly.'

'Do not put yourself to the trouble, ma'am,' said the Beau, breathing a little faster. 'I am in your debt, and will recover the glass upon my way out.'

'Oh, but it is not the least trouble in the world!' declared Miss Thane, rising, and going to the door. 'I can place my hand upon it in a trice!'

'You are too good.' He bowed, and followed her to the coffee-room.

She checked for an instant on the threshold, for the room was not, as she had expected to find it, empty. A powerful-looking man in a blue coat and buckskins was seated on the settle by the fire, warming his feet and refreshing himself from a mug of ale. He turned his head as Miss Thane came in, and although he did not look at her for more than a couple of seconds, she had an uncomfortable feeling that the look was not quite as casual as it seemed to be. She caught Eustacie's eye, and found it brimful of warning. Comforting herself with the reflection that even if the stranger were in Beau Lavenham's pay, there was no fear of either of them finding the quizzing-glass, she tripped forward to the fireplace. 'I know just where he put it,' she informed the Beau over her shoulder. 'This end it was – no! Well, that is the oddest thing! I could have sworn—— Do you reach up your arm, Mr. Lavenham: you are taller than I am.'

The Beau, who did not need this encouragement, ran his hand the length of the mantelpiece. 'You are mistaken, ma'am,' he said, his voice suddenly harsh. 'It is not here!'

'But it must be!' she said. 'I am positive it was put there. Someone must have moved it!' An idea seemed to strike her. She said: 'I wonder, did your valet take it? He was here this morning, you know, and stayed for quite some time. I could not imagine what he was about! Depend upon it, he must have discovered it, and you will find it awaiting you at the Dower House.'

He had turned pale, and said with his eyes fixed on her face: 'My valet? You said my valet was in this room to-day?'

'Yes, indeed he was,' averred Miss Thane unblushingly. 'Of course, I never dreamed the glass was what he was looking for, or I would have shown him at once where it was. All's well that ends well, however. You may be sure he has it safe.'

Eustacie, lost in admiration of Miss Thane's tactics, watched the smile vanish completely from the Beau's face. An expression half of doubt, half of dismay took its place; it was plain that while he suspected Miss Thane of prevaricating, he was unable to banish from his mind as impossible the thought that his valet, guessing that the quizzing-glass held a vital secret, might have come to search for it on his own account. She saw his hand open and close, and his lips straighten to a thin, ugly line, and was observing these signs of mental perturbation with critical interest when she became aware of being addressed by the stranger on the settle.

'Very cold day, ma'am,' he remarked, with the unmistakable air of one whose habit it was to enter into chat with anybody who crossed his path.

Eustacie glanced at him with a certain amount of misgiving. She supposed that the landlord of an inn could hardly refuse to allow a customer to drink his ale in the coffee-room if he wished to, but she could not help feeling that Nye might have contrived on this occasion at least to have lured him into the tap-room and to have kept him there under his own eye. On the other hand, it was, of course, possible that the man was known to Nye. She replied civilly: 'Yes, very cold.'

'Bitter wind blowing outside,' pursued the stranger. 'Ah well, it's seasonable, ain't it, ma'am? We hadn't ought to complain. Begging your pardon, sir, if I might put another log of wood on the fire—— Thank you, sir!'

The Beau, who was standing by the basket containing wood, moved to allow the stranger to approach it.

'That's the worst of a wood fire,' said the stranger, selecting a suitable log. 'They fall away to nothing in less than no time, don't they, sir? But we'll have a nice blaze in a minute, you'll see.' He bent to pick up another log, and said in a surprised tone: 'Well! and what might this be, all amongst the wood?' He straightened himself as he spoke, and Miss Thane saw that he was holding the Beau's quizzing-glass in his hand.

For a moment it seemed to her that she could neither speak nor think. While her eyes remained riveted to the glass her brain whirled. Had not Sir Tristram taken charge of the glass? Could he have been guilty of the unpardonable carelessness of mislaying it? How did it come to be in the wood-basket? And what in heaven's name was one to do?

She pulled herself together, met Eustacie's eyes across the room, and saw them as startled as she felt sure her own must be. She became aware of the stranger's voice, marvelling with amiable fatuity at the queer places things would get to, to be sure, and suddenly realized why Nye had left a stranger alone in the coffee-room, and what his purpose must be. She shot a warning frown at Eustacie, still standing at the foot of the stairs, and said: 'Why, there it is! Well, of all the fortunate happenings!'

The Beau held out his hand. It was shaking a little. He said: 'Thank you. That is mine.'

The stranger looked rather doubtfully at him. 'Yours, is it, sir? Well, if you say so, I'm sure it is so, but maybe I'd best give it to the landlord – not meaning any offence, your Honour, but seeing as it's a valuable kind of a trinket, and me having found it.'

A fixed smile was on the Beau's lips. He said: 'Quite unnecessary, I assure you. You will perceive that it is of unusual design. I could not mistake it.'

The stranger turned it over in his hand. 'Well, of course, sir, if you say so——' he began undecidedly.

'My good fellow,' interrupted the Beau. 'You must have seen me look for something upon the mantelshelf a minute ago. Your scruples are quite absurd, believe me. Anyone will tell you that that glass belongs to me. Be good enough to give it to me, if you please.'

'Oh yes, certainly that is Mr. Lavenham's quizzing-glass!' said Miss Thane. 'There can be no doubt!'

The stranger advanced, holding the glass out to the Beau. He grasped it, and in that instant a suspicion of the trap into which he had walked seemed to flash into his brain, and he sprang back, glaring at the man before him.

'Then, in the name of the Law I arrest you, Basil Lavenham, for the wilful murder of Matthew John Plunkett!' said the stranger.

Before he had finished speaking the Beau had whipped a pistol from his pocket and levelled it. The smile on his lips had became a ghastly grimace, but it still lingered. He said, quick and low: 'Stand where you are! If you move you are a dead man!' and began to back towards the door.

The Bow Street Runner stood still perforce. Miss Thane, standing a little behind the Beau, perceived that the moment for a display of heroism had arrived, and in one swift movement got between the Beau and the door. In the same instant Eustacie shrieked: 'Nye! *A moi!*'

The Beau, keeping his would-be captor covered, reached the door, and Miss Thane, behind him, caught his arm and bore it downwards with all her strength. He was taken unawares, gave a snarl of fury, and wrenching free from her clutch struck at her with his clenched fist. The blow landed on her temple, and Miss Thane subsided in an inanimate heap on the floor.

* * * * * *

She became aware of a throbbing pain in her head, of the smell of Hungary Water, and of the feel of a wet cloth across her brow. 'Oh dear!' she said faintly. 'The quizzing-glass! Did he get away?'

'By no means,' replied a calm voice. 'There is nothing to worry you: we have him safely held.'

Miss Thane ventured to open her eyes. Sir Tristram was sitting on the edge of the couch in the parlour on which she had been laid, bathing her forehead. 'Oh, it's you!' said Miss Thane.

'Yes,'' said Sir Tristram.

'I knew you must have returned,' murmured Miss Thane.

He replied in his cool way: 'If you knew that, what in the world possessed you to try and stop the Beau? He had no hope of escaping. I was outside with a Runner to take him if he broke from Townsend.'

'Well, pray how was I to know that?' demanded Miss Thane.

'I imagined you might have guessed it.'

She closed her eyes again, saying with dignity: 'I have the headache.'

He sounded amused. 'That is not very surprising, since you were hit on the head.'

A rustle of skirts heralded Eustacie's approach. Miss Thane opened her eyes again and smiled. 'Oh, you are better!' said Eustacie. '*Ma pauvre*, I thought he had killed you! And I must tell you that he wrenched open the door and stepped backwards right into Tristram's arms! It was of all things the most exciting! And, do you know, he tried to throw the quizzing-glass into the fire, which was entirely stupid, because that made it quite certain that he knew where the ring was hid. I do think that this has been the most delightful adventure!'

'So it has,' agreed Miss Thane. 'Positively *épatant*! What have you done with the Beau, and where is Ludovic?'

'Oh, the Runners took Basil away in a chaise, and as for Ludovic, Nye has gone to let him out of the cellar.'

Miss Thane sighed. 'Well, I suppose it is all for the best, but you know I cannot help feeling disappointed. I had quite made up my mind to it that Sir Tristram had absconded with the talisman ring, and I had thought of several famous schemes for recovering it. I never knew anyone so provoking!'

'Yes,' agreed Eustacie. 'I must say, that is true. He is very provoking, but one must be just, *enfin*, and own that he has been very clever and useful.'

Miss Thane turned her head to look up at Sir Tristram. 'I wish you will tell me what you did,' she said. 'You were not on the Brighton mail, were you? Is it possible that you rode here *ventre à terre*?'

'No,' replied Sir Tristram. 'I came post.'

Miss Thane seemed to abandon interest in his proceedings.

'Bringing with me,' continued Sir Tristram, 'a couple of Bow Street Runners. When we arrived here I learned from Nye that by some stroke of good fortune the Beau was actually in the house. I had been wondering how we were to prevail upon him to own the quizzing-glass, and the difficulties of luring him to this place without letting him get wind of a trap seemed to me to be quite considerable. When we heard that he was already here, it was easy to set our trap. The only thing I feared was that one or other of you might put him on his guard by showing surprise at seeing the quizzing-glass. You are to be congratulated on concealing your emotions so well.'

'At first,' confessed Eustacie, 'I was entirely *bouleversée*, and quite unable to speak. Then Sarah frowned at me, and I thought it would be better to remain silent. *I* thought the Runner was one of Basil's men, did not you, Sarah?'

'Yes, I did at first,' replied Miss Thane. 'But when he picked up the glass I knew Sir Tristram must be at the back of it. Is Ludovic safe now? Will he be able to take his place in the world again?'

'Yes, there can be no doubt of that. Basil lost his head, and his attempt to dispose of the ring was a complete betrayal. How do you feel, Miss Thane?'

'Very uneasy,' she replied. 'I believe there is a lump on my forehead.'

'It is already much less pronounced than it was,' said Sir Tristram consolingly.

Miss Thane regarded him with misgiving. 'Tell me at once, have I a black eye?' she said.

'No, not yet.'

She gave a shriek. 'Not *yet*? Do you mean that I shall have one?'

'I should think it highly probable,' he said, a laugh in his voice.

'Bring me the hartshorn!' begged Miss Thane in failing accents, and once more closing her eyes.

'Certainly,' said Sir Tristram. 'Eustacie, fetch the hartshorn.'

'She does not really want it, you know,' explained Eustacie. 'She is jesting.'

'Nevertheless, fetch it,' said Sir Tristram.

'*Eh bien!*' Eustacie shrugged, and went away to look for it.

Miss Thane opened her eyes again, and looked at Sir Tristram with even more misgiving than before.

'Sarah,' said Sir Tristram, 'I have a very important question to put to you. How many seasons have you spent at Almack's?'

Miss Thane gazed at him with an expression of outrage in her face, and said: 'Tristram, are you daring – actually daring – to choose this out of all other moments to make me an offer?'

'Yes,' replied Sir Tristram. 'I am. Why not?'

Miss Thane sat up. 'Have you *no* sense of romance?' she demanded. 'I won't – no, I *won't* be proposed to with my hair falling down my back, a bandage round my head, and very likely a black eye as well! It is quite monstrous of you!'

He smiled. 'Indeed, you will. You look delightfully. Will you marry me?'

'I have wronged you,' said Miss Thane, much moved. 'If you think I look delightfully at this present, you must be a great deal more romantic than I had supposed.'

'It is a long time now since I have been able to look at you without thinking how very beautiful you are,' said Sir Tristram simply.

'Oh!' said Miss Thane, blushing, 'you forget yourself! Do, pray, recollect that you do not look for romance in marriage! Remember your previous disillusionment! This will never do!'

'I see that I shall not easily be allowed to forget that nonsense,' said Sir Tristram, taking her in his arms. 'Now be serious for one moment, Sarah! Will you marry me?'

'To be honest with you,' said Miss Thane, with the utmost gravity, 'I have been meaning to marry you these ten days and more!'

A moment later Eustacie came into the room with Sir Hugh at her heels. She checked on the threshold in round-eyed amazement, but Sir Hugh merely said: 'Oh, so you're back, are you?'

'Yes,' said Shield, releasing Miss Thane. 'Have I your permission to pay my addresses to your sister?'

'Oh, certainly, my dear fellow, by all means! Not that it's anything to do with me, you know. She's her own mistress now. What have you done to your head, Sally?'

'Ludovic's wicked cousin knocked me down,' explained Miss Thane. 'I have had a very exciting afternoon, throwing myself into the breach, and being stunned, and then having an offer of marriage made to me.'

'I thought there was a devilish amount of noise going on downstairs,' remarked Sir Hugh. 'It's time we finished with this cousin of Ludovic's. I'll bring an action against him for assaulting you.'

'An excellent notion, my dear, but the Crown is already bringing an action against him for murdering Sir Matthew Plunkett.'

'Never heard of him,' said Sir Hugh. 'Not that I'm against it, mind you. A fellow who creeps about in a demmed loo-mask——'

'Sir Matthew Plunkett,' said Miss Thane patiently, 'is the man Ludovic was accused of murdering two years ago. You must know that Ludovic will now be able to stop living in the cellar, and take up his rightful position at Lavenham Court.'

'Well, I must say I'm glad to hear that,' said Sir Hugh. 'It never seemed to me healthy for him to be spending all his time in the cellar. I think if it's true that he's going to come into his inheritance, I'll go and speak to him about that horse before it slips my memory.'

He left the room as he spoke. Eustacie, finding her tongue, blurted out: 'But, Sarah, do you *want* to marry Tristram?'

Miss Thane's eyes twinkled. 'My love, when a female reaches my advanced years, she cannot be picking and choosing, you know. She must be content with the first respectable offer she receives.'

'Oh, now I know that you are laughing at me!' Eustacie said. 'But I do not understand it. I find it quite extraordinary!'

'The truth is,' said Miss Thane confidentially, 'that I cannot any longer bear his odious way of calling me ma'am. There was no other means of putting an end to it.'

'But, Sarah, consider! You are romantic, and he is not romantic at all!'

'I know,' replied Miss Thane, 'but I assure you I mean to come to an understanding with him before the knot is tied. . . . Either I have his solemn promise to ride *ventre à terre* to my death-bed or there will be no marriage!'

'It shall be included in the marriage vow,' said Sir Tristram.

Eustacie, looking from one to the other, made a discovery. '*Mon Dieu*, it is not a *mariage de convenance* at all! You are in love, *enfin*!' she exclaimed.

The
Gambling Man

Catherine
Cookson

THE CONNORS

PADDY CONNOR *a steelworker*
RUTH CONNOR *his wife*
RORY CONNOR *their elder son, a rent collector*
JIMMY CONNOR *their younger son, apprenticed to a boat builder*
NELLIE BURKE *their only daughter, married to Charlie Burke*
LIZZIE O'DOWD *Paddy Connor's half-cousin*

THE WAGGETTS

BILL WAGGETT *a widowed docker*
JANIE WAGGETT *his daughter, a nursemaid and engaged to marry Rory Connor*
GRAN WAGGETT *his mother*

THE LEARYS

COLLUM LEARY *a coal miner*
KATHLEEN LEARY *his wife*
Nine surviving children of whom three have emigrated to America

JOHN GEORGE ARMSTRONG *Rory's friend and fellow rent collector*

SEPTIMUS KEAN *a property owner*
CHARLOTTE KEAN *his only daughter*

PART ONE

CHAPTER 1

1875 RORY CONNOR

Tyne Dock was deserted. It was Sunday and the hour when the long dusk was ending and the night beginning. Moreover, it was bitterly cold and the first flat flakes of snow were falling at spaced intervals, dropping to rest in their white purity on the greasy, coal-dust, spit-smeared flags.

The five arches leading from the dock gates towards the Jarrow Road showed streaks of dull green water running down from their domes. Beneath the arches the silence and desolation of the docks was intensified; they, too, seemed to be resting, drawing breath as it were, before taking again the weight of the wagons which, with the dawn, would rumble over four of them from the coal staithes that lay beyond the brick wall linking them together. Beyond the fifth arch the road divided, one section mounting to Simonside, the other leading to Jarrow.

The road to Jarrow was a grim road, a desolate road, and a stretch of it bordered the slakes at East Jarrow, the great open stretch of mud which in turn bordered the river Tyne.

There was nothing grim about the road to Simonside, for as soon as you mounted the bank Tyne Dock and East Jarrow were forgotten, and you were in the country. Up and up the hill you went and there to the left, lying back in their well-tended gardens, were large houses; past the farm, and now you were among green fields and open land as far as the eye could see. Of course, if you looked back you would glimpse the masts of the ships lying all along the river, but looking ahead even in the falling twilight you knew this was a pleasant place, a place different from Tyne Dock, or East Jarrow, or Jarrow itself; this was the country. The road, like any country road, was rough, and the farther you walked along it the narrower it became until finally petering out into a mere cart track running between fields.

Strangers were always surprised when, walking along this track, they came upon the cottages. There were three cottages, but they were approached by a single gate leading from the track and bordered on each side by an untidy tangled hedge of hawthorn and bramble.

The cottages lay in a slight hollow about twenty feet from the gate, and half this distance was covered by a brick path which then divided into three uneven parts, each leading to a cottage door. The cottages were numbered 1, 2 and 3 but were always called No. 1 The Cottages, No. 2 The Cottages, and No. 3 The Cottages.

In No. 1 lived the Waggetts, in No. 2 The Connors, and in No. 3 the Learys. But, as this was Sunday, all the Waggett family and three of the Learys were in the Connors' cottage, and they were playing cards.

'In the name of God, did you ever see the likes! He's won again. How much is it I owe you this time?'

'Twelve and fourpence.'

'Twelve an' fourpence! Will you have it now or will you wait till ye get it?'

'I'll wait till I get it.'

'Ta, you've got a kind heart. Although you're a rent man you've got a kind heart. I'll say that for you, Rory.'

'Ah, shut up Bill. Are you goin' to have another game?'

'No, begod! I'm not. I've only half a dozen monkey nuts left, an' Janie there loves monkey nuts. Don't you, lass?'

Bill Waggett turned round from the table and looked towards his only daughter, who was sitting with the women who were gathered to one side of the fire cutting clippings for a mat, and Janie laughed back at him, saying, 'Aw, let him have the monkey nuts; 'cos if you don't, he'll have your shirt.' She now exchanged a deep knowing look with Rory Connor, who had half turned from the table, and when he said, 'Do you want me to come there and skelp your lug?' she tossed her head and cried back at him, 'Try it on, lad. Try it on.' And all those about the fire laughed as if she had said something extremely witty.

Her grannie laughed, her wrinkled lips drawn back from her toothless gums, her mouth wide and her tongue flicking in and out with the action of the aged; she laughed as she said, 'That's it. That's it. Start the way you mean to go on. Married sixty-five years me afore he went; never lifted a hand to me; didn't get the chance.' The cavity of her mouth became wider.

Ruth Connor laughed, but hers was a quiet, subdued sound that seemed to suit her small, thin body and her pointed face and black hair combed back from the middle parting over each side of her head.

Her daughter, Nellie, laughed. Nellie had been married for three years and her name now was Mrs Burke. Nellie, like her mother, was small and thin but her hair was fair. The word puny would describe her whole appearance.

And Lizzie O'Dowd laughed. Lizzie O'Dowd was of the Connor family. She was Paddy Connor's half-cousin. She was now forty-one years old but had lived with them since she had come over from Ireland at the age of seventeen. Lizzie's laugh was big, deep and hearty; her body was fat, her hair brown and thick; her eyes brown and round. Lizzie O'Dowd looked entirely different from the rest of the women seated near the fire, particularly the last, who was Kathleen Leary from No. 3 The Cottages. Kathleen's laugh had a weary sound. Perhaps it was because after bearing sixteen children her body was tired. It was no consolation that seven were dead and the eldest three in America for she still had six at home and the youngest was but two years old.

It was now Paddy Connor, Rory's father, who said, 'You were talkin' of another game, lad. Well then, come on, get on with it.'

Paddy was a steelworker in Palmer's shipyard in Jarrow. For the past fifteen years he had worked in the blast furnaces, and every inch of skin on his face was red, a dull red, like overcooked beetroot. He had three children, Rory being the eldest was twenty-three.

Rory was taller than his father. He was thickset with a head that inclined to be square. He did not take after either his mother or his father in looks for his hair was a dark brown and his skin, although thick of texture, was fresh looking. His eyes, too, were brown but of a much deeper tone than his hair. His lips were not full as might have been expected to go with the shape of his face but were thin and wide. Even in his shirt sleeves he looked smart, and cleaner than the rest of the men seated around the table.

Jimmy, the younger son, had fair hair that sprang like fine silk from double crowns on his head. His face had the young look of a boy of fourteen yet he was nineteen years old. His skin was as fair as his hair and his grey eyes seemed over-big for his face. His body looked straight and well formed, until he stood up, and then you saw that his legs were badly bowed, so much so that he was known as Bandy Connor.

Paddy's third child was Nellie, Mrs Burke, who was next in age to Rory.

Bill Waggett from No. 1 The Cottages, the son of Gran Waggett and the father of Janie, worked in the docks. He was fifty years old but could have been taken for sixty. His wife had died six years before, bearing her seventh child. Janie was the only one they had managed to rear and he adored her.

Bill's love for her had been such that he did not demand that she stay at home to keep house for him when his wife died but had let her go into service as a nursemaid, even though this meant that once again he would be treated as a young nipper by his mother who was then in her seventy-ninth year. But he, like all those in the cottages, gave her respect if only for the fact that now at eighty-five she still did a full day's work.

Collum Leary was a miner. He was now forty-eight but had been down the pit since he was seven years old. His initiation had been to sit twelve hours a day in total blackness. At eight he had graduated to crawling on his hands and knees with a chain between his legs, which was attached to a bogie load of coal, while his blood brother pushed it from behind. He could not remember his mother, only his father who had come from Ireland when he himself was a boy. The nearest Collum had ever got to Ireland was the Irish quarter in Jarrow and as he himself said, who would bother crossing the seas when almost every man-jack of them were on your doorstep?

Collum at forty-eight was a wizened, prematurely aged man who carried the trade-mark of his following on his skin, for his face and body were scarred as with pocks by blue marks left by the imprint of the coal. But Collum was happy. He went to confession once a twelve-month, and now and again he would follow it by Communion, and he did his duty by God as the priest dictated and saw to it that his wife gave birth every year, at least almost every year. Those years in which she failed to become pregnant were the times he took Communion.

'How's the shipbuilding goin', Jimmy?' Collum Leary now poked his head forward across the table.

'Oh, grand, fine, Mr Leary.'

'When are you goin' to build your own boat?'

'That'll be the day, but I will sometime.' Jimmy nodded now. Then catching Rory's eye, he smiled widely. 'I said I will, an' I will, won't I, Rory?' The boy appealed to his older brother as to one in authority.

Rory, shuffling the cards, glanced sideways at Jimmy and there was a softness in his expression that wasn't usual except when perhaps he looked at Janie.

'You'll soon be out of your time, won't you, Jimmy?'

Jimmy now turned towards Bill Waggett, answering, 'Aye, beginnin' of the year, Mr Waggett. And that's what I'm feared of. They turn you out, you know, once your time's up.'

'Aw, they won't turn you out.' Bill Waggett pursed his lips. 'You hear things around the docks you know; there's more things come up on the tide than rotten cabbages. I hear tell you're the best 'prentice Baker's ever had in his yard; a natural they say you are, Jimmy; mould a bit of wood with your hands, they say.'

'Aw, go on with you.' Jimmy turned his head to the side, his lips pressed tight but his whole face failing to suppress his pleasure at the compliment. Then looking at Bill Waggett again and his expression changing, he said, 'But I'll tell you somethin', I wouldn't be able to finish me time if old Baker saw what I was doin' at this minute.'

'You mean havin' a game?' Rory had stopped shuffling the pack and Jimmy nodded at him, saying, 'Aye. Well, you know what some of them's like. But now there's a notice come out. Didn't I tell you?'

'No, you didn't. A notice? What kind of a notice?'

'Well it says that anybody that's found playin' cards on a Sunday'll lose their jobs, an' if you know about somebody having a game an' don't let on, why then you'll lose your job an' all.'

Rory slapped his hand of cards on to the table. 'Is that a fact?'

'Aye, Rory.'

'My God!' Rory now looked round at the rest of the men, and they stared back at him without speaking until his father said, 'You don't know you're born, lad.' There was a slight touch of resentment in the tone and the look they exchanged had no friendliness in it. Then Paddy, nodding towards Bill Waggett, said, 'What did you tell me the other day about when you worked in the soda works, Bill?'

'Oh that. Well' – Bill brought his eyes to rest on Rory – 'couldn't breathe there. If you were a few minutes late you were fined, and if it was a quarter of an hour, like it might be in winter when you couldn't fight your way through the snow, why man, they stopped a quarter day's pay. And if you dared to talk about your work outside you were fined ten bob the first time, then given the push if it happened twice. That's a fact. It is, it is. An' you might be sayin' nowt of any account. And if anybody covered up for you when you were late . . . oh my God! they were in for it. You know what? They had to pay the fine, the same fine as you paid. You were treated like a lot of bairns: back-chat the foreman and it was half a dollar fine. My God! I had to get out of there. You see, Rory, as your da says, you don't know you're born being a rent collector. Your da did something for you lettin' you learn to read. By! aye, he did. It's somethin' when you can earn your livin' without dirtyin' your hands.'

Rory was flicking the cards over the flowered oilcloth that covered the wooden table. His head was lowered and his lids were lowered, the expression in his eyes was hidden, but his lips were set straight.

Jimmy, as always sensing his brother's mood, turned to Collum Leary and said. 'It's a pity our Rory isn't in America along with your Michael and James and on one of them boats that ply the river, like Michael said, where they can gamble in the open.'

'Aye, it is that, Jimmy,' Collum laughed at him. 'He'd make his fortune.' He turned and pushed Rory in the shoulder with his doubled fist, adding, 'Why don't you go to America, Rory, now why don't you?'

'I just might, I just might.' Rory was now fanning out the cards in his hand. 'It would suit me that, down to the ground it would. A gamblin' boat. . . .'

'Gamblin', cards, fortunes made in America, that's all you hear.' With the exception of Rory the men turned and looked towards Lizzie O'Dowd, where she had risen from her chair, and she nodded at them, continuing, 'Nobody is ever satisfied. Take what God sends an' be thankful.' Then her tone changing, she laughed as she added. 'He's gona send you cold brisket this minute. Who wants pickled onions with it?'

There were gabbled answers and laughter from the table and when she turned away and walked down the room past the chiffonier, past the dess-bed that stood in an alcove, and into the scullery, Janie, too, turned and followed her into the cluttered cramped space and closed the door after her.

Hunching her shoulders upwards against the cold, Janie picked up a knife and began cutting thick slices off a large crusty loaf. She had almost finished cutting the bread before she spoke. Her head still bent, she said quietly, 'Don't worry, Lizzie, he won't go to America.'

'Aw, I know that, lass, I know that. It's me temper gets the better of me.' She turned from hacking lumps of meat from the brisket bone and, looking full at Janie, she said, 'It's funny, isn't it, it's funny, but you understand, lass, don't you?'

'Aye, I understand, Lizzie. Aw, don't worry, he understands an' all.'

'I wish I could think so.'

'He does, he does.'

Lizzie now put the knife down on the table and, bringing one plump hand up, she pressed it tightly across her chin as she remarked, 'I'm not a bad woman, Janie, I never was.'

'Aw, Lizzie, Lizzie.' Janie, her arms outstretched now, put them around the fat body of Lizzie O'Dowd, whom she had known and loved since she was a child; even before her own mother had died she had loved Lizzie O'Dowd as if she were a second mother, or perhaps she had placed her first, she was never quite certain in her own mind; and now, their cheeks pressed close for a moment, she whispered, 'It'll all come right. It'll all come right in the end, you'll see.'

'Aye, yes. Yes, you're right, lass.' Lizzie turned her head away as she roughly swept the tears from her cheeks with the side of her finger. Then picking up the knife again and her head bowed once more, she muttered, 'I think the world of Ruth an' I always have. She's the best of women. . . . Life isn't easy, Janie.'

'I know it isn't, Lizzie. And Ruth's fond of you, you know she is. She couldn't do without you. None of us could do without you.'

'Ah, lass.' Lizzie was smiling now, a denigrating smile. 'Everybody can be done without.' She gave a short laugh. 'Have a walk around the cemetery the next time you're out.'

'Aw, Lizzie –' Janie was leaning against her shoulder now laughing – 'you're the limit. You know, every time I feel down I think of you.'

'Huh, that's a left-handed compliment if ever I heard one: When you're down you think of me. You can't get much lower than down, can you?'

'You!' Janie now pushed her. 'You know what I mean. Look, is that enough bread?'

'That! It wouldn't fill a holey tooth; you'd better start on another loaf. . . . How is that nice family of yours?'

'Oh, lovely as always, lovely, Eeh! you know I often wonder what would have become of me, I mean what kind of job I would've got in the end. I'd likely have landed up in some factory, like most others, if I hadn't had that bit of luck. Life's so different there, the furniture, the food, everything. The way they talk, the master and mistress, I mean. Do you understand, Lizzie? You know I'm not bein' an upstart but I like bein' there. Mind you, that's not to say I don't like comin' home; I love coming home, even when I know me grannie is goin' to choke me with words and her bloomin' old sayin's. Eeh! the things that she remembers.' They were laughing again. Then she ended, 'But there's different kinds of life . . . I mean livin', Lizzie. You know what I mean?'

'Aye, lass, I know what you mean, although I've never lived any other kind of life but this and I don't want to, not for meself I don't, but for you and . . . and others. Yes, yes, I know what you mean.' She now placed portions of the meat on the slices of dry bread which she then stacked on a plate. Patting the last one, she exclaimed, 'Well now, let's go and feed the five thousand an' find out if it's tea they want or if they're goin' to get the cans on.'

In the kitchen once more, Lizzie slapped down the heaped plate of meat and bread in the middle of the table, saying, 'Is it tea or are you gettin' the cans on?'

The men glanced furtively from one to the other, their eyes asking a question. Then Paddy and Bill turned simultaneously and looked towards the women, and as usual it was Lizzie who answered them, crying loudly now, 'There's none of us goin' trapesing down there the night an' it fit to cut the lugs off you. If you want your beer there's the cans.' She thrust out her thick arm and pointed towards four assorted cans, their lids dangling by pieces of string from the handles.

The men made no answer but still continued to look towards the women, and then Ruth spoke. Quietly and in levelled tones, she said, 'It's Sunday.'

The men sighed and turned back to the table again, and Bill Waggett muttered under his breath, 'An' that's that then. Bloody Sunday. You know' – he glanced up from the cards and, catching Jimmy's attention, he nodded at him, saying softly, 'I hate Sundays. I always have hated Sundays ever since I was a lad 'cos she kept me going harder on a Sunday than when I was at work.' He had inclined his head backwards towards the fire-place and had hardly finished speaking when his mother, her dewlap chin wobbling, cried across the room, 'Lazy bugger! you always were. Wouldn't even kick when you were born; slid out like a dead fly on hot fat.'

As the roars of laughter filled the kitchen Bill Waggett turned towards his mother and yelled, 'That's a fine thing to say; you should be ashamed of yersel.' He now looked towards Ruth as if apologizing, but she was being forced to smile, and Ruth rarely smiled or laughed at ribaldry.

'Remember the day he was born. Old Mrs Waggett had got their attention now. 'Me mother an' me grannie pulled him out, an' I remember me grannie's very words. "Like a Saturday night rabbit he is," she said. You know' – she turned towards Janie – 'when the last of the rabbits are left in the market, all weary skin an' bone? "You'll never rear him," she said; "he'll go along with the other five." But I never had no luck, he didn't.'

She now glanced in impish affection towards her son, where he was sitting, his head bowed, moving it slowly from side to side. The movement had a despairing finality about it. His mother had started and it would take some kind of an event to stop her, especially when as now she had the ears of everyone in the room. He could never understand why people liked listening to her.

'And it was me own mother who looked at him lying across her hands an' said, "I don't think you need worry about the press gang ever chasin' him, Nancy." An' you know somethin'? The press gang nearly got me dad once. Around seventeen ninety it was. I'm not sure of the year, one, two or three, but I do know that all the lads of the Tyne, the sailors like, put their heads together; they were havin' no more of it. They ran the press gang out of the town, North Shields that is, not this side. Then in come the regiment. Barricaded the town, they did, an' forced the lads on board the ships. But me dad managed to get over to this side of the water; he said himself he never knew how.'

'He walked on it.'

There were loud guffaws of laughter now and Gran cried back at her son, 'Aye, an' he could have done that an' all, for at one time you could walk across the river. Oh aye, they once made a bridge with boats, me mother said, and laid planks over 'em, and a whole regiment passed over. The river's changed.' She nodded from one to the other. 'You know, me grannie once told me they caught so much salmon on the Tyne that it was sold at a farthin' a pound. It was, it was. Can you believe that? A farthin' a pound!'

'Yes, yes, Gran.' All except her son were nodding at her.

'And I don't need to go as far back as me grannie's or even me mother's time to remember the great shoals of fish that were caught in these waters. An' there were nowt but keels and sailin' ships takin' the coal away then. None of your Palmer's iron boats. What did you say, our Bill?' She frowned towards her son. '"Oh my God!" that's what you said. Well, I'm glad you think of Him as yours.'

She joined in the titter that now went round the room. Then nodding her head from one to the other, she went on, 'Talkin' of coal. I can remember as far back as when Simon Temple opened his pit at Jarrow. I was only eight at the time but by! I remember that do. The militia was marching, the bands playing, an' when he got to Shields market the lads pulled the horses from his carriage and drew him themselves. His sons were with him and his old dad. They pulled them all the way to the Don Bridge, where the gentlemen of Jarrow met him. And that was the day they laid the stone for the school for the bairns of his workmen. By! I remember it as if it was yesterday. Simon Temple.' She shook her head and lapsed for a moment into the memory of one of the rare days of jollification in her childhood.

In the pause that followed Collum Leary put in, 'Simon Temple. Aye, an' all the bloody coal owners. Grand lads, grand fellows, great gentlemen. Oh aye, especially when they're shedding crocodile tears over the dead. Ninety-nine men and lads lost in the Fellon pit and over twenty at Harrington. . . .'

'That was a long time ago, Collum.' Grannie Waggett thrust her chin out at the small man who had usurped her position of storyteller and he turned on her, no longer jocular as he cried, 'Don't be daft, Gran. It's happenin' almost every month in one pit or t'other. Don't be daft, woman.'

'Leave be. Leave be.' It was the first time Kathleen Leary had spoken and her husband looked at her as he repeated, 'Leave be, leave be, you say. Bloody coal owners!'

The mood of the kitchen had changed as it nearly always did when the subject of work was brought up, whether it was Paddy Connor talking of the steel works or Bill Waggett of the conditions in the docks, or Collum Leary of the soul destroying work in the mines; and nearly always it was on a Sunday when the atmosphere would become charged with bitterness because nearly always on a Sunday Grannie Waggett was present.

'Come on, Gran.' Janie had taken hold of her grandmother's arm.

'What! What you after? Leave me be.'

'It's time we were goin' in.' Janie nodded towards the wall. 'An' I'll soon be making for the road.'

Grannie Waggett stared up into Janie's face for a moment. Then her head nodding, she said, 'Aye, aye, lass; I forgot you'll soon be making for the road. Well –' She pulled herself up out of the chair saying now, 'Where's me shawl?'

Janie brought the big black shawl from where it had been draped over the head of a three-seated wooden saddle standing against the far wall pressed between a battered chest of drawers and a surprisingly fine Dutch wardrobe.

The old woman now nodded, first to Ruth, then to Nellie, then to Lizzie, and finally to Kathleen Leary, and to each she said, 'So long,' and each answered her kindly, saying, 'So long, Gran,' and as she made for the door with Janie behind her, Lizzie called to her, 'Put the oven shelf in the bed, you'll need it the night.'

'I will, I will, Oh my God! look at that,' she cried, as she opened the door. 'It's comin' down thicker than ever.' She turned her head and looked into the room again. 'We're in for it, another window-sill winter. I can smell it.'

Janie had taken an old coat from the back of the door and as she hugged it around her she glanced back towards the table and Rory, and when she said, 'Half an hour?' he smiled and nodded at her.

'Go on, Gran, go on; you'll blow them all out.' Janie went to press her grandmother on to the outer step, but the old lady resisted firmly, saying, 'Stop a minute. Stop a minute. Look, there's somebody coming in at the gate.'

Janie went to her side and peered into the darkness. Then again looking back into the room, she cried, 'It's John George.'

Rising slowly from the table and coming towards the door, Rory said, 'He wasn't coming the night; he mustn't have been able to see her.'

'Hello, John George.'

'Hello there, Janie.' John George Armstrong stood scraping his boots on the iron ring attached to the wall as he added, 'Hello there, Gran.'

And Gran's reply was, 'Well, come on in if you're comin' an' let us out, else I'll be frozen stiffer than a corpse.'

Janie now pressed her grannie none too gently over the step and as she passed John George she said, 'See you later, John George.'

'Aye, see you later, Janie,' he replied before entering the kitchen and closing the door behind him and replying to a barrage of greetings.

Having hung his coat and hard hat on the back of the door he took his place at the table, and Rory asked briefly, 'What went wrong?'

'Oh, the usual. . . . You playing cards?' The obvious statement was a polite way of telling the company that he didn't wish to discuss the reason for his unexpected presence among them tonight, and they accepted this.

'Want to come in?'

'What do you think?'

As John George and Rory exchanged a tight smile Bill Waggett said, 'You'd better tighten you belt, lad, an' hang on to your trousers 'cos he's in form the night. Cleared me out of monkey nuts.'

'No!'

'Oh aye. We were sayin' he should go to America and make his fortune on one of them boats.'

'He needn't go as far as that, Mr Waggett, there's plenty of games goin' on in Shields and across the water, and they tell me that fortunes are made up in Newcastle.'

'Gamblin'! That's all anybody hears in this house, gamblin'. Do you want a mug of tea?' Lizzie was bending over John George, and he turned his long thin face up to her and smiled at her kindly as he answered, 'It would be grand, Lizzie.'

'Have you had anything to eat?'

'I've had me tea.'

'When was that?'

'Oh. Oh, not so long ago.'

'Have you a corner for a bite?'

'I've always got a corner for a bite, Lizzie.' Again he smiled kindly at her, and she pushed him roughly, saying, 'Death warmed up, that's what you look like. Good food's lost on you. Where does it go? You haven't a pick on your bones.'

'Thoroughbreds are always lean, Lizzie.'

As she turned and walked away towards the scullery she said, 'They should have put a brick on yer head when you were young to make you grow sideways instead of up.'

The game proceeded with its usual banter until the door opened again and Janie entered, fully dressed now for the road in a long brown cloth coat to which was attached a shoulder cape of the same material. It was an elegant coat and like all the clothes she now wore had been passed on to her from her mistress. Her hat, a brown velour, with a small flat brim, was perched high on the top of her head, and its colour merged with the shining coils of her hair. The hat was held in place by two velvet ribbons coming from beneath the brim and tied under her chin. She had fine woollen gloves on her hands. The only articles of her apparel which did not point to taste were her boots. These were heavy-looking and buttoned at the side. It was very unfortunate, Janie considered, that her feet should be two sizes bigger than her mistress's, yet she always comforted herself with the thought that her skirt and coat covered most parts of her boots and there was only ever the toes showing, except when she was crossing the muddy roads and the wheels of the carts and carriages were spraying clarts all over the place.

'Eeh! by! you look bonny.' Lizzie came towards her, but before reaching
her she turned to Rory, who was rising from the table, saying, 'You going
to keep her waiting all night? Get a move on.'

The quick jerk of Rory's head, the flash of his eyes and the further
straightening of his lips caused Janie to say quickly, 'There's plenty of
time, there's plenty of time. I've got a full hour afore I'm due in. Look, it's
only eight o'clock.'

'It'll take you all that to walk from here to Westoe an' the streets
covered.'

'No, it won't, Lizzie. When I get goin' George Wilson, the Newcastle
walker, or me grannie's fusiliers aren't in it.' She now swung her arms and
did a standing march and ended, 'Grenadier Waggett, the woman walker
from Wallsend!' Then stopping abruptly amid the laughter, she looked to
where John George was taking his coat from the back of the door, and she
asked flatly, 'You're not comin' surely? You haven't been here five
minutes.'

'I've got to get back, Janie, me Uncle Willy's not too good.'

'Was he ever?'

The aside came from Lizzie and as Ruth went to admonish her with a
quick shake of her head Rory turned on her a look that could only be
described as rage, for it was contorting his features. He did not shout at
her, but his low tone conveyed his feelings more than if he had bawled as
he said. 'Will you hold your tongue, woman, an' mind your own business
for once!'

Strangely Lizzie did not turn on him, but she looked at him levelly for a
moment and countered his anger with almost a placid expression as she
said. 'I've spent me life mindin' me own business, lad, an' me own
business is to take care of those I'm concerned for, and I'm concerned for
John George there. That uncle and aunt of his live off him. And what I'm
sayin' now I've said afore to his face, haven't I John George?'

'You have that, Lizzie. And I like you mindin' me business, it's a
comforter.'

'There you are.' She nodded towards Rory, who now had his back to
her as he made his way down the long narrow room towards the ladder at
the end that led into the loft, which place was Jimmy's and his bedroom
and had been since they were children, one end of it at one time having
been curtained off to accommodate Nellie.

With no further words, Lizzie now went into the scullery, and Janie
began saying her good-byes. When she came to Nellie she bent over her
and said below her breath, 'You all right, Nellie?'

'Aye. Aye, Janie, I'm all right.'

Janie stared down into the peaked face; she knew Nellie wasn't all right, she had never been all right since she married. Nellie's marriage frightened her. Charlie Burke had courted Nellie for four years and was never off the doorstep, and Sunday after Sunday they had laughed and larked on like bairns in this very room. But not any more, not since she had been married but a few months. It was something to do with – the bedroom. Neither her grannie nor Lizzie had spoken to her about it and, of course, it went without saying that Ruth wouldn't mention any such thing. But from little bits that she had overheard between Lizzie and her grannie she knew Nellie's trouble lay in – the bedroom, and the fact that she had not fallen with a bairn and her all of three years married. Charlie Burke rarely came up to the house any more on a Sunday. Of course he had an excuse; he worked on the coal boats and so could be called out at any time to take a load up the river.

Janie now went into the kitchen to say good-bye to Lizzie.

Lizzie was standing with her hands holding the rim of the tin dish that rested on a little table under the window, which sloped to the side as if following the line of the roof.

'I'm off then Lizzie.'

Without turning and her voice thick and holding a slight tremor, Lizzie said in answer, 'He's a bloody upstart. Do you know that, Janie? He's a bloody snot. I'm sorry to say this, lass, but he is.'

'He's not; you know he's not, Lizzie.' She shook her head at the older woman. 'An' you're as much to blame as he is. Now yes you are.' She bent sideways and wagged her finger into the fat face, and Lizzie, her eyes blinking rapidly, put out her hand and touched the cream skin that glowed with health and youth and said, 'Lass, you're too good for him. And it isn't the day or yesterday I've said it, now is it? He's damned lucky.'

'So am I, Lizzie.'

'Aw, lass.' Lizzie smiled wryly. 'You'd say thank you if you were dished up with a meat puddin' made of lights, you would that.'

'Well, and why not? And it wouldn't be the first time I've eaten lights.'

They pushed against each other with their hands; then Janie said, 'Remember that starving Christmas? How old was I? Ten, eleven? No work, strikes, trouble. Eeh! we had lights all right then. Me grannie cooked them seven different ways every week.' She paused and they looked at each other. 'Bye-bye, Lizzie.'

Spontaneously now Janie put her arms around Lizzie and kissed her, and Lizzie hugged her to herself. It was an unusual demonstration of affection. People didn't go kissing and clarting on in public, it wasn't proper; everybody knew that, even among engaged couples kissing and clarting on was kept for the dark country lanes, or if you were from the town, and common, a back lane or shop doorway; the only proper place for kissing and clarting on was a front room, if you had one; if not, well then you had to wait for the bedroom, as every respectable person knew. She was going to wait for the bedroom, by aye she was that, even although she wasn't all that taken with what she understood happened in the bedroom.

She now disengaged herself and went hurriedly from the scullery, leaving Lizzie once more gripping each side of the tin dish.

Rory and John George were already dressed for outdoors and waiting for her, Rory, although not short by any means, being all of five foot ten, looking small against John George's lean six foot.

John George wore a black overcoat that had not been made for him. Although the length was correct, being well below his knees, the shoulders were too broad, and the sleeves too short, his hands and arms hanging so far out of them that they drew attention to their thin nakedness. There was a distinct crack above the toecap of one of his well-polished boots and a patch in a similar place on the other. His hard hat was well brushed but had a slight greeny tinge to it. His whole appearance gave the impression of clean seediness, yet his position as rent collector in the firm of Septimus Kean was superior to that of Rory, for whereas Rory had only worked for Mr Kean for four years John George had been with him for eight. Now, at twenty-two years of age and a year younger than Rory, he showed none of the other's comparative opulence for Rory wore a dark grey overcoat over a blue suit, and he had a collar to his shirt, and he did not wear his scarf like a muffler but overlapping on his chest like a business gentleman would have worn it. And although he wore a cap – he only wore his hard hat for business – it wasn't like a working man's cap, perhaps it was only the angle at which he wore it that made it appear different.

Looking at him as always with a feeling of pride welling in her, Janie thought, He can get himself up as good as the master.

'Well then, off you go.' Ruth seemed to come to the fore for the first time. She escorted them all to the door and there she patted Janie on the back, saying, 'Until next Sunday then, lass?'

'Yes, Mrs Connor, until next Sunday. You'll give a look in on her?' She nodded towards the next cottage and Ruth said, 'Of course, of course. Don't worry about her. You know' – she smiled faintly – 'I think she'll still be here when we're all pushing the daisies up.'

'I shouldn't wonder.' Janie went out laughing, calling over her shoulder. 'Ta-rah. Ta-rah everybody. Ta-rah.'

Out in the black darkness they had difficulty in picking their way in single file down the narrow rutted lane. When they reached the broader road they stopped for a moment and Rory, kicking the snow aside with his foot, said, 'By! it's thick. If it goes on like this we'll have a happy day the morrow, eh?'

'I'd rather have it than rain,' John George replied; 'at least it's dry for a time. It's the wet that gets me down, day after day, day after day.'

'Here, hang on.' Rory now pulled Janie close to him and linked her arm in his. 'It's comin' down thicker than ever. Can't even see a light in the docks. We'll find ourselves in the ditch if we're not careful.'

Stumbling on, her side now pressed close to Rory's, Janie began to giggle; then turning her head, she cried, 'Where are you, John George?'

'I'm here.' The voice came from behind them and she answered, 'Give me your hand. Come on.'

As she put her hand out gropingly and felt John George grip it, Rory said, 'Let him fend for himself, he's big enough. You keep your feet, else I'm tellin' you we'll be in the ditch.'

It took them all of twenty minutes before they reached Tyne Dock, and there, taking shelter under the last arch, they stopped and drew their breath, and Janie, looking towards a street lamp opposite the dock gates, said, 'Isn't it nice to see a light?'

'And you can just see it and that's all. Come on, we'd better be goin'. It's no use standin', we soon won't be able to get through.'

As Rory went to pull Janie forward she checked him, saying, 'Look, wait a minute. It's daft, you know, you walkin' all the way to Westoe, you've only got to tramp all the way back. It isn't so bad in the town 'cos there's the lights, but from the bottom of the bank up to our place . . . well, we've just had some, haven't we? An' if it keeps on, as you say it'll get worse underfoot, so what's the sense of trapesing all the way there with me when John George's place is only five minutes away?'

'She's right, Rory. It's daft to tramp down all the way to Westoe for it'll be another couple of hours afore you get back. And then with it coming down like this. Well, as Janie says . . .'

Rory peered from one to the other before he answered, 'Imagine the reception I'd get if I told them back there I'd left you at the arches. They'd wipe the kitchen with me.'

'But you're not leavin' me at the arches; John George'll see me right to the door. Look.' She turned and pushed John George away, saying, 'Go on, walk on a bit, I'll catch up with you in a minute at the Dock gates.'

When John George walked swiftly from the shelter of the arch Rory called, 'Hold your hand a minute . . .'

'Now just you look here.' Janie pulled at the lapels of his coat. 'Don't be such a fathead; I'd rather know you were safely back home in the dry than have you set me to the door.'

'But I won't see you for another week.'

'That didn't seem to bother you all afternoon, 'cos you've done nowt but play cards.'

'Well, what can you do back there? I ask you, what can you do? There's no place to talk and I couldn't ask you out in the freezing cold or they'd've been at me. And I wanted to talk to you, seriously like 'cos it's . . . it's time we thought about doin' something. Don't you think it is?'

She kept her head on the level, her eyes looking into his as she replied, 'If you want a straight answer, Mr Connor, aye, I do.'

'Aw, Janie!' He pulled her roughly to him and pressed his mouth on hers and when she overbalanced and her back touched the curved wall of the arch she pulled herself from him, saying, 'Eeh! me coat, it'll get all muck.'

'Blast your coat!'

Her voice soft now, she said, 'Aye, blast me coat,' then she put her mouth to his again and they stood, their arms gripped tight around each other, their faces merged.

When again she withdrew herself from him he was trembling and he gulped in his throat before saying, 'Think about it this week, will you?'

'It's you that's got to do the thinking, Rory. We've got to get a place an' furniture 'cos there's one thing I can tell you sure, I'm not livin' in with me dad and grannie. I'm not startin' that way up in the loft. I want a house that I can make nice with things an' that . . .'

'As if I would ask you. What do you take me for?'

'I'm only tellin' you, I want a decent place . . .'

'I'm with you there all the way. I'm not for one room an' a shakydown either, I can tell you that . . . I've got something in me napper.'

'Gamblin'?'

'Well, aye. And don't say it like that; I haven't done too badly out of it, have I now? But what I'm after is to get set on in a good school . . . A big school. And there's plenty about. But you've got to be in the know.'

'What! be in the know afore you can get into a gamblin' school?' Her voice was scornful. 'Why, you've been up at Boldon Colliery where they have schools . . .'

'Aye in the back yards an' in the wash-houses. I know all about Boldon Colliery and the games there, but they're tin pot compared to what I'm after. The places I mean are where you start with a pound, not with a penny hoping to win a tanner. Oh, aye, I know, there's times when there's been ten pounds in a kitty, but them times are few and far between I'm telling you. No, what I'm after is getting set on in a real school, but it's difficult because of the polis, they're always on the look out – it's a tricky business even for the back-laners. That's funny,' he laughed, 'a tricky business, but it is. Remember what Jimmy said the night about notices in the works? They try everything to catch you out: spies, plain-clothes bobbies, touts. It's odd, you know; they don't run you in for drinking, but you touch a card or flick a coin and you're for it . . . Anyway, as I said, I've got something in me napper, and if it works out . . .'

'Be careful, Rory. I . . . I get worried about your gamin'. Even years ago when you used to play chucks and always won, I used to wonder how you did it. And it used to worry me; I mean 'cos you always won.'

'I don't always win now.'

'You do pretty often, even if it's only me da's monkey nuts.'

They both made small audible sounds, then moved aside to let a couple of men pass. And now she said, 'I'll have to be goin', John George'll get soaking wet . . . Eeh! I always feel sorry for John George.'

'Your pity's wasted, he's too soft to clag holes with, I'm always telling him. It's right what she said' – he jerked his head – 'those two old leeches suck him dry. He gets two shillings a week more than me and yet look at him, you'd think he got his togs from Paddy's market. And he might as well for he picks them up from the second-hand stalls. And this lass he's after . . . he would pick on a ranter, wouldn't he?'

'Well, he's not a Catholic.'

'No, I know he's not. He's not anything in that line, but he goes and takes up with one from the narrowest end of the Non-conformists, Baptist-cum-Methodist-cum . . .'

'What's she like?'

'I don't know.'

'Doesn't he talk about her at all?'

'Oh, he never stops talkin' about her. By the sound of it she should be a nun.'

'Oh Rory!'

'She should, she's so bloomin' good by all his accounts. She's been unpaid housekeeper to a sick mother, her dad, two sisters and a brother since she was ten. And now she's twenty, and she daresn't move across the door for fear of her old man. He even escorts his other two lasses to work. They're in a chemist's shop and he's there when it closes to fetch them home.'

'What is he?'

'He's got a little tailor's business, so I understand. But look, forget about John George for a minute. Come here.' Once again they were close, and when finally they parted he said, 'Remember what I said. Think on it and we'll settle it next Sunday, eh?'

'Yes, Rory.' Her voice was soft. 'I'm ready anytime you are, I've been ready for a long time. Oh, a long time . . . I want a home of me own . . .'

He took her face gently between his hands and as gently kissed her, and she, after staring at him for a moment, turned swiftly and ran from under the arch and over the snow-covered flags until she came to John George, who was standing pressed tight against the dock wall. She did not speak to him and together they turned and hurried on, past a line of bars arrayed on the opposite side of the road, and so into Eldon Street.

Her throat was full. It was strange but she always wanted to cry when Rory was tender with her. Generally, there was a fierceness about his love-making that frightened her at times, it was when he was tender that she loved him best.

'Daft of him wanting to come all this way.'

'Yes, it was, John George.'

'Of course I was just thinking that if I hadn't have come along he would have taken you all the way, and that, after all, was what he wanted. I'm blind about some things some times.'

She was kind enough to say, 'Not you, John George,' for she had thought it a bit short-sighted of him to accompany them in the first place, and she added, 'Don't worry. And you know what? We're goin' to settle something next Sunday.'

'You are? Oh, I'm glad, Janie. I'm glad. I've thought for a long time he should have a place of his own 'cos he doesn't seen quite happy back there. And yet I can't understand it for they're a good family, all of them, and I like nothing better than being among them.'

'Oh! What makes you think that? What makes you think he's not happy at home, John George?'

'Well, he's surly like at times. And I get vexed inside when I hear the way he speaks to Lizzie 'cos she's a nice body, isn't she . . . Lizzie? I like her . . . motherly, comfortable. Yet . . . yet at times he treats her like dirt. And I can't understand it, 'cos he's not like that outside, I mean when he's collecting; he's civility's own self, and all the women like him. You know that, don't you? All the women like him, 'cos he's got a way with him. But the way he speaks to Lizzie . . .'

Janie paused in her walk and, putting her hand on John George's arm, she drew him to a stop. Then flicking the falling snow away from her eyes, she asked quietly, 'Don't you know why he goes on at Lizzie like that?'

'No.'

'He's never told you?'

'No.'

'You mean he's never told you an' you've been workin' with him and coming up to the house for . . . how many years?'

'Four and over.'

'Eeh! I can't believe it. I thought you knew.'

'Knew what?'

'Well, that . . . that Lizzie, she's . . . she's his mother.'

'*Lizzie?*' He bent his long length down to her. 'Lizzie Rory's mother? No! How does that come about? I don't believe it.'

'It's true. It's true. Come on, don't let us stand here, we'll be soaked.'

'What . . . what about Mrs Connor? I mean . . . his mother . . . I mean.'

'It's all very simple, John George, when you know the ins and outs of it. You see they were married, Mr and Mrs Connor for six years an' there was no sign of any bairn. Then Mr Connor gets a letter from Ireland from a half-cousin he had never seen. Her name was Lizzie O'Dowd. Her ma and da had died – as far as I can gather from starvation. It was one of those times when the taties went bad, you know, and this lass was left with nobody, and she asked if she could come over here and would he find her a job. Everybody seemed to be comin' to England, particularly to Jarrow. They were leaving Ireland in boatloads. So what does Mr Connor do but say come right over. By the way, she had got the priest to write 'cos she couldn't write a scribe and Mr Connor went to a fellow in Jarrow who made a sort of livin' at writing letters an' sent her the answer. It was this by the way, Mr Connor having to go an' get this letter written, that later made him see to it that Rory could read and write. Anyway, Lizzie O'Dowd arrives at the cottage. She's seventeen an' bonny, although you mightn't think it by the look of her now. But I'm goin' by what me grannie told me. And what's more she was full of life and gay like. Anyway, the long and the short of it is that she and Mr Connor . . . Well, I don't need to tell you any more, do I? And so Rory came about. But this is the funny part about it. Almost a year later Ruth had her first bairn. That was Nellie. And then she had another. That was Jimmy. Would you believe it? After nothing for seven years! Eeh! it was odd. And, of course, we were all brought up as one family. You could say the three families in the row were all dragged up together.'

As she laughed John George said solemnly, 'You surprise me, Janie. It's quite a gliff.'

'But you don't think any the worse of Lizzie, do you?'

'Me think any the worse of . . . ? Don't be daft. Of course I don't. But at the same time I'm back where I started for I understand less now than I did afore, Rory speaking to her like that and her his mother.'

'But he didn't always know that she was his mother. It was funny that.' She was silent for a moment, before going on, 'There was us, all the squad of the Learys, me da, me ma, and me grannie. Well, you know me grannie, her tongue would clip clouts. But nobody, not one of us, ever hinted to him that Mrs Connor wasn't his mother, it never struck us. I think we sort of thought that he knew, that somebody must have told him earlier on. But nobody had; not until six years ago when he was seventeen and it was Lizzie herself who let the cat out of the bag. You know, Lizzie is one of those women who can't carry drink. Give her a couple of gins and she's away; she'll argue with her own fingernails after a couple of gins. And it was on a New Year's Eve, and you know what it's like on a New Year's Eve. She got as full as a gun an' started bubbling, and Rory, who up till that time had been very fond of her, even close to her, when she hadn't got a drink on her, 'cos this is another funny thing about him, he can't stand women in drink. Well, I don't remember much about it 'cos I was only a lass at the time, but as I recall, we were all in the Connors' kitchen. It was around three o'clock in the morning and I was nearly asleep when I heard Lizzie blurting out, "Don't speak to me like that, you young . . . !" She called him a name. And then she yelled, "I'm your mother! Her there, Ruth there, never had it in her to give breath to a deaf mute till I went an' had you." And that was that. From then on he never has been able to stand her. An' the pity of it is she loves him. He went missing for a week after that. Then he turned up one night half starved, frozen, and in the end he had the pneumonia. He had been sleeping rough, and in January mind. It's a wonder it didn't kill him. Now do you begin to understand?'

'I'm flabbergasted, Janie. To think that I've known him all this time and he's never let on. And we talk you know, we do; I thought we knew everything there was to know about each other. Me, I tell him everything.' The tall length drooped forward. His head bent against the driving snow, he muttered now, 'I'm that fond of Rory, Janie, 'cos, well, he's all I'd like to be and never will.'

'You're all right as you are, John George; I wouldn't have you changed.' Her voice was loud and strong in his defence.

'You wouldn't, Janie?' The question was almost eager, and she answered, 'No, I wouldn't, John George, because your heart's in the right place. An' that's something to be proud of.'

They walked on some way in silence now before she said quietly, 'I hope you don't mind me askin', but the lass you're gone on, why don't you bring her up to the kitchen?'

He didn't answer immediately but took her arm and led her across the road and up the street towards the beginning of Westoe and the select section of the town, where the big houses were bordered by their white railings and the roads were broad enough to take two carriages passing, and he said now, 'I wish I could, oh I wish I could 'cos she's nice, Janie, and bonny. Not as bonny as you, but she's bonny. And she's had a life of it. Aye, one hell of a life. And still has. Her da's got religion on the brain I think. Her mother's bedridden, and, you know, they spend Sunday praying round her bed, taking turns. The only time she's allowed out is on a Saturday afternoon when she's sent to Gateshead to visit an aunt who's dying and who seems to have a bit of money. Her da want to make sure of who she's leaving it to and as he can't go up himself and the other two lasses are in jobs – there was a brother, Leonard, but he ran off to sea, and good luck to him I say – Anyway, Maggie is allowed to go to Gateshead on a Saturday afternoon. That's how I met her first, on one of me Saturday train jaunts.'

'You go on a train to Gateshead every Saturday? I didn't know that. Eeh! on a train . . .'

'Well' – he laughed self-consciously – 'not every Saturday, only when funds allow. And then not to Gateshead, but Newcastle. I take the train up half-way, say to Pelaw, and walk the rest. I love Newcastle. Aw, lad, if I had the money I'd live there; I wouldn't mind rent collecting around Newcastle.'

'Aren't there any slums up there then?'

'Oh aye, Janie, plenty. But I don't look at the slums, it's the buildings I look at. There's some beautiful places, Janie. Haven't you ever been to Newcastle?'

'No, I've been across the water to North Shields and Cullercoats, and once I went as far as Felling on this side, but no, I've never been to either Gateshead or Newcastle.'

'Rory should take you up, he should take you to a theatre.'

'There's a good theatre here, I mean in Shields.'

'Oh aye, it's all right, but it isn't like Newcastle.'

'They get the same turns, only a little later.'

'Oh, I'm not thinkin' about the turns, nothing like that, it's the buildings you know. I suppose it was a wrong thing to say that he should take you to a theatre, but I think he should take you up to Newcastle to see the lovely places there, the streets and buildings.'

'I never knew you liked that kind of thing, John George?'

'Oh aye, an' have ever since I was a lad. It was me da who started it. On holiday week-ends we'd walk up there. Me mother never came, she couldn't stand the distance and she wasn't interested in buildings. It was because of me da's interest in buildings and such that I was taught to read and write. He was standing looking up at a lovely front door once. They're called Regency. It was off Westgate Hill; it was a bonny piece of work with a lovely fanlight and the windows above had iron balconies to them when a man came alongside of us and started crackin'. And it turned out he worked in an architect's office and he seemed over the moon when he knew me da was interested in masonry and such and was leading me along the same lines. That was the first time I heard the name Grainger mentioned. He was the great builder of Newcastle. And John Dobson, he used to design for Grainger and others. I'd heard of the Grainger Market, and had been through it, but you don't think of who built these places. And then there's Grey Street. Eeh! there's a street for you. The best time to see it is on a Sunday when there's no carts or carriages packing it out and few people about. By! it's a sight. As me da once said, that's what one man's imagination could do for a town.'

Janie now blew at the snow that was dusting her lips and turned her head towards him and blinked as she said, 'You're a surprise packet you are, John George. Do you ever talk to Rory about it?'

'Aye, sometimes. But Rory's not really interested in Newcastle or buildings and such.'

'No, no, he's not.' Janie's voice held a dull note now as she added, 'Cards, that's Rory's interest, cards. Eeh! he seems to think of nothing else.'

'He thinks of you.'

'Aye, he does, I must admit.' She was smiling at him through the falling snow and she added now, 'You've got me interested in Newcastle. I'll tell him . . . I'll tell him he's got to take me up.'

'Do that, Janie. Aye, do that. Tell him you want to see Jesmond. By! Jesmond's bonny. And the houses on the way . . . Eeh! lad, you see nothing like them here.'

'I think I'd like to see the bridges. I heard me da say there's some fine bridges. Funny me never ever havin' seen Newcastle and it only seven miles off. And there's me grannie. She worked there at one time, she was in service at a place overlooking the river. She used to keep talking about the boats laden down with coal going up to London. It was funny, she never liked Newcastle. She still speaks of the people there as if they were foreigners; she's always sayin' they kept the South Shields men down, wouldn't let them have their own shipping rights or nothing until a few years back. It's funny when you come to think of it, John George, we know more about the people from Ireland, like the Learys and Rory's folks, than we do about them up in Newcastle. I'm beginning to see the sense of some of me grannie's sayings; she always used to be saying, "You could be closer to a square head from Sweden than you could to a man with a barrow from Jarrow."'

John George laughed now, saying, 'I've never heard that one afore.'

'Oh, I think it's one of me grannie's make-up ones. You know, half the things she says I think she makes up. If she had ever been able to read or write she would have been a story teller. I've said that to her. Oh –' She sighed now and shook her gloved hands to bring the circulation back into her fingers as she said, 'we're nearly there.' Then on a little giggle, she added, 'If the missis was to see you she'd think I was leading a double life and she'd raise the riot act on me.'

As they stopped before a side gate that was picked out by the light from a street lamp she looked at John George, now blowing on his hands, and said with deep concern, 'Oh, you must be frozen stiff, John George. And no gloves.'

'Gloves!' His voice was high. 'You can see me wearin' gloves, I'd be taken for a dandy.'

'Don't be silly. You need gloves, especially goin' round in this weather, scribbling in rent books. At least you want mittens. I'll knit you a pair.'

He stood looking down on her for a long moment before saying, 'Well, if you knit me a pair of mittens, Janie, I'll wear them.'

'That's a bargain?'

'That's a bargain.'

'Thanks for comin' all this way, John George.'

'It's been my pleasure, Janie.'

'I . . . I hope you see your girl next week.'

'I hope so an' all. I . . . I'd like you to meet her. You'd like her, I know you'd like her, and what's more, well, being you you'd bring her out, 'cos she's quiet. You have that habit, you know, of bringing people out, making people talk. You got me talkin' the night all right about Newcastle.'

Janie stood for a moment blinking up at him and slightly embarrassed and affected by the tenderness of this lanky, kindly young fellow. His simple talking was having the same effect on her as Rory's gentle touch had done. She felt near tears, she had the silly desire to lean forward and kiss him on the cheek just like a sister might. But that was daft, there was no such thing as sisterly kisses. That was another thing her grannie had said and she believed her. There were mothers' kisses and lovers' kisses but no sisterly kisses, not between a man and woman who weren't related anyway . . . Yet the master kissed his sister-in-law, she had seen him. Eeh! what was she standing here for? She said in a rush, 'Good night, John George. And thanks again, I'll see you next Sunday. Ta-rah.'

'Ta-rah, Janie.'

She hurried up the side path, but before opening the kitchen door she glanced back towards the gate and saw the dim outline of his figure silhouetted against the lamplight, and she waved to it; and he waved back; then she went into the house . . .

Mrs Tyler, the cook, turned from her seat before the fire, looked at Janie, then looked at the clock above the mantelpiece before saying, 'You've just made it.'

'There's three minutes to go yet.' Her retort was perky.

She wasn't very fond of Mrs Tyler. She had only been cook in the Buckhams' household for eighteen months but from the first she had acted as if she had grown up with the family. And what was more, Janie knew she was jealous of her own standing with the master and mistress.

The cook never said anything outright to her but she would talk at her through Bessie Rice, the housemaid, making asides such as 'Some people take advantage of good nature, they don't know their place. Don't you ever get like that, Bessie now. In Lady Beckett's household, where I did my trainin', the nursemaid might have her quarters up on the attic floor but below stairs she was considered bottom cellar steps. Of course, a governess was different. They were educated like. Why, in Lady Beckett's the still-room maid sat well above the nursemaid.'

On the occasion when this particular remark was made, Janie had had more than enough of Lady Beckett for one day and so, walking out of the kitchen, she remarked to no one in particular, 'Lady Betty's backside!'

Of course she should never have said such a thing and she regretted it as soon as she was out of the door, and before she had reached the nursery she knew that the cook was knocking on the parlour door asking to speak to the mistress. Ten minutes later the mistress was up in the nursery looking terribly, terribly hurt as she said, 'Janie, I'm surprised at what the cook has been telling me. You must not use such expressions, because they may become a habit. Now just imagine what would happen if you said something like that in front of the children.' She had gulped and stood speechless before the young woman who had shown her nothing but kindness and when the mistress had gone she had laid her head in her arms on the table and cried her heart out until young Master David had started to cry with her, and then Margaret, and lastly the baby.

She looked back on that day as the most miserable in her life, and yet when she went to bed that night she had had to bury her head in the pillow to smother her laughter. Having earlier decided that feeling as she did she'd get no rest, she had gone downstairs to apologize to the mistress and to tell her that never again would she use such an expression in her house, and that she need not have any fear that the childrens' minds would ever be sullied by one word that she would utter.

She had reached the main landing when she was stopped by the sound of smothered laughter coming from the mistress's bedroom. The door was ajar and she could hear the master saying, 'Stop it. Stop it, Alicia, I can't hear you . . . what did she say?'

She had become still and stiff within an arm's length of the door as her mistress's voice came to her spluttering with laughter the while she made an effort to repeat slowly: 'She . . . said . . . you . . . can . . . kiss . . . Lady

... Beckett's ... backside.'

'She didn't!'

The laughter was joined now, high, spluttering; it was the kind of laughter that one heard in the Connors' kitchen when Lizzie said something funny.

'Well done, Waggett!'

There was more laughter, then the master's voice again saying, 'I can't stand Tyler. You want to get rid of her.'

'Oh, she's a good cook; I can't do that. David. And Janie mustn't be allowed to say things like that. But oh, I don't know how I kept my face straight.'

She had backed slowly towards the stairs, and when she reached the nursery floor her face split into one wide amazed grin; yet her mind was saying indignantly, 'I didn't say that. It's just like cook to stretch things. But eeh! the master, I've never heard him laugh like that afore. Nor the missis. They sounded like a young couple.'

It wasn't until she was in bed that she thought to herself, Well, I suppose they are a young couple. Yet at the same time it was strange to her to realize that people of their class could laugh together, spluttering laughter; for they always acted so very correct in front of other folk, even when the sister came. But then the sister was married to a man who had a cousin with a title, a sir, or a lord, or something, and, of course, she wouldn't expect them to act in any way but refinedly. But, anyway, they had laughed, and the mistress actually repeated what she herself had said, only, of course, with a bit added on by the cook.

And that night she had told herself yet once again that she liked her master and mistress, she did, she did, and she would do anything for them. And as she had recalled their laughter the bubbling had grown inside her, and to stop an hysterical outburst she had turned and pressed her face tightly into the pillow. And her last thought before going to sleep had been, I'll have them roaring in the kitchen next Sunday. And she had.

CHAPTER 2

It was the Saturday before Christmas; the sky lay low over the town and the masts of the ships were lost in grey mist.

Rory shivered as he walked up the church bank and entered Jarrow. He passed the row of whitewashed cottages, then went on towards the main thoroughfare of Ellison Street. He hated this walk; he hated Saturday mornings; Saturday mornings meant Pilbey Street and Saltbank Row. Pilbery Street was bad enough but the Row was worse.

He had six calls in Pilbey Street and fifteen in the Row, and as always when he entered the street he steeled himself, put on a grim expression and squared his shoulders, while at the same time thinking, Old Kean and those other landlords he represents should be lynched for daring to ask rent for these places.

For four years now he had collected the rents in these two streets. In the ordinary way he should have collected them on Monday, Tuesday or Wednesday because on these days he came this way collecting, and right on into Hebburn, but you couldn't get a penny out of anybody in Pilbey Street or the Row on any other day but a Saturday morning. And you were lucky if you managed to get anything then; it was only fear of the bums that made them tip up.

He lifted the iron knocker and rapped on the paint-cracked knobless door. There was a noise of children either fighting or playing coming from behind it, and after a few minutes it was opened and three pairs of eyes from three filthy faces peered up at him. All had running noses, all had scabs around their mouths and styes on their eyes. The eldest, about five, said in the voice of an adult, 'Aw, the rent man.' Then scrambling away through the room with the others following him, he shouted, 'The rent man, Ma! 'Tis the rent man, Ma!'

'Tell the bugger I'm not in.'

The woman's voice came clearly to Rory and when the child came back and, looking up at him, said, 'She's not in,' Rory looked down on the child and as if addressing an adult said, 'Tell her the bugger wants the rent, and somethin' off the back, or else it's the bums Monday.'

The child gazed at him for a moment longer before once more scrambling away through the room, and when his thin high voice came back to him, saying, 'He says, the bugger wants the rent,' Rory closed his eyes, bowed his head and pressed his hand over his mouth, knowing that it would be fatal to let a smile appear on his face with the two pairs of eyes surveying him. If he once cracked a smile in this street he'd never get a penny.

It was almost three minutes later when the woman stood before him. She had a black shawl crossed over her sagging breasts, the ends were tucked into a filthy ragged skirt, and in a whining tone and a smile widening her flat face she exclaimed, 'Aw begod! it's you, Mr Connor. Is it the rent you're after? Well now. Well now. You know it's near Christmas it is, and you know what Christmas is for money. Chews it, it does, chews it. An' look at the bairns. There's not a stitch to their arses an' himself been out of work these last three weeks.'

Without seeming to move a muscle of his face Rory said, 'He's in the rolling mills and never lost a day this six months, I've checked. You're ten weeks in arrears not countin' the day. Give me five shillings and I'll say nothing more 'til next week when I want the same and every week after that until you get your book clear. If not, I go to Palmer's and he'll get the push.'

It was an idle threat, yet she half believed him because rent men had power, rent men were rich; rent men were a different species, not really human.

They stared at each other. Then the smile sliding from her face, she turned abruptly from him and went through the room, shouting, 'You Willy! You Willy!' And the eldest child followed her, to return a moment later with two half-crowns and the rent book.

Rory took the money, signed the book, marked it in his own hard-backed pocket ledger, then went on to the next house. Here he pushed open the bottom door and called up the dark well of the staircase, 'Rent!' and after a moment a man's voice came back to him shouting, 'Fetch it up.'

His nose wrinkled in distaste. If he had a penny for every time that worn-out quip had been thrown at him he considered he'd be able to buy a house of his own. After a moment of silence he again shouted, 'Rent, or it's the bums Monday.'

The moleskin-trousered bulky figure appeared on the stairhead and after throwing the rent book and a half-crown down the stairs he yelled, 'You know what you and the bloody bums can do, don't you?' then as Rory picked up the money and the book and entered in the amount the man proceeded to elaborate on what he and the bums could do.

Without uttering a word now Rory threw the book on to the bottom stair, looked up at the man still standing on the landing, then turned about and went towards the end of the street.

There was no answer whatever from the next three doors he knocked on, but he had scarcely raised the knocker on the fourth when it was opened and Mrs Fawcett stood there, her rent book in one hand, the half-crown extended in the other, and without any greeting she began,

'You won't get any change out of them lot.' She nodded to one side of her. 'Nor to this one next door.' Her head moved the other way. 'Off to Shields they are, the lot of them, to the market and they won't come back with a penny, not if I know them. Lazy Irish scum. And I'll tell you somethin'.' She leant her peevish face towards him. 'Her, Flaherty, she's got her front room packed with beds, and lettin' them out by the shift; as one lot staggers out another lot drops in. Great Irish navvies with not a drop on their faces from Monday mornin' till Saturda' night, but Sunday, oh, that's different, away to Mass they are, and straight out and into the bars. Disgrace!'

Rory closed her rent book, handed it to her, looked at her straight in the eye, then turned and walked away. He did not bother knocking at the door next to hers for he believed what she had said, they were all away on a spending spree. It was odd, she was the only good payer in the street; she'd always had a clear rent book; but of the lot of them, scum Irish they might be, he preferred any one of them to Mrs Fawcett.

Pilbey Street was bad but Saltbank Row was worse. Here it was the stench that got him. The dry middens at the back of the Row, dry being a mere courtesy title, seeped away under the stone floors of the two-roomed cottages, and the dirt in front of the cottages was always wet to the feet. In winter the stench was bad enough but in summer it was unbearable. Why the Town Corporation did not condemn the place he didn't know. Vested interests he supposed; in any case anything was good enough for the Irish immigrants, and they didn't seem to mind, for as it was well known they had been used to sleeping among the pigs and the chickens in their tiny hovel huts over in Ireland.

Yet there were Irish in the town among Palmer's men whom he had heard were buying their own houses. That had come from old Kean himself, and the old boy didn't like it.

His own father had worked in Palmer's for years, but there was no sign of him being able to buy his own house. Likely because he didn't want to; his father spent as he went, he ate well and drank as much as he could hold almost every day in the week, because his body was so dried up with the heat from the furnaces.

Drinking was one thing he didn't blame his father for, but he did blame him for his carry-on with her . . . Lizzie. He supposed it was by way of compensation that he'd had him sent to the penny school but he didn't thank him for that either, for he hadn't attended long enough to take in much beyond reading, writing and reckoning up. When funds were low the last thing to be considered was the penny fee. And he wouldn't go to school without it. Nor would his father have his name put down on the parish list so that he could send him free – not him.

Anyway, his reading and writing had enabled him finally to become a rent collector with a wage of fifteen shillings a week. He was told from all quarters that he was damned lucky to be in such a job. Fifteen shillings for neither bending his back nor soiling his hands. And his employer, more than others, emphasized this statement.

Mr Kean owned about half the cottages in Saltbank Row, and the rent of each was two shillings a week, but when he reached the end of the Row all he had in the back section of his leather bag was twenty-five shillings and sixpence.

It was just turned twelve o'clock when he reached the main street and joined the stream of men pouring out of Palmer's and the various side streets which led to different yards on the river. They were like streams of black lava joining the main flow, faces grey, froth-specked with their sweat. He was carried along in the throng until he reached the church bank again by which time the blackness had dwindled into individual pockets of men.

He reckoned he should be back at the office by one o'clock. He never carried a watch, not on his rounds, because it could be nicked in the time he blinked an eyelid. A gang of lads supposedly playing Tiggy could rough you up. He had seen it done. But he told himself as he paused for a moment on the Don bridge and looked down at the narrow mud-walled banks of the river that there was no immediate hurry today, for old Kean was off on one of his duty trips to Hexham to see his old father. When this happened the day's takings were locked up until Monday. Saturday's takings didn't amount to very much, not on his part anyway. John George took more, for he did the Tyne Dock area and the better part of Stanhope Road.

He was getting a bit worried about John George. There was something on his mind; he supposed it was that damned ranter's lass he had taken up with. Only last night he had told him to think hard about this business, for being her father's daughter, she might turn out to be a chip off the old block and be 'God-mad' like the rest of them.

The whole of Shields was becoming 'God-mad'; there was chapels springing up all over the place and the more of them there were the greater the outcry against drink and gambling. And them that made the fuss, what were they? Bloody hypocrites half of them. Oh, he knew a thing or two about some of them. That's why he had warned John George.

As he walked on into Tyne Dock he forgot about John George and his troubles for his mind was taken up with the evening's prospects. He had heard tell of a square-head, a Swede who lived down Corstorphine Town way. He was known as Fair Square; he did summer trips there and back to Norway and Sweden, but in the winter he stayed put somewhere along the waterfront and ran a school, so he understood, and not just an ordinary one, a big one, for captains and such. But as little Joe, the tout, had said, they didn't often let foreigners in . . . That was funny that was, a Swede calling an Englishman a foreigner, and in his own town at that. Anyway, little Joe had promised to work him in somewhere.

He felt a stir of excitement in his stomach at the thought of getting set-in in a big school; none of your tanner pitch and tosses or find the lady, but banker with a kitty up to twenty pounds a go. By, that was talking. Twenty pounds a go. Once in there it wouldn't be long afore he could set up house – he and Janie, setting up house. He wanted to get married, he ached for Janie. And that was the right word, ached. At night he would toss and turn until he would have to get up and put the soles of his feet on the ice-cold square of lino that stood between the beds.

He'd see her the morrow. Just to be with her lifted him out of the doldrums; just to look at her pulled at his heart, 'cos she was bonny, beautiful. And he wasn't spending the whole afternoon the morrow playing cards for monkey nuts. Huh! He wondered why he let himself in for it Sunday after Sunday. No, hail, rain or shine they'd go out up the lanes, and he'd settle things in his own way. Aye he would.

'Rory! Rory!'

He turned swiftly and looked up the dock bank to see John George pushing his way through a press of men towards him, and when he came up Rory stared at him saying, 'You're late, aren't you? You're generally done around twelve.'

'I know, but there was an accident back there at the Boldon Lane toll-gate. I helped to sort the carts out. A young lad got crushed. Toll's finished next year they say, an' a good thing an' all.'

'Getting into a throng with money in your bag, you must be mad . . . And where did you get that?'

Rory was now looking John George over from head to foot. 'You knock somebody down?'

Stroking the lapels of a thick brown overcoat that, although a little short, fitted his thin body, John George said, 'I picked it up last Saturday in Newcastle, in the market.'

'What did you give for it?'

'Half a dollar.'

'Well you weren't robbed, it's good material. You should have got yourself some boots while you were on.' He glanced down at the cracked toecaps. 'It's a wonder the old fellow hasn't spotted them and pulled you up. You know what he is for appearances.'

'I'm going to see about a pair the day when I'm up there.'

'You're going to Newcastle again?'

'Aye.' John George now turned his head and smiled at Rory 'I'm meeting her on the three o'clock train an' I'm going to show her round. Look' – he thrust his hand into the overcoat pocket, then brought out a small box wrapped in tissue paper – 'I bought her this for Christmas. What do you think of it?'

When Rory took the lid off the box and looked at the heartshaped locket and chain he stared as it for some seconds before turning to John George again and asking quietly, 'What did you give for it?'

'Not . . . not what it's worth, it's second-hand. It's a good one.'

'What did you give for it?'

'Seven and six.'

'Seven and six! Are you mad? How can you afford seven and six? You tell me that your Aunt Meg needs every penny to keep the house goin' and three bob's as much as you can keep back.'

'Well, it's . . . it's true. But . . . but I worked out a system.'

'You worked out a system, you!' Rory screwed up his face. 'You worked out a system! On what? Tell me on what?'

'Aw, not now, man, not now. I'll . . . I'll tell you after . . . later on. I wanted to have a word with you about something else . . . You see I'm thinking of moving, trying to get a better job. I could never hope to get Maggie away on the wage I've got and having to see to them at home and . . .'

'Where could you get a better job than what you've got?'

'There's places in Newcastle.'

'Aye, I know there's places in Newcastle, but them chaps don't get even as much as we do. There's no trade unions yelling for us. I'm not satisfied, but I know damn well that if I want more money I won't get it at rent clerking. Look, are you in some kind of fix?'

'No, no.' John George shook his head too vigorously and Rory, eyeing him from the side, shook his head also. They walked on in silence, taking short cuts until they came to the market, then they wound their way between the conglomeration of stalls, turned down a narrow side lane known as Tangard Street, and past what appeared to be the window of an empty shop, except that the bottom half, which was painted black, had written across it: Septimus Kean, Estate Agent, Valuer, and Rent Collector. Next to the window was a heavy door with a brass knob that had never seen polish, and above it a keyhole.

As John George was about to insert his key into the lock the door was pulled open from inside and they were both confronted by Mr Kean himself.

'Oh! . . . Oh! Mr Kean. We thought you were away.'

The small, heavy-jowled man looked at Rory and barked, 'Evidently.

Do you know what time it is?' He pulled out a watch, snapped open the case and turned the face towards Rory. 'Ten minutes past one. When the cat's away the mice can play.'

'But we finish at one.' Rory's voice was harsh, the muscles of his neck were standing out and his face was flushed with sudden temper.

'Be careful, Connor, be careful. Mind who you're speaking to. You know what happens to cheeky individuals; there's never an empty place that cannot be filled. I know that you're finished at one, and damned lucky you are to be finished at one, but you should have been back here before one and your book settled, and then you could have been finished at one . . . And what's the matter with you?' He was now glaring at John George. 'You sick or something?'

John George gulped, shook his head, and remained standing where he was on the threshold of the door.

And this caused Mr Kean to yell, 'Well, come in, man! What's come over you? Close the door before we're all blown out. And let me have your books; I want to get away.'

With this, Mr Kean turned about and went through a door into another room. The door was half glass, but it was clear glass, clear in order that the master could look through it at any time and see that his two clerks weren't idling at their desks.

'What is it? What's the matter?' Rory had taken hold of John George's shoulder. 'You look like death, what is it?'

John George gulped twice in his throat before he whispered, 'Lend . . . lend me ten bob.'

'Lend you ten bob?'

'Aye. Look, just for now, I'll have it for you Monday mornin'. Just . . . just lend it me. Aw, Rory, lend it me. For God's sake, lend it me.'

Rory looked towards the glass door and as he put his hand into his pocket, he hissed, 'You were paid last night.'

'Aye, I know, but I'll explain, I'll explain in a minute or two.' The hand he held out was trembling and when Rory put the gold half sovereign on to the palm John George's fingers pressed over it tightly for a moment before swiftly dropping it into the leather bag which he still held in his hand.

'*Come on, come on.*'

They exchanged glances before John George turned away and almost stumbled across the room and into his master's office.

Rory remained gazing at the half open door . . . He was on the fiddle. The damn fool was on the fiddle. It was that lass. God, if he hadn't been here and old Kean had found him ten shillings short!

Mr Kean's voice came bawling out of the room again, saying, 'What the matter with you, Armstrong? You look as if you're going to throw up.'

Then John George's voice, thin and trembling, 'Bit of a chill, sir. Got a cold I think.'

There was a pause, then Mr Kean's observation: 'That coat's new, isn't it? You shouldn't feel cold in that. About time you did smarten yourself up. Bad impression to go around the doors looking like a rag man.' Another pause before his voice again rasped, 'Mrs Arnold, she's paid nothing off the back for four weeks. Why haven't you seen to it?'

'She been bad. She . . . she took to her bed a few weeks ago. But she says she'll clear it up soon because her girl's got set on across the water at Haggie's . . . the Ropery you know.'

'Yes, I know, I know the Ropery. And I know the type that works there. She'll likely drink her pay before she gets back across the water. She's got others working, hasn't she?'

'Yes. Yes, she's got a lad down the pit. But . . . but he's only a nipper, he's not getting more than tenpence a day. She's . . . she's had hard times since her man went.'

'That's neither my business nor yours, I don't want the family history, I only want the rent and the back rent. Now you see to it. You're getting slack, Armstrong. I've noticed it of late.'

There followed another silence before John George returned to the outer office, his face looking bleak, his eyes wide and in their depth a misery that caused Rory to turn away, pick up his bag and go into the other room.

When he had placed the money from the bag on the table, Mr Kean separated each single coin with his forefinger, then after counting them he raised his eyes without lifting his head and said, 'You mean to tell me this is the result of a morning's work?'

'It was Saltbank Row and Pilbey Street.'

'I know damned well it was Saltbank Row and Pilbey Street, it's always Saltbank Row and Pilbey Street on a Saturday, but what I'm saying to you is, do you mean to tell me that's all you got out of them?'

Rory moved one lip over the other before replying, 'It's always the same near Christmas.'

'Look!' The thick neck was thrust forward, then the head went back on the shoulders and Mr Kean directed an enraged stare on to Rory's grim face as he cried, 'One gives me family histories, the other festival dates as excuses. Now look, I'm telling you they're not good enough, neither one nor the other, Christmas or no Christmas. If that sum' – he now dug his finger on to one coin after another – 'if it isn't doubled at the next collection then there'll be a lot of barrows needed to shift their muck. You tell them that from me. And that's final.' Again he stabbed the coins. 'Double that amount or it's the bums for the lot of 'em.'

When Rory turned abruptly from the table Mr Kean barked at him,

'Answer me when I'm speaking to you!'

Rory stopped, but it was a few seconds before he turned to face Mr Kean again, and then he said slowly, 'Yes, sir.'

Seconds again passed before Mr Kean said, 'There's going to be changes here, Connor,' and again Rory said, 'Yes, sir.'

'Get yourself out.'

The buttons on Rory's coat strained as he drew in a deep breath before turning round and leaving the room, closing the door after him.

John George was standing by his narrow, high desk. A little colour had returned to his face and he was about to speak when the outer door opened and they both looked towards it and at Miss Charlotte Kean.

Charlotte was Kean's only child but she bore no resemblance to him, being tall, extremely tall for a woman, all of five foot eight and thin with it. Moreover, she had what was commonly called a neb on her. Her nose was large; her mouth, too, was large but in proportion to her face. Her eyes were a greeny grey and her hair was black. She was an ugly young woman yet in some strange way she had just missed being beautiful for each feature taken by itself was good even though, together, one cancelled another out. Her features gave the impression of strength, even of masculinity. It was understood in the office that she knew as much about the business as did her father, yet she rarely came here. Rory hadn't seen her but half a dozen times in four years, and each appearance had given him material for jokes in the kitchen, especially at the Sunday gatherings.

He had from time to time openly teased John George about her. John George had said he felt sorry for her, because a young woman like her had little chance of being married. His words had proved true, for here she was at twenty-eight and still on the shelf.

But there was one thing his master's daughter possessed that he couldn't make game of, in fact it had the power to make him feel ill at ease, and that was her voice. There was no hint of the Tyneside twang about it. This he understood had come about by her being sent away to one of those posh schools when she was no more than ten, from which she hadn't come back to Shields for good until she was turned seventeen.

She gave them no greeting – one didn't greet clerks – but stared at Rory before demanding briefly, 'My father in?'

'Yes, miss.' Rory inclined his head towards the door.

She stood for a moment longer looking from one to the other. Then her eyes resting once more on Rory, she surveyed him from head to toe, as he said bitterly afterwards, 'Like some bloody buyer at a livestock show.' But he wasn't going to be intimidated by any look she could cast over him, and so he returned it. His eyes ranged from her fur-trimmed hat down over her grey velour coat with its brown fur collar, right to her feet encased in

narrow-toed brown kid boots. He had noticed her feet before. They were
so narrow he wondered how she balanced on them, how she got boots to fit
them. But when you had money you could be fitted from top to toe and
inside an' all, but he'd like to bet with that face her habit shirts would be
made of calico, unbleached at that, no lace camisoles for her. Anyway, she
had nothing to push in them.

As she went towards the door he looked at her back. It was like a
ramrod, she wasn't like a woman at all. He beckoned to John George, who
seemed to be glued to his desk, and as he opened the door he heard her say,
'You'll be late for the ferry, I came with the trap. Come along or you'll
never get there.'

The old man always went by ferry up to Newcastle; he didn't like the
trains although he had to take one from Newcastle to Hexham. When he
went on his usual trips there he generally left early on a Saturday. What
had stopped him this time? Anyway, whatever had stopped him had also
nearly stopped John George's breath.

They were crossing the market again before he said, 'Well now, come
on, spit it out.'

'I'll . . . I'll give you it back, I . . . I can give you six bob of it now. I'll get
it from home and . . . and the rest on Monday.'

'What were you up to?'

'Aw' – John George wagged his head from side to side – 'I . . . I wanted
to give Maggie something and it had to be the day, it's the only time I can
see her. I mightn't see her again until after the holiday and so, thinkin' he
wouldn't be in till Monday, I . . . I took the loan of ten bob out of the . . .'

'You bloody fool!'

'Aye, I know, I know I am.'

'But . . . but how did you expect to put it back by Monday if you haven't
got it now?'

'Aw well, man' – again his head was wagging – 'I . . . I usually put me
good suit in and me watch and bits of things . . .'

'You usually do? You mean you've done this afore?'

John George nodded his head slowly. 'Aye. Aye, a few times. The times
that he goes off at the week-ends and doesn't count up till Monday. I . . . I
thought I'd drop down dead when I saw him standing there.'

'You deserve to drop down dead, you bloody fool you. Do you know he
could have you up? And he's the one to do it an' all; he'd have you along
the line afore you could whistle. You must be up the pole, man.'

'I think I'll go up the pole soon if things don't change.'

'What you want to do is to pull yourself together, get things worked out
straight. Leave your Uncle Willy and Aunt Meg, he's able to work, he's
nothin' but a scrounger, and take a place on your own.'

'What!' John George turned his face sharply towards him. 'Take the furniture amd leave them with three bare rooms or tell him to get out? What you don't understand, Rory, is that there's such a thing as gratitude. I don't forget that they were both good to me mother after me da died, aye, and long afore that; and they helped to nurse him the two years he lay bedridden.'

'Well, they've been damned well paid for it since, if you ask me . . . All right then, say you can't do anything about them, an' you want that lass . . . well then, ask her to marry you and bring her into the house.'

'That's easier said than done. If I took her away her father would likely go straight to old Kean and denounce me.' He now put his hand to his brow, which, in spite of the raw cold, was running with sweat, and muttered, 'But I'll have to do something, and soon, 'cos . . . oh my God! I'm in a right pickle . . . Rory.'

'Aye, I'm still here, what is it?'

'There's something else.'

'Aw.' Rory now closed his eyes and put his hand across his mouth, then grabbed at his hard hat to save it from being whipped by the wind from his head. 'Well, go on.'

'It doesn't matter. Another time, another time; you're not in the mood . . . Look –' he pointed suddenly – 'Isn't that Jimmy?'

They were passing the road that led to the Mill Dam and the river front. Rory stopped and said, 'Yes that's our Jimmy . . . Jimmy!' he shouted down the lane, and Jimmy who had been walking with his eyes cast down looked upwards, then came dashing up the slope at his wobbling gait.

'Why, fancy seein' you, I mean both of you. An' I was just thinking of you, our Rory.'

'You were? Why? You another one that wants a sub?'

'No, man.' Jimmy laughed. 'But I was thinkin' that when I got home I'd ask you to come down here again. Now wasn't that funny.'

'I can't see much to laugh at in that, not yet anyway.'

'Well, it was something I wanted to show you down on the front.' He nodded towards the river. 'Come on.' He again indicated the river with his head, then added, 'And you an' all, John George.'

'I can't, Jimmy, I'm sorry. I'm . . . I'm on me way home.'

'Aw, all right, John George, I understand, it's your day for Newcastle.' He laughed.

John George didn't laugh with him, but he repeated, 'Aye. Aye, Jimmy, it's me day for Newcastle.' Then nodding at him, he said, 'Be seeing you. So long. And so long, Rory. Aw, I forgot. What about the other, I mean . . . ?'

'Leave it till Monday. And mind, don't do any more damn fool things until then.'

'I'll try not to. But what's done's done. Nevertheless thanks, thanks. You'll have it on Monday. So long.'

'So long.'

'What's up with him?' Jimmy asked as they went down towards the road that bordered the river.

'He's been a damned fool, he's mad.'

'What's he been and gone and done?'

'Nothing . . . I'll tell you some other time. What do you want me down here for?'

'I want to show you something.'

'A boat?'

'Aye, a boat. An' something more than that.'

Rory looked down into the young face. It was always hard for him to believe that Jimmy was nineteen years old, for he still looked upon him as a nipper. He was more than fond of Jimmy, half-brothers though they were; he liked him the best of the bunch.

'Where we going?'

'Just along the front, then down the Cut.'

'There's nothing but warehouses along there.'

'Aye, I know. But past them, past Snowdon's, on a bit, you'll see.'

After some walking they had turned from the road that bordered the warehouse and wharf-strewn river front and were clambering over what looked like a piece of spare ground except that it was dotted here and there with mounds of rusty chains, anchors and the keels and ribs of small decaying boats, when Jimmy, squeezing his way between a narrow aperture in a rough fence made up of oddments of thick black timber, said, 'Through here.'

Rory had some difficulty in squeezing himself between the planks, but when once through he looked about him on to what appeared to be a miniature boatyard. A half-finished skeleton of a small boat was lying aslant some rough stocks and around it lay pieces of wood of all shapes and sizes. A few feet beyond the boat was the beginning of a slipway bordered by a jetty and he walked towards the edge of it and leant over the rail and looked down into the water; then there he turned and surveyed the building at the far end of the yard.

It wasn't unlike any of the other warehouses cluttering the river bank except that it had three windows in the upper part of it, and they were big windows, one on each side of the door and one fitting into the apex of the roof. There was no name on the front of the structure like there was on the rest of the boatyards and warehouses, and Rory now turned and looked into Jimmy's bright eyes and said, 'Well?'

'It's a little boatyard.'

'I can see that but I wouldn't say it was a prosperous one. You're not going to leave Baker's for here, are you?'

'No, man, no. I'm not going to leave Baker's at all. I wish I could. At the same time I'm terrified of being stood off. No, I just want you to see it.'

'Why?'

'Oh, 'cos . . . it's up for sale.'

'Up for sale?'

'Aye.'

'Well, what's that got to do with us?'

'Nowt . . . nowt, man.'

Rory watched the light slowly fade from Jimmy's face. He watched him turn away and look at the river, then up at the house, and lastly at the boat on the stocks, and he said softly now, 'I know what you're thinkin', but it's like a dream, lad, that's all, it can never come true.'

'I know.'

'Then what did you bring me here for?'

'I just wanted you to see it, just to show you.'

'What good is that going to do you or anybody else?'

'Well, I just wanted to show you that a man could start on almost nowt an' build up. They've done it all along the river. The Pittie Brothers, they started from nowt. A sculler among the three of them, and now they've got the run of the place, or they think they have. But there's always room for another one or two. Some say the keelman's day is over since they've widened the river and the boats can go farther up and pick up their coal straight from the staithes, but as Mr Kilpatrick used to say there's other things to be carted besides coal. Anyway, I'd never aim to be a keelman 'cos it's as tight to get in as a secret society, an' they're a tough lot, by aye! Nor do I want to build keels, with a cabin an' hold, 'cos it takes all of three men to manage a keel. No; but I've got something in me mind's eye; it'd be under thirty foot but with space for timber, packages and such, something I could manage meself or, at a push, just two of us. Mr Kilpatrick used to say he could design . . .'

'Who's Mr Kilpatrick?'

'The old fellow who owned this place.'

'Did you know him?'

'Aye, in a way. I used to pop in in me bait time. He's always given me tips, things that you don't come by only by experience. He used to take the wood from the river' – he pointed to the wood scattered around the boat – 'and when he was finished with it, it was as good as new. He had a way with wood. He said I had an' all.'

'And he's dead?'

'Aye.'

'Who's sellin' it then?'

'His son. Well, he's selling the goodwill.'

'Goodwill!' Rory gave a short laugh. 'What goodwill is there here? The back end of a boat and wood you can pick up from the river.'

'There's a house up there and there's some decent pieces of furniture in it. And then there's his tools. And he's got a bond on the place for the next ten years.'

'You mean it's just rented?'

'Aye.'

'How much is it a week?'

'Three and a tanner.'

'Huh!' The sound was sarcastic. 'They're not asking much, three and a tanner for this!'

'But everything is included. And a permit to ferry stuff up and down the river.'

'And what's the son wanting for it?'

'Thirty-five pounds.'

'*What!*' It was a shout. 'You havin' me on?'

'No, I'm not, that's cheap. There's the boat, and all the wood. And you haven't seen his tools. Then there's the furniture. There's three rooms up there, I've been in them. He used to give me a cup of tea now and again. He lived on his own. They're big rooms. You don't get much of an idea from here.'

'But there's no boat, he must have had a boat.'

'Aye, his son took that.'

'That son knows what he's doing. Has he been pumping you?'

'No. Why no, man, why would he pump me? Only that he knew I used to talk to his old man. He came here once or twice when I was in the yard and when he saw me t'other day he told me. He said –' Now Jimmy turned away and walked up towards the house, his body seeming to rock more than his bowed legs and Rory called after him, 'Well, go, finish telling me what he said.'

'It doesn't matter; as you said, it's a dream.' And now he swung round and stabbed his finger towards Rory as he ended, 'But some day, mark my words, I'll make it come true. I don't know how but I will. I'll have a place of me own where I can build a boat an' ply a trade. You'll see. You'll see.'

'All right, all right.' Rory walked towards him now. 'No need to bawl your head off.'

'You bawled first.'

'Well, I had a right.' He now passed Jimmy and walked up and into the end of the slipway, over which the building extended, and looked towards the ladder that was fixed to the wall and ended in a trap-door, and he called back over his shoulder in an amused tone, 'Is this how you get in?'

'No, of course, it isn't,' Jimmy said scornfully; 'there's steps up and a door, you saw them. But –' And now his eyes were bright again as he went on, 'I can show you inside, I know how to get in through the hatch.'

'What we waitin' for, then, if it's going to cost us nothin'? So go on, get up.'

The desire was strong in him to please this brother of his and to keep his dream alive for a little longer. He watched him run up the vertical ladder with the agility of a monkey. He saw him put his flat hand in the middle of the trap-door, jerk it twice to the side, and then push it upwards. He stood at the foot of the ladder and watched him disappear through the hole. Then he was climbing upwards, but with no agility. He wasn't used to crawling up walls he told himself.

When he emerged into the room he straightened up and looked about him but said nothing. Just as Jimmy had said, there were some good pieces of furniture here. He was amazed at the comfort of the room. The whole floor space was covered with rope mats fashioned in intricate patterns. There was a high-barred fireplace with an oven to the side of it and a hook above it for a spit or kettle. A good chest of drawers stood against one wall, and by it a black oak chest with brass bindings. There was a big oval table with a central leg in the middle of the room, and the top had been polished to show the grain. There were three straight-backed wooden chairs and a rocking chair, and all around the walls hung relics from ships: brass compasses, wheels, old charts. He walked slowly towards the door that led into the next room. It was a bedroom. There was a plank bed in one corner but slung between the walls was a hammock. And here was another seaman's chest, not a common seaman's chest but something that a man of captain's rank might have used, and taking up most of the opposite end of the room was a tallboy.

'It's good stuff, isn't it? Look at his tools.' Jimmy heaved up the lid of the chest to show an array of shining tools hung meticulously in order around the sides of the chest.

'Aye, it's good stuff. He was no dock scum was your Mr Kilpatrick. Everything orderly and shipshape.'

'Of course he wasn't dock scum. He was a gentleman . . . well, I mean not gentry, but a gentleman. He had been to sea in his young days, ran off, so he told me. His people were comfortable. They took his son when his wife died, that's why the son doesn't want anything to do with the water front. He's in business, drapery.'

'What's up above?'

'It's a long room, it runs over both of these. It's full of all kinds of things, maps and papers and books and things. He could read. Oh, he was a great reader.'

Rory looked down on Jimmy. He looked at him for a long moment before he was able to say, 'I'm sorry.'

'What've you to be sorry for?' Jimmy had turned away and walked towards the window where he stood looking out on to the river.

'You know what I'm sorry for, I'm sorry you can't have it. If I had the money I'd buy it for you this minute, I would.'

He watched his brother's face slowly turn towards him. The expression was soft again, his tone warm. 'I know you would. That's why I wanted you to see it an' to hear you say that, 'cos I know if you had it you would give it me, lend it me.'

Rory went and sat in the rocking chair and began to push himself slowly backwards and forwards. Thirty-five pounds. A few nights of good play somewhere and he could make that. He once made thirteen pounds at one sitting, but had lost it afore he left. But if he were to win again he'd smilingly take his leave. That's if he wasn't playing against sailors, for some of them would cut you up for tuppence.

Suddenly jumping up from the chair, he said, 'Come on.'

'Where?'

'Never mind where. Just come on, let's get out of here.' But before dropping down through the trap-door he looked about him once again as he thought, It'll kill two birds with the one stone. Janie. Janie would love it here, she would be in her element. There was the room up there, that would do Jimmy. He closed his eyes and shook his head. He was getting as barmy as Jimmy . . . But there was nothing like trying.

When they were out of the yard and on the road again he stopped and, looking down at Jimmy, said, 'Now I want you to go straight home. You can say that you saw me, and I was with a fellow. We . . . we were going to see the turns later on. Aye, that's what to say, say we were going to the theatre later on.'

'You're goin' in a game?'

'Aye, if I can find a good one.'

'Aw, Rory.'

'Now, now, don't get bright-eyed, nowt may come of it. But I'll have a try. And if we could put something down to secure it –' he punched Jimmy on the shoulder – 'the fellow might wait, take it in bits like, eh? If he's not short of a bob he could wait, couldn't he? And it isn't everybody that's going to jump at a place like that. But . . . but as I said, don't get too bright-eyed. Just tell them what I told you, and if I shouldn't be back afore they go to bed, tell them . . . well, tell them not to wait up.'

'Aye, Rory, aye, I'll do that. And . . . and you be careful.'

'What have I got to be careful of?'

'You hear things, I mean along the front, about the schools an' things.

There are some rough customers about.'

'I'm a bit of one meself.'

'You're all right.'

They looked at each other, the undersized bow-legged boy with the angelic face and his thick-set straight-backed, arrogantly attractive-looking half-brother, and each liked what he saw: Rory, the blind admiration in the boy's face, and Jimmy, the strength, determination and apparent fearlessness in this man he loved above all others.

'Go on with you, go on.' Rory thrust out his hand, and Jimmy turned away. Again he was running, and not until he had disappeared from view into the main thoroughfare did Rory swing about and stride along the waterfront in the direction of the pier. But before he came to the high bank known as the Lawe, on which stood the superior houses with their view of the sea and the North and South piers, and which were occupied by ships' captains and respectable merchants of the town, he turned off and into a street which, from its disreputable appearance, should never have been allowed to lie at the skirt of such a neighbourhood as the Lawe. There were only eight houses in this street and they all had walled back yards and all the doors were locked. It was on the third yard door that he knocked, a sharp knock, rat-tat a-tat, tat-tat, and after some minutes it was furtively opened by a man hardly bigger than a dwarf.

'Hello, Joe.'

'Oh. Oh, it's you, Mr Connor?'

'Aye, Joe. I want a word with you.'

'Oh well, Mr Connor, I'm off on a message you see.' He brought his two unusually long and fine-shaped hands in a sweeping movement down the front of his short coat, and Rory, nodding, smiled and said, 'Aye, you've got your best toggery on, must be some special message.'

He had never before seen little Joe dressed like this. He had never imagined he had any other clothes but the greasy little moleskin trousers and the old broadcloth coat he usually wore. Not that he couldn't afford to buy a new suit because he must do pretty well on the side; besides being a bookie's runner, little Joe could be called upon to negotiate odd jobs, very odd jobs, along the waterfront. Last year it was said he almost went along the line when two lasses went missing. They couldn't prove anything against him for he was a wily little beggar. But the case recalled the outcry of a few years earlier when some lasses were shipped off. Afterwards of course this line of business had of necessity quietened down for a time, but nature being what it is a demand for young lasses, especially young white lasses, was always there, and so was Joe.

He said to him now, 'I want you to get me some place the night, Joe, like you promised. But no back-yard doss.'

'Aw, it'll take time, Mr Connor, an' I told you.' He came out into the lane now and pulled the door closed, and as he walked away Rory suited his steps to the shorter ones.

'Now you can if you like, Joe. You said . . .'

'I told you, Mr Connor, it takes time that kind of thing. And they're on to us . . . coppers; they're hot all round the place.'

'You have ways and means, you know you have, Joe. An' I'd make it worth your while, you know that.'

'Oh, I know that, Mr Connor. You're not tight when it comes to payin' up. Oh, I know that. And if I could, I would . . . There's Riley's.'

'I don't like that lot, I told you last time.'

'Well, I'll admit it, they're a bit rough.'

'And twisted.'

'Aw well, you see, I don't play meself, Mr Connor, so I wouldn't know.'

'There's other places, Joe.'

'But you've got to be known, Mr Connor, an' . . . an' it's me livelihood you know.'

'You could do it, Joe.'

And so the conversation went on, flattery pressing against caution; but by the time they parted caution had won.

'I'm sorry, Mr Connor, but . . . but I'll let you know. I'll take a walk around your office as soon as I can manage anything for you. That's a promise; it is.'

Rory nodded, and as he stood and watched the small shambling figure hurry away and disappear around the bottom of the street he repeated bitterly, 'That's a promise.' Then he asked himself the question, 'Where's he off to, rigged out like that?' He wouldn't need to dress up to go round his usual haunts. He was going some place special?

As if he had been pushed from behind he sprang forward, but when he came out into the main street he slowed to a walk. Little Joe was well ahead, but he kept him in sight until he turned into Fowler Street.

There he was impeded in his walking by a number of people who had stepped hastily up to the pavement from the road to allow a private coach and a dray-cart to pass each other. There were angry shouts and strong language among those who had their clothes bespattered with mud, and as he didn't want his own mucked up, he kept as near as he could to the wall, and because of the press he was only just in time to see little Joe turn off into Ogle Terrace.

Ogle Terrace, apart from Westoe, was in the best end of the town. Who was he going to see up there? On the small figure hurried until at the top of Plynlimmon Way he disappeared from view.

Rory, now about to set off at a run towards the end of the terrace, was impeded for a second time by a party of ladies coming through an iron gateway and making for a carriage standing at the kerb.

When he eventually reached the top corner of Plynlimmon Way there was no sight of little Joe.

He stood breathing deeply, working things out. Joe wouldn't have had access to a front door, not around here he wouldn't, yet it was into one of these houses he had disappeared. So the place to wait was the back lane.

The back lane was cleaner than many front streets. It was servant territory this, at least two or three maids to a house, hired coaches from the livery stables for the owners and trips abroad in the fashionable months. And little Joe was in one of these houses delivering a message. He was on to something here.

When a back door opened and a man wearing a leather-fronted waistcoat swept some dust into the back lane, he did a brisk walk past the end of the lane and as briskly returned. The man was no longer in sight, all the back gates were closed. He moved up slowly now, past the first one, and the second, then stood between it and the third. It was as he paused that the third door opened and out stepped little Joe.

The small man stood perfectly still and gazed at Rory with a pained expression before he said, 'You shouldn't've, Mr Connor. Now you shouldn't've. You don't know what you're at.' He cast a glance back to the door he had just closed, then hurried on down the lane. And Rory hurried with him.

They were in the main street before the little man slowed his pace, and then Rory said, 'Well now, Joe, what about it?'

And again Joe said, his tone surly now, 'You don't know what you're at, you don't.'

'I know what I'm at Joe.' Rory's voice was grim. 'The buggers that live along there are like those in their mansions up Westoe, they run this town; they control the polis, the shippin', they own the breweries, an' have fingers in the glassworks, chemical works . . . Aye, the chemical works on the Jarrow road. There's one in Ogle Terrace who's on the board. You forget I'm a rent collector, Joe. There's no rent collected in this area. No, they're all owned. But I know about them. Who doesn't? By the morrow I'll find out who's in that particular number and that's all I'll need to know because now I know he's on the fiddle. What is it, Joe? Gamin' or girls . . . lasses?'

'Mr Connor, you'd better mind yourself, aye you'd better.' Little Joe's voice held a note of awe now. 'You want to be careful what you say, he's . . .'

'Aye, aye, I've got the message, Joe, he's powerful. Well now, let's sort this thing out, eh? He's one of two things: he's a man who likes a game or he's a man who runs a game. We'll leave the lasses out of it for the time being, eh? Now havin' the kind of mind I have, Joe, I would say he's a man who runs a game, and likely in that house, 'cos if he wanted to go some place else for a game he wouldn't need you as a runner. A man in his position would have a key to open any door, even the ones in Newcastle. And there's some big games there, aren't there, Joe? No pitch an' toss, Joe, it's Twenty-Ones, or Black Jack, whatever name they care to call it; isn't it, Joe?'

He looked down on the little man, and although the twilight was bringing with it an icy blast Joe was sweating. He now said in some agitation, 'Let's get out of this crush.'

'Anything you say, Joe. Where you makin' for now?'

'I've got to go up Mile End Road.'

'Another message?'

'No, no.' The little man now turned on him and, his tone for the first time really nasty, he said, 'An' there's one thing I'm gona tell you. Whatever comes of this you'd better not let on 'cos . . . an' I'm not funnin', Mr Connor, with what I'm about to say, but things could happen, aye, things could happen.'

'I've no doubt of it, Joe.'

'Don't be funny, Mr Connor.'

'I'm not being funny, Joe, believe you me. Things are happenin' all the time along the waterfront an' I should imagine in Plynlimmon Way an' all. Now, you know me, Joe, I'm as good as me word. If I've owed you a couple of bob in the past you've got it, haven't you, with a bit tacked on? And I've never had a win on a race but I've seen you all right, haven't I? And I haven't got a loose tongue either. So look, Joe.' He stopped and bent down to the little man. 'All I want from you is to get me set on in a decent school.'

'They go in for big stakes, Mr Connor.' The little fellow's voice was quiet again.

'That's what I want, Joe.'

'But you haven't got that kind of ready. You couldn't start in some of them under ten quid, an' that's so much hen grit.'

'You say some of them, there must be a few who start on less. I'll come to t'others later on. Aye, Joe, the big ones, I'll come to them later on, but in the meantime . . .'

The little man blinked, gnawed at his lip, looked down to the cobbles on which they were standing, as if considering. Then his eyes narrowing, he squinted up into Rory's face, saying conspiratorially, 'There's one in Corstorphine Town I might manage; it's not all that cop but they can rise to five quid a night.'

'It'll do to start with, Joe.'

'An' you'll say nowt about?' He jerked his head backwards.

'No, Joe, I'll say nowt about. . .' Now Rory imitated Joe's gesture, then added, 'Until you take me in there.'

'That'll be the day, Mr Connor.'

'Aye, that'll be the day, Joe. An' it mightn't be far ahead.'

'You worry me, Mr Connor.'

'I won't get you into any trouble, Joe, don't you worry.' Rory's tone was kindly now.

'Oh, it isn't that that worries me, it's what'll happen to you, if you take a wrong step. You don't know this game, Mr Connor.'

'I can play cards, Joe.'

'Aye, I've heard tell you can. But there's rules, Mr Connor, rules.'

'I'll stick to the rules, Joe.'

'But what if you come up against those who don't stick to them, Mr Connor?'

'I'll deal with them when I come to them, Joe. Now this place in Corstorphine Town.'

'What time is it now?' Joe looked up into the darkening sky, then stated, 'On four I should say.'

'Aye, on four, Joe.'

'Well on seven, meet me at the dock gates.'

'Seven, Joe, at the dock gates. I'll be there. And thanks.' He bent down to him. 'You won't regret it. I'll see to you, you won't regret it.'

Once again Rory watched the little man hurry away, his feet, like those of a child, almost tripping over each other. Then almost on the point of a run himself he made for home.

When he entered the kitchen Jimmy stared at him, exclaiming almost on a stutter, 'I told them –' he indicated both his mother and Lizzie with a wave of his hand – 'I told them you met a fellow an' you were going to . . . to see the turns.'

'So I am, but it was so bloomin' cold walkin' around waiting, he's gone home for his tea. I was going to ask him up but thought the better of it. But I wouldn't mind something.' He looked towards Ruth. 'I'm froze inside and out. I'm meeting him at seven again.'

'Aw –' Jimmy smiled broadly now – 'you're meeting him at seven? And you're going to see the turns?'

'Aye, we're going to see the turns.'

As Lizzie, walking into the scullery, repeated as if to herself, 'Going to see the turns,' Rory cast a hard glance towards her. She knew what turns he was going to see; you couldn't hoodwink her, blast her. But Ruth believed him. She came to him now, smiling and saying, 'Give me your coat and come to the fire; I'll have something on the table for you in a minute or so.'

He grinned at Ruth. He liked her, aye, you could say he loved her. Why couldn't she have been his mother? Blast the other one. And blast his da. They were a couple of whoring nowts. Aw, what did it matter? He had got his foot in, and Jimmy would get his yard, and he and Janie would be married and they would live in that house overlooking the water. And Jimmy would build up a business and he would help him. Aye, with every spare minute he had he'd help him. He knew nowt about boats but he'd learn, he was quick to learn anything, and he'd have his game and he'd have Janie. Aye, he'd have Janie.

It did not occur to him that he had placed her after the game.

CHAPTER 3

All the while she kept looking from one to the other of them, but they remained smilingly silent. Then she burst out, 'But the money! You've got the money to buy this?' Flinging both arms wide as with joy she gazed about the long room.

'Well –' Rory pursed his lips – 'enough, enough to put down as a deposit.'

'He didn't get in till six this mornin'.' Jimmy was nodding up at her, and she turned to Rory and said, 'Gamin'?'

'Yes. Yes, Miss Waggett, that's what they call it, gamin'.'

'And you won?'

'I wouldn't be here showing you this else.'

'How much?'

'Ah well' – he looked away to the side – 'Almost eleven pounds at the beginning, but' – he gnawed on his lips for a moment – 'I couldn't manage to get away then, I had to stay on and play. But I was six up anyway when I left.'

'Six pounds?'

'Aye, six pounds.'

'And this place is costin' thirty-five?'

'Aye. But five pounds'll act as a starter. Jimmy's goin' to get the address of the son and I'll write to him the morrow.'

There was silence between them for a moment until Rory, looking at Janie's profile, said, 'What is it?'

'The waterfront, it's . . . it's mostly scum down here.'

'Not this end.'

She turned to Jimmy, 'No?'

'No, they're respectable businesses. You know, woodyards, repair shops, an' things like that. An' there's very few live above the shops. There's nobody on yon side of us, an' just that bit of rough land on the other. Eeh!' he laughed, 'I'm sayin' us, as if we had it already . . .'

'What do you think? Rory was gazing at her.

'Eeh!' She walked the length of the room, put her hand out and touched the chest of drawers, then the brass hinges on the oak chest, then the table, and lastly the rocking chair, and her eyes bright, she looked from one to the other and said, 'Eeh! it's amazing. You would never think from the outside it could be like this 'cos it looks ramshackle. But it's lovely, homely.'

'Look in t'other room.'

She went into the bedroom, then laughed and said, 'That'll come down for a start.'

She was pointing to the hammock, and Rory answered teasingly, 'No. Why, no. Our Jimmy's going to swing in that and we'll lie underneath.'

'Aw you!' Jimmy pushed at the air with his flat hand, then said, 'I'll be upstairs, I'll make that grand. Come on, come on up and have a look. Can you manage the ladder?'

Janie managed the ladder, and then she was standing under the sloping roof looking from one end of the attic to the other and she exclaimed again, 'Eeh! my ! did you ever see so many bits of paper and maps and books and things? There's more books here than there are in the master's cases in his study.'

'Aye.' Jimmy now walked up and down the room as if he were already in possession of the place, saying, 'By the time I get this lot sorted out I'll be able to read all right.'

'Talkin' of reading.' Janie turned to Rory. 'The mistress is having a teacher come in for the children, sort of part time daily governess. She said I could sit in with them. What do you think of that?'

'You won't be sittin' in with them long enough to learn the alphabet. And anyway, I'll teach you all you want to know once I get you here, an' you won't have any spare time for reading.'

'Rory!' She glanced in mock indignation from him to Jimmy, and Jimmy, his head slightly bowed and his lids lowered, made for the ladder, muttering, 'I'm goin' to see if there's any wood drifted up.'

Alone together, they looked at each other; then with a swift movement he pulled her into his arms and kissed her. He kissed her long and hard and, her eyes closed tightly, she responded to him, that was until his hand slid to her buttocks, and then with an effort she slowly but firmly withdrew from him, and they stood, their faces red and hot, staring at each other.

'I want you, Janie.' His voice was thick.

Her eyes were closed again and her head was nodding in small jerks and her fingers were moving round her lips wiping the moisture from them as she muttered softly through them, 'I know, I know, but ... but not until ... no, no, not until. I'd ... be frightened.'

'There's nothing to be frightened of. You know me, you're the only one for me, always have been, an' ever will be. There's nothing to be frightened ...'

'I know, I know, Rory, but I can't, I daren't.' She was flapping both hands at him now. 'There's me da, an' me grannie, and all the others.'

He was making to hold her again. 'Nothing'll happen, just once.'

'Aw –' she now actually laughed in his face – 'me grannie's always told me, she fell the first night. An' you can, you can ... Eeh!' She now pressed her fingers tightly across her mouth. 'I shouldn't be talkin' like this. You shouldn't make me talk like this. It isn't proper, we're ... we're not married.'

'Don't be daft, we're as good as married. I tell you there's only you, there's only ...'

'No, Rory, no, not until it's done.' She thrust his hands away. 'I mean proper like in the church, signed and sealed. No, no, I'm sorry. I love you, oh, I do love you, Rory, I've loved you all me life. I've never even thought of another lad an' I'm twenty. I can't tell you how I love you, it eats me up, but even so I want to start proper like so you won't be able to throw anythin' back at me after.'

'What you talking about?' He had her by the shoulders now actually shaking her. 'Me throw anything back at you? Actually thinking I'd do a thing like that?'

'You're a man and they all do. Me grannie ...'

'Blast your grannie! Blast her to hell's flames! She's old. Things were different in her day.'

'Not that. That wasn't any different. Never will be. It's the only thing a woman's really looked down on for. Even if you were to steal you wouldn't have a stamp put on you like you would have if ... if you had a bairn.'

'You won't have ...'

'Rory, no. I tell you no. We've waited this long, what's a few more months?'

'I could be dead, you could be dead.'

'We'll have to take a chance on that.'

'You know, Janie, you're hard; there's a hard streak in you, always has been about some things ...'

'I'm not.' Her voice was trembling. 'I'm not hard.'

'Yes you are. . . .'

'I'm not. I'm not.'

'All right, all right. Aw, don't cry. I'm sorry, I am. Don't cry.'

'I'm not hard.'

'No, you're not, you're lovely . . . It's all right. Look, it's all right; I just want to hold you.'

When his arms went about her she jerked herself from his hold once more and going to the window, stood stiffly looking down on to the river, and he stood as stiffly watching her. Only his jaw moved as his teeth ground against each other.

She drew in a deep breath now and, her head turning from one side to the other, she looked up and down the river. As far as her eyes could see both to the right and to the left the banks were lined with craft, ships of all types and sizes, from little scullers, wherries and tugs to great funnelled boats, and here and there a masted ship, its lines standing out separated and graceful from the great iron hulks alongside.

Rory now came slowly to the window and, putting his arm around her shoulders and his manner softened, he said, 'Look. Look along there. You see that boat with a figurehead on it – there's a fine lass for you . . . Look at her bust, I bet that's one of Thomas Anderson's pieces, and I'll bet he enjoyed makin' it.'

'Rory!'

He hugged her to him now and laughed, then said, 'There's the ferry boat right along there going off to Newcastle . . . one of the pleasure trips likely. Think on that, eh? We could take a trip up to Newcastle on a Sunday, and in the week there'll always be somethin' for you to look at. The river's alive during the week.'

She turned her head towards him now and said, 'You said the rent's three and six?'

'Aye.'

'You won't get anything from Jimmy, not until he gets set-in.'

'I know, I know that. But we'll manage. I'll still be workin'. I'll keep on until we really do get set-in and make a business of it. I mightn't be able to build a boat but I'll be able to steer one, and I can shovel coal and hump bales with the rest of them. I didn't always scribble in a rent book you know; I did me stint in the Jarrow chemical works, and in the bottle works afore that.'

'I know, I know, but I was just thinkin'. Something the mistress said.'

'What did she say?'

'Well –' she turned from him and walked down the length of the room – 'she doesn't want me to leave, I know that, she said as much.' She swung round again. 'Do you know she even said to me face that she'd miss me.

Fancy her sayin' that.'

'Of course she'll miss you, anybody would.' He came close to her again and held her face between his hands. 'I'd miss you. If I ever lost you I'd miss you. God, how I'd miss you! Oh, Janie.'

'Don't . . . not for a minute. Listen.' She pushed his hands from under her oxters now and said, 'Would you demand I be at home all day?'

'I don't know about demand, but I'd want you at home all day. Aye, of course I would. Who's to do the cooking and the washing and the like? What are you gettin' at?'

'Well, it was something the mistress said. She said she had been thinking about raising me wage . . .'

'Ah, that was just a feeler. Now look, she's not going to put you off, is she?'

'No, no, she's not. She knows I'm goin' to be married. Oh, she knows that, but what she said was, if . . . if I could come for a while, daily like, until the children got a bit bigger and used to somebody else, because well, as she said, they were fond of me, the bairns. And she would arrange for Bessie to have my room and sleep next to them at night and I needn't be there until eight in the morning, and I could leave at half-six after I got them to bed.'

He swung away from her, his arms raised above his head, his hands flapping towards the low roof, and he flapped them until he reached the end of the room and turned about and once more was standing in front of her. And then, thrusting his head forward, he said, 'Look, you're going to be married, you're going to start married life the way we mean to go on. You'll be me wife, an' I just don't want you from half-past six or seven at night till eight in the morning, I want you here all the time. I want you here when I come in at dinner-time an' at tea-time.'

'She'll give me three shillings a week. It's not to be sneezed at, it would nearly pay the rent.'

'Look. Look, we'll manage. A few more games like last night, even if nothing bigger, and I can spit in the eye of old Kean . . . and your master and mistress.'

'Don't talk like that!' She was indignant now. 'Spittin' in their eye! They've been good to me, better than anybody in me life. I've been lucky. Why, I must be the best-treated servant in this town, or in any other. She's kept me in clothes. And don't forget –' she was now wagging her head at him – 'when things were rough a few years ago with their damned strikes and such, she gave me a loaded basket every week-end. And your own belly would have been empty many a time if I hadn't have brought it. Meat, flour, sugar . . .'

'All right, all right; have you got to be grateful for a little kindness all your life? Anyway, it was nothing to them. The only time that kind of charity has any meaning is when the giver has to do without themselves. She likely throws as much in the midden every week.'

'We haven't got a midden, as you call it.'

'You know what I mean.'

Both their voices were lowering now and in a broken tone she replied, 'No, I don't know what you mean. There's things about you I don't understand, never have.'

He didn't move towards her but turned his head on his shoulder and looked sideways at her for some seconds before saying, 'You said you loved me.'

'Aye, aye, I did, but you can love somebody and not understand them. I might as well tell you I don't understand how you're always taken up so much with cards. It's a mania with you, and I shouldn't be surprised that when we're married you'll be like the rest of them; the others go out every night to the pubs but you'll go out to your gamin'.'

'I'll only go gamin' when I want money to get you things.'

'That'll be your excuse, you'll go gamin' because you can't stop gamin', it's like something in your blood. Even as far back as when we went gathering rose hips you wanted to bet on how many you could hold in your fist.'

They were staring at each other now, and he said, 'You don't want to come here then?'

'Aw yes, yes. Aw Rory.' She went swiftly towards him and leant against him. Then after a moment she muttered, 'I want to be where you are, but . . . but at the same time I feel I owe them something. You don't see them as I do. But . . . but don't worry, I'll tell her.'

He looked at her softly now as he said, 'It wouldn't work. And anyway I want me wife to meself, I don't want her to be like the scum, gutting fish, or going tatie pickin' to make ends meet. I want to take care of you, I want a home of me own, with bairns and me wife at the fireside.'

She nodded at him, saying, 'You're right, Rory, you're right,' while at the same time the disconcerting mental picture of Kathleen Leary flashed across the screen of her mind. Mrs Leary had borne sixteen children and she was worn out, tired and worn out, and she knew that Rory was the kind of man who'd give her sixteen children if he could. Well, that was life, wasn't it? Yes, but she wasn't sure if she was going to like that kind of life. She drew herself gently from him now and made for the trap door, saying, 'I'll have to get started on some sewing, I haven't got all that much in me chest.'

As he took her hand to help her down on to the first step she looked up at him and said, 'The mistress is goin' to give me me bed linen. I didn't tell you, did I?'

'No.'

'Well, she is. And that'll be something, won't it?'

'Aye, that'll be something.'

As he looked down into her face he stopped himself from adding, 'She can keep her bloody bed linen, I'll make enough afore long to smother you in bed linen.'

CHAPTER 4

Rory didn't make enough money in a very short time to smother Janie in bed linen. By the third week of the New Year he had managed to acquire only a further eight pounds and this after four Saturday nights' sittings. And the reason wasn't because of his bad play or ill luck, it was because he was playing against fiddlers, cheats, a small gang who worked together and stood by each other like the close-knit members of a family.

Well, he was finished with the Corstorphine Town lot, and he had told little Joe either he got him into a good school or he himself would do a little investigating into No. 3 Plynlimmon Way. He could have told him he had already done some investigating and that the occupier, a Mr Nickle, was a shipowner. Even if not in an ostentatious way, nevertheless he was big enough to be a member of the shipowners' association, known as the Coal Trade Committee, which had its club and meeting room in a house on the Lawe. Moreover, he was understood to have shares in a number of businesses in the town, including those which dealt not only with the victualling of ships with bread and beef but also in ships' chandlery. And then there was the tallow factory, and many other smaller businesses. In his favour it could be said that he subscribed to such causes as distressed seamen and their families. And at times there were many of these; the bars along the waterfront were not always full, nor the long dance rooms attached to them in which the sailors jigged with the women they picked up.

Mr Nickle had also been a strong advocate for better sewerage, especially since the outbreak of cholera in '66, and the smallpox outbreak in 1870. He had helped, too, to bring about the new Scavenging Department under the Borough Engineer. Before this the removal of the filth of the town had been left to contractors.

Oh, Mr Nickle was a good man, Rory wasn't saying a thing against him, but Mr Nickle had a failing which was looked at askance by the temperance societies and the respectable members of the community.

And although Rory himself thought none the less of Mr Nickle, for if the

crowned heads could gamble . . . and it was well known that Bertie, the
Prince of Wales, was a lad at the game, why not Mr Nickle, and why not
Rory Connor, or any working man for that matter? But it was the same
injustice here, one law for the rich, another for the poor. Yet these
sentiments did not deter him from harassing, or even threatening little
Joe, nor did little Joe see any injustice in Mr Connor's treatment of him.
He had a rough-hewn philosophy: there were gents of all grades, there
were the high gents, middle gents, and the lower gents. Mr Connor was of
the lower gents, but his money was as good as anybody else's and often he
was more generous than the middle gents. The real toffs were open
handed, and the waterfront gamblers were free with their money when
they had it, but the middle gents were mean, and although Mr Nickle was
prominent in the town and lived in one of the best ends he was, to little Joe,
a middle gent, in the upper bracket of that section maybe, but still a
middle gent. But he was a man who had power, as had those who worked
for him, and they could be nasty at times.

Little Joe was worried for Mr Connor, but apparently Mr Connor
wasn't worried for himself. In a way Joe admired a fellow like Mr Connor;
he admired his pluck because it was something he hadn't much of himself.

So it was that little Joe spoke to Mr Nickle's man. Mr Nickle's man was
a kind of valet-cum-butler-cum-doorman, and his wife was Mr Nickle's
housekeeper, and his two daughters were Mr Nickle's parlour-maid and
housemaid respectively. Altogether it was another close-knit family.
There was no Mrs Nickle, she had died some years previously.

Little Joe did not lie about Mr Connor's position, that is not exactly.
What he said was, he was a gent in the property business. Also, that he
played a good hand and was very discreet. He had known him for some
years and had set him on in schools along the waterfront, and he had
added that, as he understood that two of Mr Nickle's friends had passed
away recently, he had stressed the word friends, he wondered if Mr Nickle
was looking for a little new blood. One thing he told Mr Nickle's man he
could assure his master of, and that was Mr Connor was no sponger.

Mr Nickle's man said he would see what could be done. What he meant
was he would look into Mr Connor's mode of business. He did.

When next little Joe met Rory all he could say was, 'I've got you set-in
for a game in a place in Ocean Road, just near the Workhouse.'

'Do you think you'll make it the night, Rory?' Jimmy asked under his
breath as he stood near the door watching Rory pull on his overcoat.

'I'll have a damned good try, I can't say better. It's a new place; I'll
have to see how the land lies, won't I?'

'You'll find yourself lying under the land if you're not careful.'

Rory turned his dark gaze on to Lizzie where she sat at one side of a long mat frame jabbing a steel progger into the stretched hessian. He watched her thrust in a clipping of rag, pull it tightly down from underneath with her left hand, then jab the progger in again before he said, 'You'd put the kibosh on God, you would.'

Ruth looked up from where she was sitting at the other side of the frame. In the lamplight her face appeared delicate and sad, and she shook her head at him, it was a gentle movement, before she said, 'Just take care of yourself that's all.'

'I've always had to, haven't I?'

'Aw, there speaks the big fellow who brought himself up. Suckled yourself from your own breasts you did.'

Rory now grabbed his hard hat which Jimmy was holding towards him, then wrenching open the door, he went out.

It was a fine night. The air was sharp, the black sky was high and star-filled. He could even make out the gate because of their brightness, and also with the help of the light from Learys' window. They never drew their blinds, the Learys.

He picked his way carefully down the narrow lane so that he shouldn't splash his boots. He had also taken the precaution of bringing a piece of rag with him in order to wipe them before he should enter this new place because the houses in King Street and down Ocean Road were mostly decent places.

The rage that Lizzie always managed to evoke in him had subsided by the time he reached Leam Lane and entered the docks. And he decided that if there was a cab about he'd take a lift. But then it wasn't very likely there'd be one around the docks, unless it was an empty one coming back from some place.

He didn't find a cab, so he had to walk all the way down to Ocean Road, a good couple of miles.

Although the streets were full of people and the roads still packed with traffic, but mostly flat carts, drays and barrows now, he kept to the main thoroughfare because the bairns seemed to go mad on a Saturday night up the side streets, and in some parts lower down in the town one of their Saturday night games was to see which of them could knock your hat off with a handful of clarts. The devil's own imps some of them were. Once he would have laughed at their antics, but not since the time he'd had a dead kitten slapped across his face.

The market place was like a beehive; the stalls illuminated with naphtha flares held every description of food, household goods, and clothing; the latter mostly second, third and fourth hand. The smells were mixed and pungent, and mostly strong, especially those emanating from the fish and meat stalls.

In King Street the gas lamps were ablaze. People stood under them in groups, while others gazed into the shop windows. Saturday night was a popular night for window-gazing and there was no hurry to buy even if you wanted to; the supplies never ran out and most of the shops were open until ten o'clock, some later.

He stopped within a few yards of his destination. He had come down here last night to make sure of the number. It was a corner house, not all that prosperous looking but not seedy. He stopped and rubbed his boots vigorously with the rag, then threw it into the gutter, after which he straightened his coat, tilted his hard hat slightly to the side, pulled at the false starched cuffs that were pinned to the ends of his blue-striped flannelette shirt sleeves, then, following little Joe's directions, he went round the corner, down some area steps, and knocked on the door.

He was surprised when it was opened by a maid, a maid of all work by the look of her, but nevertheless a maid.

'Aye?' She peered up at him in the fluttering light from a naked gas jar attached to a bracket sticking out from the wall opposite the door, and in answer he said what Joe had told him to say. 'Me name's Connor. Little Joe sent me.'

'Oh aye. Come in.'

He followed her into a room which by its appearance was a kitchen and, after closing the door, she said, 'Stay a minute'; then left him. A few minutes later she returned, accompanied by a man. He was a middle-aged half-caste, an Arab one, he surmised. It was his hair and his nostrils which indicated his origin. He looked Rory up and down, then said in a thick Geordie accent that was at variance with his appearance, 'Little Joe said you wanted a set-in. That right?'

'That's right.'

'You've got the ready?'

'Enough.'

'Show us.'

Rory stared back into the dull eyes; then slowly he lifted up the tail of his coat, put his hand in his inside pocket and brought out a handful of coins, among which were a number of sovereigns and half-sovereigns. Without speaking he thrust his hand almost into the other man's chest.

The man looked down on it, nodded and said briefly 'Aye.' Then turning about, he said, 'Come on.'

As they passed from the kitchen into the narrow passage the man said over his shoulder, 'You'll be expected to stand your turn with the cans. Little Joe tell you?'

Little Joe hadn't told him but he said, 'I'll stand me turn.'

The man now led the way into another room, and Rory saw at once that it was used as a storage place for some commodity that was packed in wooden boxes. A number of such were arrayed along one wall. The only window in the place was boarded up. There was an old-fashioned stove at one side of the room packed high with blazing coals, and the room was lit by two bracket gas lamps. There were six men in the room besides Rory's companion and himself; four of them were in a game at the table, the other two were looking on. The players didn't look up but the two spectators turned towards Rory and the half-caste with a jerk of his head said, 'This's who I was tellin' you about. Connor –' he turned to Rory – 'What's your first name?'

'Rory.'

'What!'

'Ror-ry.'

'Funny name. Haven't heard that afore.'

The two spectators at the table nodded towards Rory and he nodded back at them. Then the man with arm outstretched named the players one after the other for Rory's benefit.

Rory didn't take much heed to the names until the word Pittie was repeated twice. Dan Pittie and Sam Pittie. The two brothers almost simultaneously glanced up at him, nodded, then turned their attention to the game again.

Rory, standing awkwardly to the side of the fireplace, looked from one to the other of the men, then brought his attention back to the two Pitties. They looked like twins. They were bullet-headed men, heavy-shouldered but short. These must be the fellows, together with a third one, who Jimmy said had started the keel business from nothing. They looked a tough pair, different from their partners at the table, who didn't look river-front types; the elder of the two could have been Mr Kean; he wasn't unlike him, and was dressed in much the same fashion.

Well, he had certainly moved up one from Corstorphine Town, because, for a start, they were playing Twenty-Ones, but as yet he didn't know whether he liked the promotion or not; he certainly didn't like the half-caste. But he wasn't here to like or dislike any of them, he was here to double the money in his pocket and then see that he got safely outside with it. On the last thought he looked from the half-caste to the Pittie brothers again and thought it would take him to keep his wits about him. Aye . . . aye, it would that.

CHAPTER 5

'You're tellin' me she's in the family way?'

'Don't put it like that, man.'

'How do you expect me to put it? You bloody fool you, how did you manage it? On the ferry or in the train? . . . All right, all right.' He thrust John George's raised arm aside. 'But I mean just what I say, for you've seen her for an hour or so a week, so you've told me, when you've taken her around Newcastle making a tour of ancient buildings. From the Central Station into Jesmond Dene, there doesn't seem to be one you've missed, so that's why I ask you . . . Aw, man . . .'

They were standing on a piece of open land. A building was being erected to one side of it while at the other old houses were being knocked down. There was a thin drizzle of rain falling, the whole scene was dismal and it matched John George's dejected appearance. His thin shoulders were hunched, his head hung down, his gaze was directed towards the leather bag in his hand but without seeing it. He mumbled now, 'It's all right. Don't worry, I'll manage. I'm sorry I asked you; you'll want everything you can lay hands on to get the yard, I know.'

'It isn't that. You can have the two pounds, but what good's that going to do you in this fix, I ask you. It's a drop in the ocean and what'll happen when she tells her folks?'

John George raised his eyes and looked up into the grey sky. 'God! . . . I just don't know. He'll be for murdering her. He's an awful man from what I can gather. I want to get her out of there afore he finds out.'

'How far is she?'

'Over . . . over three months.'

'Well, it won't be long then will it afore he twigs something?'

Rory shook his head, then put his hand into his back pocket, pulled out a small bag and extracted from it two sovereigns, and as he did so his teeth ground tightly together. This was putting him in a fix, he'd had just five pounds left to make a start the night, and it could be a big night, now he was left with only three.

He hadn't won anything that first Saturday night down in the cellar but he hadn't lost either, he had broken even. And the following week he had just managed to clear three pounds ten; the week after he was nine pounds up at one o'clock in the morning, but by the time he left it had been reduced to four pounds, and even then they hadn't liked it. No, none of them had liked it, the Pittie brothers least of all.

Last week when he had cleared six he said he was calling it a day and, aiming to be jocular, had added, and a night. It was the elder of the Pittie brothers who had looked at him and said, 'No, not yet, lad.' But he had risen to his feet, gathered his winnings up and stared back at the other man as he replied, grimly, 'Aye, right now, lad. Nobody's going to tell me when I come or go. I'll be along next week and you can have your own back then, but I'm off now.'

There had followed an odd silence in the room, it was a kind of rustling silence as one man after the other at the table moved in his seat. 'So long,' he had said, and not until he was up the steps and into the street did he breathe freely. For a moment he had thought they were going to do him. He had decided then that that was the last time he would go there.

Three times this week he had tried to find little Joe but with no success. He was keeping out of his way apparently, so there was nothing for it if he wanted a game but to show up in the cellar again the night.

He never went with less than five pounds on him and he'd had a job to scrape that up today because during the week he had, by putting twelve pounds ten down, cleared half the cost of the boat yard, and signed an agreement that the other seventeen pounds ten was to be paid within six weeks, and he knew, his luck holding out and as long as he didn't get into a crooked game, he would clear that. One thing about them in the cellar, they played a straight game. Anyway, they had so far.

But if he went in with only three and lost that in a run, well then, the sparks would fly. He'd have to put his thinking cap on. Oh, this bloody fool of a fellow.

As he handed the two sovereigns to John George and received his muttered thanks he asked himself where he could lay his hands on a couple of quid. It was no good asking any of them back in the house. His dad usually blew half his wages before he got home; by the time he had cleared the slate for the drinks he had run up during the week Ruth was lucky if there was ten shillings left on the mantelpiece for her. There was Janie; she had a bit saved but he doubted if it would be as much as two pounds. Anyway, he wouldn't be able to see her until the morrow and that would be too late. Oh, he'd like to take his hand and knock some damn sense into John George Armstrong.

They were walking on now, cutting through the side streets towards the market and the office, and they didn't exchange a word. When they reached the office door they cast a glance at each other out of habit as if to say, Now for it once again, but when the door didn't move under Rory's push he shook it, then, looking at John George, said, 'That's funny.'

'Use your key. Aw, here's mine.'

John George pushed the key into the lock and they went into the office and looked about them. The door to the far room was closed but on the front of the first desk was pinned a notice and they both bent down and read it. There was no heading, it just said, 'Been called away, my father has died. Lock up takings. My daughter will collect on Monday.' There was no signature.

They straightened up and looked at each other; then Rory jerked his head as he said, 'Well, this's one blessin' in disguise, for I've had the worst morning in years. He'd have gone through the roof.'

'Funny that,' John George smiled weakly; 'my takings are up the day, over four pounds. About fifteen of them paid something off the back and there wasn't one closed door.'

'That's a record.'

'Aye.' John George now went towards the inner office, saying, 'I hope he hasn't forgot to leave the key for the box.'

Standing behind Mr Kean's desk and, having opened the top drawer on the right-hand side, John George put his hand into the back of it and withdrew a key; then going to an iron box safe that was screwed down on to a bench table in the corner of the room he unlocked it. He now took out the money from his bag, put the sovereigns into piles of five and placed them in a neat row on the top shelf with the smaller change in front of them, and after placing his book to the side of the compartment he stepped back and let Rory put his takings on the bottom shelf.

As John George locked the door he remarked, 'One day he'll get a proper safe.'

'It would be a waste of money, it's never in there long enough for anybody to get at it.'

'It'll lie in there over the week-end, and has done afore.'

'Well, that's his look-out. Come on.'

John George now replaced the key in the back of the drawer; then they both left, locking the outer door behind them.

As they walked towards Laygate, Rory said stiffly, 'What you going to do about this other business, have you got anything in mind?'

'Aye. Aye, I have. I'm going to ask her the day. I'm going to ask her to just walk out and come to our place. She can stay hidden up there until we can get married in the registry office.'

'Registry office?'

'Aye, registry office. It's just as bindin' as any place else.'

'It isn't the same.'

'Well, it'll have to do for us.'

'Aw, man.' Rory shook his head slowly. 'You let people walk over you; you're so bloomin' soft.'

'I'm as God made me, we can't help being what we are.'

'You can help being a bloody fool, you're not a bairn.'

'Well, what do you expect me to do, leave her?'

'You needn't shout unless you want the whole street to know.'

They walked on in silence until simultaneously they both stopped at the place where their roads divided.

'See you Monday then.' Rory's tone was kindly now and John George, looking at him, said, 'Aye, see you Monday. And thanks Rory. I'll pay you back, I promise I'll pay you back.'

'I'm not afraid of that, you always have.'

'Aw . . . I wish, I wish I was like you, Rory. You're right, I'm too soft to clag holes with, no gumption. I can never say no.'

It was on the tip of Rory's tongue to come back with the retort, 'And neither can your lass apparently.' Janie had said no, and she'd kept both feet on the ground when she said it an' all. But what he said and generously was, 'People like you for what you are. You're a good bloke.' He made a small movement with his fist. 'I'll tell you something. You're better liked than me, especially up in our house. It's John George this, an' John George that.'

'A, go on, man, stop pulling me leg. But it's nice of you to say it nevertheless, and as I said –' he patted his pocket – 'I won't forget this.'

'That's all right, man. So long, and good luck.'

'So long . . . so long, Rory. And thanks. Thanks again.'

They went their ways, neither dreaming he would never see the other again.

When Rory went into the cellar that same evening he had eight pounds in his pocket.

The Pittie brothers were already at the table, but the two men partnering them were unknown to Rory until he realized that one of them was the third Pittie brother. He was a man almost a head taller than the other two. His nose was flattened and looked boneless. This was the one who was good with his fists, so he had heard, but by the look of him he wasn't all that good for his face looked like a battered pluck. The fourth man looked not much bigger than little Joe and he had a foxy look, but he was well put on. His suit, made of some kind of tweed, looked quite fancy, as did his pearl-buttoned waistcoat. During the course of conversation later in the evening he discovered that he was from across the water in North Shields and was manager of a blacking factory.

Rory kicked his heels for almost an hour before he got set-in at the table, for after the game they spent quite some time drinking beer and eating meat sandwiches. Although he always stood his share in buying the beer he drank little of it and tonight less than usual, for he wanted to keep his wits about him. Some part of him was worried at the presence of the third Pittie brother, it was creating a small niggling fear at the back of his mind.

The big Pittie was dealer. He shuffled the cards in a slow ponderous way until Rory wanted to say, 'Get on with it'; then of a sudden he spoke. 'You aimin' to buy old Kilpatrick's yard I hear?'

Rory was startled, and he must have shown it for the big fellow jerked his chin upwards as he said, 'Oh, you can't keep nowt secret on the waterfront; there's more than scum comes in on the tide . . . Your young 'un works at Baker's, don't he?'

'Aye. Yes, he works at Baker's.'

'What does he expect to do at Kilpatrick's, build a bloody battleship?'

The three brothers now let out a combined bellow and the thin man in the fancy waistcoat laughed with them, although it was evident he didn't know what all this was about.

Rory's lower jaw moved from one side to the other before he said, 'He's going to build scullers and small keel-like boats.'

'Keel-like boats. Huh!' It was the youngest of the Pittie's speaking now. 'Where's he gona put them?'

'Where they belong, on the river.'

'By God! he'll be lucky, you can hardly get a plank atween the boats now. And what's he gonna do with the keel-like boats when he gets them on the water, eh?'

'Same as you, work them, or sell them.'

As the three pairs of eyes became fixed on him he told himself to go steady, these fellows meant business, they weren't here the night only for the game. He kept his gaze steady on them as he said, 'Well now, since you know what I have in mind, are we going to play?'

The big fellow returned to his shuffling. Then he dealt. When Rory picked up his cards he thought, Bad start, good finish.

And so it would seem. He lost the first game, won the next two, lost the next one, then won three in a row. By one o'clock in the morning he had a small pile of sovereigns and a larger pile of silver to his hand. Between then and two o'clock the pile went down a little before starting again to increase steadily.

At the end of a game when the man in the fancy waistcoat had no money in front of him he said he must be going. He had, he said, lost enough for one night and what was more he'd have to find somebody to scull him across the river. And at this time of the morning whoever he found would certainly make him stump up, and what he had left, he thought, was just about enough to carry him over.

When Rory, too, also voiced that he must be on his way there were loud, even angry cries from the table.

'Aw, no, no, lad,' said the big fellow. 'Fair's fair. You've taken all our bloody money so give us a chance to get a bit of it back, eh? We've to get across the river an' all.' There was laughter at this, but it was without mirth.

And so another game started, and long before it finished the uneasy sickly feeling in the pit of Rory's stomach had grown into what he hated to admit was actual fear.

Another hour passed and it was towards the end of a game when things were once again going in Rory's favour that the youngest Pittie brother began speaking of Jimmy as if he were continuing the conversation that had centred around him earlier in the play.

'Your young 'un's bandy,' he said. 'Bandy Connor they call him along the front . . . Saw him from the boat t'other day. Drive a horse and cart through his legs you could.' He now punched his brother in the side of the chest and the brother guffawed: 'Aye, his mother must have had him astride a donkey.'

Any reference to the shape of Jimmy's legs had always maddened Rory; he had fought more fights on Jimmy's account than he had on his own. But now, although there was a rage rising in him that for the moment combated his fear, he warned himself to go steady, for they were up to something. They were like three bull terriers out to bait a bull. He was no bull, but they were bull terriers all right.

The stories of their past doings flicked across the surface of his mind and increased his rising apprehension, yet did not subdue his rage, even while the cautionary voice kept saying, 'Careful, careful, let them get on with it. Get yourself outside, let them get on with it.'

When he made no reply to the taunt, one after another, the three brothers laid down their cards and looked at him, and he at them. Then slowly he placed his cards side by side on the table.

. The three Pitties and the half-caste stared at his cards and they did not lift their eyes when his hand went out and drew the money from the centre of the table towards him. Not until he pushed his chair back and got to his feet did one of them speak. It was the youngest brother. 'You goin' then?' he said.

'Aye.' Rory moved his head slowly downwards.

'You've had a good night.'

'You all had the same chance.'

'I would argue about that.'

'Would you?'

'I think you had a trick or two up your sleeve.'

'What! Then search me if you've got a mind.'

'Aw, no need for that, I wasn't meanin' the actual cards. But you're a bit of a clever bugger, aren't you?'

'I'm bucked that you think so.' He stood buttoning his coat, and noted that the half-caste was no longer in the room. He picked up his hat from a side table and went towards the door, saying, 'So long then.'

The brothers didn't speak. When he pulled at the door it didn't open. He tugged at it twice before turning and looking back into the room. The three men had risen from the table. He stared at them and now the fear swept over him like a huge wave and his stomach heaved.

'What you standing there for? Can't you get out?'

The big fellow was approaching him, his arms hanging loosely at his sides. But strangely it wasn't the fellow's arms or his face that Rory looked at, but his feet. He hadn't noticed them before. They were enormous feet encased in thick hob-nailed boots. The boots had the dull sheen of tallow on them with which they had likely been greased.

When the arms sprang up and grabbed at his shoulders Rory struck out, right, then left; right, then left, but his blows were the wild desperate punches used in the back lanes or among the lads in a scrap, as often happened in a work's yard.

He remembered hearing the big fellow laugh just before the great fist struck his jaw and seemed to snap his head from his body.

He was on the floor now and he screamed when the boot caught him in the groin. Then he was on his feet again, somebody holding him while another belted into him, the big fellow. They left it all to the big fellow. He was still struggling to hit out but like a child swapping flies when the blow came under his chin, and once more he was on his back. But this time he knew nothing about it. He didn't feel them going through his pockets, nor when the three of them used their feet on him. He was quite unaware of being hoisted across the big fellow's shoulder and being carried past the half-caste who was standing in the doorway now and up the area steps into the dark side street, then through the back alleyways towards the river.

That he didn't reach the river was due to the appearance of two bulky figures coming through a cut between the warehouses. One was a dark-cloaked priest who had been to a ship to give the last rites to a dying sailor. The man accompanying him was the dead man's friend who was seeing the priest safely back into the town. But to the three brothers their shapes indicated two burly sailors or night-watchmen, and both types could do some dirty fighting on their own, so with a heave they threw the limp body among a tangle of river refuse, broken spars, boxes, and decaying fruit and vegetable, and minutes later the priest and the sailor passed within six feet of it and went on their way.

CHAPTER 6

They were all in the kitchen, Bill Waggett, Gran and Janie – Janie still had her outdoor things on; Collum Leary and Kathleen and with them now was their son Pat; Paddy Connor, Ruth, Jimmy; and lastly Lizzie; and it was Lizzie who, looking at young Pat Leary said, 'Talk sense, lad. 'Tis three o'clock on Sunday afternoon an' he left the house round six last night. Who would be playin' cards all that time I ask you?'

'It's true, Lizzie. 'Tis true. I've heard of games goin' on for twenty-four hours. They win an' lose, win an' lose.'

'He would never stay all this time; something's happened him.'

Nobody contradicted her now but they all turned and looked at Janie who, with fingers pressed tightly against her lower lip, said, 'You should have gone down and told the polis.'

'What should we tell the polis, lass?' Paddy Connor now asked her quietly. 'That me son was out gamin' last night an' hasn't come back? All right, they'll say, let's find him an' push him along the line. Where was he gamin'? I don't know, says I. Lass –' his voice was still gentle – 'we've thought of everything.'

Grannie Waggett, who was the only one seated, now turned in her chair and, her pale eyes sweeping the company, she said, 'If you want my advice the lot of you, you'll stop frashin'. It's as Pat there says, he's got into a game. He's gamin' mad, always has been. It affects some folks like that, like a poison in their blood. Some blokes take to drink, others to whorin' . . .'

'Gran!'

The old woman flashed a look on Janie. 'Whorin' I said, an' whorin' I mean, an' for my part I'd rather have either of them than one that takes to gamin', 'cos with them you're sure of a roof over your head some time, but not with a gamer for he'd gamble the shift off your back an' you inside it. There was this gentleman who used to come to the house when I was in service in Newcastle. Real gentleman, carriage an' pair, fancy wife, mansion, he had. One day he had everything, next day nowt. I tell you, me girl –' she turned and stabbed her finger towards Janie – 'you want to put your foot down right from the start or get used to livin' in the open, for I tell you, you won't be sure of a roof . . .'

'Be quiet, Ma.'

Grannie Waggett turned on her son. 'Don't you tell me to be quiet.'

'Be quiet all of you, please.' It was Ruth speaking gently. 'What I think should be done is somebody should go down to the Infirmary, the new

Infirmary. If anything had happened to him they'd take him there.'

'And make a fool of themselves askin'.'

Ruth now looked at her husband. 'I don't mind lookin' a fool, I'll go.'

'No, Ma.' Jimmy who had not opened his mouth so far went towards the bottom of the ladder now, saying, 'I'll go, I'll change me things an' I'll go.'

As he mounted upwards Collum said, 'It's odd it is that he made no mention of whereabouts he'd be, now isn't it? But then again perhaps it isn't; if he'd got set on in a big school the least said the soonest mended, for you can't be too careful: the polis just need a whisper and it's up their nose it goes like a sniff to a bloodhound.'

Up in the loft Jimmy went straight to a long wooden box and took out his Sunday coat and trousers, but he didn't get into them immediately. For quite some minutes he stood with them gripped tight against his chest, his eyes closed, his lips moving as he muttered to himself, 'Oh dear God! don't let nowt happen our Rory. Please, please don't let nowt happen him.'

As he came down the ladder again, Janie said, 'I'll go with you.' But he shook his head at her. 'No, no, I'll be better on me own. Well, what I mean is, I can get around the waterfront. If he's not in the hospital I can get around and ask.'

'Be careful.'

He turned to Lizzie and nodded, saying, 'Aye, aye,' and as he went to let himself out, Ruth followed him and, opening the door for him, said quietly. 'Don't stay late, not in the dark, not around there.'

'All right, Ma.' He nodded at her, then went out.

He ran most of the way into Shields and wasn't out of breath. He took no notice of the urchins who shouted after him:

> 'Bow-legged billy,
> Bandy-randy,
> One eye up the chimney, the other in the pot,
> Poor little sod, yer ma's given you the lot.'

At one time the rhyme used to hurt him but he was inured to it now. Nothing could hurt him, he told himself, except that something should happen to their Rory. He'd want to peg out himself if anything happened to their Rory. What was more, if it had already happened he would be to blame because if he hadn't yarped on about the boatyard Rory wouldn't have gone gambling . . . But, aye, he would, he would always gamble. But not at this new place, this big place he had gone to these past few Saturdays. He hadn't let on where it was. He had asked him, but the laughing answer had been, 'Ask no questions and you'll get no lies . . .'

The porter at the Infirmary said, 'No, lad, nobody with the name of Connor's been brought in the day. Then they don't bring people in on a Sunday less it's accidents like.'

'Well, I was thinkin' it could've been an accident.'

'Well, there's no Connor here, lad. Neither mister nor missis.'

'Ta . . . thanks.' He didn't know whether he was disappointed or relieved.

He was going down the gravel drive when the porter's voice hailed him, saying, 'Just a minute! There's a fella, but I hope it isn't the one you're lookin' for. There was a bloke brought in round dinner-time, no name on him, nothing. He was found on the waterfront. Not a sailor. His clothes were respectable, what was left of them, but I expect by now he's kicked the bucket.'

Jimmy walked slowly back towards the man, saying as he went, 'What's he like?'

'Oh, lad, his own mother wouldn't be able to recognize him, he's been bashed about worse than anybody I've seen afore.'

'Had he brown hair, thick, wavy. . . . ?'

'Whatever colour this fellow's hair once was, lad, I couldn't say, but the day it was dark red, caked with blood.'

Jimmy stood looking up at the man, his mouth slightly agape. Then closing it, the words came dredged through his lips as he said, 'Could . . . could I see him, this . . . this fella?'

'Well. Well, I'll ask the sister. Come on back.'

'Sit there a minute,' he said a moment later, pointing to a polished wooden chair standing against the painted brick wall of the lobby.

Jimmy sat down, glad to get off his legs. He was feeling weak, faint, and frightened, very frightened.

The porter came back and beckoned to him. Then with his hand on Jimmy's shoulder, he pointed and said, 'Go down there, lad, to the end of the corridor, turn left, an' you'll see the sister.'

The sister was tall and thin. She put him in mind of John George. He had to put his head back to look up at her. She said to him, 'You're looking for your brother?'

'Aye, miss.'

'How old is he?'

'Twenty-three, comin' up twenty-four next month.'

'There's a young man in there,' she nodded towards the wall. 'He's in a very bad state, he's been badly beaten. But . . . but you may be able to recognize him, if he is your brother.'

She turned away, and Jimmy followed her towards the figure lying on the bed. It was very still. The head was swathed in bandages, the face completely distorted with bruises. He found himself gasping for breath. He had once seen a man taken from the river. He was all blue, bluey black and bloated. He had been dead for days, they said. This man on the bed could be dead an' all. He didn't know if it was their Rory. The sister was whispering something in his ear and he turned and looked dazedly at her. Then he whispered back as he pointed to his thumb. 'He had a wart atween his finger an' thumb towards the front. He'd always had it.'

The sister gently picked up the limp hand from the counterpane and turned it over; then she looked at Jimmy as he stared down at the flat hard wart that Rory had for years picked and scraped at in an effort to rid himself of it.

The sister drew him backwards away from the bed, and when they were in the corridor again she still kept her hand on his shoulder as she endeavoured to soothe him, saying, 'There now. There now.'

The tears were choking him. Although they were flooding down his face they were packing his gullet, he couldn't breathe.

She took him into a room and said, 'Where do you live?'

When he was unable to answer she asked, 'In the town?'

He shook his head.

'Tyne Dock?'

He brought out between gasps, 'Up . . . up Simonside.'

'Oh, that's a long way.'

He dried his face now on his sleeve, then took a clean rag from his pocket and blew his nose. After some minutes he looked up at her and said, 'I'll bring me ma and da,' then added, 'Will he . . . ?'

She said kindly, 'I don't know, he's very low. He could see the morning, but then again I don't know.'

He nodded at her, then walked slowly from the room. But in the corridor he turned and looked back at her and said, 'Ta,' and she smiled faintly at him.

He didn't run immediately, he walked from the gates to where the road turned into Westoe and as he looked down it he thought of Janie. Poor Janie. Poor all of them. In their different ways they'd all miss him, miss him like hell. He had been different from them, different from his da and Mr Waggett and Mr Leary, and all the women had looked up to him. He had become something, a rent collector. There were very few people from their walk of life who rose to rent collectors . . . And himself? He stopped in the street. If Rory went then his own life would come to an end. Not even boats would bring him any comfort. This feeling he had for Rory was not just admiration because he had got on in the world, it was love, because he was the only being he'd really be able to love. He had another love, but that was in a secret dream. He'd never have a lass of his own for no lass would look the side he was on; but that hadn't mattered so very much because there'd always be Rory.

As if he were starting a race he sprang forward and ran. He ran until he thought his heart would burst, for it was uphill at the way after he left the docks, and when finally he staggered into the kitchen he dropped on to the floor and held his side against the painful stitch before he could speak to them all hanging over him. And when he did speak it was to Janie he addressed himself.

They walked quickly, almost on the point of a run, all the way back with him into Shields in the dark, Paddy, Ruth, Lizzie and Janie, and for hours they all waited in the little side room. It was against the rules, but the night sister had taken pity on them and brought them in out of the cold.

Janie left the Infirmary around eleven o'clock to slip back to her place, and the look on her face checked the upbraiding from the cook and her master and mistress. The master and mistress were deeply concerned over the incident and gave her leave to visit the hospital first thing in the morning.

Fortunately it was not more than five minutes' walk from the house, they said, so she was to go upstairs and rest, as she would need all her strength to face the future.

It was a term that ordinary people used when a man had died and a woman was left to fend for herself and her family with no hope of help but the questionable charity of the Poor House. It was as if Rory were already gone. Well, the family expected he would go before dawn, didn't they? Men in his condition usually went out about three in the morning.

She asked politely if she could go back now because she'd like to be with him when he went.

Her master and mistress held a short conference in the drawing-room and then they gave her their permission.

Rory passed the critical time of 3 a.m. He was still breathing at five o'clock in the morning, but the night sister informed them now that he might remain in a coma for days and that they should go home.

Ruth and Paddy nodded at her in obedience because they both knew that Paddy must get to work; and Ruth said to Janie, 'You must get back an' all, lass. Don't take too much advantage an' they'll let you out again.' And Janie, numb with agony, could only nod to this sound advice. But Lizzie refused to budge. Here she was, she said, and here she'd remain until she knew he was either going or staying. And Jimmy said he'd stay too, until it was time to go to work.

So Ruth and Paddy nodded a silent good-bye to Janie when their ways

parted at Westoe and walked without exchanging a word through the
dark streets that were already filling with men on their way to the
shipyards, the docks, and farther into Jarrow to Palmer's. But when they
had passed through the arches and came to where the road divided Paddy
said, 'I'd better go straight on up else I'll be late.'

'You've got your good suit on.'

'Bugger me good suit!'

Ruth peered at him through the darkness before she said quietly, 'If he
goes things'll be tight, think on that. There'll be less for beer and nowt for
clothes. I depended on him.'

'Aw, woman!' He swung away from her now and made for the Simonside road, saying over his shoulder, 'Then stop skittering behind, put a
move on. If they dock me half an hour it'll be less on the mantelpiece, so
think on.'

Think on, he said. She had thought on for years. She had thought on the
pain of life that you managed to work off during the daytime, but which
pressed on you in the night and settled around your heart, causing wind,
the relief of which brought no ease. She had loved him in the early years,
but after Rory was born she hated him. Yet her hate hadn't spread over
Lizzie. Strange that, she had always liked Lizzie. Still did. She couldn't
imagine life without Lizzie. When Nellie was born a little wonder had
entered her life, yet she had actually fought him against the conception.
Every time he had tried to touch her she had fought him. Sometimes she
conquered because he became weary of the struggle, but at other times
after a hard day at the wash tub and baking and cleaning, because she'd
had it all to do herself then as Lizzie went out daily doing for the people
down the bank, she would surrender from sheer exhaustion. When Jimmy
came life ran smoothly for a time. She felt happy she had a son; that he
should have rickets didn't matter so much. As he grew his legs would
straighten. So she had thought at first. Then came the day when hate rose
in her for Paddy again. It was when he tried once more to take Lizzie. She
had come in from next door and found them struggling there in the open
on the mat and the bairns locked in the scullery. There had been no need
for Lizzie to protest 'I want none of him, Ruth, I want none of him,' the
scratches on his face bore out her statement.

From then on the dess bed in the kitchen became a battleground.
Finally he brought the priest to her; and she was forced to do her duty in
the fear of everlasting hell and damnation.

She had never asked herself why Lizzie had stayed with them all these
years because where would a single woman go with a bairn? Anyway, it
was his responsibility to see that she was taken care of after giving her a
child.

And now that child was lying back there battered and on his way to death. What would Lizzie do without him? He had scorned her since the day he learned she was his mother. But it hadn't altered her love for him; the only thing it had done was put an edge to her tongue every time she spoke to him. Funny, but she envied Lizzie. Although she knew she had Rory's affection, she envied her, for she was his mother.

Rory regained consciousness at eight o'clock on the Monday morning. Lizzie was by his side and he looked at her without recognition, and when his lips moved painfully she put her ear down to him and all she could make out was one word, which she repeated a number of times and in an anguished tone. 'Aye. Aye, lad,' she said, 'It is a pity. It is a pity. Indeed it is a pity.'

He would rally, they said, so she must leave the ward but she could come back in the afternoon.

Without protest now she left the hospital. But she didn't go straight home. She found her way to the Catholic church, which she had never been in before; on her yearly visits she patronized the Jarrow one. She waited until the Mass was finished, and then approaching the priest without showing the awe due to his station and infallibility, she told him that her son was dying in the Infirmary and would he see that he got the last rites. The priest asked her where she was from and other particulars. He showed her no sympathy, he didn't like her manner, she was a brusque woman and she did not afford him the reverence that her kind usually bestowed on him, nor did she slip anything into his hand, but she did say that if her son went she would buy a mass for him.

He watched her leave the church without putting a halfpenny in the poor box.

The priest's feelings for Lizzie were amply reciprocated. She told herself she didn't like him, he wasn't a patch on the Jarrow ones. But then she supposed it didn't make much difference who sent you over to the other side as long as there was one of them to see that you were properly prepared for the journey.

It was around half-past one when Lizzie, about to pick up her shawl for the journey back to the hospital, glanced out of the cottage window, then stopped and said, 'Here's John George; he must have heard.'

By the time John George reached the door she had opened it and, looking at his white drawn face, said quickly, 'Come in, lad. Come in.'

He came in. He stood in the middle of the room looking from one to the other; then as he was about to speak Ruth said softly. 'You've heard then, John George?' and he repeated 'Heard?'

'Aye, about Rory.'

'Rory? I . . . I came up to find him.'

'You don't know then?'

He turned to Lizzie. 'Know what, Lizzie? What . . . what's happened him?' He shook his head, then asked again. 'What's happened him?'

'Oh lad!' Lizzie now put her hand to her brow. 'You mean to say you haven't heard? Jimmy was going to tell Mr Kean at break time.'

'Mr Kean?'

'Aye, sit down, lad.' Ruth now put her hand out and pressed John George into a chair, and he looked at her dumbly as he said, 'Mr Kean's not there. Miss Kean, she . . . she came for a while.' He nodded his head slowly now, then asked stiffly, 'Rory. Where is he?'

'He's down in the hospital, John George. He was beaten up, beaten unto death something terrible.'

When John George now slumped forward over the table and dropped his head into his hands both womem came close to him and Lizzie murmured, 'Aye, lad, aye, I know how you feel.'

After a while he raised his head and looked from one to the other and said dully, 'He' dead then?'

'No.' Lizzie shook her head from side to side. 'But he's as near to it as makes no matter. It'll be one of God's rare miracles if he ever recovers, an' if he does only He knows what'll be left of him . . . Was Mr Kean asking for him?'

It seemed now that he had difficulty in speaking for he gulped in his throat a number of times before repeating, 'He wasn't there, won't be; won't be back till the night, his father died.'

'Ah, God rest his soul. Aye, you did say he wasn't there. Well, you can tell him when you do see him that it'll be some time afore Rory collects any more rents, that's if ever. It's God's blessin' he hadn't any collection on him when they did him. Whatever they took from him, an' that was every penny, it was his own.'

John George's head was bent again and he now made a groaning sound.

'Will you come in along of me and see him, I'm on me way? It's the Infirmary.'

He rose to his feet, and stared at her, then like someone in a daze, he turned and made for the door.

'Aren't you stayin' for a cup of tea, lad?' It was Ruth speaking now.

He didn't answer her except to make a slight movement with his head, then he went out leaving the door open behind him.

They both stood and watched him go down the path. And when he was out of sight they looked at each other in some amazement, and Lizzie said, 'It's broken him; he thought the world of Rory. It's made him look like death itself.'

'Get your shawl on and go after him.' Ruth pointed to where the shawl was lying across the foot of Lizzie's bed which was inset in the alcove. But Lizzie shook her head, saying, 'He wants no company, something about him said he wants no company.' She moved her head slowly now as she stared back at Ruth. 'God knows, this has hit everyone of us but in some strange way him most of all. It's strange, it is that. Did you see his face, the look on it? It was as if he himself was facing death. Me heart's breakin' at this minute over me own, yet there's room for sorrow in me for that lad. Poor John George.'

CHAPTER 7

Janie sat by the bed and gazed down on the face that she had always thought was the best looking of any lad in the town and she wondered if it would ever go back into shape again. Oh, she hoped it would, for, being Rory, he'd hate to be marked for life. And she couldn't stand the thought either of him being disfigured; but as long as he was alive that's all that really mattered. And he was alive, and fighting to keep alive.

He had opened his eyes once and looked at her and she thought that he had recognized her, but she wasn't sure. His lips were moving continuously but all he kept saying was 'Pity. Pity.' There must be something on his mind that was making him think it was a pity, and she thought too that it was the greatest of pities that he had ever gone gaming because she had no doubt but that he had been followed from wherever he had played, and been robbed, and by somebody in the know; likely one of them he had played against. But as Jimmy said last night, they mustn't breathe a word of it because if it got to Mr Kean's ears that would be the finish of his rent collecting. You couldn't be a gambler and a rent collector . . . And then there was this business of John George.

Eeh! she was glad to the heart that Rory didn't know about that because that would really have been the finish of him. Of all the fools on this earth John George was the biggest. She couldn't really believe it, and if the master hadn't told her himself she wouldn't have, but the master's partner dealt with Mr Kean's business. Odd, but she hadn't known that afore. But still, she asked herself, why should she? Anyway, he had pricked his ears up when he heard that one of Mr Kean's men had swindled him because, as he said, he knew that her intended worked for Mr Kean.

Rory's head moved slightly on the pillow, his eyelids flickered, and she bent over him and said softly, 'Rory, it's Janie. How you feelin', Rory?'

'Pity,' he said. 'Pity.'

The tears welled up in her eyes and rolled down her cheeks and she whispered, 'Oh, Rory, come back from wherever you are.' Then she said softly, 'I've got to go now, I've got to get back, but I'll come again the night. The mistress says I can take an hour off in the afternoon and evening. It's good of her.' She spoke as if he could understand her, then she stood up, whispering softly, 'Bye-bye, dear. Bye-bye.'

Five minutes later she was turning off the main road and into Westoe when she saw the two dark-clothed figures of Ruth and Lizzie approaching. She ran towards them, and immediately they asked together, 'You've been?'

'Aye, yes.'

'Any change?'

She looked at Lizzie and shook her head, then said, 'He opened his eyes but . . . but I don't think he knew me, he just keeps sayin' that word, pity, pity . . . Have . . . have you heard about John George?'

'John George? Was he in?'

'No, Mrs Connor –' she always gave Ruth her full title – 'he's . . . he's been taken.'

'Taken?' They both screwed up their faces while they looked back at her.

'Yes, for stealin'.'

'John George!' Again they spoke simultaneously.

She nodded her head slowly. 'Five pounds ten, and . . . and he's been at it for some time.'

They were speechless. Their mouths fell into a gape as they listened. 'Mr Kean was away and Miss Kean came early on, earlier than usual to collect the money. She was on her way to some place or other an' she just called in on the off-chance. She had her father's key and she opened the box and . . . and there was five pounds ten short from what was in his book. Apparently he had been doin' a fiddle.'

'No! Not John George.' Ruth was holding the brim of her black straw hat tightly in her fist.

'Yes. Aye, I couldn't believe it either. It made me sick, but the master, he heard it all in the office. The solicitors, you know. He . . . he said he was a stupid fellow. I . . . I put a word in for him I did. I said I'd always found him nice, a really nice fella, and he said, 'He's been crafty, Janie. He's admitted to using this trick every time he was sure Mr Kean wasn't goin' to collect the Saturday takings.' Apparently he would nip something out then put it back on the Monday mornin' early, but this time he was too late. And then he said nobody but a stupid man would admit to doing this in the past, then try to deny that he had taken five pounds ten. He wanted to say it was only ten shillings, and he had that on him to put back . . . He had just been to the pawn. They found the ticket on him.'

'Oh God Almighty! what'll happen next? Rory and now John George, an' all within three days. It isn't possible. But this accounts for his face, the look on his face when he came up yesterday. Eeh! God above.' Lizzie began rocking herself.

'It's this lass that he's caught on to, Lizzie.' Janie nodded slowly. 'Rory said he was barmy about her. He bought her a locket an' chain at Christmas and he takes her by the ferry or train to Newcastle every week, then round the buildings. He's daft about buildings. I never knew that till he told me one night. Then last week he gave her tea in some place. Yes, he did, he took her out to tea. And not in no cheap cafe neither, a place off Grey Street. An' Rory said Grey Street's classy.'

'Women can be the ruin of a man in more ways than one.' Lizzie's head was bobbing up and down now. 'But no matter, I'm sorry for him, to the very heart of me I'm sorry for him 'cos I liked John George. He had somethin' about him, a gentleness, not like a man usually has.'

Ruth asked quietly, 'Do you know when he'll be tried, Janie?'

'No, but I mean to find out.'

'Somebody should go down and see him, he's got nobody I understand, only those two old 'un's. And you know, it isn't so much laziness with them –' Ruth turned now and shook her head at Lizzie – 'it isn't, Lizzie, it's the rheumatics. And this'll put the finish to them, it'll be the House for them. Dear, dear Lord!'– Ruth never said God – 'You've got to ask why these things happen.'

The three of them stood looking at each other for a moment. Then Janie said, 'I've got to go now, but I'm gettin' out the night an' all. The mistress said I can have an hour in the afternoon and in the evenin's. She's good, isn't she?'

They nodded at her, and Lizzie agreed. 'Aye, she's unusual in that way. Bye-bye then, lass.'

'Bye-bye.' She nodded from one to the other, then again said, 'Bye-bye,' before running across the road and almost into a horse that was pulling a fruit cart, and as Lizzie watched her she said, 'It only needed her to get herself knocked down and that would have been three of them. Everythin' happens in threes, so I wonder what's next?

CHAPTER 8

Janie had never before been in a court. She sat on the bench nearest the wall. At the far end of the room, right opposite to her, was the magistrate; in front of him were a number of dark-clothed men. They kept moving from one to the other, they all had papers in their hands. At times they would bend over a table and point to the papers. The last prisoner had got a month for begging, and now they were calling out the name: 'John George Armstrong! John George Armstrong!'

As if emerging out of a cellar John George appeared. The box in which he stood came only to his hips, but the upper part of him seemed to have shrunk, his shoulders were stooped, his head hung forward, his face was the colour of clay. One of the dark-suited men began to talk. Janie only half listened to him, for her eyes were riveted on John George, almost willing him to look at her, to let him know there was someone here who was concerned for him. Poor John George! Oh, poor John George!

. . . 'He did on the twenty-fourth day of January steal from his employer, Septimus Kean, Esquire, of Birchingham House, Westoe, the sum of five pounds ten shillings . . .'

The next words were lost to Janie as she watched John George close his eyes and shake his head. It was as if he were saying, 'No, no.' Then the man on the floor was mentioning Miss Kean's name . . . 'She pointed out to the accused the discrepancy between his entries in the ledger and the amount of money in the safe.'

Rory had always said they hadn't a safe, not a proper one. She looked towards Miss Kean. She could only see her profile but she gathered that she was thin and would likely be tall when she stood up. She wore a pill-box hat of green velvet perched on the top of her hair. She looked to have a lot of hair, dark, perhaps it was padded. Even the mistress padded her hair at the back, especially when she was going out to some function.

'The accused argued with her that he was only ten shillings short and he had the amount in his pocket, and he had intended to replace it. He asked her to recount the money. This she did. He then admitted to having helped himself on various previous occasions to small sums but said he always replaced them. He insisted that there was only ten shillings missing. He then tried to persuade her to accept the ten shillings and not mention the matter to her father . . . When taken into custody he said . . .'

Oh John George! Why had he been so daft? Why? It was that girl. If she ever met her she'd give her the length of her tongue, she would that, and when Rory came to himself and heard this he'd go mad, he would that. But it would be some time before they could tell Rory anything.

The magistrate was talking now about trusting employers being taken advantage of, about men like the prisoner being made an example of; about some men being nothing more than sneak thieves and that the respectable citizens of this town had to be protected from them.

'Do you plead guilty or not guilty?'

'I . . . I didn't take five pounds, sir.'

'Answer the question. Do you plead guilty or not guilty?'

'I didn't take five . . .' John George's voice trailed away. There was talk between the magistrate and one of the men on the floor, then Janie's mouth opened wide when the magistrate said, 'I sentence you to a total of twelve months. . . .'

She shot to her feet and actually put her hand up to try to attract John George's attention, but he never raised his head.

A few minutes later she stood by the door of the Court House. The tears were running down her face. Her hour was nearly up and she wanted to call in at the hospital. That's where she was supposed to be. She didn't know what she would have done or said if the master had been in the court, but he wasn't there. Oh, John George! Poor John George!

A policeman came through the door and looked at her. He had seen her in the court room, he had seen her lift her hand to the prisoner. He said, not unkindly, 'He got off lightly. I've known him give three years, especially when they've been at it as long as he has. He always lays it on thick when he's dealin' with men who should know better. He had the responsibility of money you know an' he should have known better. Anyway, what's a year?' He smiled down at her, and she said, 'Would . . . could . . . do you ever allow anybody to see them for a minute?'

'Well now. Aye, yes, it's done. He stared at her, then said quickly, 'Come on. Come this way. Hurry up; they'll be movin' them in next to no time. There's more than a few for Durham the day and he'll be among them I suppose.'

She followed him at a trot and when he came to an abrupt stop she almost bumped into his back. He opened a door and she glimpsed a number of men, definitely prisoners, for the stamp was on their faces, and three uniformed policemen.

Her guide must have been someone in authority, a sergeant or someone like that, she thought, for he nodded to the officers and said, 'Armstrong for a minute, I'll be with him.'

'Armstrong!' one of the policemen bawled, and John George turned about and faced the door. And when the policeman thumbed over his shoulder he walked through it and out into the corridor.

The sergeant now looked at him. Then, nodding towards Janie, said, 'Two minutes, and mind, don't try anything. Understand?' He poked his face towards John George, and John George stared dumbly back at him for a moment before turning to Janie.

'Hello, John George.' It was a silly thing to say but she couldn't think of anything else at the moment.

'Hello, Janie.'

'Oh!' Now as the tears poured from her eyes her tongue became loosened and she gabbled, 'I'm so sorry, John George. Why? Why? We're all sorry. We'll come an' see you, we will. There'll be visitin' times. I'll ask.'

'Janie!' His voice sounded calm, then again he said 'Janie!' and she said, 'Yes, John George?'

'Listen. Will you go and see Maggie? She won't know, at least I don't think so, not until she reads the papers. She's . . . she's going to have a bairn, Janie, she'll need somebody.'

She put her hand tightly across her mouth and her eyes widened and she muttered, 'Oh, John George.'

'Time's up. That's enough.'

'Janie! Janie! listen. Believe me; I never took the five pounds. Ten shillings aye, but never the five pounds. You tell that to Rory, will you? Tell that to Rory.'

'Yes, yes, I will, John George. Yes I will. Good-bye. Good-bye, John George.'

She watched him going back into the room. She couldn't see the policeman now but she inclined her head towards him and said, 'Ta, thanks.'

He walked with her along the stone passage and to the door, and there he said, 'Don't worry. As I said, what's a year? And you can visit him once a month.' Then bending towards her he said, 'What are you to him? I thought you were his wife, but I hope not after what I heard . . . You his sister?'

'No, only . . . only a friend.'

He nodded at her, then said, 'Well, he won't need any friends for the next twelve months, but he will after.'

'Ta-rah,' she said.

'Ta-rah, lass,' he said, and as she walked away he watched her. He was puzzled by her relationship to the prisoner. Just a friend, she had said.

She walked so slowly from the Court House that she hadn't time to call in at the hospital and when she arrived in the kitchen she was crying so much that the cook called the mistress, and the mistress said, 'Oh, I'm sorry, I'm sorry, Janie,' and she answered her through her tears, 'No, 'tisn't . . . 'tisn't that, he's . . . he's still as he was. It's . . . it's John George. I know I shouldn't have but I went to the court, ma'am, and he got a year.'

Her mistress's manner altered, her face stiffened. 'You're a very silly girl, Janie,' she said. 'The master will be very annoyed with you. Court rooms are no places for women, young women, girls. I, too, am very annoyed with you. I gave you the time off to visit your fiancé. That man's a scamp, a thieving scamp. I'm surprised your fiancé didn't find it out before . . . . What sentence did he get?'

'A year, ma'am.'

'That was nothing really, nothing. If he had been an ordinary labouring man, one could have understood him stealing, but he was in a position of trust, and when such men betray their trust they deserve heavy sentences. Dry your eyes now. Go upstairs and see to the children. I'm very displeased with you, Janie.'

Janie went upstairs and she was immediately surrounded by the children.

Why was she crying? Had their mama been cross with her?

She nodded her head while they clung to her and the girls began to cry with her. Yes, their mama had been cross with her, but strangely it wasn't affecting her. Another time she would have been thrown into despair by just a sharp word from her mistress. At this moment she did not even think of Rory, for Rory had turned the corner, they said, and was on the mend, but her thoughts were entirely with John George. His face haunted her. The fact that he had told her that he had got a girl into trouble had shocked her, but what had shocked her even more was his mental condition, for she felt he must be going wrong in the head to admit that he took the ten shillings but not the five pounds. Poor John George! Poor John George! And Rory would go mad when he knew.

CHAPTER 9

A fortnight later they brought Rory home in a cab actually paid for by Miss Kean. Miss Kean had visited the hospital three times. The last time Rory had been propped up in bed and had stared at her and listened silently as she gave him a message from her father.

He was not to worry, his post was there for him when he was ready to return. And what was more, her father was promoting him to Mr Armstrong's place. Her father had taken on a new man, but he was oldish and couldn't cover half the district. Nevertheless, he was honest and honest men were hard to come by. Her father had always known that but now it had been proved to him.

Miss Kean had then asked, 'Have you any idea who attacked you?' and all Rory did was to make one small movement with his head. He had stared fixedly at Miss Kean and she had smiled at him and said, 'I hope you enjoy the grapes, Mr Connor, and will soon be well.' Again he had made a small movement with his head. It was then she said, 'When you are ready to return home a cab will be provided.'

His mind was now clear and working normally and it kept telling him there was this thing he had to face up to and it was no use trying to ignore it, or hoping it would slip back into the muzziness that he had lain in during the first days of his recovery when they had kept saying to him, all of them, the nurses, the doctor, Ruth, his dad, her, Janie, all of them, 'Don't worry, take it slowly. Every day you'll improve. It's a miracle. It's a miracle.'

Although after the third day he had stopped saying the word 'Pity' aloud it was still filling the back of his mind. Whenever he closed his eyes he saw the big feet coming towards him; that's all he remembered, the big feet. He couldn't remember where they had hit him first, whether it was on the head or in the groin or in his ribs; they had broken his ribs. For days he had found it difficult to breathe, now it was easier. His body, although black and blue from head to foot, and with abrasions almost too numerous to count, was no longer a torment to him, just a big sore pile of flesh. He did not know what he looked like, only that his face seemed spread as wide as his shoulders.

He didn't see his reflection until he reached home. When they helped him over the step he made straight for the mantelpiece. Although Ruth tried to check him he thrust her gently aside then leant forward and looked at his face in the oblong mottled mirror. His nose was still straight but his eyes looked as if they were lying in pockets of mouldy fat. Almost two inches of his hair had been shaved off close to the scalp above his left ear and a zig-zag scar ran down to just in front of the ear itself.

'Your face'll be all right, don't worry.'

He turned and looked at Ruth but said nothing, and she went on, 'The dess-bed's ready for you, you can't do the ladder yet. We'll sleep upstairs.'

He said slowly now, like an old man might, 'I'll manage the ladder.'

'No,' she said, 'it's all arranged. Don't worry. Now come on, sit yourself down.' She led him towards the high-backed wooden chair, and he found he was glad to sit down, for his legs were giving way beneath him.

He said again, 'I'll make the ladder,' and as he spoke he watched Lizzie go into the scullery. It was as if she could read his mind; he didn't want to lie in the same room with her, although she lay in the box bed behind the curtains. He couldn't help his feelings towards her. He knew that she had been good to him over the past weeks, trudging down every day to the hospital, and he hadn't given her a kind word, not even when he could speak he hadn't given her a kind word. It was odd but he couldn't forgive her for depriving him of the woman he thought to be his mother. But what odds, what odds where he slept; wherever he slept his mind would be with him, and his mind was giving him hell. They thought he wasn't capable of thinking straight yet, and he wasn't going to enlighten them because he would need to have some excuse for his future actions.

Nobody had mentioned John George to him, not one of them had spoken his name, but the fact that he had never been near him spoke for them. Something had happened to him and he had a good idea what it was; in fact, he was certain of what it was. And he also knew that he himself wasn't going to do anything about it. He couldn't. God! he just couldn't.

'Here, drink that up.' Lizzie was handing him a cup of tea, which he took from her hand without looking at her and said, 'Ta.'

'It was good of old Kean,' she said, 'to send a cab for you. He can't be as black as he's painted. And his daughter comin' to the hospital. God, but she's plain that one, stylish but plain. Anyway, he must value you.'

'Huh!' Even the jerking of his head was a painful action, which caused him to put his hand on his neck and move his head from side to side, while Lizzie concluded, 'Aye well, you know him better than me, but I would say deeds speak for themselves.'

When Lizzie took his empty cup from him and went to refill it, Ruth, poking the fire, said, 'I'll have to start a bakin',' and she turned and glanced towards him. 'It's good to have you home again, lad. We can get down to normal now.'

He nodded his head and smiled weakly at her but didn't speak. It was odd. Over the past weeks he had longed to be home, away from the cold painted walls and clinical cleanliness of the hospital, but looking about him now, the kitchen, which had always appeared large, for it was made up of two rooms knocked into one, seemed small, cluttered and shabby. He hadn't thought of it before as shabby, he hadn't thought of a lot of things before. He hadn't thought he was cowardly before. Afraid, aye, but not cowardly. But deep in his heart now he knew he was, both cowardly and afraid.

He had always been afraid of enclosed spaces. He supposed that was why he left doors open; and why he had jumped at the collecting job, because he'd be working outside most of the time in the open. He had always been terrified of being shut in. He could take his mind back to the incident that must have created the fear. The Leary's lads next door were always full of devilment, and having dragged a coffin-like box they had found floating on the Jarrow slacks all the way down the East Jarrow road and up the Simonside bank, they had to find a use for it before breaking it up for the fire, so the older ones had chased the young ones, and it was himself they had caught, and they had put him in the box and nailed the lid on. At first he had screamed, then become so petrified that his voice had frozen inside him. When they shouted at him from the outside he had been incapable of answering; then, fearful of what they had done, they fumbled in their efforts to wrench the heavy lid off.

When eventually they tipped him from the box he was as stiff as a corpse itself, and not until he had vomited, after the grown-ups had thumped him on the back and rubbed him, did he start to cry. He'd had nightmares for years afterwards, and night after night had walked in his sleep, through the trap door and down the ladder. But having reached the kitchen door that led outside he would always wake up, then scamper back to bed where he would lie shivering until finally cold gave place to heat and he would fall into sweaty sleep.

But since starting collecting, he'd hardly had a nightmare and he hadn't sleep-walked for years. But what now, and in the weeks ahead?

Jimmy came in at half-past six and stood just inside the door and stared towards the dess-bed where Rory was sitting propped up, and he grinned widely and said, 'Aw, lad, it's good to see you home again,' then went slowly towards the bed. 'How you feelin'?'

'Oh, well, you know, a hundred per cent, less ninety.'

'Aye, but you're home and you'll soon be on your feet again. And you know somethin'?' He sat on the edge of the bed. 'I've seen him, Mr Kilpatrick. I told him how things stood, an' you know what he said? He said the rest can be paid so much a month. If you could clear it off in a year he'd be satisfied.'

'He said that?'

'Aye.'

'Oh well –' Rory sighed – 'that's something. Yes –' he nodded at Jimmy – 'that's something. We can go ahead now, can't we?'

'You know, he came to the yard for me 'cos he was down that way on business. And Mr Baker wanted to know what he was about 'cos I had to leave me work for five minutes, and so I told him.' Jimmy pulled a face. 'He wasn't pleased. Well, I knew he wouldn't be. You know what he said? He said he had intended keepin' me on an givin' me a rise . . . That for a tale. He asked what we were givin' for it and when I told him he said we were being done, paying that for the goodwill when it was just a few sticks of furniture and half an old patched sculler. One of the lads told me that he had seen him round there himself lookin', an' what he bet was that the old fellow was after the place for himself. Anyway, we scotched him.' He jerked his head and grinned widely, then added, 'Eeh! man, I'm excited. I never thought, I never thought.' He leant forward and put his hand on Rory's. 'And if it wasn't for what happened you we'd be over the moon, wouldn't we?'

'Aye, well, we can still be over the moon now.'

'Get off the side of that bed with your mucky clothes on!'

'Aw, Lizzie.' Jimmy rose to evade her hand and he laughed at her as he said, 'You're a grousy woman,' and when she made to go for him he ran into the scullery, his body swaying and his laughter touched with glee.

Jimmy was happy, Ruth was happy, and, of course, Lizzie was happy; and Janie would be happy; everybody was happy . . . except himself . . . and John George. John George. God Almighty, John George!

Yes, Janie was happy at the news that they had got the yard, for this meant she could be married any time now. Yet her excitement seemed to have been stirred rather by the fact that she had been granted a full day's leave next Thursday. She sat by the bed gazing at Rory as she gave him the news. He wasn't actually in bed, just lying on top of it fully dressed. His legs and ribs still ached, and so the bed was left down during the day so that he could rest upon it.

Janie glanced from him to the Sunday company, all assembled as usual, and she hunched her shoulders at them as she said, 'I told a fib, well, only a little one. I told her, the missis, it would need time to clear up the place an' put it to rights an' suggested like if I could have a full day. But you know what I wanted the day for? I thought we'd go up to Durham and –' She clapped her hand over her mouth, then stared at Rory before looking back at the others again and saying, 'Eeh! I forgot.' Again she was looking into Rory's unblinking stare and, taking his hand, she said softly, 'We . . . we didn't tell you, 'cos you were so bad, and you wouldn't have been able to take it in.' She gave him an apologetic look now. 'I mean, with your head bein' knocked about an' that. And we knew that if you had been all right you would have asked for him, you know. Now, Rory, don't be upset.' She gripped his hands tightly. 'John George's been a silly lad. It's all through that lass. You know, you said he was daft. Well, he was, and . . . and he took some money. He meant to put it back. I don't know whether you knew or not but he had been on the fiddle for a long time and so . . . and so he was caught and' – her head drooped to one side as she shook it – 'he was sent along the line. He's in Durh . . . Oh, Rory . . .'

They were all gathered round the bed now looking down on him. The sweat was pouring from him and Lizzie cried at them, 'Get back! the lot of you's an' give him air.' She looked angrily across the bed at Janie. 'You shouldn't have given it him like that.'

'I'm sorry. I know, but . . . well, he had to know some time, Lizzie.'

'He'll be all right. He'll be all right.' Ruth was wiping the sweat from his brow and the bald patch on his head. 'It's just weakness. It's like how he used to be after the nightmares. Go on –' she motioned the men towards the table – 'get on with your game.'

'Bad that,' said Grannie Waggett. 'Bad. Don't like it. Bad sign.'

'Anybody can have sweats, Gran.' Jimmy's voice was small, his tone tentative, and she bent forward from her chair and wagged, her bony finger at him, saying, 'Nay, lad, not everybody, women but not men. Bad look out if all men had sweats. Always a sign of summit, a man havin' sweats. I remember me grannie when she worked for those high-ups in Newcastle sayin' how the son got sweats. Young he was an' the heir. Lots of money, lots of money. He started havin' sweats after the night he went out to see Newcastle lit up for the first time. Oil lamps they had. Eighteen and twelve was it, or eleven, or thirteen? I don't know, but he got sweats. Caught a chill he did going from one to the other gazin' at 'em, got the consumption . . .'

'Gran!'

'Aye, Ruth . . . Well, I was just sayin' about me grannie an' the young fellow an' the things she told me. Do you know what the bloody Duke of Northumberland did with a pile of money? Gave it to buildin' a jail or court or summat, an' poor folks . . .'

'Look, come on in home.' Bill Waggett was bending over his mother, tugging at her arm now, and she cried at him, 'Leave be, you big galoot!'

'You're comin' in home, Rory wants a bit of peace an' quiet.'

'Rory likes a bit of crack, an' I've said nowt.'

'Go on, Gran.' Janie was at her side now pleading.

Spluttering and upbraiding, the old woman allowed her son to lead her from the cottage. And this was the signal for the Learys, too, to take their leave, although it was but six o'clock in the evening, and a Sunday, the day of the week they all looked forward to for a game and a bit crack.

The house free from the visitors, as if at a given signal Jimmy went up the ladder into the loft, and his father followed him, while Lizzie and Ruth disappeared into the scullery, leaving Janie alone with Rory.

She had pulled her chair up towards the head of the bed, and, bending towards him, she asked tenderly, 'You feeling better?'

He nodded at her.

'I knew when it came it would be a shock, I'm sorry.'

He made no motion but continued to stare at her.

'I . . . I thought we should go up and see him on Thursday. It'll be the only chance we have, he's allowed visitors once a month . . . All right, all right.'

She watched his head now moving backwards and forwards against the supporting pillows, and when he muttered something she put her face close to his and whispered, 'What do you say?'

'I . . . I can't.'

'We'd take the ferry up to Newcastle an' then the train. It . . . it might do you good, I mean the journey.'

'I can't; don't keep on.'

She looked at him for a moment before she said, 'You don't want to see him?'

'I . . . I can't go there.'

'But why, Rory? He's . . . he's your friend. And if you had seen him in the court that day, why . . .'

Again he was shaking his head. His eyes, screwed up tightly now, were lost in the discoloured puffed flesh.

She sat back and stared at him in deep sadness. She couldn't understand it. She knew he wasn't himself yet, but that he wouldn't make an effort to go and see John George, and him shut up in that place . . . well, she just couldn't understand it.

When he looked at her again and saw the expression on her face, he said through clenched teeth, 'Don't keep on, Janie. I'm sorry but . . . but I can't. You know I've always had a horror of them places. You know how I can't stand being shut in, the doors and things. I'd be feared of making a fool of meself. You know?'

The last two words were a plea and although in a small way she understood his fear of being shut in, she thought that he might have tried to overcome it for this once, just to see John George and ease his plight.

She said softly, 'Somebody should go; he's got nobody, nobody in the world.'

He muttered something now and she said, 'What?'

'You go.'

'Me! On me own, all that way? I've never been in a train in me life, and never on the ferry alone, I haven't.'

'Take one of them with you.' He motioned his head towards the scullery. And now she nodded at him and said, 'Aye, yes, I could do that. I'll ask them.' She stared at him a full minute before she rose from the chair and went into the scullery.

Both Lizzie and Ruth turned towards her and waited for her to speak. She looked from one to the other and said, 'He won't, I mean he can't come up to Durham with me to see John George, he doesn't feel up to it . . . not yet. If it had been later. But . . . but it's early days you know.' She nodded at them, then added, 'Would one of you?'

Ruth looked at her sadly and said, 'I couldn't, lass, I couldn't leave the house an' him an' them all to see to. Now Lizzie here –'

'What! me? God Almighty! Ruth, me go to Durham! I've never been as far as Shields Market in ten years. As for going on a train I wouldn't trust me life in one of 'em. And another thing, lass.' Her voice dropped. 'I haven't got the proper clothes for a journey.'

'They're all right, Lizzie, the ones you've got. There's your good shawl. You could put it round your shoulders. An' Ruth would lend you her bonnet, wouldn't you, Ruth?'

'Oh, she could have me bonnet, and me coat an' all, but it wouldn't fit her. But go on, it'll do you good.' She was nodding at Lizzie now. 'You've hardly been across the doors except to the hospital –' she paused but didn't add, 'since you came from over the water' but said 'in years. It's an awful place to have to be goin' to but the journey would be like a holiday for you.'

'I'd like to see John George.' Lizzie's voice was quiet now. 'Poor lad. A fool to himself, always was. He used to slip me a copper on a Sunday even though I knew he hadn't two pennies to rub against one another. And I didn't want to take it, but if I didn't he'd leave it there.' She pointed to the corner of the little window-sill. 'He'd drop it in the tin pot. The Sunday there wasn't tuppence in there I knew that his funds were low indeed. Aye, lass, I'll come along o' you. I'll likely look a sketch an' put you to shame, but if you don't mind, I don't, lass.'

Janie now laughed as she put out her hand towards Lizzie and said, 'I wouldn't mind bein' seen with you in your shift, Lizzie,' and Ruth said, 'Oh! Janie, Janie,' and Lizzie said, 'You're a good lass, Janie. You've got what money can't buy, a heart. Aye, you have that.'

It took some minutes before Janie could speak to John George. It was Lizzie who spoke first. 'Hello there, lad,' she said, and he answered, 'Hello, Lizzie. Oh hello, Lizzie,' in just such a tone as he would have used when holding out his hands towards her. But there was the grid between them.

'Hello, Janie.'

There was a great hard lump in her throat. The tears were blinding her but through them the blurred outline of his haggard features tore at her heart. 'How . . . how are you, John George?'

'Well . . . well, you know, Janie, not too bad, not too bad. Rough with the smooth, Janie, you know. Rough with the smooth. How . . . how is everybody back there?'

'All right. All right, John George. Rory, he . . . he couldn't make it, John George, he's still shaky on his legs after the knockin' about, like they told you. Eeh! he was knocked about, we never thought he'd live. He would have been here else. He'll come later, next time.'

John George made no reply to Janie's mumbled discourse but he looked towards Lizzie and she, nodding at him, added, 'Aye, he'll come along later. He sent his regards.'

'Did he?' He was addressing Janie again.

'Aye.'

'What did he say, Janie?'

'What was that, John George?'

He leant farther towards the grid. 'I said what did Rory say?'

'Oh, well.' She sniffed, then wiped her eyes with her handkerchief before mumbling, 'He said to keep your pecker up an' . . . an' everything would work out once you get back.'

'He said that?' He was holding her gaze and she didn't reply immediately, so that when she did say 'Aye,' it carried no conviction to him.

'We've brought you a fadge of new bread an' odds an' ends.' Lizzie now pointed to the parcel and he said, 'Oh, ta, Lizzie. It's kind of you; you're always kind.'

'Ah, lad, talkin' of being kind, that's what's put you here the day, being kind. Aw, lad.'

They both looked at the bent head now; then when it jerked up sharply they were startled by the vehemence of his next words. 'I didn't take five pounds, I didn't! Believe me. Will you believe me?' He was staring now at Janie. 'I did take the ten bob. As I said, I'd done it afore but managed to put it back on the Monday morning, you know after going to the pawn.' He glanced towards Lizzie now as if she would understand the latter bit. Then looking at Janie again, he said, 'Tell him, will you? Say to him, John George said he didn't take the five pounds. Will you, Janie?'

It was some seconds before she answered, 'Aye. Yes, I will. Don't upset yourself, John George. Yes, I will, an' he'll believe you. Rory'll believe you.'

His eyes were staring into hers and his lips moved soundlessly for a moment before he brought out, 'Did you go and see Maggie, Janie?'

Janie, flustered now, said, 'Why, no; I couldn't, John George, 'cos you didn't tell me where she lived.'

Just as he put his doubled fist to his brow and bowed his head a bell rang, and as if he had been progged by something sharp he rose quickly to his feet, then gabbled, 'Horsley Terrace . . . twenty-four. Go, will you Janie?'

'Yes, John George. Yes, John George.' They were both on their feet now.

'Ta, thanks. Thank you both. I'll never forget you. Will you come again? . . . Come again, will you?'

They watched him form into a line with the others before they turned away.

Outside the gates they didn't look at each other or speak, and when Lizzie, after crossing the road, leaned against the wall of a cottage and buried her face in her hands Janie, crying again, put her arms about her and having turned her from the wall, led her along the street and into the town. And still neither of them spoke.

PART TWO

CHAPTER 1

MISS KEAN

Rory stood before the desk and looked down at Charlotte Kean and said, 'I'm sorry to hear about your father.'

'It's a severe chill, but he'll soon be about again. As I told you, you are to take Armstrong's place and you will naturally receive the same wage as he was getting . . . You don't look fully recovered yourself, Mr Connor. Are you feeling quite well?'

'Yes. Yes, miss, I'm quite all right.'

'I think you had better sit down.' She pointed with an imperious finger towards a chair, and he looked at her in surprise for a moment before taking the seat and muttering, 'Thank you.'

'As I told you, we took on a new man.'

He noticed that she said 'we' as if she, too, were running the business.

'He was the best of those who applied; with so many people out of work in the town you would have thought there would have been a better selection. If it had been for the working-class trades I suppose we would have been swamped.'

He was surprised to know that rent collecting didn't come under the heading of working-class trade, yet on the other hand he knew that if they had been in the town, in either Tyne Dock or Shields, he wouldn't have been able to hob-nob with neighbours such as the Learys or the Waggetts; the distinction between the white collar and the muffler was sharply defined in the towns.

'My father suggests that you take over the Shields area completely. Mr Taylor can do the Jarrow district, particularly the Saturday morning collection.' She smiled thinly at him now. 'As he says, it's a shame to waste a good man there . . . He has a high opinion of your expertise, Mr Connor.'

Well, this was news to him. Shock upon shock. If things had been different he would have been roaring inside, and later he would have told John George and . . . Like a steel trap a shutter came down on his thinking and he forced himself to say, 'That's very nice to know, miss.'

She was still smiling at him, and as he looked at her he thought, as Lizzie had said, God! but she's plain. It didn't seem fair somehow that a

woman looking like her should have been given all the chances. Education, money, the lot. Now if Janie had been to a fine school, and could have
afforded to dress like this one did, well, there would've been no one to
touch her.

As he stared across the desk at the bowed head and the thin moving
hand – she was writing out his district – he commented to himself that
everything she had on matched, from her fancy hat that was a dull red
colour to the stiff ribboned bow on the neck of her dress. Her green coat
was open and showed a woollen dress that took its tone from the hat, but
had a row of green buttons down to her waist. He could see the bustle of
the dress pushing out the deep pleats of the coat. It took money to dress in
colours and style like that. The old man seemingly didn't keep her short of
cash.

When she rose to her feet he stood up, and when she came round the
desk she said, 'I can leave everything in your hands then, Mr Connor?'
She handed him a sheet of paper.

'Yes, miss.'

'I've got to go now. Mr Taylor should be in at any moment.' She turned
the face of the fob watch that was pinned to the breast of her dress and
looked at it. 'It isn't quite nine yet, make yourself known to him. And this
evening, and until my father is fully recovered, I would like you to bring
the takings to the house. You know where it is?'

'Yes, I know where it is.'

'Yes, he knew where it was. He had caught a glimpse of it from the
gates. He knew that it had been occupied by Kean's father and his
grandfather, but that's all he knew about it, for he had never been asked to
call there on any pretext. But what he did know was that all the Keans had
been men who had made money and that the present one was a bully.
More than once, when he has stood in this office and been spoken to like a
dog, he'd had the desire to ram his fist into his employer's podgy face.

'Good morning then, Mr Connor.'

'Good morning, miss.'

He went before her and opened the outer door, then stood for a second
watching her walking down the alley towards the street. She carried
herself as straight as a soldier; her step was more of a march than a walk,
and she swung her arms; she didn't walk at all like women in her position
usually did, or should.

He closed the door, then looked around the office and through into the
inner room. Then walking slowly into it, he sat in the chair behind the
desk, cocked his head to the side and, speaking to an imaginary figure
sitting opposite, he said, 'Now, Mr Taylor, I will assign you to the Jarrow
district.' Oh yes, he would always speak civilly to subordinates because,

after all, he was a subordinate himself once, wasn't he? A mere rent collector. But now. He looked round the office. He was master of all he surveyed.

Huh! This was the time to laugh, if only he had someone to laugh with.

When he heard the outer door open he got quickly to his feet and went round the desk.

He looked at the clean but shabbily dressed figure standing, hat in hand, before him, and he said quietly, 'You, Mr Taylor?'

'Yes, sir.' The old man inclined his head, and Rory, now making a derogatory sound in his throat, said, 'You needn't sir me, Mr Taylor. I'm just like yourself, a roundsman. Me name's Connor. The old man – Mr Kean – is in bed with a cold. His daughter's just been along. She says you're to take my district.'

'Anything you say, Mr Connor. Anything you say.'

God! had he sounded as servile as this when he was confronted by Kean? There should be a law of some kind against bringing men to their knees.

As he stared at the old man it came to him that everything in his life had changed. And it was to go on changing. How, he didn't know, he only knew that things would never again be as they were.

It was half-past five when he made his way from the office to Birchingham House in Westoe, and it was raining, a fine chilling soaking rain.

The house was not in what was usually called the village, nor did it stand among those that had sprung up to run parallel with that part of Shields that lay along the river, nor was it one of a small number that remained aloof in their vast grounds. But it was of that section the social standing of which was determined by its size, the number of servants it supported, and whether its owner hired or owned his carriages.

And Birchingham House had another distinction. Although it stood in only two acres of ground it was situated on the side road that led off the main road to Harton and to two substantial estates, one belonging to a mine owner, the other to a gentleman who was known to own at least six iron ships that plied their trade from the Tyne.

The histories of the houses of the notabilities of the town were known to the nobodies of the town; and the notabilities themselves formed a topic of gossip, not only in the bars that lined the river-front, but also in the superior clubs and societies that flourished in the town.

But the situation of his master's house or of his master himself had not up till this moment impressed Rory with any significance. Kean, to him, had been just a money-grabbing skinflint who owned rows of property, particularly in Jarrow, which should have been pulled down years ago, and streets in Shields that were fast dropping into decay for want of repair. Yet in this respect he admitted Kean was no worse than any of the landlords he represented.

Now, as he neared the house in the dark and saw the front steps leading to it lighted by two bracket lamps, he stopped for a moment and peered at it through the rain. It was big. There were ten windows along the front of it alone. Moreover, it was three-storey. He couldn't quite make out the top one, only that there was a gleam of glass up there. Likely attics. There was a carriage standing on the drive at the foot of the steps and he paused near it to look up at the driver sitting huddled deep in a cloaked coat. The man hadn't noticed him; he seemed to be asleep.

He hesitated. Should he go to the front door or the back door? Damn it all, why not the front! Why not!

He went up the steps and pulled the bell.

The door was answered by a maid. She was wearing a starched apron over a black alpaca dress. The bib of the apron had a wide, stiff frill that continued over the straps on her shoulders. She had a starched cap on her head and the strings from it looked as stiff as the cap itself and were tied under her chin in a bow. She was evidently flustered and said, 'Yes, yes. Who is it?'

'I'm Mr Connor. Miss Kean told me to come. I've brought the takings.'

'Oh! Oh!' She looked from one side to the other, then said, 'Well, you'd better come in.' And she stood aside and let him pass her into the small lobby, then opened another door into a hall, which he noted immediately was as big as the kitchen at home.

'Stay there,' she said, 'an' I'll tell her, that's if she can come, the master's had a turn. They've had to send for the doctor again. He's right bad.' She nodded at him, then made for the stairs that led from the hallway in a half spiral and disappeared from view.

He stood looking around him, frankly amazed at what he saw. To the right of the staircase was a side table with a lamp on it. He noted that it was oil, not gas. Yet they had gas outside. The soft light from it illuminated a large oil painting on the wall showing the head and shoulders of a man: he had a broad, flat face, and the high collar was wedged into the jowls below his chin; he had a white fringe of hair above his ears, the rest of his head was bald; his eyes were round and bright and seemed to be looking with stern condemnation at the visitor. Rory did not need to guess that this was an ancestor of Mr Kean, and also that the lamp was there as a sort of illuminated commemoration to do him honour.

A cabinet stood against the wall at the far side of the stairs. He had never seen the like of it before, not even in a picture. It was glass-fronted and made of yellowish wood picked out in gold; the legs were spindly with fancy cross-bars connecting the four of them. It had two shelves. The top one held figures, some single, some in groups; the lower shelf had glass goblets standing on it. From what he could see at this distance they were etched with paintings.

There were a number of doors going off all round the hall, and the thick red carpet he was standing on reached to the walls on all sides except where one door was deeply inset in an alcove and had a step down to it.

He felt his mouth closing when he heard the rustle of a gown on the stairs and saw Charlotte Kean coming down towards him. Her face wore a worried expression. She said immediately, 'My father has taken a turn for the worse, we are very concerned. Will you come this way?'

Without a word he followed her down the step and through the door that was set in the alcove and found himself in an office, but an office very different from the one in Tangard Street. The room in a way was a pattern of the hall, thick carpet, highly polished desk, the top strewn with papers and ledgers. There were paintings on all the walls except that which was taken up with two long windows over which the curtains had not been drawn.

He watched her turn up the gas light; the mantle, encased in its fancy globe gave out a soft light and set the room in a warm glow.

He couldn't understand the feeling he was experiencing. He didn't know whether it was envy, admiration, or respect, that kind of grudging respect the symbols of wealth evoke. He only knew that the feeling was making him feel all arms and legs.

'Sit down, Mr Connor.'

This was the second time in one day she had invited him to be seated.

He hesitated to take the leather chair that she had proffered; instead, looking down at the bag he had placed on the desk, he opened it for her and took out a number of smaller bags and the two pocket ledgers, which he placed before her, saying, 'I've counted everything, it's in order.'

She glanced up at him, 'Thank you.' Then with her hand she indicated the chair again. And now he sat down and watched her as she emptied each bag and counted the money, then checked it against the books.

In the gaslight and with her expression troubled as it was, she looked different from what she had done in the stark grey light this morning, softer somehow.

The money counted, she returned the books to the bag; then rising, she stood looking at him for a moment before saying, 'I'm sure I can trust you, Mr Connor, to see to things in the office until my father is better. I . . . I may not be able to get along. You see' – she waved her hand over the desk – 'there is so much other business to see to. And he wants me with him all the time.'

'Don't worry about the office, miss, everything will be all right there. And . . . and Mr Taylor seems a steady enough man.'

'Thank you, Mr Connor.'

'I'm sorry about your father.'

'I'm sure you are.'

He stared back into her face. There was that something in her tone. Another time he would have said to himself, Now how does she mean that?

He opened the door to let her pass out into the hall, and there she turned to him and asked, 'Is it still raining?'

'Yes. Yes, it was when I came in.'

'You have a long walk home. Go into the kitchen and they will give you something to drink.'

Crumbs from the rich man's table. Soup kitchens run by lady bountifuls. Clogs for the barefoot. Why was he thinking like this? She only meant to be kind, and he answered as if he thought she was. 'Thank you, miss, but I'd rather get home.'

'But you don't look too well yourself, Mr Connor.'

'I'm all right, miss. Thank you all the same. Good night, miss.'

'Good night, Mr Connor.'

The maid appeared from the shadows and let him out. He walked down the steps and along the curving drive into the road, feeling like some beggar who had been given alms. He felt deflated, insignificant, sort of lost. It was that house.

He walked through the rain all the way back to the beginning of Westoe, down through Laygate and on to Tyne Dock, through the arches and the last long trek up Simonside Bank into the country and the cottage.

Opening the door, he staggered in and dropped into a chair without taking off his sodden coat, and he made no protest when Lizzie tugged his boots from his feet while Ruth loosened his scarf and coat and held him up while she pulled them from him.

He had no need to pretend tonight that he was ill, at least physically, for the first day's work had taken it out of him, and the trail back from Westoe had been the last straw.

When later in the evening Jimmy, by way of comfort, whispered to him, 'When we go to the yard it'll be easier for you, you could cut from the office to the boatyard in five minutes,' he nodded at him while at the same time thinking, not without scorn, The boatyard! With thirty-five pounds he could have got himself a mortgage on a decent house. Slowly it came to him the reason why he had allowed himself to become saddled with the boatyard. It wasn't only because he wanted to kill two birds with one stone: marry Janie and give Jimmy something of his own to live and work for; it was because he wanted to get away from here, from the kitchen; and now from their concern for his mental state, which must be bad, so they thought, when he still wouldn't go and see his best friend, and him in prison.

Only last night when he said good-bye to Janie the rooms over the boatyard had appeared to him like a haven. And later, as he lay awake staring into the blackness listening to Jimmy's untroubled breathing, he had thought, Once we get there, once I'm married, I'll see it all different-ly. Then like a child and with no semblance of Rory Connor, he had buried his face in the pillow and cried from deep within him. 'I'll make it up to him when he comes out. I'll make him understand. He'll see I could do nothing about it at the time 'cos I was too bad. He'll understand. Being John George, he'll understand. And I'll make it up to him, I will. I will.'

But now, after his visit to Birchingham House, he was seeing the boat house for what it was, a tumbledown riverside shack, and he thought, I must have been mad to pay thirty-five pounds for the goodwill of that. Look where it's landed me. And the gate shut once again on his thinking as an inner voice said, 'Aye; and John George.'

CHAPTER 2

They were married on the Saturday after Easter. It was a quiet affair in that they hadn't a big ceilidh. They went by brake to the Catholic church in Jarrow, together with Ruth, Paddy, Lizzie, Jimmy, and Bill Waggett. A great deal of tact and persuasion had to be used on Gran Waggett in order that she should stay behind. Who was going to help Kathleen Leary with the tables? And anyway, Kathleen being who she was needed somebody to direct her, and who better than Gran herself?

Janie's wedding finery was plain but good, for her flounced grey coat had once belonged to her mistress, as had also the blue flowered cotton dress she wore underneath. Her blue straw hat she had bought herself, and her new brown buttoned boots too.

She was trembling as she knelt at the altar rails, but then the church was icy cold and the priest himself looked blue in the face and weary into the bargain. He mumbled the questions: Wilt thou have this man? Wilt thou have this woman? And they in turn mumbled back.

After they had signed their names and Rory had kissed her in front of them all they left the church and got into the brake again, which was now surrounded by a crowd of screaming children shouting 'Hoy a ha'penny oot! Hoy a ha'penny oot!'

They had come prepared with ha'pennies. Ruth and Lizzie and Jimmy threw out from both sides of the brake; but they were soon finished and when there were no more forthcoming the shouts that followed them now were, 'Shabby weddin' . . . shabby weddin',' and then the concerted chorus of:

> Fleas in yer blankets,
> No lid on your netty,
> To the poor house you're headin',
> Shabby weddin', shabby weddin'.

The fathers laughed and Ruth clicked her tongue and Lizzie said, 'If I was out there I'd skite the hunger off them. By God! I would.' But Janie and Rory just smiled, and Jimmy, sitting silently at the top end of the brake, his hands dangling between his knees, looked at them, and part of him was happy, and part of him, a deep hidden part, was aching.

Out of decency Jimmy did not immediately go down to the yard. The young married couple were to have the place to themselves until Monday, and on Monday morning the new pattern of life was to begin, for Janie had had her way and was continuing to go daily to the Buckhams'.

Of course, in the back of her mind she knew that the three shillings had been a great inducement to Rory seeing her side of the matter, for now that he wasn't gaming there was no way to supplement his income, and what was more, as she had pointed out, he would be expected to give a bit of help at home since he was depriving them of both his own and Jimmy's money. So the arrangement was that, until Jimmy got some orders, for his sculler was almost finished, then she would continue to go daily to her place . . .

Having clambered up the steps in the dark and unlocked the door and dropped their bundles and a bass hamper on to the floor, they clung to each other in the darkness, gasping and laughing after the exertion of humping the baggage from where the cart had dropped them at the far end of the road.

'Where's the candle?'

'On the mantelpiece of course.' She was still laughing.

He struck a match and lit the candle, then held it up as he looked towards the table on which the lamp stood.

When the lamp was lit he said, 'Well, there you are now, home sweet home.'

Janie stood and looked about her. 'I'll have to get stuck in here at nights,' she said.

'Well, if you will go working in the day-time, Mrs Connor.' He pulled her to him again and they stood pressed close looking silently now into each other's face. 'Happy?'

She smiled softly, 'Ever so.'

'It's not going to be an easy life.'

'Huh! what do I care about that as long as we're together. Easy life?' She shook her head. 'I'd go fish guttin' if I could help you, an' you know how I hate guttin' fish, even when we used to get them for practically nowt from the quay. Do you remember walkin' all the way down into Shields and getting a huge basketful for threepence?'

'Only because they were on the point of going rotten.'

'Ger-away with you . . . Do you want something to eat?'

'No.'

'You're not hungry?'

'Not for food.'

Her lips pressed tightly together; she closed her eyes and bowed her head.

He now put his hands up to her hair and unpinned her hat and throwing it aside, unbuttoned her coat.

'I'll have to get these bundles unpacked and . . . and tidied up.'

He went on undoing the buttons. 'There's all day the morrow and the next day and the next, all our life to undo bundles . . .'

'Hie! what're you doin'? That's me good coat. Look, it's on the floor.'

'Leave it on the floor; there's more to follow.'

'Rory! Rory! the bed isn't made up.'

'The bed is made up, I saw to it.'

'Oh Rory! . . . An' I'm cold, I'm cold, I'm cold. I'll have to get me nightie.'

'You're not going to need a nightie.'

'Aw, Rory! . . . Eeh!' She let out a squeal as, dressed only in her knickers and shift, he swung her up into his arms and carried her through into the bedroom and dropped her on to the bed. She lay there just where he had dropped her and in the dim light reflected from the kitchen she watched him throw off his clothes.

When he jumped on to the bed beside her she squealed and said, 'Ech! the lamp.'

'The lamp can wait.'

They were pressed close, but she was protesting slightly, she didn't want to be rushed. She was a bit afraid of this thing. If she could only make him take it quietly – lead up to it sort of. Her grannie had said it hurt like hell. His lips were moving round her face when she murmured, in a futile effort to stem his ardour, 'Oh Rory, Rory. I'll never be happier than I am at this minute. It's been a wonderful day, hasn't it? . . . They were all so

good, an' they enjoyed themselves, didn't they? I bet they'll keep up the
jollification all night.' She moaned softly as his hands moved over her;
then, her voice trailing weakly away, she ended, 'If-only-John-George-
had-been-there . . .'

His hands ceased their groping, his lips became still on her breast and
she screamed out now as he actually pushed her from him with such force
that her shoulders hit the wall as he yelled at her 'God Almighty! can't you
give him a rest? What've you got to bring him up now for, at this minute?
You did it on purpose. *You did!*'

In the silence that followed he listened to her gasping. Then she was in
his arms again and he was rocking her. 'Oh lass, I'm sorry, I'm sorry. I
didn't mean it. Did I hurt you? I'm sorry, I'm sorry. It was only, well, you
know, I've waited so long . . . And, and . . .'

When she didn't answer him, or make any sound, he said softly, 'Janie.
Janie. Say something.'

What she said was, 'It's all right. It's all right.'

'I love you. I love you, Janie. Aw, I love you. If I lost you I'd go mad,
barmy.'

'It's all right. It's all right, you won't lose me.'

'Will you always love me?'

'Always.'

'You promise?'

'Aye, I promise.'

'I'll never love anybody in me life but you, I couldn't. Aw, Janie, Janie
. . .'

Later in the night when the light was out and he was asleep she lay still
in his arms but wide awake. It hadn't been like she had expected, not in
any way. Perhaps she wasn't goin' to like that kind of thing after all. Her
grannie said some didn't, while others couldn't get enough. Well she'd
never be one of those, she was sure of that already. Perhaps it was spoiled
for her when he threw her against the wall because she had mentioned
John George.

It was most strange how he reacted now whenever John George's name
was mentioned. She could understand him not wanting to go to the prison, him having this feeling about being shut in, but she couldn't work out
in her own mind why he never spoke of John George. And when the name
was mentioned by anybody else he would remain silent. But to act like
he had done the night just because . . . Well, she was flabbergasted.

Her grannie, as part of the advice she had given her on marriage last
Sunday, had said, 'If he want any funny business, out of the ordinary like,
and some of them do, you never know till the door's closed on you, you
have none of it. An' if he raises his hand to you, go for the poker. Always

leave it handy. Start the way you mean to go on 'cos with the best of them, butter wouldn't melt in their mouths afore they get you in that room. But once there, it's like Adam and Eve racing around the Garden of Eden every night. An' if you cross your fingers and say skinch, or in other words, hold your horses, lad, I've had enough, they bring the priest to you, an' he reads the riot act. "Supply your man's needs," he says, "or it's Hell fire and brimstone for you." So off you gallop again, even when your belly's hangin' down to your knees.'

She had laughed at her grannie and with her grannie. She had put her arms around the old woman and they had rocked together until the tears had run down their faces, and the last words she had said to her were, 'Don't worry, Gran, nowt like that'll happen to me. It's Rory I'm marrying, and I know Rory. I should do, there's only a thin wall divided us for years.'

But now they hadn't been hours married afore he had tossed her against a wall, and tossed her he had because he had hurt her shoulder and it was still paining. Life was funny . . . odd.

CHAPTER 3

Septimus Kean died, and Rory continued to take the day's collections to the house for some four weeks after Mr Kean had been buried, and each time Miss Kean received him in what she called the office. But on this particular Friday night she met him in the hall and said to him, 'Just leave the bag on the office table, Mr Connor, we'll see to that later. By the way, are you in a hurry?'

He was in a hurry, he was in a hurry to get home to Janie, to sit before the fire and put his feet up and talk with Jimmy, and hear if he had managed to get an order, and to find out if any of the Pitties had been about again . . . The Pitties. He'd give his right arm, literally, if he could get his own back on the Pitties. There was a deep acid hate in him for the Pitties. And it would appear they hadn't finished with him for they had been spying about the place. He knew that to get a start on the river Jimmy would have to take the droppings, but if it lay with the Pitties he wouldn't get even the droppings. They were beasts, dangerous beasts. By God he'd give anything to get one over on them.

He answered her, 'Oh no, not at all.'

'There is something I wish to discuss with you. I'm about to have a cup of tea, would you care to join me?'

Old Kean's daughter asking him to join her in a cup of tea! Well! Well!

He could scarcely believe his ears. Things were looking up. By lad, they were.

In the hall she said to the maid, 'Take Mr Connor's coat and hat.'

Then he was following her to the end of the hall, and into a long room. There was a big fire blazing in the grate to the right of them. It was a fancy grate with a black iron basket. It had a marble mantelpiece with, at each end, an urn-shaped vase standing on it, and above the mantelpiece was another large oil painting of yet another past Kean.

At first glance the prominent colour of the room seemed to be brown. The couch drawn up before the fire and the two big side chairs were covered with a brown corded material. The furniture was a shining brown. There were three small tables with knick-knacks on them. A piece of furniture that looked like a sideboard but like no sideboard he'd ever seen before had silver candlesticks on it. The velvet curtains hanging at the windows were green with a brown bobble fringe and were supported from a cornice pole as thick as his upper arm.

'Sit down, Mr Connor.' She motioned him towards one of the big chairs and he sat down, then watched her pull a handbell to the side of the fireplace.

When the door opened she turned to the maid, not the same one who had opened the door to him, and said, 'I'll have tea now, Jessie; please bring two cups.'

The girl bent her knee, then went out.

He noticed that although her tone was uppish, as always, she had said 'Please.'

He watched her as she sat back in the corner of the couch. She made a movement with her legs and for a moment he thought that she was actually going to cross them. But what she did was cross her feet, and as she did so her black skirt rode above her ankles and he saw the bones pressing through what must have been silk stockings . . . She certainly looked after herself in the way of dress did this one. She was in mourning but her mourning was silk.

'I will come to the point, Mr Connor. I have a proposition to make to you.'

'A proposition?' His eyes widened slightly.

'I don't know whether you are aware that property dealing was only one of my father's interests.' She did not wait for him to comment on this but went on, 'Among other things, he had interests in a number of growing concerns and, since my grandfather died, other small businesses have come into the family. Do you know the Wrighton Tallow Works?'

'I've heard of them.'

'Well, my grandfather owned the works and naturally they fell to my father, and unfortunately, I say unfortunately, because of the loss of my father they are now my concern . . . How far have you advanced in book-keeping Mr Connor?'

'Advanced?' He blinked at her. 'What . . . what do you rightly mean, miss?'

'What I mean is, have you studied any further than that which is required to tot up rent accounts? Have you thought of your own advancement in this line, such as that of becoming a fully fledged clerk in a bank, or to a solicitor, say?'

'No, miss.' The answer was curt, his tone cold. 'The opportunities didn't provide themselves.' He knew too late that he should have said present, not provide.

'Opportunities are there for the taking, Mr Connor. This town offers great opportunities to those who are willing to take advantage of them. It isn't only the shipyards and the boat buildery and such who offer apprenticeships in particular crafts; there are the arts.'

The arts! He narrowed his eyes at her. What was she getting at? Was she having him on, trying to get a bit of amusement out of him? The arts! Why didn't she come to the point?

She came to the point by saying, 'I have in mind that I need a manager, Mr Connor, someone who is capable not only of taking charge of the property side of my affairs but who could assist me in the running of my other businesses. There are places that need to be visited, books to be gone over. Of course I have my accountant and my solicitor but these are there only for the final totalling at the year's end, and for advice should I need it. But there is so much to be seen to in between times and my father used to attend to this side of affairs, for you know, if a warehouse or business is not visited regularly those in charge become slack.' She stared at him without speaking for almost a full minute before saying, 'Would you consider taking on this post if, and when, you became qualified to do so? You would, of course, need a little training.'

His heart was thumping against his ribs causing his breath to catch in his throat. He couldn't take it in. She was proposing that he should be her manager. He was peering at her through the narrow slits of his eyes now, he was puzzled. Why wasn't she advertising for somebody right away if the burden of the businesses was so great on her?

As if she were reading his thoughts she said, 'I have no doubt I could get someone to fill this post almost immediately, but then the person would be strange to me, and . . . and I don't mix easily. What I mean is, I take a long time in getting to know people.'

They were staring at each other through the fading light, and in silence again. It was she who broke it, her voice low now, ordinary sounding, no

uppishness to it. 'I . . . I have known you for some time, Mr Connor, and
have always thought that you should be capable of much better things
than mere rent collecting.'

Before he could answer the door opened and the maid entered pushing
a tea trolley.

When the trolley was by the side of the couch she looked at the maid and
said, 'I'll see to it, Jessie. I'll ring when I need you.'

'Yes, miss.' Again the dip of the knee.

'Do you take sugar, Mr Connor?'

'No. No, thank you.'

'That is unusual; men usually like a lot of sugar.'

He watched her pour the weak-looking tea from a small silver teapot
and add milk to it from a matching jug, and when a few minutes later he
sipped at it he thought, My God! dish-water.

'Oh, I'm sorry, I didn't ask what tea you preferred. You see, they're so
used to bringing me China; I'll ring and get some . . .'

'Oh no, please don't. It's nice, it's only different. And' – he grinned now
at her – 'you can understand I'm not used to havin' China tea.'

She actually laughed now, and he noticed that it changed her face and
made her almost pleasant-looking, except that her nose remained just as
sharp. 'I hope it will be a taste you will learn to acquire in the future.'

He doubted it but he nodded at her, smiling in return.

He took the buttered scone she proffered him and found it good, and
had another, and by the time he had eaten a cake that melted in his mouth
he was laughing inside, thinking, By gum! they just want to see me now,
all them in the kitchen. They just want to see me now. And wait till I tell
Janie. My! who would believe it? She had asked if he was willing to learn
to manage her affairs. God! just give him the chance. By lad! he had fallen
on his feet at last. It wouldn't matter now if the boatyard never made a go
of it. But he hoped it would, for Jimmy's sake. He mentioned the boatyard
to her now. It was when she said, 'I mustn't keep you any longer, Mr
Connor, you have a long walk home. But I will leave you to think over my
proposition. Perhaps tomorrow evening you will tell me what you have
decided. If your answer is favourable I can put you in touch with a man
who would teach you book-keeping and the rudiments of management.
And perhaps you could attend night school. But we can discuss that later.'

He rose to his feet, saying, 'I'm not more than ten minutes' hard tramp
from my home now; I'm . . . I'm on the waterfront.'

She raised her eyebrows as she repeated, 'The waterfront?'

'Yes.' He squared his shoulders. 'I became interested in a boatyard, a
very small one mind.' He smiled as he nodded at her. 'A pocket handkerchief, some folks would call it, but nevertheless it's big enough to make a

keel and scullers and such like. There's a house of sorts attached. I . . . I
took it for my brother. He's served his time in boat building, small boats
that is, the same line, scullers, wherries and such, and it's always been his
dream to have a place of his own where he could build. So I heard of this
concern. The man had died, and . . . and it was going reasonable, so I took
a chance.'

Her face was stretching into a wide smile, her lips were apart showing a
set of strong white teeth. 'Well, well!' She inclined her head towards him.
'I wasn't wrong, was I? You do have business acumen. Where is this
place?'

'Oh, it's yon side of the mill dam. It's so small you wouldn't be able to
see it, not among all the other yards along there. It used to belong to a Mr
Kilpatrick.'

'Kilpatrick?' She shook her head. 'I don't recall hearing the name. But
. . . but I'm very interested in your enterprise. I must come and see it some
time.'

'Yes, yes, do that.'

She walked with him to the door and although the maid was standing
ready to open it she herself let him out, saying, 'Good night, Mr Connor.
We will reopen this subject tomorrow evening.'

'Yes, as you say, miss. Good night.'

He was walking down the drive . . . no, marching down the drive.

'We will reopen this subject tomorrow evening.'

Indeed, indeed, we will.

Would you believe it?

They said the age of miracles was past.

Would he go to night school?

He'd go to hell and sit on a hot gridiron to please her.

But on the road he slowed his pace and again asked himself why she had
picked him. And he gave himself her own answer. She didn't mix and it
took her a long time to get to know people. Aye. Aye well, he could
understand that. She wasn't the kind that most people would take to. No
looks and too smart up top for most men, he supposed, for he had the idea
she'd be brainy. And that would apply to her effect on women an' all.

Hip-hip-hooray! He wanted to throw his hat in the air. Things were
happening. They were happening all the time. Janie! Here I come . . . A
manager!

What wage would he get?

He'd have to leave that to her of course but he'd know the morrow night.

CHAPTER 4

Janie left the Buckhams' with the mistress's words racing round in her mind. 'Well, you have a month to think it over, Janie,' she had said. 'It would be wonderful for you and it'll only be for three weeks. And just think, in all your life you might never have the opportunity to go abroad again. And the children would love to have you with them, you know that.'

Yes, Janie knew that, but she also knew that she was being asked to go to keep the children out of the way and let the master and mistress enjoy their holiday in France.

She had said she would talk to her husband about it, but she already knew what his answer would be. He hated the idea of her being out every day and if it wasn't that he had needed her wages he would have put his foot down before now. But with this new development and Miss Kean offering to make him manager, well, she knew that her days at the Buckham's were numbered; in fact, she could have given in her notice this morning.

There was something else on her mind. She had promised John George she would go and see that lass of his, but with one thing and another she had never had time. But tonight Rory would be late, for even now he'd be in Westoe clinching the matter, and so she told herself why not clear her conscience and go round and see that girl. She must be all of six months' gone.

When she reached the end of the road she did not, automatically, turn right and cut down to the river but went into a jumble of side streets and towards Horsley Terrace.

They were, she considered, nice houses in the terrace, respectable. It was number twenty-four; it had three steps up to the front door and an iron railing cutting off four feet of garden. She went up the steps and rapped on the door with the knocker. When it was opened she stared at the young woman in front of her. She wasn't pregnant. 'Could . . . could I speak with Miss Maggie Ridley please?'

The young woman cast a quick glance over her shoulder, then stepped towards her, pulling the door half closed behind her.

'She not here.'

'Oh, I had a message for her.'

The girl's eyes widened. 'A message? Who from?'

'Well, he's . . . he's a friend of hers.'

The young woman stared at her for a moment, then poked her face forward, hissing, 'Well, if it's the friend I think it is you can tell him that she's married. Tell him that.'

'Married?'

'That's what I said.'

'Oh, well' – Janie was nodding her head now – 'In a way I'm glad to hear it. I . . . I hope she'll be happy.'

The face looking into hers seemed to crumple and now the whispered tone was soft and laden with sadness as she said, 'He . . . he was a friend of, of my father's, he's a widower with a grown-up family.'

In the look they exchanged there was no need to say any more.

Janie now nodded towards the young woman and said, 'Thank you, I'll . . . I'll tell him,' then turned and went down the steps. Poor John George! And the poor lass. A dead old man likely. The very thought of it was mucky, nasty.

Rory hadn't returned when she got in, but Jimmy was there with the kettle boiling and the table set, and immediately he said, 'Sit down and put your feet up.'

'I'm not tired.'

'Well, you should be. And you will be afore the night's out, I've put the washing in soak.'

'Thanks, Jimmy. Any news?'

'Aye, Mr Pearson, you know Pearson's Warehouse, I went in and asked him the day. I said I'd carry anything. He joked at first and said he had heard they were wantin' a battleship towed from Palmer's. And then he said there were one or two bits he wanted sending across to Norway.' He laughed, then went on excitedly, 'But after that he said, "Well, lad, I'll see what I can do for you." He said he believed in passing work around, there was too many monopolies gettin' a hold in the town. I've got to look in the morrow.'

'Oh Jimmy, that's grand.' She took hold of his hand. 'Eeh! you just want a start. And when I'm home all day I could give you a hand, I could, I'm good at lumpin' stuff. And I could learn to stccr an' all . . . But I'd better learn to swim afore that.' She pushed at him and he laughed with her, saying, 'Aye, but if they had to learn to swim afore they learned to row a boat on this river it would be empty; hardly any sailors swim.'

'Go on!'

'It's a fact.'

'Eeh! well, I'll chance it, I'll steer for you, or hoist the sail, 'cos have you thought you'll need another hand?' At the sound of footsteps she turned her head quickly away from him and towards the door, and she was on her feet when Rory entered the room, and she saw immediately that he was in great high fettle.

'It's settled then?'

'Out of me way, Mrs Connor.' He struck a pose and marched down the room as if he were carrying a swagger stick, and when he reached Jimmy he slapped the top of his own hat, saying, 'Touch yer peak, boy. Touch yer peak.'

Then they were all clinging together laughing, and he swung them round in a circle, shouting:

> 'Ring a ring o' roses,
> Keels, scullers and posies,
> Managers, managers,
> All fall down.'

'But we're all going up!' He pulled them to a stop and, looking into Janie's laughing face, he added, 'Up! Up! We're going up, lass; nothing's going to stop us. She's for me, why God only knows, but she's the ladder on which we're going to climb. You take that from me. All of us' – he punched Jimmy on the head – 'all of us . . . She's got influence, fingers in all pies, and that includes this river an' all. We're going up, lad.'

Later, when in bed together and closely wrapped against each other, he said to her, 'You haven't seemed as over the moon as I thought you would be. There's something on your mind, isn't there?'

She didn't answer, and when he insisted, 'Come on,' she said, 'There's two things on me mind, Rory, but if I mention them they'll both cause rows, so I'd better not, had I?'

He was quiet for a moment before saying, 'Go on, tell me. I won't go off the deep end, whatever they are . . . I promise, whatever they are.'

It was a long moment before she said, 'Well mind, don't forget what you said.'

He waited, and then her voice a whisper she began, 'The missis, she wants me to go with them to France for a holiday. Of course, it's only to keep the bairns out of the way, I know, but she keeps tellin' me that I won't get the chance again . . .'

'Who says you won't get the chance again? They're not the only ones who can go to France. You're not goin'. You told her you're not going? All right, all right, I'm not going to get me neb up about it, but you did tell her you weren't going'?'

'I said I didn't think you would hear of it.'

'That's right I won't. And you can also tell her when you're on, that you're putting your notice in . . . Well now, the other thing?' He waited.

'I went the night to take a message to . . . to John George's lass. She's . . . she's married.'

'Married!'

'Yes, to an old man, a widower with a grown-up family.'

'It's . . . it's the best thing.' She could hardly hear his voice but she was relieved that he had kept his promise and hadn't gone for her for mentioning John George or his affairs. And now, a minute later, he was mumbling into her neck, 'When he comes out I'll set him up. I've . . . I've always meant to do something for him but now I can, I'll set him up properly in something.'

'Oh, Rory, Rory. Aw, that's . . . that's my Rory. I knew you would. Aw ta, thanks, lad, thanks. I'll tell the missis the morrow straight out, I'll tell her me husband's put his foot down and said no France and that I'll have to be givin' in me notice shortly. Oh, Rory, Rory . . .'

In the middle of the night she was wakened by him crying out. His arms were flaying about and when she put her hand on his head it came away wet with sweat and she cried at him, 'Rory! Rory! wake up,' but he continued to thrash about in the bed, gabbling out words from which she could distinguish bits of the conversation that they'd had last night. 'I'll make it up to John George, I will, I will. I always meant to.' Then he began to shout, ' 'Twas being shut in, 'twas being shut in.'

When she finally managed to wake him he spluttered, 'What's it? What's-the-matter?' Then putting his hand to his head, he added, 'I was dreamin' . . . Was I talking?'

'Just jabbering. It was all the excitement.'

'Aye, yes,' he said, 'all the excitement. By! I'm wringing.'

'Yes, you are. Lie down, right down under the clothes here.' She drew him towards her and held him closely, soothing him as if he were a child, until he went to sleep again.

CHAPTER 5

On three afternoons and three evenings of each of the next three weeks Rory visited Mr Dryden, to be coached in the matter of accountancy and business management.

Mr Dryden had in his early years been in accountancy, and later had become a solicitor's clerk, and the reports he gave to Miss Kean on the progress of his pupil were most encouraging. 'He shows great acumen,' he told her. 'I think you have made a wise choice,' he told her. But he also told his friends with a smirk that old Kean's daughter had taken on a protégé. Ha! Ha! they said. Well, she wasn't likely to get a husband, so she had to resort to a pastime. Yet, as some of them remarked, she ought to have known her place and picked her pastime from a grade higher than that of rent collectors, and this one by all accounts wasn't a skin away from a common labouring man. If it wasn't that the fellow was already married you could put another version to it, for as had already been demonstrated in one or two instances she was a strong-headed young woman who took little heed of people's opinions. Look what she was like on committees. She had got herself talked about more than once for openly defying the male opinion. Of course, this was due to the type of education she'd been given. She had been sent away, hadn't she? To the south somewhere, hadn't she? That was her mother's doing. So . . . well, what could you expect?

Rory was not unaware of Mr Dryden's personal opinion of him. He gauged it in the condescending tone the old man used when speaking to him. But what did it matter, he could put up with that.

He was now receiving the handsome sum of twenty-five shillings a week, with the promise of it being raised when he should finally take over his duties. He'd had glimpses into what these would be during the past few days when he had seen the number of properties in Hexham and Gateshead, and the haberdashery and hatters shops that had been left by Grandfather Kean. All this besides the business old Kean himself had had on the side.

He became more and more amazed when he thought of what his late employer must have been worth. Yet never a night had he missed, winter or summer, coming to the office to pick up the takings, except when he was called away to visit his father. He had never, not to his knowledge, taken a holiday all the time he had been there, and yet he was rolling in money.

He wondered what she would be worth altogether. If she ever married, some man would come in for a packet. But apart from her not being the kind to take a man's fancy he thought she was too independent to think that way. No one, he considered, could be as business-like as her without having the abilities of a man in her make-up . . .

It was Saturday morning and he had brought the takings from his two men – he thought of them as his now. She had allowed him to choose the second man himself. This fellow was young and hadn't done any rent collecting before but he had been to school continuously up till he was fourteen, and that was something to start on. Moreover, he was bright and eager and in need of work. He felt he had made a good choice. And he told her so. 'Patterson's doing well,' he said. 'Gettin' round quickly. And so far he's allowed nobody to take advantage of him, you know, soft-soap him.'

'Good.' She smiled at him from across the desk; then she said, 'I would like you to accompany me to Hexham on Monday.'

'Hexham?' He moved his head downwards while keeping his eyes on her. 'Very well.' He sometimes omitted to say miss, but she had never pulled him up for it.

'I think it's time you saw the places you're going to be responsible for.'

'Aye, yes, of course.' He'd have to stop himself saying aye.

'By the way –' she was still smiling at him – 'I should like to come and see your boatyard. I'm very interested in it. I may be of some assistance in supplying freight – in a small way. Would this afternoon be convenient?'

He thought quickly. What was the place like, was it tidy? Was there any washing hanging about? No, Janie had cleared the ironing up last night and scrubbed out last thing.

He nodded at her, saying, 'Yes, that'll be all right with me. Me wife won't be in because she works until four on a Saturday, she's nursemaid at the Buckhams in Westoe, but you'll be welcome to see . . .'

'Your . . . wife?' The words came from deep within her chest and were separate as if they were strange and she had never spoken them before.

'Yes. Yes, miss, me wife . . .' His voice trailed off for he was amazed to see the colour flooding up over her face like a great blush.

'I . . . I wasn't aware that you were married, Mr Connor . . . Since when?'

'Well, well –' he moved uneasily in the chair – 'just recently, miss. I didn't like to mention it to you at the time because the date was fixed for shortly after your father's funeral. I couldn't change it, but it didn't seem proper to . . .'

Her eyes were shaded now as she looked down towards the desk and on to her hands which were lying flat on the blotter, one on each side of the ledger that he had placed before her. Her back was straight, her body looked rigid. She said cooly, 'You should have informed me of your change of situation, Mr Connor.'

'I . . . I didn't think it was of any importance.'

'No importance!' She did not look at him, but now her eyes flicked over the table as if searching for some paper or other. 'A married man cannot give the attention to business that the single man can, for instance, he hasn't the time.'

'Oh, I have all the time . . .'

'Or the interest.' She had raised her eyes to his now. The colour had seeped from her face leaving it moist and grey. 'This alters matters, Mr Connor.'

He stared at her, his voice gruff now as he said, 'I don't understand, I can't see why.'

'You can't? Well then, if you can't then I am mistaken in the intelligence I credited you with.'

His back was as straight as hers now, his face grim.

As she held his gaze he thought, No, no I'd be barmy to think that. I haven't got such a bloody big head on me as that. No! No! Yet it was pretty evident that the fact that he was married had upset her. She was likely one of these people who didn't believe in marriage, there were such about; there was one lived in the end house down the lane. She dressed like a man and it was said that she handled a horse and a boat as well as any man, but she looked half man. This one didn't. Although she had a business head on her shoulders she dressed very much as a woman of fashion might. He couldn't make her out. No, by God! he couldn't.

He said now, 'I can assure you, miss, me being married won't make any difference to my work. I'll give you my time and loyalty . . .'

'But as I have indicated, Mr Connor, only a certain amount of time and an equal amount of your loyalty . . . a married man has responsibilities. We can discuss the matter later. Mr Dryden has been paid in advance for your quarter's tuition, you will continue to go to him. That'll be all at present, Mr Connor. Good day.'

He rose stiffly from the chair. 'Good day . . . miss.'

The maid let him out; she smiled at him broadly. 'Good day, sir,' she said.

He had acquired the title since it was known Miss Kean was sending him for training to be her manager and there was a significant deference in the servants' manners towards him now. She kept six altogether, with the gardener-cum-coachman. He answered her civilly, saying, 'Good day,' but as usual he did not address her by name. His position wasn't such that he felt he could do so yet.

Out on the drive he walked slowly, and at one point he actually stopped and said to himself, No! No! And before he entered the main thoroughfare he again slowed his walk and exclaimed aloud now, 'Don't be a fool!'

He had no false modesty about his personal attraction. He knew that many a back door would have been left open for him if he had just raised an eyebrow or answered a gleam in a hungry woman's eyes. He didn't class himself as particularly handsome but was aware that he had something which was of greater appeal. If he had been asked to define it he would have found it impossible; he only knew that women were aware of him. And he had liked the knowledge, it gave him what he called a lift. But at the same time he knew there was but one woman for him.

But he couldn't get away from the fact that she had done what she had for him because she thought he was single. Now the question was, why? Why?

Yet again he shook his head at himself and said no, no. Why, the woman must be worth a fortune, and although she was as plain as a pikestaff there were men in the town who, he thought, would more than likely overlook such a minor handicap in order to get their hands on what she owned. Doubtless, some were already trying, for twice of late there had been carriages on the drive and he had seen sombre-clothed gentlemen descending towards them as he approached the house. And he recalled now, they had looked at him pretty hard.

But coming to know her as he had done over the past weeks, he imagined she would have all her wits about her with regard to such suitors who would be only after the main chance. She was the kind of woman who would do the choosing rather than be chosen, and apart from her face she had a lot on her side to enable her to do the choosing . . . *Had she been going to choose him?*

He didn't answer himself this time with, 'No! No!' but walked on, muttering instead, 'God Almighty! it's unbelievable.'

'You're quiet the night. Nothing wrong is there? And what made you go back to the office this afternoon?'

'Oh, I had some work to get through. It's been a heavy week, and I've got that Pittie mob on me mind. Did he say he's seen them around the day?'

'No. He only stayed in for a few minutes after I got home, I told you. He said he was goin' down to collect some wood he had roped together.'

'But that was this afternoon. It's dark, he should be back by now. I'd better take a walk out and see if he's comin'.'

He looked towards her where she was kneading dough in a brown earthenware dish, then went out and down the steps into the yard. There was a moon riding high, raced by white scudding clouds. He walked to the end of the little jetty and looked along each side of the river where boats large and small were moored. He liked the river at night when it was quiet like this, but he had made up his mind, at least he had done until this morning, that it wouldn't be long before he moved Janie away from this quarter and into a decent house in the town. He had thought Jimmy could stay on here, Jimmy wouldn't mind living on his own, for he was self-sufficient was Jimmy. But now things had changed. This morning's business had blown his schemes away into dust.

He'd had the feeling of late that he was galloping towards some place but he didn't know where. So many strange things had happened over the past months. He wasn't even wearing the same kind of clothes he wore a few weeks ago for she had hinted not only that he should get a new suit but where he should go to buy it. However, he hadn't patronised the shop she suggested; he hadn't, he told himself, enough money as yet for that kind of tailoring. Nevertheless, he had got himself a decent suit, with a high waistcoat and the jacket flared, and the very cut of it had lifted him out of the rent collector's class. But now the rosy future had suddenly died on him. What would she say on Monday? . . . Well, he'd have to wait and see, that's all he could do.

He heard a soft splash and saw the minute figure of Jimmy steering the boat towards the jetty. He bent down and grabbed the rope that Jimmy threw to him, then said, 'You all right? Where you been all day? What's taken you so long?'

'The wood I'd had piled up, it was scattered, some back in the river, all over. I had a job collectin' it again.'

'The Pitties?'

'I shouldn't wonder. I don't think it could be bairns, it would have been too heavy for them.'

'Well, leave it where it is till the mornin', we'll sort it out then.'

When Jimmy had made fast his boat and was standing on the quay he peered at Rory saying, 'What's up? You look as if you'd lost a tanner and found a threepenny bit. Anything wrong?'

'No, no, nothing. How about you?'

'Oh well, they were around early on in the mornin' again, two of them. They moored just opposite and sat lookin' across, just starin'. But I went on with me work, and I stood for a time and stared back. Then they went off.' And he added, 'If they try anything I'll go straight and tell the river polis.'

'It'll likely be too late then. The only thing is be careful and don't be such a bloody fool stayin' out in the dark. They're not likely to try anything in the daylight, but give them a chance in the dark, and you're asking for it.'

All Jimmy replied to this was, 'Aye. By! I'm hungry,' and ran up the steps, and when he opened the door he sniffed loudly and said, 'Ooh! that smells good.'

Janie turned to him from the table, saying, 'Aye well, now you'll have to wait a bit, we've had to wait for you.'

'I'm hungry, woman.'

'Are you ever anything else?' she laughed at him. 'Well, there's some fresh teacakes there, tuck into them.'

As he broke a hot teacake in two, he asked, 'What's for supper?'

'Finny haddy.'

'Good, and hurry up with it.'

She thrust out her arm to clip his ear, but he dodged the blow and went and sat himself on the steel fender with his back to the oven and laughed and chatted as he ate.

Looking at him, Rory knew a sudden spasm of envy as he thought, he was born bowed, but he was born happy. Why can't I be like him? But then the answer to that one was, they had different mothers. He hadn't

thought along these lines for some time now; it was odd but it was only
when he was faced with trouble that he let his bitterness against Lizzie
have rein.

Of a sudden he said to neither of them in particular, 'Will we have to go
home the morrow again?'

Both Janie and Jimmy turned a quick glance on him and it was Janie
who said, 'Of course we'll have to go home the morrow. We always do,
don't we? It's Sunday.'

'That's what I mean, we always do. Couldn't we do something different, take a trip up the river or something? We've got our own boat.'

'But they'll be expectin' us. It won't be Sunday for them if we don't go
up; they'll all be there.'

'Aye, they'll all be there.' His voice trailed away on a sigh and he turned
and went into the bedroom while Janie and Jimmy exchanged another
look and Jimmy said under his breath, 'Something's wrong. I twigged it
right away.'

'You think so?' Janie whispered back.

'Aye, don't you?'

'Well, I did think he was a bit quiet, but when I asked him he said
everything was all right.'

'Aye, that's what he says, but there's something up. I'm tellin' you,
there's something up.'

When, in the middle of the night, Janie was again woken from her sleep by
Rory's voice, not mumbling this time but shouting, she hissed at him,
'Ssh! ssh! Wake up. What it it?'

But he went on, louder now, 'I'll make it up to you, I will . . . I know . . .
I know, but I couldn't.'

'Rory! Rory! wake up.'

'Five pounds. I had it, I had it. You're to blame.'

'Rory! do you hear me?' She was trying to shake him.

'Wha'? Wha'?' He half woke and grabbed at her hands, then almost at
the same time threw her aside, crying. 'What was the good of two of us
doin' time! I'm not goin' in there, so don't keep on. You won't get me in
there, not for five pounds, or fifty. Five clarty pounds. Five clarty pounds.
If I'd had the chance I'd have put it back, I would. I . . . would . . .' His
voice trailed away and he fell back on the pillows.

Janie sat bolt upright in the bed staring down through the darkness, not
on to Rory but towards where her hands were gripping the quilt . . . *That
was it then. That was it*! It should have been as clear as daylight from the
beginning.

She saw John George's face through the grid saying, 'Tell Rory that, will you? Tell him I didn't take the five pounds.' And what John George was actually saying was, 'Tell him to own up.' She couldn't believe it, yet she knew it was true. He had let John George, his good friend, go to that stinking place alone. It was true he couldn't have done much about it at first, but after he regained consciousness in hospital he must have known. That's why he hadn't asked for John George. It should have been one of the first things he mentioned. 'What's the matter with John George?' he should have said. 'Why hasn't he come to see me?'

No, she couldn't believe it, she couldn't. But she had to. She now turned her head towards the bulk lying beside her and instinctively hitched herself away from it towards the wall. But the next move she made was almost like that of an animal, for she pounced on him and, her hands gripping his shoulders, she cried, 'Wake up! Wake up!'

'Wha'? What's-it? What's-up? What's-wrong?'

'Get up. Get up.'

As he pulled himself up in the bed she climbed over him, grabbed the matches from the table and lit the candle, and all the while he was repeating, 'What is it? What's the matter?'

The candle lit, she held it upwards and gazed down into his blinking eyes.

'What's up with you? You gone mad or something?'

'Aye, I've gone mad, flamin' mad; bloody well flamin' mad.'

She sounded like Lizzie and her grannie rolled into one. He pushed the clothes back from the bed but didn't get up, he just peered at her. 'What the hell's up with you, woman?'

'You ask me that! Well, you've just had a nightmare an' you've just cleared up somethin' that's been puzzling me for a long time. *You*! Do you know what I could do to you this minute? I could spit in your eye, Rory Connor. I could spit in your eye.'

He now leant his stiff body back against the wall. He'd had a nightmare, he'd been talking. He was sweating, yet cold, it was always cold on the river at night. With a thrust of his arm he pushed her aside and got out of the bed and pulled his trousers on over his linings, but didn't speak; and neither did she. But when he went towards the door to go into the other room she followed him, holding the candle high, and she watched him grab the matches from the mantelpiece and light the lamp. When it was aflame he turned and looked at her and said quietly, 'Well, now you know.'

'Aye, I know. And how you can stand there and say it like that God alone knows. My God! to think you let John George take the rap for you . . .'

He turned on her. His voice low and angry, he said, 'He didn't take the rap for me, he took it for himself. He'd have been caught out sooner or later; he'd been at it for months.'

'Aye, he might have, but only for a few shillings at a time not five pounds.'

'No, not for a few shillings, a pound and more. I'd warned him.'

'You warned him!' Her voice was full of scorn. 'But you went and did the same, and for no little sum either. It was for your five pounds he got put away for the year, not for the little bits.'

'It wasn't. I tell you it wasn't.'

'Oh, shut up! Don't try to stuff me like you've been doin' yourself. That's what you've been tellin' yourself all along, isn't it, to ease your conscience? But your conscience wouldn't be eased, would it? Remember our first night in this place. You nearly knocked me through the wall 'cos I mentioned his name. I should have twigged then.'

'Aye, yes, you should.' His tone was flat now, weary-sounding. 'And if you had, it would have been over and done with, I'd have gone through less.'

'Gone through less! You talkin' about goin' through anything, what about John George?'

'Damn John George!' He was shouting now. 'I tell you he would have gone along the line in any case.'

'You'll keep tellin' yourself that till the day you die, yet you don't believe it because the other night you promised to set him up when he came out. Eeh! –' she now shook her head mockingly at him – 'that was kind of you, wasn't it? And I nearly went on me knees to you for it.'

'Janie –' he came towards her – 'try to understand. You . . . you know how I feel about being locked in, and I was bad at the time. I was bad. God! I nearly died. And that was no make game, I couldn't think clearly not for weeks after.'

As his hand came out towards her she sprang back from it, saying, 'Don't touch me, Rory Connor. Don't touch me, not until you get yourself down to that station and tell them the truth.'

'*What*!' The word carried a high surprised note of utter astonishment. 'You'd have me go along the line now?'

'Aye, I would, and be able to live with you when you came out. It isn't the pinchin' of the five pounds that worries me, an' if nobody had suffered through it I would have said, "Good for you if you can get off with it," but not now, not the way things are; not when that lad's back there. And you know something? When I think of it he could have potched you, he could have said you were the only other one who had a key. He could have said you were a gambling man and would sell your own mother. Oh aye –' she wagged her head now – 'you would sell your real mother for less than five pounds any day in the week, wouldn't you? Poor Lizzie . . .'

The blow that caught her across the mouth sent her staggering, and at the same moment Jimmy came rushing down the ladder. Without a word he went to her where she was leaning against the chest-of-drawers, her back arched, her hand across her mouth, and he put his arm around her waist as he looked towards Rory and said, 'You'll regret that, our Rory. There'll come a day when you'll be sorry for that.'

'You mind your own bloody business. And get out of this.'

'I'll not. I've heard enough to make me as sick as she is. I can't believe it of you, I just can't. And to John George of all people. He'd have laid down his life for you.'

Rory turned from the pair and stumbled to the mantelpiece and, gripping its edge, he stared down into the banked-down fire. That he was more upset by Jimmy's reactions than by Janie's didn't surprise him, for he knew he represented a sort of hero to his brother. He had never done one outstanding thing to deserve it but he had accepted his worship over the years, and found comfort in it, but now Jimmy had turned on him.

God Almighty! why did everything happen to him at once? Her, yesterday, blaming him for being married, now this with Janie; and not only Janie, Jimmy. Yet he knew that if, come daylight, he took himself along to the polis station they'd both be with him every inch of the road. But he couldn't, he knew he couldn't go and tell them the truth. Apart from his fear of imprisonment look what he stood to lose, his job; and not only that but the good name that would help him to get another. Never again would he be allowed to handle money once he had been along the line. And this place would go, Jimmy's yard. Had he thought of that? He swung round now, crying at them, 'All right, if I was to give meself up, what would happen? No more yard for you, Jimmy boy, your dream gone up in smoke. Did you think of that?'

'No, but now you mention it, it wouldn't be the end of me, I could always get me other job back. And I can always go home again. Don't let that stop you. Don't try to use me in that way, our Rory.'

'And her, what's gona happen to her then?' He was speaking of Janie as if she weren't sitting by the table with her face buried in her hands, and Jimmy answered, 'She won't be any worse off than she was afore, she's always got her place.'

'Aw, to hell's flames with the lot of you!' He flung his arm wide as if sweeping them out of the room. 'What do you know about anything? Own up and be a good boy and I'll stand by you. You know nowt, the pair of you, the lot of you, you're ignorant, you can't see beyond your bloody noses. There's swindlin' going on every day. Respectable men, men looked up to in this town twisting with every breath. And you'd have me ruin meself for five pounds.'

'It's not the five . . .'

'Be quiet, Jimmy! Be quiet!' Janie's voice was low. 'You won't get anywhere with him 'cos he'll keep on about the five pounds, he'll try to hoodwink you like he's hoodwinked himself. Well –' she rose from the table – 'I know what I'm gona do.' She walked slowly into the bedroom and they both gazed after her. When the door banged behind her Jimmy made for the ladder and without another word mounted it and disappeared through the trap door.

Rory stared about the empty room for a moment, then turning towards the mantelshelf again he bowed his head on it and slowly beat his fist against the rough wall above it.

CHAPTER 6

'Why, lass, it's the chance in a lifetime. In a boat cruising? My! my! round France. By! the master's brother must have plenty of money to own a boat like that.'

'I think it's his wife who has the money, he married a French lady.'

'And you tell us it's a sort of castle they live in?'

'Yes, that's what the missis says.'

'We'll miss you, lass.' Lizzie sat back on her heels from where she had been kneeling sweeping the fallen cinders underneath the grate and she looked hard at Janie as she said, 'I know it's only for three weeks, but what puzzles me is him lettin' you go at all. Didn't he kick up a shindy?'

Janie turned away and looked towards Ruth where she was coming out of the scullery carrying plates of thickly cut bread, and she answered, 'Yes, a bit. But then he's taken up with his new position an' such, and . . . and often doesn't get in till late.'

'Aye.' Lizzie pulled her bulk upright and bent to her sweeping once again. 'His new position. By! he's fallen on his feet if anybody has. It was a whole day's blessin' when old Kean died, you could say.'

'You're off first thing in the mornin' then, lass?'

Janie nodded towards Ruth and said, 'Yes, we've got to be in Newcastle by eight o'clock; we're goin' up by carriage.'

'Then all the way to London by train.' Ruth shook her head. 'It's amazing, wonderful; the sights you'll see. It would have been a great pity if you hadn't taken the opportunity; such a thing as this only comes once in a lifetime . . . And you won't stay for a bite to eat?'

'I can't, thanks all the same, there's so much to do, to see to you know.

And that reminds me. I needn't ask you, need I, to see to me grannie?'

'Aw, lass –' Ruth pulled a face at her – 'you know that goes without sayin'. At least you should.'

'Aye, I know. And thanks, thanks to both of you.' She cast her glance between them, then looking at Lizzie, who had now risen to her feet, she said, 'Well, I'd better say ta-rah,' and the next moment she was hugging Lizzie, and Lizzie was holding her tight and saying brokenly, 'Now don't cry, there's nowt to cry about, goin' on a holiday . . . Don't. Don't lass.'

'There, there.' She was enfolded in Ruth's arms now and Lizzie was patting her shoulder. Then swiftly pulling herself away from them, she grabbed up her bag from a chair and ran out of the cottage.

It was Ruth who, having closed the door after her, came back to the centre of the room and looking at Lizzie said, 'Well, what do you make of it?'

'What can I make of it? There's somethin' wrong, and has been for weeks past, if you ask me. He's hardly been across the door. Jimmy, look what he was like the last time he was here, no high-falutin' talk of boats and cargoes and contracts an' such like.'

'Whatever it is, it doesn't lie just atween the both of them, not when Jimmy's concerned in it.'

'No, you're right there.' Lizzie nodded. 'And it couldn't be just marriage rows. Jimmy would take those in his stride, havin' been brought up on them.' She smiled faintly. 'No, whatever it is, it's somethin' big and bad. I'm worried.'

'In a couple of days' time we could take a walk down and tidy up and do a bit of baking and such like. What do you say, Lizzie?'

'That's a sensible idea. Aye, we could do that, and we might winkle out something while we're there.'

'It could be. It could be.'

'Things are changin', Ruth. Folks and places, everything.'

Ruth came to her now and, tapping her arm gently, said, 'Don't worry about him, he'll straighten things out. Whatever trouble there is he'll straighten things out. He's your own son, being such he's bound to be sensible at bottom.'

'You're a good woman, Ruth, none better.'

They turned sadly away from each other now and went about their respective duties in the kitchen.

Janie had been gone ten days and his world was empty. If she were to appear before him at this minute he would say to her, 'All right, I'll go, I'll go now, as long as I know you'll be here, the old Janie, waiting for me when I come out.' His mind was like a battlefield, he was fighting love and hate, and recrimination and bitterness.

The recrimination was mostly against his employer. He had seen her only twice in the past three weeks. He still took the takings to the house in the evenings but his orders were to leave them in the study and to call for the books the next morning.

During their two meetings there had been no discussion about future plans of any kind. Her manner had been cool and formal, her tone one that he recalled from her visits to the office years ago. It was the tone in which orders were issued and brooked no questions.

But although in one breath he was telling himself that if Janie were here now he would do what she asked, in the next he was asking himself what was going to happen when she did return. After the night of the show-down she had slept up in the loft, and Jimmy had slept on a shaky-down in the kitchen. Would it go on like that until he gave in? He could have asserted his rights as many a man before him had done by well-directed blows, but the fact that he had hit her once was enough; that alone had created a barrier between them. She wasn't the type of girl who would stand knocking about, she had too much spirit, and he was ashamed, deeply ashamed of having struck her. He had acted no better than his father whom, at bottom, he despised.

It was Saturday again. He hated Saturdays, Sundays more so. He hadn't gone up home since she had left, but they had been down here, at least Ruth and she had. They had cleaned up and cooked, and spoken to each other as if they were back in the kitchen. They hadn't asked any questions regarding how he felt about her going away, which pointed more forcibly than words to the fact that they were aware that something was wrong.

Then there was Jimmy. Jimmy was making him wild, sitting for hours at night scratching away with a pencil on bits of paper and never opening his mouth. He had turned on him the other night and cried, 'If anyone's to blame for this business it's you. Who pestered me into buying this bloody ramshackle affair, eh? Who?' and snatching up a miniature wooden ship's wheel from the mantelshelf he had flung it against the far wall, where it had splintered into a dozen pieces, and Jimmy, after looking down on the fragments with a sort of tearful sadness, had gone up the ladder, leaving him to increased misery.

He stood at the window now looking down on to the yard. The sun was glinting on the water; there were boats plying up and down the river; on the slipway Jimmy had set the keel of a new boat in the small stocks and he was working on it now. In the ordinary way he would have been down there helping him, they would have been exchanging jokes about what they would do when they had the monopoly of the river, or grinding their teeth at the Pitties and their tactics.

As he looked down on Jimmy's fair head, he was suddenly brought forward with a jerk, for there, coming round the side of the building, was Ruth and his da and Lizzie. It wasn't the fact that they'd all turned up together to visit him, it was the expression on their faces that was riveting his attention for both Lizzie and Ruth were crying, openly crying as they talked rapidly to Jimmy, and his da was now holding out a paper to Jimmy. He watched Jimmy reading it, shake his head, then put his hand to his brow before turning and looking up at the window. Then they were all looking up at the window.

He didn't step back but stared down at them as they remained still, their postures seemingly frozen into a group of statuary. He noticed that Lizzie was wearing her old shawl, and old it was, green in parts. And Ruth too was in a shawl; she nearly always wore a bonnet. And they both still had their aprons on.

He moved from the window and went to the door and, having opened it, looked down the steps at them. They came towards him. It was his father who mounted first, and he said to him, 'What's up?' But Paddy didn't answer, he just walked into the room, followed by Ruth and Lizzie and, lastly, Jimmy.

Rory's gaze travelled from one to the other, then came to rest on Jimmy who was gripping the paper with both hands and staring at him.

He did not repeat his question to Jimmy, but took the paper from him and began to read.

> 'It is with deep regret that we hear of the terrible tragedy that has overtaken a Shields family on holiday on the coast of France. Mr Charles Buckham, his wife, three children, and their nursemaid Mrs Jane Connor, together with Mr Buckham's brother, are feared lost, after their yacht was caught in a great storm. Mrs Buckham's body and that of one child were washed ashore, together with pieces of wreckage from the boat. There is little hope of any survivors. Two other boats were wrecked at the same time, with a total loss of twenty-six lives. Mr Charles Buckham was a prominent member . . .'

Someone must have brought a chair forward for him to sit on because when next he looked at them they were standing in a half-circle before him and they were all crying, even his da. His own eyes were dry; his whole body was dry, he was being shrivelled up; his mind had stopped working except for a section which oozed pain and ran like a burning acid down into his heart, and there it was etching out her name: Janie. Janie.

'Janie. Janie,' he said the name aloud and turned and saw Lizzie lift up her white apron and fling it over her head, and when she began to moan like a banshee he made no protest because the sound was finding an echo within himself. 'Janie. Janie. Aw, Janie, don't go, Janie. Don't be dead, Janie. Come back to me, Janie. Don't leave me. Don't leave me. I'll see about John George, honest to God I promise, now, right now. Oh, Janie.'

'Give him a drop out of the bottle.'

Paddy put his hand into his inside pocket and drew out a flat flask of whisky and, picking up a cup, he almost half-filled it. Then handing it to Rory, he said, 'Get it down you, lad. Get it down you. You need to be fortified. God knows you need to be fortified.'

When Lizzie suddenly cried, 'Why does God bring disasters like this to us? What have we ever done to Him?' Paddy turned on her, hissing, 'Whist! woman. It's questions like that that bring on disasters.'

Her wailing increased, and she cried, 'It's the third thing. I said there would be three, didn't I? Didn't I? An' I told Andrews the polis when he brought the paper up, didn't I, didn't I?'

'Oh Janie, Janie. Come back, Janie. Just let me look on you once more.' It was sayings like that that brought disaster his da had just said. He was ignorant. They were all ignorant. That's what he had said to Janie, they were all ignorant. And he had compared their talk, their ways, and their dwelling, the dwelling that he had known since birth, with Charlotte Kean and her fine house. Yes their ignorance was a warm ignorance, it was something you didn't have to live up to; pretence fell through it like water through a sieve. Their ignorance was a solid foundation on which he could lean. He was leaning against it now, his head tucked against warm, thick flesh, nor when he realized it was Lizzie's flesh, his mother's flesh, did he push it away. In this moment he needed ignorance, he needed love, he needed warmth, he needed so many things to make up for the loss of Janie.

'Aw, Janie, Janie. I'm sorry, Janie. I'm sorry, Janie.'

CHAPTER 7

Charlotte Kean did not read the paper until late on the Saturday evening. She had returned from Hexham about seven o'clock feeling tired, irritable and lonely. After a meal she had gone into the office with the intention of doing some work on the mass of papers that always awaited her on the desk, but after sitting down she stared in front of her for a moment before closing her eyes and letting her body slump into the depths of the leather chair.

How much longer could she go on like this? She'd asked herself the same question numbers of times over the past weeks. There was a remedy, in fact two. But the cure offered by either Mr Henry Bolton or Mr George Pearson was worse, she imagined, than her present disease. Henry Bolton was forty-eight and a widower. George Pearson would never see fifty again. She wasn't foolish enough to think that either of them had fallen in love with her. She would go as far as to say that they didn't even like her, considering her ways too advanced by half, having heard her opinions from across a committee table. But since the death of both her father and her grandfather they had almost raced each other to the house.

No. No. Never.

She rose from the desk. She was a spinster and she'd remain a spinster. The wild fantastic dream she'd had was only that, a wild fantastic dream. She had humiliated herself because of her dream; she had been willing to be publicly humiliated because of her dream.

She went from the office and upstairs to her room, the room that until a few weeks ago had been her father's. It was the largest bedroom in the house and faced the garden and shortly after he died she had it completely redecorated and had made it her own. She knew that the servants had been slightly shocked by such seeming lack of respect for the dead but she didn't care what servants thought, or anyone else for that matter.

It was very odd, she mused, as she slowly took off her day clothes and got into a housegown, a new acquisition and another thing that had shocked the servants, for it wasn't black or brown, or even grey, but a startling pink, and its material was velvet. Yes, it was very odd, but there was no one for whose opinion she cared one jot. And more sadly still, there was no one who cared one jot about what happened to her. She hadn't a close relative left in the world, nor had she a close friend. There were those in the town who would claim her as a friend, more so now, but to her they were no more than acquaintances.

She sat before the mirror and unpinned her hair and the two dark, shining plaits fell down over her shoulders and almost to her waist. As her fingers undid each twist the hair seemed to spring into a life of its own and when, taking a brush, she stroked it from the crown down to its ends it covered her like a cloak.

The brush poised to the side of her face, she stared at herself in the mirror. It was a waste on her; it should have been doled out to some pretty woman and it would have made her beautiful, whereas on her head it only seemed to emphasize the plainness of her features. She leant forward and stared at her reflection. How was it that two eyes, a nose, and a mouth could transform one face into attractiveness while leaving another desolate of any appeal? She was not misshapen in any way, yet look at her. She dressed well, she had a taste for dress, she knew the right things to wear but the impression they afforded stopped at her neck. She had even resorted to the artifice of toilet powder, and in secret had applied rouge to her lips and cheeks with the result that she looked nothing better, she imagined, than a street woman.

She rose and glanced towards the bed. Were she to go to bed now she wouldn't sleep. She couldn't read in bed at all. This was the outcome, she supposed, of being taught to read while sitting in a straight-backed chair. Her father had enforced this rule and the teachers at the school to which her mother had sent her were of a like mind too. When she was young her idea of heaven had been to curl up on the rug before the fire and read a book, but when finally she had returned home from school she had found no pleasure in this form of relaxation.

She decided to go down to the drawing-room and play the piano for a while. This often had the power to soothe her nerves. Then she would take a bath, after which she might get to sleep without thinking.

It was as she was crossing the hall that she noticed the local paper neatly folded, together with a magazine, lying on a salver on the side table. She picked up both and went on into the drawing-room. But before laying them down she glanced at the newspaper's headlines: Shield Family Lost at Sea.

'It is with deep regret that we hear of the terrible tragedy that has overtaken a Shields family on holiday on the coast of France. Mr Charles Buckham, his wife, three children and their nursemaid, Mrs Jane Connor, together with Mr Buckham's brother are feared lost, after their yacht was caught in a great storm. Mrs Buckham's body and that of one child were washed ashore, together with pieces of wreckage from the boat. There is little hope of any survivors . . .'
Mrs Jane Connor, nursemaid.
Mrs Jane Connor, nursemaid.

He had said she was nursemaid to the Buckhams. Yes, yes, it was the

Buckhams of Westoe. She knew him, Charles Buckham, and she had met his wife a number of times, and . . . and there couldn't be two nursemaids by the name of Jane Connor.

He hadn't said his wife had gone away, but then she hadn't spoken to him for weeks, not since he had startled her by saying he was married.

She was sorry, very sorry . . .

Was she?

Of course she was, it was a terrible thing. Could she go to him now and tell him? What time was it? She swung round and looked at the clock on the mantelpiece. Quarter-to-nine. It was still light, yet she didn't know exactly where the place was; but it was on the waterfront and would be dark by the time she got there.

She found herself walking up and down the room. Her stomach was churning with excitement. She said again, 'What a tragedy! A terrible tragedy. And those poor young children.'

She suddenly stopped her pacing and, dropping into a chair bent her body forward until her breasts were almost touching her knees. She mustn't make herself ridiculous; nothing had altered, things stood as they had done a few minutes earlier.

Slowly she drew herself up and, taking in deep draughts of air, said to herself, 'You can call tomorrow morning. It will be quite in order then for you to go and offer your condolences. He's in your employ and naturally you have his concern at heart. Go and have a bath now and go to bed; you can do nothing until tomorrow.'

She had a bath and she went to bed, but it was almost dawn before she finally fell asleep. And she was still asleep when the maid came in with her early morning tea at eight o'clock.

She hardly gave herself time to drink the tea before she was out of bed dressing, and at nine o'clock she left the house, presumably to go to an early service. She had informed Jessie that she wouldn't need the carriage, it was a fine morning and she preferred to walk.

The only answer Jessie could give to this was 'Yes, miss,' but the expression on her face told Charlotte that she considered that by breaking yet another rule she was letting the prestige of the family down; no one of any importance in this district went to church on foot.

Because the occasion demanded sobriety she had dressed in the black outfit she had worn to her father's funeral and so she wasn't conspicuous as she made her way from the residential quarter of Westoe to the long district lining the waterfront. Yet she did not pass without notice for she was tall and slim and her walk was purposeful as if she knew where she was going. But on this occasion she didn't, at least not precisely.

Having almost reached the Lawe she stopped an old riverside man and asked him if he could direct her to Mr Connor's boatyard.

'Connor's boatyard? Never knew no boatyard by that name along this stretch, ma'am. No Connor's boatyard along here.'

'It's . . . it's a small yard, I understand.'

'Big or small, ma'am, none of that name.'

'Mr Connor has only recently taken the yard over.'

'Small yard, taken it over?' The old man rubbed the stubble on his chin and said, 'Oh aye, now I come to think of it, it's old Barney Kilpatrick's place. Oh aye, I heard tell of a young 'un startin' up there. Takes some grit and guts to start on your own along this stretch. Well now, ma'am, you turn yourself round and go back yonder till you pass a space full of lumber, bits of boats . . . odds and ends. There's a cut at yon side atween a set of pailings, the gate into Kilpatrick's place is but a few steps down there.'

'Thank you. Thank you very much.'

'You're welcome, ma'am. You're welcome.'

She walked swiftly back along the potholed road, followed the directions the old man had given her and within a few minutes found herself opposite a wooden gate in a high fence of black sleepers.

The gate opened at a touch and she went through and stood for a moment looking at the ramshackle building before her. There were steps leading up to a door and, having mounted them, she knocked gently and waited. After a short interval she knocked again, harder now, and after knocking a third time she tried the handle and found the door locked.

She descended the steps and looked about her. There was evidence of a small boat being built. She walked into the slipway, then out again and stood looking up at the windows. She could see the place as a boatyard, even though it was very small, but as a residence, never. She gave a slight shudder. Being almost on the river's edge it would be overrun with rats and so damp. And he lived here and had spoken of it with enthusiasm!

Where was he now? Most likely at his parents' house. Of course, that's where he would be. Well, she couldn't go there . . . or could she?

'You mustn't. You mustn't.'

She walked out of the yard, closing the gate behind her, and again she chastised herself, sternly now. 'You mustn't. You mustn't. Please retain some sense of decorum.'

But it was such a long time until tomorrow. Would he come to work? Well, the only thing she could do was to wait and see, and if he didn't put in an appearance, then she would go to his home. It would seem quite in order to do so then.

She walked slowly back through the town. People were making their way to the churches. There were a number of carriages in the market place adjacent to St. Hilda's. She wondered for a moment whether she should go in there, then decided not to. What would she pray for? She mustn't be a hypocrite. She'd always prided herself on being honest, at least to herself. She went to church, but she was no churchwoman. She knew why more than half the congregation attended her own particular church. Their reasons were various, but had nothing to do with God and worship: to see and be seen; to make connections. It was an established fact that it did one no harm in the business world to belong to a congregation, especially if you paid substantially for your pew and had your name inscribed on a silver name-plate.

In her loneliest moments she warned herself against cynicism knowing that if she didn't want to lose those few people who termed themselves her friends she must keep her radical opinions to herself. But oh, she had thought so often how wonderful it would be, how comforting to have someone with whom she could talk plainly. A male. Oh, yes a male, someone like . . .

When had she first thought of him in that way? All her life seemingly. Don't be ridiculous. Well, four and a half years was a lifetime.

Sunday was a long day, and on Monday morning she was awake early and dressed for outdoors by eight o'clock, and by a quarter to nine she was seated behind the desk in the inner office in Tangard Street.

If he were coming to work he would come here to see to the men. If he didn't put in an appearance, well she must see to them, and once they were settled she would go on to Simonside and offer her condolences . . .

He came into the office at ten minutes to nine and she was shocked at the sight of him, and sad, truly sad; yet at the same time envious of a woman who, by her going, could pile the years almost overnight on a man.

She rose swiftly from the chair, then came round the desk and stood in front of him, saying, and with sincere feeling, 'I'm so sorry. Now you shouldn't have come, I didn't expect you. You . . . you must go home and stay there as long as you feel it is necessary; there's no hurry, I can see to things . . .'

She watched him wet his lips before saying in a voice so unlike his own in that it was quiet, like that of a sick man bereft of strength, 'I'd . . . I'd much rather be at work, if you don't mind.'

'Well —' she shook her head slowly — 'it's as you wish. But . . . but you don't look well. And . . . and haven't you got . . .? Well, aren't there things you must see to officially?'

'No.' He shook his head. 'We . . . I went on Saturday. The police said they'd let me know if they heard anything further. Mr . . . Mr Buckham's father has gone over, I'm to see him when he comes back.'

'Oh.' She stared into his face. It was grey, lifeless. She realized as she looked at him that his appeal did not come from his looks at all, as one might imagine, as she herself had imagined years ago, but from the vitality within, from the bumptiousness and the arrogance that was part of his nature. At the moment there was no life either in his face or in his body. But, of course, it was to be understood this was only temporary; he was under shock, he would revive . . . she would see that he revived. The decision he had taken to come straight to work was the best possible thing he could have done.

She said now, 'Then I can leave you?'

'Yes.'

She picked up her bag and gloves from the desk, and turning to him again, she said, 'If you wish you may send Mr Taylor with the collection.'

'Thanks.' He inclined his head towards her.

'Are you staying with your parents?'

'No.' He shook his head. 'I've been with them over the weekend but I'm going back to the boatyard.'

She said with some concern now, 'Do you think it wise for you to be alone at this time?'

'My brother will be with me.'

'Oh.' She stared at him; then again she said, 'I'm deeply sorry.'

He made no reply but turned from her and she had to stop herself from going to him for she imagined he was about to cry, and if she were to see him cry . . . She turned hastily and went out.

Alone now he stood staring down at the desk as if he had never seen it before, as if he were surprised to find it there; then going behind it, he sat down and, drawing a handkerchief from his pocket, wiped it quickly round his face before blowing his nose. He had said he'd be better at work. He'd never be better anywhere, anytime, but being here was better than remaining in the kitchen. He'd go mad if he had to listen to any more talk of Janie. Since Saturday night they had talked about her, wailed about her, cried about her, and he too had cried and wailed, but inside. To them it was as if she were lying in the coffin in the corner of the room. They had drunk their beer and had their tots of whisky as if they were holding a wake. They had sat up all night, the Learys and her da and grannie, and his own father and Ruth and Jimmy . . . and her. Nellie had come and her husband with her. And that had been another thing that had nearly driven him mad, when Nellie announced through her tears that she was pregnant at last, and her, his big slob of a slavering mother, had cried, 'That's God's way. That's God's way, when He shuts one door He opens another.' Another day among them and he would have gone out of his mind.

There was only one good thing that had come out of it, he and Jimmy were back where they were before. Nothing had been said but Jimmy hadn't left his side since Saturday, not even during the night, the longest night of his life. All Saturday night he had sat by his side up in the loft, and last night too, and it was he who had said early this morning, 'Let's get back away home, eh?' It was odd that Jimmy should think of the boatyard as home rather than the place in which he had been brought up. But Janie had made it home.

He thought with shame and guilt of how he had begun to compare it with Charlotte Kean's place. God, he wouldn't swop it for a palace decked with diamonds at this moment if Janie was in it.

Aw Janie. Janie. Oh! God, and they had parted like strangers. The last words he spoke to her were, 'You are hard. I said it afore in this very house and I say it again, there's a hard streak in you.'

She had gazed at him and replied, 'Aye, perhaps you're right.'

Then she was gone, and when the door closed on her he had beaten his fists against his head.

Why the hell was he standing there! Why didn't he go after her and drag her back by the scruff of the neck? He was her husband, wasn't he? He had his rights – was he a man? No other bloody man in the town would have put up with what he had these past two weeks, they would have knocked the daylights out of her. Why was he standing here?

Back in the cottages they referred to him, behind his back, as 'the big fella', and he had come to think of himself, and not without pride as 'a gambling man'. But what in effect was he? He . . . he was nothing more than a nowt who couldn't keep his wife, a nowt who had let a little chit of a lass best him. Had it happened to John George he would have said, 'Well, what do you expect?'

. . . John George!

This morning he had taken up a jug and hurled it almost at the same place at which he had thrown the ship's wheel. It was because of him he was in this pickle.

Janie! Janie! How am I to go on?

There was a knock on the door and Mr Taylor entered and provided him with the answer . . . work. It was either that or the river.

PART THREE

CHAPTER 1

THE BARGAIN

In 1877 those who were enlightened by reading newspapers discussed among other things such topics as Disraeli proclaiming Queen Victoria Empress of India and seeing to it that she had the adulation of Indian princes and African chiefs. But for the ordinary man and woman in towns such as South Shields, there were other happenings that struck nearer home, very much nearer home.

The sea which provided most of the inhabitants with a livelihood also created havoc and disaster. There was that awful night in December last year when three vessels were wrecked and the sea, still unsatisfied, had engulfed and destroyed another two later in the day, and all under the eyes of horrified townspeople who could only watch helplessly. Even though the Volunteer Life Brigade did heroic work, many lives were lost.

Such tragedies had the power to unite the townspeople, at least for a time. Rich and poor alike mingled in their sorrow until the poor, once again forgetting their place in God's scheme of things, protested against their lot. And how did they protest? They protested through societies called trade unions.

Since the first national union of the Amalgamated Society of Engineers had been founded in 1851, in every town in the country where skilled workers were employed trade unions had sprung up, to the fear and consternation of the middle classes who looked upon them as a network of secret societies, whose sole purpose was to intimidate honest citizens, plot to confiscate their property, cause explosions and mob violence and bring the country to total revolution if they were allowed to get the upper hand.

The County of Durham was a hotbed of such people. They agitated in mines, in steel works, in shipbuilding yards, in factories, and it was even whispered they tried to inveigle young women into their ranks; and not only those, let it be understood, from the common herd, but women of education and property.

Such a one who was suspected in South Shields was Miss Charlotte Kean. She wasn't accused openly of supporting trade unions because than that would be ridiculous, for she not only held shares in some quite big concerns but owned outright a number of small ones. No, they weren't accusing her of giving her sympathy to the quarter that would eventually precipitate her ruin through business, but what they did say was, she pushed her nose into too many cultural activities in the town, activities that had hitherto been inaugurated and worked mainly by gentlemen, such as the Public Library that had been opened four years previously.

This grand building could boast its eight thousand two hundred volumes only because of generous donations from men like the Stephensons, and Mr Williamson, and Mr Moore. What was more, the library had grown out of the Mechanics' Institute and the Working Men's Club, and this joint establishment had its origins in the Literary, Mechanical and Scientific Institution which was one of the earliest mechanics' institutions in the kingdom, having come into being in the November of 1825.

And who had created such places of learning? *Men*, gentlemen of the town, not women, or even ladies. Why the efforts of the gentlemen of the town had made The Working Men's Club and Institution so popular that in 1865 they'd had to seek new premises yet once again, premises large enough to contain now not only a newsroom and library but two classrooms and a conversation and smoking room, besides rooms for bagatelle, chess and draughts, and, progress and modernity being their aim, a large space was set off in the yard for the game of quoits.

For such progress men, and men only, could be given the credit. But now there were people like Charlotte Kean pushing their way into committees and advocating, of all things, that the library should be open seven days a week. Did you ever hear of such a suggestion that the Lord's Day should be so desecrated! She had been quoted as saying, if the wine and gin shops can remain open on a Sunday why not a reading room? One gentleman had been applauded for replying that God's house should be the reading room for a Sunday.

Then there was the matter of education. She would have made a ruling that no fee be charged for schooling and that a poor child should have admission to a high-class teaching establishment merely on his proven intelligence.

Some gentlemen of the town were amused by Miss Kean's attitude and said, Well, at least credit should be given her for having the mentality of a man. However, the majority saw her as a potential danger both to their domestic and business power. To light a fire you needed tinder, and she was the equivalent to a modern matchstick. Look how she was flaunting all female decorum by parading that upstart of a rent collector around the county. Not only had she made him into her manager but she took him everywhere as her personal escort. She was making a name for herself and not one to be proud of. By, if her father had still been alive it would never have happened. He had made a mistake by allowing her to become involved with the business in the first place, because she had developed what was commonly termed a business head. She was remarkable in that way. But they didn't like remarkable women, neither those who were against her nor those who were for her. No, they didn't hold with remarkable women. This was a man's town, a seafaring town; women had their place in it, and they would be honoured as long as they kept their places; but they wanted no remarkable women, at least not the kind who tended to match them in the world of commerce.

Her manager, too, had his reservations about his employer, and the things she got up to. Yet he granted, and not grudgingly, that she *was* a remarkable woman. Odd in some ways, but nevertheless remarkable.

A year had passed since the news of Janie's death and the old saying of time being a great healer had proved itself true yet once again, for Rory, over the past months, had come up out of despair and settled on a plane of not ordinary but, what was for him, extraordinary living.

Though Janie still remained in his heart as a memory the ache for her was less. Even in the night when he felt the miss of her he no longer experienced the body-searing agony and the longing for her presence.

Two things had helped towards his easement. The first was the combination of Jimmy and the yard, and the second – or should he have placed her first? – was Charlotte Kean.

When, six months ago, he had taken up the position as her manager she had raised his wage – salary she called it now – to three pounds a week. It was incredible. Never in his life had he dreamed of ever being able to earn three pounds a week. To get that much and ten times more by gambling, oh yes, he had dreamed of that, but never as an earned wage. And did he earn it? Was the work he was doing worth three pounds a week, going to the town office in the morning, then around ten o'clock up to the house and the office there, he at one side of the table, she at the other?

'What would you advise in a case like this, Mr Connor?'

The first time she had pushed a letter across the table towards him he had stared at her blankly before reading it. It was from her solicitor advising her that a certain new chemical company was about to float its shares, and suggesting that she would do well to consider buying.

Utterly out of his depths Rory had continued to stare at her, for he sensed in that moment that a great deal depended on how he answered her. And so, holding her gaze, he said, 'I can't advise you for I know nothin' whatever about such matters;' but had then added, 'as yet.'

She hadn't lowered her eyes when she replied, 'Then you must learn . . . that is if you want to learn. Do you, Mr Connor?'

'Yes . . . yes, I want to learn all right.'

'Well, that's settled,' she had said. 'We know now where we stand, don't we?' And then she had smiled at him, after which she had rung the bell, and when Jessie opened the door she had said, 'We'll have some refreshment now, Jessie.'

And that was the pattern he followed on the days he didn't go to Hexham or Gateshead or over the water to Wallsend to cast an eye over her interests, until two months ago, when the pattern had changed and she began to accompany him.

Journeying by train, they would sit side by side in the first-class carriage. He helped her in and out of cabs, he opened doors for her, he obeyed her commands in all ways, except that he would refuse her invitation to stay for a meal after he had delivered the takings of an evening, or when they had returned from one of their supervising trips. The reason he gave was a truthful one, his brother expected him, he was alone.

When he first gave her this reason she looked at him with a sideward glance and asked, 'How old is your brother?'

'Coming up twenty.'

'Twenty! And he needs your protection at night?'

And he answered flatly and stiffly, 'Yes, he does. Only last week a boat he had started to build was smashed up to bits, and it could be him next.'

'Oh!' She showed interest. 'Did you inform the police?'

'No.'

'Have you any idea who did it, and why?'

'Yes, both; I know who did it, and why. There's a family on the river who run the wherries, three brothers called Pittie . . .'

'Ah! Ah! the Pitties.' She had nodded her head.

'You've heard of them?'

'Yes, yes, I've heard the name before. And I also know of some of their activities.'

'Well, you know what they're like then.'

'Yes, I've a pretty good idea. And –' she had nodded and added, 'I can see the reason why you must be with your brother at night. But you, too, must be careful. What they've done once they can do again.'

His head had jerked in her direction as he asked, 'What do you mean?'

'Well, they could break up another boat.'

'Oh. Oh yes; yes they could.'

So he had stayed at home every night, including Saturdays, up till recently when, the urge rearing once more, he had joined a game, not on the waterfront, nor in the town, but away on the outskirts in Boldon.

It was odd how he had come to be reintroduced to the Boldon house for he had forgotten he had ever played there. He was in the train going to

Gateshead when a 'find the lady' trickster took him for a mug. He had
followed him into the compartment at Shields, then got on talking with a
supposedly complete stranger who boarded the train at Tyne Dock,
whom he very convincingly inveigled into 'finding the lady', and, of
course, let him win, all the while making a great fuss about his own bad
luck, before turning to Rory and saying, 'What about you, sir? It was then
that Rory had turned a scornful glance on the man and replied, 'Don't
come it with me. That dodge is as old as me whiskers.'

For a moment he had thought the pair of them were going to set about
him. Then the one who had supposedly just won peered at him and said,
'Why I know you, I've played in with you. Didn't you use to go up to
Telfords' in Boldon?'

Yes, he had played in the Telfords' wash-house, and in their kitchen,
and once up in the roof lying on his belly.

From that meeting the urge had come on him again, not that it had ever
really left him. But he had played no games, even for monkey nuts since
Janie had gone.

So he had got in touch with the Telfords again and he went to Boldon on
a Saturday night, where it could be simply Black Jack or pitch and toss.
Sometimes the Telford men went farther afield to a barn for a cock fight,
but he himself would always cry off this. He didn't mind a bit of rabbit
coursing but he didn't like to see the fowls, especially the bantams, being
torn to shreds with steel spurs. To his mind it wasn't sporting.

His winnings rarely went beyond five pounds, but neither did his losses.
It didn't matter so much now about the stake as long as he could sit down
to a game with men who were serious about it.

But now, at this present time, he was also vitally aware that he was
playing in another kind of game, and this game worried him.

He looked back to the particular Saturday morning when, having told
her he was married, her reaction had made him jump to conclusions
which caused him to chastise himself for being a big-headed fool. But he
chastised himself no longer.

He saw the situation he was in now as the biggest gamble of his life.
There were two players only at this table and inevitably one would have to
show his hand. Well, it wouldn't, it couldn't be him, it could never be him
for more reasons than one. *Him* marry Charlotte Kean, a woman years
older than himself and looking, as she did, as shapeless as a clothes prop,
and with a face as plain as the dock wall! True, she had a nice voice . . .
and a mind. Oh aye, she had a mind all right. And she was good company.
Yes, of late he had certainly been discovering that. She could talk about all
kinds of things, and he had realized that by listening to her he too could
learn. She could make a very good friend; yet even so there could be no

such thing between him and her for two reasons: on his part, you didn't, in his class, make friends with a woman, oh no, unless you wanted one thing from her: on her part, it wasn't a friend she wanted, it was a man, a husband.

Oh, he knew where things were leading. And he wouldn't hoodwink himself, he was tempted all right. Oh aye, he was both tempted and flattered. At nights he would lie thinking of what it would mean to live in Birchingham House in the select end of Westoe and to be in control of all those properties and businesses, all that money. My God! just to think of it. And he would be in control, wouldn't he? What was the wife's was the husband's surely. And there she was, willing, more than willing, to let him take control, him, Rory Connor, once rent collector from No. 2 The Cottages, Simonside. It was fantastic, unbelievable.

And them up in the kitchen, what would they say if he took this step? Lord! the place wouldn't hold them. No, he was wrong there. It wouldn't affect Ruth. As for her, his mother, after one look at Charlotte Kean she would be more than likely to say, 'My God! everything must be paid for.' She had a way with her tongue of stating plain facts. It would be his da who would brag. Every man in his shop would know, and it would be talked of in every pub in Jarrow from the church bank to the far end of Ellison Street.

But what would Bill Waggett say?

Ah, what the hell did it matter! It wouldn't happen. It couldn't. He couldn't do it. He wouldn't do it. Anyway, he was all right as he was. Jimmy wasn't doing so bad; he'd do better if it wasn't for them blasted Pitties. By, he'd get his own back on them if it was the last thing he did in life. Hardly a day passed but that he didn't think of them, when he would grab at this or that idea to get even with them. And he would, he would. He'd get a lead one day, and by God, when he did, let them look out! . . . He could have a lead now, right away. With money you had power, and it needed power to potch the Pitties. All he had to do was to say, 'Thank you kindly, Miss Kean, I'll be your man,' and he was home, safe home from the stormy sea, with chests full to the top.

But what would he really say? He knew what he'd say. 'I'm sorry, miss, but it wouldn't work.'

And, strangely, he realized that when he should say the latter he would be sorry, for, banter as he would, and did, about her in his mind there was a part of him that was sorry for her, and it had been growing of late. He pitied her lonely state, and he understood it because of the loneliness within himself. But although her kind of loneliness had gone on for years and she was weary of it, she was not yet resigned to it. That was why she had set her sights on him.

But why him? People of her station usually classed the likes of him as muck beneath their feet. And what was more, just think how she'd be talked about if anything should come of it. Lord! any link up with him would set the town on fire.

He was already vaguely aware that sly looks were being cast in their direction. When they were last in Durham to look over some property along the river bank they had gone to an inn to eat. She had chosen it, she said, because she thought he would like it; it was a man's place, oak-trestle tables, hefty beams, meat pudding and ale. And he would have liked it if it hadn't been in Durham . . . the gaol was in Durham.

Well, he had done what he could in that direction. He had tried to make reparation; he had given Jimmy ten pounds and sent him up to visit John George and to ask him if he would come and see him when he came out. But Jimmy had returned with the ten pounds; John George was already out and they couldn't tell him where he had gone. For days afterwards he had expected a visit from him, but John George hadn't come. So he told himself that the business was closed; he had done his best. It was only in his recurring nightmare, when he would relive the awakening to Janie shouting at him, did he realize that his best hadn't been good enough and that John George would be with him like an unhealed wound until the end of his days.

But on that day in the inn in Durham, two Shields' men – gentlemen – had come to their table to speak to Charlotte Kean, and she had introduced him to them. They were Mr Allington and a Mr Spencer. He knew of both of them. Allington was a solicitor, and Spencer owned a number of small grocery shops. He had started with one about fifteen years ago, and now they had spread into Jarrow and beyond.

After the first acknowledgment, they hadn't addressed him again until they were bidding her good-bye, and then they had merely inclined their heads towards him. Oh, he knew where he stood with the gentlemen of the town. He was an upstart rent man.

Then came the day when Charlotte Kean showed her hand and brought an abrupt end to the game by laying her cards face up on the table.

They had returned from Newcastle where she had been to see, of all things, an iron foundry with a view to taking a part share in it. The journey had been taken against the advice of her solicitor. The Tyneside foundries, he had said, were unable to produce iron as cheaply as they once had done; the railways had killed the iron trade in this part of the country. But she had explained, and to Rory himself, that she could not follow her solicitor's reasoning, for, as she saw it, people would always want iron stoves, kitchen grates, fenders, and railings of all kinds, from those that enclosed parks to small private gates; and then there were bedsteads and safes and such-like. She went on to say she wasn't thinking of competing with Palmer's and making ships but merely of supplying household requisites. What did he think?

He had answered her bluntly, as always, for he had learned that she preferred the truth, at least in most things. 'I think that I agree with Mr Hardy; he knows what he's talking about.'

'And you think I don't?'

'Well, I wouldn't say that you know very much about the iron trade.'

'You are aware that I read a great deal?'

'Yes, I'm aware of that, but as I understand it it takes more than reading to get an insight into such trades; the workings of them go deeper than books.'

'The workings might, but I would leave the workings to managers and men, of course.'

He shrugged his shoulders slightly and smiled as he said, 'Well, I won't say you know best, but what I will say is, you'll do what you want in the long run.'

That he could speak to her in this fashion was evidence of how far they had travelled in their association over the past year. He now rarely used the term miss, and although from time to time she would call him Mr Connor, it was usually done when in the presence of servants; at other times she addressed him without using his name at all.

Whatever her servants thought of the situation they treated their mistress's new manager with respect, even deference, which at one time would have amused him. At one time, too, such subservient attitudes would have given him material for mimicry and a big joke in the kitchen; in fact, his association with Miss Charlotte Kean would have been one big joke. At one time, but not now. Anyway, Sundays were different now. He did not always visit the cottage on a Sunday, he went up only on Jimmy's urging. He did not ask himself why he had turned against the Sunday gatherings, but he knew that the general opinion was he had become too big for his boots. And that could very well be near the truth, for he admitted to himself that the more he saw of the Westoe side of life the less he liked that in which he had been brought up.

He had, on this day, gone through a mental battle which left him thinking he didn't know which end of him was up. It was the anniversary of Janie's death, and there was no fierce ache left in him, and he felt there should be. He should, in some way, have held a sort of memorial service, at least within himself, but what had he done? Gone up to Newcastle, walked blithely by his employer's side as she paraded around a foundry, sat with her at a meal, which she called lunch, at the Royal Exchange

Hotel; then had waited like a docile husband while she went shopping in Bainbridge's. He had sauntered with her through the Haymarket, where they had stopped and examined almost every article in the ironmongery store. Then she had said they would go to the Assembly Rooms and he wondered what her object was, until, standing outside, she looked at the building and said almost sadly, 'My mother once danced in there. She often told me about it. It was the highlight of her life; she was taken there by a gentleman – and they danced the whole evening through.'

When she had turned her face towards him he had ended for her, flippantly, 'And they married and lived happy ever after.'

'No, she married my father.'

What could he make of that?

Her last call was at Mawson & Swan's in Grey Street, where she purchased a number of books.

By the time they reached the railway station he likened himself to a donkey, he was so loaded down under parcels, and he thanked God he wasn't likely to come across anyone he knew. When they arrived at Shields she hired a cab, and they drove through the drizzling rain to the house, and into warmth and comfort and elegance.

Elegance was another new word he had of late added to his vocabulary; it was the only word to describe this house, its furniture and the comforts of it.

'Ah, isn't it nice to be home?' She had returned from upstairs, where she had evidently combed her hair and applied some talcum powder to her face for her chin had the same appearance as Ruth's had when she wiped it with a floured hand.

'It's an awful night; you must have something before you go, something to eat that is. Did Mr Taylor bring the takings?'

'Yes; I've checked them, they're all right.'

This was a new departure; he no longer went to the office to collect the rents. Mr Taylor had been promoted and so came each evening to the house.

On the days she did not send him off on tours of inspection he would receive the money from the old man, count it, then check the books, and never did he hand them back to him but he saw himself as he was a year ago, a younger edition of this man. That was the only difference, a younger edition; the old man's insecurity did not make his own position in comparison appear strong, quite the reverse.

Only a week ago he had felt he could play his hand for a good while yet, but today, the anniversary of Janie's death, he had a feeling in his bones that soon all the cards would be laid face up, and as always they would show a winner and a loser; there could never be two winners in any game . . .

Why not?

Oh my God! He'd been through it all before, hadn't he, night after
night? He was what he was, that was why not.

Below his outer covering, his jaunty aggressive air, the look that gave
nothing away while at the same time suggesting that what it had to hide
was of value, behind all this, only he himself knew the frailties of his
character. Yet, in this particular case, he wasn't going to be weak enough
– or did he mean strong enough? – to cheat at this game and let her be the
winner.

And again he told himself he had to stop hoodwinking himself on this
point too, because it wasn't really the moral issue that would prevent him
from letting her win, but the fact that he didn't think he was up to paying
the stake. It was too high. Yet he liked her. Oh aye, it was very odd to
admit, but he liked her. He liked being with her; she was good company,
except at those times when she made him feel so small that he imagined
she could see him crawling around her feet. Once or twice she had done
this when he had dared to contradict her on some point with regard to the
business. And yet she never took that high hand with him when they were
in company. At such times she always deferred to him as a woman might
to her husband, or her boss.

She was a funny character; he couldn't get to the bottom of her. He had
never known anyone in his life so knowledgeable or so self-possessed. But
then, never in his life had he been in contact with women of her class.

'You will stay for something to eat?'

He hesitated, then said, 'Yes. Yes, thank you.'

'Good.' She smiled at him, put her hand to her hair and stroked it
upwards and back from her forehead; then she said, 'Don't sit on the edge
of that chair as if you were waiting to take off in a race.'

His jaw tightened, his pleasant expression vanished. This was the kind
of thing that maddened him.

'Oh! Oh, I'm sorry.'

Now she was sitting forward on the edge of the couch leaning towards
him. 'Please don't be annoyed. I have the unfortunate habit of phrasing
my requests in the manner of orders.' She made a small deprecating
movement with her head. 'I . . . I must try to grow out of it. All I intended
to say was, please relax, be comfortable . . . make yourself at home.' The
last words ended on a low note.

After a moment he slid slowly back into the chair and smiled ruefully at
her.

Settling herself back once again on the couch, she stared at him before
saying, still in a low tone, 'I'm going to call you . . . No' – she lifted her
hand – 'again my phrasing is wrong. What I mean to say is, may I call you

by your Christian name?'

He did not answer but stared at her, unblinking.

She was looking down at her hands now where they were joined on her lap, her fingers making stroking movements between the knuckles. 'You see, I . . . I want to talk to you this evening about . . . about something important, if you can afford me the time after dinner. Which reminds me. Would you mind ringing the bell, please?'

He rose slowly to his feet and pulled the bell by the side of the fireplace, and they didn't speak until the maid appeared; then she said, 'Mr Connor will be staying for dinner, Jessie. How long will it be?'

'Well . . . well, it's ready now, miss, but' – The girl cast a glance in Rory's direction, then added, 'Say five minutes' time, miss?'

'Very well, Jessie, thank you.'

When the door was closed on the maid, she said, 'I have never seen you smoke, do you smoke?'

'Yes. I have a draw at nights.'

'My father never smoked. I like the smell of tobacco. About . . . about your Christian name. What does the R stand for . . . Robert?'

'No, Rory.'

'Roar-y. What is it short for?'

'Nothin' that I know of. I was christened Rory.'

'Roar-y.' She mouthed the word, then said, 'I like it. My name, as you know, is Charlotte. My father once said it was a very suitable name for me.' Her head drooped again. 'He was an unkind man, a nasty man, a mean nasty man.'

He could say nothing to this. He was so amazed at her frankness he just sat staring at her, until she said, 'Would you care to go upstairs and wash?' He blinked rapidly, swallowed, wetted his lips, and as he drew himself up from the chair answered, 'Yes. Yes, thank you.'

She did not rise from the couch but looked up at him. 'The bathroom is the third door on the right of the landing.'

He inclined his head towards her, walked out of the drawing-room, across the hall and up the stairs. This was the first time he had been upstairs and he guessed it would be the last.

After closing the bathroom door behind him he stood looking about him in amazement. A full length iron bath stood on four ornamental legs. At one end of it were two shining brass taps, at the foot was a shelf and, on it, an array of coloured bottles and fancy boxes. To the left stood a wash basin, and to the left of that again a towel rack on which hung gleaming white towels. In the wall opposite the bath was a door, and when he slowly pushed this open he found he was looking down into a porcelain toilet, not a dry midden as outside the cottage, or a bucket in a lean-to on the waterfront, but something that looked too shiningly clean to be put to the use it was intended for.

A few minutes later as he stood washing his hands, not from any idea of hygiene, but simply because he wanted to see the bowl fill with water, he thought, I'm a blasted fool. That's what I am, a blasted fool. I could use this every day. I could eat downstairs in that dining-room every day. I could sit in that drawing-room, aye, and smoke every day. And I could sleep up here in one of these rooms every . . . He did not finish the sentence but dried his hands, gave one last look around the bathroom, then went downstairs.

The meal was over and once again they were sitting in the drawing-room.

He had hardly opened his mouth from the moment he had entered the dining-room until he left it. Talk about arms and legs; he could have been a wood louse, and he felt sure he had appeared just about as much at home too at that table as one might have done. Nor had it helped matters that she had been quiet an' all. She usually kept the conversation going, even giving herself the answers, and now here they were and the game had come to an end, the cards were face up.

He felt sorry. In so many different ways he felt sorry, but most of all he knew that at this moment he was feeling sorry for her because he could see from her face, and her attitude, that she, too, was in a bit of a spot, and he was wishing, sincerely wishing that it could have been possible for him to help her out of it, when she spoke.

Sitting perfectly still, staring straight ahead as if she were concentrating on the picture of her grandfather above the mantelpiece, she said, 'I . . . I really don't know how to begin, but this thing must be brought into the open. You . . . you are aware of that as much as I am, aren't you?' It was some seconds before she turned her head towards him, and now such were his feelings of pity that he couldn't hold her gaze. He looked down on his hands, as she herself had done earlier and, like hers, his fingers rubbed against each other.

She was speaking again, softly now, her voice scarcely above a whisper. 'I am putting you in a very embarrassing situation. I'm aware of that. Even if your feelings were such that you wanted to put a certain question to me, you wouldn't under the circumstances have the courage to do so, but let me tell you one thing immediately. I know that you have no wish to put that question to me. If you agree to what I am going to ask of you, I won't be under the illusion it is through any personal attraction, but that it will be for what my offer can bring to you in the way of advantages.'

His head was up now. 'I don't want advantages that way.'

'Thank you at least for that.' As she made a deep obeisance with her head towards him, he put in quickly, 'Don't get me wrong. What I meant was –' He shook his head, bit hard down on his lip as he found it impossible to explain what he meant, and she said, 'I know what you meant, but . . . but you haven't yet heard my proposition.'

She turned her face away and once again stared at the picture as she went on, 'Suppose I were to ask you to marry me, you would . . . you would, on the face of it I know, refuse, forgoing all the advantages that would go with such a suggestion, but suppose I were to say to you that this would be no ordinary marriage, that I . . . I would expect nothing from you that an ordinary wife would from her husband. You could have your own apartments, all I would ask for is . . . is your companionship, and your presence in this house, of which . . . of which you would be the master.' She again turned her face towards him.

He was sitting bolt upright in the chair now; his eyes were wide and his mouth slightly open. He said under his breath, 'That would be the poor end of the stick for you, wouldn't it?'

'Poor end of the stick?' She gave a short laugh. 'Well, if I would be quite satisfied with the poor end of the stick, shouldn't that be enough for you?'

He shook his head. 'No! No! It wouldn't be right, for as I see it you wouldn't be gettin' any more out of me than you do now. . . . So why not let things be as they are?'

There now came upon them an embarrassing silence, before she said, 'Because I need companionship, male companionship. Not just anyone, someone, an individual, someone whom I consider special, and . . . and I chose you. What is more, I feel I know you, I know you very well. I know that you like this house, you like this way of living, I know that you could learn to appreciate finer things. Not that I dislike the roughness in you; no, it is part of your attraction, your bumptiousness, your arrogance. It is more difficult to be arrogant when you have nothing to be arrogant about than when you have something.'

His face took on its blank look. This was the kind of clever talk that maddened him, and he had no way of hitting back except by using the arrogance she was on about. He said gruffly, 'You seem to think you know a lot about me, everything in fact.'

'No, not everything, but quite a bit. I've always given myself the credit of being able to read character. I know a lot of things about a lot of people, especially in this town, and I know what a good many of them are saying at this very moment – and about us.'

'About us?'

'Oh yes, yes, about us. Don't you know that we're being talked about? Don't you know they're saying –' she now dropped into the local inflexion which patterned the speech of even many of the better-off of the townsfolk

– "What d'you think, eh? Kean's daughter and the rent collector. And her five years older than him and as plain as a pikestaff. She's brazen, that's what she is, she's buying him. And, of course, he's willing to be bought. He's no fool, who would turn down that chance? She should be ashamed of herself though, using her money as bait. You can't blame the fellow. And you know, this didn't start the day, or yesterday; they were going at it when his wife was alive"? . . . That's what they're saying.'

His face was burning, the colour suffusing it was almost scarlet.

'Oh, please don't get upset about it; you must have been aware that our association would cause a minor scandal?'

'I wasn't!' His answer was vehement. 'If. . . if I'd thought they'd been saying that I . . . I wouldn't have gone on. I . . . I was your manager. Anyway, if you knew this, why didn't put put a stop to it? Why did you let it go on?'

'Oh . . . huh! Why? Well, to tell you the truth, it made me all the more determined to go on. I don't care a fig for their chatter. What are they after all, the majority of them? Braggarts, strutting little nonentities, men who have clawed their way up over the dead bodies of miners, or of their factory workers. Oh, there are a good many hypocrites in this town. I could reel them off, sanctimonious individuals, leading double lives. You know, you'd think Newcastle was at the other end of the world, and it is for some of them, keeping their second homes . . . It is very strange you know but women talk to me, they confide in me; perhaps it's because to them I'm unfeminine. But anyway –' she tossed her head to the side – 'I have no room to speak, at least on the point of clawing one's way up, for what did my father do for anyone except himself? And for that matter what have I done but talk? But this is where you come in. I have thought that with you I might begin to do things for other people. I –' her voice dropped – 'I might become so at peace with myself that I could turn my thoughts on to the needs of others, and there are many in need in this town. And you know that better than I do, because you have been on that side of the wall. You have had to say "Yes, sir", and "No, sir", and of course –' she nodded at him – ' "Yes, miss", and "No, miss", and it's only recently and only through you that I have realized how people such as you, in your position, must feel.'

She now rose from the couch abruptly and, going to the mantelpiece, she put her hands on it and looked down into the fire as she muttered, 'I am not saying this in order to make the future appear more attractive. If . . . if closer association with me would be intolerable to you, very well, you have only to say so.'

'And what if I did, what then?' The question was quiet, soft, and her answer equally so. 'I don't know, because . . . because I haven't allowed myself to look into the future and face the desolation there.'

As he stared up at her he thought, She's remarkable. By aye, she's a remarkable woman. He had never imagined anyone talking as frankly as she had done; no man would ever have been as honest. He said softly, 'Will you give me time to think it over?'

'*No!*'

The word was barked and it brought him to his feet as if it had been the crack of a gun. He watched her march down the room, then back again towards him. At the head of the couch she stopped, and he saw her fingers dig into the upholstery as she said tersely, 'It must be now, yes or no. I . . . I cannot go on in uncertainty. I . . . I'm not asking anything from you but to come into this house and stay with me as a . . . a friend, a companion. You don't believe it now, but you'll find out there's more lasting happiness stems from friendship than has ever done from love. I know you don't love me, couldn't love me, and never will . . . No! No! Don't protest.' She lifted her hand. 'Let us start from the beginning being honest. When you lost your wife I knew that you must have loved her deeply, and that kind of love only happens once, but there are other emotions comparable with love. A man can have them towards a woman and be happy. That can also apply to a woman, although' – She swallowed deeply in her throat here before ending, 'In most cases she needs to love even if she's not loved in return.'

God, he was hot, sweating. What could he say? What could he do? Strangely, he knew what he had the desire to do, and it was scattering to the winds all his previous decisions, for at this moment he wanted to go behind that couch and put his arms about her, comfort her. Just that, comfort her. Nothing else, just comfort her. Then why wasn't he doing it?

He was surprised to hear himself saying in a voice that sounded quite ordinary, 'Come and sit down.' He was holding his hand out to her, and slowly she put hers into it. Then he drew her round the head of the couch and on to its seat, and still with her hand in his he sat beside her, and as he looked at her an excitement rose in him. He seemed to be drawing it from her. Aye yes, that was the other word he wanted for what he felt for her, excitement. It was almost akin to the feeling he got when he was in a good game. He hadn't been aware of it, but that was why he had liked to be in her company, liked to hear her talk; even when she was getting her sly digs in at him, she was exciting.

If she hadn't been so tall and thin and plain what was happening now would likely have happened months ago. But now he realized that her thinking, her voice, her manner, the way she dressed, all the things she did were in a way a compensation for her looks. In fact, they formed a kind of cloak over them because there had been times lately when in her company

that he had forgotten how she looked. He hadn't realized this until now.
Suddenly he felt at ease with her as he'd never done before. He knew he
could talk to her now, aye and comfort her. He bent towards her and said,
'Can I tell you something?'

Her eyes had a moisture in them when she answered, 'I'm eager to hear
whatever you have to say, Rory.'

'It's going to be difficult for me to put into words 'cos you see I haven't
your gift, your gift of the gab.' He wagged the hand that was within his.
'You know you've got the gift of the gab, don't you? But there's one thing,
when you open your mouth something meaningful always comes out.
That's the difference between you an' me . . . and the likes of me. But I . . .
I want to tell you, I've been learnin' these months past. There's not a day
gone by when I've been with you but I haven't learned something from
you. It mightn't show, it still hasn't covered up me aggressiveness.' Again
he shook her hand. 'And I want to tell you something more. I've liked
being with you . . . I mean, I do like being with you. You won't believe
this, but well, I . . . I find you sort of exciting. I've never known any other
woman like you. Well, I wouldn't, would I, not coming from my quarter?
Mind, I must say at this point that Janie was a fine girl and I was happy
with her. I've got to say that; you said a minute ago let's be honest. Yet, at
the same time, I've got to admit she wasn't excitin'. Lovable aye, but not
excitin'. Looking back, I see that Janie had little to teach me, only perhaps
thoughtfulness for others; she could get really worked up over other
people's problems, you know, and after all, that's no small thing, is it?'

'No, it isn't . . . Rory.'

'Yes?'

'What is the answer you're giving me? I . . . I want to hear it in . . . in
definite terms. You are kind now but I don't know whether it is merely to
soothe me. I want to hear you say, "Yes, Charlotte," or "No, Charlotte." '

Their hands were still joined, their knees almost touching, their faces
not more than two feet apart, and he knew that if he said no, his life would
in some way become empty, barren, and not only because he might no
longer have admittance to this house.

'. . . Yes . . . Charlotte.'

He watched her close her eyes. When she opened them they were
bright; in any other face they would have been starry.

'It's a bargain.'

'Aye, it's a bargain.'

As he uttered the words he again had a vivid mental picture of the
kitchen. He could see his dad, Ruth, her, and Jimmy, all staring at him, all
saying, 'What, her, Miss Kean! Never! . . . What about Janie?'

He said suddenly, 'I'm not going to make any excuses about me people;

I'm not going to hide them; you'll have to meet them.'

'I'll be pleased to, very pleased to. I've never had any people of my own.'

He said suddenly on a laugh, 'You know something? I'll never make excuses to you, I'll always tell you the truth. That's a promise. It'll likely not always please you . . .'

'It won't.' She was pulling a long face at him now and her laughter was high, slightly out of control as she said, 'It certainly won't if you tell me you are going out gambling every night.'

When his eyes widened and his lips fell apart her laughter increased and she cried with the air of a young teasing girl, which lay awkwardly on her, 'Didn't I tell you I know most things about most people in this town?'

His face straight and his voice flat, he asked, 'How did you know about that?'

'Deduction, and the one word you kept repeating when you were in hospital. When I first saw you, you said again and again, "Pittie. Pittie. Pittie". The second time I visited you you were still saying it.'

'I was?'

'Yes, and you know when a man gets beaten up as you were there's nearly always something behind it. A footpad might have hit you on the head and knocked you senseless, but then I don't think he would have kicked you within an inch of death's door. After thinking about it, I realized you were telling everyone the name of your assailants, but no one seemed to be taking any notice, they thought you were saying, "Isn't it a pity?" when what you were really doing was giving them the name of the men who attacked you, the Pittie brothers. The Pittie brothers are well-known scoundrels, besides being dirty gamblers. They were fined for gambling some short time ago.'

'Huh! Huh!' A smile was spreading over his face, widening his mouth. He now put his head back on his shoulders and laughed until his body shook, and she laughed with him.

His chest was heaving and he was still laughing when he looked into her face again and said, 'I've thought it, but now I'll say it, you're a remarkable woman.'

'Oh, please don't judge my intelligence on the face that I recognized something that should have been staring everyone in the face, the police into the bargain. Yet at the same time I don't think the police were as stupid as they made out to be, but when they asked you had you seen the assailant or assailants, I was given to understand you said no, you had been attacked while walking down a side street.'

He screwed up his eyes at her now and, his face serious, he asked, 'But . . . but how could you know that I gambled?'

She stared at him for a long moment before saying, and seriously now, 'A short while ago you said you'd always tell me the truth. I understood, of course, that you were referring to the future, but now I'm going to ask you: Is there anything further you want to tell me, anything, about your past say?'

For a moment he wondered if she were referring to his birth. He stared into her eyes, then gulped in his throat as he thought, She can't know about the other business, else I wouldn't be here now.

'Think hard before you answer.'

He felt the colour flooding his face again. They were staring into each other's eyes. His body was sweating; it was as if he were having a nightmare in broad daylight. His voice was a gruff whisper when he said, 'Well, knowin' what you know, or think you know, why am I sitting here now?'

Her voice was equally low as she replied, 'I'll answer that in a moment when you answer my question.'

His gaze riveted on her, he pondered. If she didn't know, if she wasn't referring to John George's business then what he was about to say would likely put the kibosh on her proposal. But if it was that she was hinting at, then indeed, aye, by God! indeed she was a remarkable woman.

He closed his eyes for a moment, lowered his head, and turned it to the side before he muttered, as if he were in the confessional box: 'I took the five pounds that John George did time for. I went back that night and helped meself, but like him I expected to be there first thing on the Monday morning to return it. If . . . if I had been there and you had caught me I would have stood me rap along of him, but by the time I knew what had happened I was sick and weak, and petrified at the thought of prison.' His head still to the side, he jerked his neck out of his collar before going on, 'I . . . I have a fear on me, always have had since I was nailed down in a box as a child. I fear being shut in, I can't stand being behind closed doors of any kind. I . . . I should have come forward, I know, but there it is, I didn't . . . Is that what you want to know?'

There was a long pause and when she made no reply he looked at her again and said 'You knew this all along?'

'No, not from the beginning,' she shook her head slowly. 'But in the court I felt the man was speaking the truth and I recalled his amazement when I mentioned that not ten shillings but five pounds ten was missing. He was so astonished he couldn't speak. But in any case, five pounds ten or ten shillings he had to be brought to book, for, as he admitted, he had been tampering with the books for some long time, and as he also admitted, not only for ten shillings at a time either.'

All this time their hands had been joined and he looked down on them as he asked quietly, 'Why am I here now? Tell me that. Knowing all this about me, why am I here now?'

She now withdrew her hands from his and, rising to her feet, went towards the fire and once again looked at the picture above the mantelpiece. Then she wetted her lips twice and drew in a long breath before she said softly, 'I . . . I happened to care for you . . . This, of course, wipes out all my fine talk about friendship et cetera, but you see –' again she wetted her lips – 'I've loved you since the first time I saw you in my father's office. It was just like that, quickly, the most sudden thing in my life. I remember thinking, that's the kind of man I would like to marry if it were possible. I knew it was a preposterous desire, quite hopeless, utterly hopeless. My father would never never have countenanced it. Strangely, he didn't like you. But then he liked so few people, and if I'd shown the slightest interest in you, even mentioned your name in a kindly fashion, he would have dismissed you.'

She turned and looked at him. 'I'm a fraud, but I really did not intend that you should know this. I . . . I was going to acquire you under false pretences. But . . . but it makes no difference to the bargain. That can remain as it stands. But –' she laughed selfconsciously – 'so much for all my fine platonic talk. You know, Rory, the emotions are not measured in proportion to one's looks: if that were so all the beauties in the world would be passionate lovers, but from what I have gauged from my reading they're often very cold women. My . . . my emotions don't match my looks, Rory, but as I said the bargain stands: you give me your friendship and protection as a husband, I will give you what . . . well, what I cannot help giving you.'

He rose from the couch and went slowly towards her, and he stared into her face before he said softly, 'There must be a dozen men in this town who'd be only too glad to have married you, and would serve you better than I'll ever be able to.'

'Doubtless, doubtless.' She nodded slowly at him. 'But you see, and here we come to the question of truth again, they would have been marrying me for one thing, my money, and they would likely have been men with whom I couldn't bargain. In their cases I would most assuredly have wished them to have their own apartments, but in their cases they would assuredly not have complied, for let us face the fact that most men's needs do not require the stimulus of love. . . .'

Slowly and firmly now he put his arms about her and drew her thin form towards him, and when he felt her taut body relax against him, and her head bury itself in his shoulder, he put his face into the dark coils of her hair and murmured, 'Don't. There, there, don't cry. Please don't cry. I'll . . . I'll make you happy, Charlotte. I promise I'll make you happy.'

He didn't know how he was going to do it. The only thing he was sure of in this fantastic moment was that he'd have a damned good try.

CHAPTER 2

He stood in the kitchen at the end of the long table, while they, like a combating force, stood at the other end, Ruth, his father, and Lizzie. Jimmy stood to the side towards the middle of the table, his face pale, anxious, his eyes darting between them like a troubled referee.

'Well, you can say something, can't you?' His voice re-echoed through the timbers in the roof.

It was his father who spoke. Quietly he said, 'Janie's hardly cold.'

'Janie's been dead over a year, a year and three weeks to be exact.'

'Huh! Well.' Paddy broke away from the group and walked towards the fireplace and, picking up a clay pipe from the mantelpiece, he bent and tapped it on the hob, knocking out the doddle as he said, 'you're doin' well for yersel, there's that much to be said. Aye, aye. They used to say old Kean could buy Shields, that is the parts Cookson hadn't bought up. Money grabbers, the lot of them! . . .'

'It wasn't the money . . .'

'Well, begod! it couldn't be her face.'

Rory swung round and glared at Lizzie. It looked for a moment as if he would spring down the table and strike her. Their eyes held across the distance before she snapped her gaze from his and, swinging round, went towards the scullery, muttering, 'My God! My God! What next!'

The anger in him blinded him for a moment. Any other family in the town, any other family from here to Newcastle, would, he imagined, have fallen on his neck for making such a match, but not his family, aw no. In their ignorance they thought you must keep loyal to the dead, if not for ever, then for a decent period of years.

His vision clearing, he glared now at Ruth. She was usually the one to see both sides of everything, but she wasn't seeing his side of this, there was a stricken look on her face. He put his hands on the table and leant towards her now as he cried, 'You didn't condemn her da, did you –' he jerked his head back in the direction of the cottage next door – 'when he went off and lived with his woman in Jarrow after Gran died. He couldn't wait. Six weeks, that's all he stayed there alone, six weeks. But you said nothin' about that. And I'm marrying her. Do you hear?' He flashed a glance towards his father's bent head. 'I'm not taking her on the side. And one at a time'll be enough for me.'

There was no sound in the kitchen. Paddy hadn't moved, Ruth hadn't moved, Lizzie hadn't burst into the room from the scullery. He stood breathing deeply. Then looking at Jimmy, he yelled, 'I came here, you know I came here to say that she wanted to meet them. My God! she didn't know what she was askin' . . . Well, it doesn't matter. I know where I stand now; you'll want me afore I'll want you, the lot of you.' And on this he turned round and marched out of the room.

Before the door had crashed closed Lizzie appeared in the kitchen. Paddy turned from the fireplace, and Ruth, putting her hand out towards Jimmy as if she were pushing him, said quickly and in a choked voice, 'Go after him. Stay with him. Tell . . . tell him it'll be all right.'

She was now pressing Jimmy towards the door. 'Tell . . . tell him I understand, and . . . and she'll be welcome. Tell him that, she'll be welcome.'

Jimmy didn't speak but, grabbing up his cap, he pulled it tight down on his head, then ran wobbling down the path and out of the gate, calling, 'Rory! Rory!'

He was at the top of the bank before he caught up with Rory.

'Aw, man, hold your hand a minute. It's . . . it's no use gettin' in a paddy. I . . . I told you afore we come it would give them a gliff; it gave me a gliff, not only . . . not because of Janie, but . . .'

'But what?' Rory pulled up so suddenly that Jimmy went on a couple of steps before turning to him and looking up at him and saying fearlessly, 'You want the truth? All right, you'll get it. She's different, older; plain, as Lizzie said, plain an' . . .'

'Aye, go on.' Rory's voice came from deep within his throat.

'Well . . . All right then, I'll say it, I will, I'll say it, she's a different class from you. You'll you'll be like a fish out of water.'

Rory, his voice a tone quieter now, bent over Jimmy and said slowly, 'Did you feel like a fish out of water last night when you met her?'

Jimmy tossed his head, blinked, then turned and walked on, Rory with him now, and after a moment, he answered, 'No, 'cos . . . 'cos I felt she had set out to make me like her. But I won't be livin' with her.' He now turned his head up to Rory. 'That's the difference, I won't have to live her life and meet her kind of people. I won't have to live up to her.'

'And you think I can't?'

Jimmy's head swayed from one side to the other following the motion of his body, and he said, 'Aye, just that.'

'Thanks. Thanks very much.'

'I . . . I didn't mean it nasty, man, no more than they meant to be nasty.'

'Huh! They didn't mean to be nasty? My God! You must have ten skins. You were there, you were there, man, weren't you?'

Jimmy didn't answer for a while, and then he said quietly, 'Me ma says she'll be welcome; you can bring her and she'll be welcome.'

'Like hell I will! Take her up there among that bigoted tribe? Not on your bloody life. Well –' he squared his shoulders and his step quickened and his arms swung wider – 'why should I worry me head, they're the losers, they've potched themselves. I could have put them all on their feet, I could have set them all up, set them up for life.' He cast a hard glance down now on Jimmy and demanded, 'Do you know how much I'll be worth when I marry her? Have you any idea? I'll be a rich man, 'cos she's rollin', and I'll be in control. Just think on that.'

'Aye well, good for you, I hope it keeps fine for you.'

The colloquial saying which was for ever on Lizzie's tongue caused Rory to screw up his eyes tightly for a moment.

I hope it keeps fine for you.

Would he ever do anything right in this world? Would he ever do anything to please anybody? . . . Well, he was pleasing her, wasn't he? He had never seen a woman so openly happy in his life as he had her these past three weeks. Her happiness was embarrassing; aye, and humbling, making him say to himself each night when he left her, I'll repay her in some way, and he would, he would, and to hell with the rest of them. The kitchen had seen him for the last time, he'd go to that registry office whenever she liked and he'd show them, by God! he'd show them. He would let them see if he could live up to her or not.

I hope it keeps fine for you.

And Janie was dead!

CHAPTER 3

He let himself in through the front door, but as he opened the door leading from the lobby into the hall Jessie was there to close it for him.

'What a night, sir. Eeh! you are wet.' As she took his hat and thick tweed coat from him he bent towards her and said in a conspiratorial whisper, 'Well, don't shout it out, Jessie, or I'll have to take cough mixture.'

'Oh, sir.' She giggled and shook her head, then said, 'The mistress is upstairs,' and as he nodded at her and went towards the staircase she hissed after him, 'Your boots, sir.'

He looked down at his damp feet, then jerking his chin upwards and biting on his bottom lip like a boy caught in a misdemeanour he sat down on the hall chair and unlaced his boots. He then took his house shoes from her hand and pulled them on, and as he rose he bent towards her again and said in a whisper, 'Between you all I'll end up in a blanket.'

Again she giggled, before turning away towards the kitchen to inform the cook that the master was in. She liked the master, she did; the house had been different altogether since he had come into it. He might have come from the bottom end of nowhere but he didn't act uppish. And what's more, he had made the mistress into a new woman. By! aye, he had that. She had never seen such a change in anybody. Nor had she seen such a change in the house. Everybody was infected; as cook said, they'd all got the smit . . .

On opening the bedroom door he almost pushed her over and he put out his arm swiftly to catch her, saying, 'Why are you standin' behind the door?'

'I wasn't standing behind the door, Mr Connor, I was about to open the door.'

She put her face up to his and he kissed her gently on the lips.

'I didn't hear you come in.'

'Well, you wouldn't.' He shook his head from side to side. 'Jessie carried me from the front door to the foot of the stairs, made me put my slippers on, and told me to be a good boy.'

She shook his arm and smiled at him; then she unloosened his tie as she asked, 'How did things go?'

He now pressed her from him and on to the long padded velvet stool set before the dressing table, and as he stood back from her he took off his coat and tugged the narrow tie from his high collar; then turned and as he walked towards the wardrobe that filled almost one entire wall, he pulled his shirt over his head, saying, 'Very well. Very well. I've enjoyed meself the day.' He looked over his shoulder.

'More so than usual?'

'Oh, much more so than usual.'

He now took from the wardrobe drawer a silk shirt with a wide soft collar, put it on, then divested himself of his trousers and, after selecting another pair from a rack, he stepped into them, while she watched him in silence and with seeming pleasure. Lastly, he donned a matching coat, then returned towards her, saying, 'I met someone I've been hoping to meet for a long time.'

'Lady or gentleman?'

He gave her a twisted smile now before answering, 'Gentleman.'

'Oh –' She placed her hand on her heart now, saying, 'My rage is subsiding, please proceed.'

He gave a small laugh, then sat down beside her on the stool. 'Do you know a man named Nickle?'

'Nickle? I know two men by the name of Nickle, Mr Frank Nickle and Mr John Nickle, but they're not related. Which one did you meet?'

'Oh, I'm not sure. This one lives in Plynlimmon Way.'

'Oh, that's Mr Frank Nickle. Why have you wanted to meet him? I'm sure you would have nothing in common.'

'That's where you're wrong . . . What do you know of him?'

She put her head on one side as if considering, then said, 'I know I don't care much for him, yet I have nothing against him except that I don't think he was kind to his wife. I met her twice. It was shortly after I came back from school, Mother was alive. We went to dinner there once, and she came here. She was a sad woman. I think she was afraid of him. Yes –' she nodded – 'looking back, I think she was afraid of him. I don't think Mother had much time for him either, but they were all members of the same church and . . . What are you laughing at?'

'Oh, there's the bell for dinner. I'll tell you after.'

'You'll tell me now.'

He stared at her for a moment, then said quietly, 'I'll tell you later, Mrs Connor.'

She bit on her lip to stop herself from laughing, bowed her head slightly, then, holding her hand out to him, rose from the seat. When he didn't immediately follow suit she said, 'Would you mind accompanying me down to dinner, Mr Connor?'

'Not at all, Mrs Connor.' He did rise now and gave her his arm, and she laid her head against his for a moment and they went out and down the stairs and into the dining-room like a young couple who were so in love that they couldn't bear to be separated even while going into a meal . . .

They had been married for five months now and Rory had grown so used to this way of life that it was hard at times for him to imagine he had ever lived any other. He was dressed as became a man of means; he ate like a man of means; he was beginning to enter the society of the town as should a man of means, because twice lately they had been asked out to dinner, and only four days ago he had played host to ten guests at this very table.

As day followed day he became more surprised at himself; he had never thought he would have adapted so quickly and so easily. Even Jimmy had said recently, 'It's amazing how you've learned to pass yourself. You'll be hobnobbing with Lord Cole next.'

He had laughed and said, 'I shouldn't be at all surprised at that either, lad,' at the same time knowing that while he might have gained access to certain houses in the town, there were still those whose doors would never be open to the one-time rent man, and among the latter were certain members of her church.

She'd tried to get him to church. He should attend for two reasons, she had laughingly said, in God's cause, and the cause of business. But no, he had put his foot down firmly here. He couldn't be that kind of a hypocrite. He had been brought up a Catholic and although he had never been through a church door for years, except when the banns were called and on the day he was married, he'd been born one and he would die one, he wasn't going to become a turncoat.

He was happy as he had never expected to be happy again in his life. It was a different kind of happiness, a steady, settled sort of happiness; a happiness made up partly of material things, partly of gratitude, and . . . and something else. It wasn't love, but at the same time it came into that category, yet he couldn't put a name to it. But he liked her, he liked her a lot, and he admired her. Strangely, he had ceased to be sorry for her. He couldn't imagine now why he'd ever been sorry for her. And strangely too, he was more at ease in her company than he had ever been with anyone in his own family, apart from Jimmy that was . . . He hadn't always been at ease with Janie. It was funny that, but he hadn't. No, he couldn't put a name to the feeling he had for Charlotte, he only knew that he liked being with her and that this was the life for him. He had fallen on his feet and he meant to see that they carried him firmly into the future . . .

The meal over and in the drawing-room, she sat by his side on the couch and watched him begin the process of filling his pipe – This liberty had even shocked the servants. No gentleman smoked in a drawing-room, but there, the mistress allowed it – and now she said, 'Well, I'm waiting. What have you discovered about Mr Nickle that has filled you with glee?'

'Glee?'

'Yes, glee. It's been oozing out of you since you came in.'

'He's a good churchman, isn't he?'

'Yes, as churchmen go, he's a good churchman.'

'A highly respected member of the community.' He pressed the tobacco down into the wide bowl of his red-wood pipe.

'What is it?' She put her hand out and slapped his knee playfully, and he looked at her steadily for a minute before he said flatly, 'He's a two-faced hypocrite.'

'Oh, is that all? Well, he's not alone in this town, is he?'

'He runs a gaming house.'

Now she was startled. 'Mr Nickle running a gaming house? You're dreaming, Rory.'

'Oh no. Oh no, Charlotte, Rory isn't dreaming,' he mimicked her. 'Rory once tried to get into Mr Nickle's gaming house, but he was politely warned off, then recommended to a house in King Street. And you know what happened to Rory in King Street, don't you?'

'You can't mean it?' Her face was straight and his also, and his tone was deep and bitter when he answered, 'I do. And it's not only gaming he's interested in when he can frighten little Joe . . .'

'Who's little Joe?'

'He's a bookie's runner, you know, one who goes round taking bets. But he's many more things besides, some things that it would be dangerous to look into. Not that he could do much on his own. But those who hire him could, such as our Mr Nickle. You know –' he now rose and went to the fire and lit a spill and after drawing on his pipe came back towards her, saying, 'You know, I wouldn't have told you. I mean I wouldn't have given him away, only I met him the day across the water in Crawford's. He was doing the same as I was, getting the lay of the land, seeing if the place was worth buying, and he talked loudly to Crawford for my benefit about the stupidity of competing against rope works just farther up the river, such as Haggie's. And all the while he eyed me. Yet he ignored me, completely ignored me. Then Crawford, who's as blunt as an old hammer, said, "Aw well, if that's your opinion of the place you're not interested, are you? So what about you, Mr Connor, you think the same?" "No," I said, "I'm here to talk business." And on that the old fellow turned his back on our Mr Nickle and walked with me into the office, leaving his highness black in the face. And that's why I'm oozing glee, as you call it, 'cos Crawford's askin' much less than we thought. I told him we weren't thinking of rope, but a foundry, at least material from it to make household goods.'

'Good. Good.' She put her hand out towards him, and he held it and went on, 'And later, I saw his highness in the hotel when I was having a meal, and again he cut me dead. Now I could've understood such an attitude from any number of men in this town, and took it, but not from him, not knowin' what I know about him. Because it isn't only gambling, it's lasses.'

'Lasses?'

'Yes, there's quite a number of lasses disappear now and again.'

'Oh no! Rory, he . . . he wouldn't.'

'He would, and he does. Little Joe, the fellow I mentioned, was very much afraid of our Mr Nickle, and a game on the side wouldn't have caused him to sweat so much so that he got washed and cleaned up afore going to his back door. I'd never known little Joe so clean in his life as when I saw him that day, the day I found out about Nickle . . . Look.' He tugged her towards him. 'I've thought of something. Do you think you could invite him here to dinner?'

'Invite him here?'

'That's what I said. Say your husband would very much like to meet him.'

'But after he's cut you, do you think . . . ?'

'Aye. Aye, I do. Invite him in a way that he'll think twice about refusing . . . Put that something in your voice . . . You can do it.'

'Blackmail?'

'Aye. Yes, if you like.'

She began to smile slowly, then she nodded at him. 'Yes, I see your point. Yes, I'll invite him. If I'm not mistaken I'll be meeting him next week; he's a member of the Church Council. We'll likely be sitting side by side in the vestry. Yes –' she laughed outright now – 'I'll invite him here, and enjoy it . . . that's if he accepts the invitation.'

'He will, after you've put it over in your own way . . . Huh! it's a funny life.' He leant back in the couch and she twisted her body round and looked fully at him.

'How are you finding it?'

'Finding what?'

'Life, this funny life.'

Taking the pipe from his mouth, he said, 'I'm liking this life fine, Mrs Connor. I never dreamed I'd like it so well.'

'I wish I were beautiful.' Her voice was low, and he pulled her suddenly towards him and encircled her with his arm, saying, 'You've got qualities that beat beauty any day in the week. You're the best-dressed woman in the town, too. Moreover, you've got something up top.'

'Something up top?' Her face was partly smothered against his shoulder. 'I'd willingly be an empty-headed simpering nincompoop if only I . . . I looked different.'

Quickly now he thrust her from him and said harshly and with sincerity, 'Well, I can tell you this much, you wouldn't be sitting where you are now, or at least I wouldn't be sitting where I am now, if you were an empty-headed nincompoop.'

'Oh, Rory.' She flung herself against him as any young girl might, and he lay back holding her tightly to him.

Hardly a week passed but he had to reassure her with regard to her looks. It seemed that she was becoming more conscious of her plainness as time went on, and yet strangely, he himself was actually becoming less aware of her lack of beauty as the days passed; there were even times when her whole face took on an attractive quality. Then there was her voice. Her voice was beautiful. He never tired listening to it, even when she was in one of her haughty moods, which were becoming rarer.

She was saying, 'You've never asked what I've been doing all day today?'

'What have you been doing all day today?'

'Nothing. Nothing much. But . . . but I have two things to tell you.'

'Two things? Well, get on with them. What are they?'

She pulled herself gently from his arms, saying now, 'Don't be disturbed, but Jimmy came this afternoon. One . . . one of the boats has been sunk . . .'

He was sitting on the edge of the couch now. 'Why . . . why, didn't you tell me this afore?'

She placed her hands on his shoulders, saying, 'Be quiet. Don't get agitated. I've seen to it.'

'Where's Jimmy now?'

'Where he always is, in the boathouse.'

'Look, I'd better go down, he shouldn't be there alone. I'll . . .'

'I told you I've seen to it. Mr Richardson is staying there with him.'

'The boat . . . what happened to the boat?'

'A plank had been levered from the bottom.'

'And it would have been full. He was transporting for Watson yesterday.'

'Yes, it had on the usual cargo.'

'And it all went to the bottom?'

'They salvaged it. I went back with Jimmy; you hadn't been gone half an hour.'

He pulled himself up from the couch and began to pace back and forth in front of the fire, grinding out between his teeth, 'Those bloody Pitties!' He never apologized for swearing in front of her, nor did she ever reprimand him. 'If they're not stopped they'll do murder. Something's got to be done.' He was standing in front of her, looking down at her now, and she said quietly, 'Something will be done; I've seen to that as well. I . . . I called on the Chief Constable. I told him of our suspicions. Of course you cannot accuse anyone unless you have absolute proof, but I knew by the little he said that he was well aware of the Pitties' activities and would be as pleased as us to convict them. And he said something that I found very interesting. He ended by saying it was difficult of course to catch little fish when they were protected by big fish. What do you make of that?'

He rubbed his hand tightly along his jawbone. 'What do I make of it? Just that it links up with what I was saying earlier: there are some respectable people in this town leading double lives . . . big fish behind little fish.' He narrowed his eyes at her. 'Who would be protectin' the Pitties? Only somebody who wants to use them. And what would they use them for? What's their job? Running freight, anything from contraband whisky, silk, baccy, or men . . .'

'Or maidens? As you were saying earlier.'

He nodded at her. 'Aye, men or maidens, anything.' He bowed his head and shook it for a moment before saying, 'What I'm really frightened of is, if they should go for Jimmy. He's no match for any of them, although he's got plenty of guts. But guts aren't much use against them lot, it's guile you want.'

'If you are so worried about him then you must make him come here to sleep.'

He gave a weak smile and put his hand out and touched her shoulder, saying, 'That's nice of you, kind, but I doubt if he would.'

'Why not? He's got over his shyness of me, he's even, I think, beginning to like me. It gives me hope that your family may well follow suit.'

He turned from her and went towards the mantelpiece. And now he looked up into the face of her great-grandfather, and he thought, That'll be the day. That pig-headed lot. Even Ruth was included in his thoughts now.

Jimmy, acting as a kind of go-between, had arranged that he should take her up one Saturday, and because she also demanded it, but much against the grain, he had complied. And what had happened? Nothing. She had sat there trying to talk her way into their good books, and how had they responded? By staring at her as if she were a curio.

Later, she had remarked, 'I think your mother is a gentle creature.'

His mother. That was one secret he had kept to himself. She knew eveything about him but that, and he couldn't bring himself to tell her that the slight, quiet, little woman, with a dignity that was all her own, was not his mother. His mother was the woman he had introduced to her by merely remarking, 'This is Lizzie', and explaining later that she was his father's cousin. Why was it that some things were impossible to admit to? He felt as guilty at being Lizzie's son as if it were he himself who had perpetrated the sin of his conception.

Damn them! Let them get on with it. It was Jimmy he was worried about, and those bloody Pitties were beginning to scare him. Little fish protected by big fish!

He turned to her. 'I'm goin' down,' he said.

'All right.' She rose from the couch. 'I'll go with you.'

'You'll do nothing of the sort. It's coming down whole water now.'

'If you're going down there tonight I'm going with you.'

He closed his eyes for a moment; he knew that tone. 'Well, get your things on.' His voice was almost a growl.

As she was walking towards the door, she said, 'I'll tell Stoddard.'

'No, no.' He came to her side. 'You don't want to get the carriage out at this time of night. And he'll be settled down. I meant to walk.'

'All right, we'll walk.'

'Oh, woman!'

'Oh, man!' She smiled at him and tweaked his nose, then left the room smiling.

Half an hour later they went up the steps and into the boathouse and startled Jimmy and Mr Richardson who were playing cards.

'Oh, hello.' Jimmy slid to his feet; then looking from one to the other, he asked, 'Anything wrong?'

'Not at our end; what about this end? What's this I'm hearin'?'

'Oh that.' Jimmy nodded, then said, 'Well, it's done one thing.' He was looking at Charlotte now. 'The river polis have been past here three times to my knowledge this afternoon. That's . . . that's with you going down there. Hardly seen them afore. That should warn the bug . . . beggars off for a bit.'

'Aye, for a bit.' Rory pulled a chair towards Charlotte. She sat down, and what she said was, 'Have you plenty to eat?'

'Oh aye.' Jimmy smiled at her. 'Lizzie's been down this afternoon an' baked. She feeds me up as if I was carryin' tw . . .' He swallowed and the colour flushed up over his pale face as he amended Lizzie's description of pregnancy, carrying twins for eighteen months, with 'cartin' coals to Newcastle.'

As he looked at Charlotte he saw that her eyes were bright, twinkling. She had twigged what he was about to say. It was funny but he liked her, he liked her better every time he met her. He could see now what had got their Rory. When you got to know her you forgot she was nothing to look at. He had said so to Lizzie this very afternoon when she was on about Rory, but she had come back at him, saying, 'You another one that's got a short memory? I thought you used to think the world of Janie.' Well, yes he had, but Janie was dead. And he had said that to her an' all, but what had she come back again with, that the dead should live on in the memory. She was a hard nut was Lizzie, she didn't give Rory any credit for making life easier for the lot of them. Three pounds every week he sent up there; they had never been so well off in all their lives. New clothes they had, new bedding, and they ate like fighting cocks. If Lizzie kept on, and his ma too didn't really soften towards Charlotte – he wasn't concerned about his da's opinion – he'd give them the length of his tongue one of these days, he'd tell them straight out. 'Well,' he'd say, 'if you think like you do, you shouldn't be takin' his money.' Aye, he would, he'd say that. And what would they say? 'It isn't his money, it's hers' . . . Well, it didn't matter whose it was, they were taking it and showing no gratitude. For himself he was grateful. By lad! he was grateful. Three boats he had, but one without a bottom to it.

He said to her, 'Will you have a cup of tea?'

'No, thank you, Jimmy. We . . . we just came to see that everything was all right.' She smiled from him to Mr Richardson.

Mr Richardson was a burly man in his forties. He had worked in

Baker's yard alongside Jimmy but had gladly made the move to here when Rory offered him five shillings a week more than he was getting there. He was a married man with a family, so the arrangement of keeping Jimmy company at nights could not be a permanent one.

'We're grateful for you staying, Mr Richardson,' she said.

'Do anything I can, ma'am.'

'Thank you. We won't forget it, Mr Richardson.'

The man nodded and smiled widely. Then she rose to her feet and, looking at Rory, said, 'Well now, are you satisfied?'

Before he could answer she turned her head towards Jimmy, saying, 'The trouble with your brother, Jimmy, is he won't recognize the fact that you are a young man no longer an apprentice.'

Jimmy laughed back at her, saying, 'Well, we'll have to show him, won't we? You tell him when you see him I'll take him on any day in the week an' knock the stuffin' out of him. You tell him that, will you?'

Rory now thrust out his fist and punched Jimmy gently on the head saying, 'You've always been a daft lad; you always will be.'

'Daft? Huh! Who's daft comin' down this end in the black dark an' it pourin'. Don't you think you're askin' for trouble yourself, walking along the dockside, an' not alone either?' He nodded towards Charlotte.

'She came along to protect me. Can you imagine anybody tacklin' me when she's there?' He now took hold of Charlotte's arm and led her towards the door as she tut-tutted and cast a reproving glance up at him.

'Keep that door bolted, mind.'

'Aye. Don't you worry.' Jimmy smiled quietly at Rory.

The farewells over, they took the lantern and went down the steps and made their way through the stinging rain on to the road and along the waterfront, and as they hurried through what, even in daytime, was known to be an unsavoury thoroughfare Rory thought. He was right, I was crazy to let her come, and at this time of night.

And so he didn't breathe easily until they emerged into the main street, and there she said to him, 'Now you can relax.'

He did not reply, only heaved a telling sigh as he thought for the countless time, There's no doubt about it, she's remarkable.

His mind more at ease now with regard to Jimmy, he said, 'There were two things you were going to tell me the night. Well, let's have the second one now.'

'No, not now; it will have to wait until we get out of this, the rain is choking me.'

'Serves you right; you would have your own way.'

'Far better have my own way than sit worrying until you returned.'

'You're a fool of a woman. You know that, don't you?'

'Yes, I know that, I've known it now for five months and three days.'
'Oh, Charlotte!' He pressed her arm closer to his side.

She had taken a bath and was now dressed in a pale grey chiffon night-dress with matching negligee. It was night attire which one might have expected to see on a picture postcard such as sailors brought over from foreign countries, like France, on which were painted ladies in flowing robes, their voluptuousness alone signifying their lack of virtue.

He had now become used to seeing her dressed, or undressed, like this. His own night attire not only would have caused the women in the kitchen to throw their aprons over their heads, but would have raised the eyebrows of many a smart gentleman in the town, for his nightshirt was a pale blue colour, the flannel being so fine as to be almost like cashmere. Moreover, it had cuffs that turned back and were hemmed with fancy braid, as was the deep collar. It, and a dozen more like it, were one of the many presents she had given him. And to hide his embarrassment he had made a great joke the first time he had worn one, but now he never even thought of his nightshirts, even when a fresh one was put out for him every other night.

As he pulled this one over his head he called to her, 'I'm waiting.'
'So am I.'

When her flat reply came back to him he bit on his lip, closed his eyes, tossed his head backwards and laughed silently. She was a star turn really. Who would have thought her like it?

He went from the dressing-room into the bedroom smiling. She wasn't in bed but was sitting on the edge of it, and at this moment she looked ethereal in the soft glow of the lamplight. He had the idea that if he opened the windows the wind that was blowing in gusts around the house would waft her away. He sat down beside her on the bed and, adopting an attitude of patience, he crossed his slippered feet, crossed his arms and stared ahead.

'Are you feeling strong?'
'Strong? In what way?' He turned his head sharply to look at her.
'Oh, in all ways.'
'Look, what is it?' He twisted his body round until he was facing her. 'Stop beating about the bush; what have you got up your sleeve now?'

She gave a little rippling laugh that might have issued from the lips of some dainty creature, then said, 'Nothing up my sleeve. No, decidedly not up my sleeve; I happen to have become pregnant.'
'Preg . . . *pregnant*?'

As his mouth fell into a gape she nodded at him and said, 'Yes, you know, "A woman with child" is how the Bible puts it.'

He drew in a long breath that lifted his shoulders outward. She was pregnant, she was with child, as she had said. Well, well. He had the desire to laugh. He stopped himself. She was going to have a bairn. Charlotte was going to have a bairn. And he had given it to her . . . Well, what was surprising about that? With all that had happened these past months why should he be surprised, for if anyone had worked for a bairn she had? He would never forget the first night in this bed. He had thought to treat her tenderly because right up to the moment they had first stood outside that door there, she had given him the chance to take advantage of the agreement she had first suggested; in fact, she had stood blocking his way into the room as she said, 'I won't hold it against you. Believe me, I won't hold it against you.' And what had he done? He had put his hand behind her and turned the knob. And she had entered with her head down like some shy bride, and he had told himself again that it was as little as he could do to be kind to her, to ease her torment, and make her happy. And he had made her happy. Aye by God! he had made her happy. And himself too. She had been surprising enough as a companion, but as a wife she had enlightened him in ways that he had never thought possible, because she had loved him. Aye, it was she who had done the loving. Up till then he hadn't been aware that he had never been loved. He had loved Janie. A better term for it would be, he had taken Janie. And she had let him, but she had never loved him in the way he was loved now. Perhaps it was his own fault that things had not worked out that way with Janie, it was the business of John George coming between them on that first night. He had known a few other women before Janie. On his first year of rent collecting there had been one in Jarrow – her man went to sea – but what she had wanted was comfort not love. Then another had been no better than she should be, she had given him what she would give anybody at a shilling a go.

No, he had never been loved until Charlotte loved him. It was amazing to him how or from where she had gained her knowledge, for one thing was certain, he was the first man she'd had in her life. Perhaps it was instinctive. Whatever it was, it was comforting. And now, now she was saying . . . 'Huh! . . . Huh! . . . Huh!'

He was holding her tightly to him. They fell backwards on to the bed and he rolled her to and fro, and they laughed together; then, his mouth covering hers, he kissed her long and hard.

When finally he pulled her upright the ribbon had fallen from her hair and it was loose about her shoulders and he took a handful of the black silkiness and rubbed it up and down his cheek.

'You're pleased?'

'Oh! Charlotte, what more can you give me?'

'One every year until I grow fat. I'd love to grow fat.'

'I don't want you fat, I want you just as you are.' And in this moment he was speaking the truth. He now took her face between his hands and watched her thin nostrils quiver. Her eyes were soft and full of love for him, and he said, 'You're the finest woman I've ever known, and ever will know.'

And she said, 'I love you.'

He could not say, 'And me you,' but he took her in his arms and held her tightly.

PART FOUR

CHAPTER 1

THE RESURRECTION

The foreign-looking young woman handed her ticket to the ticket collector, stared at him for a moment, then passed through the barrier. She was the last of a dozen people to leave the platform and his look followed her. She was a foreigner. He could tell by her dress; she had strange-looking clogs on her feet and a black cloak hung from her shoulders right down to the top of them. She had a contraption on her head that was part hat, part shawl, with a fringe, and strings from it, like pieces of frayed twine, were knotted under her chin. Another odd thing about her was, although her skin was brown her hair was white and frizzy, like that of an old Negro's, yet her face was that of a young woman. She reminded him of a man that used to live near him who had white hair and pink eyes. They said he was an albino. He had been an oddity.

When the young woman reached the main thoroughfare she seemed slightly bemused; the traffic was so thick, and the Saturday evening crowd were pushing and shoving. She stepped into the gutter and the mud went over the top of her clogs. She stared at one face after another as if she had never been in a crowd before, as if she had never seen people before.

She walked on like someone in a daze. She skirted the stalls in the market place and when she heard a boat horn hooting she stopped and looked down the narrow lane that led to the ferry, then she went on again.

She was half-way down the bank that dropped steeply to the river when again she stopped. And now she put her hand inside her cloak and pressed it against her ribs. Then she turned her head upwards and gazed into the fading light.

Two men paused in their walking and looked at her, and she brought her head down and stared back at them. And when they looked at each other in a questioning way she ran swiftly down the bank away from them, her clogs clip-clopping against the cobbles.

On the river-front now, she hurried in a purposeful way along it until she came to where had stood the square of waste land, and here she looked about her in some perplexity, for the ground was now railed in, its railings joining those which surrounded the boatyard. Her steps slowed as she approached the alleyway; the light was almost gone, and when she went to open the gate and found it locked, she rattled it, then knocked on it, waited a moment, and, now almost in a frenzy, took her fist and banged on it.

When there was still no reply she looked up and down the alleyway before hurrying towards the far end where it terminated at the river wall; and now she did what she had done a number of times before when Jimmy had bolted the gate from the inside, she gripped the last post of the fence where it hung out over the river and swung herself round it, and so entered the boatyard.

Now she stood perfectly still looking up towards the house. There was a light in the window of the long room. Again she put her hand inside her cloak and placed it over her ribs, then slowly she went towards the steps and mounted them. She didn't open the door but knocked on it.

She heard the footsteps coming across the wooden floor towards it, but it didn't open. A voice said, 'Who's there?'

She waited a second before answering, 'Open the door, Jimmy.'

There was complete silence all about her now, no movement from inside the room. She said again, 'Open the door, Jimmy, please. Please open the door.'

Again there was no answer. She heard the steps moving away from the door. She turned her head and saw the curtains pulled to the side; she saw the outline of Jimmy's white face pressed against the pane. She held out her hand towards it.

She didn't hear the footsteps return to the door; nor was there any other sound, not even any movement from the river. It seemed to her that she was dead again. Her voice high now, beseeching, she called, 'Jimmy! Jimmy, it's me. Open the door. Please open the door.'

When at last the door opened it seemed it did so of its own accord; it swung wide and there was no one in the opening. She stepped over the threshold and looked along the room to where Jimmy was backing slowly along the side of the table towards its far end, and she stood with the door in her hand and said, almost in a whimper, 'Don't be frightened, Jimmy, I'm . . . I'm not a ghost. It's . . . it's me, Janie. I . . . I've been bad. I . . . I wasn't drowned.' She closed the door, then leant her back against it and slowly slid down on to the floor and slumped on to her side.

Jimmy gazed at the crumpled figure but didn't move. He had never been so terrified in all his life, he wanted to run, jump out of the window, get away from it . . . her. Yet . . . yet it was Janie's voice, and she said she was Janie. That's all he had to go on, for from what he could see of her, her skin was like an Arab's and her hair was white. Janie had been bonny, and her skin was as fair as a peach and her hair brown, lovely brown.

When she moved and spoke again, he started.

'Give me a drink, Jimmy, tea, anything.'

As if mesmerized now, he went to the hob and picked up the teapot that had been stewing there for the past hour, and with a hand that shook he filled a cup, spooned in some sugar, then slowly advanced towards her.

He watched her pulling herself to her feet, and as he stood with the cup in his hand, staring wildly at her, she passed him and went towards a chair, and after a moment she held out her hand and took the cup from him, and although the tea was scalding she gulped at it, then asked, 'Where's Rory?'

The gasp he gave brought her leaning towards him, and she asked softly, 'Nothin' . . . nothin's happened him?'

His head moved as if in a shudder and then he spoke for the first time. 'Where've you been?' he said.

'I . . . I was washed up there. I don't remember anything about it but they told me . . . at least after a long time when the priest came over the hills; he could speak English. The fishing-boat, it found me off Le Palais. I was clinging to this wood and they thought I was dead. I must have been in the water for a long time swept by a current, they said, and . . . and when I came to meself I didn't know who I was. I . . . I never knew who I was till a month ago.'

'Just a month ago?'

'Aye.' She nodded slowly.

He gulped twice before he asked, 'Well, how did you get on? Who did you think you were?'

'Nobody; I just couldn't remember anything except vaguely. I seemed to remember holding a child. I told the priest that, and when he came next, he only came twice a year, he said he had inquired along the coast and he'd heard of nobody who had lost a wife and child. There had been great storms that year and lots of boats had been sunk. He told me to be patient an' me memory'd come back and I'd know who I was. It . . . it was Henri who brought it back.'

'Who's Henry?'

'He was madame's son. They're all fisherfolk, she looked after me. Life was very hard for them all, so very hard, much . . . much harder than here.' She looked slowly around the room. 'I . . . I remember how I used to talk about guttin' fish as being something lowly. I had to learn to gut fish. They all worked so hard from mornin' till night. It was a case of fish or die. You don't know.' She shook her head in wide movements. 'But they were kind and . . . and they were happy.'

Jimmy gulped. His mind was racing. This was Janie. It was Janie all right. Eeh! God, what would happen? Why couldn't she have stayed where she was? What was he saying? He muttered now, 'How did you get your memory back?'

'It was through Henri, he couldn't understand about me not wantin' to learn to swim. The young ones swam, it was their one pleasure, and this day he . . . he came behind me and pushed me off the rock. It . . . it was as I hit the water it all came back. He was sorry, very sorry I mean that it had come back.' She looked down towards the table and up again suddenly. 'Where's Rory? Is he up home?'

Jimmy turned from her. He was shaking his head wildly now. He lifted up the teapot from the hob, put it down again, then, swinging round towards her, he said, 'You've . . . you've been away nearly . . . nearly two years, Janie, things've happened.'

She rose slowly to her feet. 'What things? What kind of things?'

'Well . . . well, this is goin' to be another shock to you. I'm . . . I'm sorry, Janie. It wasn't that he wasn't cut up, he nearly went mad. And . . . and it was likely 'cos he was so lonely he did it, but –' now his voice faded to a mere whisper, and he bowed his head before finishing, 'he got married again.'

She turned her ear slightly towards him as if she hadn't heard aright; then her mouth opened and closed, but she didn't speak. She sat down with a sudden plop, and once more she looked around the room. Then she asked simply, 'Who to?'

Jimmy now put his hand across his mouth. He knew before he said the name that this would be even harder for her to understand.

'Who to?' She was shouting now, screaming at him.

If he had had any doubts before that this was Janie they were dispelled.

'Miss . . . Miss Kean.'

'What!' She was on her feet coming towards him, and he actually backed from her in fear.

'You're jokin'?'

'No, no, I'm not, Janie. No.' He stopped at the foot of the ladder and she stopped too. With one wild sweep she unhooked the clasp of her cloak and flung it aside, then she tore the bonnet from her head and flung it on to the cloak. And now she walked back to the table, and she leant over it as she cried, 'Money! Money! He married her for money. He couldn't get it by gamin', but he had to have it some way.'

'No, no, it wasn't like that . . .'

She swung round and was facing him again, and he noted with surprise that her figure was no longer plump, it was almost as flat as Charlotte Kean's had been before her body started to swell with the bairn. Eeh! and that was another thing, the bairn. Oh my God! Where would this end? He said now harshly, 'It's nearly two years, you've got to remember that. He . . . he was her manager, and . . . and she was lonely.'

'Lonely? Lonely?' She started to laugh; then thrusting her white head forward, she demanded, 'Where's he now? Living in the big house? Huh! Well, his stay's goin' to be short, isn't it, Jimmy? He can't have two wives, can he?'

'He didn't know, you can't blame him.'

'Can't blame him? Huh! I was the only woman he'd ever wanted in his life, the only one he would ever love until he died. You . . . you know nowt about it. Can't blame him, you say!'

'You should never've gone; it was your own fault, you going on that holiday. I . . . I told him he shouldn't have let you.'

'But he did, he did let me, Jimmy. What he should have done the day I left was come after me and knock hell out of me an' made me stay. But he didn't, did he? He let me go.'

'You know why he let you go. It was because of John George, that business an' you sticking out and wanting him to go and give himself up. You're as much to blame as he is, Janie, about that. But . . . but he's not to blame for marryin' again, 'cos how was he to know? He waited a year, over a year.'

'That was kind of him. Well now, what are we going to do, Jimmy, eh? You'll have to go and tell him that his wife's come back. That's it . . . just go an' tell him that his wife's come back.'

He stared at her. This was Janie all right, but it was a different Janie; not only was she changed in looks but in her manner, her ways, and as he stared at her he couldn't imagine any disaster great enough to change a woman's appearance as hers had been changed.

She saw his eyes on her hair and she said quietly now, 'I mean it, Jimmy. You'd better go and tell him. And . . . and tell him what to expect, will you?' She put her hand up towards her head. 'I . . . I lost all me hair. I was bald, as bald as any man, and . . . and they rubbed grease in, fish fat, an' . . . an' this is how it grew. And . . . and living out in the open in the sun and the wind I became like them, all brown 'cos of me fair skin likely.'

She sat down suddenly on a chair and, placing her elbows on the table, she lowered her face into her hands.

'Don't cry, Janie, don't cry.' He moved to the other side of the table. And now she looked up at him dry-eyed and said, 'I'm not cryin', Jimmy. That's another thing, I can't cry. I should cry about the children and the master and mistress and how I look, but something stops me . . . Go and fetch him, Jimmy.'

'I . . . I can't, Janie. It would . . .'

'It would what?'

'He'd . . . he'd get a gliff.'

'Well, if he doesn't come to me, I'll have to go to him. He'll get a gliff in any case, and he'd far better meet me here than . . . than up home . . .

What's the matter? . . . What is it now?'

'Your grannie, Janie, she's . . .'

'Aw no!' She dropped her head to the side and screwed up her eyes, then after a moment said, 'When?'

'Last year, after . . . shortly after she heard the news.'

'And me da?'

'He . . . he went to Jarrow to live with . . . he took lodgings in Jarrow. There's new people in the house, an old couple. An' the Learys have gone an'll. I never thought they'd ever move but he started work in St Hilda's Colliery, and it's too far for him to trek in the winter. They live down here now in High Shields. It's all changed up there.' He wanted to keep talking in a hopeless effort against what she was going to say next, but she stopped him with a lift of her hand as she leant back in the chair and drew in long draughts of breath, then said, 'I don't think I can stand much more. And I'm so tired; I haven't been to sleep for . . . aw, it seems days . . . Go and fetch him, Jimmy.'

The command was soft, but firm and brooked no argument. He stared at her for a moment longer; then grabbing his coat and cap from the back of the door, he dragged them on and rushed out. But once down in the yard he didn't run; instead, he stood gripping the staunch post that supported the end of the house as he muttered to himself, 'Eeh! my God! What's gona happen?'

CHAPTER 2

Charlotte straightened the silk cravat at Rory's neck, dusted an invisible speck from the shoulder of his black suit, and finally ran her fingers lightly over the top of his oiled hair, and then, standing slightly back from him, she said, 'To my mind you're wasted on a gaming table.'

'I'm never wasted on a gaming table.' He pressed his lips together, jerked his chin to the side and winked at her.

Her face becoming serious now, she said, 'Be careful. The more I hear of that man, Nickle, the more perturbed I become.'

'Well, you couldn't ask for a quieter, better mannered or refined gentleman, now could you?'

'No; that makes him all the more sinister. It's really unbelievable when you think of it, but I'm glad that he knows I'm aware of what he is. I wish I had been there when he put his tentative question: "Your wife, of course, knows nothing of our little . . . shall we say excursions into chance?"'

He took up a haughty stance and mimicked, '"Sir, my wife knows everything; she's a remarkable woman." And she is that.' He put out his hand and slapped the raised dome of her stomach, and she laughed and tut-tutted as she in return slapped at his hand. Then her manner becoming serious again, she said, 'Well, there's one thing I can be assured of, he won't try any of his underhand business on you, because if he wants to silence you he'll also have to silence me. Who are you expecting tonight?'

'Who knows! My, my! It gets more surprising. You should have seen the look on Veneer's face when he saw me there, in the Newcastle rooms I mean. I thought he was going to pass out. I nearly did meself an' all. I couldn't believe me eyes. Him, a staunch supporter of the Temperance League! They would burn him at the stake if they knew. Just imagine the ladies of this town who wave the banners for temperance getting wind of what their Mr Veneer's up to . . . And you know something? I'd gather the kindling for them; I never could stand him. I remember your father once sending me on some business to his office. He spoke to me as if I were so much clarts. Sorry, madam.' He pulled a face at her. 'Mud from the gutter.'

She was now standing in front of him holding his face firmly between her hands, and she said with deep pride, 'Well, we've shown them. You've outwitted two of them already in business deals, and that's only a beginning. What's more, you're the most fashionably dressed, best-looking man in the town, or the county for that matter.' She tossed her head.

He didn't preen himself at her praise, but he said, 'I keep sayin' you're a remarkable woman, and you are. Every day that passes I discover something more remarkable about you. The very fact that you raised no protest at my gaming amazes me.'

'What is one evening a week? As long as your failings only embrace cards and wine I'll be content.'

He bent towards her now and kissed her gently on her lips, then said, 'You can rest assured, Mrs Connor, that these shall be the limit of my failings. But now for orders.' His manner changed, his voice took on a sterner note. 'You are not to wait up for me, do you hear? Stoddard will pick me up at twelve, and when I get in I shall expect to find you in bed and fast asleep. If I don't, then there's going to be trouble.'

'What will you do?'

He stared at her for a moment before replying, 'I'll take up the other vice.'

'No, don't say that.' There was no flippancy in her tone now. 'Not even in joke say you'll take up the third vice. That's something I couldn't bear.'

'You silly woman, don't you ever believe anything I say?'

'I want to.'

'Well, what can I say to make you believe it?'

She looked into his eyes. They were smiling kindly at her and she only just prevented herself from blurting out, 'Say that you love me. Oh, say that you love me.'

'Go on.' She pushed him from the room and into the hall. It was she who helped him into his coat and handed him his hat and scarf. Then she stood at the top of the steps and watched him go down them and into the carriage, and she waved to him and he waved back. Then stretching out his legs, he leant his head against the leather upholstery and sighed a deep contented sigh.

They were nearing the gate when the carriage was brought to an abrupt halt and he heard Stoddard shouting, 'Whoa! Whoa, there!' then add, 'Who's you?'

He pulled down the window and looked out, and there in the light of the carriage lamps he saw Jimmy. Quickly opening the door, he called to the driver, 'It's all right, Stoddard,' then to Jimmy, 'Get in. What's up? What's happened?'

As the carriage jerked forward again Jimmy bounced back on the seat, and again Rory demanded, 'What is it? What's happened now? Have they sunk another one?'

'No.' Jimmy shook his head. 'It's nowt to do with the boats.'

'Well, what is it? Something wrong at home?' Rory's inquiry was quiet, and when again Jimmy shook his head, he said almost angrily, 'Well, spit it out, unless you've just come for a chat.'

'I haven't just come for a chat, and . . . and I've been hangin' around for nearly an hour waitin', waitin' to see if you'd come out on your own.'

'Why?' Rory was sitting forward on the seat now. Their knees were touching. He peered into Jimmy's white face, demanding, 'Come on, whatever it is, tell us.'

'You're going to get a gliff, Rory.'

'A gliff?'

'Aye, you'll . . . you'll never believe it. You'd . . . you'd better brace yourself. It's . . . it's something you won't be able to take in.' When he stopped, Rory said quietly, 'Well, tell us.'

'It's . . . it's Janie.'

Jimmy's voice had been so soft that Rory thought he couldn't possibly have heard aright; Jimmy's words had been distorted, he imagined, by the grinding of the carriage wheels, so he said loudly, 'What did you say?'

'I said, it's Janie.'

'Janie?' A sudden cold sweat swept over his body and his own voice was scarcely audible now when he asked, 'What . . . what about Janie?'

'She's . . . she's back. She's . . . she's not dead, she wasn't drowned . . .'

Rory didn't utter a word, no protest, nothing, but his body fell back and his head once more touched the upholstery, and as if he had been shot into a nightmare again he listened to Jimmy's voice saying, 'I was petrified. It was her voice, but . . . but I wouldn't open the door at first. And then . . . and then when I saw her, I still didn't believe it was her. She's . . . she's changed. Nobody . . . nobody would recognize her. It . . . it was the shock. Her hair's gone white, and her skin, her skin's all brown like an Arab's in Corstorphine Town. It's the sun, she said. She's . . . she's been in some place in France miles off the beaten track. She talks about a priest comin' once every six months. She's changed, aye. I knew you'd get a gliff but . . . but I had to come. If . . . if I hadn't she would have turned up herself. Eeh! she's changed. What'll you do, Rory? What'll you do?'

His world was spinning about him. He watched it spiralling upwards and away, taking with it the new way of living and the prestige it had brought to him. Sir, he was called, Master. She had given him everything a woman could possibly give a man, a home, wealth, position, and now a child. He had never been so happy in his life as he had been since he married her; and his feelings for her were growing deeper every day. You couldn't live with a woman like that and receive so much from her and give nothing in return; something had been growing in him, and last night he had almost told her what it was, he had almost put a name to it. He had never thought he would be able to say to another woman, I love you. That kind of thing didn't happen twice, he had told himself. No; and he was right, that kind of thing didn't happen twice. But there were different kinds of love. It was even appearing to him that what he was feeling now would grow into a bigger love, a better love, a fuller love. Charlotte had said there were better marriages based on friendship than on professions of eternal love.

He had once sworn eternal love for Janie, but he knew now that that had been the outcome of a boy's love, the outcome of use, the outcome of growing up together, seeing no one beyond her . . .

She couldn't be back. She couldn't. No! No! Life couldn't play him a trick like that. He had gone to the Justice before he married Charlotte and the Justice had told him it was all right to marry again. "Drowned, presumed dead," was what he had said. And she was dead. She had been dead to him for nearly two years now, and he didn't want her resurrected.

God Almighty! What was he saying? What was he thinking? He'd go mad.

'Rory. Rory.' Jimmy was sitting by his side now, shaking his arm. 'Are you all right? I . . . I knew it'd give you a gliff; she . . . she scared me out of me wits. What are you gona do?'

'What?'

'I said what are you gona do?'

He shook his head. What was he going to do?

'She's back in the boathouse; she wants to see you.'

He stared dumbly at Jimmy for a time, then like someone drunk he leant forward and tapped on the roof of the carriage with his silver-mounted walking stick, and lowering the window again, he leant out and said, 'We'll get off here, Stoddard; I . . . I've a little business to attend to.'

A few minutes later Stoddard was opening the carriage door and pulling down the step, and when they alighted he said, 'Twelve o'clock, sir?'

'What? Oh. Oh yes; yes, thank you.'

'Good night, sir.'

'Good . . . Good night, Stoddard.'

He walked away, Jimmy by his side, but when the carriage had disappeared into the darkness he stopped under a street lamp and, peering down at Jimmy, said, 'What, in the name of God, am I going to do in a case like this?'

'I . . . I don't know, Rory.'

They walked on again, automatically taking the direction towards the river and the boatyard, and they didn't stop until they had actually entered the yard, and then Rory, standing still, looked up at the lighted window, then down on Jimmy, before turning about and walking towards the end of the jetty. And there he gripped the rail and leant over it and stared down into the dark, murky water.

Jimmy approached him slowly and stood by his side for a moment before saying, 'You've got to get it over, man.'

Rory now pressed a finger and thumb on his eyeballs as if trying to blot out the nightmare. His whole being was in a state of panic. He knew he should be rushing up those steps back there, bursting open the door and crying, 'Janie! Janie!' but all he wanted to do was to turn and run back through the town and into Westoe and up that private road into his house, *his house*, and cry, 'Charlotte! Charlotte!'

'Come on, man.'

At the touch of Jimmy's hand he turned about and went across the yard and up the steps. Jimmy had been behind him, but it was he who had to come to the fore and opened the door. Then Rory stepped into the room.

The woman was standing by the table. The lamplight was full on her. She was no more like the Janie he remembered than he himself was like Jimmy there. His heart leapt at the thought that it was a trick. Somebody imagined they were on to something and were codding him. They had heard he was in the money. He cast a quick glance in Jimmy's direction as if to say, How could you be taken in? before moving slowly up the room towards the woman. When he was within a yard of her he stopped and the

hope that had risen in him flowed away like liquid from a broken cask for
they were Janie's eyes he was looking into. They were the only recognizable things about her, her eyes. As Jimmy had said, her skin was like that
of an Arab and her hair was the colour of driven snow, and curly,
close-cropped, curly.

Janie, in her turn, was looking at him in much the same way, for he was
no more the Rory that she had known than she was the Janie he had
known. Before her stood a well-dressed gentleman, better dressed in fact
than she had ever seen the master, for this man was stylish with it; even his
face was different, even his skin was different, smooth, clean-shaven,
showing no blue trace of stubble about his chin and cheeks and upper lip.

Her heart hardened further at the sight of him and at the fact that he
didn't put out a hand to touch her.

'Janie.'

'Aye, it's me. And you're over the moon to . . . to see me.' There was a
break in the last words.

'I thought . . . we all thought . . .'

'Aye, I know what you thought, but . . . but it isn't all that long, it isn't
two years. You couldn't wait, could you? But then you're a gamblin' man,
you couldn't miss a chance not even on a long shot.'

He bowed his head and covered his eyes with his hand, muttering now,
'What can I say?'

'I don't know, but knowin' you, you'll have some excuse. Anyway, it's
paid off, hasn't it? You always said you'd play your cards right one day.'
She turned her back on him and walked to the end of the table and sat
down.

He now drew his hand down over his face, stretching the skin, and he
looked at her sitting staring at him accusingly. Jimmy had said she had
changed, and she had, and in all ways. She looked like some peasant
woman who had lived in the wilds all her life. The dark skirt she was
wearing was similar to that worn by the fishwives, only it looked as if she
had never stepped out of it for years. Her blouse was of a coarse striped
material and on her feet she had clogs. Why, she had never worn clogs
even when she was a child and things were pretty tight. Her boots then,
like his own, had been cobbled until they were nothing but patches, but
she had never worn clogs.

Aw, poor Janie . . . Poor all of them . . . Poor Charlotte. Oh my God!
Charlotte.

'I'm sorry I came back.' Her voice was high now. 'I've upset your nice
little life, haven't I? But I am back, and alive, so what you going to do
about it? You'll have to tell her, won't you? Your Miss Kean . . . My God!
You marryin' her of all people! *Her*! But then you'd do anything to make

money, wouldn't you?'

'I didn't marry her for . . .' The words sprang out of his mouth of their own volition and he clenched his teeth and bowed his head, while he was aware that she had risen to her feet again.

Now she was nodding at him, her head swinging like that of a golliwog up and down, up and down, before she said, 'Well, well! This is something to know. You didn't marry her for her money. Huh! You're tellin' me you didn't marry her for her money. So you married her because you wanted her? You wanted *her*, that lanky string of water, her that you used to make fun of?'

'*Shut up*! My God! it's as Jimmy said, you're different, you're changed. And yet not all that. No, not all that. Looking back, you had a hard streak in you; I sensed it years ago. And aye, it's true what I said, I . . . I didn't marry her for her money, but it's also true that I didn't marry her 'cos . . . 'cos I was in love with her.' He swallowed deeply and turned his head to the side and, his voice a mutter now, he said, 'She was lonely. I was lonely. That's . . . that's how it was.'

'And how is it now?'

He couldn't answer because it was wonderful now, or at least it had been.

'You can't say, can you? My God, it's a pity I didn't die. Aye, that's what you're thinkin', isn't it? Eeh! I wouldn't have believed it. I wouldn't, I wouldn't.' She was holding her head in her hands now, her body rocking. Then of a sudden she stopped and glared at him as she said, 'Well, she'll have to be told, won't she? She'll have to be told that you can have only one wife.'

As he stared back at her he was repeating her words, 'I wouldn't have believed it,' for he couldn't believe what he was recognizing at this moment, that it could be possible for a man to change in such a short time as two years and look at a woman he had once loved and say to himself, 'Yes, only one wife, and it's not going to be you, not if I can help it' – What was he thinking? What was he thinking?

He was trapped. Standing before him was his wife, his legal wife, and he'd have to tell Charlotte that his wife had come back and that she herself had no claim to him and the child in her couldn't take his name. He couldn't do it. What was more, he wouldn't do it. He heard his voice saying now, clearly and firmly, 'I can't tell her.'

'You what!'

'I said I can't tell her, she's going to have a ch . . . bairn.' He had almost said child, so much had even his vocabulary changed.

There was complete silence in the room, until Jimmy moved. He had been standing at the side of the fireplace and now his foot jerked and he kicked the brass fender, which caused them both to look towards him. And then she said, 'Well, it's going to be hard on her, isn't it, bringing up a bairh without a father? But then, her way will be smoothed, money's a great compensation. Oh yes, money's a great compensation. You can make things happen when you've got money. I had four sovereigns. The mistress give them to me to buy presents for you all to bring home. I put them in me little bag, an' you know me an' me little bag. Whenever I changed I used to pin it under me skirt, and when they found me there was me little bag still pinned under me skirt. But I didn't know anything about it until I got me memory back. Madame, the old woman I lived with, had taken it, but when I came to meself and wanted to come home and didn't know how, the son put the bag into me hand. He was very honest, the son, and so I travelled in luxury all the way here. First, in the bottom of a cart with pigs; then for miles on foot, sleeping on the floors of mucky inns; then the boat; and lastly, the back end of the train, like a cattle-truck; and –' and now she screamed at him – 'you're no more sorry for me than you would be for a mangy dog lying in the gutter. The only thing you're worried about is that I've come back and your grand life is to be brought to an end. Well, if you don't tell her, I will; I'm not gona be pushed aside, I'm gona have me place.'

'Janie. Janie.' His voice was soft, pleading, and she stopped her ranting and stared at him, her face quivering but her eyes still dry. 'I'll . . . I'll do what I think is right. In . . . in the end I'll do what I think is right. But give me a little time, will you? A few days, time to sort things out, to . . . to get used to –' He gulped in his throat. 'You can have what money you want . . .'

'I don't want your money. Anyway, 'tisn't *your* money, you've never worked for it, it's her money.'

'I do work for it, begod! and hard at that.' His voice was loud now, harsh. 'I work harder now than ever I've done in me life. And now I'm goin' to tell you something, an' it's this. Don't push me; don't drive me too far. This . . . this has come as a surprise. Try to understand that, but remember I'm still Rory Connor and I won't be pushed.' He paused for a moment, then ended, 'I'll . . . I'll be back the morrow night,' and on this he swung round on his heel and went out.

Jimmy, casting a look at Janie, where she was standing now, her hands hanging limply by her side and her mouth open, turned and followed him. In the yard he saw the dim outline of Rory standing where he himself had stood earlier in the evening against the stanchion post, and he went up to him and put his hand on his arm, and held it for a moment before saying. 'I'm sorry, Rory. I'm sorry to the heart of me, but . . . but you can't blame her.'

'What am I going to do, Jimmy?' The question came out as a groan.

'I don't know, Rory. Honest to God, I don't know. Charlotte 'll be in a state. I'm sorry, I mean I'm sorry for Charlotte.'

'I . . . I can't leave her, I can't leave Charlotte. There's her condition and . . . Oh dear God! what am I goin' to do? Look, Jimmy.' He bent down to him. 'Persuade her to stay here out of the way, don't let her go up home. Look, give her this.' He thrust his hand into an inner pocket and, pulling out a chamois leather bag, emptied a number of sovereigns on to Jimmy's palm. 'Make her get some decent clothes; she looks like something that's just been dug up. I could never imagine her letting herself go like that, could you?'

'No. No, Rory. I told you, she's . . . she's changed. She must have gone through it. You'll have to remember that, she must have gone through it.'

'Aye, and now she's going to make us all go through it.'

As he moved across the yard Jimmy went with him, saying, 'Where you makin' for? Where were you going'?

'To a game.'

'Game? Does Charlotte know?'

Rory stopped again and said quietly, 'Aye, Charlotte knows and she doesn't mind. As long as I'm happy, doing something that makes me happy, she doesn't mind; all she minds is that she'll ever lose me. Funny, isn't it?'

They peered at each other through the darkness. 'Where you goin' now, back home?'

'No, no, I'll . . . I'll have to go on to the game. They're expecting me, and if I didn't turn up something would be said. Anyway, I've got to think. I'm . . . I'm nearly out of me mind.'

Jimmy made no reply to this and Rory, touching him on the shoulder by way of farewell, went up the yard and out of the gate.

He did not go straight to Plynlimmon Way but walked for a good half-hour, and when at last he arrived at the house Frank Nickle greeted him with, 'Well, Connor, we thought you weren't coming, we've been waiting some –' he drew from the pocket of his spotted grey waistcoat a gold lever watch attached to a chain across his chest – 'three quarters of an hour.'

'I . . . I was held up.'

'Are you all right? Are you unwell?'

'Just . . . just a bit off colour.'

'No trouble, I hope?'

'No trouble.'

'Then let us begin.'

Nickle's tone was peremptory, it was putting him back into the servant class as far as he dared allow it. That the man hated him he was well aware, for he knew he was cornered, and had done since the night he came to dinner. But he also knew that he'd have to be careful of him in all ways. However, at this moment Nickle and his nefarious doings seemed of very minor importance.

They went into what was known as the smoking room. It was part office and part what could be considered a gentleman's rest room, being furnished mostly with leather chairs, a desk, and a small square table, besides four single chairs.

The two men present were smoking cigars and they greeted Rory cordially, speaking generally, while Frank Nickle lifted a china centrepiece from the square table, laid it aside, then opened the top of the table which was cut in the shape of an envelope, each piece being covered with green baize. This done, they all took their seats around the table and Nickle, producing the cards from a hidden drawer underneath, the game began . . .

Three hours later Rory rose from the table almost twenty pounds poorer. At one time in the evening he had been thirty pounds to the good.

He left before the others, and at the door Frank Nickle, smiling his thin smile, said, 'You weren't your usual brilliant self tonight, Connor.'

'No, I think I'm in for a cold.'

'That's a pity. Give my regards to your lady wife.' The large pallid face now took on a slight sneer. 'Tell her not to slap her little boy too hard for losing.'

He had the urge to lift his hand and punch the man on the mouth. But wait, he told himself, wait. Give him time, and he would do it, but in another way. He left without further words, went down the pathway through the iron gate and to the road where the carriage was waiting.

Nickle had suggested covertly that it was unwise to come by carriage, servants talked . . . ordinary servants, and to this Rory had replied that Stoddard was no ordinary servant, he was as loyal as Nickle's own. And anyway, wasn't he visiting the house for a 'Gentlemen's Evening'? They were common enough. How could one discuss the finer points of business if it weren't for 'Gentlemen's Evenings'?

When he arrived home Charlotte was in bed, but she wasn't asleep, and when, bending over her, he kissed her she pushed him slightly away from her, but holding him by the shoulders, she said, 'What is it? What's happened?'

'Nothing.'

'Oh, come, come Rory, you . . . you looked strained. Something happened at Nickle's?'

'No.' He pulled himself from her. 'Only that I lost . . . twenty pounds.'

'Oh!' She lay back on her pillows. 'Hurt pride. Twenty pounds, quite a sum. But still I suppose you must let them have their turn. If you won every time they would say you were cheating.'

'Yes, yes.' When he went into the adjoining room to undress she called to him anxiously, 'There's nóthing else wrong, is there? I mean, he didn't say anything, there wasn't any unpleasantness?'

'No, no; he wasn't more unpleasant than usual. He was born unpleasant.'

'Yes, yes, indeed.'

In bed he did not love her but he held her very tightly in his arms and muttered into her hair, 'Oh, Charlotte. Charlotte.'

It was a long time before he went to sleep, but even then she was still awake, although she had pretended to be asleep for some time past. There was something wrong; she could sense it. By now she knew every shade of his mood and expression. Her love for him was so deep that she imagined herself buried inside him.

At four o'clock in the morning she was woken up by his screaming. He was having a nightmare, the first he had had since his marriage.

CHAPTER 4

Three days passed before Charlotte tackled him openly and very forcibly. 'What is it?' she said. 'Something is wrong. Now –' she closed her eyes and lifted her hand upwards – 'it's no use you telling me, Rory, that there's nothing amiss. Please give me credit for being capable of using my eyes and my ears if not my other senses. There *is* something wrong, and I must know what it is. Rory, I must know what it is.'

When he didn't answer but turned away and walked down the length of the drawing-room towards the window she said, 'You're going out again tonight; you have been out for the last two nights supposedly to see Jimmy. When I was passing that way today I called in . . .'

'You what!' He swung round and faced her.

She stared at him over the distance before rising to her feet and saying slowly, 'I said I called in to see Jimmy. Why should that startle you? I have done that before, but what puzzled me today, and what's puzzling me now, is that you are both reacting in the same way. I asked him if he was feeling unwell and he said, no. I asked him if there had been any more tampering with the boats, he said, no . . . Rory, come here.'

When he made no move towards her, she went swiftly up the room and, putting her arms about him, she demanded, 'Look at me. Please, look at me,' and when he lifted his head, she said, 'Whatever it is, it cannot be so awful that you can't tell me. And whatever it is, it's leaving its mark on you, you look ill. Come.' She drew him down the room and towards the fire, and when they were seated on the couch she said, softly now, 'Tell me, Rory, please. Whatever it is, please tell me. You said once you would always speak the truth to me. Nothing must stand between us, Rory. Is it that man, John George? Is he blackmailing you? After all I did for him is he . . .?'

'Oh no! No! Oh God, I wish I could say he was, I wish that's all it was, John George. John George wouldn't blackmail anybody, not even to save his life. I know that, don't I? . . . Charlotte –' he now gathered her hands tightly between his own and held them against his breast – 'I've . . . I've wanted to say this to you for some time past, but . . . but I didn't think I could convince you because, to tell you the truth, when . . . when all this first started between you and me, I never thought it would ever be possible, but Charlotte . . . Charlotte, my dear, I . . . I've grown to care for you, love you . . .'

'Oh Ror-y, Ror-y.' She made a slow movement with her head, then pressed her lips tightly together as he went on, 'I want you to know this and believe it, for . . . for what I'm going to tell you now is going to come as a great shock. If it were possible to keep it from you I would, especially now when the last thing in the world I want you to have is worry, or shock, but . . . Aw God! how can I tell you?' When he turned his head to the side she whispered. 'Rory. Rory, please; whatever it is, listen to me, look at me, whatever it is, whatever you've done, it won't alter my feelings for you, not by one little iota.'

He was looking at her again. 'I haven't done anything, Charlotte, not knowingly. It's like this.' He swallowed deeply on a long breath. 'The other night, Saturday, when you sent me out so gaily to the game, Jimmy was waiting at the bottom of the drive. He . . . he had news for me . . .'

He stopped speaking. He couldn't say it but gazed at her, and she didn't say, 'What news?' but remained still, very still as if she knew what was coming.

. . . 'He told me something amazing, staggering. I . . . I couldn't believe it, but . . . but Janie, she had come back . . . *Charlotte! Charlotte!*'

As she lay back against the couch he watched the colour drain from her face until she had the appearance of someone who had just died, and he took her by the shoulders and shook her, crying again, 'Charlotte! Charlotte! it's all right. Listen, listen, it's all right, I won't leave you, I promise I won't leave you. I know she can claim through law that . . . that she's still my wife, but . . . but after seeing her, hearing her . . . I don't know, I don't know.' He lowered his head, 'She's no more like the woman I married than . . .'

Charlotte had made a small groaning sound, and now he gathered her
limp body into his arms and, stroking her hair, he muttered, 'Believe me.
Believe me, Charlotte, I'll never leave you. No matter what happens I'll
never leave you unless .. unless you want me to . . .'

. . . 'Unless I want you to? Her voice was scarcely audible. 'How . . .
how can you say such a thing? I'd want you near me even if I knew you
were a murderer, or a madman. Nothing you could do, nothing, nothing
would ever make me want to be separated from you.'

'Oh my dear! My dear!'

They were holding each other tightly now and, her mouth pressed
against his cheek, she was murmuring, 'How . . . how are you going to go
about it? Does . . . does she know?'

He released her and sat slowly back against the couch. 'I'm . . . I'm
going down to tell her tonight.'

'Where is she?'

'In the boathouse.'

'Yes, yes, of course, she would be there. That is why Jimmy was so
concerned. It is strange but . . . but already I seem to have lost a family. I
liked Jimmy, I liked him very much indeed. I . . . I had great plans for
him, a new yard. I had been looking about on my own. It . . . it was to be a
surprise for you, and your . . . your people. I thought they were coming to
accept me, particularly your aunt, for it was she who from the beginning
appeared the most distant. But these past few weeks, in fact only last
Thursday when I met her in the boathouse, she was cooking for Jimmy,
and she made a joke with me, and for the first time she didn't address me
as ma'am . . . and now . . . Oh! Oh, Rory!' She turned and buried her face
in his shoulder, and when her body began to shake with her sobbing his
heart experienced an agony the like of which hitherto he hadn't imagined
he was capable of feeling. It was only the second time he had heard her
cry. She wasn't the weeping type; she was so strong, so self-assured; she
was in command of herself and of him and of everyone else.

As he held her tightly to him he dwelt for a moment on the strangeness
of life and what two years could do to a man's feelings, and he realized that
no man could really trust himself and say that what he was feeling today
he would still feel tomorrow. A few moments ago he had told Charlotte he
loved her and would never leave her; two years ago he had told Janie that
he loved her and she would always and ever be the only one in his life.
What was a man made of when he could change like this? It was past him,
he couldn't understand it. Yet there was one thing at the moment he was
certain of, and that was that he no longer wanted Janie but he did want
Charlotte, and that what he felt for her wasn't mere gratitude but love, a

love that owed nothing to externals but sprang from somewhere deep within him, a place that up till now he hadn't known existed.

CHAPTER 4

Janie had refused to take the money that Rory had left. Not until she was back in her rightful place, she had said, would she take a penny from him.

'But Janie,' Jimmy had pleaded, 'you can't go round looking like that, and . . . and all your clothes . . . well, they were given away, the Learys got them.'

'Why can't I go round like this, Jimmy? This is what I've worn for the last two years, and as I said, when I'm back in me rightful place then I'll take money from him for clothes.'

On that night one of the first things she asked when he had come back into the room was, 'What's happened to John George?'

'Oh,' Jimmy had answered, 'John George's all right. He has a newspaper shop in Newcastle . . . and that lass is with him. When he got out he came back and saw her, and she left the man. Her father went after her and threatened both of them, but she said it was no good she wouldn't go back. They're all right,' he had ended.

She had looked at him hard as she asked, 'How did he come by the paper shop?'

'Well.' Jimmy had brought one foot up on to his knee and massaged his ankle vigorously while he said, 'It was her . . . Charlotte, she saw to it.'

'*She* saw to it? You mean to say, after sendin' him along the line she set him up in a shop?'

'Aye.'

'And he let her?'

'Oh aye, he held no grudge. That's John George, you know. He's too good to be true really, or soft, it's how you take him. But she found out where he was, and she went up to him and talked with him and . . . and well, that was that . . . She's kind, Janie.'

She had looked hard at him as she said, 'I don't know about kind, but one thing's clear, she's wily. She's bought the lot of you. You're for her, aren't you, Jimmy? Hook, line and sinker you're for her. And I'll bet you'll be telling me next that all them in the kitchen are at her feet an' all.'

'Oh no, Janie, oh no. There was hell to pay. They . . . they didn't speak to him for ages.'

Slightly mollified, she held out her hands towards the blaze, then said quietly, 'He doesn't want me now, Jimmy. You can see it; he doesn't want me.'

And Jimmy could make no reply to this by way of comfort . . .

Nor could he the next night after Rory had gone, nor last night, because each time they met they seemed to become further apart. They were like two boxers who hated each other. Even if Rory were to leave Charlotte he couldn't see them ever living together again. He began to wonder why she was insisting on it.

He had just come in from the yard and the sight of her cooking a meal caused him to say, 'Lizzie . . . Lizzie 'll be down the morrow; she . . . she comes to bake. What you gona do, Janie?'

'What do you think?' She went on cutting thick slices from a piece of streaky bacon.

'Well, you'll give her a gliff.'

'We've all had gliffs, Jimmy.' Still continuing slicing the bacon, she didn't look up as she said, 'You didn't mention it, but I suppose her ladyship's been supportin' them up there an' all?'

It was some seconds before he answered, 'Rory has, and it's his own money, 'cos as he said he works hard for it. And he does, Janie. He travels about a lot, seein' . . . seein' to different businesses and things . . . and he studies . . .'

'Studies!' She raised her head and looked at him scornfully. 'Rory Connor studies! What? New tricks in the card game?'

'Don't be so bitter, Janie.'

She flung the knife down so hard on to the table that it bounced off on to the floor, and, leaning towards him, she cried, 'Jimmy, have you any idea how I feel, comin' back here and finding I'm not wanted by nobody? *Nobody*. Oh –' she moved her head slowly from shoulder to shoulder – 'how I wish I'd never got me memory back. Do you know something? I was happy back there. The life was hard, but they were good people, jolly, and they took to me.' She now looked down towards the table. 'There's something else I'll tell you. There was a man there, the son . . . he wanted to marry me. There were few young ones in the village and they had to go miles and miles to reach the next settlement. But . . . but I still had me wedding ring on' – she held out her hand – 'and I said I must be married to somebody. They all worked it out that I'd been with me husband and child and they must have been both drowned 'cos I kept talking about the child afore I came round, so the priest said. He was on one of his visits when I was picked up. It was Miss Victoria. And . . . and then Henri pushed me off the rock and when I came up out of the water I remembered. They were all strange to me. I looked at them an' saw them as I hadn't afore, rough fisherfolk, rougher than anything you see round here, livin' from hand to mouth. They only had two old boats atween the lot of them. It was his, Henri's boat, that picked me up. He' – Her voice trailed away now, as she ended, 'He sort of felt I belonged to him 'cos of that.'

When she raised her eyes again to Jimmy she said softly, 'They all came and saw me off. They walked the five miles with me to where we met the priest and he took me on to the next village in the cart. And you know something? He warned me, the priest. He warned me that things would've changed. And do you know what I said to him, Jimmy? I said to him, "Well I know, Father, of one who won't have changed, me husband . . ."'

It was half an hour later when they'd almost finished the meal that Jimmy, scraping the fat from his plate with a piece of bread, said tentatively, 'What'll happen, Janie, if . . . if he won't leave her?'

'He's got to leave her. He's got no other option, it's the law.'

'Janie –' He chewed on the fat-soaked piece of bread, swallowed it, then said, 'Rory's never cared much for the law. I mean he hasn't bothered about what people think. What if he says, I mean 'cos of the bairn comin', "To hell with the law!" and stays with her, what then?'

'What then? Well, she'll be living in sin won't she? And she's prominent in the town, and the gentry won't stand for that, not in the open they won't. Things can happen on the side, but if it came out in court that he wouldn't take me back, and me his wife, and he went on living with her, why neither of them would dare show their faces. There's things that can be done and things that can't be done, especially in Westoe; it isn't like along the river-front here. And he'll find that out. Oh aye, he'll find that out.'

It was at this point in the conversation that the door opened and Rory entered. She did not turn and look at him, and he walked slowly towards the fireplace.

Jimmy, rising flustered from the table, said, 'Hello there.'

Rory nodded towards him, but gave him no reply. He had taken off his hat and was holding it in one hand which was hanging by his side; then looking at Janie he said, 'Do you think we could talk quietly?'

'That's up to you.' She did not even glance towards him.

'I've . . . I've made a decision.'

She said nothing, but waited, and he glanced towards Jimmy, whose eyes were tight on him. Before he spoke again he stretched his chin up out of the collar of his overcoat. 'I'm not going to leave her, Janie.'

She made no move in any way, no sign.

'You'll take me to court as is your right, and I'll maintain you, and well too, as is also your right, but . . . but she's carrying my child and I'm not leaving her.'

Now she did turn towards him and, like a wild cat, she spat her words at him. 'You're a swine! Do you know that? You're a rotten, bloody swine, Rory Connor! And, as I said to Jimmy, you do this and you won't be able to lift your head up in this town. Aye, and I'll see you don't, I'll take you to court. By God! I will. It'll be in all the papers; both you an' her'll have to hide yourselves afore they've finished with you. And her money won't save you, not from this disgrace it won't . . .'

As he stared back into her face which was livid with passion, he thought, even if Charlotte were to die at this minute I wouldn't go back to her; I could never live with her again. His thoughts, swirling back over the past, tried to find the man he had been, the man who had loved this woman, the man who had sworn always to love her, but in vain. And so he said, 'Do what you think you have to do; if it'll make you feel any better go the whole hog; but I'd like to remind you that Shields isn't the only town on the planet. The world is wide and when you have money you can settle where you like.' He felt no compunction now at throwing his money at her.

He stared at her a moment longer. She was not recognizable to him; the white hair, the brown skin, even her eyes were no longer Janie's. He pulled on his hat, saying, 'Well, that's that; the rest is up to you,' and, turning, went out; and as he always did on these visits, Jimmy followed him into the yard.

It was a bright evening; the twilight was long in passing. They walked side by side down to the end of the yard and stood against the railing bordering the river. The moored boats were bobbing on the water beneath them. They stood looking down into them, until he asked, 'Do you blame me?'

There was a short pause before Jimmy answered, 'No, not really, Rory, no. But . . . but I'm sorry for her. I can see her side of it an' all.'

'Well, I would expect you to 'cos she has got a side. And I'm sorry for her too. At this moment I'm sorry for us all.'

He looked up and down the river as he said, 'Things were going so fine. I was riding high, I was me own man. Even with Charlotte's money I was me own man, because I knew I was making meself felt in the business.' He looked down at Jimmy. 'You know, as I said, we could go away. I thought of that as I came along. We could move to any place in the country, but somehow I don't want to leave this town. And I know she doesn't. But anyway, no matter where we go we'll see you're all right.'

'Aw . . . aw, don't worry about me, Rory, I'll get through. And you've done more than enough already. By the way, I didn't tell you, 'cos you've got enough on your plate, but those buggers down there must have been up to something last night. I heard somebody in the yard, more than one. I . . . I thought they were comin' under the house, and then a patrol boat came up and stopped – it stops most nights – and I heard nothing after that. I . . . I was a bit scared.'

'Get Richardson to come along and stay with you.'

'Aye, I will, but I think I must look for somebody else, somebody single. You see, he's got his wife and family.'

'You do that. Tell them they'll be well paid.'

Jimmy nodded; then he asked quietly, 'What's going to happen her . . . Janie? I mean, will she want to go on livin' here? It's awkward. She says she's going up home the night or the morrow. Well, if she does she might decide to stay up there.'

'Home? Huh!' Rory tossed his head back. 'They'll have a field day with this. Our dear Lizzie will come out with all the sayings back to Noah: As ye sow so shall ye reap; Pride goes before a fall; Big heid small hat. Oh, I can hear her.'

'I . . . I don't think so, Rory. You know, I've always meant to say this to you, but you don't see Lizzie as she really is. She's all right is Lizzie, and I've never been able to understand why you still hold it against her. And I look at it this way: after what's happened to you if you don't see her side now you never will.'

'Aye. Aye, I suppose you're right . . . Well, I'll be off. I . . . I won't come back as long as she's here. Come up, will you, whenever you can and let me know how things are going? I'll want to know when I'm to expect the authorities.'

'All right, Rory, I'll let you know. Tell Charlotte I wish her well, and I'm sorry . . .'

'I will; she'll be grateful. So long then.'

'So long, Rory, so long.'

They looked at each other for a moment longer, then Rory turned away and walked slowly out of the yard.

Jimmy waited a while before returning to the house, and it was as he mounted the steps that he heard her crying. When he entered the room he saw her, her face buried in her arms on the table, her body shaking.

He did not go to her but went and sat by the side of the fire and, following his habit, he brought his foot on to his knee again and stroked his ankle vigorously. It would do her good, he told himself, to cry it out. Perhaps it would wash away some of the bitterness in her.

After a moment he slid his foot off his knee and looked down at the triangular shape made by his legs; he had always hated them for from the beginning they had erased any hope of him ever finding a lass of his own; no lass wanted to be seen walking the streets alongside him. He had gone through a lot of body torment, and occasionally he still did, but these feelings he mostly sublimated in his affection for the family and his love for Rory . . . Aye, and her sitting behind him there.

But now at this particular moment as he looked down at his legs he was in a way grateful to them, for because of them he would never experience the agony that Rory, Janie and Charlotte were enduring at this minute.

Life was funny, it handed out compensations in very odd ways.

CHAPTER 5

'You're sure, darling, quite sure.'

'I'm as sure as I will be of anything in me life.'

'You won't regret it. I'll never let you regret it for one moment.'

'There'll be a hell of a rumpus. As she said, we won't be able to lift our heads up in the town . . . Should we leave?'

'No, no, we won't leave . . . we won't leave. We married in good faith; she has no children by you, I'm to have your child. We are as it were the victims of circumstance.'

'They won't look at it that way. You know as well as I do what they'll say. He's on to a good thing, that's what they'll say. He's not going to give all that up and go back to rent collectin', or some such.'

'Do you mind very much what they say?'

He thought for a moment before answering, 'Yes, I do, because . . . because it won't be true. I'm staying with you now for one reason only, although I can't say I haven't got used to all this –' he spread his arms wide – 'but if I had retained any feeling for her, as it once was, say, this wouldn't have mattered.'

'I know that . . . Oh, why had this to happen? We were so happy, so content; there was only one thing missing in my life.'

'One thing?'

'Yes, and then you gave it to me earlier this evening . . . You said you loved me.'

'Oh, Charlotte!' He put his hand out and caught hers.

'When do you think she'll take proceedings?'

'Tomorrow likely. The mood I left her in, she'll waste no time. But you know something? In spite of all I know is going to happen, the scandal, the gossip, the papers, the lot: "Woman returns from the dead. Husband, married again, refuses to acknowledge her" – You can see them, can't you, the headlines? – Well, in spite of it all, the moment I came back, the moment I stepped through the door and saw you sitting there I had the oddest feeling. It was strange, very strange. I can't remember feeling anything like it before. It was a feeling . . . well, I can't put a name to it, a sort of joy. No, no –' he shook his head – 'I shouldn't say joy . . . Certainty? No, I really can't put a name to it, but I knew that everything was going to turn out all right. I thought, in a way it's a good job it's happened; we'll start a new life, you and me and him – or her.' He placed his hand gently across the mound of her stomach, and she put her two hands on top of his and as she pressed them downwards she looked into his face and said, 'I love you, I adore you. Blasphemy that, isn't it? But to me you are my God.'

He now dropped on to his knees and, burying his face in her lap, murmured, 'Charlotte, Charlotte, I'll want no other but you ever, believe me . . .'

When there came the tap on the drawing-room door he turned round hastily and knelt before the fire and busied himself attending to it as Charlotte called, 'Come in.'

Jessie closed the door softly behind her, came up the room, and, standing at the edge of the couch, she said, 'There's . . . there's a man at the door, sir. He . . . he says he would like to speak to you.'

'A man?' Rory got to his feet thinking, My God she hasn't lost much time. 'Did he give you his name?'

'No, sir. He just said it was important, and . . . and he must speak with you. He's a little man, very little, sir.'

A little man, very little. Who did he know who was very little? Only little Joe.

'Where is he now?'

'I've . . . I've left him in the lobby, sir. He's . . . he's a workman type.'

He looked down towards Charlotte. Then went swiftly past Jessie.

When he opened the hall door and looked into the lobby he was looking down on to little Joe.

'Evenin', Mr Connor.'

'Hello, Joe. What's brought you here?' His voice was stiff.

'Mr Connor, I'd . . . I'd like a word with you.'

'I don't need to be set-on any longer, Joe, you should know that.' His tone held a slight bitterness.

'Tisn't about that, Mr Connor. I . . . I think you'd better hear me, and in private like; it's . . . it's important, very, I should say.'

Rory hesitated a moment, then said, 'Come away in.' He opened the door and let the little fellow pass him. He watched him as his eyes darted around the hall. Then he led the way to the office. Once there, he seated himself behind the desk and, motioning to a chair, said, 'Sit yourself down,' and when Joe was seated he said, 'Well, let's have it.'

'I thought you should know, Mr Connor, but . . . but afore I tell you anythin' I want you to believe that I wasn't in on the other business when they done you over. They're a dirty crew an' they've got me where they want me, the Pitties an' him – Nickle. But . . . but there's some things I don't stand for, and if they knew I was here the night me life wouldn't be worth tuppence. But . . . but I thought you should know.'

'Know what?'

'Well.' Joe stretched his feet downwards until his toes touched the carpet; then he leant forward towards the desk and, gripping it, he said under his breath, 'They're up to something. I just got wind of it a while ago. They're gona get at you through your brother. I've . . . I've seen him. He's not much bigger than me, and he's got his own handicap, and . . . and I didn't think it was fair 'cos of that, so I thought I'd come and tell you, 'cos you always played straight by me, never mean like some of them. And . . . and after that business when you didn't drag me into it, and you could 'ave, oh aye, you could 'ave, I thought to meself, if ever . . .'

'Get on with it, Joe. What are they up to?'

Joe now brought his hands from the table and, joining them together, he pressed them between his knees before he announced, 'They're gona burn you out.'

'*Burn me out*? Here?'

'Oh no, not here; they wouldn't dare come up this way. No, the boatyard and the boathouse. Steve Mackin let it drop. They'd been to him for paraffin.'

'What!' Rory was on his feet and around the desk. 'When?'

'Oh, late on's afternoon. I . . . I was payin' him a bet and he said, "Poor little bastard."' Joe now looked from one side to the other as if to apologize to someone for his language, then went on, 'I said, "Who?" and he said, "Connor. Little bandy Connor. But what can you do against those three buggers?"'

Rory was going towards the door now. 'What time was this?'

'Oh, an hour gone or more. I took a stroll by that way 'cos I thought if I saw him, I mean your brother, I would tip him off to keep clear like, but I saw big Pittie standing at the corner. He was talking to a fellow, just idling like, standing chattin'. But he doesn't live down that end, and so I thought it wasn't fair, Mr Connor, an' so I came . . .'

They were in the hall now and the drawing-room door was opening. 'What is it?'

'I . . . I've got to go down to the boatyard. Nothing, nothing.'

Charlotte came up to him as he was taking his coat from the hall wardrobe and again she asked, 'What is it?' then added, 'Oh, what is it now, Rory?'

Nothing.' He turned to her, a faint smile on his face. 'This chap here, well –' he thumbed towards Joe – 'he's been kind enough to come and give me a warning. The Pitties mean business; I think they're going to loosen the boats.'

'Don't go.' Her voice was stiff now. 'Don't go, please. Let us go straight to the station; the police will deal with it.'

'Now, now.' He put his hands on her shoulder and turned her about, then led her towards and into the drawing-room. Once inside he closed the door, then whispered to her, 'Now look, it's nothing. All right, all right –' he silenced her – 'I'll get the police. I promise I'll get the police.'

'It's dark; anything could happen; it's dark.'

'Look, nothing's going to happen. Richardson'll be there with him. He's a tough fellow is Richardson. Now look, I've got to go. You stay where you are.'

'No, let me come with you. Please let me . . .'

'No. No. Now don't you dare move out of here.' He opened the door and called, 'Jessie!' and when the maid appeared he said, 'See that your mistress doesn't leave the house until I get back. Now, that's an order.'

The girl looked from one to the other, then said, 'Yes, sir. Yes, sir.'

He turned again to Charlotte and, putting his hand out, he cupped her chin and squeezed it before hurrying towards the door, where little Joe was standing.

The little fellow cast a glance back towards Charlotte, touched his forelock and said, 'Evenin', ma'am,' and she replied, 'Good evening.' Then he sidled out quickly after Rory.

They hadn't reached the bottom of the steps before Charlotte's voice came after them, crying, 'Wait for the carriage!'

'I don't need the carriage. Go back inside. Do what you're told. His voice trailed away as he hurried down the drive.

Once in the lane, he began to run and little Joe kept up with him, but by the time they had reached Westoe village the little fellow was lagging far behind.

Fire. It only needed a can of oil and a match and the whole place would go up like dried hay lit by lightning, and they mightn't be able to get out in time. If Jimmy was up in the loft he could be choked with smoke. There were so many books and papers there, and all that wood, oiled wood inside and out, and the tarred beams underneath in the covered slipway . . . **He'd** kill those Pitties; one or all of them he'd kill them. It had to come **sooner or** later; it was either them or him. If they hurt Jimmy . . . And she **was there** an' all, Janie. To come back from the dead and then be burned alive. And that's what could happen, if they'd both gone to bed. Those buggers! They were murderers, maniacs.

He was racing down the back towards the market. Dark-clothed figures stopped and looked after him, then looked ahead to see if he was being chased.

It was as he turned into the Cut that he smelt the smoke, and then he looked up and saw the reflection of the flames. Like a wild horse he tore down to the waterfront and along it. But he was too late. He knew before he reached the crowd that he was too late.

The place was alive with people. He pushed and thrust and yelled to try to get through them. But they were packed tight and all staring upwards towards the flaming mass inside the railings.

Dashing back, he climbed the stout sleepers that he'd had put up to encase the spare land they had bought only a few months earlier. When he dropped on to the other side he saw men dragging a hawser from a river boat, and he ran, scrambling and falling over the debris, yelling, 'Jimmy! Jimmy!'

He grabbed hold of a man's arm. 'Are they out?'

'Who, mate?'

'Me . . . me brother.' He was looking wildly around him. 'And . . . and Janie.'

'There's nobody in there, man. Anyway, look at it, nothin' could live long in that, they'd be choked with the smoke afore now.'

'Jimmy! Jimmy!'

He was hanging over the rail yelling down into the wherries when a woman appeared. She swung round the end post from the passage and he stared into her face, made pink now by the reflection from the fire. 'Janie!' He gripped her arms. 'Where's . . . where's Jimmy?'

'Jimmy? I . . . I left him. I left him here. I've been up home.'

'Oh my God!'

He turned now towards the house and gazed upwards. It looked like a huge torch. Flames were coming out of the two bottom windows but only smoke out of the upper one. As he stared there came the sound of breaking glass. It could have been caused by the heat but instinctively he swung round to Janie, and there flashed between them a knowing glance. Then she put her hand over her mouth as she cried, 'God Almighty, Jimmy!'

He raced towards the steps, but as he attempted to mount them the heat beat him back. To the side of him two men were playing a hose that spurted intermittent water into one of the bottom windows. His hand was gripping the stanchion of the balustrade over which a sack was lying; it was the hessian hood that Jimmy wore when working in the rain. Tearing it from the railing he dashed towards the men and pulling the hose downwards he saturated the sack; then, throwing it over his head, he went up the steps again, and into the house.

Everything that was wood inside was alight. The floor felt like slippery wet mush beneath his feet. Blindly he flew over it and to the ladder. One side of it was already burning but he was up it in a second and had thrust the trap-door open.

The room was full of smoke, but through it he saw the glow of the burning bookcase at the far end. Coughing and choking he dropped flat on the floor and pulled himself towards the window, and there his groping hands touched the limp body, and it wasn't until he went to drag it towards the trap door that he realized that both Jimmy's hands and feet were bound. There was no time to unloosen them. So gripping him under the armpits, he pulled him backwards towards the trap-door, but there he had to pause and stuff the wet hessian into his mouth and squeeze the water down his throat to stop himself from choking.

To descend the ladder he had to get on to his knees, then hoist Jimmy's slight body on to his shoulder. By now he wasn't really conscious of his actions, one followed the other in automatic frenzy. Even the agony of gripping the burning rungs didn't penetrate his mind.

The room now was one inferno of hissing flame and smoke; his coat was alight, as was Jimmy's guernsey. Half-way along the room he felt the floor giving way, and as his feet sank he threw himself and his burden in the direction where he thought the door was. His lungs were bursting, his whole body seemed to be burning as furiously as the room.

One hand groping blindly, he felt for the opening, and found it. The steps were below. He let Jimmy slide to the ground. He was choking. He was choking. Dimly he was aware of yells and screams and at the same time he felt the whole building shudder. That was all he remembered.

He was alive when they raised the burning beam from him, then beat the fire out of his clothes.

When they carried him to where Jimmy was lying covered with coats, Janie stumbled by his side, and when she went to take his blackened hand, his skin came away on her palm.

As if totally unconscious of the turmoil in the yard she knelt between the two men with whom she had been brought up, and she groaned aloud.

Someone went to raise her up but she pushed the hands aside. The voices were floating over her: 'We must get him to the hospital. Get a stretcher, a door, anything.' Then there followed a period of time before a voice said, 'Here, Mrs Connor. He's here, Mrs Connor,' and she lifted her head to see a tall figure dropping on to her knees at the other side of the man who was her husband. She stared at the woman who was putting her arm under Rory's shoulders and crying to him, such words, endearing words that she had never heard said aloud before. 'Oh my darling, my darling, dearest, dearest. Oh Rory, Rory, my love, my love.' Such private words all mixed up with moans.

Janie felt herself lifted aside, almost pushed aside by a policeman. He was directing the lifting of Jimmy on to a stretcher. When they went to take up Rory they had to loosen the woman's hands from him, and she heard the voices again saying, 'We must get him to hospital.' And now the woman's voice, 'No, no, he must go home. Both of them, they must come home. I . . . I have the carriage.'

'They'll never get in a carriage, ma'am.' It was a policeman speaking.

'A cart then, a cart, anything. They must come home.'

There were more voices, more confusion, then a discussion between three uniformed men.

When they carried the two still forms out of the yard Janie followed them. They crossed the waste land to avoid the fire which was now merely a mass of blazing wood to where, on the road stood a flat coal cart that had been commandeered. She watched them putting the two stretchers on to it, and as it moved away she saw the woman walk closely by its side. Then the driver got down from a carriage that was standing by the kerb in the road and ran to her. She watched her shake her head at him, and he went back and mounted the carriage and drove it behind the cart. And Janie followed the carriage.

Even when it turned into the drive and up towards the house she followed it. She stopped only when it moved away to the side, past the cart and towards the stables. She watched the men who had accompanied the cart lifting the stretchers off it. She watched the servants running up and down the steps. Then everyone disappeared into the house, and for a few minutes she was standing alone looking at the lighted windows, until the coachman came racing down the steps, rushed into the yard, turned the carriage and put the horses into a gallop and went past her.

Then again she was alone for a time and she stood staring unblinking at the house. She did not move when the carter and three other men came down the steps and mounted the cart and rode away.

She did not know how long she stood there before she saw the carriage return and the doctor, carrying his leather bag, get out and hurry into the house, but she imagined that it was near on two hours before he came out of the house again.

As he went to get into the carriage she seemed to come out of a trance and, stumbling towards him, asked, 'Please, please. How is he? How are they?'

The doctor looked her up and down, her odd hat, her cloak, her clogs. She looked like a field peasant from the last century, and not a peasant of this country either. He peered at her for a moment before he answered, 'The young man will survive but Mr Connor is very very ill, seriously so.' He made an abrupt movement with his head, then stepped up into the carriage, and the driver, after giving her a hard stare, mounted the box, turned the carriage and was about to drive away when a servant came running down the steps, calling, 'Will! Will!' When the coachman pulled the horses up, the servant, gripping the side handle, looked up at him and said quickly, 'The mistress, she says, you're to go straight on after dropping the doctor and . . . and bring the master's people. You know where.'

'Aye. Aye.' The coachman nodded and cracked his whip and the horses once again sped down the drive.

The servant now looked at the woman standing to the side of the balustrade. 'Do you want something?' she asked.

Janie shook her head.

'Did . . . did you come with them?'

Janie nodded once.

The servant now looked her up and down. She had never seen anyone dressed like her, she looked a sketch, like a tramp, except that her face didn't look like that of a tramp for it was young, but she looked odd, foreign, brown skin and white hair sticking out from under that funny hat. She said, 'What do you want then?'

'Just to know how they are.'

The voice, although low and trembling, was reassuring to the servant. She might look foreign but she was definitely from these parts.

'They're bad. The master's very bad and . . . and the mistress is demented. The master's brother, he'll pull through. Come back in the mornin' if you want to hear any more. Do . . . do you know them?'

'Aye.'

'Aw . . . well, come back in the mornin'.'

As the servant went up the steps Janie turned away, but only until she had heard the click of the door; then she stopped and took up her position again, staring at the two upper brightly lit windows.

CHAPTER 6

Rory lay swathed in white oiled linen. His face was the same tone as the bandages. At five o'clock this morning he had regained consciousness and he had looked into Charlotte's face, and she had murmured, 'My dearest. Oh, my dearest.'

As yet he wasn't conscious of the pain and so had tried to smile at her, but as he did so it was as if the muscles of his face had released a spring, for his body became shot with agony. He closed his eyes and groaned and turned his head to the side, and when he opened his eyes again he imagined he was dreaming, because now he was looking into Lizzie's face.

And he could see her more clearly than she could him, for her face was awash with tears. But she was crying silently.

Vaguely he thought, she generally moans like an Irish banshee when she cried . . . then, What's she doing here? He turned his head towards Charlotte again and her face seemed to give him the answer. He was that bad. Yes, he was bad. This pain. He couldn't stand this pain. He'd yell out. Oh God! God! what had happened him? The fire. The Pitties! The Pitties. They were murderers. He had always meant to get the Pitties but they had got him and Jimmy . . . Jimmy . . . Jimmy . . .

He said the name a number of times in his head before it reached his lips. '*Jimmy.*'

'He's all right, darling. Jimmy's all right. He's . . . he's in the other room, quite close. He's all right. Go to sleep, darling, rest.'

'Char-lotte.'

'Yes, my dear?'

The words were again tumbling about in his mind, jumping over streams of fire, fire that came up from his finger nails into his shoulders and down into his chest. His chest was tight; he could hardly breathe but he wanted to tell her, he wanted to tell her again, make her understand, make her believe, press it deep into her that he loved her. He wanted to leave her comfort . . . What did he mean? Leave her comfort. Was he finished? Had they finally done for him? Was he going out? No. No. He could put up a fight. Aye, aye, like always he could put up a fight, play his hand well. If only the burning would stop. If he could jump in the river, take all his clothes off and jump in the river.

'Char-lotte.'

'Go to sleep, darling. Rest, rest. Go to sleep.'

Yes, he would go to sleep. That's how he would fight it. He would survive; and he'd get the Pitties. Little Joe, he'd make Little Joe speak out . . . and about Nickle. God! Nickle. It was him who was the big fish, aye he was the big fish . . . Aw, God Almighty. Oh! oh, the pain . . . He only needed thirty-five pounds to get the boatyard for Jimmy. If he could get set into a good game he'd make it in two or three goes. He wanted to give Jimmy something to make up for those lousy legs he was stuck with . . . Somebody was scorching him . . . burning him up . . .

'Drink this.'

The liquid sizzled as it hit the fire within him, then like a miracle it gradually dampened it down . . .

'He'll sleep for a while, lass.'

Lizzie took the glass from Charlotte's hand and placed it on a side table and, coming round the bed, she said, 'Come away and rest yourself.'

'No, no; I can't leave him.'

'He doesn't need you now, he needs nobody for the time being. It's when he wakes again and that won't be long, come away.'

Charlotte dragged her eyes from the face on the pillow and looked up into the round crumpled face of the woman she had come to think of as Rory's aunt. Then obediently she rose from the chair and went towards the other room, and Lizzie, following her, said, 'I would change me clothes if I was you and have a wash, then go downstairs and have a bite to eat. If you don't, you'll find yourself lying there along of him, and you won't be much use to him then, will you?'

Charlotte turned and stared at the fat woman. She spoke so much sense in her offhand way. She nodded at her but didn't speak.

Lizzie now closed the door and walked back to the bed and, sitting down, stared at her son, at the son who hadn't given her a kind word for years. As a boy he had liked her and teased her, as a man he had insulted her, scorned her, even hated her, but all the while, through all the phases, she had loved him. And now her heart was in ribbons. He was the only thing she had of her own flesh and he was on his way out.

On the day he was born when he had lain on her arm and first grabbed at her breast she had thought, He's strong; he'll hold the reins through life all right. And everything he had done since seemed to have pointed the same way, for he had earned a copper here and there since he was seven. And hadn't he been sent to school? And hadn't he been given full-time work afore he was fourteen? And then to jump from factory into the high position of a rent man. Moreover he had been the best dressed rent man in the town because he made enough out of his gaming to keep himself well rigged out and still have a shilling or two in his pocket. Then his latest bit of luck, marrying into this house. Who would ever have believed that would have come about? He'd always had the luck of a gambling man.

Aye, but she hadn't to forget that a gambling man's luck went both ways. And she had thought of that at tea-time yesterday when that ghost walked in the door. How she stopped herself from collapsing she'd never know. Only the fact that Ruth was on the verge of it herself had saved her, for to see Janie standing there, the Janie that wasn't Janie, except when she spoke. God in heaven! Never in all her born days had she had such a shock. And nothing that would happen to her in this life or the next would equal it. But a couple of hours later, as she watched Janie go down the path looking like something from another world, she asked God to forgive her for the thoughts that were passing through her mind, for there had been no welcome in her heart for this Janie, whose only aim in life now seemed to be the ruin of the man she had once loved, and whose wife she still was. Aye, that was a fact none of them could get over, whose wife she still was. And that poor soul back there in the room carrying a child. Well, as she had always said, God's ways were strange but if you waited long enough He solved your problems. But dear, dear God, she wished He could have solved this one in some other way than to take her flesh, the only flesh she would ever call her own.

When the door opened behind her she rose to her feet, and going towards Charlotte, she said, 'I'll call Ruth and the young maid, an' I'll come down along of you and put me feet up for a short while.'

Charlotte passed her and walked to the bed, and, bending over it, she laid her lips gently on the white sweat-laden brow, and as she went to mop his face Lizzie took her arm and said, 'Come. No more, not now. And them nurses should be here by daylight.'

Out on the landing, Jessie was sitting on a chair by the side of the door, and Charlotte said to her, 'Sit by the bed, Jessie, please. I'll . . . I'll be back in a few moments.'

'Yes, ma'am.'

The girl disappeared into the room and Charlotte crossed the landing and gently opened the door opposite, and Ruth turned from her vigil beside Jimmy's bed and asked in a whisper, 'How is he?'

'Asleep.' She went to the foot of the bed and, looking at Jimmy, she said softly, 'His hair will grow again, it's only at the back. He's sleeping naturally.' Then she asked, as if begging a favour, 'Would you sit with Rory just in case he should wake? Jessie's there, but . . . but I'd rather –' She waved her hand vaguely. 'You could leave the door open in case Jimmy calls.'

Ruth stared up at her for a moment, then looked at Lizzie before she said, 'Aye, yes, of course' . . .

In the drawing-room, Charlotte sat on the couch, her hands gripped tightly in front of her, and stared at the fire, and when the door opened and Lizzie came from the kitchen carrying a tray of tea and a plate of bread and butter she did not show any surprise.

The time that had passed since nine o'clock last night was filled with so many strange incidents that it seemed to have covered a lifetime, and that this woman should go into her kitchen and make tea seemed a natural thing to do; it was as if she had always done it.

It seemed to Charlotte from the moment she had knelt beside Rory last night that she had lived and died again and again, for each time she thought Rory had drawn his last breath she had gone with him. That he would soon take his final breath one part of her mind accepted, but the other fought hysterically against it, yelling at it, screaming at it: No, no! Fight for him, will him to remain alive. You can't let him go. Tell him that he must not go, he must not leave you; talk to his spirit, get below his mind, grasp his will, infuse your strength into him. He can't. He can't.

He must not die . . .

'Here, drink that up and eat this bit of bread.'

'No, thank you. I . . . I couldn't eat.'

'You've got to eat something. If nothin' else you need to keep the wind off your stomach when you're carryin' or you'll know about it.'

'I'm sorry, I couldn't eat. But you . . . please, please help yourself.'

'Me? Aw, I've no need to eat.' Lizzie sighed as she sat down on the edge of a chair. There followed a few moments of silence before Charlotte, wide-eyed, turned to her and said, 'What do you think?'

'Well, lass, where there's life there's hope they say. As long as he's breathin' he's got a chance, but if you want my opinion, it's a slim one. He was always a gamblin' man, but he's on a long shot now.' She put her cup down on a side table and her tightly pressed lips trembled.

Again there was silence until Lizzie said quietly, 'It's not me intention to trouble you at this time, for God knows you've got enough on your plate, but . . . but I think there's somethin' you should know 'cos there's only you can do anything about it . . . Janie. She's been outside all night sittin' in the stables, your coachman says. He doesn't know who she is of course. He told one of your lasses that there was a strange woman there and she wouldn't go, she was one of his relatives he thought.'

Lizzie now watched Charlotte rise to her feet and, her hands clasped tightly in front of her, go towards the fire and stand looking down into it, and she said to her, 'When she walked into the kitchen last night I was for droppin' down dead meself.'

Charlotte's head was moving in small jerks. The woman, the girl, his wife . . . his one-time wife in her stables? She had a vague memory of seeing a black huddled figure kneeling at Rory's side in the yard, then again when they had lifted him on to the cart, and for a moment she had glimpsed it again in the shadows of the drive. What must she do? Would Rory want to see her? He had once loved her . . . She couldn't bear that thought; he was hers, wholly hers. The happiness she had experienced with him in the months past was so deep, so strong, that the essence of it covered all time back to her beginning and would spread over the years to her end, and beyond. And he loved her, he had said it. He had put it into words, not lightly like some unfledged puppy as he had been when he married his childhood playmate, but as a man who didn't admit his feelings lightly. So what place had that girl in their lives? What was more, he had told her he wanted none of her . . .

'If he had been taken to the hospital she would have seen him, she would have claimed the right.'

Charlotte swung round. Her face dark now, she glared at the fat woman, and for a moment she forgot that she knew her as Rory's aunt.

She was just a fat woman, a common fat woman, ignorant. What did she know about rights?

'Don't frash yourself, 'cos you know as well as I do the law would say she had a right. They would take no heed that his feelings had changed.' She nodded now at Charlotte. 'Oh, aye, Janie told me he wouldn't go back to her, he had told her so to her face, and that must have been hard to stomach. So havin' the satisfaction that he wanted you, and seemingly not just for what you could give him, it should be in your heart, and it wouldn't do you any harm, to let her have a glimpse of him.'

'I can't.'

Lizzie now got to her feet and heaved a sigh before she said, 'Well, if you can't, you can't, but I'd like to remind you of one thing, or point it out, so to speak. As I see it, you should be holding nothing against her. You've got nothin' to forgive her for except for being alive. She's done nothin' willingly to you. The boot's on the other foot. Oh aye –' she dropped her chin on to her chest – 'it was all done in good faith, legal you might say, but nevertheless it was done. How would you feel this minute if you were in her place? Would you be sitting all night in the stables hoping to catch a glimpse of him afore he went?'

Charlotte sat slowly down on the couch again and, bending her long body forward, she gripped her hands between her knees.

It was some time, almost five minutes later when she whispered, 'Take her up. But . . . but I mustn't see her; I . . . I will stay here for half an hour. That is, if . . . if he doesn't need me.'

She was somewhat surprised when she received no answer. Turning her head to the side, she saw Lizzie walking slowly down the room. She was a strange woman, forthright, domineering, and she had no respect for class . . . of any kind. Yet there was something about her, a comfort.

She lay back on the couch and strained her ears now to the sounds coming from the hall. She heard nothing for some minutes, then the front door being closed and the soft padding of footsteps across the hall towards the stairs brought her upright. She was going up the stairs, that girl, his wife, she was going up to their bedroom, to hers and Rory's bedroom. And she would be thinking she was going to see her husband. *No! No, not her husband,* never any more. Hadn't he told her she could do what she liked but he'd never return to her?

She'd be by his bedside now looking at him, remembering their love, those first days in the boathouse.

'*My wife won't be there, miss, but you're welcome.*'

She was back sitting behind the desk again looking at him as he told her he was married.

She almost sprang to her feet now. She couldn't bear it, she couldn't bear that girl being up there alone with him. She must show herself. She must let her see that she was the one he had chosen to stay with, not someone who was seven years her junior, or young and beautiful, but her, as she was . . . herself.

She was out of the drawing-room and running up the stairs, and she almost burst into the bedroom, then came to a dead stop and stared at the three women standing round the bed, his mother, his aunt and the person in the black cloak who wasn't a beautiful young girl but a strange-looking creature with dark skin and white frizzy hair; she was young admittedly, but she could see no beauty in her, no appeal.

She walked slowly up to that side of the bed by which Ruth stood and she stared across into the eyes of the girl called Janie. The eyes looked sad, weary, yet at the same time defiant.

A movement of Rory's head brought their attention from each other and on to him. He was awake and looking at them.

If there had been any doubt in Rory's mind that he was near his end it was now dispelled. Janie and Charlotte together. Through the fire in his body was now threaded a great feeling of sadness. He wanted to cry at the fact that this was one game he was going to lose. The cards were all face up, and his showed all black . . . dead black. But still he had played his hand, hadn't he? The game had been short but it hadn't been without excitement. No, no, it hadn't. But now it was over . . . almost. He wished the end would get a move on because he couldn't stand this pain much longer without screaming out his agony. Why didn't they give him something, a good dose, that laudanum . . . laudanum . . . laudanum . . .

He was looking into Janie's eyes now. They were as he remembered them in those far-off days before they were married when she was happy, because she had never really been happy after, had she? It was funny, but in a way Janie hadn't been made for marriage. She looked it, she had the body for it, but she hadn't been made for marriage, whereas Charlotte. Ah! Charlotte.

Charlotte's face was close above his. He was looking up into her eyes. Charlotte. Charlotte was remarkable. Charlotte could forgive sins. She was like all the priests rolled into one. There'd been a priest here last night, hadn't there? He couldn't really remember. Well, if there had been he knew who would have brought him . . . A dose . . . Why didn't they give him something?

'Darling.'

It was nice to be called darling . . . Oh God! the pain. Why the hell didn't they give him something? . . . Janie had never called him darling. She had said she loved him, that was all. But there was more to love than that, there was a language. Charlotte knew the language. Charlotte . . .

Should he fight the pain, try to stay? He could hardly breathe . . . If only they'd give him something.

He closed his eyes for a second; when he opened them again he was looking at Lizzie. There was something in her face that was in none of the others. What was it? Why had he hated her so? It seemed so stupid now. Why had he blamed her as he had done? If there had been anybody to blame it was his father. Where was his father? He was surrounded by women. Where was his father? Where was Jimmy? They'd said Jimmy was near. Jimmy was all right. And his father? His father had a bad leg; his father had been burnt at the blast furnace . . . He had been burnt . . . *Burnt. Burnt.* He was back in the boathouse gasping, struggling. The floor was giving way. He slid Jimmy from his shoulder. He was getting out, he was getting out . . .

'He's asleep again. Leave him be, let him rest.' Lizzie moved from the bed as she spoke, and Ruth followed her, leaving Janie and Charlotte standing one on each side.

Janie looked down on the man whose face was contorted with agony. She did not see him as the virile young man she had married, nor yet as the boy she had grown up with, but she saw him as the stranger, dressed as a gentleman, who had confronted her in the boathouse. Not even when he had looked into her eyes and recognized her a moment ago had she glimpsed the old Rory, but had seen him as someone who had transported himself into another world and made that world fit him – and having won that world, so to speak, and being Rory Connor, he was determined to hang on to his winnings.

She was the first to turn away from the bed. She knew she had looked at the face on the pillow for the last time and she could not, even to herself, describe how she felt.

As Charlotte watched her walking towards the door she was amazed that the turmoil in her mind had disappeared; she was feeling no jealousy against the girl now, no hate. Amazingly she was experiencing a feeling of pity for her. As Lizzie had said, put yourself in her place; she was the one who had been rejected.

She bent over Rory now and, the tears blinding her, she gently wiped the sweat from his face, murmuring all the while, 'Oh my dearest, my dearest.'

When the door opened and Jessie entered she said brokenly, 'I . . . I won't be a moment. If the master should wake call me immediately,' and Jessie whispered, 'Yes, ma'am,' and took her seat beside the bed once more.

On the landing she stood for a moment drying her face and endeavouring to overcome the choking sensation that was rising from the anguish in her heart, as it cried, 'Oh Rory, what am I to do without you? Oh my darling, how am I to go on now? Don't leave me. Please, please don't leave me.' Yet as she descended the stairs she knew it was a hopeless cry.

In the hall she showed her surprise when she saw Ruth in her cape and tying on her bonnet. Going to her, she murmured, 'You're not leaving? You, you can't . . .'

Ruth swallowed deeply before she said, 'Just for . . . for a short while; I'm takin' Janie back home. And there's me husband, he's got to be seen to. He can do nothing with his leg as it is. I'll be back later in the mornin'.'

'I'll call the carriage for you then.' There was a stiffness in her tone.

'That would be kind.'

'But why?' Charlotte was now looking at Ruth with a deeply puzzled expression. 'I . . . I should have thought you'd have let Lizzie go back and take care of things . . . Being his mother, you would have –' she paused as Ruth, nodding at her now, put in quietly, 'Aye, yes, I know you're thinkin', it's a mother's place to be at her son's side at a time like this. Well, he'll have his mother with him. For you see, lass, I'm not his mother, 'tis Lizzie.'

'What!' The exclamation was soft.

'Yes, 'tis Lizzie who's his mother.'

'But . . . but I don't understand. He's never, I mean he's got such a regard for you, I'm . . .'

'Aye, it is a bit bewilderin' and it's a long story, but put simply, me husband gave Lizzie a child when she was but seventeen. Rory regarded me as his mother for years and when he found out I wasn't and it was Lizzie who had borne him he turned against her. I'm not surprised that you didn't know. It's something very strange in his nature that he should be ashamed of her, for she's a good woman, and she's suffered at his hands. I shouldn't say it at this stage, but to be fair I must; many another would have turned on him as he did on her, but all she did was give him the length of her tongue. Her heart remained the same towards him always. She's a good woman is Lizzie . . . So there it is, lass, that's the truth of it. Well, I'll be away now, but I'll be back.'

When the door had closed on her Charlotte remained standing. The hall to herself, she looked about it; then in a kind of bewilderment she walked down the step into the office and, sitting behind the desk, she put her forearms on it and patted the leather top gently with her fingers. He had admitted to her the theft of the five pounds; he had told her everything about himself; he had confessed his weaknesses, and boasted of his strength; yet he had kept the matter of his birth to himself as if it were a shameful secret. *Why?* Why couldn't he have told her this? She felt a momentary hurt that he should have kept it from her. She had wondered at times at him calling his mother, Ruth. He had appeared very fond of the gentle-voiced, quiet little woman, even proud of her. And yet of the two women she was the lesser in all ways, body, brain, intelligence. She remembered that Rory had once referred to Lizzie as ignorant, and she had replied that she should imagine her ignorance was merely the lack of opportunity for her mind always seemed lively.

It was strange, she thought in this moment, that he could never have realized that all the best in him stemmed from Lizzie – for now she could see he was a replica of her, in bulk, character, obstinacy, bumptiousness . . . loving. Her capacity for loving was even greater than his, for, having been rejected, she had gone on loving.

There came a knock on the door and when she said, 'Come in,' it opened and Lizzie stood on the threshold.

'I was wondering where you were, I couldn't see you. You mustn't sit by yourself there broodin', it'll do no good. Come on now out of this.'

Like a child obeying a mother, Charlotte rose from the chair and went towards Lizzie. Then standing in front of her, she looked into her eyes and said quietly, 'I've just learned that you're his mother. Oh, Lizzie. Lizzie.'

'Aye.' Lizzie's head was drooping. 'I'm his mother an' he's always hated the fact, but nevertheless, it was something he could do nowt about. I am what I am, and he was all I had of me own flesh and blood an' I clung to him; even when he threw me off I clung to him.'

'Oh, Lizzie, my dear.' When she put her arms around Lizzie, Lizzie held her tightly against her breast, and neither of them was capable of further words, but they cried together.

It was three days later when Rory died. He was unconscious for the last twelve hours and the final faint words he spoke had been to Charlotte. 'If it's a lad, call him after me,' he murmured.

She didn't know how she forced herself to whisper, 'And if it should be a girl?'

He had looked at her for some time before he gasped, 'I'll . . . I'll leave that to you.'

It was odd but she had hoped he would have said, 'Name her Lizzie,' for then it would have told her of his own peace of mind, but he said, 'I'll leave it to you.' His very last words were, 'Thank you, my dear . . . for everything.'

Through a thick mist she gazed down on to the face of the man who had brought her to life, who had made her body live, and filled it with new life – his life. She was carrying him inside of her; he wasn't dead; her Rory would never die.

When she fainted across his inert body they thought for a moment that she had gone with him.

CHAPTER 7

Rory's funeral was such that might have been accorded to a prominent member of the town for the sympathy of the town had been directed towards him through the newspaper reports of how he had been fatally injured in saving his brother from the blazing building, and the likelihood that charges, not only of arson, but of murder or manslaughter as well, would soon be made against local men now being questioned by the police.

No breath of scandal. No mention of former wife reappearing.

Other reports gave the names of the town's notable citizens who had attended the funeral. Mr Frank Nickle's name was not on it. Mr Nickle had been called abroad on business.

Two of the Pittie Brothers had already been taken into custody. The police were hunting the third. And there were rumours that one of the brothers was implicating others, whose names had not yet been disclosed. Not only the local papers, but those in Newcastle as well carried the story of how there had been attempts to monopolize the river trade, and that Mr Connor's boats had not only been set adrift, but also been sunk when they were full of cargo.

The reports made Jimmy's little boats appear the size of tramp steamers or tea clippers, and himself as a thriving young businessman.

The private carriages had stretched the entire length of the road passing Westoe village and far beyond. The occupants were all male. In fact, the entire cortège was male, with one exception. Mrs Connor was present at her husband's funeral and what made her presence even more embarrassing to the gentlemen mourners was that it was whispered she was someway gone in pregnancy. She wore a black silk coat and a fashionable hat with widow's weeds flowing low down at the back but reaching no farther than her chest at the front. She was a remarkable woman really . . . nothing to look at personally, but sort of remarkable, a kind of law unto herself.

Another thing that was remarkable, but only to the occupants of the kitchen, was that John George had been present at the burial, but had not shown his face to condole with them nor had he spoken with Paddy who had struggled to the cemetery on sticks. All except Jimmy said they couldn't make him out. But then prison changed a man, and likely he was deeply ashamed, and of more than one thing, for was he not now living with another man's wife?

Poor John George, they said. Yet in all their minds was the faint niggling question, Who was the poorer? John George was alive; Rory, the tough gambling man, was dead.

And this was exactly what had passed through Jimmy's mind when he had seen John George standing against the wall of an outbuilding in the cemetery.

It happened that as they left the grave-side he had become separated from Charlotte. He'd had to make way for gentlemen who had ranked themselves on each side of her. He could not see his father, and so he walked on alone, weighed down with the pain in his heart and the sense of utter desolation, and wondering how he was going to live through the endless days ahead.

It was as he crossed an intersecting path that he saw in the distance the unmistakable lanky figure of John George. He was standing alone, head bowed, and his very stance seemed to be portraying his own feelings.

Without hesitating, he went towards him; but not until he was almost in front of him did John George raise his head.

For almost a full minute they looked at each other without speaking. Then it was Jimmy who said, 'I'm glad you came, John George.'

John George swallowed deeply, wet his lips, sniffed, then brought out a handkerchief and rubbed it roughly around his face before mumbling, 'I'm sorry, Jimmy, sorry to the heart.'

'Aye, I knew you'd feel like that, John George. In spite of everything I knew you'd have it in your heart to forgive him.'

'Oh, that.' John George shook his head vigorously, then bowed it again before ending. 'Oh, that was over and done with a long time ago.'

'It's like you to say that, John George. You were always a good chap.'

'No, not good, just weak, Jimmy. And you know, in a funny sort of way I feel responsible for . . .'

'*No*! Don't be silly, John George.' Jimmy cut in. 'Now don't get that into your head. It's me, if anybody, who should shoulder the blame for Rory's going. It's me. If I hadn't wanted the damned boatyard he'd be here the day. Aye, he would.'

'No, no, don't blame yourself, Jimmy. It was just one of those things. Life's made up of them when you think about it, isn't it?' He paused, then asked softly, 'How's she, Miss . . . I mean his wife? How's she taking it?'

'Oh, hard, though she's puttin' a face on it to outsiders. She was more than fond of him you know.'

'Aye. Yes, I guessed that. Yet it came as a surprise when I heard they'd married. But I got a bigger surprise when she sought me out. I couldn't take it in. After all . . . well, you know, doing what I did, and the case and things. I'd imagined she was like her father. You knew about what she did for me, like setting me up?'

'Yes, John George.'

'And you didn't hold it against me for taking it?'

'Why, no, man. Why, no; I was glad; it showed you held no hard feelings.'

'Some wouldn't see it that way. What did they think about it in the kitchen?'

'Oh, they just thought it was kind of her; they don't know the true ins and outs of it, John George.'

Again they stared at each other without speaking. Then John George said, 'Well, they'll never hear it from me, Jimmy. I've never let on to a soul, not even to Maggie.'

'Thanks, John George. You're one in a thousand.'

'No, just soft, I suppose. He used to say I was soft.' He turned and looked over the headstones in the direction of the grave, but there was no rancour in his words. Then looking at Jimmy again, he said, 'It's eased me somewhat, Jimmy, to have a word with you. I hope I'll see you again.'

'Me an' all, John George. Aye, I'd like that. I'll come up sometime, if you don't mind.'

'You'd be more than welcome, Jimmy, more than welcome.'

'Well, I've got to go now, they'll likely be waiting and I'll be holding up the carriages. So long, John George.' Jimmy held out his hand.

John George gripped it. 'So long, Jimmy.'

They now nodded at each other, then simultaneously turned away, John George in the direction of the grave and Jimmy towards the gates, the carriage and Charlotte, and the coming night, which seemed the first he was about to spend without Rory, for up till now his body had lain in the house.

It was as he crossed the intersecting path again that he saw Stoddard hurrying towards him.

'Oh, there you are, sir. The mistress was wondering.'

'I'm sorry. I saw an old friend of . . . of my brother's. I . . . I had to have a word . . .'

'Yes, sir. Of course, sir.'

It was funny to be called sir, he'd never get used to it like Rory had.

They were making their way through small groups of men in order to reach the gates and the carriage beyond when he saw her. Perhaps it was because of the strong contrast in dress that the weirdly garbed figure standing in the shadow of the cypress tree stood out. Both Jimmy and Stoddard looked towards it, and Jimmy almost came to a stop and would once again have diverted had not Stoddard said quietly, 'The mistress is waiting, sir.'

'Oh yes, yes.' Poor Janie. What must she be feeling at this moment? Rory's wife, his real wife after all was said and done, hidden away like a criminal. But she had come; despite the protests she had come. Her presence would surely cause comment.

So thought Stoddard. But then, as he told himself yet again what he had said to the staff last night, it was a lucky family that hadn't someone they were ashamed to own because of their oddities. It happened in the highest society, and certainly in the lowest, and you couldn't blame the master or his folks for not wanting to bring that creature to the fore.

CHAPTER 8

They were gathered in the kitchen. Paddy sitting by the fire with his leg propped up on a chair; Ruth sitting opposite to him, a half-made shirt lying on her lap, her hands resting on top of it; Jimmy sitting by the corner of the table, and Lizzie standing by the table to the side of him, while Janie stood at the end of it facing them all.

She was dressed as she had been since she came back; even, within doors she kept the strange hat on her head. She looked from one to the other as she said, 'You're blamin' me for taking it, aren't you? After the stand I made you think I should have thrown the money back in her face?'

'No, no.' They all said it in different ways, shakes of the head, movements of the hands, mutters, but their protests didn't sound convincing to her, and now, her voice raised, she said, 'You took from her. It was all right for you to take from her, all of you. And what had she done to you? Nowt.'

'Nobody's sayin' you shouldn't 've taken it, Janie. We're just sad like that you still feel this way about things.'

She turned and looked at Jimmy, and her body seemed to slump inside the cloak. She said now flatly, 'How would any of you have felt, I ask you? Look at yourselves. Would you have acted any differently? And don't forget, I could have gone to the polis station, I could have said who I was? I could have blown the whole thing into the open, but I didn't, I kept quiet, I didn't even go and see me da. I kept out of his way even when I saw him at the funeral. And I won't see him now, 'cos he'd open his mouth. It would only be natural. But . . . but when she sent for me and . . . and she knew I was going back there, she asked if she could do anything for me and I said aye, yes, she could. I told her, I told her what it was like there. They had nothing or next to nothing. The boats were dropping to bits. It . . . it was she who named the sum. Five hundred, she said, and I didn't say, yes, aye, or nay.'

'You mean she gave you five hundred straightaway like that?' Paddy was peering at her through narrowed lids.

'No, she gave me a paper. I've . . . I've got to go to a French bank. She's puttin' four hundred and fifty pounds in there; she gave me the rest in sovereigns.'

'And after that, lass, you still haven't got a good word in yer belly for her?'

She dropped her eyes from Lizzie's gaze, then said, 'I can't be like you all, fallin' on her neck.'

'Nobody's fell on her neck.'

She turned and looked at Jimmy. 'No, you didn't fall on her neck, Jimmy, just into her arms. You were as bad as Rory. I've got to say it, it's funny what money can do, by aye, it is. I wouldn't 've believed it.'

'Well, you're not turnin' your nose up at it, are you. Janie?'

'No, no, I'm not, Jimmy, but as I look at it now I'm only takin' what's due to me, 'cos as things were he would have had to support me. And in the long run it would have cost him more than five hundred pounds 'cos I'm likely to live a long time.'

They all stared at her, Ruth, Lizzie, Paddy and Jimmy. This was the little girl who had grown up next door. This was the young lass, the kindly young lass, who had cared for her grannie, who had been full of high spirits and kindliness. Each in his own way was realizing what life could do to any one of them. Each in his own way knew a moment of understanding, and so it was Ruth who spoke first, saying, 'well, wherever you go, lass, whatever you do, our good wishes 'll go with you. Our memories are long; we'll always remember you.' She did not add 'as you once were.'

'Aye, that goes for me an' all.' Paddy was nodding at her. 'We've had some good times together, Janie, and in this very kitchen. I'll think back on 'em, Janie.'

Lizzie's face and voice was soft as she said, 'As you say, you'll live a long time, lass, and you'll marry and have a sturdy family, an' when you do, name some of them after us, eh?'

Janie's head was up, her lips were tight pressed together, her eyes were wide and bright; then as the tears sprang from them, they came around her, patting her, comforting her; even Paddy hobbled from his chair, saying, 'There, lass. There, lass.'

'I've . . . I've got to go.'

'Yes, yes, you've got to go.' Ruth dried her eyes and smiled. 'And have a safe journey, lass. It's a long way to go, across the sea to another country. Aren't you feared?'

'No.' Janie shook her head as she blew her nose. 'I know me way, an' I won't have to ride in the cattle trucks.' She smiled weakly, and Lizzie said somewhat tentatively now, 'Why didn't you get yourself a decent rig-out, lass, to go back with?'

'No, Lizzie, no.' Again she shook her head. 'I came like this and that's how I'm goin' back. And . . . and you see, they wouldn't understand, not if I went back dressed up. I'll . . . I'll be one of them again like this. But at the same time I've seen things, and I know things what they don't, and I'll be able to help . . . It's funny, isn't it, how life works out?'

As she looked from one to the other they saw a glimpse of the old Janie, and they smiled tenderly at her.

'Eeh! well, I'll be away. I've got to get the train.'

She backed from them now and, with the exception of Jimmy, they didn't move towards her, not even to come to the door. Jimmy opened the door for her, and with one backward glance at them she went out, and he followed her down the path. At the gate he said, 'Look, wait a minute, I'll go back and get me coat and come down with you to the station.'

'No. No, Jimmy. Thanks all the same. Anyway, you're in no fit state to be about yet, never mind walking to the station.'

He took her hand and they stared at each other. 'Be happy, Janie. Try to forget all that's happened. And . . . and another thing I'd like to say, thank you for not letting on to them' – he jerked his head back towards the cottage – 'about, well, you know what, the John George business.'

She stared at him blankly. This was the second time those very words had been said to her within a short space.

Yesterday she had stood in that beautiful room and thought to herself with still remaining bitterness, I can see why he didn't want to come back, for who'd want to give up all this for a boathouse, ignoring the fact that it was the tall black-garbed, sad-looking woman facing her who had been the magnet that had kept him there. Nor had she softened towards her when, in open generosity Charlotte had said, 'I understand how you feel for he was such a wonderful man,' but she had blurted out before she could check herself, 'You didn't know him long enough to know what he was like . . . really like.'

'I did know what he was really like.' Charlotte's tone had altered to tartness.

She had stared hard at the woman before retorting, 'I shouldn't say it at this time, but I doubt it,' and the answer she received was 'You needn't, for I knew my husband' – the last word was stressed – 'better than most. I was aware of all his weaknesses. I knew everything about him before I married him . . . with the exception of one thing . . .'

'Yes, and I know what that was,' she had said. 'He wouldn't let on about that.'

It had appeared as if they were fighting.

'Do you?'

'Aye.'

'Well, tell me what you think it was,' said Charlotte.

She had become flustered at this. 'It was his business,' she said. 'It's over, it's best left alone.' Then she had stood there amazed as she listened to the woman saying, 'You are referring to the John George Armstrong affair and Rory taking the five pounds and letting his friend shoulder the blame for the whole amount, aren't you?'

She had gaped at her, then whispered, 'He told you that?'

'Yes, he did, I already knew all about it. I had pieced things together from the events that followed the court case.'

'And you did nothin', I mean to get John George off?'

'He had been stealing for some time. His sentence would have been the same . . .'

She had stared open-mouthed at the woman, she couldn't understand her. She was a lady yet such were her feelings for a fellow like Rory that she had treated as nothing something that she herself had thought of as a crime and condemned him wholesale for. In fact, so big was it in her eyes that she saw it now as the cause of all that had happened to her – all the heartache and the hardship.

She hadn't been able to understand her own feelings at that moment for strange thoughts had galloped about in her mind. She had made a mistake somewhere. Had she ever loved Rory? Of course, she had. But not like this woman had loved him. Perhaps her own mistake lay in that she had liked too many people, and it had sort of watered down her love; whereas this woman had concentrated all her feelings in one direction and had gained Rory's love in return . . . she hadn't bought him. It seemed to be the last bitter pill she had to swallow.

. . . 'The only thing he kept from me was the fact that Lizzie is his mother.'

'That?'

'Yes.'

'Well, he always was ashamed of it. Yet I couldn't understand why 'cos Lizzie's all right.'

'Yes, Lizzie's all right.'

She had asked her to sit down after that, and then she had offered her the money. But even when she took it she still couldn't like her, or soften towards her . . .

. . . 'You all right, Janie?'

'Aye, Jimmy.'

'Try to forgive and forget.'

'Aye, I will. It'll take time, but I will, Jimmy. I'll marry. I'll marry Henri. I liked him well enough, but that isn't lovin'. Still, we've got to take what we get, haven't we?'

'You'll be happy enough, Janie.'

'Aye, well, think on me sometimes, Jimmy.'

'There'll never be a time when I won't, Janie.' He leant towards her and they kissed quietly, then, her head bowed, she turned swiftly from him and went through the gate and down the narrow path and became lost from his view in the hedgerows.

For quite some time he stood bent over the gate-post. He had been in love with her since he was a lad. During the time Rory courted her he had lived with a special kind of pain, but when he had lain in the loft above them he had suffered an agony for a time because he had loved them both. Now in a way they were both dead, for the Janie he had loved was no more. She hadn't just disappeared down the road; paradoxically she had died when she had come back to life and showed herself as a strange creature that night in the boathouse. Her resurrection had freed him. Life was odd. Indeed it was. As she had said, it was funny how it worked out.

He knew that a different kind of life lay before him. Charlotte was setting him up in a new boatyard and, what was more, she wanted him to take an interest in business.

Yes, a new kind of life was opening up before him, but whatever it offered it would be empty, for Rory was no longer in it. He ached for Rory, and night following night he cried silently while he wished that God had taken him too . . . or instead. Aye, instead. Why hadn't he died instead, for he wouldn't have been missed like Rory was? He had emptied so many lives by his going, Charlotte's, Janie's, Lizzie's, his ma's, aye and even his da's, all their lives were empty now . . . Yet free from the scandal that his living would have created. It was funny, weird. In a way it was like the outcome of Lizzie's saying, leave it to God and He'll work it out.

He went up the path and into the kitchen that housed the old life.

CHAPTER 9

They were all in the kitchen again, but now they were waiting for the carriage to take them on what had become for all of them, up till now, one of their twice-weekly visits to Birchingham House.

Ruth stood facing Lizzie and Jimmy as, spreading her hands wide, she said, 'Don't worry about me, I'll have me house to meself for once an' –' she nodded towards Paddy – 'I've got your dad to look after.'

'But both of us goin', ma?' Jimmy screwed up his face at her.

'Well, now look at it this way, lad.' Ruth's tone was unusually brisk.

'You're goin' into business, and it's on the waterfront, practically at the end of it. Now, unless you're going to have a carriage and pair for yourself, you can't make that trek twice a day. Now Westoe's on your doorstep so to speak. And there's always the week-ends, you can come home at the week-ends. As for you, Lizzie.' She turned her gaze on Lizzie. 'You know, if you speak the truth, you're breakin' your neck to stay down there; you can't wait for that child to be born.'

'What you talkin' about, woman? Breakin' me neck!' Lizzie jerked her chin upwards.

'I know what I'm talkin' about and you know what I'm talkin' about. And you've lost weight. The flesh is droppin' off you.'

'Huh!' Lizzie put her forearms under her breasts and humped them upwards. That should worry you. You've told me for years I'm too fat. And anyway, what do you think Charlotte will have to say about all this?'

'Charlotte will welcome you with open arms, the both of yous, she needs you. Remember the last time we saw her as we went out the door, remember the look on her face? She was lost. She's no family of her own, she needs family.'

'The likes of me?' Lizzie now thumped her chest.

'Yes, the likes of you. Who better? Now stop sayin' one thing and thinkin' another. Go and pack a few odds and ends. And you an' all, Jimmy. Now both of yous, and let me have me own way for once in me own house with me own life. I've never had much say in anything, have I? Now, have I?' She turned and looked towards her husband who was staring at her, and he smiled; then nodding from Lizzie to Jimmy, he said, 'She's right, she's right, she's had the poor end of the stick. Do what she says and let's have peace.'

Stoddard was a little surprised when the two leather-strapped bass hampers were handed to him to be placed on the seat beside him, but then so many surprising things had happened of late that he was taking them in his stride now.

Three quarters of an hour later, when the carriage drew up on the drive, he helped Mrs O'Dowd, as she was known to the servants, down the steps; then taking up the hampers, he followed her and the young gentleman up towards his mistress who was waiting at the door. As the greetings were being exchanged he handed the hampers to the maid, and she took them into the hall and set them down, and when Charlotte glanced at them, Lizzie, taking off her coat, said, 'Aye, you might look at them; you're in for a shock.'

A few minutes later, seated in the drawing-room, Lizzie asked softly, 'Well, how you feeling now, lass?' and it was some seconds before

Charlotte, clasping and unclasping her hands, replied, 'If I'm to speak the truth, Lizzie, desolate, utterly, utterly desolate.' Her voice broke and she swallowed deeply before ending, 'It gets worse, I, I miss him more every day. I was lonely before but, but never like this.'

Lizzie, pulling herself up from the deep chair, went and sat beside her on the couch and, taking her hand, patted it as she said, 'Aye, and . . . and it'll be like this for some time. I know. Oh aye, I know 'cos I've a world of emptiness inside here.' She placed her hand on her ribs. 'But it'll ease, lass; it'll ease; it won't go altogether, it'll change into something else, but it'll ease. We couldn't go on livin' if it didn't. So in the meantime we've put our heads together, haven't we, Jimmy?' She looked towards Jimmy, where he sat rubbing one lip tightly over the other and he nodded, 'And this is what we thought. But mind, it's just up to you, It's up to you to say. But seeing that in a short while Jimmy'll be working on the waterfront, well, as Ruth pointed out, it's a trek and a half right back to the cottage twice a day, and in all weathers. And –' she gave a little smile now – 'she also reminded him that he hadn't got a carriage and pair yet, and that he's have to shank it, so she wondered if you wouldn't mind puttin' him up here for a while, 'cos . . .'

'Oh, yes. *Oh, yes,* Jimmy.' Charlotte leant eagerly towards him, holding out her hand, and Jimmy grasped it. And now with tears on her voice she said, 'Oh, I'm so grateful. But . . . but your mother?'

'Oh, she's all right.' Jimmy's voice was a little unsteady as he replied. 'She has me da, and I'll be poppin' up there every now and again. She's all right.'

'Oh, thank you. Thank you.' Now Charlotte looked at Lizzie, and Lizzie said, 'An' that's not all, there's me.' She now dug her thumb in between her breasts. 'I've got nothin' to do with meself, I'm sittin' picking me nails half me time, an' I thought, well, if she can put up with me I'll stay until the child comes 'cos I've a mind to be the first to see me grandson, or me granddaughter, or twins, or triplets, whatever comes.'

'Oh, Lizzie! Lizzie!' Charlotte now turned and buried her face in the deep flesh of Lizzie's shoulder, and Lizzie, stroking her hair, muttered, 'There now. There now. Now stop it. It's the worst thing you can do to bubble your eyes out. Grannie Wagget used to say that you should never cry when you're carryin' a child 'cos you're takin' away the water it swims in.' She gave a broken laugh here, then said, 'There now. There now. Come on, dry your eyes. What you want is a cup of tea.' She turned towards Jimmy, saying, 'Pull that bell there, Jimmy, an' ring for tea.' Then with the tears still in her eyes, she laughed as she lifted Charlotte's face towards her, saying, 'Did you ever hear anythin' like it in your life? Me, Lizzie O'Dowd, saying ring for tea. What's the world comin' to, I ask you?'

Charlotte stared back into the face of the mother of her beloved. Two years ago she had been alone, but since then she had experienced love, and such love she knew she would never know again. But on the day she had bargained for Rory's love she had said to him that there were many kinds of love, and it was being proved to her now at this moment.

When Lizzie said to her, 'If you don't watch out I'll take over, I'm made like that. Ring for tea, I said, just as if I was born to it. I tell you!' Charlotte put out her hand and cupped the plump cheek, and what she said now and what she was to say for many years ahead was, 'Oh, Lizzie! Lizzie! My dear Lizzie.'

The King's Pleasure

Norah Lofts

For JULIET O'HEA who shares Katharine's faith, kindliness, and determination.

A BALLAD FOR KATHARINE OF ARAGON (From UNION STREET by CHARLES CAUSLEY)

The Queen of Castile has a daughter
Who won't come home again
She lies in the grey cathedral
Under the arms of Spain
O the Queen of Castile has a daughter
Torn out by the roots
Her lovely breast in a cold stone chest
Under the farmer's boots.

CHAPTER 1

Mules, everybody agreed, were more sure-footed, so Isabella of Spain rode on a mule, her heavily pregnant body wrapped in a rain-repellent leather cloak, on her head a hood of the same material, her feet encased in a pair of boots similar to those worn by foot soldiers. The winter rains had set in and the roads which through the long hot summer had been ankle-deep in dust were now over hoof deep in mud, sticky as glue. Every time the mule put a foot down there was a squelching sound, every time it lifted one there was a plop. Sometimes, under the smooth shining surface of the mud, there was a dip; then the mule stumbled, recovered itself with a jerk and a heave and plodded on: sometimes, under a mere skim of mud there was a boulder, thrown in to fill a hole visible last summer; striking one of these the mule stumbled again; recovered and plodded on. Each time this happened Isabella felt like a woman holding a basketful of eggs riding on a seesaw; after each jolt the question, All right? Ah well? Yes, thanks be to God, no harm done. The child, so soon to be born, would be her tenth; four were alive, thank God; few mothers had been so blessed; but with every stumble and jolt she knew a small fear – not here, please God, not in the open, in the rain. Alcalá de Henares is not so far away; the road is bad, the going slow, but please, I beseech thee, let me arrive, settle into the place prepared for me and there let the child be born.

She was Queen; she could have ridden comfortably in a litter slung between two mules, or carried on the shoulders of willing men, but to do so would have been a concession to female weakness, and she scorned it. God had called her to take a man's place in the world, and handicapped as she had been by her female body, she had taken that place, filled it adequately, done as much as, or more than, any man could have done – all by the help of God. She must not weaken now.

In everything Isabella could see the hand of God, working slowly, sometimes obscurely but to a sure end. Because there was no male heir she had become Queen of Castile, and she had married Ferdinand of Aragon, thus uniting the two kingdoms and making them strong enough to attempt to drive out the Moors who had occupied the south of the Iberian peninsula for six hundred years. She did not deceive herself; Ferdinand might look upon the campaign, now in its fifth year, as a means to increase his own power; for her it was a Crusade, Christian against infidel, as urgent and important as any Crusade waged centuries earlier to free the Holy Land. For Isabella, Spain was holy land and to wage the war of freedom she had ridden, slept, eaten, suffered and endured alongside her army, showing fortitude in the face of hardship and in defeat a certain grim cheerfulness which communicated itself to the men.

The army, with one of its hardest and most successful campaigns behind it, was moving into winter quarters, making on this drear day for the bleak upland town of Alcalá de Henares, where there was a palace of a sort. It was a comfortless place, ancient, ill-heated and in poor repair; its owner, the Bishop of Toledo, used it only once a year when he made his visitation, and he took good care that this should be neither in winter nor in summer, but in late spring or early autumn when, for a brief period the weather was tolerable. He was always preceded by a baggage train, laden with hangings and cushions and soft feather bedding, silverware and little luxuries in the way of food. The Queen of Castile could have taken similar precautions, but she never did. The horses, mules and donkeys in her train were laden enough without carting a lot of useless gear from place to place. Even her personal luggage was kept to the minimum; with her always were her suit of armour, her riding clothes, three changes of linen and two dresses, one plain and simple made of Flemish cloth, the other very fine, a rich reddish purple silk, so boned and padded and embroidered that it was almost as stiff as armour. Both were old; she had other things to do with her money than to buy fripperies. Yet she was an elegant woman, with narrow feet and delicate hands, white and well kept; her hair, once golden, now silver-gilt, was washed every other Monday, even when, as often happened, Monday had seen fighting renewed. She had a fastidious nose and in her youth had used and liked a perfume distilled from roses; but the trick of making it was a secret, brought to Spain by the Moors when they came out of the east and as soon as she knew her destiny she had abandoned its use, making do with the simpler preparation made from crushed lavender, native to Spain.

On this day her few clothes, her few toilet necessities were all contained in a brassbound hide box, which also held everything that a baby might need. The enforced parsimony was evident there, too. For the new baby nothing new. The baby clothes had served many times already; for Isabella, Juan, Joanna and Maria and babies who had died young; well washed and bleached by the summer sun in the south, they would serve again for the child who would, God willing, be born in the Bishop's palace at Alcalá de Henares. Not in the rain and the mud, the birth precipitated by a fall.

Isabella hoped for another son. The one she had already, Juan, had survived the danger period of infancy and first youth and was now seven years old, healthy, intelligent, charming, God be thanked; but he was only one life, only one heir; life was so full of threats; another boy would be a kind of security; and if this child were a boy, and if Juan lived, the younger one could become a cleric – perhaps even Pope.

Jerking along, in increasing discomfort, the leather cloak growing heavier and then porous so that finally the wetness seeped through to her skin, Isabella cheered herself with thoughts of the future. Juan King of a united Spain, with not a Moor left alive in it; Carlos – for so she would name this child, should it be a boy, on the Papal throne, and all her daughters married to kings, linking Spain, so long isolated, to Europe, carrying their Spanish piety and good manners with them.

To her second son, if God so favoured her, she would say, 'You were almost born in a saddle.' She would not say that if this child were a girl. She had learned from a long, hard experience what turns of speech appealed to men and what to women. She had been compelled to speak both languages and could switch from one to the other without conscious thought. When her husband, Ferdinand, who had been at the rear of the long train, urging on the laggards, brought his horse alongside her mule and asked how she did, she said:

'Mules are somewhat overrated; but at least I am still in one piece.'

He laughed. A woman would have been more sympathetic, would have said things like 'Poor lady!' or 'How courageous you are, madam.' *Weakening* words. The sort that she had resisted for years.

Ferdinand said, 'Not long now. That fellow who broke his ankle and was heaved up on top of one of the baggage wagons just told me that he could see the roofs. Then the road dipped and he lost sight of them again, but in less than an hour we should be there.'

They were there in less than an hour. The Bishop's palace was as stark, as bare as she remembered it; but it was a suitable place for the birth of a child who, if a boy, would be obliged to subjugate the flesh, at least for a time, and if a girl would be the fourth daughter, with all the really advantageous marriages made before it was her turn, and might become a nun.

Freed of the mule's movements and relieved of her sodden clothes and heavy boots, the Queen felt better and derided herself for her fears of a somewhat premature delivery. She proceeded in her usual, orderly way, moving slowly but purposely. First a visit to the little chapel, ill-lit and cold as a tomb, where she knelt and thanked God that the journey had been completed without mishap save for a broken ankle and one wagon wheel smashed; she prayed that God would forgive her for the lack of complete faith that had made her fears possible. Then to more mundane matters. First of all – before the children, even, the need to make certain that every man would sleep under cover in this night of wind and rain.

The Bishop's palace, like every other palace where Isabella had stayed in the last four years, was virtually a barracks, only a few private rooms reserved for the Royal Family and its immediate entourage; but even so, and with every outbuilding brought into service, it was still necessary to find outside billets for a great number of soldiers, and a senior officer had been sent on ahead to make arrangements. The Queen knew how ordinary people felt about having soldiers thrust upon them, but it was a necessity in winter and it was the turn of the people up here in the northwest to assume their part of the burden; the towns and villages to the south, near the fighting front, had stripped themselves to keep the army fed during spring and summer; that was what made these long winter journeys an essential part of the year's routine. Isabella had done her best to instil a crusading spirit into her army; men were forbidden to loot or to meddle with respectable females; they knew that their Queen disapproved of drunkenness and of the use of foul language. On the whole her rules and her wishes were regarded, but there were exceptions which distressed her less than might have been supposed; it was an army of men, not of monks, that she had gathered and she was shrewd enough to realise that the men who sometimes broke rules were not necessarily the worst soldiers.

'Every man has a roof over his head?' she asked.

'Yes, your Grace.' The officer added – for unless the queen was in childbed tomorrow, she would be out and about, inspecting and criticising, and he did not want his efforts underrated: 'Of a sort. It was not easy. Since last year a dozen houses at least have become untenanted and have fallen into total disrepair; and at the lower end of the town there is a sickness.'

'Plague?' Isabella asked sharply, prepared to move on tomorrow if this were so. Of all diseases the plague was most to be dreaded; even the bodies of the dead emitted a fatal contagion.

'No, madam. I was not myself sure, but the surgeon-in-chief whom I consulted as soon as he arrived, assures me that it is not. The sick are fevered, restless and raving, but they show no signs of plague. I ordered the area to be cordoned off and placed out of bounds. It contains several wineshops and . . . other places.'

'You did well,' she said. She knew what he meant by other places. Again regrettable, but what could one do? Take an ordinary man away from his family, deprive him of most of life's comfort, expose him to the constant danger of death, and could you blame him for snatching at a passing pleasure? You could not. Nor were the women themselves, the rather pathetic camp followers or the homebound ones who welcomed an army's arrival in their town, much to be blamed. They were so *poor*. The poverty of her people was a matter of great concern to Isabella; she could distinguish between poverty accepted as a way of life, for the glory of God, by certain religious orders, and poverty inflicted by circumstance. Over the greater part of Castile, and of Aragon, the soil was poor and the climate inclement, veering between too-cold winters and too-hot-and-dry summers. North of the Pyrénées was France, very fertile and rich, and farther north still England where green grass was plentiful all the year round and there were – it was said – more sheep than people. The wool of these sheep was shipped to Flanders where it was made into cloth, a saleable commodity. In this lucrative two-way trade Spain could take no part. It was a pity, but it was a situation which would not last forever. Next year, please God, the rich Moorish provinces would be restored to Spain; minerals, vineyards, orange and lemon groves . . . And at the very back of her mind there was another thought.

There was a Genoese sailor, a man called Christopher Columbus, wandering about the courts of Europe, searching for a patron who would fit out an expedition to enable him to prove his contention that the world was a globe, not a flat surface and that by travelling towards the west he could reach the rich, fabulous world of the Indies whence came by slow, expensive, overland route or by Portuguese caravel things like sugar and cloves and cinnamon and ginger and precious stones. It sounded a fantastic idea, but no more fantastic than that a woman should be Queen of Castile in her own right and called to wage the last Crusade. And win it. She meant to, if she lived. She visualised the last Moorish King driven out of Granada, fleeing back to Africa, where the Moors belonged; she visualised herself just able to afford this westward voyage which might conceivably end in the East and bring the wealth of the Indies, where even kitchen utensils were – they said – made of silver and gold, under the control of Spain. To God nothing was impossible.

The matter of the soldiers' comfort dealt with – not without reason they regarded her as The Mother, and so referred to her – she turned her attention to those to whom she was actually mother. They were, so far as the building and its amenities allowed, comfortably installed. There was the Infanta Isabella, fifteen years old, very solemn and, even Isabella admitted, pompous; an admirable girl in a way, but once she had so exasperated her mother that Isabella had said, 'You talk to me as though you were my mother-in-law!' The younger Isabella's destiny was settled; she would be Queen of Portugal, and her solemnity, pomposity and complete lack of humour would make her a most excellent queen; she had been reared and educated for the position. Isabella the Queen of Castile had always been aware of her own faulty education – she had become Queen through the premature death of her stepbrother and been obliged to learn Latin, the language in which all legal and diplomatic matters were phrased, in a hurried three weeks. As a result she had paid particular attention to her children's education.

Juan, as the heir, already had his own establishment, a separate little court for which Isabella had lain down the rules and which, even on journeys like this one, ran smoothly. All well, Isabella thought, and moved on to the more cramped quarters where her two younger daughters and their attendants were housed. Maria, the baby of the family until the new one came, was settling down to sleep, almost too drowsy to be aware of her mother's presence; Joanna, who was six, was giving trouble; not for the first time. She had rejected her supper and now refused to go to bed.

Isabella endeavoured to be an impartial mother and outwardly achieved this aim, but Joanna, so beautiful, so precocious and so strange, was her favourite daughter, almost as much loved as the only son. Deep concern and apprehension lay at the root of this preference. It was impossible for Isabella to look upon her second daughter and not remember that her own mother had been mad and had passed the last years of her life under restraint. But I am sane, she told herself whenever that memory struck; and then immediately she would think of things like left-handedness, stammering, a colouring of eyes or hair skipping one generation. To any of her other children, on this evening she would have administered a rebuke, an admonition; to Joanna she said:

'Come here and tell me what is the matter.'

She sat herself on a hard wooden stool and would have taken Joanna on to her lap – but she had no lap these days, instead she put her arm around the child and pulled her close, held her firmly, aware of vibrating tremor.

'We have all had a hard day,' she said in her calm, low voice. 'It is unkind of you, Joanna, to make things more difficult.'

'I know. I am sorry.'

'Then why do you do it?'

'It is a bad place, Mother. Not a place to eat and sleep in. A place to go away from. Could we not go away? Now.'

'It is cold, and not very comfortable,' Isabella said. 'But it is better than being out in the night and the rain. *I* think it is a good place, Joanna. *I* was very glad to arrive here. *I* shall eat my supper and go to bed and be grateful to God for the food and the resting place. You should do the same. Come along now, eat just a little and then go to bed like my good, sensible little girl.'

'I can't,' Joanna said with a violent shudder. 'Not here.'

'Why not?'

'Because of the coffin.'

'What coffin?'

'The brown one.'

Despite all her faith, despite her practical and rational mind, Isabella felt a little superstitious shiver. She had long ago, before she bore her first child, given orders that no money should be wasted on her funeral, should she die. Masses for her soul, yes, they must be asked for, paid for, but no mummers, no black plumes; and a simple wooden casket, such as every peasant somehow managed to afford. It would be brown.

More to herself than to Joanna she said:

'This is nonsense! You were so tired that you fell asleep on your feet and dreamed. Making such a fuss about nothing, about a dream! And if you are not hungry, I am,' she said, fighting off fear as she had done so many times before: she was thirty-four years old; women who did not die in their early child-bearing years often did later on, in their thirties; and the last months had been strenuous, the last ride not one that a woman so far advanced in pregancy should have attempted. But if she died, she died; God ruled; it might not be His wish that she should live and drive the Moors from Granada and send the Genoese sailor on his westward voyage. It was all in God's hands and she must leave it there. What was left to her own mere human agency was to see that this distressed child ate something and went to bed.

'Come,' she said, heaving her laden body up; 'you can share my supper if you promise, afterwards, to go straight to bed.'

Always the same, the lady governess thought sourly; the normal child, sound in mind and wind and limb was taken for granted, the less normal one pampered and spoiled.

Isabella, watching the child eat and become restored, even merry, thought about life and death, soldiers, children, the vast responsibility which lay upon a woman called upon to play a man's part in the world without owning a man's impregnable body. Tonight, tomorrow or perhaps the next day, she and the task she had to set herself, might end in the bloody and painful business of giving birth. But if so – the brown coffin – all the will of God, not to be questioned or disputed.

CHAPTER 2

The baby was born on December 16th and was a girl. Isabella was disappointed that the dynasty had not been reinforced by the birth of another prince, but since God in His infinite wisdom had given a daughter instead of a son, she accepted His decision with cheerfulness.

Her moment's superstitious fear, which Joanna's mention of a brown coffin had evoked, was not in the least justified; it was a comparatively easy birth; the baby throve and in a short time Isabella was on her feet again, resuming the duties of Queen, army commandant and mother. But while she lay in bed, recovering, she had time to think and some of her thoughts centred about Joanna who, at six, should now be outgrowing childish fancies. Princesses were born to a definite destiny, that of making marriages which bolstered political alliances and their characters must be trained for the purpose; to allow a king's daughter to grow up fanciful, wilful and unpredictable could make trouble in the future and was certainly not kind. Princesses must be stolid, placid, adaptable. Joanna might be steadied by responsibility; so, from the first, Isabella placed upon her some of the duties of caring for the new baby. 'If she cries, you must try to soothe her. When she is older you must amuse her. You must always think of her welfare and comfort before your own.' She intended the duties to be merely nominal, a means of occupying Joanna's attention, but Joanna, in whom there was a capacity for boundless, blind devotion, took them seriously and sometimes annoyed both ladies-in-waiting and nursemaids by her officiousness; sometimes there were complaints and appeals to the Queen who could always point out that in general Joanna's behaviour had greatly improved and that while she was fussing around the baby nobody else needed to.

Isabella had had an English grandmother, Katharine of Lancaster, and for her she named her fourth daughter; an act of sentiment rather than policy; England and connections with England – except in the way of trade – were worthless now. The Wars of the Roses had ravaged the country and decimated its nobility, and since August the country had been ruled by an upstart Welshman whose only claim to the throne was through his great-grandfather, a bastard later legitimised but excluded from inheriting the crown. There were men with better claims, there were pretenders and it seemed highly unlikely that Henry Tudor would be King of England for long. When Isabella, taking her brief rest, looked at her fourth daughter and speculated about her future she never once visualised her as Queen of turbulent England; there were steadier thrones. And in her heart Isabella still felt that this child, born in the very middle of a Catholic Crusade, might show a vocation for the religious life. Such things must be left to God; what must not be left to God, since He must not be bothered with such petty details, was the matter of rehousing twenty men lodged in a barn that had lost its roof in a recent storm; dealing with a soldier accused of rape, the non-delivery of a consignment of grain, promised from nearby Aragon, Ferdinand's own Kingdom. Tact must be exercised there; Ferdinand was still very Aragonese in his thinking; Castile was his because he had married her, Queen of Castile, but Aragon was not hers, even to criticise. Perhaps, when she was up and about again and capable of looking into the matter closely she could find, somewhere involved, a Jew who could be made culpable. Jews had no nationality; they could be blamed with impunity . . . There were dozens of such things to be seen to.

Katharine, as she emerged from baby to identifiable child, was, Isabella rejoiced to see, going to be pretty; not beautiful like Joanna who had a fragile, vulnerable loveliness of a flower, but pretty; she had clear large eyes, grey, tinged with green, her eyebrows were thin and arched, her hair, darkening from childish silver-gilt became brown, with a russet red shade in it, her complexion was fair and unblemished and she had inherited her mother's grace, and ability to look elegant without extraneous trimmings. Her temperament was as satisfactory as her appearance; less stolid than the Infanta's or Maria's, less volatile than Joanna's.

For Katharine, making every day another step out of babyhood into ordinary life, the centre and pivot of her life was, for years, Joanna, slavishly devoted so far as physical matters were concerned; she would change plates if her portion of any dish seemed preferable to that given to Katharine; for Katharine always the rosiest apple, the juiciest orange. From Joanna, Katharine received her first lessons, plodding away to learn things which Joanna had mastered in an hour. 'You are *slow*,' Joanna sometimes said impatiently and Katharine came to realise that, compared with Joanna whose acceptance or rejectance of everything was instant, she was indeed slow. 'But I never forget anything,' she said, not defensively, but humbly – offering her good memory as a sop.

The lessons, the lives, the food they ate, the beds they slept in were all subjected to the progress of the war. Isabella, intent to do her duty by everyone, to oversee everything, dragged her family along behind the army. The war went on; there were tedious journeys, uncomfortable lodgings, scanty meals. Always Joanna was there, presiding over Katharine's destiny not like a mother – Mother was waging war on the Moors – but like the good fairy in the stories which Joanna would tell on the long jogging journeys. Joanna was a wonderful storyteller, though sometimes her tales had a frightening element in them that would have scratched Katharine's nerves and made her afraid of the dark, of thunder and several other things but for the fact that Joanna herself seemed so fearless, and Joanna was always there.

The shocking fact that Joanna would not always be there broke upon Katharine on what was, apart from this revelation, a gay and glorious occasion, their sister Isabella's betrothal to Alfonso of Portugal. Isabella was so much their senior, and so sedate that she had played little part in their lives; but she had always been there, and soon she would not be; she would go to live in Portugal.

'You won't ever get married and go away, will you?' Katharine asked anxiously.

'Of course I shall,' Joanna said with a rapt look. 'I shall live in Burgundy, and in Brussels and Vienna. I'm looking . . .' she broke off, seeing Katharine's face. 'Not yet,' she said hastily. 'Years and years . . .' But Katharine was facing for the first time in her life the truth that no human relationship is permanent; she was already, in her mind, bereaved; so she wept with the noisy abandon of a five-year-old. Doña Elvira said sternly, 'What behaviour! Tears on such a day bring ill luck to the bride.' Katharine choked and blinked.

'Joanna, will you have me to live with you whenever you go?'

'I couldn't. You'll be married yourself. You'll have to live in England. In London.' That sounded somewhat meagre after Burgundy, Brussels and Vienna, so Joanna ferreted about in her mind and produced another place name. 'And Windsor, I think.'

'Oh. Oh dear. What a pity.'

'Yes, it is,' said Joanna, worldly wise at eleven years old. 'But, you see, there are four of us and you are the youngest . . .' That again sounded condescending, so she added, 'Your husband has a nice name though – Arthur; like the King in the book; the one with the Round Table and all the brave knights.' She had read the story in a battered manuscript from her mother's library and retold the tales, much simplified. Not that this English Arthur would be much like the one in the legend; for one thing he was a year younger than Katharine and said to be delicate and he had no breeding. Joanna had a sharp ear for gossip and had mastered the art of being unobtrusive if she chose; things had been said in her presence because she was not noticed or because she was regarded as too young to comprehend. She knew that the King, her father, had not much wanted a marriage alliance with England, and had rejected the first advances; then for some reason that she did not understand, all political, to do with France and Italy, he had changed his mind. It seemed that the King of England had been offended by the rebuffs and now demanded, with Katharine, a dowry that Mother said was extortionate, but admitted must be paid. It could be afforded once Granada was conquered and the war over. It could be more easily afforded because Joanna herself needed no dowry at all. The Emperor Maximilian planned to marry his daughter Margaret to Juan, at the same time as he married his son, Philip, to Joanna. So there had been a mutual abandonment of dowries. Joanna knew that hers would be the most splendid match of them all and she felt sorry for Katharine who would have to live in a small island where, when it was not raining it was foggy.

'And you'll be rich,' she said, still intent upon comforting Katharine. 'The King of England is very rich and very, very mean. When he dies Arthur will inherit a great fortune.'

She had no very clear idea of what a great fortune meant, and Katharine who was never to have any financial sense at all, understood even less. But it sounded nice, and young as they were, both little girls – like everyone else closely connected with Queen Isabella – knew what it meant to be poor. War was a costly business; cannon and cannon balls and chain shot, and gunpowder and scaling ladders and a hundred other things must come before new dresses or shoes.

'If I am to be rich,' Katharine said, 'I shall buy some horses, and come to visit you.'

'I will visit you, too. Though I shall not be rich. My father-in-law squanders and borrows and does not repay. Mother said so. But if I can get a horse I will come.'

It was typical of their upbringing that horses should be almost a standard of currency. They had spent more than one night in a wagon from which the horses had been unhitched in order to be harnessed to a gun carriage; they had seen knights in armour made temporarily as useless as tortoises because their horses had been killed. They had heard it said of a beleaguered city – And now they are eating their horses! A good sign; soon that city would yield.

War with its privations, its horrid sights, its occasional glories, its setbacks, was for years their natural environment because Isabella was conscious of her duty as a warrior and as mother. She never willingly allowed them to be in danger; she had them housed and fed as well as she could and gave them as much attention as possible. But she was engaged in what she regarded as a Holy War and that came first.

Lodged behind the lines, in places to which any man who might be expected to survive in order to fight on another day was brought and roughly cared for, the children became accustomed to the sight of maimed men, and dying men. The Moors had devices as yet unknown to the west. One of them was a thing no bigger than a pear, with a fuse of tow; this when thrown exploded and stuck to the object against which it exploded.

A knight in armour, hit by one of these things, could be roasted alive; or, hacked out in time, be horribly scarred. And there were men with hands and arms lopped off, men holding their bowels in their hands against the gaping stomach wounds. There were dead men too.

Katharine was still a child when she realised what a dead man meant. She had never seen Alfonso of Portugal, but he died, and Isabella came back to Spain, all muffled in black, pale and weeping.

Mother said, 'You must all be kind to Isabella; she has suffered a great loss.'

Joanna said, 'To lose a husband must be the worst thing . . .'

Katharine thought: And every dead man we have seen carried past meant as much to some woman . . .

It was a thought to put away, prickling and uncomfortable and not to be shared. Who would understand?

There was another thought, running alongside, more personal and immediate.

'Joanna, I cried that day in Seville and Doña Elvira said tears brought ill luck to the bride. Am I responsible for this?'

'How could you be, stupid one? Doña Elvira has a sharp tongue. Had you laughed she might have said the same. Men die when God wills. And you need not grieve for Isabella. I will tell you, but it is secret. You must not say a word. Promise. She is to have another husband. Alfonso's cousin, Manoel, who is now King of Portugal. *She* says she would sooner be a nun, but Mother thinks that by the time the arrangements are completed, she will have come to her senses.'

But what about all the other dead men and the women who wept?

There was little time for such thought. Granada fell, and Katharine stood, in her best dress, holding Joanna's hand and watched the last Moors ride, defeated, out of the palace-fortress of the Alhambra. And when the Te Deum had been sung in the building, only this day snatched back from Allah and Mahomet, they had the whole, fabulous fairy tale place to explore. Flowers and fountains, marble floors, terraces. A different and very wonderful world.

And then, in no time at all, another wonderful and amazing thing; a visit to Barcelona to welcome home the Genoese sailor, Christopher Columbus, whom Mother, despite all her other commitments had furnished out with three little ships so that he could go out and test his theory that the world was a globe and that by going west he could reach the east, the Indies.

'Nobody else in the whole of Europe,' Joanna said, gripping Katharine's hand hard, 'would give him a hearing, leave alone a ducat. Mother did. And she was right.'

So it seemed; the swaggering little Admiral believed that he had proved his theory; he had brought back specimens of strange birds and beasts, most of them stuffed, but monkeys and parrots still alive, and six wild brown Indians, painted and clad in feathers. Of the great wealth in gold and silver of the East he brought on this trip only sample quantities; but it was there. Spain would one day be as rich as Portugal; and since Spanish ships would sail to the west, while the Portuguese held to the old sea road around the tip of Africa, the friendliness between the countries would not be impaired.

Now that the main war was over – though the conquered province was far from completely subdued – a more settled and normal way of life was possible and Isabella brought attention to bear upon her daughter's education. They were more thoroughly instructed in academic subjects than most princesses of the time, and they must also learn domestic skills, spinning, weaving, plain sewing. Then there were the social arts, singing, dancing, playing the lute, doing fine embroidery, mastering the rules of precedence and etiquette, learning how to behave with grace and dignity even in trying circumstances. Joanna would be Empress one day, and Katharine Queen of England. They must be fitted for their high positions. For Maria no definite plans had yet been made, but she, too, must be ready for the position to which God would undoubtedly call her.

CHAPTER 3

With so much to learn and so much happening, time went all too fast and the thing which Katharine so dreaded, the parting with Joanna, came about. Joanna sailed away to Flanders to marry Philip. She went gladly, already romantically in love with the young man so well-favoured that he was called Philip the Handsome.

Katharine said gloomily, 'You are glad to go. Leaving me does not make you sad at all. The thought of parting from you breaks my heart.'

'Only because you are too young to understand. You will, in time. When you are fourteen, fifteen. Sisters love each other and hold one another dear, but that is not enough. Men and women belong together. Besides, there will be the visits to look forward to. Where is that map? Look, when I am in Flanders and you are in England, we shall be close.' She pointed to the seemingly negligible stretch of water.

'Mother never has time to go visiting.'

'Mother is different.'

Mother was now busy with the expulsion of all Jews from Spain; with preparations for Juan's wedding to Margaret of Flanders who was to set out at about that same time as Joanna left; and with arrangements for the widowed Isabella to marry Manoel of Portugal. But she had time to notice Katharine's glum looks, and as for everything, a remedy to suggest.

'There is no need to go about with the melancholy air. You will still have Maria.' The very close association between Joanna and Katharine had left Maria somewhat isolated, a fact which, when Isabella had time to notice it, had drawn admonitions. It was true that Maria was a self-contained child, inclined to be dull, but being always left out of things did not improve matters. 'What is more, you will soon have another sister, Margaret. She may be homesick at first and our ways may seem strange to her. You must behave to her as you wish Margaret Tudor to behave to you when you go to England.'

It was sound, sensible advice and kindly meant but Katharine spurned it. It simply showed how little grown-ups understood. For one thing nobody could ever take Joanna's place; and for another, if she made a close bond with Margaret there would be another wrench when she herself went to England. She would try to be kind to Margaret, to take a little more notice of Maria, and naturally she would continue to love her mother. But when she thought the matter over she decided that she would never wholeheartedly love anyone again until she was married. Men and women, as Joanna said, belonged together, and the husband-and-wife relationship seemed the only safe and durable one.

There was evidence of this before her eyes. Few people could be less fundamentally alike than her father and mother and sharp disputes between them were frequent. Partly this was the result of circumstance; it was all too easy for Father to accuse Mother of favouring Castile and all things Castilian and Mother to retort that she could say the same about him and his Aragonese. Yet all differences seemed to blow over; they continued to work together and plan together and as far as their various duties allowed, to be together. That was the kind of link with another human being which she craved; and she hoped that she would find it with Arthur Tudor.

Margaret arrived; she was pretty enough and gay – Mother said giddy – but with a gaiety quite different from Joanna's. She had not, by Spanish standards, been well-brought up and seemed not to mind; she made no secret of the fact that she thought the Spanish Court old-fashioned and dull and pompous. She decried even the Spanish dresses, complaining that they made it impossible to move one's arms. 'And is it necessary to move one's arms? One is not expected to go hay-making in a satin gown,' Isabella said coldly.

'When I am Queen I shall alter everything,' Margaret said to

Katharine. That sounded rather shocking. And on another day, Margaret said something even worse. 'The Queen, your mother, can afford to behave as though she had no legs. She can throw off these pompous rules whenever she is tired of them. She has only to start a war and she can dress like a man and enjoy a man's freedom.'

'The Queen, my mother, has never started a war in her life,' Katharine said fiercely. 'But, once involved she has never lost one.'

Since that could not be said of Margaret's father, the Emperor, the argument ended there. Yet, despite the fact that there was no great fondness between them, Margaret, indirectly, influenced Katharine in a way that possibly shaped her whole life.

The young couple had been married only a short time when preparations were made for the journey to Alcantara where Isabella was for the second time, to cross the border into Portugal. Katharine was to go with her father and mother, and two days before they were due to start she developed a rash. Smallpox, everybody said, except Mother, who, taking a look said, 'Nonsense. She has eaten something that disagreed with her.' Then, because everyone else seemed dubious and frightened, Katharine was wrapped in a blanket and carried into Isabella's bedroom and put on a couch, given a long drink of goat's milk, and presently fell asleep.

She woke to the sound of voices; Father and Mother in argument; one almost always knew because in dispute Father's voice grew shrill and sharp, Mother's deep and gruff.

'Don't say nonsense to me,' Father said. 'It is fact. Look at peasants, scraping and saving to get married at thirty, or soldiers who have to weather four or five campaigns. What they do in bed never hurts them; the young of the rich often die within a year or two.'

'Give me one example.'

'I could give a dozen. They're said to die of other ills; but the truth is they've spent their vital forces and so fall easy prey. You'd be well advised to bring the girl to Alcantara and give him a rest.'

'They would not agree to be parted.'

'They'd obey a direct order. You could say you wanted Margaret as part of Isabella's train. Promise her half a dozen new dresses.'

'Whom God hath joined let no man put asunder.'

'Give me patience! Who spoke of sundering them? All I say is, give him a rest. They're young and she's an insatiable bitch. He's thinner and paler and his cough is worse.'

'Then the doctors must examine him. And also give their opinion upon the other matter.'

'Is that not what I began by saying? Sometimes ... You are supposed to be an intelligent woman . . . I said, did I not, that Dr. de La Sa told me that in his opinion the marriage should not have been consummated for a year.'

'In less than a year I hope there will be a child.'

'There may well be. A child without a father.'

'Nonsense.'

'Will you not say nonsense to me? I am not one of your mercenaries. I am your husband.'

'You should remember that more often.'

Even inside the sheltering blanket Katharine felt the sense of danger threatening, something violent about to happen. But nothing did.

'Will you order Margaret to come with us to Alcantara?'

'No. And if you do I shall countermand the order. This is Castile.'

'Then if the boy kills himself . . .' Father said. She heard the rapid footsteps, the slammed door. There was a silence so deep that for a moment or two Katharine thought both her parents had gone. Mother could move almost soundlessly. Then there were hands, gentle about the blanket. Katharine pretended to be newly awakened. Such pretence she knew was the equivalent of a lie; it must be confessed and she would do penance.

'And how is the smallpox?' Isabella asked, peering closely.

The rash had vanished. Mother, as always, had been right.

But not about Juan.

That was the terrible fact which left its indelible stamp on Katharine's mind.

They were still making merry on the frontier; even the younger Isabella seemed happy again and restored, when word was brought that Juan, in Salamanca, was very ill, dying, dead.

'If the boy kills himself . . .'

After that things were never quite the same, Juan's death was, Katharine admitted to herself, to her a lesser matter than Joanna's departure because their lives had been less closely intertwined; but he was her brother, handsome, amiable whenever they met, and to think that anyone should die so young was sad.

It was sad, too, to see the effect upon Mother, the lightly silvered hair growing white almost perceptibly from day to day, the step heavier, the shoulders a little bowed.

For Spain, plunged into grief as it was, there was still a dynastic hope. Margaret was pregnant. Mother's wish for a child within a year seemed likely to be fulfilled. But the child was born prematurely, dead. Spain had no heir.

Then in Portugal, Isabella gave birth to a son who was named Miguel. That she died in childbed nobody seemed to notice much. Women, especially Princesses, were, Katharine reflected, like soldiers, expendable. Miguel lived for two years, heir apparent to Portugal and Spain. Then he fell ill of a childish ailment and died. Fortunately for everbody's peace of mind, just before he did so, Joanna, in faraway Ghent, had borne a son who was named Charles and who, if he lived, would inherit more territory than any other man in the modern world. Flanders, Burgundy, Austria, Spain and the expanding colonies in the west, in what people were beginning to recognise as a new world.

A new world was opening out, new ideas, some of them very strange, were spreading; but the old ideas still had power. One was that Spain and Portugal must be linked by marriage. The period of mourning for Isabella was hardly over before plans were afoot for Maria to take her place. Could Manoel marry his deceased wife's sister? Yes, if the Pope made a special dispensation. Couriers began to hurry between Spain and Rome and presently the necessary permission arrived. With the same solemn pomp as had twice accompanied Isabella to the border, Maria went to marriage and Queendom.

Katharine and her mother spent the next winter alone in Granada. Ferdinand had combated his grief at Juan's death by an increased activity and could usually contrive some good reason for being wherever Isabella was not. He blamed her for the boy's death and then, when his own sorrow eased, was displeased by her continued melancholy which he considered excessive. She never abandoned her mourning clothes, and now wore, under the black, the rough habit of a Franciscan nun.

In December 1500 Katharine was fifteen and it had been arranged that she was to leave for England as soon after her fifteenth birthday as the weather made travel possible and when the new year came found herself looking forward to the prospect of getting away and at the same time accusing herself of heartlessness. When she was gone her mother would be lonely indeed.

Nobody who was not forced to it would set out on such a journey in January or February and the March gales were notorious; but April came and May and Isabella's only mention of plans was a negative one; there was plague in the north and travel would be unwise at present.

'Would it not be possible for me to leave from Huelva? Or even cross into Portugal and sail from Lisbon?'

'You are so eager to be gone?'

'I am not anxious to leave *you*, or Spain. I dread the parting. But the Prince of Wales writes more and more impatiently.' Arthur wrote in Latin, good enough but less perfect than her own – a fact that she found touching – and he wrote how much he looked forward to her coming; he said he already looked upon her as his wife; he hoped that the gales would not be prolonged this year.

Isabella's Ambassador to England, Dr. Puebla, had also written, urging that the Princess should leave for England soon: the King of England mentioned the matter at every interview and seemed to be growing suspicious.

'I have been betrothed for twelve years,' Katharine said, as Isabella sat silent. 'And I must go, sooner or later.'

'Not unless you wish,' Isabella said, to Katharine's astonishment. 'I have been thinking. I want what is best for you.'

Katharine's heart gave a little jerk. A change of plan – which meant a change in political attitudes – at this late hour! And she so accustomed to regarding herself as Princess of Wales; so ready to love Arthur who was young, and sounded friendly. But there was nothing she could do. Princesses had as little say in their own destinies as hounds and horses. She waited for her mother's next words with breathless trepidation, remembering something that now seemed to have an ominous significance – amongst all the things she had learned English was not included. Had this withdrawal been planned all along?

Isabella stood up and began to walk about in a characteristic attitude, her fingers linked, tips upwards, her head bent, her shoulders hunched. Katharine rose immediately.

'Sit down, child. Sit down. Words come to me more easily when I am on my feet. The truth is, and I see it more and more clearly as time goes by, this is a false, hollow world and any woman is well out of it. I suppose that on the face of it I have been luckier than most. But I can say frankly that had I my time over again I should do differently. I should go into a convent and devote myself entirely to the worship of God. Would you prefer that to marriage?'

'Become a nun? Mother, I should hate it!' Too violent, too vehement. 'I have no vocation. I am not good enough. I try to be good, to love God and please Him, to obey the laws of the Church . . . But to take the veil . . . I never once thought about it.'

'Then think about it now . . . I am not trying to persuade you; I am offering you a choice that I think no girl in your situation has ever been offered before. An opportunity to abandon the world before it betrays you. As it will . . . it will . . . I know. I speak of what I know. Win a war and prepare for another! Here we are in the Alhambra but Granada is not subdued. Bear children, they die, or are sold away like calves. And men – I'll warrant that your father is now in some hunting lodge, with a fat peasant girl whose name he may know tonight but will not remember tomorrow.'

It was like seeing a great fortress crumble and collapse under the fire of culverins. Mother, a woman who had managed so well in a world made for and by men. Mother, indomitable, resourceful, proud.

But she is growing old, and I am young. I want to be married and have children. I love fine clothes and jewels, and music and dancing and gay company.

'Think about it,' Isabella said again. 'Of all my children you are most like me and for that reason I wish to spare you. I bore ten children, three are now alive. I sent Columbus out and what did it profit me? The whole thing ended in a sordid little quarrel over who should govern in a place that is not the India he thought to find. Child, there is nothing, nothing in *this* world that once taken in the hand is worth handling.'

Katharine was too young and uninformed to know that her mother was suffering from the menopause and singularly unfortunate in that it had coincided with the loss of a son, the death of a daughter and a grandchild and presently with a husband's infidelity.

She said, very gently, 'Mother, I think that those God chooses for a religious life, He calls. Had He called you the Infidel would still rule here. And I do not feel any desire to be a nun.'

'Then I pity you. You will have the whole world to deal with,' Isabella said.

Next day it seemed that this dispirited conversation had never taken place. Activity began; stuff for dresses, ladies and maids in waiting to be chosen, the silver plate and jewels that were part of the dowry to be selected and packed, the escort to ride with her to Corunna picked. Isabella, who wished that she had abandoned the world before it had a chance to betray her, saw to it that Katharine, going to face the world, went well provided.

She took with her, in coin and goods the worth of half her dowry, the other half was to follow; she took a household of sixty people including Doña Elvira who had been chosen as her duenna. She took twelve huge chests containing her clothes and linen.

She also took what she had been born with and what fifteen years had taught her. She was deeply, but not fanatically pious; she had a fixed aversion to war; she had the born Spaniard's Francophobia; she had a longing for a relationship that would be permanent; she knew that for a future Queen to bear sons was a matter of paramount importance. She went with hope and goodwill. She was healthy, pretty, accomplished and affectionate.

In bright summer weather the Queen of Castile's daughter set sail for England, and all the auguries were good.

CHAPTER 4

Henry Tudor rode towards Dogmersfield, a palace belonging to the Bishop of Bath, some forty-five miles out of London, at which, at last, *at last*, the Princess of Spain who was to be his daughter-in-law, had arrived.

It was now the second week in November, the weather was foul, the road deep in mire. Henry's mood matched the road and the weather. He was deeply suspicious about this whole business; it had been too long coming to the boil. The girl had been supposed to set out as soon as travel was feasible after her fifteenth birthday – that was eleven months ago; she had left Granada in May, sailed from Corunna in August, met with bad weather and needed the services of an English pilot from Devon to get her on her way again. She had landed in Plymouth in early October and been met, there, and at each stage of her journey, by the local officials and gentry whom Henry ordered to show her hospitality and every possible civility. The fact remained that no one had yet seen her, close to and face to face. There was a female official known as a duenna, a veritable tiger, who had so far managed to stand between the Princess and even the lords under whose roofs she had lodged; and when Henry had demanded of his own household steward, Lord Willoughby de Broke, sent to meet the girl at Exeter, 'Well, what is she like?' the answer had been, 'Your Grace, it would be difficult for me to say. She was so shrouded and beveiled in Spanish fashion. About so high.'

Henry knew that Ferdinand of Aragon was not to be trusted; in his mind he always thought of him as 'that fox beyond the Pyrénées', and he hated him because in those early, unsure days Ferdinand had shown, by his rejection of the first marriage offers that he thought little of England and had no confidence in Henry's ability to keep his throne. He'd changed his mind – but only because it suited him, and he had paid, or would pay, in good hard cash for that earlier hesitation; but it did occur to Henry as delay followed delay that Ferdinand might have outwitted him after all and sold him what he called 'a pig in a poke'. This Katharine was, after all the eleventh child, and any family of more than three was likely to produce one member in some way defective; since the betrothal was made this girl's brother had died, somewhat mysteriously; a sister had died in childbed and there were some very curious stories going the rounds about the sister who had married Philip of Burgundy, wrong in the head they said.

Whom to believe; what to believe? His own emissaries to Spain had reported favourably about the Princess. Deluded? Bribed? Well, he intended to see for himself; and if the girl had, as he rather thought she might, a hare lip, a squint, one shoulder or one hip higher than the other he'd turn her, her duenna, the vast expensive household which Spanish dignity demanded, back to Plymouth and though it was November that clever Devon pilot, what was his name? Stephen Brett – who'd brought her into Plymouth, could take her back. England was no longer in need of a Spanish alliance. It had been arranged, and he, busy with a thousand other things, involved with the complete reconstruction of a country broken by civil war, had let the thing ride. It was still a good match and the dowry he had demanded was something to be considered; but the keeping at a distance, the mention of veils and such flummery, alerted him. So despite the rheumatism which was beginning to trouble his bones, he rode out to see for himself; to interpose his judgment between Arthur and any kind of disillusionment. Arthur was already romantically and imaginatively in love with his Spanish princess and Arthur was so consti-tuted that if he saw her and she was maimed or infirm he would simply love her more than ever. Arthur was – his father admitted it – given to the most costly extravagance of all, pity. For Arthur always the lame dog. If the delay, which Henry believed to be a bit of Ferdinand's cagey policy, meant, as he suspected, that Ferdinand had hesitated to put his goods on the counter, it was better that Arthur saw the merchandise. Send Arthur, who was, after all, Prince of Wales, on an official errand that would take two days, and ride out to see for himself.

He swung himself, stiff and chilled, out of the saddle in the courtyard at Dogmersfield and was met by Doña Elvira and the Archbishop of Santiago, rigid as statues. He realised that his arrival, unannounced, unheralded, was no surprise to them; it should have been; but by now he was accustomed to the way that news could be spread. Let a tax assessor set foot in a village anywhere in England and the word was out, silver was whipped off sideboards and dropped into wells, pigs and cattle driven into the woods; a plodding peasant ploughing a field, tending sheep, or indoors nursing a broken leg could still, in some mysterious way, communicate with others of his kind and issue the signal, 'Danger.' He was not astonished to be met and greeted, very correctly; but he was annoyed, and his suspicions were deepened, when he was told that he could not see the Princess. Doña Elvira, in French – which he understood, having spent much of his youth in exile in Brittany – explained the rigid Spanish rule. Until the wedding, nobody, not even the prospective bridegroom, could see the bride unveiled. The Archbishop, in sonorous Latin, confirmed this.

Henry's mood splintered; despite himself he was impressed by Doña Elvira who did not look like a woman who would lend herself to a shifty trick, but then, wouldn't Ferdinand know that and select her purposely?

And he was aware of being a parvenue, ruling with a firm hand and sound good sense over a Court where such niceties of etiquette played little part, the stateliness of the English Court had vanished with the Plantagenets; he himself had no time for such rubbish, but confronted with it felt reluctantly that it was the product of an older and more dignified régime than his own. There was another thing too – the Archbishop spoke Latin as though he had been born to it; Henry's, like Isabella's, had been acquired for practical use only. Henry felt inferior, but only for a moment; he had come up the hard way and was a hard man. And he was King of England. He said it, addressing himself to the duenna,

'Madam, I am King of England. The only rules observed here are those I make myself. I wish to see the Princess.'

Doña Elvira turned to the Archbishop and spoke a few words in Spanish; he answered in the same tongue. Then she said:

'Your Grace, I deeply regret that it is impossible. The Princess is weary from her journey and has retired.'

'Then I'll see her in her nightshift,' Henry said. The best way, really; there were ways of padding clothes to disguise deformities.

They looked shocked and stunned. Then the duenna said:

'It will take a few minutes,' and rustled away. Henry moved to the fire where his wet clothes began to steam. He was on his own ground, the Archbishop, in a sense, his guest; he knew that he should make some attempt at conversation, but had no intention of exposing his faulty Latin any more than was absolutely necessary. For a second he regretted not having brought some of *his* clerics with him; Cardinal Morton, Archbishop of Canterbury, was a match for any of his kind in the world.

Doña Elvira opened the door of the adjoining room, and made a sign, curtseyed as Henry passed her in the doorway, and stood aside.

Katharine curtseyed, too. Henry, without speaking looked at her, closely and calculatingly as though she were a horse he had been offered in sale. The gauzy, voluminous veil which had so far defeated curious English eyes, was thrown back away from her face; her shoulders and hips were level, in fact she stood well, holding her head high; there was no blemish on her face, not even the sallowness associated with Spanish blood, her complexion was fair, a clear pink and white; her eyes were grey, shy yet quite steady under his deliberate, assessing stare. For a girl not yet sixteen she was very well grown, somewhat taller than de Broke had indicated.

Relief and delight swept through him; a proper, royal Princess; if he'd had her made to his own specifications, he couldn't have been more satisfied. In the English fashion he leaned forward, kissed her cheek and said, 'Welcome to England.'

He saw that the phrase was meaningless to her. You'd have thought that in twelve years, knowing she was destined for England, they'd have seen that she learned English. He repeated his welcome in French: and that she appeared to understand, for her face lighted with a smile and she inclined her head a little; but she said nothing and the horrible suspicion struck him that there might lie the truth; poor girl, she was dumb! That would never do; such afflictions ran in families, imagine the next heir to England being dumb, unable to hold his own in a Council Chamber.

He half-turned and shot a question at Doña Elvira: 'Can she speak at all?'

'The Princess of Wales,' the duenna said frigidly, 'is taken by surprise at your insistence to see her . . .' Her black eyes raked Henry from top to toe, his filthy, muddy riding clothes, still faintly steaming, the ancient battered hat awkwardly snatched off under his arm. The words *and by your appearance* hung on the air.

'My French deserted me, your Grace,' Katharine said, recovering it. She had learned it from her sister-in-law. 'It is most kind of your Grace to ride so far and in such bad weather in order to welcome me in person.' She smiled again and Henry smiled back at her. The smile changed his face entirely, rearranging the harsh lines which determination, anxiety and self-discipline had engraved on his weathered skin. They took, in that moment, an odd liking to one another.

Henry was no sentimentalist and his imagination in some respects was limited, but he realised that the girl would wish to see her bridegroom, not her father-in-law.

'Arthur may arrive this evening,' he said. 'Or he may not. He had a longer journey and the going is foul. But he is eager to see you – as I was – and will ride hard.'

'I look forward to our meeting,' she said, and smiled again. As with Henry the smile made a difference. In repose her face inclined towards the solemn and the effort of recalling her French made it rather more solemn, just as it stiffened her diction. But smiles were interchangeable currency. Smiling, Henry said:

'I'm hungry. You must be too. I'll clean up a bit and then we'll eat roast beef together, eh?'

'That will be most pleasant, your Grace,' she said.

Roast beef was the national dish; it could only be eaten in a country where there was so much rain that there was enough grass to nourish cattle all through the summer, so that they could grow to maturity. In places where pastures were dry and scorched by mid-May calves must be either slaughtered, or starve to death and were brought to the table as veal. The English obviously thought very highly of roast beef; it had been served at every place where she had stayed since her arrival in Plymouth.

But this evening the roast beef had a different flavour because of the company in which it was eaten.

Arthur arrived within the hour. It disturbed Henry to realise that had his worst suspicions been well-founded, he would have only an hour to work in; he'd counted on twenty-four hours at least. As it was, all was well. He was able to take the hand of his son, the hand of the Princess from Spain and bring them together with complete satisfaction. In Arthur the Yorkist and Lancastrian blood ran side by side, unifying England; in his bride ran the blood of ancient royalty; brought together they would found a dynasty the like of which England, the like of which no country in the world had ever seen.

In their rather stiff little letters to one another Katharine and Arthur had made vows of love and each was in love with the idea of being in love; now, brought face to face, they felt a mutual disappointment. Katharine thought: 'Oh, but he's a mere child; Arthur noted with dismay that she was at least five inches taller than he was. He had known that she was a year older, but on the whole females were smaller than males and he had hoped for a tiny bride. He consoled himself by the thought that she was very pretty, in all but those extra inches, the princess of every boy's dreams; and perhaps she had finished growing while he might any day begin to shoot up. It was not the first time that he had been made aware of his lack of stature; his brother Henry, four years his junior, was almost as tall as he was, and a great deal more sturdy.

Both of them, inwardly ashamed of their disappointment, took great pains to be pleasing, and paid one another compliments in Latin, and made little jokes and laughed, all under the King's pleased, benevolent eye. Arthur was both intelligent and well-educated and Henry felt a self-made man's pride in his son's accomplishments, was pleased to think that the boy's upbringing had been so different from his own. And the fact that Arthur was small and slight and took small interest in weapons and their use did not matter much; he would never be obliged to fight for his crown. The turbulent era was over; the boy would inherit a united England, at peace from border to border. Nevertheless, the thought occurred to the father, as it had occurred before: it was a pity that *physically* his two sons could not have changed places; Arthur, who would be King, had the physique of the churchman, Harry, destined for the Church, was plainly built for kingship. 'That great boy,' as his father called him in the frequent moments of annoyance, was as much too large for his age as his brother was too small; not overgrown, a word that suggested lankiness or awkwardness, Harry was beautifully proportioned, was already an excellent horseman and a useful performer in the tiltyard as well as in the tennis court. Arthur was mild-tempered; Harry in a rage was something to see. Now and again Henry felt that his second son would find his priest's vows of continence hard to keep, but this was all part of the plan. The whole business of the Wars of the Roses went back to the fact that Edward III had several sons, who had most of them had sons, a too great a proliferation of putative heirs in any emergency. Henry did not intend to have his Tudor dynasty go by that road. Arthur was heir; Harry would be Archbishop of Canterbury and any child he sired – some clerics did have children – would be smuggled away into obscurity.

After supper Katharine – without consulting Doña Elvira – asked Arthur if he would like to see some Spanish dances. He said eagerly that he would. Dancing was not a pastime that he enjoyed, but he liked watching it. So the room was cleared and some musicians found and Katharine danced, in Spanish fashion, with one of her ladies, Maria de Rojas, as once she had danced with Joanna. Henry, watching and applauding and approving thought – And they said she was so weary she had gone to bed; one cannot believe a word they say.

Doña Elvira, supervising Katharine's disrobing, apologised for the intrusion upon Katharine's privacy, using the apology as an opening for the expression of her displeasure.

'One has always been given to understand that the English were without manners. That their King should be such a boor I did not expect. Coming into this room in a state that no mere courier in Spain would dare to present himself.'

'I think it was because he already looks upon me as one of his family,' Katharine said. Rallying from her disappointment she had enjoyed herself that evening, had basked in Henry's approval and in Arthur's admiration, had felt curiously free and gay for the first time in years.

'If that is so,' Doña Elvira said sternly, 'he is wrong. Until the final benediction upon your marriage has been pronounced neither he, nor his son, should have seen you unveiled; and certainly they should not have been invited to watch you dance.'

'That was my fault,' Katharine admitted; but something had taken possession of her; the result of the air, the rain, the roast beef? 'They came to welcome me and I wished to please them. And I did.'

She had pleased them, and she was glad. She could, she felt, afford to ignore Doña Elvira's carping and criticism. In a few days she would be a married woman; she would not need a duenna . . .

In a few days she was married, in circumstances of such pomp and splendour and lavish expenditure as London had not seen for many years. The King of England knew that he was regarded as parsimonious, and if that was the word applied to a man who disliked waste of money, very well, he was parsimonious and to hell with those who used the word deridingly. But, like many miserly people, when he wished to spend he spent with élan. Delighted with the prize which his son had drawn in the royal-marriage lottery, he hurried back to London, issued orders, opened his purse. Katharine walked to her wedding in St. Paul's along a great platform, hung with fine red worsted cloth, so that she was in full view of all the throng. Leading her along by the hand was Arthur's brother, the Duke of York, called Harry in the family to distinguish him from his father.

He was ten years old; six years younger than she was, four and a half years younger than Arthur of whom, at first meeting, she had thought: Oh, but he's a mere child; but although Harry was maybe an inch shorter than Arthur, he bulked larger in his white satin suit, trimmed with gold; and he had an astonishing confidence of manner. Ten years old, a child, performing one of his first public official duties and doing it as though he had done it twenty times, fifty times before.

He took her hand in his. With that attention to some irrelevant detail that is possible in moments of nervous tension, she noticed that he had well-shaped hands, with square palms and long fingers. The one that held hers gave signs of rough usage, the skin peeling away from what had recently been blisters in two places and one knuckle badly grazed.

They stood for a moment, alone at the end of the elevated platform, with the eyes of the massed congregation upon them. The space they must walk to reach the end, where another, transverse platform bore the King and the Queen, the Lord Mayor of London and the priests who would officiate, looked endless.

'Your hand is very cold,' Harry said in his excellent Latin. 'Are you afraid?'

'A little,' she confessed.

'There is no need to be. They are only people.' The hard brown hand tightened on hers reassuringly. 'All we have to do is keep in step. Now, left foot first . . .'

It occurred to her that he enjoyed being looked at and admired; but the calm ease of his manner and the clasp of his hand restored her confidence. At the end of the platform he released her hand, made a low bow and stood back, watching with bitter, unchildlike envy while his brother Arthur and the pretty Princess were made man and wife.

Why had he not been the first-born? He knew – it was impossible that he should not know – that he was in every way more suitable to be King one day than Arthur was, or ever could be. Arthur was shy with people, whereas he, disdaining most of them, got on well with everybody; Arthur was always tired, his own energy was boundless: Arthur was inept at games and sports, he was good, and intended to be better: Arthur was so retiring that even now, on his wedding day, he cut no figure at all; the one whom all these people would remember, and talk about afterwards was the Duke of York who would never have a wedding of his own. The second son, destined for the Church.

He bore no grudge against Arthur, of whom he was fond and towards whom he often extended a somewhat condescending protectiveness; his resentment was against Fate; Arthur should have been the second son, or a girl – he'd have made a splendid girl. Harry had been obliged to comfort him over this night's business, which Arthur confessed to dreading. 'That public putting to bed, all those lewd jokes . . .'

'You need only to laugh. And then . . . think of afterwards. It is said to be . . . not unpleasant.'

Arthur, dreading the preliminaries, dreaded the afterwards even more. He was in love with his pretty, amiable bride, but, in the secrecy of his heart, he admitted, not in that way. To talk to, walk with, sing with, confide in, spoil a little, a special kind of sister who would belong to him and never be given away in marriage. Still, he realised that he was caught in the dynastic mill and must just do his best as occasion rose.

After the long and exhausting ceremony, there was the ride to Baynard's Castle, properly cleansed and aired, and with a great bed with fine new hangings set in a chamber spread with rushes brought all the way from Suffolk and unique in that when trodden upon they emitted a pleasant odour. The bedding procedure was preceded by a feast, interrupted by music and singing and the antics of dwarfs and jugglers. Most people, by the end of it, were a little tipsy: in the maelstrom of noisy merriment the Prince and Princess of Wales sat in a small patch of quietude and Katharine saw Arthur begin to wilt. The flush was still on his smooth cheeks, but it had contracted into patches, almost circular, on each cheekbone; the rest of his face was chalky white except for smudges of fatigue below the eyes.

She said, 'It will not be long now, Arthur,' and realised that this would-be comforting statement was open to misinterpretation. 'I have seldom been so tired in my life,' she said, exaggerating. She knew then that had it been her fortune to have for a husband a man, full grown, strong and tough, the Arthur of the stories, she would now be entertaining very different feelings; a little fear perhaps, but a pleasurable fear, a looking forward to the culmination of a wedding day, the great day in a woman's life. As it was she knew that towards Arthur her feelings were maternal; she, the mother, merely wished to get this bone-weary child to bed and see him fall into a recuperative sleep.

The moment came at last; the bawdy jokes, the hearty good wishes all done, the curtains drawn round the great bed, the room silent and the well-trampled rushes giving up their scent. Katharine remembered how sometimes, towards the end of one of those long journeys across Spain, Joanna, playing the mother, would put out her arm and pull the sleepy head on to her shoulder. How comfortable it had been.

She did the same thing; putting her arm around the slight, tense, too-hot body, cradling the golden head on her shoulder, kissing the brow — a little alarmed to find it so damp.

'Sleep,' she said. 'Sleep well, my dear one.'

He said, 'Just for a little. The crowds and the noise . . . I revive as quickly as I tire; I have great recuperative power. If I close my eyes and lie still for a few moments . . . all will be as it should be.'

'All is,' she assured him. She felt him go limp.

She lay awake long enough to think how like, in build and colouring, Arthur was to her brother Juan — though Juan, being older than she was, had never seemed like a child to her. And Juan had exhausted his strength, killed himself, over the business of getting Margaret with child. Father himself had said so, accusing Mother, anxious to blame in his first grief. That, she made up her mind, there and then, was *not* going to happen to Arthur. They would wait. With this decision made, being young and healthy and tired, she fell asleep herself.

They both slept until morning. Arthur, conscious of having failed in his duty, apologised, thus endearing himself to her even more. Poor child! She told him — and there was apology in her voice, too, of her overnight thoughts; she pleaded the case of Juan and Margaret: 'We are married,' she said, 'nothing could make us more so. Nothing. But we should wait.'

Nothing could have suited him better; the warm intimacy of the shared bed, the scent of her hair; the status of being a married man . . . and all without the thing which he did not yet want to do, did not yet feel able to do. A sister who was more than a sister.

'But they will know,' he said, 'and mock me.'

'This is between ourselves; who could possibly know?'

'Those who make the bed,' he said miserably, aware that his comfortable, shrouded place was not the whole of the world, 'I think . . . I have been told . . . they will look . . . there should be a little blood.'

Nobody had told her that. How astonishing!

'Yours? Or mine?'

'Yours.'

'Those who come looking shall find what they seek,' she said. She pushed back the bedcurtains and reached for the knife which lay beside the dish, piled high with apples and pears on the side table. Not her hand, that would show; her foot. She jabbed at her heel, judging that to be the less sensitive part.

The first bedmaker to witness this proof of deflowering thought: 'What a lot! But they're different to us, them Spaniards!'

Arthur, completely reassured because his pretty princess understood him so well and was the other self he had always longed for, moved a farther step away from the reality of life, his position and his duty and threw himself into the part. When the first gentlemen, a bit thick-headed and bleary-eyed, cautiously opened the door of the marriage chamber, he called to them, before they did anything else, to bring him something to drink. 'Marriage is thirsty work,' he said.

The Prince of Wales was expected to keep Christmas at Ludlow. Katharine had not been alone in remembering her brother Juan and Margaret. There was a suggestion that she should remain with her father-and mother-in-law and that Arthur should go to Ludlow alone. But that seemed a cruel decision to make; the two young people were so plainly in love; Arthur seemed no worse for his marital exertions. So they left for the west together and Arthur enjoyed showing Katharine the romantic, still almost untamed country whose title they bore, and she told him about Granada, Madrid, Corunna. He promised, with the wild west wind howling about Ludlow, to build her, one day, a palace the equal of the Alhambra, the tender plants, the orange and lemon trees all under glass.

Then, late in March, coming back from a meeting of the Council – a thing of pretence, a sop to Welsh pride, all major decisions being taken at Westminster – Arthur said that his head ached and that his throat was sore. It was nothing, he said, he would be better in the morning, but he allowed himself to be persuaded to go to bed, with a cup of hot, well-spiced wine to drink and a hot brick at his feet. He had a restless night, alternately shivering and sweating: in the morning his fever was high and his doctor bled him in the left foot and advised that he should have nothing to drink since liquid encouraged the sweating. Denied so much as a sip of water, Arthur still sweated and burned and shivered, and through an endless day Katharine sat by the bed, holding his hand, stroking his head, replacing the covers his tossing disarranged. The doctor padded in and out with a pill to be swallowed, a plaster to be applied; he bled the patient from his right arm; he was aware of his heavy responsibility, this sick boy was the King's son; no effort must be spared. He wished that this had happened in London, where he could have called upon colleagues to share the burden – and if things went wrong, the blame. There was a doctor in Ludlow, but he himself had the sweating sickness, which had been rife in the town for some time.

In the evening Arthur asserted himself, perhaps for the first time in his life.

'I will not die of thirst,' he said in a low croaking voice. 'I want some water, cold, straight from the well.'

'My lord, you must not . . .'

The Tudor temper flashed. 'It is not for you to tell me what I must or must not. I want cold water and I want it *now*!'

Katharine herself held the cup for him, urging him to sip slowly, now and then moving the cup away, 'Enough, darling, enough,' but his hot damp fingers closed on her wrist, 'More. I could drink a gallon.'

When, two days later, the heir to the throne lay dead, the doctor attributed his death to the drinking of cold well water and if asked to give the *true* reason for the Prince's demise, would have said, 'his own wilfulness'. But such things could not be said to Kings, about the sons of Kings. He dismissed the whole business of the sweating sickness and the gulping of ice-cold water from his mind; the courier who set out on the 3rd of April to carry the news to London, was instructed to tell the bereaved father and mother that their son had died 'of a consumption'.

Katharine was in no position to dispute the verdict; smitten down by the same sickness – her head had been aching and her throat very sore when she held the water to Arthur – but in a different form because she had more vitality and made a series of recoveries, suffered a series of relapses. She was still in bed and very weak when Arthur's coffin, so light that it seemed to confirm the verdict of a consumption, a disease which wasted, was carried out of Ludlow and by easy stages to burial at Worcester. It was May, warm and sunny, when in her widow's garb she set out for London and the world where the death of a boy had changed everything.

CHAPTER 5

The King of England said, 'Surely, the most preposterous suggestion ever made. It would take that fox, Ferdinand, to put forth such a proposal of bare-faced robbery. Is he mad? Send her home with that half of her dowry that has been paid; *and* pay her her dower rights as Dowager Princess of Wales; that is a third of the revenues of Wales, Chester and Cornwall. And what the wedding cost me . . .' He thought furiously of the fountains spouting wine, the food for all comers, the prizes for the jousting, the complete refurbishing of Baynard's Castle. And all for what? A marriage that had lasted four months. 'To this,' he said, slapping his hands on the paper, 'I shall never agree.'

Cardinal Morton, whose financial genius had made his King the richest monarch in Europe, said:

'I am inclined to think, Your Grace, that this proposition was not intended to be taken seriously. When Dr. Puebla took it from his pouch there was another paper – you know how they interfold – which he stuffed back hastily. And he looked very sly.'

'His eyes are so set that facing a loaf of bread he would look sly. If this is not a serious proposition, what is it? Apart from being something any brigand would blush at?'

'I can only think, Sire, that the intention was to shock so that another proposal, perhaps equally shocking, but in a different way, might seem acceptable. That is my guess. I cannot know.'

'If anything could be as shocking as this, but different, I should be interested, very interested, to see it. Have him in.'

Dr. Puebla came in. He had been the Spanish Ambassador to England for many years; he had negotiated the betrothal between Arthur and Katharine. He was a Jew and though it might seem strange to other people that Isabella, busy driving the Jews from Spain, should maintain one as her chosen representative in a country of growing importance, Dr. Puebla did not find it strange at all. When, because money was needed for other purposes, his salary was not paid, he never whined or grumbled; in a free busy town like London, any man who was conversant with law, could stand on his two feet and had the use of his tongue, could make a living. In lean times he had supported himself and his staff; and he had a modest little fortune, every penny of it honestly made, safely tucked away. And he was clever.

He came in, bowed very low to the King, less low but low enough to the Cardinal.

'This, Dr. Puebla,' Henry said, tapping the paper again, 'is a ridiculous proposal.'

With a nice mingling of surprise and reproach in his tone, Puebla said:

'I am grieved that Your Grace should think so. It is in accord with the terms of the marriage settlement.'

'We then visualised a long marriage and the Princess's revenue being spent in England, to the benefit of the country from which it derived.'

'The circumstances are sad indeed. But – if I may say so – it was not the fault of Princess Katharine that her married life should be of such short duration.'

'She is now sixteen years old. She could be drawing this vast income for the next fifty years!' The thought agitated him.

'The purpose of all marriage settlements is to provide for the female, whatever circumstances may arise.'

'She is a pretty girl; still young; very amiable. She will marry again,' Henry said brusquely. 'You may inform your master that I – more generous than he – will excuse him the payment of the other half of her dowry. With that in her hand she will make some man a very desirable wife. And that is my last word on the subject.'

Dr. Puebla took a swift, almost imperceptible glance at Cardinal Morton's face. The Cardinal gave a slight nod of the head. It is the last word.

'Men set such ridiculous store by virginity,' Dr. Puebla said plaintively. 'The Princess is all that you say . . . but to put it coarsely, she is now secondhand. However, I will inform my master, and Queen Isabella, of Your Grace's decision.'

He hurried away to the large, ancient, draughty house in the Strand where Katharine and her suite were now installed. It was called Durham House because it belonged to the Bishop of Durham who never used it, having other and more comfortable residences. Puebla hoped to avoid any meeting with Doña Elvira whom he disliked as much as she disliked him, and who was now back in full charge of the Princess and her household, and this he managed and made for the apartment of Father Alessandra, Katharine's confessor who had been with her at Ludlow.

'It is,' he said, after a few preliminaries, 'a question of Her Highness's future. I suppose there could be no doubt that the marriage was consummated?'

'That surely is a question that should be put to her duenna. Once the Sacrament of Marriage has been performed marital acts are not subject to the confessional – and even if they were they would be under the seal.'

'But you know, as well as I do, that Doña Elvira would not tell me the time of day correctly.'

'Nor me. She has such a jealous and domineering disposition that she wishes to be High Highness's duenna, controller of her household, her confessor and Spanish Ambassador, all in one.'

The mutual enmity made for a feeling of fellowship between them.

'You cannot help me then? The question is of some importance.' The second paper in his pouch, unread by anyone but himself, was concerned with the importance.

'Naturally, I have heard things, in the ordinary way,' Father Alessandra said. 'I do not go about with my eyes and ears shut. You may take it from me that the marriage *was* consummated.'

'Oh dear.'

'You sound displeased, Dr. Puebla.'

'It makes things a trifle more difficult. And the poor boy was so young, so frail.'

'He was married. He would recognise his duty. And so would the Princess.'

'Yes, yes, of course. Naturally.'

Dr. Puebla hurried away to write a letter to Spain, telling Ferdinand and Isabella that their first suggestion had been rejected out of hand; and that he had it on the best authority that the marriage between Katharine and Arthur had been consummated.

He had slightly exceeded his duty. Queen Isabella, like Father Alessandra, felt that such a question should be left to Doña Elvira.

Katharine had been glad enough to escape from the strict, sharp-tongued woman with her insistence upon strict Spanish etiquette. After the exceptionally free life at Ludlow as a married woman, it was hard to be obliged to return to tutelage and supervision. But Isabella in a letter expressing sympathy – though sorrow came to all – after urging her daughter to be brave and resigned to the will of God, had added that she was to place herself entirely in Doña Elvira's hands and never to forget that a young widow must be even more discreet in her behaviour than an unmarried girl.

'Your Highness,' Doña Elvira said one day. 'There is something which I should know. Are you with child?'

Blushing, Katharine said, 'No. Would that I were.' Sometimes it seemed to her that restraint had been mistaken; poor Arthur with so short a time to live; and a baby would have been something . . . 'I know what you think, Doña Elvira . . .' The blush deepened. 'Remember, I was ill. I was bled every day, sometimes twice. The rhythm was disturbed. I am sure that this month . . .'

'Did you and the late prince of Wales live together as husband and wife?'

'How can you ask that? You know that we were hardly apart for an hour from the moment we were married until . . . he died.' She was still in a weak, morbid state and her eyes filled with tears as she thought: Oh, poor little boy, poor little boy; he promised to build me a palace like the Alhambra; he had so many plans for the future.

'Then how can you be so sure that this disturbance of rhythm is due to your indisposition,' Doña Elvira asked, pressing her point home.

Katharine was now crying.

'He was so young; and not sturdy. I remembered my brother and what was said when he died. So . . . so we agreed to wait. It was his wish, as well as mine. We said a year . . . And now, notwithstanding, he is dead. And he was so kind and clever and amiable, the child would have been . . . like him . . .'

It would also have been heir to England and you as his mother, would have had status; your future would have been assured, Doña Elvira thought, almost annoyed by Katharine's ignoring of the *real* situation. Unworldliness in others always affronted her. Still the information which she had extracted, was satisfactory; men set such a ridiculous value on virginity. She hastened to write to Queen Isabella. She wrote in good faith; after all virginity was a physical state, capable of investigation and proof or disproof and when Doña Elvira wrote, 'She shared a bed with a sick boy and is still as virgin as when she came from the womb,' she was certain that she was writing the truth.

Katharine, immured behind the double screen of mourning and etiquette, almost her only visitor her mother-in-law, Queen Elizabeth, ailing and prematurely aged and heartbroken over Arthur's death, totally ignorant or oblivious to what was going on in the wider world, was spared all knowledge of what was going on outside the walls of Durham House. She knew that her confessor, Father Alessandra, had been recalled but she did not know that he was recalled in disgrace because he was the originator of the story that she and Arthur had been man and wife in fact as well as name. Dr. Puebla – to Doña Elvira's immense digust – was not recalled; he was far too useful.

Nobody told Katharine anything; she lived in a muted world. Even to stand by the window and look into the Strand where life went on, busy, avid, noisy and colourful was, by Doña Elvira's decree, ill-advised; a widow should show no interest in the outer world; or play cards; make or listen to any cheerful tune or even to seem to enjoy her food.

On the farther side of the double screen arrangements, the ultimate result of which none of the arrangers in their wildest dreams could have envisaged, were going on. The day came when Dr. Puebla produced, for the inspection of Henry and Cardinal Morton, Ferdinand's and Isabella's alternative suggestion – a marriage between Katharine and the boy who was now Prince of Wales.

'Agreed to,' Dr. Puebla said, touching the King in his most vulnerable spot, 'this would ensure that the half-dowry, already paid, remained in England and also the revenues to which, by law, the Princess is entitled.'

'It would also involve a vast amount of legislation,' Henry said, tempted, but cautious. 'She was Arthur's wife. A Papal dispensation would be necessary.'

'Such a dispensation was obtained, Your Grace, when Princess Maria of Spain married the King of Portugal, formerly wedded to her sister who died.'

'She is almost seventeen years old. My boy is twelve. In view of what happened to my elder son I could not consent to any marriage for Harry until he is sixteen. Dr. Puebla, the ages are too disparate.'

'The Prince of Wales – the late Prince of Wales – did not die of overmuch exertion in the marital bed, Your Grace. Nor of the consumption often associated with such activities. I beg you to forgive me if I speak frankly. I have gone into this matter. He died of drinking water, cold from the well, when the sweating sickness was on him. And the marriage was never consummated. I admit that once I thought otherwise, but I was misled. The Princess is a virgin. She is by law entitled to the half-dowry, already paid; and to her revenues under the marriage settlement. A most enviable match for any man. Even – permit me to say it – for the Prince of Wales, so different from his brother, at twelve almost a man.'

He had hit Henry in his next most vulnerable spot. The King, who was also a father, had been almost ashamed of the pride he had felt, since poor Arthur's death, in presenting Harry to the people. This boy never tired, was never upset by what he ate, was never shy or reticent; was able, it seemed, to endear himself without effort to great nobles, sober tradesmen and humble peasants alike. It was sad about Arthur, but he was safe in the keeping of God and perhaps it was as well that he was out of a world in which he had never seemed really at home; Harry was better equipped to assume the burden of monarchy which Henry nowadays sometimes felt to be heavy.

'The fact remains that he is only twelve,' Henry said curtly. He was not disposed to take this second proposal too willingly; the terms of the first had been too harsh. 'I will agree that a dispensation be applied for. It may not be granted. In the interim I think that the Princess should renounce her revenue rights. I shall allow her . . .' he hesitated, reckoning swiftly; she had a ridiculously large suite, 'a hundred pounds a month. That should pay her household expenses and anything over she can spend on fripperies.'

Not ungenerous, Dr. Puebla reflected; though the value of money was rapidly depreciating. It was paradoxical; the Spanish galleons now beat their way from the New World which Columbus had discovered almost by mistake, and they carried much silver, some gold, some precious stones; the wealth of the world appeared to have increased, but a pound bought less than it did even a year ago, and there were times when he thought: If this goes on what I have gathered and hoarded against my old age will barely suffice. Perhaps Henry, King of England, felt the same about his stored-up fortune.

'I will inform my master, Your Grace. A moratorium upon the dower revenues, in return for an allowance of a hundred pounds a month. And, if the Pope grants the dispensation, a betrothal between the Prince of

Wales and the Princess.'

The two people most nearly concerned in this bargaining were not consulted or informed directly; but the knowledge seeped in. Katharine thought: Another child; more waiting; even if Julius gives the dispensation, I shall be over twenty when I hold my first child in my arms; twenty was, by Spanish standards, old. But it was her mother's and father's wish that she should remain in England and wait, and she recognised their authority.

The Prince of Wales, still very busy adjusting himself to the change in his future, saw himself as peculiarly blessed. Even the beautiful Princess from Spain, the possession of whom, God forgive him, he had once envied poor Arthur, would one day be his. One day . . .

The waiting time was not, even for Katharine, completely dull. Once her period of mourning was over she was welcome at Court and went to Greenwich, Richmond and Windsor, to take her place as third lady in the realm in brave style, even though her dresses had to be furbished up and her attendants were growing shabby. Her allowance did not permit any expenditure on fripperies and the table at Durham House was often sparsely set.

The position of first lady was Elizabeth's, that was indisputable, she was Queen of England; in next order of precedence Katharine should have held place; but there was the old – and now hideous, though people said that in her day she had been beautiful – Countess of Richmond, the King's mother; jabbing the stick between which she leaned to relieve her lameness into the floor as though she were piercing an enemy, she always forced herself forward.

'It is entirely wrong,' Doña Elvira said. 'Your Highness should assert yourself more positively. That old woman was never Queen, or Princess of Wales. It is against all the rules that she should precede you as she does.'

Katharine said, 'But she *is* old and to her it matters. Whether I go second or third makes no difference to me. I enjoy the occasions.' To a more sympathetic hearer she would have mentioned the items that she had enjoyed; but Doña Elvira would have said again, as she once had, 'I fear that Your Highness has a frivolous mind.' The remark had been wounding: to herself Katharine admitted that she liked the massed candles, the gay music, the brightly coloured clothes and sparkling jewels, enjoyed the food, especially after a spell of short commons in Durham House. Am I frivolous? We made merry at Ludlow and there was no rebuke. Is it wrong to be happy for an hour? To be happy for an hour in a world where – let it be faced – happiness was a rare commodity and misery abounded; the blind and crippled begging at every street corner;

unwanted babies flung out to die – nuns of the Franciscan Order set out regularly between nine o'clock and midnight to collect the abandoned from rubbish heaps. In such a world was it wrong to snatch an hour's joy?

And it was not that one lacked personal cause for grief. On Candlemas Day in the year 1503, Queen Elizabeth bore the child about whom she had, throughout her pregnancy, spoken to Katharine. 'I had two sons; one for the Throne, one for the Church. Arthur died and Harry's future was changed. I hope that this child will be a boy and live to take what was Harry's place.'

'I hope so, too. And I will pray . . .' Katharine said.

But the child was a girl, hurriedly christened Catherine, the English version of Katharine's name, which was a compliment. Nine days later Elizabeth and the girl child she had borne were dead. Elizabeth died on her birthday; she was thirty-seven.

The Court was plunged into mourning; and from this mourning the King never truly emerged; there were no more festivities which Doña Elvira could deem frivolous; and within a month or two Katharine realised that the King's demeanour towards herself had changed. He could no longer afford to support her in a separate establishment, he said. In future she must regard herself as part of his Court; and since accommodation was everywhere limited, her suite must be much reduced.

It astonished her to learn how many of her Spaniards had been homesick, staying on this alien land, this abominable climate out of loyalty to herself. She tried to push the thought aside, but it would intrude, that a few of them had come with her in the hope of position and power, and instead of receiving the rich pickings which a Princess of Wales could be expected to have in her gift, they had been relegated to live meagrely, to be ill-clad and to shiver in ill-heated rooms. She was not sorry to say goodbye to her duenna.

With the King so low in spirits and his parsimony growing, life had few glittering occasions; an exception was the ceremony of her betrothal to the Prince of Wales. The necessary dispensation for their marriage was to be granted – though it would take months to arrive.

She felt that the occasion justified a new dress, and chose blue velvet, the low cut, square neckline and the sleeves edged with embroidery in silver thread and studded with pearls. She was eighteen years old and absurdly anxious not to look old to the eyes of her bridegroom-to-be, or to the eyes of the beholders; she was glad to think that since her arrival in England she had not grown in height; Harry had grown enormously, so much so that this time when he took her hand and they stood side by side, their two heads, so similarly russet, were almost level. And the fashion of the day made the boy, bulky as he was, seem even more full-grown. Tunics were padded, especially about the shoulders and sleeves, and then slashed, as though they were at bursting point, the insets of a contrasting colour. Harry on this day wore white satin, slashed over gold, and his confidence, his curious facility for attracting attention, to woo and at the same time appear to be unconscious of the crowd – as he had said, 'they are only people' – made him the focus for all eyes.

His hand was broader and harder, but still warm and steadying and this time the touch of it held a possessiveness. This is ridiculous, she told herself, a boy of twelve! But something that had never moved in her before woke and stirred. She crushed it down; later, at the banqueting table, where they were seated side by side, it reared again, when he said:

'I beg you – forgive my lack of years. No man can choose his date of birth. Could I have chosen mine I should now be twenty; and ready to take you to bed forthwith.'

She blushed hotly and he laughed; the blue of his eyes hard and brilliant as enamel between lashes that were thick, but short and bristly. On his upper lip, cheek and chin, there was a reddish golden fuzz.

'They say four years,' he went on, 'but if I can persuade the King, my father, it will be less.'

He was a little beside himself. There was something heady in the thought that the will of God and the will of Harry Tudor were in such accord.

After this satisfactory if rather disturbing meeting, they saw each other seldom. The Prince was often out of London, entertaining, or being entertained. The King grew grumpier and more miserly. More than once Katharine was made painfully aware that the second half of her dowry had never been paid and that this was resented. Two of her ladies-in-waiting, who had remained in England because marriages loomed, needed the dowries which they had every right to expect, even from a Dowager Princess of Wales. Where was the money to come from? Katharine suggested selling or pawning some of her silver plate and jewels, but Dr. Puebla said that would be unwise since they constituted part of the half-dowry that had been paid. She wrote to her mother, not a letter of complaint, but a statement of her situation, and added the comment that it was a long time since she had a letter from her. Weeks later when the news came that Isabella was dead, some remorseful tears mingled with those of grief. In retrospect the calm, dispassionate letter looked like one long grumble.

Isabella of Castile had died worn out by worry and work. She had achieved much, but not enough. She had known for some time that her days were numbered – and when she died Spain would be divided again. Joanna would inherit Castile, and some very disquieting stories had reached her concerning her eldest surviving daughter. Joanna's passion for her husband, Philip the Handsome, seemed to amount to mania. His infidelities maddened her; she had attacked one of his mistresses with a pair of scissors and would have killed her if not prevented. A dog of which he was particularly fond she had killed, because he caressed it. What kind of Queen of Castile would she make? Isabella was concerned, too, for Katharine. On what was to be her deathbed she was shown a copy of the Papal dispensation, legalising the marriage between Katharine and the young Prince of Wales. Satisfactory? It was what had been requested; His Holiness had granted the request and it was not for a good Catholic to question. Yet she did. Had too much attention been paid to material things; to financial arrangements? to the trade treaty that was part of the marriage contract? She had always been obliged to be practical; in her earlier years had delighted in managing, contriving, outwitting, out-bargaining. And now it all seemed a waste of energy . . .

Isabella died and, far away in England, Katharine felt her death, first as a grief and then, in its repercussions, as a damage.

The nub of the matter was that Ferdinand did not propose to hand over Castile to Joanna and her husband without a struggle and since he must prepare for war he could not afford to pay the now long overdue half of Katharine's dowry; this displeased Henry; so did the fact that the privileges and concessions granted to English traders in Spain were withdrawn without warning; so that a crowd of English sailors and merchants came back from Seville declaring that they were 'all lost and ruined'.

At the same time, the Emperor Maximilian, seeing that his son Philip and his daughter-in-law might have to fight for Castile, began looking around for friends, and making advances to Henry of England. Philip and Joanna had a daughter, Eleanor, nearer in age to the Prince of Wales. How would it be if a marriage were arranged between them?

Henry studied this from all angles; there was the matter of age; the fact that a dispensation had been necessary for the betrothal between Katharine and Harry; the fact that Eleanor's father would inherit the widest territory in Europe – and probably be elected as Emperor, as well. As a father-in-law far more desirable and useful than foxy Ferdinand.

The result of his deliberations was a deterioration in his treatment of Katharine; she was still attached to the Court but no longer part of it and in every place to which it moved, her accommodation became worse and less suitable to her rank. She was seldom invited to take part in any ceremony or share any festivity and she never saw the Prince of Wales at all. She was even poorer than she had been at Durham House, and but for the fact that Dr. Puebla liked her and considered her badly used, so that he spent his own money on comforts, she would have had no wine on her table, and sometimes no fuel for her hearth.

On a cold evening in December 1505 as they rose from the supper table, Henry said to Harry, 'I wish to talk to you.'

'Now, Sire? We were about to dance.'

The question was just one more small sign of the not-completely filial behaviour which Henry had observed lately. The boy now fourteen and a half, almost full grown, was beginning to have a will of his own; and of course he was spoilt, everywhere deferred to because of his rank, his good looks and his accomplishments. In the old days boys of his age would have commanded their own armies, Henry remembered; Harry could not be ruled like a schoolboy much longer. Tonight he must be.

Henry said, 'You can dance later,' and led the way into a small room where a great fire burned. The close warm atmosphere was suitable to the ageing man with his thinning blood, oppressive to the young man who, given permission to sit, unbuttoned his tunic and loosened his collar, revealing his thick muscular neck.

'Philip of Burgundy and his wife are coming here next month,' Henry began.

Harry imagined that he knew why. His marriage to Katharine was to be brought forward and they were coming to attend it.

Henry's next words were a shock. 'They are coming to discuss the possibility of your betrothal to their daughter, Eleanor.'

'But I am betrothed already. To Katharine.'

'That can be got round. I no longer regard it as a suitable match for you.'

'In God's name, why not?'

'If you ask properly, you may be answered,' Henry said crushingly.

'May I ask why not?'

'Ferdinand is no longer of importance. If he tries to keep Castile he will have to fight for it. When he dies Joanna will inherit Aragon, too. A firm link with Philip will be advantageous.'

'How? May I ask in what way?'

'A useful ally.'

'England needs none,' Harry said proudly. 'It is they who need us.' And would do, more and more, when he came into his own and could spend some of that hoarded treasure on fitting out armies and restoring the navy, now a pitiable affair of rotting old hulks.

'And it could be good for trade.'

The intensely blue eyes blazed. Harry said contemptuously:

'Huckster talk! And where does it lead? Katharine and I joined hands, and there was a trade treaty. Broken immediately. The marriages of Kings should not be concerned with the sale of a few ells of cloth! To my eye the best cloth – the best chamberpot for that matter – will find its own market, regardless of who marries whom.'

Yes, Henry thought – but not altogether without pride – there speaks the boy who has never lacked; never gone without his supper in order to have his horse shod, or his sword tuned, or a hinge in his armour mended. We work and plan and set them up and then they look down from the place where we have put them and call us huckster.

'You throw my one bad bargain in my face. Think of the dozen good ones I have made. For England. For you. Think of this. The most powerful ruler in Europe will be your father-in-law; you will have a *young*, and I believe beautiful, bride, and a marriage whose legitimacy can never be questioned.'

'Who would dare to question this one? His Holiness gave permission for Katharine and the . . .'

There was something about the way in which he said her name.

'A betrothal can be cancelled. Now listen to me. You will stand up before witnesses and solemnly declare that your present betrothal was made when you were too young to know what it was about; and that now that you do know, you refuse to ratify it.'

The moment of outright defiance, foreseen by the father, had come.

'I will not do it,' Harry said. 'I knew what I was doing when I gave Katharine my hand and plighted my troth. And I stand by it.'

The King rose, went to the hearth and kicked a log into place and then stood, back to the fire, his shoulders hunched.

'Katharine,' he said, very slowly and distinctly, 'is my widowed daughter-in-law. Her dowry was never fully paid; she is my ward and my pensioner. *Mine to dispose of.* Must I wear the crown day and night to remind you that I am King of England? If you are going to talk and behave like some lovesick shepherd boy, dispose of her I will. I'll marry her myself if needs be.'

Old, almost fifty, round-shouldered, shrivelled and with a cough! In bed with, married to, the pretty Princess from Spain. Revolting.

But have a care. He is King of England.

'I should hardly have thought that, unfit as a bride for me, she would be fit for Your Grace. And another dispensation would be needed.'

'They are easily come by, these days.'

'And what must I do to prove that I am not a lovesick shepherd boy?'

'Stand up and renounce your betrothal. Privately. No need to inform the world as yet. And look and act agreeably when Philip and I discuss the possibility of marriage between you and his daughter. That at present is all that is required – except a little more awareness, Harry, that I am your father and anxious, in all respects, to do my best for you.'

To capitulate too easily, having said, 'I will not do it,' might give rise to suspicion. And worse than that it might reveal what was in one's mind. And his mind was set like stone.

'I know,' he said, giving his most charming smile. 'And I suppose I have much to learn about betrothals and treaties and the political game in which they are used as cards. I am learning now what heirs from birth learn while they are still lisping.'

Disarmed and reassured, Henry said, 'Go to your dancing, boy.'

Harry went, away from the music, towards his own apartments; loitering and scowling.

Then, holding his right wrist with his left hand, he went into a room where a yawning page waited.

'Tom, can you handle a pen at all?'

'I am reckoned to write a good clear hand, Your Highness.'

'I strained my wrist at tennis this afternoon. Sit down and write, and make it plain. Begin: Matthew, my good friend . . .' It was a letter such as any young man might write to another; news of himself and of London; mention of the fact that Philip of Burgundy and the Queen of Castile, sister to the Princess of Wales, were coming to England: unwisely choosing January for the Channel crossing. 'Now,' he said, 'take a new line. Write—You may in the next few weeks, hear some strange tales. Take nothing to heart. Between you and me all is well and ever shall be, as I hope shortly to show.' He paused.

'Thank you, Tom; that is all.'

'Is it writ to Your Highness's satisfaction?' Who knew? A page who could write might become a scribe, a secretary.

'Very well done. I can make shift to sign and seal it. You may go.

Left alone he took his knife and cut off the part of the paper that held the genuine message; then he cut from the rest four words of Katharine's title. He folded the half letter and applied the wax lavishly, pressing the slip that bore her name into the wax and testing that it held. It was a very necessary communication, but it must be anonymous. Women tended to hoard and cherish things; to show letters to other women; or leave them lying about. He wished Katharine to be reassured; but he had no intention of provoking his father into keeping that truly shocking threat. He had a feeling that she would understand; she might even – and he smiled at the thought – finding the message where he intended to place it – think that it had fallen by some miracle.

Katharine found the letter in her place in chapel next morning. She did not open it. Before you approached God or put yourself into a position in which God could approach you, you must empty your mind of all distractions and mundane matters. Her mind was already distracted by the news, heard overnight, that Joanna was coming to England. The girlish promise, given long ago, was, after all, to be kept.

To Arthur she had described Joanna and spoken of her desire to make a visit to her sister and to be visited by her. Arthur had understood, as he understood everything, and planning for the future he was never to know, had included the visits in his plans. All his plans had gone with him to the grave.

Katharine, a widow, with no assured position and little money could not go visiting, or extend invitations. But now Joanna was coming. At last there would be someone to talk to without any reserve. Katharine had two very devoted ladies, still, but it had always seemed to her to be lacking in dignity to discuss with them the petty humiliations to which she was subjected, or her shortage of funds, or even the fact that she was never allowed to see the Prince of Wales, to whom she was, after all, betrothed. To Joanna she could tell all these things; Joanna was older, cleverer, might be able to advise her; might even lend her some money.

When she opened the letter she was puzzled. There was no signature; the writing resembled none she had ever seen. She recognised the goodwill in the message; someone wished to reassure her; there was also a hint that soon she would hear something calculated to disturb her. She did not connect this with the coming visit, for it was common knowledge that Philip and Joanna had been negotiating with Henry about the marriage of their son, Charles, to his daughter, Mary Tudor. They were coming to complete the talks in person, and to discuss the accompanying trade treaty. And how could that affect Katharine? 'Between you and me all is well . . .' The only person between whom and herself there was anything that she could think of was the Prince of Wales; it was not his writing and he would have signed his name.

The Court, including Katharine, moved to Windsor and waited. Philip had chosen one of the worst months of the year for a Channel crossing and the voyage had been hideous. Some of the escorting vessels were wrecked, and when the royal couple finally landed at Melcombe Regis Philip was certain that he had been spared from drowning only because at a crucial moment he had vowed that if he lived he would give his own weight in silver to two religious houses.

He arrived at Windsor alone: Joanna he said was so ill and exhausted that she was unable to travel. Actually they had had one of their most virulent quarrels and she had refused to accompany him.

Katharine, admitted to the ceremony of welcome, waited for a moment and then approached Henry:

'Your Grace, I ask permission to go to Melcombe Regis, to see my sister and help to tend her.'

Before Henry could answer, Philip said:

'That would be *most* inadvisable,' with so much emphasis that both the King and Katharine looked at him with startled enquiry.

'She may already be on her way. She is not seriously indisposed.' Nothing wrong with her except bad temper! 'She has great recuperative power. And it would be a pity if you missed one another on the road.'

With a tenacity towards her own ends that she hardly ever displayed, Katharine addressed herself to Henry.

'I should need only two horses. I would take my own man, Francisco Filipez.' Expense need cause him no concern. But Henry had heard the emphasis in Philip's voice and said:

'No, no. It would be better for you to wait here in readiness to greet her.'

There was no more to be said.

Katharine waited. Joanna did not come; nor did she send any message. Worried by the silence Katharine repeated her request to be allowed to set out, and this time Henry could plead, with some truth, the inclement weather and the state of the roads. He had now learned from Philip how *most* inadvisable it would be to allow the two sisters to meet before Joanna had come to her senses and given in.

'And,' Henry said to Katharine, 'I could ill spare you. On an occasion like this a Court needs a chief lady.'

There was some truth in that. Henry had thrown off his melancholy and, once again, his parsimony. For ten days Philip was royally entertained. Outside the great grey pile of Windsor, snowstorms obliterated the daylight, substantiating Henry's argument that Joanna was weather-bound somewhere and that if Katharine set out she would be weather-bound too; but inside great fires and thousands of candles blazed and there were feasts and games and dancing. Young Mary Tudor showed her skill with the lute – a skill largely acquired from Katharine; and for the first time in many months Katharine found herself in the company of the Prince of Wales whose manner to her was polite but exceedingly formal – except on one occasion when, commanded by the King, she and Maria de Moreto had given a display of dancing in the Spanish style; the same dance that she had performed, years ago, with lighter feet and a lighter heart, at Dogmersfield, under Doña Elvira's cold and disapproving eye.

Harry jumped up and said, 'I would like to try it. Show me.'

Philip and Henry, who in the intervals had had long, entirely satisfactory talks, could well afford to sit and laugh.

The true style of Spanish dancing could not be acquired in ten minutes and Harry seemed to be out of his element; clumsy. It involved the minimum of physical contact and for that reason woman could dance with woman and man with man. But under cover of the music Harry said, 'Believe nothing that you hear . . . old men sit in corners and plot.' And then, having set everybody laughing, he called to the musicians:

'Enough. This is no dance for me.' He stood still and held out his hand.

'I thank you for your patience with me. One day I shall do better.'

The same warm, reassuring clasp and a glance, no more, from the intensely blue eyes.

'My Lord of Burgundy, I yield place to you,' Henry said. Philip of Burgundy stood up and came forward. Harry went and sat by his father.

Old men sit in corners and plot. Perhaps to the Prince of Wales Philip of Burgundy seemed old; but he was only twenty-seven, handsome and vigorous; and ten days of jollity, out of his wife's ambience, with everything going well, had given a patina of happiness and self-confidence to his physical attractions. Katharine thought, dispassionately, that if Charles, off-spring of Philip and Joanna, inherited a tenth of his parents' charm and good looks, Mary Tudor could count herself fortunate.

On the tenth day, coincident with an improvement in the weather and exactly twenty-four hours before Philip was due to leave, Joanna arrived.

Any other woman, so pared to the bone, would have been hideous; there were hollows in her cheeks and at her temples and her hands, held to the fire, looked transparent; she contrived to be breathtakingly beautiful. Her eyes, greener than Katharine's, had a feverish brilliance; her skin was like cream satin, her mouth as red as rosehips. Even the King of England who at fifty seemed to be an old man, stared at her with admiration and responded to her animated chatter with smiles.

Her husband watched this display of charm with some apprehension; Joanna's moods were unpredictable and could change more swiftly than the wind. In the tossing ship she was the one person who had shown no panic at all; she had crouched at his feet, her arms around his knees, saying that she did not mind drowning so long as they drowned together: a few hours afterwards she was screaming abuse at him and refusing to set out for Windsor. However, ten days' separation had been as much as she could bear and that she had come at all seemed to hint that she had changed her mind on the subject over which they had quarrelled. He could only hope that she would not let slip something indiscreet.

'And is this,' Joanna said, looking around with a shiver, 'the best that that old goat can do for you?'

Katharine, accustomed to inferior accommodation, looked around as though seeing her bedroom for the first time.

'This is not so bad as some of my lodgings. At least it has a hearth. Sit here, close to the fire. Oh, I have longed to see you; and now the time together is so short. I wanted to come to where you were, but for some reason the idea found no favour.'

Joanna's eyes glinted.

'And I suppose Philip said, every day, that I should arrive tomorrow. Running after him like a bitch cringing on its belly; begging to be forgiven. I always have, in the past. But this time I stayed away ten whole days; to show him that I could live without him.'

'Then you were not . . . not really ill?'

'I am never ill; at least not in the ordinary way. I suffer from one mortal complaint – its name is Philip of Burgundy. I longed to see you, Katharine, of course I counted every wasted day . . . but we had such a quarrel.' She put up one delicate hand and pushed back her hair and looked distraught. 'Did you and . . .' For a horrified second she had forgotten the name of the boy Katharine had married '. . . Arthur ever quarrel?'

'I thank God, no. Never an unkind word.'

'No time,' Joanna said. 'Philip and I had a year, a wonderful year. Then he ceased to love me and began to torment me. Deliberately. He is a fiend, Katharine, a fiend.'

To Katharine he had seemed to be a handsome, good-humoured, rather bovine young man, anxious to please and easily pleased.

'And lately I have had to be so careful,' Joanna went on, lifting her hair again. 'Because now he is trying to get rid of me. He is so clever. He thinks I am blind. But I know. I see through him. He wishes to drive me mad; he would like me to be shut up in one of those houses where nuns act as gaolers to the demented. Then he would have Castile, a new mistress every week and his damned hounds. So you see, I have to be very careful. At that place with the strange name – Melcombe Regis? – he took me by surprise and put me in a rage. But I held out ten days. That should balance things.' She laughed: and again pushed her hair back: the gesture was as regular and as meaningless as the twitch that affected some people's eyes and made them seem to be winking. And the laughter, like the accusations, had a hollow sound. This was not the Joanna to whom Katharine had planned to talk, of whom she meant to ask advice, and perhaps borrow money. When she was not speaking or smiling or laughing, Joanna wore a look of settled melancholy. She had always tended, Katharine remembered, to extremes, too easily exhilarated, too easily downcast.

It was difficult to know what to say; yet something must be said.

'Are you in such good health, Joanna? You are very thin. When one ails one tends to take to heart things that are not important. This notion that Philip is ill-intentioned . . . I thought he greeted you with great affection.'

The green eyes narrowed and glinted.

'He was relieved to see me. He knew that this time he had gone too far. Also he was anxious to placate me.' That gesture again. 'Listen; I will tell you what happened at Melcombe Regis. Then you can judge of his intentions. I will name no names. There is a person of whom I am very fond, but we have not met for years and my life has been very full and to be honest the person had become a name, little more. Some time ago, in the midst of many other plans and arrangements – you can have little idea of what one is called upon to deal with and consider, Philip mentioned, quite casually, something which would affect . . . this person, in a most damaging way. I made no protest; I may even have agreed; it is sometimes difficult to remember.' The hand went to the hair. 'It was not, in any case a plan likely to come to anything. Then . . . we had, as you will have heard, a terrible voyage. I forced myself to calm, but I expected to drown at any moment and at such times one looks back over life and remembers. I realised that this person was very dear to me. While I was feeling thus – we were no sooner on land and our clothes changed – Philip spoke again of his plan and his determination to carry it out. I did protest then; I said I would not be a party to it. *And* I saw what he was trying to do – so to upset and torment me that I should behave like a lunatic in England, in front of English witnesses. He has often said that I am mad and should be locked up – but those who know me well do not agree with him. I have friends . . . but not in England . . . You see in these quarrels he speaks soberly, he says *terrible* things in a soft voice, with a smile sometimes. In itself that is maddening.'

And so, did you but know it, is that regular movement of hand to hair.

'I cried, I went on my knees and beseeched him not to do this thing. He took no notice – he never does. Then I said that I would prevent it. I am Queen of Castile *now*, he as yet is only Duke of Burgundy. And then he said that if I moved a finger or said a word he would never sleep with me again. Knowing how I love him, he said that to me. And I said I would not come with him to Windsor. To love someone who does not care a fig for you is a very terrible thing, Katharine. I pray you may be spared it. But – there again; Philip says only the Devil would heed any prayers of mine . . .' Abruptly she began to cry, as unrestrainedly as a child, but bitterly.

So beautiful, so lively; so rich in worldly goods; and so unhappy. For whether Philip were actually unkind or not she believed him to be, which was almost as bad.

Katharine dragged her stool near to Joanna's chair and put her arm around the frail, sob-shaken figure.

'Cry on my shoulder,' she said. 'Perhaps things will look better now that you have told somebody.' Perhaps Joanna also lacked somebody in whom to confide completely. *I* meant to tell her things which I could tell no one else; but what have I to tell? Little slights, lack of money, a sense of having been relegated. Nothing.

Presently she said, 'You have your children, darling.'

'They are *his* too. To dispose of as he likes.' Joanna lifted her head and gave Katharine a peculiar look. 'I am never allowed . . . not even over Charles' riding. His pony was far too fat – in Flanders they are – and his legs grew more and more bowed. I said he should not ride for a year; or have a less fat pony. Philip just laughed and took him riding for hours every day. Now he will be bow-legged all his life – and none too tall to begin with. And of course, Charles thinks that I tried to interfere with his pleasure and when Philip says that Eleanor is the most beautiful girl in the world and I say that it is not a thing to be said to a child, vain enough already, she thinks I am decrying her. So they love their father and hate me, and would be glad to see me shut away.'

More than the report of the quarrel at Melcombe Regis – a nameless person whom Philip planned to damage and Joanna tried to protect, just possibly someone of whom Philip had cause to be jealous? – this telling of domestic bickering showed just how unhappy this seemingly promising marriage had proved to be. After thinking it over, Katharine said:

'Perhaps it ill becomes me to say because what I have been called upon to bear is by comparison nothing; but if you could be calmer, Joanna. To become excited; to laugh and cry too readily, to show rage . . . it never serves. I have found . . . I know that my experience has been different . . . but with the little humiliations over the dowry and other things, I always say to myself: You *are* Princess of Wales, behave with dignity. You are so much more. You are Queen of Castile and if you could cultivate calm even Philip, if his intentions are as bad as you suspect, would pause. He would have no ground . . . do you see what I mean?'

'Calm,' Joanna said using the word as though it were the name of some vice. 'You speak to me of calm!' The last tears had vanished from her eyes which gleamed with positive malice. 'Now, show me. Let me see how calm you can be when I tell you that you were the person over whom Philip and I quarrelled ten days ago at Melcombe Regis.'

She jumped up and went to the far side of the hearth, hugging herself with her arms and looking dangerous, and desperate and mad.

'But you said, just now, that Philip planned to damage . . .'

'And is it not damage to propose that your betrothal to the Prince of

Wales should be ignored and that he should marry our daughter, Eleanor?'

Katharine remained calm, so calm and still and so deathly pale that Joanna thought: I have killed her; she will fall from the stool. Fright banished hysteria and she ran forward and knelt, holding Katharine by the shoulders.

'I should not have said it. Katharine, forgive me. I was against it, I begged and implored . . .'

'You were right to tell me,' Katharine said.

'But not like that. Not as a taunt. You see. You said calm and I thought . . . There are times when *I* think I am mad.'

Her hands were very hot. Katharine shrugged herself away from their clutch.

'Sit in the chair, Joanna. I need no support. I am not even much surprised.' Her voice was firm, though her lips were white. 'I have felt, for some time, something wrong. The way I have been treated. This explains . . .'

It explained the unsigned letter in an anonymous hand; it explained that warm, reassuring handclasp. Harry was young, in no position to defy his father; but he had wanted her to know: 'Between you and me all is well and ever shall be.' I thank you for your patience with me. One day I shall do better.'

'There will be,' Joanna said eagerly, 'another match for you and you can trust me to see that it is a good one . . . someone suitable and agreeable. And Katharine, I do beg you, I beg you urgently, say nothing of this. He said that if I made a sign or breathed a word he would never sleep with me again. And that I could not bear. The last ten days . . .'

'Trust me. I shall say nothing. I shall wait.'

Joanna, with another lightning change of mood, said:

'You spoke of calm and assuredly you have set me an example.'

It was one by which she had little opportunity to profit. Within a few months Philip the Handsome was dead and the brown coffin was a reality. It was of bronze.

Their last months had been spent in Castile, where, because Joanna was rightful Queen, and beautiful and capable – if she set her mind to it – of charming all comers, Philip had deferred to her, and stayed close, not flaunting his infidelities and not taunting her. The brief time of revived happiness made her grief the worse. She refused to have the coffin lid fastened down. Wherever she went it went, in a litter carried by horses all draped in black and with black feathers on their heads; about it monks, in relays, chanted. And at each stopping place, all over Castile, where the rightful heiress had come to show herself to the people, the lid of the coffin must be lifted and Joanna, who should have been asserting her rights, wooing partisans and reminding everyone that she was Isabella's daughter, knelt, sometimes weeping, sometimes praying, but more often staring in a kind of wild ecstasy upon the great handsome man, now a corpse, embalmed but deteriorating, the husband who was now hers, and hers alone.

It was Ferdinand, her father, who finally, not without cause, had her put away into a house where nuns acted as gaolers for the insane.

CHAPTER 6

Katharine waited. Nothing happened and nothing was said. In June 1507 Harry had his sixteenth birthday and the time for their marriage had arrived, if the contract were going to be honoured. After that hope dwindled; there seemed no reason why she should not spend the rest of her days as Henry's unwelcome pensioner, poorly housed, shabbily dressed, sometimes so short of food for her household finally she was obliged to pawn the plate and the jewels that were supposed to be part of her dowry. The other half was never paid. She wrote repeatedly to her father, who never answered. An ambassador who espoused her cause and told Ferdinand that his daughter's circumstances did little credit to Spain, was sharply told that it was Castile's duty to pay the rest of the dowry, Aragon could not be held responsible.

Sometimes she thought that honour was a virtue that had vanished from the earth; her own betrothal had been ignored; there was now talk of Charles' betrothal to Mary being broken so that he could marry a French princess whose dowry was Brittany; and Henry VII, prematurely old and in failing health, had professed himself willing to marry poor Joanna, 'mad or not'. It was a wrong-headed world and perhaps she was as well out of it; often left behind now when the Court moved. She sewed a great deal, read, observed her religious duties scrupulously, made music and played cards with the members of her small household.

The spring of 1509, coming in with the early flowers and the young leaves on the trees and the cuckoo calling, found her at Greenwich. The Court had moved to Richmond.

Only the King knew that he had gone to Richmond, his favourite palace, the place with which he had once shared a name, to die. Everybody knew that he was in ill health and had a troublesome cough and little appetite; what else was wrong with him he kept to himself having lost faith in physicians who, for all their nostrums, purgings and bleedings, had not cured his cough. He intended to die if he could arrange it, without their troublesome attentions.

From Richmond he unobtrusively made preparations for death. Throughout the length and breadth of England there were religious houses, once flourishing, now fallen into decay, with three or four old monks or nuns controlling and mismanaging hundreds of acres, potentially valuable, or drawing the revenues of country markets, levying tolls on bridges. The wealth could be better employed and in a few days the King, aided by Wolsey, his Almoner, and watched by his son, gave the order for the funds of several to be diverted and used to build a great hospital in Bath and to provide daily alms for the poor in chosen places. There was a touch of miserliness, as well as good commonsense about even these final charities. But he said, privately to Wolsey, that he wished ten thousand Masses to be said for his soul, and paid for out of his personal money; and in order that other prayers, freely offered from gratitude and goodwill should be said on his behalf, he ordered a general gaol deliverance, a pardon for all those who had broken his laws.

And even so, Death caught him unawares. April the 21st was a beautiful day, warm as June and dry; his cough was alleviated, his heart laboured less; even his secret symptom which he had taken such pains to conceal, seemed slightly abated. He told himself that this morning he felt well enough to have the serious talk with Harry which he had been deferring from day to day. So, having despatched the morning's business from his bed, he was helped into his old robe and slippers and sent for his son. As usual his eyes brightened at the sight of him.

'Lend me your arm, Harry, and I can make shift to walk in the garden. It is such a fair morning. And I feel better.'

'I am glad to hear it,' Harry said; but he offered his arm with reluctance. His father's arm had grown thin as a stick, and though he frequently complained of feeling cold, his skin held an unnatural heat. His coughing fits were distressing – but digusting too, producing quantities of mucus. And lately there had gathered about him a curious odour, the smell of age and decay. Harry had an inordinate hatred of anything less than perfect health, perfect form. Many men of position had dwarfs and freaks about them constantly and seemed to find them amusing, he was revolted by them; and if, as often happened, amongst the crowds which he loved – and who loved him – there was at the forefront a blind man, or a cripple or a man lacking a limb, he would, after a glance, look away. 'Give him a shilling and tell him to stand back.' Decrepitude repulsed him too. He had a poet's susceptibility linked to a vast egoism; brought face to face with any proof that a man could not be strong and healthy, handsome and young forever, the one cried, 'No! No!'; the other whimpered, 'Me too? One day? God forfend!'

But he offered Henry his arm and suffered a whiff of what he privately called the smell of old dog. Through his own padded sleeve and the sleeve of the robe he could feel the contact of the sharp bone, and soon the heat, against his own healthy flesh. Old, sick men, he thought, should be content to stay in bed. And then, instantly, he was penitent. Poor old man!

'In which direction, Sire?'

'The seat under the yew. I have something to say – for your ear alone.'

The river sparkled and flashed in the sun; the daffodils had broken and in the grass under the trees just beyond the formality of the laid-out garden the bluebells were in bud, a deeper blue than the open flowers would be.

'It is as warm as June,' Harry said.

'In June you will be eighteen; that is what I want to talk . . .'

He seemed to stagger, sagged for a second very heavily against Harry's arm and then fell away, and would have fallen to the ground had Harry not quickly changed position, caught and held him.

Dead. Here in my arms. And no one within sight. He is my father; he is King of England. I cannot lay him down, here on the path. I must hold, I must carry . . . He lifted his father – heavier weight than one would have expected from his emaciated state – and stumbled towards the palace, and as he went he shouted in a voice that seemed too loud to be used in the presence of death.

Help came, and the founder of the Tudor dynasty was carried to his bed. He was not dead, yet.

For hours, through a noonday and an afternoon phenomenally warm, the next King of England stood or sat, generally in the window embrasure, while the physicians and the priests came and went. Now and again he wept, remembering how his father, confirmed miser that he was, had never been mean to him: thinking of the young man who had fought his way to the throne, made a marriage that linked red rose to white and healed the sores of the Civil War; loved his wife, begotten children. Reduced to this! Me too? One day?

He knew that death was not the end. The soul, its fleshly envelope cast off, lived on. There was the Judgment; Purgatory, Heaven, Hell. There would be the resurrection of the body, the communion of saints and the life everlasting. All men must die; on the day of one's birth the death warrant was signed. One knew that, but, aged not yet eighteen, on an April day, it was a thing hard to accept.

From the bed, suddenly the King, whom the physicians had given up and the priests regarded as a soul properly despatched on its journey, said, 'Harry!'

'I am here,' Harry said, hurrying forward. The dying man had spoken his son's name in a loud, clear voice but his next words were so weak and blurred that the boy, leaning over the bed, could hardly hear.

'Mistake, Harry . . . the Spanish girl . . . a bad thing. Free . . . let her go . . . Arthur . . . Choose . . . choose . . .' He made a noise like the beginning of a coughing fit, but no cough came. Henry, King of England, was dead.

The room stank of death and there was no purpose in staying in it. The body could be left to those whose business it was. Tomorrow they would be crying, 'The King is dead; long live the King,' and he would be Henry VIII of England, a figure in two overlapping pageants, one mourning the dead, the other acclaiming the living.

Outside was the April light, tender, lingering. A little time to himself, who could grudge it? And, if they did . . . he was King now. And he needed to take the taste of death out of his mouth, to plunge without a moment's delay into something that was an assurance of life, death's opposite.

Katharine and Maria de Moreto had taken their sewing into the garden, the fine warm day having coincided with the day when the stables were raked out. The work they had been doing was not interesting; they both loved embroidery – stoles, altar cloths, vestments, bold, glowing colours mixed with gold and silver threads, but such materials were costly. This had been a mending day and both were secretly relieved when the light began to fail and the first chill of sunset set a term to it. They pushed their needles into the little pad stuffed with sawdust which absorbed moisture and prevented rusting, and wound the unused thread on the spools. They folded the shifts and petticoats.

'It is a pile,' Katharine said, 'we have been busy.' Mended up, patched and darned, frayed edges cut off and rehemmed. 'I will carry some.'

'It is not right,' Maria de Moreto said. A Princess should not act as porter; and whatever was said or not said, done or not done, one thing was sure; the Princess Katharine was the Princess Katharine and Maria de Moreto her waiting lady – since the marriage and departure of Maria de Salinas, her favourite lady and closest companion.

'By what ruling?' Katharine asked and took up half the pile of mended linen.

They were halfway along the avenue of pleached limes whose leaves, in the one warm day, had expanded into a translucent greenness when Harry entered it, walking swiftly with great strides. Katharine stopped, her heart jolting.

'The Prince of Wales,' she said. 'Here take these,' She turned and pushed the mended things – evidence of poverty and makeshift – on top of the pile Maria was already carrying. She wished that she had been wearing her better dress, and her golden collar – her mother's last gift from which she would never be parted, no matter what the necessity. For, if ever dignity were needed, it was now. She was certain that within the next few minutes her fortitude would meet its final test. She was about to be discarded . . . Everything pointed that way. The fragile little hope, based on a cryptic message and a few words and a handclasp, had long since died. He was too young in a world where old men were powerful, with their schemes and their plots. And Joanna had warned her.

She advanced slowly, holding her head high; he came on quickly. When they were face to face she made him the most elaborate curtsey, holding her skirts, faded and shabby, into the prescribed fanlike shape, bowing her head. He took her by the elbows, pulled her up and kissed her; on the brow, knocking her headdress back. He said, very simply, 'My lady,' slipped his hands down her arms and took hers and stood looking at her with admiration, with love, with possessive greed, with curiosity. Under the stare she coloured. In him the life force, life-giving, life-begetting, sprang violently, defying death and the misery of the last few hours. He was able to say, almost casually:

'My father, the King, is dead.'

She remembered, not the unkindness and neglect of recent years, but her welcome to England and the early approval and kindness.

'I am very sorry, my lord.'

Answering something in his own mind, he said:

'He was fifty-five. And old before his time.'

Me too? No! No! I shall not be old at fifty-five. I shall not ruin my eyes or hunch my shoulders brooding over figures in a countinghouse. At fifty-five I shall still be in my prime; aye and at sixty-five. What was that story some Venetian merchants told, vowing it true; some Turk had lived to be a hundred and ten.

'I have not come to speak of sad things. Or of the past. We must speak of the future.'

He was making little of his grief, but she saw that his eyes were reddened and his cheekbones glazed by tears shed earlier. Wine heartened and comforted; she was glad to think that she had a little left of Dr. Puebla's last gift.

'Will you come and take a little wine with me, my lord?'

'Gladly. And except when you must, do not call me that. You are my lady. I am your servant. Your humble, loving servant; soon to be your husband.'

Her blush deepened and he knew how right he had been to leave Richmond where death presided to come here, where a look, a word could make a girl change colour.

He had heard and understood his father's last words but he had decided to ignore them; they ran counter to his will. He had been patient, very cautious in his behaviour, wily in his evasions of other betrothals; he did not intend to forgo his reward.

He let go one of her hands and holding the other fell in beside her and they walked to the end of the lime walk as once, years ago, they had walked along the raised platform of St. Paul's; a precious, envious ten-year-old and a fairy princess from Spain.

At the end of the walk she made to go in the direction of her humble apartments.

'This way,' he said. 'As I came through I rattled the lazybones, and told them to make ready.'

The Queen's apartments had not been used since his mother died. There was a musty smell in the air. But the servants left in charge, prepared to doze their time away for months, perhaps for the whole summer, had stirred themselves. The thickest dust had been swept from the surfaces of tables and chests and a newly lighted fire crackled on the hearth. Henry looked round and was satisfied that his order had been obeyed. He was King of England. For the next fifty years, God willing, his word would be law.

'We must wait six weeks, for decency. And then a wedding without display. Where would you wish it to be?'

'Here. If that would suit you . . .'

'Anything that you wish suits me – except the waiting. We have waited long enough.'

'Then in the little Oratory of the Observant Friars on the palace wall.'

'So it shall be. And to make up for the humble wedding, we will have a coronation of the utmost magnificence,' he said. 'On . . . on Midsummer Day.'

The April evening lingered and darkened; the cuckoo called for the last time but the doves mourned on a little longer. At Richmond those whose duty it was prepared the corpse for burial. Couriers rode hard carrying news of the death. Wolsey made one of his rapid, conservative reckonings and came to the conclusion that with his throne Henry VIII would inherit a fortune of two million pounds in cash money, as well as all the other assets. *Together with his brother's wife*, thought the statesman-cleric, who would have wished things otherwise. In the room which smelt of the past the two young people looked to the future. Six weeks was nothing to those who had learned to wait. They had waited. Both of them believed that the outcome of their waiting was the will of God.

'White satin,' Henry said. 'All white; no colour, even in your jewels – that can come after. There is a coronet called the Orient Crown, all of pearls. The palfreys of your litter must be all white and maids in white dresses shall line the streets. You shall go to your coronation as a bride.'

He had learned – or perhaps had been born knowing – that what the ordinary man saw with his eyes made more impact than that which he heard with his ears. He was anxious that all beholders on the Coronation Day should see Katharine as a virgin. There were still a few old-fashioned people, his grandmother, Countess of Richmond, among them, who chose to believe that Katharine had been Arthur's wife in truth; that Doña Elvira and Father Alessandra between them had muddled things and that Pope Julius had been misled. These people, in the short time allowed them, counselled delay, spoke of the difference in age, calling it six years, spoke of indecent haste, spoke of other, better alliances, even spoke of the yet unfully paid dowry.

They all strengthened his determination. It pleased him to think that England had no need to make an alliance by marriage, that he had no need to bother about a dowry. He had no inkling of it but the pattern of his life was set – he the giver, rich and powerful, conferring favour with a flick of the finger, altering everything with a word. Before he died he was to have, after Katharine, five other wives and not one of them either import-ant in her own right, or rich, four of them his own subjects. But Katharine was his first love and she offered him his first chance to play King Cophetua; it delighted him to take her from poor apartments and set her on the throne; to load her with jewels and replace her worn shabby gowns with the richest and most gorgeous apparel obtainable. Those who directly or indirectly decried her thwarted their own purpose.

'And your hair must hang loose; though I shall be jealous of every man who eyes it. Beautiful hair, wonderful hair.' He took a handful of it and wound it about his throat.

She was so dazzled with it all – it was like being let out of a dark prison into the sunshine – that his object in presenting her on her first public appearance as Queen, decked in the symbols of virginity, escaped her. Had he suggested that she wear sack-cloth and wooden shoes, she would not have questioned his whim. She was completely subjugated by him and so much in love that she felt wicked. Was it right sometimes to forget even God? To be so carnally inclined?

When the old Countess of Richmond and the Princess Mary, both of whom had avoided her for months, came with offers of friendship she found herself looking at the old woman and thinking: Did you ever know such joy? and at the young one: Will you ever know it? The answer was no. There never had been, was not, and never would be, a lover like Henry.

By the ordinary people the marriage had been welcomed. With them Katharine enjoyed a mysterious popularity. The English did not take kindly to foreigners, and there were times – especially when the trade with Spain was dishonoured – when it was not safe for a Spaniard to walk the streets of London; but Katharine was pretty, in un-Spanish fashion; she had been widowed tragically early; and of late years she had been ill-done-by. English sympathy for the underdog was awakened. And there were all the elements of a romantic tale in the handsome prince honouring his betrothal as soon as his old father – obviously the obstacle – was dead. It was right, and it was also symbolic, part of all the new reign promised, youth in the ascendant, less taxes and restrictions, more splendour.

So the crowds roared themselves hoarse as the pretty Princess dressed like a bride rode to her coronation through streets hung with bright cloth and tapestries and cloth of gold. She was even more beautiful than she had been eight years earlier, and looked, they said, not a day over eighteen.

Katharine was aware that in half a year she would be twenty-four. She also knew that in return for all this adulation, she owed the crowd something – an heir to the throne. Please God, this would be a fruitful marriage and that she would be pregnant soon.

The celebrations were hardly over before she was with child and able to say to Henry – as soon as she was certain: 'Dearest, you must not play any more tricks on me . . .' He loved dressing up and bursting into her apartments, followed by a group of young men, all disguised, as Moors, as Saracens, as Robin Hood and his merry men. She was never surprised or deceived, but she delighted in the pretence of being and receiving them as the occasion seemed to demand. Frivolity had played so small a part in her life.

'Sweetheart, *when*?'

'I think in *our* month, April.'

Joanna's married happiness had ended when Philip turned from her when she was pregnant: Katharine, seeing her figure grow bulky and her face puffy, knew some anxiety. But Henry never veered. He could have been a middle-aged father watching over a pregnant daughter. When she could no longer dance he would sit beside her and watch until she urged him to join in; then he would dance, never more than once with any lady, and at the end of each measure, come back to her side with a question, was she comfortable, tiring, too hot, too cold? The musicians were instructed not to play too loudly; and never any sad songs; the ballad mongers were to bring no story that would hurt a lady's tender heart. No woman, Katharine was sure, ever had a more cherished, peaceful pregnancy.

They kept Christmas at Richmond, and on the seventh day of the festivities, she was at table when the pain struck. Nothing; I have been overeating. Again; and it is not in my stomach. Akin to, but worse than, the pains I used to have each month, the pains love cured. July; and this is the first of January. Do I imagine? No!

'I must retire,' she said.

No real cause for panic; I was premature; Joanna once told me that I was almost born on muleback; and I lived. He will live.

She said, 'Heap up the fire, warm blankets.' Born untimely into a winter world he would need comfort and great care.

But what the last violent wrench of pain brought into the world needed no warmth, no cosseting. A female, stillborn.

Katharine bowed to the will of God. He ruled all and had chosen, for some reason that it would be heresy even to question, to bring this pregnancy to nothing. But she was disappointed and feared that Henry would be.

Henry proved that he was unique among men.

'I am sorry. But we are young. There will be others. It is a pity that you have nothing to show for your pains. Poor Kate, all to do again.' He held her hand, he kissed her and when she was up and about again, planned things to divert and amuse her. In after years when she heard him called 'cruel', her mind might accept the word; her heart never did; she had seen him kind and cheerful in circumstances in which many a man – not a King awaiting the birth of his heir – would have been gloomy, reproachful or merely indifferent.

The ordinary people stood by her too. The few, very few, women who could write, sent letters, all on the one theme. 'I lost three before I bore one living, a great boy I have now.' Most of the messages were verbal, 'Tell Her Grace not to worry. I lost my first . . . my second . . . my third.' 'I was hard on forty when I bore my John, after three slips.'

The seemingly boundless goodwill – actually proof of the fact that once the English, from titled lady to fishwife, had taken up an attitude, were loath to let it go – cheered and heartened her. February; March; and the Court very gay, full of visitors, attracted as though by a magnet; a Renaissance Court, but at the same time safe and orderly.

In April – our month – she was pregnant again. This time . . . God, God, please . . .

A year to the very day; on the first of January in the year of our Lord

1511, this time properly prepared, in a room with new hangings, all embroidered with the initials H and K, she was brought to bed, properly attended, and delivered of a living child, a boy.

'A boy, thanks be to God,' the midwife said, as much satisfaction in her voice as if she had begotten and borne him.

The child's first wailing cry was that of dynasty, sounding through Richmond, beyond and beyond. Bell-ringers leaned on their ropes and rocked ancient steeples; bonfires were lighted; people danced in the streets. A prince, a prince; one day to be Henry the Ninth. All England – not yet emerged from the celebration of Christmas into the workaday world – went mad.

And once again Henry showed himself to be unique. From the congratulations, the feastings, the planning for the most splendid christening any child had ever had, he removed himself to go, in midwinter, to a most inclement region of his realm; to stay in what he called 'my little palace of Barsham', which was indeed a small and inconvenient if beautiful house; to cast off his shoes in the Slipper Chapel and walk, barefoot, to the Shrine of Our Lady at Walsingham, in order to give thanks to God for this great blessing.

'I wish I could go with you,' Katharine said. 'Lay my eternal gratitude, and my gift, with your own, at her feet.'

'I will.'

'I shall go myself, as soon as I am well enough.'

'To be well, you must eat well,' he said solicitously: 'Dish after dish you pick at and send away. Is there nothing of which you could eat heartily?'

'Salad,' she said. 'With a dish of salad I could outeat you.'

Some Spanish dish, he supposed. Bearing the word carefully in the forefront of his mind he went and found Wolsey who knew a little about everything.

'Thomas, what is salad?'

'A dish, Your Grace.'

'I know. What made of? How cooked? The Queen has expressed a desire for it.'

'A desire which cannot, alas, be gratified. Not in England nowadays.'

'Why not *nowadays*?'

'Once,' Wolsey said, 'there were salad gardens all along the banks of the Thames. They ran to ruin, or so I understand, during the late wars. And sheep are more profitable.'

'It grows then?' Henry asked with interest. 'Order me a salad garden at each palace and manor.'

'Even so – in mid-winter. Though I believe that in Flanders they grow lettuces and carrots and such things all the year round, under glass to save them from the frost.'

'Then we, too, will have glass. Meantime order what is needed from Flanders.'

'But Your Grace it would be withered and dead . . .'

'Why? A great tree can be transplanted if the roots are dug out wide enough. I want a salad garden dug up, entire, and shipped here with all possible speed. I want some Flemings who understand such things. We will have a whole house of glass if necessary. You see to it. I am on my way to Walsingham. I hope to find a dish of the stuff on my table when I come back.'

Katharine must have whatever she wanted: but there was more to it than that. Wolsey's words about the late wars underlined a fact – the later Plantagenet kings had enjoyed a standard of luxury never since attained. During those wars England had dropped behind a little, and not yet caught up because his father cared nothing for such things. He would alter all that. Imagine a King of England obliged to send to Flanders for a dish of salad!

Thomas Wolsey, humbly born, the son of a butcher and grazier at Ipswich, had reached his present position, King's Almoner, by industry and attention to duty. The post in itself was not important; but even in the elder Henry's time he had begun to twist it to his own ends. No former Almoner had been so often consulted, taken into such confidence. The younger Henry had inherited him, relied upon him, had already made him a member of his Council; said to others, 'Wolsey will see to it,' to Wolsey, 'I leave it to you.' Wolsey, in the service of his King, and in the interests of his own inordinate ambition, was prepared to work twenty hours a day and to achieve the impossible without breathing hard or allowing the sweat to show. Promotion would come.

By the twentieth of February the Court was at Westminster. All the royal residences were a little too small for the number of people who must be accommodated and each in turn must be used, then vacated and cleaned and aired; regular movement was the habit. But because it was winter it had been decided to leave the baby Prince of Wales with his household, his wet nurse and his paraphernalia at Richmond.

To leave him was a wrench and for the first time Katharine understood why her mother had dragged tired, hungry children from battle front to winter quarters and back again. Poor Mother, she had tried to compound her duty as parent with her duty as Queen. Her own was by comparison a small problem; the baby was in good hands and it was necessary that she should take her place as Queen of England at the great – the most resplendent tournament – planned to take place at Westminster in honour of her son's birth.

The tournament had been splendid. Henry – disguise again – had ridden in the lists as Sir Loyal Heart, wearing her sleeve. Sleeves had now become of such importance that they were garments in themselves, detachable and interchangeable. Ladies, prewarned, had three made so that one could be given to the favoured knight without leaving one of their own arms bared.

She sat in the ladies' gallery overlooking the tourney ground and saw Sir Loyal Heart, wearing her sleeve, white slashed with rose, challenge and defeat all comers.

Later she sat at the table, on the dais of the great hall, and watched what anyone who was not conversant with the English would have thought to be a dangerous riot. Dozens of young men, most of them apprentices, broke into the hall, snatched food from the lower tables, drained wine cups, twitched away gold lace and even jewels from women, and buttons from men.

'It is their way of showing their pleasure,' Henry said, and jumped down to join in the mêlée. They stripped him too. The fun might have lasted another hour had he not remembered the dish of salad; when he did, he called the guard, his Beefeaters, and had the hall cleared.

He came back to the table, in his shirt, all aglow.

'My doublet has gone for honour and largess,' he said, laughing. Then Francisco Filipez, her own server, one of those who had lived through the lean days with her, set a great dish of crisp young lettuce, carrots the size of a little finger, sliced cucumber, tiny radishes like rubies, all gleaming with oil, between her and Henry.

At the same time the Duke of Buckingham, whose turn to take the honour it was, moved into position behind Henry with a bowl and a towel. It was a dish that called for the washing of hands.

'So,' Henry said. 'Now let me see you outeat me.'

There was a little commotion behind the screen at the door. Henry said, 'If it is the mob returned, tell the yeomen to lay about with intent.'

Buckingham jumped down, made his way to the door, vanished behind the screen.

Somebody said, 'Holy Mother of God!' and from the lower end of the hall a stunned silence spread like an incoming tide.

Buckingham, making his way through those who had heard, through those who were passing the word, had a face bleached white as bone. When he reached the dais, standing at a lower level, looking up, his face contorted; tears sprang from his eyes.

'The prince is dead,' he said.

There were many princes in the world; but only one over whose demise Lord Buckingham would weep.

CHAPTER 8

This time she was stunned by grief, bewilderment and remorse. She knew that everything that happened in the world happened because it was God's will, and being the will of God the child would have died had she leaned over his cradle. Yet the thought was unavoidable: There was I, making merry at Westminster while my child drew his last breath at Richmond.

Henry was grieved but still stout-hearted; the child had lived for fifty-two days, that gave hope for the future. There was still no hint of reproach in his manner towards her; nothing but kindness and the desire to comfort.

'Grieving,' he said sensibly, 'will not bring the boy back; and too much misery could undermine your health, upon which the next child depends.'

He thought she spent too long on her knees in cold chapels, fasted too often and too severely. He was himself conscientious about his religious duties and attended Mass every day; but he did not kneel for hours as Katharine did, praying for and hoping for enlightenment as to where she had been at fault to deserve such punishment.

His response to his loss was to think about it as little as possible; to look towards the future, surround himself with good company and allow himself no time for brooding. He was a man, he needed an heir; but his whole life was not centred, as Katharine's was, on a lunar cycle: Am I? Am I not? Perhaps next time.

Also the future into which he looked was different; this year he would have his twentieth birthday; she her twenty-sixth.

The year passed, and the next, without any sign of what she hoped for; otherwise they were full and happy; and in 1513 Henry paid her the highest compliment which a King could pay his Queen.

War against France had long been talked of. Louis XII had encroached in Italy and Henry and Ferdinand could persuade themselves that in attacking him they were defending the Pope. Both had other motives; Ferdinand his own interests and ambitions in Italy, Henry the ancient claim of the Kings of England to the throne of France. Also war, he felt, would be as exhilarating as any tournament.

'When I go to France,' he told Katharine, 'I shall leave you as Regent.'

'I hope that war may be avoided,' she said. He was disappointed.

'No Queen has been Regent since Edward the Third appointed Philippa to be his Regent when he went to France.'

She had by this time acquired some knowledge of English history.

'The Scots attacked *then*. The Battle of Neville's Cross?'

'They are unlikely to do so this time. James of Scotland is my brother-in-law; we have a treaty. Is it fear of the Scots that makes you look so grave?'

'No. If I look grave it is at the thought of your absence; and of the dangers that you will face.'

He laughed.

'Danger? From whom? Old Louis of France? One of his knights? When no man in England has yet unhorsed me.'

'There are other dangers. I have seen war. For every man who falls on the field three die of disease – sickness flourishes where men live close, and another dies of privation.'

The mention of disease woke his horror of it.

'I shall not live close. As for the rest, there will be no privation in this war. Wolsey is ordering the provender; biscuits, cheese, dried fish, twenty-five thousand oxen, all prime beasts, will be slaughtered and salted down. And no man of my thirty thousand will spend a night under a hedge or a haystack. There will be tents for all. And what is more, we take the Twelve Apostles with us.'

'In what form?'

'Twelve great guns, now being cast; each bears the name and the image of an Apostle.' The knight's sword, the yeoman's bow still had their part to play, but a modern King, planning a modern war, must have modern weapons. Henry spoke with childish pride about his cannon, and indeed he and his friends wore, all that spring, the air of boys planning an outing, they were a generation too young to have known war and when they thought of it they thought in terms of glory; there'd be some blood shed, mostly French, and exciting opportunities to show off skill and courage.

'This, you will see, will be my glorious year,' Henry said. 'And before I leave, I hope to get you with child again.' He could still make her blush.

She hoped that she was pregnant – too early to speak of it, too soon to be quite sure – when she rode down to Dover to see Henry and his host embark. The fleet was the largest ever to leave England; four hundred ships waited in the June sunshine to carry the men, the armour, the horses, the pavilions of the nobles, the tents, the cannon, the provisions. It was a momentous occasion; it was a splendid show; but as she stood for a little while on the beach after Henry had gone aboard, she felt the onset of loneliness – they had been much together in the last four years, far closer than most couples of any rank; fear for his safety – she knew what war was; and a heavy sense of responsibility – for even Wolsey had gone with his King and here she was, in charge of England with two old men, Sir Thomas Lovell, left behind to advise her, and the Earl of Surrey, who was to take charge of the northern border in case the Scots should attack despite the treaty.

She withheld her tears until she was riding, between them, on the way back to London. Then the thought – the wind carries him in one direction, this horse carries me in another and who knows what may happen before we meet again – brought the tears.

She said, 'Forgive me, my lords, I know . . . a great occasion . . . not to be marred by weeping . . .' There was a faint echo there, from the past; tears on a wedding day, ill luck to the bride . . . Tears at embarkation. Bad luck to those who sailed? God forbid.

Neither of the old men answered her and she thought that their silence was evidence of disapproval; she looked at each apologetically. They were both weeping too.

'To be left behind, with cripples and dotards,' the old Earl said. 'I am seventy years old, but I can still ride as hard and fight as well as any youngster. I need no tent to lie in, or beef in a cask. In my day a soldier had the sky for a roof and lived on what he could find.' Scorn quenched his tears. 'Pretty popinjays. I could outlive any three of them and I take it amiss that my very experience should disqualify me.'

'It did not,' Katharine said vehemently. 'It was because of your experience, because you could ride and fight with the best that His Grace chose you to guard the border. The rearguard must be the best – or so I have heard my mother say.'

Sir Thomas Lovell said nothing. Her Grace might take amiss any complaint. But he felt in the same way; there'd be a victory to match or eclipse Agincourt, and here was he, left behind with cripples, dotards and *women*.

'The border is quiet as a graveyard,' Surrey said.

And so let it stay, please God. Let nothing happen while Henry is absent. Let me sit at Greenwich and feel this child grow; and in March bear a boy, hardier than the other.

The old men wished otherwise. Let the King of Scots ignore that marriage link and the treaty; let the trumpets sound, let the warning beacons blaze; give us a chance to show that the years have toughened, not weakened us. *Let us show what old men can do?*

It was their wish, not Katharine's, which was fulfilled. As soon as the King of England and the pick of his nobility were safely engaged across the Channel, the Scots, following the old pattern moved southwards. The border, that quiet graveyard, sprang into life again. Surrey halted the invasion which made mock of all marriage alliances and treaties, at Norham, and Katharine as Captain-General called out all available reserves. Men older than Surrey snatched down weapons that had hung on their walls, unused since the Battle of Bosworth Field, heaved themselves on to horses, relatively as old, pastured for years, and rode north. And with them went apprentices from every town and city, some armed only with the tools of their trade, yardsticks, butchers' knives.

To her own surprise Katharine found herself capable of making rousing, patriotic speeches; God's hand, she said, moved in support of those who fought to protect their homeland. She reminded them that the English had always been the most valorous of nations. The old men and the boys went to war with these heartening words in their ears. Those who survived remembered.

She was definitely pregnant now, nauseated at the most inconvenient and unexpected moments. When she said that she must go to York, a rallying point, Maria de Moreto protested.

'It is two hundred miles; five days at least in the saddle. Your Grace, in this state, it is impossible.'

'My mother did longer journeys; on worse roads.'

And lost several babies that way. Not a thing one could say forthright.

'His Grace, when he returns would wish to find you in good health, a child on its way . . .'

'I must go, Maria. I promised to lead them. They look to me.'

Amidst it all she wrote to Henry, as she had done regularly, once a week since his departure; she sent him fresh linen and many admonitions about changing his clothes if he were caught in the rain or became overheated. Her worst fears for his safety were lulled; the French had avoided rather than courted a face-to-face conflict and the only engagement of any importance was called the Battle of the Spurs because the French knights had prodded their horses into headlong flight. To Katharine who knew what real war was, what was going on in France, the exchange of prisoners, the ransoms, Henry firing with his own hand one of the Twelve Apostles, seemed to be that she had imagined it, an exercise in chivalry. She was engaged in a real war.

Things her mother had said came into memory: 'An army must have something to fall upon. Men run, but a wall or a fence will steady them and they will turn and fight again.'

York, Katharine thought, must be what Surrey's men had to fall back upon. She would be there, with the cannon taken from the Tower.

Fresh recruits fell in at every market square and at every crossroads and by the time she reached Buckingham she had a sizeable army; the country men came armed with sickles, scythes and hay forks.

She held to another of Isabella's axioms – leader and men should be as little separated as possible – and lodged in the one inn of the town. She was hardly installed there when there was a commotion, first in the street, then in the yard. She thought: Quarrelling already! It was, she knew, the curse of armies such as this, seasoned soldiers reserved their spleen for the enemy. She went to the window that overlooked the yard and saw a horse with hanging head, heaving flanks and sweat-streaked hide standing just inside the gateway, while a young man thrust his way through the throng that gathered round him and shouted:

'Hinder me not. I must tell the Queen.'

News from France! Her heart halted; the crowded yard swirled in a grey blur. She caught at the window sill to steady herself and called into the greyness:

'Tell me *quickly*.'

'A great battle. A great victory, Your Grace.'

'And the King?'

'Well, when last I heard. This battle was against the Scots.'

Her sight cleared and there was the yard, full of men with their faces lifted up towards the window where she stood; country faces, bronzed from harvesting, paler townsmen's faces, and the face of the young man in tawny, all striped, paper white where the sweat had run freely, grey where the dust had gathered.

'Come up,' she said, 'and tell me all.'

He was as nearly exhausted as the horse which had carried him on the last stage of his wild ride, but, unlike the horse, he knew the worth of the message he bore and the necessity of delivering it properly. On the six stairs that led to the Queen's room he wiped his face on his sleeve so that when he knelt before her he seemed to wear a mask, all greyish, with blazing pale eyes.

The news he brought was wonderful. Never in the long history of war between English and Scots had such a decisive victory been won by either side. The veteran Earl of Surrey had pushed the Scots back to the foothills of the Cheviot Hills and there, by a cunning deployment of his forces, surrounded them. James of Scotland was dead, cut almost to pieces, nine thousand lay dead on the field.

'They will remember Flodden, Madam.'

And so shall I; that moment by the window . . .

'What is your name?'

'Harry Percy, Your Grace. I am son to the Earl of Northumberland. Too young for France, they said: but I was at Flodden.' The grey mask twitched into a sardonic grin. 'And because I ride so light, honoured to bring the news.'

Well, wars were fought to be won; and one must think that decisive victories were less wasteful of men than long drawn-out wars of attrition, skirmishes and sieges.

But how was Margaret of Scotland feeling at this moment? As I would feel at hearing that Henry was dead, cut almost to pieces . . . and for every one of those nine thousand dead men some woman weeps.

She was sickened; but she had learned lately that a resolute ignoring of bodily weakness helped. Fix the mind, the inward eye upon something extraneous, even a thing so trivial as a milestone, or the clink of a loose horseshoe, and the bad moment passed. She fixed her eye and her mind on the thing which the boy wore, knotted around his waist like a sash; a piece of cloth, crudely dyed, the colours at odds with the tawny doublet.

'What is that that you wear?'

'Oh, this? I took it from the Scot I killed, Your Grace. He wore things of more value – but I did not wish to profit . . . All Scots carry these, cloak, blanket, pillow, for most the only equipment, besides arms, that they have.' As he spoke he unknotted the sash and shook it out, astonishingly wide.

'It is your trophy,' she said, 'but might I ask it of you? I could send it to His Grace. It would look well as a banner.'

He began to smooth out the creases, 'Had I known that it was to be so honoured, I would have carried it more carefully. Folded and wrapped.'

'It does very well,' she said.

'Oh,' he said with a remembering look, 'there was something I was to ask Your Grace. My lord of Surrey wished to know what to do with the body of the King of Scots.'

Nausea again.

'It should be embalmed. The place and time of interment will be for His Grace to decide.'

James had played false, but he was King. He was also Henry's brother-in-law; he would be buried with due pomp.

And now the makeshift army could go home; some regretfully, some, already homesick, most gladly. She had no need to push on to York. She could sit down and write letters.

'I will write to the Earl of Surrey and despatch my letter tomorrow. Not by you. I think you should rest for a day.'

He was affronted.

'Your Grace, I am not tired. A little sleep and a fresh horse . . .'

There was something immensely touching about boys of that age; fifteen? sixteen? So much touchy pride, such an anxiety to prove themselves the equal of men. Please God she would mother such a one.

She wrote to the Earl of Surrey, jokingly reminding him about the importance of the rearguard and congratulating him upon the wonderful victory. Then she wrote to Henry, telling him the news, but careful not to make Flodden sound superior, or even equal to the Battle of the Spurs. Of James IV she wrote: 'It should have been better for him to have been at peace than to have this reward.' And she told Henry that she was sending him a Scots coat – the only name that her tired mind could fix upon – to hang from his banner. And then she thought that, spared the further fighting and the ride to York or beyond, she would make her way back to London by way of Walsingham and she ended her letter, 'And now I go to our Lady at Walsingham.'

It was a woman's place. It was said that when the Saracens overran the Holy Land, the Virgin was grieved to see her little house at Nazareth fall into infidel hands and had appeared to a Norman lady in Norfolk and asked her to build a replica, giving specific instructions. Angelic hands had helped in the building and in the inmost sanctuary there was a little flask, filled with the milk from the breast that had nursed the Saviour of the world – still liquid after more than fifteen hundred years.

It was the season of pilgrimage; humble and unassuming she took her place with the rest and prayed for a child, a living boy, lusty . . . Holy Mother of God, not my need alone, England's need . . .

There were dozens, hundreds of them, helping with the last harvesting, brown-faced, barefoot little boys. And in and around Walsingham more of them, eager to hold a horse's head, eager to carry the shoes one must discard, eager to sell the crude, yet oddly pleasing images of clay or wood. The world that September seemed full of little boys.

It was still September when she miscarried.

One must not give way to despair; it ranked with gluttony, avarice and anger amongst the deadly sins. She knew that she must not dwell upon the loss of some part of her flesh, a little red lumpish thing, no bigger than a pear; but she had looked forward to greeting Henry with the news. Oh God, why? What have I done?

Henry came back, safe and well, full of his exploits; as loving as ever, and yet, she sometimes felt, subtly changed. Over two matters that autumn he surprised her by showing a ruthless streak. One was the disposal of the corpse of the King of Scots. She spoke of it, thought he had forgotten and reminded him. 'Why bother about him? He stabbed me in the back. Let him rot.' The embalmed body was bundled away into a lumber room. The other matter was the marriage that was to seal the peace between France and England; a marriage between Henry's sister Mary, and Louis XII. Mary was eighteen, old enough to have a mind of her own, too old to be easily compliant; at the same time too young for an old, ailing man. She wept and protested, made what seemed to Katharine pitiable little attempts at defiance. Henry was adamant.

'Take her aside,' he told Katharine, 'and make her see sense.'

'She is in love, Henry; that makes it harder.'

'Unworldly, girlish nonsense about Charles Brandon. She is a princess not a lovesick . . .' He halted abruptly and his face took on a curious remembering look; but whatever he remembered seemed to make him more irascible. 'This mopish atmosphere wearies me. Tell her, if she weeps again in my presence, I shall send her to Hatfield until she sails for France.'

The reference to a mopish atmosphere was a little disturbing. It was true that since his return she found it more and more difficult to match his exuberant high spirits; some of the pranks, once so amusing, seemed silly; the days of hunting, a pastime she had adopted eagerly because it meant being with him, she now found exhausting and every now and then, even when she was making merry, the thought would strike, like a cold draught – twenty-eight and I have no child. But, disturbed or not, she risked one more protest on Mary's behalf.

'She is eighteen; and at that age one's heart can be set. As we know.' Surely that would move him. It did not.

'A different thing altogether,' he said, 'and you are not to encourage her.'

Mary, without encouragement from Katharine, struck her own bargain. In every marriage ceremony there came a moment when the bride could say, 'I do' or 'I do not'.

'And I will say I do not, loud and clear, in Notre Dame, unless you promise me that when the old man dies – I hope it may be soon – I can choose my second husband myself.'

She made other conditions, too; she would have only English women and girls about her. Prospective candidates for the honour of accompanying the Princess Mary to France came to Court to be inspected and approved. One was Sir Thomas Boleyn's second daughter, Anne; among the fair, pink-cheeked young creatures, her colouring marked her out; darker than any Spaniard; not pretty, but with a certain grace. Katharine noticed her, a changeling child . . .

Mary left for France in October 1514. Two months later Katharine gave birth to a boy, born living, dead within a few hours. He had not even been christened; nameless he went to join other unbaptised infants in Limbo. The will of God? Yes, she must cling to that because beyond there was nothing but darkness and chaos; and a mind that might, all too easily, run distraught. Why? Why? She asked God and there was no answer; but when, mourning, she put the question, perhaps for the twentieth time, to Maria de Moreto, Maria said:

'The blame lies elsewhere, Madam. It is not *your* punishment; it is *his*. And well deserved.'

Her voice was hard; she was a hard woman. She had been born, eighth child; fifth daughter into a family of the kind which only Spain could produce. Immensely proud, wretchedly poor. In such a family sons, handsome enough, might make advantageous marriages, or, clever enough, attain some official post; daughters without dower, but with some looks, might make marriages, not altogether mésalliances. But even the most determined and resourceful parents grew old and lost hope and energy. By the time that Maria was twelve she was acting as page to her brothers, even polishing armour at times, and as maid to her pretty sisters. Servants were plentiful enough in the unproductive countryside in which her father's crumbling castle stood, but they expected to be fed, and whenever there was a shortage the old man would go stamping and shouting through the kitchens and stables, driving them out. 'Look to God to provide for you, not to me.' They fled; and presently, finding God's rations even shorter than their master's, they drifted back. In the interim periods Maria did the menial work.

One of her brothers, who had attained not the hoped-for good marriage, but a minor appointment in Isabella's Court, remembered his little sister with gratitude, and when Katharine's suite was being gathered, had mentioned her name. So she had come to England. She was rather less than a year older than Katharine, but she was hard, sour and intolerant.

Katharine said, 'And what has His Grace done to deserve such punishment? Missed a Mass? Eaten meat on a fast day?'

Too late, Maria realised what her outburst meant. *She*, if she answered the question, must cause distress to the mistress she adored. She said primly:

'I spoke inadvisedly. It is not for me to criticise His Grace.'

'But you did! Now, you will sit on that stool and you will explain what you meant. If His Grace is at fault, there is a remedy. He is as anxious as I am.'

In moments of emotion her voice always deepened, as her mother's did. It was like a man's, like the voice of the fearsome old father who had dominated Maria de Moreto's youth. It woke fear's memory. Maria turned pale, was glad to take the stool.

'One must be to blame. And it is not Your Grace; so pious, charitable, wearing the rough habit under the silk and the velvet, going to Walsingham again, and to Canterbury. Therefore it must be His Grace. That was all . . .' She let her voice trail off and she managed to produce the smile, sick, sly false which had been her defence in another time another world.

'You meant more than that, Maria,' Katharine said.

Well, Maria thought, better the knowledge than the whispers, the sly looks. Sooner or later someone will tell her.

'It gives me sorrow to say this, Your Grace. But I ask myself, what blessing can a man expect on his own marriage when he sins with another man's wife?'

Katharine turned pale, but she remained calm and her expression showed more astonishment than shock or anger or hurt. It was, quite simply, unbelievable. Men did often seek, in another woman's arms, something they failed to find in their wives'; but not Henry. It had been a consolation for her childlessness that the love between them had never ceased to be lively and fresh. After six years, no lessening of passion or pleasure. A perfect relationship, she would have said, in bed and out of it.

'Maria, are you *sure*? People spread such wicked . . .'

She saw by Maria's face that it was true.

'Who is she?'

'She was born Elizabeth Blount,' Maria, born Maria de Moreto, said with contempt in her voice. 'She married Sir Gilbert Taillebois and followed him to the war. At least to Calais where the King met her. Now she has a manor, called Jericho. In Essex.'

That had the ring of truth. Henry often went in that direction, his destinations variable, Brentwood, Romford, Tilbury; and always he had had some reason for going alone.

'Calais. That was months ago. *Has she borne his child?*'

'Not yet.'

'And everybody knew. Except me.'

'Know is too firm a word. Whispers. Rumours. Jokes about the walls of Jericho falling. I made it my business to find out. Your Grace wearing your knees to the bone . . . And it is true, I swear it. So you need no longer ask *why*. God has His ways of punishing men; and the innocent suffer with the guilty.'

'One lapse, Maria,' Katharine said defensively. 'His Grace was absent almost four months. And in *France* . . .' A Spaniard, speaking to a Spaniard, had no need to complete the sentence. Of all peoples the French were the most easy-going in such matters.

A natural curiosity made itself felt.

'What is she like? Very pretty? Very young?'

'Fair, they say. Somewhat plump. And with a shrew's tongue. Sharp words, spoken with a smile, can pass for wit.'

Was that the attraction? I am older than he? I have taken each loss to heart. Perhaps I have become too serious, even in my loving.

'Maria, I hope that you contradict this story whenever, wherever you may hear it. The old King was strict. His Grace had no opportunity to sow, as the English say, his wild oats. I shall make little of this, except to point out, as is my duty, that adultery is sin and imperils his soul.'

And even for that, great strength was required. The happy, the seemingly perfect relationship . . . only last night . . . He would be angered. It was plain that he had done his best to keep her in ignorance. Some men flaunted their mistresses. Kings had been known to bring their paramours to Court, splendidly dressed, dripping with jewels and forced their Queens to accept and recognise. Henry had spared her that. Or God. God knew the inmost secrets of the heart and knew what each could bear.

'Come to bed, Kate,' Henry said at last. She was overlong at her prayers and would take a chill. Katharine was praying for strength and courage, praying that Henry might not be angered and that he might take notice of what she had to say. But he could not be kept waiting forever. She rose from her knees and went to bed. Henry threw the covers back. 'Come and get warm.' He pulled her close and, holding her, blew out the candle.

After a few seconds he asked:

'What is wrong with you tonight? So long at your prayers; and now . . .?'

'I heard something today that made me sad.'

'You sadden too easily,' he said, handling her more purposefully. It was some silly little thing, he thought; she had heard of some woman giving birth to a child; or a nun dead; or an orphan sick; or one of her many protégées turning out badly. 'Nobody can bear the woes of the world.' For six years she had found refuge from woe on his breast; tonight, clutching and fondling, he felt the difference.

'Who or what made you sad today? Is it anything I can deal with?' He had lightened her grief often; once even countermanding the death sentence passed on some silly – but dangerous – boys, because she had been sad, saying that they were young, and how would their parents feel?

She said, 'It is a hard thing to say. And I beg you not to be angry.'

'Have I ever been angry with you?' He could ask that with a certain smug justification. Many a man, married for six years and with no living child would have blamed his wife, said harsh things. Many a man, let down as he had been by Ferdinand, would have said spleenish things to the man's daughter. Henry never had. He was a poet and to him more than to ordinary men, love was a beautiful, shining whole, a climate, a country, not of this world. Set apart.

Katharine said, 'No. But darling, I have never yet spoken of Elizabeth Taillebois. And now I must.'

The convulsive movement he made shook the solid bed. She waited for the rage. She knew Henry's temper. Into fury, as into everything else he threw the whole of himself, strong body, lively mind, ardent soul.

But now after what seemed a long silence, full of dread, he spoke in a muted voice.

'I hoped you would never know. It is a thing no woman – not even you – can understand. You must not even think . . .' Usually so fluent with words, he spoke haltingly. 'Unfaithful in the act; never more, Kate. Never in my heart. No love concerned. Nothing that you and I . . .' He knew that he could never hope to explain. Presently, in a more positive voice, he said, 'I am heartily sorry, sweatheart, for any pain I have caused you. Forgive me.' His hands added – And forget. It would have been easy to do; but it would be a failing in duty.

'I do. I have. But Henry, it is sin.'

'As well I know. The penances lasted longer than . . . Five Masses one day. When I should have been hunting.' He sounded plaintive; almost ill-done-by. She could imagine Dr. Langford, his confessor, growing sterner with each iteration.

'We are told,' she said gently, 'to avoid occasion for sin.'

'I do. I have tried. Then something starts; a tune, a scent, a mere thought in the mind. No woman knows . . . See,' he took her hand and guided it. 'Here we are, talking of *my* wickedness and *he* is so unruly . . . Kate, my love!'

Afterwards she wondered, whether for the good of his soul, she should have been firmer; wept perhaps, made the most of her hurt and extracted promises. She examined herself sternly, too, in another direction. Had she been right to be so pleased to hear Henry's heart was not concerned. She had believed it and been gratified, whereas, really, in the eyes of God, surely the heart's involvement was the only possible excuse.

Then she gave up thinking about it; for though Henry had made no promises and she had been too easily distracted, on that night or one soon after, what she had prayed for came about. In May, am I? In June, I think so. Then certainty.

This time she carried the child full term and on February 18, 1516, gave birth to a baby, very strong and lively; even the first cry was different; not a kittenish wail at being confronted with an alien world, but a lusty noise – Here I am! There was only one tiny flaw in the happiness; the baby was Henry's daughter, not his son.

Henry proved himself equal to the occasion. He was as pleased as though Mary had been a boy. No prince, not even the little boy who had died at Richmond, ever had a more ostentatious christening; no child ever had a more doting father. There were many men, indeed the majority of men, who would have turned away, saying, 'After all this, a mere girl!' Henry spoke proudly of 'my daughter', and would carry the baby about to take the air in the garden or to be presented to visiting notables and ambassadors who, if they valued his goodwill, were prompt and fulsome with their admiration. In his complex and sometimes contradictory character the paternal instinct was strong. Katharine was one day to learn that any child of his was an extension of himself. In addition, this little girl, solid and thriving, was a promise for the future. Next year she would have a brother.

When Henry spoke of the boy who was to come, Katharine said, 'I hope so,' or 'God grant it may be,' but as Mary survived the most dangerous period of early infancy and she herself did not become pregnant again, she sometimes wondered, in her inmost mind, whether it mattered so much. Her own mother had been a Queen, one without equal among Kings; could not this child, properly trained, well-educated, be to England what Isabella had been to Castile? The English, she realised, would have to be converted to the acceptance of a female ruler. Long ago, another Henry, dying without a son, had wished his daughter to become Queen, but the moment he was dead the young woman's male cousin had claimed the throne and there had been a civil war of such savagery that men had said that Christ and all the saints slept.

Still, things were different now; Henry I had died in 1135; this was the sixteenth century and in four hundred years fashions in thought and social attitudes underwent changes.

Whenever Katharine entertained such thoughts, sooner or later she was bound to think of Thomas More, Henry's closest *friend*. A king's society was, like an archery target, a thing of concentric circles, narrowing down. At the centre of Henry's wide ring of acquaintances, servants, jolly companions, men to be sparred with, using weapons or words, More was unique, the very centre. He was thirteen years older than Henry, but he seemed to have learned the trick of perpetual youth without missing the lessons taught by experience. He was, in intellect, one of the new men, a humanist, a disciple of Erasmus, a student of Greek – and in Greece, in classical times, women had been despised. He was good-looking, a thing which counted enormously with Henry, and he was witty, which also counted. Katharine had realised, quite soon after her arrival in England, that verbal quips, the seemingly flippant yet telling comments that provoke first laughter and then thought, could only be made in the tongue to which one was born. To More's witticisms her own response was always just that perceptible second slow.

But she liked, admired and trusted him, and in planning her daughter's future, somewhat prematurely, she counted upon his support. He had a daughter of his own, Margaret, whom he was bringing up, so far as education went, exactly as though she had been a son. And when, leaning over the infant Mary she had said to Henry, 'Children at an early age learn so easily; she must learn Latin and French as she learns English. And all the other things of which I am ignorant,' Henry had said, 'To what end? The time would be better spent in acquiring the graces.'

One evening, at the little supper table, private and intimate, she asked a bold question: 'Sir Thomas, have you found that your daughter's learning' – he had been boasting about it – 'has interfered with her acquiring of the grace desirable in a woman?'

'How could it, Your Grace? God knows His job. Every woman is born with grace. Imagine a man making a curtsey or climbing a flight of stairs, cumbered with skirts! I often think: God tried His prentice hand on man and then improved, as apprentices do, and so made woman.'

Henry said amiably, 'Tom, that is near heresy!'

'Heresy, Your Grace? *The adoption and maintaining of a belief contrary to authorised teaching.* Hardly. And what always struck me forcibly was that in Eden, whereas Adam turned about and blamed the woman whom God had made for tempting him, Eve was more moderate in her denunciation and simply said that the serpent beguiled her. She did not say: 'The serpent *whom you made*, thus shifting the blame. It is possible that when it comes to point, the female more willingly accepts responsibility? Is that a heretical question?'

'It does not answer mine, Sir Thomas,' Katharine said mildly. 'I am anxious to know because I want Mary to be thoroughly educated, but not at the expense of grace, charm, feminine accomplishments.'

'A girl,' Henry said, 'should be able to read and write; to dance well and to ride, to make herself agreeable even to those whom she does not find compatible. And if she can sew a fine seam,' he said, smiling at Katharine who had sewn so many for him, 'all the better. My sweet Kate, you have only to look in your glass to see how Mary should be modelled.'

She said, 'I thank you. A pretty compliment! But the world has widened since I was schooled. I want Mary never to be at a disadvantage.'

More's ear, always sensitive and sharpened by long hours in courtrooms where the downright lie was negligible, the half-truth, the insinuation important, informed him that between Henry and Katharine there was a difference of opinion which probably neither would have acknowledged. The Queen looked upon her daughter as heir to England; the King saw her as some man's wife.

He said: 'Wait a little and let the child be your guide. We none of us ever learned anything we did not wish to learn; and no one ever will.

Colet taught me Greek and I learned, because I wanted to read the stories; in his school at this moment there are a hundred and thirty boys, half of them have no wish to learn Greek and no amount of beating will inculcate that wish. To the child offer all things; give her what she reaches for.'

It was the kind of halfway answer to which, in his dealings with Henry, More was driven with increasing frequency. He was an honest man – so honest that he was sometimes called the only honest lawyer in London, but tact was needed in conversation with the King who was responsible for all appointments and all promotions and More had a wife and family for whom he felt responsible. In addition he was genuinely fond of Henry, admired his qualities and enjoyed his company. Occasionally, when a matter was important and no tactful answer available, he would take refuge in silence. Then Henry would say, 'Lost your tongue, Tom?' and More would say, 'No. The line of your argument,' or 'my ability to agree on this subject.'

This evening, on the subject of female education he had been honest, saying what he truly believed and in such a way as to displease neither hearer – or so he thought, but though Katharine was satisfied – offer everything was exactly what she intended to do, Henry's face took on a petulant look; he had expected more positive support. After all, he had made his *own* views plain. He cast about in his mind for a suitable way of expressing a mild displeasure and found it so easily that his face brightened into amiability again. He put down his knife and said, 'It has come to my ears, Tom, that when someone congratulated you on being in high favour with me, you replied: "Make no mistake; if my head would buy him a castle in France, he would have it." '

Where did eavesdroppers hide? Where were such gleanings marketed? More wondered. He had spoken those words, in the privacy of his own house, to a man he trusted absolutely – the man he hoped to have as a son-in-law one day. What a dangerous world!

'Yes. Those were my words. You mislike them, Sire?'

'They show small faith in me, Tom.'

'A tribute to your good sense and care for your subjects' lives. How many stout fellows' deaths would it take to capture a castle in France? Surely against them one head, even such a one as mine . . .' he laughed and spread his hands. 'Incidentally a tribute to my own good sense too. Being in favour should not make a man think himself indispensable.'

Whatever sting the reported remark had once held, it was gone. Henry said warmly, 'Not regarding yourself as indispensable renders you so to me, Tom. I would not give your head for twenty French castles!'

Just for a moment another presence seemed to hover about the table as all three who sat by it thought of another indispensable man, Cardinal

Wolsey, Archbishop of York, Bishop of London, holder of a dozen other clerical offices and the Pope's Legate in England.

Katharine thought of him with a certain dislike. Well as he had organised provisions for the army to invade France she suspected him of pro-French sympathies and of wishing that Henry had not married a Spaniard. This feeling was instinctive rather than reasonable, but it tended to make her critical of his ostentation, his extravagance and self-importance. Once the French war was over – with Flodden reckoned as part of its victory – Henry had showered favours upon Wolsey, given him three dioceses in a single year and practically ordered Pope Leo X to send the coveted Cardinal's hat to the man without whom he, King of England, could do nothing of importance. Wolsey had promptly abandoned the plain cassock which had been his wear, and the mule which had been his mount. Now, clad in scarlet satin, mounted like a prince, he outshone every noble in the land, and sometimes came near to rivalling Henry himself. His building schemes were inordinately ambitious, his hospitality royally lavish, nine hundred people were said to eat at his expense even on an ordinary day. It was possible for Isabella's daughter to think, tolerantly – The man is compensating himself for his humble birth. Possible to think – Only in England could a butcher's son rise so high. But under all such thoughts, under the personal distrust, was a more deeply rooted feeling. A man who had clambered so far by way of the Church, should be more attentive to his clerical duties. Dioceses and livings were not to be collected and held and exploited, like cattle or acres of land. Wolsey might be an administrator without equal, a diplomat of the utmost skill and cunning, a sound theologian, but he was not a good priest. Yet, whenever she reached this conclusion, a little self-distrust would round off the circle. Could it be, she wondered, that she misjudged him because she was jealous of him? Henry spent so much time with him, held him in such high esteem . . .

Henry thought of his faithful servant with complacency. It was right that the greatest King on earth should be served by the most splendid minister. He admired Wolsey's taste and style, and if he ever remembered his humble origin it was only to underline the thought that a King could make so lordly a creature out of a butcher's son. Even Wolsey's extravagances reflected glory on himself. And that a man should be able to employ his remarkable talents in a sphere so far removed from that into which he was born reflected credit on England, so different from France and Spain where all high office was the prerogative of the aristocracy. Added to all this was his complete certainty that Wolsey was utterly devoted to himself; in Wolsey there were no reserves at all. If Wolsey ever hesitated when confronted by a suggestion, or spoke a word of unpalatable advice it was not from scruple or principle but because he had the King's good at heart. There lay the difference between the two Thomases. It was possible for Henry to imagine a situation in which More would put a moral or religious consideration first. Just possible. Not that this detracted from Henry's esteem of More; in a paradoxical way it enhanced it. Henry admired integrity. As he thought his complacency grew; he was a fortunate man; an amiable wife of his choosing – and how many monarchs could claim as much? One true Thomas to use and another to enjoy. Only one thing lacking – and that would be granted in time.

Thomas More thought of Thomas Wolsey with admiration and a certain pity. It was impossible not to admire the tenacity and industry of a man who could sit down to a job at four in the morning and stay there for twelve hours, not eating, ignoring the needs of nature. Impossible not to admire a mind, so acutely intelligent, so widely informed, and gifted with such power of memory. At meetings of the Privy Council it was noticeable how when some matter was mentioned – even a matter presumably outside the man's immediate range – he could, without reference to book or paper, produce some relevant facts or what appeared to be a considered judgment. More, whose own tastes were simple, also admired the way in which Wolsey had taken to grandeur; ostentatious perhaps but always within context; never vulgar. Even his enemies – and he did not lack them, though they might snarl enviously behind his back, face to face with him, never failed to be impressed by his personal dignity. But More, who missed very little, had seen Wolsey's single weakness – a too great dependence upon the King: he had, to a dangerous degree, made Henry Tudor his god. And if for any reason his god should cease to smile, should turn away his face, or frown, what would the poor fellow have left?

Wolsey, the indispensable man, brushed against all their minds and was gone and Henry reverted to his baby daughter, and again in terms which showed Katharine that when he looked towards the future he did not visualise Mary succeeding him.

'We may pick and choose what the child shall learn,' he said; 'when it comes to whom she shall marry there is no choice. I've given this some thought of late and there is only one man fit to mate with my daughter – her cousin Charles.'

'But he is far too old,' Katharine said. 'By the time she is marriageable he will be thirty or more.'

'In his prime,' Henry said, ignoring, as usual, anything which did not exactly fit his wish. 'He is now King of Spain, when Maximilian dies he will have the Netherlands and Austria; and he is certain to be elected Emperor. Mary will be Empress.'

To both these hearers there was a touching naiveté in this confident plan-making.

'It would hardly do to count upon it,' Katharine said. 'Before Mary is half-grown Charles will be under pressure to marry and . . .' She realised what she was about to say, faltered a second and then finished the sentence, controlling her voice, 'beget an heir.' Once one admitted that a subject was too sore to be touched upon it was sore indeed.

'Mary will be worth waiting for,' Henry said. 'And if Charles should need advice as to how to resist pressure, he can apply to me. Eh, my love?' He smiled at her and she was passionately grateful to him, both for refusing to admit that the subject was sore, and for thus indirectly reminding her that he had waited for her, avoiding all other betrothals.

More, watching them, thought how mysterious were the ways of God. A loving couple, both seemingly healthy, wedded for more than eight years, dead babies, miscarriages, one living child, female. And the Queen, poor woman, past her first youth, thirty-three at this year's end; beginning to show her age, too.

Katharine was only too well aware of the way in which the gap in age between her and Henry was widening. Her glass was a constant reminder. Disappointment must be accepted and could be borne, but it left a mark. In repose her face now wore a look of settled gravity, of patient resignation. Her smile was still sweet and in moments of animation her eyes brightened into beauty again, and since the sight of Henry always pleased her, this was the face which he saw most often. But repeated pregnancies had thickened her figure and though she wore her stays tightly laced, was careful to preserve an erect posture, kept every fast day and on others ate sparingly, the slenderness of youth was gone forever. Her complexion, thanks to Maria de Moreto, was well preserved.

'My mother,' Maria said, 'kept her looks into old age.' She spoke without fondness or pride, remembering how often she had beaten eggs and oil and honey into a cosmetic paste, when they could be ill spared. Now, with more loving care, she whisked and Katharine wore the sticky mask. 'For the hands and neck, to keep them white, there is nothing like lemon juice,' Maria said. And though lemons were less easily come by in England than in Spain, they were obtained and the juice faithfully applied. Even more rare and expensive was henna, with which the prophet Mahomet was said to have dyed his beard. It was good for colouring, hiding the fading hairs and brightening the rest, but the silky lustre was not restored. In all this business of fending off the damage of the years, clothes helped. She chose more sombre colours now but the materials were always sumptuous and her fondness for jewels had not lessened. Fully garbed and bejewelled she was a magnificent, if not a youthful, figure. Sometimes she remembered her mother, too busy for vanity, caring only that her clothes should be clean and suitable to the occasion. But the lesson to be learned from that memory was plain – her mother and father had ended as a pair of working partners, and then not always in accord. It was not a relationship which she wanted to establish with Henry; never, not even when they were very old.

Presently Mary was three and there had been no sign of another child to follow next year, next year, next year. There were moments when Katharine felt that she had failed Henry, and England in not providing a prince; but neither King nor country seemed to bear her any grudge. To Henry she was still dear Kate, or my love, and he still took pleasure in her company: with the people she was still popular, the Princess who had somehow caught their unpredictable fancy, the Queen whom they knew to be good.

And there was always Mary, as satisfactory a daughter as any parents ever had. Unlike Katharine in her youth, Mary learned quickly and easily; in that way she was like poor Joanna; but there were no disquieting signs to be seen in that resemblance. Mary was sensible from the first, completely amenable and a stranger to fear. At the age of three, wearing a gown which save for its colour was an exact replica of her mother's, she would face any stranger, however impressive, make a perfect curtsey and say, in English, Latin, French or Spanish, 'Welcome to our Court.' It was a performance that never failed to charm, and to astonish, since Mary was small for her age. Her parents, who had also appointed themselves as her first teachers, would look on with pride. Katharine would think: God saw fit to deny me a son, but in His mercy gave me Mary. Henry would think: My daughter so gifted, what might my son not be?

CHAPTER 9

'As you say, a fine boy,' Elizabeth Taillebois said. 'And it is a pity that he will have no name.' A little malicious sparkle brightened her eyes. She had done what the Queen had failed to do and borne the King a son. This boy was too late to be of her dead husband's begetting.

'He will have a name,' Henry said, looking down at the cradle; 'the best, after Tudor. Fitzroy. That will be his name; Henry Fitzroy, son of the King.' His face darkened a little and he looked stubborn. 'If it pleases God to withhold from me a legitimate son, he will have titles too. Duke of Richmond: Duke of Somerset.'

More than she had hoped. Duke of Richmond was the title which the child's grandfather had carried when he won the Battle of Bosworth and made the English crown his own. As for Henry begetting a legitimate child, that possibility could be dismissed. It was three years since Princess Mary was born, and not a sign.

'That should go a little way to make up for being born a bastard,' Lady Taillebois said. 'What a pity that there is not some pretty title that means King's whore; then I could claim the honour.'

She had, not wit exactly, but a sharp, almost shrewish way of putting things which Henry found amusing. She had never had and would never have, any emotional hold on him, their relationship was quite unsentimental; she was good to go to bed with, once in a while, and she often made him laugh.

'You wrong yourself,' he said, 'Or do you? Whore implies some degree of promiscuity. I suppose,' he said, pretending doubt, 'that he is mine.'

'Mewed up here as I have been, by Your Grace's order, I fail to see whose else's he could be. A stable boy's? A gardener's?' She too pretended doubt, squinting at the child. 'I rather think not. To me he does not look like a peasant's get.'

'You are a hussy.'

'When you say that, you should add, Thank God!'

'Sometimes I do. And I do thank God for the boy . . .' This was clear proof that he was capable of begetting a son, strong and healthy. But why, in the name of God, couldn't he have been Katharine's child, born at Richmond, Prince of Wales? As soon as Henry's resignation had ceased to be mitigated by hope, a slightly rebellious element had crept into it. He never expected to be enlightened; commanding officers did not explain their motives or designs to those under them; on the other hand even a foot soldier was entitled to mutter and mumble a bit, under his breath, when faced with a situation that he could not understand. Henry muttered and mumbled to himself fairly often. This splendid child, now three months old, past the most dangerous post-birth period, and with the true Tudor red hair curling on his head, was a son whom Henry would most proudly and gladly have presented to the nation. Imagine the joy! Presumably God knew His own business best – one must believe that – but what a left-handed way of doing things! And how difficult God had made it for His true soldier! In order to give this child his due – and to show the world what Henry Tudor could produce, it would be necessary to hurt Katharine. And that he shrank from.

She was no longer the red-gold, pink-and-white princess from Spain whom he had coveted, envying Arthur, and married, defying some death bed words. She was a woman, settling down to middle-age, engrossed in the upbringing and education of her only living child. Her extreme piety sometimes bored him – he thought the wearing of a nun's habit was carrying things to extremes – but she had never done or said anything that could, in the slightest way, diminish his respect and admiration for her. She was part of his youth, the first woman he had truly loved, and she fitted him well, in many ways. Her dignity complemented his; she had a sense of occasion that matched his; she had good sense, and magnanimity. He still admired her; he still loved her, but love, like a masquer, had changed its face of late. She no longer stirred *him*, that little, most vital member, once so unruly when in near contact with her that he would assert himself, even during a scolding. He could still take her hand, kiss her, lie beside her but these touches were no longer a preliminary to bliss.

And could a man be blamed for that. *He* was not subject to the will. *He* no longer responded wholeheartedly to Elizabeth Taillebois. *He* had run off and involved himself with a woman as different from Katharine and from Elizabeth as a woman could be.

Her name was Mary Boleyn and she was the elder daughter of Sir Thomas Boleyn, one of the knights who had fought at the Battle of the Spurs. She was lovely to look at, very blonde and she never seemed to be more than half awake. Katharine was intelligent; Elizabeth was shrewd and amusing; both of them demanded some activity above the waistline. Mary Boleyn was, by comparison, a feather bed, a comfortable, almost anonymous receptacle.

There were times when Henry thought that perhaps the Turks had the right idea – God forgive him for admiring any infidel custom; but perhaps a man needed three women; one to be good with; one to be bad with; one with whom to be nothing.

Thinking these things he said to the woman who was so fit to be bad with,

'I think when he is six; able to stand up to the ceremony and comport himself properly.'

The malice shone in her eyes again. 'Naturally it will take longer than if he had been born in the right bed.' It was true that had the boy been legitimate he would not have had to wait six years for his title.

'You,' Henry said, 'will end as a shrew.'

'I hope not. I intend to be a sweet-faced lady pensioner; in a lace cap.'

That was going one step too far. Katharine had lately taken to wearing a cap made of lace petals – and very becoming it was.

'The Queen,' he said swiftly, 'will still be short of forty when this boy is six. If by then . . .' He left that sentence unfinished and went on, 'Another disrespectful remark about Her Grace and you will get no pension at all.' That was a blow in a very vulnerable area; Elizabeth had always been greedy, for gifts, for allowances, property. Still, she had given him a son, she had bolstered his belief in his own virility.

'Mind your tongue,' he said, 'and you shall have your pension.'

He thought of Mary Boleyn, curious girl, going through life like a sleepwalker; asking for nothing, refusing what was offered, even trinkets. Why? he asked. She replied in her soft, sleepy way, that to take anything from him would make her feel like a bought woman. 'Besides, people would notice, and talk. And one gaping mouth in a family is enough.'

He had tried to conduct his second extra-marital affair more discreetly even than his first. Mary Boleyn had an appointment as one of Katharine's maids-in-waiting, but it was natural enough for her to visit her father, useful, shrewd man who was seldom far from Court, except when Henry sent him on an errand. Mary went to see her father, housed not gloriously, but comfortably, wherever the Court was; the King strolled into those apartments to talk with Sir Thomas whom the old nobility called that lickspittle toady, the gentleman lackey who was not a gentleman at all. So far nobody seemed to have noticed the coincidences of the timing; he hoped nobody would. He had no wish to hurt Katharine again; and he had no wish to seem fickle. All things considered, he had been, where women were concerned, remarkably abstemious; only two mistresses in a reign of ten years; a man should be judged, not only by the temptations to which he had succumbed, but by those he had resisted. And, when he felt guilty, which was often, he remembered that he had never neglected his duty to Katharine; whenever that small, uncontrollable *he* could be forced to perform, into service he went. For one thing he had not quite abandoned hope; a woman in her late thirties, even in her forties, might still bear a child.

He intended to stay away from Jericho; Elizabeth's attraction for him was outworn and he would have been happy to give her her pension and discard her. But the child drew him. He was a doting father; he loved Mary, disappointed as he was about her sex and the fact that she seemed doomed never to have a brother; he loved Henry, born of the wrong woman, in the wrong bed. Both were extensions of himself; their colouring, shape, mental ability, amusing, graceful ways were like mirrors, reflecting his superiority. In the company of either – Mary so apt with the lute and with a phenomenal memory, speaking good, almost perfect Latin at the age of four; Henry strutting about on his hobby-horse and flourishing his little wooden sword – he could momentarily forget that Mary was a mere girl, and Henry a bastard. Afterwards, when the entrancement ended and ran full tilt into grim reality, he would think – if only . . . if only the boy had been born Prince of Wales; if only the girl had been born on the wrong side of the blanket. If only, if only . . . The stark fact remained and sooner or later he must face it. He was King, he could give the little boy a name and confer titles on him presently. Would the English people accept him as heir? It seemed improbable.

From such troubling thoughts Henry could turn his mind to other things; to the making of his Court, by the hospitality and favour extended to scholars of all nations, the most cosmopolitan and modern Court in Europe; to his own enjoyment of hunting and violent sports; to his love of music and books; and, perhaps above all, to the preservation of his position as the third, greatly sought after, power in Europe.

It was the day of the young rulers, Joanna's son, Charles V, had inherited his vast realms and been elected Emperor in 1519, when he was still only twenty; Francis of France had been twenty-one when he became King in 1515: Henry, in 1520, was still only twenty-nine and had ruled for eleven years. Between the rival powers of France and the Empire, England held the balance: between Francis and Henry there was a strong element of personal rivalry that had little to do with politics; it was even rumoured that Francis was a shade taller than Henry, and equally expert at all sports which demanded skill and courage. They were both anxious to meet.

Katharine, not really a politically minded woman, had the Spaniard's inborn distrust of France and was relieved when, just before the meeting between Henry and Francis was to take place, the Emperor proposed to visit England. She had never seen Joanna's son, but she felt that he must have inherited something of his mother's charm. Of her vagrant beauty, and the good looks that had gained his father his title of Philip the Handsome, she knew from report, that he had nothing. In her secret heart she reasoned in feminine fashion; physically Charles was no rival for Henry; therefore Henry would be more disposed to like him and to listen to him – he was said to be very reasonable and sensible – than to like Francis.

The meetings between the three young men who held Europe in their hands, were arranged for the spring and summer of 1520. Charles was to come to England in the spring; Henry was then to go to France and from there to proceed to Flanders, part of Charles' realm, for another meeting. Katharine hoped that thus a true balance would be struck. If they could meet and talk and get to understand one another, the peace of the world might be assured; and as she grew older she became even more pacifist. Her remark after Flodden and the death of the King of Scots, 'It should have been better for him to have been in peace,' expressed a conviction that had not diminished with the years.

The Emperor's visit to England was delayed by some trouble in Spain. May, the month in which England was at its most beautiful, began to expend itself in flowers and birdsong and Henry said that on the first of

June he must set out from Dover to Calais.

'*I* keep *my* promises,' he said. 'Emperor he may be; but if he delays beyond the first day of June he will find nobody to receive him.'

'Emperor he may be,' Katharine said, 'to me he is my sister's son, and to miss him by a day or two would grieve me.'

But Henry would not wait in London. There was much to see to; this peaceable visit needed almost as much preparation and foresight as the invasion of France seven years earlier had done. No Twelve Apostles but almost as many horses, knights in armour, and tents. And in addition great silk pavilions, a vast display of silver, clothes, jewels and the ladies with all their baggage. For days the shady, sunspeckled roads of Kent were crowded and the dust settled on the pale pink wild roses that wreathed the hedges. The Court took up its quarters under the roof of the Archbishop's Palace at Canterbury; the main train moved on to Dover and everything except the horses went aboard the waiting ships.

On May 26, by which time Katharine was almost desperate with anxiety, a messenger rode in to say that the Emperor's fleet had been sighted. Henry rode to Dover to greet his nephew by marriage and Katharine consulted with her ladies, and with her household officials and the Archbishop's cooks, as to what kind of meal would most please her nephew; and then turned her attention to the question of entertainment. There would be no language barrier; Henry's Latin was perfect, and no doubt, so would Charles' be; she would avoid speaking Spanish, of which Henry had a smattering but no fluency; music . . . Joanna's son would surely have an ear for a tune; and things that held a message to the eye, dancers, jugglers, contortionists.

When he arrived, side by side with Henry, her first thought was: Oh, what a poor little boy! Nothing that any ambassador or visiting Spaniard had said had really prepared her to meet – Joanna's son, Emperor – so stunted, immature-looking, ugly a creature. For the mouth, so prominent a feature in the pale face, she should, she admitted to herself afterwards, have been prepared, for on his first visit to Spain, as heir, some rude peasant shouted, 'Your Grace, keep your mouth shut. Spanish flies are very impertinent,' The remark had been reported to her and she had given it no importance; she imagined that perhaps at the time Charles had been speaking, and that the peasant was one of those who resented the linking of Spain to the Empire and eased his resentment by rudeness.

But now, face to face with her nephew, she saw the point of the remark. His lower jaw projected in such a way that he could not close his mouth properly. And even as she rustled forward to greet and embrace him she asked herself: Can he chew properly? Was I wise to order beef?

She threw her arms about him and gave the warmest, closest embrace that she had ever given anyone except her mother, her husband, the baby that had lived and the baby that had died, and bade him welcome to England.

He seemed pleased; he called her 'aunt', referred to Henry as 'my uncle'; was mannerly, unassuming, almost shy, but he never smiled, and he never laughed even when he applauded the musicians and the clowns and the jugglers. Katharine, from time to time, glanced at him, smiling herself, inviting him to smile. He never did. He praised; he said, 'This is very clever.' Or, 'It is amusing.' Or, of the music, 'It is beautiful.' But above the sagging misformed mouth the eyes very pale and rather prominent, never changed their expression, an intense stare, almost, but not quite, vacuous.

'A glum fellow,' Henry said in the privacy of their bedchamber.

She was anxious for Henry to like him, so she did not mention something that she had observed; that vacuous-seeming stare missed nothing.

'My sister was beautiful and her husband handsome. You remember them? At Windsor.'

Henry remembered; and what had happened just before that visit, and during it; the thrill which the mere touch of her hand could then convey. What happened? Where did love go?

'He had a poor start in life. His father dead, his mother crazed. And perhaps he was tired from his journey and felt at a disadvantage, being so small and plain.'

'Such as he is, we must make do with him. Mary will be Empress.'

'He will be thirty, and over, by the time she is marriageable. That worries me a little.' Otherwise it was a suitable match. It satisfied her strong family feeling; it would bring England into the strong community of the Empire, which would surely make for peace. And if, even now, she should bear a son, it would not be to his disadvantage to have the Emperor as a brother-in-law.

'The gap in their ages will be on the right side,' Henry said, unthinking; for although things had changed and *he* no longer leapt, fondness remained, and admiration and respect. Something remained when love had gone as a tree stood after the leaves had fallen. She was still his dear Kate and he had no wish to hurt her.

Charles' visit was necessarily short and Katharine took advantage of that to make it as much like a private, family visit as possible. 'We have so little time in which to discuss so many things,' she said. Even Wolsey was excluded from the meals and the conversations, and was forced to prowl about in anterooms, trying to pry out of pages and serving men some clue as to what the three royal people were discussing. He suspected Katharine of being Imperialist, as she suspected him of being Francophile and he resented the fact that now, on the very eve of the meeting between Henry and Francis, from which he hoped so much, he was being kept in ignorance of what was being said behind the closed doors.

Most of it was being said by Henry. Charles was not given to divulging what went on in his mind. Beyond saying that he was, more than anything else anxious for peace, the Emperor made a few positive statements. The pale eyes which seemed to see so little, had seen a good deal – Henry's vast vanity, amongst other things. So he asked questions, invited advice and listened, his mouth hanging open, while Henry answered, elaborated and advised. Then the astute mind set to work upon the evidence gleaned by eyes and ears and Charles realised that his uncle-by-marriage was not to be dismissed as a big, handsome, vain, self-opinionated fellow whose success so far was due to luck and to Wolsey, as people were inclined to think. Henry was shrewd and well-informed.

With the wry humour which nobody ever dreamed that he possessed, Charles thought: One cannot say that there is more in him than meets the eye, because what more could meet the eye? He conceals his real ability behind the show of bluff good-humour, vanity, pleasure-seeking and carnal appetites, just as I conceal mine . . . no, mine was concealed from the day of my birth; at this moment my uncle-by-marriage thinks me a dull fellow; my aunt believes that I am shy . . . Ha! Ha!

He had sensed Katharine's sincere goodwill from the first and so far as his cold, crippled nature allowed, was grateful for it since he, the most richly endowed man in the world, was also without question the loneliest; but he sensed also her complete subjugation to Henry's will, even to his mood. She sat, throughout these meals and conversations rather as though she were watching a tennis match, turning her head to this speaker and to that, smiling sometimes, now and then saying a few words, pleased because her husband and her nephew were getting along together so well. What she said was invariably sensible, but Charles was reasonably sure that once she was in France, as she would be in a few days' time, if Henry fell under Francis' spell, Katharine would turn Francophile too. At Guines, where Henry and Francis were to meet, if ever there was a conversation such as this, she would turn her head from one man to the other, and smile and murmur and be agreeable – as a woman should. His aunt's behaviour was impeccable, Charles admitted, but her influence was negligible. And Charles suspected that unless, at first sight, Henry and Francis took a real dislike to one another, some of their talk would be about war. These physically powerful men were inclined to look upon the battlefield as a tourney ground in which splendid prizes were to be won.

Still, Charles thought, listening and staring, he had one way of linking himself to Henry and to England that was not possible to Francis. Francis was married, he was free. Charles had little or no intention of marrying a girl almost seventeen years younger than himself, a bride for whom he must wait at least ten years; he had his duty to his Empire. But matrimony was, like everything else, a weapon and every weapon had its use. He agreed that to make public announcement of the betrothal would be absurd at this stage; and, in view of the imminent visit to France, tactless. Let it wait . . . but let it be understood, between us here, now in this room . . .

He felt a slight shiver of distaste when Katharine embraced him again and said, 'God has seen fit, so far, to withhold from me the blessing of a son, but in future I shall regard myself as your mother.' She could not know that he detested any reference, however indirect, to the mad woman who had borne him.

Charles rode away to join his fleet, now anchored off Sandwich, waiting to take him to Flanders where he hoped that Henry and Katharine would visit him when their visit to France ended. Henry and Katharine hurried down to Dover to embark for Calais.

It was seven years since Wolsey had sent to France the best-equipped, the most carefully provided for army that the world had seen, but in the interval he had not lost his eye for detail, or his sure touch. This time Henry was coming to France as a friend – but as a friend anxious to impress, eager to match hospitality and splendour with Francis, who was on his home ground.

Wolsey had seen to it all. Since March six thousand workmen – glad to be employed – had been labouring to build what was virtually a palace, but a palace out of a fairy tale, in which Henry and Katharine were to live and entertain, and a town around it to house the five thousand people, nobles and their ladies, officials and servants who accompanied them. The main pavilion and the banqueting hall were based on brick foundations, and although above they were constructed of canvas only, the canvas was supported on timbers too long for any ship to carry; they had been lashed together and floated oversea as rafts and then tugged in place by teams of sweating oxen. Everything that could be gilded or painted had been painted or gilded; glazed windows had been set into the canvas walls, and on the inside the canvas was hidden by tapestries and silk hangings and vast plaster wall pieces, mounted on wood, of biblical or allegorical scenes, brilliantly coloured.

On the opposite side of the valley the French had erected a similar palace, a matching town. Between the two, spies disguised as workmen or vendors, went to and fro, telling the French what the English were doing, or telling the English how the French were getting on. Competition and rivalry were strong long before the chief protagonists arrived. The English managed to keep one secret because only experts from London were allowed to enter a specially erected timber enclosure some few yards removed from the front of the main pavilion. When the screen was taken down, about an hour before the English King arrived, it was too late for the French either to match or out-do the marvel. It was a statue of Bacchus, said to have been brought from Italy; its bronze had been freshly gilded and it had been converted into a fountain from which three streams spouted, two of wine, one of clear water, fed from underground sources; nearby was a table furnished with cups, all of silver, so that anyone who came could quench his thirst.

But Wolsey was not only a superb organiser and an imaginative planner, he was a Cardinal, a prince of the Church, and logically, he had reserved the ultimate magnificence for the chapel which opened from the great central hall. Its ceiling and walls were lined and draped with cloth of gold, silver tissue and panels of embroidery, red roses and white silk, which matched the copes of the thirty-five priests chosen to serve there. The organ was of silver, ornamented with gold, and around the walls stood statues of the Twelve Apostles, all of gold and each as large as a well-grown child of four years. When the chapel was in use there would be real children too, three dozen young boys, the pick of all the monks' schools in England, chosen not only for their voices, but for uniformity of size, good complexion, and generally pleasing appearance. There were enough of them so that if a boy grew two inches in a fortnight, as boys sometimes did at that age, or developed spots, or lost the clarity of his voice, he could be withdrawn from the choir.

The chapel besides being the finest of the many buildings, had another distinction; it was the first known building to have been built far from the place where it was to stand. Its planning and assembling was a task which Wolsey would delegate to no one, so it had been built in England, in sections easily transportable, and then shipped to France, where workmen, like the fountain makers specially skilled, had only to put the numbered sections together and install the furnishings. They had completed the job in one day.

Wolsey had thought of everything; even the four thousand pounds of best wax needed for the making of candles; hundreds of the best sheep, calves and bullocks from English meadows awaited their last hour in French pastures; but, anxious to make this great occasion a flawless success, anxious to impress the French and to please his own beloved master, anxious that the final result of the gathering should be a lasting peace, Wolsey had overlooked one thing. Even he could not make people like one another. In Francis' suite there were knights who, only seven years earlier, had fled from the Battle of the Spurs; in Henry's rode the knights who had pursued them: 1513 was a recent memory; there were older and even harsher ones; it was the enemy who had come a-visiting; it was the enemy who was being visited. And nothing but rivalry, open or concealed, was possible between two magnificent young men, both Kings, both in their twenties, both proud and handsome, fond of show, both set to out-do the other.

The gathering known as the Field of the Cloth of Gold, partly because so much of that material was evident and partly because the French King's temporary town was sited in the Val Doré, was in essence as false and hollow as the grand pavilions where the outer canvas was painted to look like brickwork. Possibly the only genuine outcome – apart from a wary, cautious respect on either side for the power and resources of the other – was the friendship that sprang up immediately between Katharine and Queen Claude. Both were extremely pious women and neither was of a competitive nature; for the honour of their respective countries and to please their respective husbands, both must be magnificently clad, bejewelled, and attended; and generally there was no question of precedence; it was dependent upon in which canvas town they chanced to be. But early on they met in Wolsey's beautiful chapel, before the altar of God, where, in theory, all men were equal in humility. It was the privilege of the most important lady present to kiss a little tablet known as the Pax. Both hesitated and then, moved by a mutual impulse, kissed, not the Pax, but one another.

Their friendship blossomed as they sat and watched their husbands performing feats of arms in the tourney ground – not against one another, but against, with that exception, 'all comers'. Henry watching Francis, and Francis watching Henry, would each have been glad enough of a confrontation, but Wolsey had said it would be most unwise. 'Eventually, Your Grace, you would unhorse him,' he said tactfully. 'And although he might not resent it, there are those who would.'

Katharine and Claude reached that degree of intimacy where, before one of the competitive banquets over which cooks drove themselves crazy, they would pass little feminine questions across the intervening ground: 'What colour of gown and what jewels do you wish to wear this evening?' and so arrange that their colours should neither clash, nor, worse, be identical.

In Queen Claude's suite there were two English-born girls whom she had inherited from Mary Tudor when Louis XII died; most of Mary's ladies had gone home with her, but these, for reasons of their own, had not wished to, and both, being now bilingual could stay on and be useful. Each, in due time, was to be Queen of England, but who would have guessed it then? Anne Boleyn, so thin and dark, little altered, save in height, since Katharine had thought of her a changeling child amongst the fair, plump girls of Mary's suite, and Jane Seymour, fair enough but with a receding chin which the passing of the years had not improved. Katharine took pains to seek them out and speak kindly to them: and she was glad that they were in the household of good Queen Claude. Some great ladies – and some of them professedly pious – had little care for the souls or the bodies of their waiting women. In the dormitories of some palaces and magnificent houses there was enormous licence, some of them were little better than brothels. Queen Claude's ladies lived like nuns. Katharine approved, little knowing that this fact would eventually work to her own damage; that if Claude had been less strict, Anne Boleyn might have been easier game, taken, enjoyed and abandoned.

On the whole Katharine enjoyed this visit to France. There the usual crop of ugly rumours – With the King and the flower of his nobility exchanging compliments, gifts and banquets; the French fleet had secretly set sail to conquer England; ten thousand Frenchmen, skulking in the hills that ringed the Val Doré, were waiting to take Henry prisoner and hold him to ransom; both the water and the wine in the Bacchus fountain had been poisoned.

With each rumour, as it came in, her heart would jump a little; her congenital Francophobia taking over from her common sense. Henry was far calmer. Warned about the French fleet setting out for England he said, 'Nonsense! My brother of France promised Wolsey that no French ship should set sail on the Channel while we were here. And if they did, and if they landed, the militia could take care of them!' Told about the Frenchmen skulking in the hills, he said, 'This we *can* put to the test. I will ride alone, not by the direct road, but the one that skirts the hills, to pay Francis an unexpected visit.' He did so though Katharine – her distrust of the French coming uppermost – begged him not to. 'I do not believe in the hidden thousands, but two or three fanatics . . .' She had dark memories of Moorish ambushes.

But Henry rode, alone and unarmed, into Francis' camp; and came home jubilant. Next morning Francis, alone and unarmed, rode over to wish Henry good morning, and declared that he, and he alone, would hand his shirt and shave him.

On the surface it was all good-humoured and, as Claude said:

'They never completely grow up, these men. I often think that that is why God entrusted us women with the responsibility for their souls. Their minds are so easily diverted; their lusts so easily aroused. Children chasing butterflies . . . Holy Mother of God, what now?'

They were at Wolsey's table. The butcher's son from Ipswich having

feasted with the King of France and the King of England, had begged
leave to entertain them both at his and he had arranged things – he
thought – rather cleverly. There was no high table, set on a dais; there was
a round table, acknowledging neither head nor foot, set in the centre of a
round carpet which had come from Constantinople, and around it
another vast, circular table with the company seated around its outer rim.
At the inner, circular table, Wolsey sat at one place, Francis on his right,
Henry on his left – that had been prearranged; then two French Cardinals, and the two Queens whose growing friendship Wolsey had observed
with approval. 'A table with no head,' he had said to Henry, 'like that of
Arthur, at Camelot.'

Claude's question, 'What now,' had been evoked by Henry pushing
back his gilded chair, passing behind Wolsey, seizing Francis by the collar
and shouting, 'Come, you shall wrestle with me!'

For almost a fortnight he had restrained himself; in almost every move
he had made, every word he had spoken he had been guided by Wolsey's
Book of Ordinances. He had watched Francis, his junior, but more nearly
his equal than any other man he had ever seen, just as wide of shoulder,
and that irking half inch taller, match him, exploit for exploit, against *other*
men. But he was certain that had he not agreed that open confrontation
with the King of France was unwise, Francis would have been humbled.
Now, exhilarated by wine, aware that the meeting was nearing its end,
and sure that a simple wrestling match, however it ended, could rouse no
enmity, he was determined to show that though older, he was stronger
and more supple.

Francis was taken by surprise by the sudden assault, and angered by it;
he contented himself for a straining second or two in merely resisting
Henry's attempt to throw him, and then, suddenly exerting his strength to
the full, lifted and threw . . . Before eyes that were gratified or horrified, the
King of England sailed through the air and fell, full length and with a
heavy thud on the carpeted floor.

He was up instantly, face crimson, blue eyes blazing.

'Again,' he said, a trifle breathlessly, winded by the fall. But by that time
Wolsey was on his feet and between them, saying, 'My lords! My lords!'
And Claude clutched Francis by the arm, while Katharine took Henry's;
'No more, I beg you.' 'Desist, I pray you. Would you frighten us to death?'

'But he threw me!' Henry said.

'No, no!' Francis said in a loud, carrying voice. 'You threw yourself, you
resisted so stoutly. I vow I thought you had taken me with you and was
surprised to find myself left standing.'

Claude's pressure on his arm changed from entreaty to approbation.
Katharine said in Henry's ear, 'He will not risk a further bout.' Wolsey

said, 'My lords, the next dish is served.'

Francis who in the circumstances could afford to be generous, said, 'Somebody must cut my meat for me. My brother of England has pulled my arm from its socket.'

So, with amiable pretence, the meeting of the Field of the Cloth of Gold, in itself an amiable pretence, came to an end. Henry and Francis were each to reign for another twenty-seven years, and to die in the same year; their relationship was to fluctuate, now friendly, now inimical; Henry always thought of Francis, no matter against what background, as the man who had thrown him and evaded a return bout; and Francis always, in his secret mind, thought of Henry as the typical Englishman who would come up behind you and seize you by the collar.

The Emperor, silent and withdrawn, competing with nobody because there was nobody on earth with whom he must compete, sat waiting at Gravelines for the promised visit of his aunt and his uncle-by-marriage. And they, and the French, had hardly quitted the Val Doré, and men had hardly begun to shift the stuff and the symbols of splendour when one of the violent storms of early July blew up; the wind and the rain could make a sharp distinction between pretence and reality and in a short time the fairy-tale pavilions were tattered, lurching ruins, lacking entirely the sad dignity of buildings once sound and good, fallen on evil days.

CHAPTER 10

Little Henry Fitzroy, living proof that, mated to the right woman, Henry could beget a healthy boy, was two years old when his father snatched at a chance to act as a Crusader, not in armed combat against the Infidel, but as a theologian against heresy. In Germany there was an Augustinian friar named Martin Luther who for some time had been causing his superiors concern by questioning the authority of the Pope, the authority of bishops and some points of Church doctrine. Henry believed, and Katharine agreed with him, that Luther had read overmuch, and completely misinterpreted, Holy Writ which the new printing presses were pouring out in vast numbers. His own extremely revolutionary ideas were also disseminated in the new print: he held that there were only three sacraments – the Church observed seven; he did not believe in the celibacy of the clergy; he said that when the Sacrament of Holy Communion was celebrated, every communicant should take both bread and wine. Finally he nailed a list of what he called 'protests' to the door of the church in Wittenburg and hundreds of people, already prepared by his pamphlets, began to call themselves Protestants.

'He is a dangerous fellow,' Henry said. 'And his protest should be answered.'

'He has been excommunicated,' Katharine said.

'For such as he excommunication means nothing. He has already excommunicated himself. Someone should take all his arguments and refute them, one by one.'

'Someone should,' she agreed. 'Why not you?'

She was delighted to see that Henry took the suggestion seriously. The very name of Luther was anathema to her and it pleased her to think that it should be her husband who would demolish such wicked arguments. It was also important that every possible sphere of common interest between them should be cultivated. She was losing her hold over Henry's body, but they could still share the pleasures of the mind.

In writing his treatise, Henry made use of his education for the Church, his knowledge of Latin, his skill with words: he wrote swiftly and well. Katharine was capable of looking up references for him, and of copying a corrected page, and she was always willing to sit, her hands busy with the needle and listen while he read what he had written. She was free with praise: 'A splendid argument!' 'That is very clever.' As she had hoped, the project brought them together.

Two clerks made the final copies, one for the printers, one for the Pope, who when he had read *Assertium Septum Sacrementorum Contra M. Luther*, bestowed upon its author the title of Defender of the Faith. Henry proudly added it to all his other titles.

But in his heart he felt that he deserved more, a blessing from Heaven as well as from Rome He still found difficulty in believing that what he wanted was to be denied him. And it was true that in the middle of such disturbance of function as Katharine was undergoing, women did sometimes conceive.

He braced himself to make a sacrifice painful enough to deserve a near miracle. He would give up his comfortable, complaisant mistress, Mary Boleyn.

He knew that in her inarticulate way she was very fond of him and he did not underestimate the worth of what she was about to lose – himself; so he set about making the break with some consideration.

One evening he was able to say to her, 'Mary, I have found a husband for you.'

She took it calmly. Men preferred a married mistress; and in future the liaison would be conducted behind a husband-and-wife screen, instead of a father-and-daughter one. It would be better; for her father was always nagging her – Ask for this; ask for that; you stupid wench, make hay while the sun shines! Occasionally, because she would ask for nothing, he struck her.

'Who is it?' she asked with an almost total lack of interest.

'William Carey.'

'Oh no!'

'And what's wrong with him? He is of gentle birth, young, good-looking. Granted he has no estate but that can be remedied. He is fond of you, too. Elated at the prospect of marrying you.'

'He would be,' she said almost sullenly. 'He is in love with me. He would be jealous. He would not share me. It would mean the end – for us.'

'Dear Mary; it must be the end.'

'Why? What have I done?'

'Nothing. But circumstances demand it.'

He had never had to do with an hysterical woman. Katharine had taken blow after blow with dignity; Bessie Blount had allowed herself to be paid off with the cheerfulness of a mercenary at the end of a campaign; even his sister Mary, protesting against her marriage to old Louis, had not behaved like this. The sight of Mary Boleyn, so placid, undemanding and easy, tearing at the lace of her bodice, tearing at her hair, banging her head against the wall and screaming, appalled him.

'Stop it,' he said, taking her by the shoulders and shaking her into silence. 'People will think murder is being done.'

As he shook her the tears flew from her face and made dark splashes on his yellow doublet. And her nose was running. He felt for her something of the aversion he felt for the sick and the maimed.

'Will you listen to me . . . 'I'll knight him . . . You shall be Lady. I'll give him a manor and some good office.'

'Keep your gifts. You never bought me. You shall not sell me. I loved you. I love you, God help me. Go away. Get out of my sight.'

He had not taken an order from anyone since his father died.

'Very well,' he said, his tender care for her well-being and his regret at parting from her all swallowed in rage. He stamped away. If she despised his gifts, let her do without them.

Mary realised that she still had her father to face. She tidied herself and her limited mind moved from the shock of rejection to the problem of how to explain. It was with a good imitation of her usual stolidity that she said to Sir Thomas:

'William Carey has asked me to marry him. And I have accepted.'

'Without asking me!'

'He asked the King. He consented.'

'Ah!' Sir Thomas said, seeing as he thought, the whole thing. Shrewd, after all, not bothering with little benefits, waiting for the day of settlement. 'And what will your marriage portion be?'

'Nothing.'

Sir Thomas almost became hysterical himself.

'What, after all this time. All this evil talk. People saying I profited by your shame. I who carried the canopy over the Princess at her christening when you were a green girl. Nothing. You tell me nothing. In God's name, why not?'

'We love one another. We need nothing more.'

'You stupid, senseless, improvident wench! You loose-living slut! You trollop!' With each abusive word he slapped her savagely about the head. 'You could have had three manors. So marry your pauper and live on love. And starve. From me you will get nothing.'

The hoped-for, prayed-for last-minute miracle did not come about.

In May of the year 1522, when the Emperor paid his second visit to England, he noticed a change in his uncle who was far less affable than he had been two years earlier in Canterbury and at Gravelines. His aunt Katharine was, as before, kind and welcoming; the little cousin to whom he was now officially betrothed, was, at six years old, an admirable and accomplished child; but Henry had changed.

Charles, seeming to notice nothing, noticed that Wolsey was in the ascendant and Wolsey, Charles knew, was ardently Francophile. The acute political awareness which was, after his religion, the most lively thing about him, quickened in the young Emperor and made him susceptible even to a change in a tone of voice.

The moment of truth came on an evening when they were discussing Princess Mary's future. Charles had little intention of marrying a child so young, but he needed Henry's goodwill and he needed time. So plans must appear to be made.

'In three years' time,' he said, 'when she is nine. Then she must come to Spain and be reared as a Spanish princess. And she must bring with her a dowry of eighty thousand English pounds.'

'Two years ago I should have agreed,' Henry said. 'Now I consider the terms ridiculous. She will be Queen of England, she must remain in her own country. And England will be her dower . . .'

As he said that he felt sick. England, his England, part of this dullard's vast Empire. Because I have no son. No lawful son.

'I was obliged to make some concessions over the dowry and the place of residence of the Princess,' Charles said. 'There were some on my council who deplored the betrothal.'

'Why?'

'This is not pleasant for me to say. But some – good lawyers too –

professed a doubt as to her legitimacy.'

'They did *what?*'

Charles said solemnly, 'Ideas, even when repudiated, are not without effect. Within my Empire there are those who question the Pope's author-ity as a whole. This is heresy which must be put down. But in small ways . . . Nowadays even a good Catholic may ask difficult questions. I assure you, it was a good Catholic who asked whether even Papal author-ity could make lawful a man's marriage to his brother's widow.'

'Of all the outrageous . . .' Henry began and stopped. 'You say this in good faith?'

'In good faith. The man who asked the question I silenced. Forever. But the question was asked and the doubt lingers. I think therefore that over the question of the Princess's place of residence and the amount of her dowry, it would be as well not to be intransigent.'

Never, not even when thrown by Francis, had Henry known such humiliation. Not to be intransigent. To be told that by this malformed little runt!

With difficulty he mastered his fury.

'It may be that this talk is premature. By the time the child is nubile, other thoughts may prevail. If you are as earnest to root out such heretical notions as I have been and intend to be.'

'Yours is a task comparatively easy. You can have no idea what it means to govern an Empire which includes such divergent elements as most Christian Spain, and Germany, which I begin to think, was never even completely converted.'

For a moment Henry reverted to his avuncular, advice-giving role.

'Heresy must not be tolerated,' he said. 'As I see it those who rebel against one form of authority are presently likely to rebel against others. Church and Throne are one.' He added, with the sourness which Charles had noted as new, 'You may find that it pays you to be – intransigent.' He smiled as he bounced back the offensive word, but it was not a pleasant smile. Charles, ignoring the jab, went on to talk of the problem, mention-ing the Netherlands as the area most prone to disaffection; so many rich merchants, so many wealthy towns; Spain, poor and agrarian, was far more biddable; though born in Flanders, he always felt more at home in Spain . . .

*

He took his leave of his relatives and of England, without realising that into his uncle's mind he had dropped a seed which would bring forth a strange harvest.

CHAPTER 11

When Mary was nine she did not go to Spain. Instead she went to Ludlow.

Henry had thought deeply and long about the possibility of persuading the people to accept Henry Fitzroy as his heir. It would not be easy, but his own vast popularity encouraged him to think that what he willed would not be gainsaid. Wolsey's response to the suggestion was not encouraging, the Archbishop of Canterbury's even less so and the Duke of Norfolk said bluntly that it could not be done. But three men did not make up England, they did not even constitute the King's Privy Council. When the boy was six, Henry decided that a preliminary test, at least, might be made.

The boy was six, strong, big for his age, very handsome, when his father brought all his gift of showmanship to the ceremony of knighting and ennobling him. Henry Fitzroy knelt and rose to his feet, Sir Henry Fitzroy. Then he withdrew, to reappear, looking, for all his size, very small between the Dukes of Norfolk and Suffolk, and knelt again while the patent of nobility was read. When he stood up for the second time he was Duke of Richmond and Duke of Somerset, Lord Admiral of England, Keeper of the city and castle of Carlisle. And amongst the titles, spattering down like autumn leaves over the russet head of a very bored but well-mannered little boy, there were some that, for all they meant, might have been mythical. Normandy, Gascony and Aquitaine, once the provinces of English Kings, and still claimed by name, just as Henry claimed to be King of France, though only Calais remained in English possession.

As a spectacle, an occasion for rejoicing, for the rich an excuse to buy new clothes, for the poor an opportunity to eat and drink at the King's expense, the ceremony was a success, but it failed of its objective. Not one person in all that long day echoed the words that sounded in the proud father's mind – He would make a King. The boy's looks and deportment were praised, but too often there was the unwelcome addition beginning 'It is a pity . . .' or 'If only . . .'

Katharine, though Henry had never mentioned his plan to her, knew the purpose of all this; particularly significant was the title of Richmond, and of those faraway places ordinarily shared out amongst king's sons. For her it was a day of deep misery; such a sturdy, composed little boy, so obviously Henry's son. He should have been hers. But she drew comfort from the thought that God, in His infinite wisdom, working out His inscrutable purpose, intended Mary to be Queen, as He had intended Isabella to be Queen of Castile. Mary was, Katharine became every day more certain, something very special, not in looks but in intellect and disposition.

And it was plain that though Henry had not yet fully resigned himself, the people had. They showed it in subtle ways. All day all people of rank had been careful to pay particular deference to the Princess of Wales; and when the crowds, crammed with food and somewhat drunk, roared for the Duke of Richmond to show himself, the demand was no sooner met than there was another roar, incomparably more enthusiastic, 'And the Princess of Wales!' 'We want Mary!'

England had spoken. The King of England heard.

At the very end the new Duke was tired and dazed; but he wanted to say good night to the Queen. His father had occasionally brought him to Court, unofficially, and the Queen had always been very kind to him and given him sweetmeats. He had sometimes wished, in a blind childish way that she were his mother; and once he said so, 'I wish I was your little boy!' Quite the wrong thing to say; she cried and said, 'So do I!' And the second sweetmeat had not been forthcoming. She was a lady who set great store by good behaviour, but in a kind way. At home if he said or did anything amiss he was liable to be slapped.

Today he thought that he had behaved very well, and going towards the Queen at the end of it all, he hoped that she would say so. Tonight he did not want a piece of marzipan, he had eaten his fill.

Katharine sat, with Mary on one side and Lady Salisbury on the other. The Duke of Richmond knew Mary, who on his visits had sometimes played with him, putting her books or her lute aside for a little while. He took her by the hand and swung her away and went to Katharine's side and made his little bow and said, as instructed:

'I wish Your Grace good night.' Then added his own words: 'I hope you think I have been a good boy today.'

Katharine said, 'You have been a very good boy.' She put out her arm, pulled him close and kissed him in the sight of all. 'Sleep well, my lord Richmond.' He smiled up at her.

But later, alone with Henry, she said:

'He will now be about the Court and he must learn to treat Mary with respect. She is Princess of Wales.'

The emotions and strains and disappointments of the day had taken their toll; Henry's temper flared; not the hearty, noisy temper that a little shouting and stamping could dissipate; something more deadly.

'Yes,' he said, after a little pause. 'She is Princess of Wales. And I think it is high time she went to Ludlow and showed herself in her Principality.'

The boy had meant no harm; he was only six; Mary was nine; were children supposed to conform with strict Spanish etiquette? Let Mary go to Ludlow, where nobody would take her aside by swinging on her hand.

Confounded, Katharine said, 'But she is only nine! We have hardly known a day apart . . . I have supervised every moment of her days; taught her . . .'

'And done very well,' he conceded. 'But there are things that no mother can teach. Independence is one.'

'That is true. But I thought at twelve. Would twelve be not soon enough?'

'Not as things are. The Welsh are always complaining of being a mere appendage. Mary's presence at Ludlow will appease them. And there she will be treated with respect.'

She saw where she had made her error and hastened to amend it.

'I did not mean to criticise his behaviour. No other little boy in the world could have done better. I only said that he must learn . . . as all boys must.'

He was still clear-minded and fair-minded enough to realise that he was punishing Kate for the disillusions of the day. He said – and it was a lie – for which he would do penance: 'What you said had nothing to do with it. I have been minded for two months now to send Mary to Ludlow.'

'Have you chosen her governess?'

That was Kate. So reasonable. And of course, had he thought about Mary's removal he would have chosen her governess.

'Yes. The Countess of Salisbury.'

'The perfect choice,' Katharine said warmly. 'There is no one to whom I would so willingly entrust her.' Though it would mean the removal of her closest friend amongst the English ladies.

Henry, knowing this, realising so far as a man could what this day had meant to her, remembering how she kissed the young Duke, could but admire her. A woman in a million.

'I would like, with your permission, to tell Mary myself.'

'Who else should do it?' he asked. He was off to Hever, Tom Boleyn's Sussex home. He needed something to sweeten his mood after this day's doings. Mary's sister, Anne, was there, her sister but so different that it was unbelievable that they should be related; and he hoped to seduce her.

It was the second time within a brief space when Katharine had been obliged to break what she feared would be unwelcome news to Mary. On the former occasion it had been that the Emperor had broken his betrothal and was to marry another cousin, Isabella of Portugal. She had explained carefully, wondering how much a child of nine would feel rejected. She had spoken of the difference in age, of the long tradition of marriage between Spain and Portugal. She had not mentioned that Isabella of Portugal was to be the most richly endowed bride in the world. She did not herself believe that the dowry had much influenced Charles; age had; like every other monarch he needed an heir and he could not wait until he was thirty before he married.

Mary had taken the news with the utmost calm, simply saying, 'But I shall still be Queen of England.'

She took the order to go to Ludlow in much the same manner.

'I shall miss you sorely. But you will write to me?'

'Every week. And you must write to me. Not so often perhaps, because you will be busy. The Welsh chieftains are very poor, and very proud . . . I remember. If they kill a sheep it is an occasion and they make a feast of it. I found that they were pleased to be told that there was no such mutton in the world, and that is true. They like their Princess in her best gown and bejewelled. And it is essential to learn their names and say them properly. I found the names difficult. . . .'

She and Arthur had laughed, practising the names over. Madog ap Llewellyn of Meirionydd, to be distinguished from Llewellyn Ben of Senghenydd and all those Ap Rhys's. More than twenty years ago; the young Katharine as much of a ghost as the young Arthur. Laughter, friendly talk, scenery so beautiful that to one straight from Spain the lush greenery had had a fairy-tale quality. And rain almost every day. Looked back upon, the whole brief episode had a wistful, unreal quality.

'Shall I continue my Latin?'

'Yes. Master Federston will instruct you. Write to me in Latin, Mary; that will be good practice for us both.'

'I shall write a little every day. How long must I stay there?'

'Not long, darling. Just long enough to please the Welsh and eat mutton with all those who claim descent from Llewellyn Ap Rhys. And Merlin!'

Smile, child, smile.

But Mary, unsmiling drew back a pace, and with a pressing stare that resembled her father's, said:

'*Am* I being put aside to make way for the Duke of Richmond?'

'Of course not. Who put that nonsense into your head?'

'I heard it said. In a pitying voice. I do not care to be pitied – except by you, when I am ill. And I *am* being sent away.'

'Not for that reason, I assure you. Because you are Princess of Wales, and will one day be Queen of England. Nobody can ever put you aside. Nobody.'

Mary left, not very cheerfully, but the letters which came with touching regularity sounded happy and soon included a few Welsh words of greeting or farewell, strangely and phonetically spelt. All Lady Salisbury's reports were good. Her Highness invariably comported herself with grace and dignity suitable to a princess twice her age. Her health was excellent; her lessons proceeding well.

Katharine missed Mary and her favourite English lady and then settled down to what she thought life would be henceforth, a peaceful, middle-aged routine. The child-bearing years with their ardours, their hopes, disappointments and griefs were over; she had her religious observances, her public duties, her private charities; she had, if no longer Henry's love-making, his company and all the interests they shared. He seemed to have settled down, too; he made no further attempt to foist Bessie Blount's boy upon the people of England. There was no rumour of his taking any woman as his mistress. Katharine, life's zenith gone, faced the sunset with equanimity.

Presently, she realised, the business of finding a husband for Mary would need to be dealt with. Every girl needed a husband, and a Queen needed an heir. Now and then Katharine hoped that Henry, so hating the idea of England being absorbed through marriage by some other country, would consider and propose the obvious solution – Mary's marriage to Reginald Pole, the son of the Countess of Salisbury. On his mother's side he was related to the Plantagenets – the only surviving shoot of that stock whose name it was now unwise to mention, in Tudor-ruled England. But it was royal blood; marriage with him would not, for Mary, be a mésal-liance: and he was clever, bookish, pious. He was sixteen years older than Mary, but the gap would not matter so much as in the case of the Emperor, for Reginald could never be King. He would be Mary's hus-band, Consort to the Queen.

But all this could be left for the future; there was plenty of time. Katharine merely hoped that when the time came, Henry, wishing Eng-land to be an independent entity, would choose Reginald Pole rather than what seemed to be the only alternative, a French Prince. Philip of Spain, the son of the Emperor Charles and Isabella of Portugal, whom Mary was eventually to marry, was not yet born and Katharine, casting about idly in her mind saw the choice between the French and Reginald Pole and hoped that when the time came Henry would see what was best for Mary and for England.

The two English girls who had served Queen Claude had come back to England in 1523 when, for a brief time, war between England and France had seemed imminent. Jane Seymour had gone to her home, Wolf Hall, in Wiltshire, but the Duke of Norfolk had asked, almost begged, Katharine to find a place for his niece, Anne Boleyn.

'She has no real home, Your Grace; my sister died years ago, and Sir Thomas remarried – a farmer's daughter.' The Duke's dislike of his brother-in-law was undisguised. 'He has never attempted to do anything for either of his daughters; and I . . . I have my own responsibilities. But I feel sorry for the girl and thought that an appeal to you . . . Though I know,' he said deprecatingly, 'that you have a preference for good-looking women about you.'

He had stumbled by chance upon the words which immediately appealed to Katharine; who, if she had momentarily thought that Mary Boleyn's sister was one of the last people she wished to have about her, dismissed the thought immediately.

'I will make room for her,' she said.

'This one has sense in her head and has acquired accomplishments. I trust that Your Grace will find her useful.'

Having done his duty to a young relative without having to spend a penny, he retired, well satisfied with himself. Queen Katharine was always very generous to her women, and if Anne should marry – the Duke thought this unlikely, she had so few attractions – Her Grace would give her a dowry; and if she failed to find a husband, she would be safe enough; for though Katharine liked her women to be handsome, she never dismissed one simply because she was old.

So Anne Boleyn came to Court and Katharine, at first sight, thought that her looks had not improved much; and that, despite her uncle's words, she did not look like a girl who was ill-provided for. Her dresses were extremely stylish, with an individuality of their own, every colour and fashion carefully chosen to set off her one undeniable attraction, that curious elegant grace. Viewed more closely, the clothes revealed to Katharine – experienced in makeshift – that they had been remade, turned, mended. And her only ornaments were worthless; the collar, which invariably encircled her overlong neck, was of base metal, gilded over, the gilt worn away in places, studded with false gems and her one ring was set with a rather meagre piece of amber. Yet they, too, were well chosen.

Katharine was delighted when young Harry Percy, heir to the Earl of

Northumberland and a member of Wolsey's household, began to pay Mistress Boleyn marked attention. He was a handsome young man; he would one day be very rich. Many of the other ladies – not one of whom liked the newcomer – were envious, constantly asking themselves, and one another, what he could possibly see in her.

'She's not even amiable,' Maria de Moreto said. 'And that great mole on her neck and that extra finger.' Nobody had ever made a bid for Maria's hand, and no one now ever would; it was natural that she should feel envious; but others, young, pretty, even betrothed, said things just as sour. Harry Percy could marry whom he chose, why pick on her?

'He sees her with other eyes,' Katharine said. But she did snatch an opportunity to speak seriously to young Percy and to say that Anne had no mother and her father was much occupied with affairs, she felt it her duty to enquire whether his intentions were honourable; because, if not, the way he was behaving was likely to damage Mistress Boleyn's reputation. He said, with integrity shining from his eyes, as well as resounding in his voice, that his one wish in the world was to marry Mistress Boleyn. He had asked her to marry him and she had accepted; but Sir Thomas was absent from London just now; the moment he returned his consent would be asked and the betrothal announced.

'We already regard ourselves as plighted, Your Grace. I can think of no reason why Sir Thomas should object to me. We plan to be married before Christmas.'

'You brought me news of Flodden,' Katharine said. 'And in its way this is equally good news. I like my ladies to marry and be cherished. I trust that you will be very happy.'

Then something inexplicable happened. The Earl of Northumberland came hurrying down from the north; was closeted with Cardinal Wolsey and emerged to say that his son was already betrothed – had been for years – to Lady Mary Talbot, daughter of the Earl of Shrewsbury; and, a betrothal being as binding as marriage, he must marry her or no one.

Then one of Wolsey's secretaries, a man named Thomas Cromwell, had asked audience of the Queen and told her, in rather roundabout terms, that circumstances being what they were it would be easier for everyone if Mistress Boleyn retired from Court and went to her father's house at Hever.

'It seems harsh to me, Master Cromwell, that she should, in one move, lose the man who loves her *and* her place in my household.'

'So it may seem to Your Grace,' Cromwell said. He was the son of a blacksmith and to him the world had always been harsh; his first tottering steps had been taken in a place where everything was hard, heavy and dangerous. 'My lord of Northumberland would very willingly have taken his son back with him, but he refused to go and being of full age, could not well be forced. His grace and my lord Cardinal are agreed that to allow the two young people to remain in contact could have disastrous results. They might even find someone who would, in ignorance, marry them. That would cause a scandal; and worse still set the Earls of Northumberland and Shrewsbury by the ears.'

There were some people apparently who regarded betrothals as sacrosanct. In her heart Katharine held to the old ways; she could spare a thought for Lady Mary Talbot and she had no wish to see two Earls at enmity. Old Henry VII had done his best to reduce the power of his noblemen, he had forbidden them to maintain private armies, but the rules were easily avoided; every great landowner in England could still muster a force of retainers. . . .

'Very well,' Katharine said. 'I understand that Sir Thomas Boleyn is not in London.'

'He has gone to see to his estate in Norfolk. Blickling, Your Grace.'

'Then Mistress Boleyn shall go there, immediately.'

She had known humiliation and disappointment herself and could give the right due to the girl's behaviour in this crisis. No tears; no self-pity. The news had been broken to her by Lady Cuddington to whom Katharine had entrusted the unenviable task, and Anne had come and curtseyed, and asked leave to withdraw. 'Your Grace knows upon what cause.'

'I do; and believe me, I am sorry for it. God go with you.'

And Katharine had taken steps to see that the poor girl did not go unaccompanied; she had persuaded Lady Lucia Bryant to spare one of her serving women, a stern-faced but very reliable woman named Emma Arnett, to conduct Anne to Blickling in Norfolk and to hand her over to her father.

Sir Thomas had another house, Hever in Kent, and when, Katharine thought, as she did sometimes, about the girl who could wear a collar of base metal, studded with coloured glass, and a turned dress, and somehow, for all her lack of beauty, make what was tawdry seem to be real, she hoped that in Norfolk or Kent there had been some hearty, bucolic young man, one of the country squires of a breed only known in England, who would have been attracted to the girl, perhaps a little dazzled by the possibility for having as his wife a woman of little physical charm – except grace, but who had waited upon three Queens, could read and write in French as well as English, could handle the lute expertly, was equally good at the virginal, and could make an old dress look like new.

And then, in 1527, after four years, Anne Boleyn was back in London, back at Court, her sponsor this time not her uncle, but Henry himself.

'Tom Boleyn,' he said, 'has done me sterling service and I have bestowed upon him the title he coveted and to which he had a definite, though disputed right. He is now Earl of Wiltshire. His Countess is a good little creature, but humbly born and by nature shy; she will not take her place at Court – and wise she is; she cures a good ham and I understand can make butter with the best; but his daughter is not her daughter; she is . . .'

'I remember her well. Four years ago she was removed. Because Henry Percy wished to marry her. Oh yes, I remember her.'

'And you would be willing to receive her again?'

'It would be difficult not to; she left in no disgrace. The one thing is . . . she did not get along very well with the others. I could never see why.'

'Things will be easier now. As an Earl's daughter she will have her own apartments,' Henry said.

He was tired of riding to and fro between London and Hever; he had been doing it for four years. No man had ever wooed a woman so sedulously as he had wooed Anne, or been so little rewarded. Four years earlier, his fancy lightly taken, he had told Wolsey to break up that boy-and-girl nonsense; Tom Boleyn's daughter was no fit match for Northumberland's heir. That had been done and after a little space he had gone down to Hever, set on easy conquest and been rebuffed and eluded in a way that had turned fancy into infatuation. Anne had made it cruelly plain that she would never be his mistress and that, instead of cooling his ardour, had fanned it. He had only lured her back to Court by making grandiose promises, which he intended to keep: and to do that he needed Wolsey's help and full co-operation. He knew that Wolsey would not work his best on the problem if he knew that the ultimate aim was to make Tom Boleyn's daughter Queen; so care was necessary and great discretion; he had not dared to go to Hever one hundredth as often as he wished. With Anne amongst Katharine's ladies again he would at least see her, talk to her, dance with her sometimes without making himself conspicuous.

So Anne was back at Court; no longer a mere knight's daughter, but Lady Anne, daughter of an earl; and the collar she always wore was now of gold, set with real jewels; her clothes were better too; dresses of amber-coloured, or tawny velvet, or of silk, so darkly cream that it made her sallow skin look fairer than it was. She still lacked figure, no bosom at all; and she still lacked the power of endearing herself to other ladies. She was still the changeling.

Wolsey said, 'Your Grace, I see Clement's predicament; it is not easy for one Pope to go against a ruling which his predecessor gave under his leaden seal. But the Archbishop of Canterbury and I have gone very thoroughly into the matter and we have decided that there is sufficient doubt to make action feasible. The Holy See has many things to consider; we gave your great matter our undivided attention and our conclusion has been forwarded to Rome.'

'Where it will lie on a shelf, gather dust.'

'Things move slowly there,' Wolsey agreed. He knew why. He should have been the Pope – and could, would have been, but for the hidden influence of the Emperor. That influence would also operate against Henry's plea that his marriage was unlawful; the Emperor was Katharine's nephew.

'The questioning of Julius' dispensation,' he said, 'could be made unnecessary, very simply. I considered it the other night when I lay wakeful. Her Grace is, as we all know, a woman of great piety. If she could be convinced that her marriage was unlawful, she would abjure it and retire into a convent . . . There is a precedent for it. A saintly Queen of France did precisely that, and allowed her husband to remarry. It would be much the speediest way.

'I think she might do it,' Henry said, after a little pause. 'She is half a nun already; she wears the habit, under her clothes. She has a room in Greenwich, bare as a cell. She gives time and money to charities . . . My true Thomas, unfailing friend; I think you have hit on it. Will you – as Cardinal – propose it to her?'

In the eighteen years of Henry's reign Wolsey had come to power and more power by making himself indispensable, not only in great things, like the fitting out of an army or the organisation of events like the Field of the Cloth of Gold, but in innumerable, small ways. 'I will see to it.' 'Your Grace may safely leave it to me.' But now, though he had no fondness for Katharine, whom he regarded as an obstacle to his French policy, and who had once criticised his way of life, he was glad enough to be able to say, with truth and with feigned regret,

'Your Grace forgets. I am about to leave for France. Francis must be persuaded, or spurred into doing something about this Italian business. If only because while Clement is virtually the prisoner of the Emperor, he is most unlikely to give a decision favourable to you. In case the Queen spurns the suggestion we must make certain that Clement has cause for gratitude to Your Grace and the King of France.'

'Rome, falling to Charles' troops, was a stroke of ill luck for me,' Henry said.

'And for the world,' Wolsey said. 'Even for the Emperor, in the long run. Those who sacked Rome were German *landknechts*, little better than heathen, as their behaviour to nuns and monks showed.'

Momentarily *diverted* from his egocentricity, Henry said:

'The Emperor once told me himself that his German subjects were hardly Christian . . . So, must I tell her myself or would the suggestion come better from a woman?'

'What woman has Your Grace in mind?'

'The Countess of Salisbury. The Queen trusts her completely and she is back in London now.'

Wolsey looked down at his plump, well-kept hands, the great Cardinal's ring glowing on one finger.

'I should deem that unwise,' he said. 'If I know women they would end crying on one another's shoulders and saying that Julius, being Pope, could never be in error. Pious women hold extreme views.'

'As usual you are right,' Henry said gloomily. 'I must do it myself; but it is a job I have little heart for.'

Greenwich was still Katharine's favourite residence, because here Henry had met her in the lime walk and taken her from the room that smelt of the stable to the room that smelt of the past; here she had been married, and here Mary had been born. As she grew older and knew less positive happiness and occasionally felt that she had failed Henry and England, she cherished her memories more fondly.

Katharine was taking advantage of the bright light of a June morning to work upon a shirt for Henry; the linen was so fine and the stitches so small that by candlelight or on a dull day such work was impossible. When Henry came in she thought he had come to pay his courtesy morning call, a thing he never failed to do when they were under the same roof. With the shirt still in her hands she rose and curtseyed, and waited for him to seat himself. He remained on his feet and jerked his head towards her women.

'I have a private matter which I wish to discuss with you.'

She imagined that she knew what it was. The new alignment with France was to be enforced by Mary's betrothal to a French prince. Mary had in fact been in London for some time so that the French Ambassador could report upon her appearance, disposition and accomplishments.

Henry seemed to have difficulty in broaching the subject; he told her to sit down; sat down himself; jumped up and went to the window and made a comment about the fine weather.

'Is it about Mary?' she asked, resuming her stitching.

'Only indirectly. It concerns you and me.'

She looked up quickly. The light from the window fell upon his bright hair and massive figure. He ate and drank prodigiously, but he took so much hard exercise that it was muscle, not fat that made his bulk. His skin was still clear and ruddy, his eyes bright. Such a handsome man, she thought, and looked upon him with doting admiration. He saw the look, flinched and to escape it turned to the window. Speaking with his back to her he said:

'It concerns our marriage. I have thought long and hard about this, Katharine, and I beg you not to take it amiss . . . I think the dispensation should not have been given. You were my brother's wife. That is why our union has been cursed.'

The gist of it jerked out as he swung around again and met her look of bland incomprehension. Something in his mind cried: Oh, understand; make it easy for me; you with such a reputation for kindness, be kind to me!

She seemed to have been struck dumb.

'It is plainly set down in Leviticus,' he blundered on. 'If a man takes his brother's wife, they shall be childless.'

Childless? Had he gone mad? Leviticus, a set of laws laid down for Jews. Had he taken a fall and deranged his mind?

'I cannot understand,' she said. 'Ours is no childless marriage. We have Mary. Henry, are you well? Have you had a fall? There is no sense in what you are saying. No sense at all.'

'I am in my senses. I have seen the truth of the matter. So must you. We should never have married. The Pope was mistaken; the dispensation was not valid.'

'Your father and mine accepted it. So did you.'

'I was in love with you Kate, and not responsible. My father, on his deathbed, tried to warn me. I gave no heed. I was wrong then and I have been punished. For a King to have no child but a daughter is to be childless.'

'There was the boy who might have lived had he not been christened in midwinter.'

She seemed calm; only her hands, kneading at the delicate fabric which had been handled so carefully and was now being treated like a dishcloth, betrayed agitation.

'How many children are christened in winter and survive? Hundreds. I see his death as part of the curse. My conscience has wakened. I know now that I have . . . we have . . . lived in sin for eighteen years, and been punished.'

'Who put this to you, Henry? It is not true. We have not lived in sin; we have lived in the holy state of matrimony. My marriage to Arthur – as you know very well – was in name only. Pope Julius knew that and gave permission for our marriage. Who troubled your conscience with this nonsense?'

Her apparent calm angered him; he said sharply:

'It is not nonsense. Cast your mind back to Charles' last visit. You were there when he said that some of his advisers had questioned Mary's legitimacy.'

'I was *not*,' Katharine said. 'He would never have dared to say such things in my presence. If Mary is illegitimate what am I? A strumpet?'

'No, no. Perhaps you were not there. But he said it. More lately the French have raised the same question and I . . .'

'I think German lawyers, tainted with Lutheranism and the French who have never properly respected the Pope, are responsible for such talk. I think you would be well-advised to ignore it.'

'How can I? Two years ago I sent to Clement asking him to confirm or to refute Julius' dispensation. No answer has yet come. More lately the Archbishop of Canterbury and Cardinal Wolsey have gone thoroughly into the matter and say that the legality of our marriage is doubtful.'

Two years. All this going on behind her back.

'What then can be done about it? Had Clement found a flaw in the dispensation, he would surely have amended it. It rests with him.'

'With *us*. Katharine, the way is clear. We have only to admit that we were in error, that we were never married in the sight of God, and the whole thing would be undone. I would look after you well, you and Mary. You are both dear to me; I would look upon you as my sisters. My *favourite* sisters,' he added, remembering the bitter quarrels he had had with both Mary and Margaret. 'I would find a kind suitable husband for Mary and dower her well. You could revert to your title as Dowager Princess of Wales; and you could enjoy all the comfort you now have in any convent that you chose.'

'Convent!'

'It would be the best way. An acknowledgment. I thought . . . I mean of late . . .' Embarrassed he turned to the window again. 'It would be not so very different from the life you live now. It would show the world that you admitted the invalidity of our marriage. But . . . if the idea of a convent repels you, I daresay it could be managed in another way.' He needed Wolsey now. 'A public statement, perhaps, admitting that you and I were never legally married. In that case, any manor you choose. Or any palace . . .'

A small part of her confused mind, schooled by eighteen years of having no will but his, of trying to please him, was tempted to yield. Give way, please him, retain some remnant of affection. She stamped the impulse down.

'I can never consent to anything, never say a word or make a move that would make Mary, my daughter and yours, a bastard in the eyes of the world.'

'She is that already,' he said. She heard the change in his voice; the explanatory, persuasive, almost apologetic note had gone, replaced by something hard and ruthless.

'Not until Clement says so. Until he says otherwise – and if the decision had been so simple he would have declared himself by now – I am your lawful wedded wife, Mary, your lawfully begotten child, and your heir. By that I must stand.'

Something in him, not yet lost to grace, tendered its unwilling admiration; it said – A woman of quality and I recognised it from the first; a most admirable woman. But there were, in his mind, other, louder voices reminding him of Anne, that dark enchantress, waiting in the far wing of the palace, her bed for which he craved, forbidden because she would not be his mistress, only his wife, and Queen; reminding him of the slowness with which things moved in Rome; reminding him of his – and England's – need for an heir; reminding him that this summer, part of the sweet summer of life – thirty-six this month – was passing.

He said, 'If you obstruct me, I fear you will regret it.'

'And if I did not, you might regret it more. Henry, I beg you; think where this might lead. Julius gave us leave to marry. Clement must recognise the Papal authority of his predecessor, or undermine his own. If you shuffle me aside and marry the Frenchwoman whom Wolsey has chosen for you . . .'

'There is no question of that,' he said, 'until I am free.'

But he was pleased that his real intention was so well concealed.

'. . . the matter of authority will always remain,' Katharine said. 'You might well find yourself with nothing but bastards – if Clement gives you leave to marry again and half the world holds, as I do, that Julius' dispensation was good. I think you have been ill-advised.'

That was another thing to which she must hold; he had been ill-advised. It was Wolsey, so pro-French, so anti-Imperialist, thwarted because his ultimate ambition, to be Pope, had failed, who had concocted the whole abominable plot. And suddenly she saw Henry, herself, Mary, Clement, and all the thousands upon thousands of people who believed, as she did, that Popes, though subject to human weaknesses, were in their decisions inspired by Divine grace, all of us, in those plump white hands reduced to nothing but pawns in a game to be played for his advantage.

She began to cry, mopping her eyes with the shirt which she had been making for Henry, part of his birthday present.

On Henry the eighteen years of marriage, ecstatic, and then with the passing years, placid, had left their mark. As her desire to please him had been cultivated, so had his desire to cherish her. Old habits held. He said,

'Oh, for the love of God, Kate, do not cry. You know I cannot bear to see you cry.' Nor could he bear to be opposed; for eighteen years his will had been law in England. What was to be his curiously ambivalent attitude towards her was born then, when he wished to stem her tears, and wished also to beat her over the head. The whole thing could have been as easy as slipping on a glove; now it would be painful, long drawn out, and public. Anne waiting, nagging, despairing, defiant. God help any man, caught as he was, between two such stubborn women.

Katharine thought: This is a horrible world; one from which, but for Mary, I should be only too glad to retreat: and she sobbed on.

'Well, we shall see,' Henry said, unable to bear his conflicting impulses any longer; the beautiful Princess from Spain whom he had loved, who had loved him, lost and gone, even death could not be more irrevocable – *her* he wanted to hold and comfort; but she was entombed, not in stone, but in the body of this middle-aged, stubborn woman.

He went away; and for the first time there was a heaviness, a lack of liveliness in his step.

The whole interview had taken no more than fifteen, at most twenty minutes. He had put forward a proposition which she had rejected. Both were good pious Catholics and they had unleashed, in a small room, forces that were to shape and alter half a world.

Left alone, Katharine cried on, seeing what must be done, but shrinking from it; seeing what had been done and abhorring it. But tears served no purpose except to induce pity in others. She was alone, unobserved. Nobody could weep forever. And she had other resources.

She sent for the Spanish Ambassador, Don Inigo de Mendoza. Dr. Puebla she had never wholeheartedly liked; his successor had lacked tact; Mendoza was, in her opinion, as nearly ideal an ambassador as a man could be, dignified, astute, tactful. He was a member of a noble Spanish family and as a boy had been one of Isabella's pages. He had formed part of the escort which had ridden with Katharine on the first stage of her journey to England and she looked upon him as a friend. When he was appointed, she had imagined that they would have long talks together and she would hear all the intimate, trivial news from Spain. It had never come about. She had observed that, no matter how crowded the room, as soon as she and Charles' ambassador had exchanged a dozen words, Wolsey would make his way towards them and either hover, or make an interruption. She was wise enough to realise that the Cardinal suspected the possibility of connivance between a Spanish-born Queen and a Spanish ambassador – though what was there to connive about? Not to lend substance to the suspicion, however, she had never, until now, made any effort to see Mendoza in private. But this was a crisis.

She saw, by his face, his manner, that he was already informed. She had hardly begun when she stopped and said, 'You knew?'

'Your Grace, there have been rumours. In Europe for months. Lately here, even in taverns.'

'And no one saw fit – you did not see fit, Don Mendoza, to inform me?'

She sounded exactly like her mother, chiding him, years ago, for biting his nails.

'We all hoped,' he said, 'that it would blow over, without the need for Your Grace to suffer a pang. Even the ale-drinkers would spare you and I have hoped, as I have, that the Pope would give the decisive word, in your favour.'

In my favour? As though I were a criminal. What have I done?

'It was left to His Grace to inform me. To me it was a great shock. To be asked to admit, after eighteen years of happy marriage that I was never wedded at all, that my child bore the stigma of bastardy . . .' She would have wept again there, but the last tear had been wrung out of her; and the lovely June day had clouded over; she was empty, cold, wretched, greatly in need of some heartening word.

Mendoza said, 'It is all very unfortunate. Your Grace has my sympathy.' And what, at this moment, was that worth?

'I thank you,' she said, forcing herself to civility. 'But I need more. As His Grace left me he said, 'Well, we shall see.' I had raised every point I could think of, overtaken by surprise as I was; he was not convinced and those last words have an ominous ring. *His* case was submitted to Rome two years ago. Did you know that?'

'I have heard of Dr. Knight and his activities,' Mendoza admitted.

'Then some moves must be made on *my* behalf. Someone must speak for me. Whom can we send?'

'It is a matter of lawyers, Your Grace. And I am inclined to think that no English lawyer, despatched without the King's warrant, or the Cardinal's, would get farther than Abbeville, in France.' He saw the incredulous look on her face and knew that in a minute she would be thinking, probably saying, that he was imagining a state of affairs that did not exist. He said, hurried and defensive, 'The Cardinal has a long arm, Madam; and many friends in France. Last year, making my way here, with every possible letter of credit, every proof of identity about me, I was delayed, for many weeks, in Arques. The Cardinal, for some reason of his own, wished Spain and the Empire not to be represented in London. My papers were examined – by men who could not read, or pretended not to be able; my protests – and my French is fluent – were ignored or misunderstood. Eventually I was allowed to continue my journey; in the Cardinal's good time. There were many apologies for the blunder on the part of officials, too officious. But they were acting on instructions. I do not doubt that the same instructions would apply to any English lawyer who did not carry the Cardinal's blessing.'

'Then I must appeal by letter to His Holiness and to the Emperor.'

'I fear that the same fate would overtake any courier carrying such communications, Your Grace.'

She looked at him bleakly; and he stared at her, apologetic but unhelpful. She knew a swift regret for old Dr. Puebla, that resourceful man.

'Your own diplomatic correspondence?' she asked.

'I have known letters go astray in mysterious fashion. What gets through is read – I know that. Not only read but subject to tests, in case I have used invisible ink.'

She realised the weight of the forces ranged against her.

'If I may venture to offer a word of advice,' Mendoza said. 'The information reached Your Grace only this morning. When one is taken by surprise it is possible to act too hastily. A little time for reflection, perhaps, and some compromise might be reached.'

'How can one compromise over such a thing? Either I am married or I am not. One side of the case has already been under scrutiny by Rome for two years. I am not represented there . . . Thank you for coming so promptly, Don Mendoza. You have leave to go.'

'I deeply regret not being able to be helpful.'

'On the contrary, you have made me aware of danger that I did not know existed. What a pass for a country to come to! And England where the people regard themselves as the freest people in the world!'

'It happens invariably when too much power falls into the wrong hands, Madam.'

As soon as he had gone she sent for Francisco Filipez, her server. He was one of those who had come with her from Spain and had stayed. At Ludlow and for a short time afterwards he had had charge of her horses. One day at Durham House he had come to her and asked if she would allow him to become her server; and that sounded a strange request from a man, no longer young, accustomed to a different life altogether. He had explained that the climate in England did not suit him; being out of doors stiffened his joints. So she had agreed. About a week later the old King, in miserly mood, had decided that she needed no horses of her own. She had sometimes wondered whether Filipez had heard a whisper. He was an excellent server, and although he still spent much time in and around the stables, he had never once brought into her presence the slightest whiff of the odour which always reminded her of her old apartments at Greenwich where hope had so nearly died. After her marriage to Henry, with gifts to give, she had offered Filipez the post as steward at her own manor of Ampthill and he had refused it, saying, 'I would sooner stay with Your Grace. Unless, of course, you think my grizzled head incongruous.' She had hastily reassured him.

Now she said to him, with brisk practicality:

'Francisco, do you still ride?'

'Every day, Your Grace.' A man who, so long ago, had sought an indoors post!

'How long would it take you to get to Spain?' She knew that Charles was in Valladolid.

Filipez reckoned quickly; summer with long days, the roads dry and the rivers fordable.

'With good horses, sixteen, seventeen days.'

'And could you carry, in your head, a message that I dare not commit to paper?'

'My memory is good.'

'Then it remains to find a reason for your going, and for your haste. Otherwise you might be waylaid.'

He knew more about the circumstances than she had done – until ten minutes ago.

'Your Grace, who would waylay a humble man, going home to receive his dying mother's blessing?'

His mother had died so long ago that he had no memory of her and could use the name with no feeling.

The thought shot through her mind that only those who had known a hard upbringing were resourceful. Dr. Puebla, Maria de Moreto, this man; me?

She gave him her message; one for Charles himself, one for him to forward to Rome. 'You will need a passport, Francisco.'

'I shall have it, not tomorrow perhaps, but the next day, Your Grace.'

'God keep you,' she said.

In every way this had been a vile day, even weatherwise; but she was Queen of England, and in the glowering light which made the candles necessary, even on a June evening, she took her place at the supper table, the marrow of her bones quivering like jelly. But after all, nothing had *happened*; only her inner, private world had been overset, her mind rocked, her heart broken. But this was her place and she took it, beside Henry, who was surprisingly amiable. In the course of the long day he had realised that, if Katharine would not give way, sorrow, not wrath would be his best weapon; he must appear to be a man compelled by his conscience to take a course very painful to him. Alongside this reasoning, all through the day, another thought had run, a mounting anger because his sweet Kate, always so amenable and anxious to please, had defied him.

He said, halfway through the meal, with some malice in his voice:

'That server of yours has just applied for a safe conduct to Spain. He claims that his mother is dying. To me he looks somewhat old to have a mother, even dying.'

So that resource had failed too. In the bright hall, full of candles and colour, music and merriment, she felt as stranded as though she sat alone on a rock in the sea. But Filipez must be protected.

'There will be others, with similar excuses. My people will see no future here, after what was said this morning.'

'Straws show which way the wind blows,' he said sententiously. 'For your own sake you should think again. Those who take up an indefensible position must expect to stand alone.'

'I know,' she said, wondering if she could ever be more alone than at this moment.

Henry was so pleased by Filipez's apparent desertion and the opportunity it had given for the delivery of a little homily, that before he slept he had signed papers that would have ensured Filipez's safe conduct anywhere in Christendom.

A fortnight later, beating his own most optimistic estimate by two days, Filipez was in Valladolid, seeking audience of the least accessible monarch in Europe. Unshaven, caked with dust, red-eyed from lack of sleep, he said to one official after another, 'I carry an urgent message to His Imperial Highness.' 'Where is it?' they asked, prepared to take it, peruse it, judge its importance and possibly deliver it. 'In my head,' he said. Mad? Drunk? Inadmissable.

Filipez had hoped that by some miracle he could gain an audience without disclosing whence he came; it was a secret errand, but in the end, asked for the twentieth time, 'Where is it?', he pulled out of his doublet the much-handled paper which had served him so well.

'This is not the message – that is in my head,' he said again, 'but this is proof of urgency.' The black, scrawled, signature, *Henry R.* was recognised and in a short time, Filipez, on his knees before the Emperor, was repeating, word for word, the message that Katharine had entrusted to him.

Charles was not ignorant of the rumours. The King of England plans to put away his wife, remarry and beget a son. There had been no developments; and for a man upon whose shoulders such vast responsibilities weighed, there were a thousand other things to think of. Charles had as little knowledge of, as little patience with, sexual traffic as any man alive. He had been betrothed ten times; he had married his cousin, Isabella of Portugal, he had begotten an heir. His uncle-by-marriage, Henry of England, had been less fortunate in that respect and had appealed to Clement to annul his marriage and set him free to marry again. And in two years, Clement had made no move and there had appeared to be no need for Charles to concern himself.

Now here the thing was, cropping up again; in the frantic appeal from his aunt that he should send a good lawyer to represent her at Rome – a request made in this unusual fashion.

He approached the matter cautiously.

'You may stand,' he said. Filipez stiffly and with some difficulty stood. 'This is a strange approach. I have my Ambassador in London. It seems to me that the Queen, my aunt, could have communicated through the usual diplomatic channels.'

'They are blocked,' Filipez said bluntly. 'Nothing in these days goes in or out of England except what suits the Cardinal. Nothing that Her Grace wrote would have reached Your Imperial Highness.'

'Yet you were given safe conduct.'

'By accident. Have I leave to speak freely? Unless Her Grace receives help from outside England, her cause is lost because the Cardinal has set himself to ending this marriage and making a new one, between His Grace and a Princess of France.'

Behind the vacuous expression, the sharp mind sprang to attention.

'Tavern gossip?'

'My lord, I have lived in England for twenty-six years and I have learned that what the ale drinkers say, though it may be hotly contradicted, is right, nine times out of ten.'

Charles was fond of his aunt, who had been kind and maternal to him, and who had not resented the breaking of his betrothal to her daughter; but his nature was too cold, too reasonable to be moved into action by sentiment. Policy was a different matter; he had no wish to see England and France linked by marriage.

'You intend to return to England? When?'

'Tomorrow, Your Imperial Highness.'

'Then inform Her Grace that her message was delivered, and noted and that action will be taken. I shall instruct my Ambassador, by letter, to support her in her decision – and offer what comfort is possible.'

'May I . . .' Filipez hesitated; it was already late, so much time had been wasted; and it was hardly for him to suggest that the Emperor should sit late into the night writing letters . . . 'If you would allow me to carry the letter? I go faster than any courier, and with my safe conduct I get better treatment in France than anyone without it would do.'

Charles noted the significance of that remark, not with hurt to his vanity – he had little – but as a circumstance to be considered; in France Henry's signature on a passport meant more than his own!

'The letter will be ready for you in the morning. Her Grace is fortunate in her servant.'

'She has many,' Filipez said deprecatingly. 'All the people of England, save a handful of the Cardinal's men.'

Charles noted that remark too.

He wrote to Henry first, a curious letter, more forthright than was his habit, and in tone that of a father rebuking and reproaching a son who contemplated some action not only disastrous but preposterous. Then he wrote to Mendoza, telling him to seek an audience with the Queen immediately and assure her of his support and sympathy. He was sending Cardinal Quinones, a most gifted and experienced lawyer, to Rome on her behalf. The two letters were folded together and addressed to Mendoza who would present Henry's with due formality.

Filipez made the return journey in thirteen days, went straight to Katharine with the verbal message which he made sound warmer and more partisan and energetic than it had been in fact; not because he deliberately falsified it, but because thirteen days of thinking, *The Emperor is on her side*, had coloured his opinion. It was worth the twenty-seven days in the saddle to see her face light up and hear her say 'Thank God.'

He then delivered the package at Mendoza's house and went to bed for eight hours. Redressed, scoured clean, he was behind Katharine's chair that evening at suppertime.

Henry, with that personal touch, the passing interest in people's affairs which endeared him to so many, noticed and said:

'You! Back already?'

'Your Grace, I got no farther than Valladolid. There I heard that I was already too late. My mother was buried. So I turned about; and the Emperor himself honoured me by entrusting me with a package for Don Inigo de Mendoza. So I rode fast.'

'If you were a younger man, I'd say you were wasted at that job.' He ran his eye over Filipez; very spare, he'd ride light. Henry nowadays on a hunting day tired out five or six horses; but then who would wish to be like that fellow with no calves to his legs, spindle-shanked in his hose.

In the near-month of Filipez's absence, life had seemed so placid and ordinary that sometimes it seemed as though that terrible interview had never occurred. After the sidelong warning that those who took impossible stands must expect to be alone, Henry had not referred to the subject again, and except for adding to her prayers a request that Filipez might get through safely and that Charles would do what she asked, Katharine had tried to put it out of her mind. She had done what she could; there was no more to do at the moment, she must trust in God and stay calm. Even anxiety showed lack of faith. Act as though all were well and all might yet be well.

But it was strange to sit and stand by Henry's side, smile, make amiable conversation, make one of his summer progresses with him and be everywhere received as Queen, knowing all the time what was in her mind. When the first shattering shock had worn off a little, she could sort out one hurt from another and knew that the lasting wound had been dealt when he said that he had put his case to Rome two years ago. He might be justified in his doubts; she loved him and found it easy to see things from his angle; what Charles had said about Mary's legitimacy was enough to sow a seed. But before a word was said to anyone else, she, the person most nearly concerned, should have been consulted; if necessary they should *together* have asked for a Papal decision. It was impossible not to feel a sense of betrayal. It was almost equally impossible to look upon Henry as a traitor, capable of so base an action. The habit of loving and admiring him was too strong to be overcome so easily. He had remained faithful to her and to his betrothal – not without difficulty; he had remained faithful, save for two excusable lapses, to his marriage vows. Why should he suddenly be so faithless as to go behind her back in an attempt to break up their marriage? It was out of character. So how? So why?

She would reach this point in her thinking and give herself an answer. Always the same. Wolsey. Wolsey was pro-French, against her and the Spanish alliance from the first. And she could well imagine how he had gone about the work of persuading Henry that his marriage was unlawful and his sonlessness a punishment. Those plump white hands with the great Cardinal's ring gleaming steepled under the double chin, the solemn sonorous voice quoting Leviticus. It was probably Wolsey who had first said that for a King to have only a daughter was to be childless; it was the way he used words, making traps for men's minds. He had done it for years, weaving webs like a spider, leaving it to others to entangle themselves. 'Your Grace has no *legitimate* son. But you are still young. With another woman, not cursed . . .'

And why had Henry not said, 'On a woman who was not my wife I got a son.' Perhaps he had said it and Wolsey had replied with some sophistry about sin between the sheets being less culpable than sin between the ears, sin with Elizabeth Taillebois, completely unhallowed, more easily forgiven than sin with Katharine, Arthur's wife, in defiance of God's law and the more offensive for having the appearance of legality. Elizabeth Taillebois pensioned, her son provided for; Mary Boleyn married off; venial; shallow, uprooted and forgotten; her own case, as Wolsey would present it was altogether different, far closer – If thine eye offend thee, pluck it out. And whether Wolsey was the originator of the scheme or not, he was certainly the source of the secretiveness, secret motives governed him, secret methods were his tools.

It was so easy to exonerate the man she loved by blaming the one she neither liked nor respected, but now and again, clear-headed in a wakeful night she would think in a different fashion. Henry was not entirely incapable of secretiveness; he had learned to keep his own purposes concealed when his father lived; both his extra-marital affairs had been conducted with what was called in such circumstances, discretion. Was his desire to end his marriage prompted less by some words in Leviticus than a wish to take some other woman as his wife? Some young Princess, with many child-bearing years ahead of her. French if Wolsey had any say. Princess Renée. Perhaps.

She had, as yet, no knowledge of her real enemy; the one so close, lodged across the courtyard in apartments suited to an earl's daughter, mingling with the other ladies-in-waiting. Henry and Anne had been very careful – not that there was much to be careful about, Henry often thought, angrily: they were hardly ever alone in a room together. Anne was determined that nobody should say that she, like her sister, was a strumpet. Henry was anxious that neither Wolsey close at hand, nor Clement far away in Rome should know the truth. All must be cloaked until Wolsey had persuaded Clement to give the desired answer. And both Henry and Anne had another reason for behaving with great circumspection. He was determined that she should be Queen, therefore her reputation must not be smirched. Anne was afraid that if she yielded an inch the spell would be broken. Only for the seemingly unattainable did men go to impossible lengths.

On Henry with his sensual nature, and now for a long time accustomed to having his own way in most things, the strain was enormous; seeing Anne every day, sometimes many times in a day, always in a crowd, being obliged to curb even his glances; and then, in their brief, painfully contrived times alone together, sometimes permitted a kiss, a caress, but more often being teased, railed at, mocked. For Anne also felt the strain – not of thwarted passion – but of insecurity and impatience. Men would go to great lengths for the seemingly unattainable, but only for a limited time. Suppose that time spent itself while Clement still dithered. Only her maid, Emma Arnett, knew how often Anne's nerves gave way and she would have fits of hysteria, take to her bed, have to be dosed and cosseted.

And almost every day, sometimes many times in a day, she was forced to join the ladies around Katharine, the impediment in her path; the woman who could have, should have, retired with grace and made the whole thing easy, and chose not to do so.

To Katharine a form of enlightenment – almost immediately rejected – came on an apparently ordinary evening, when, as the tables were cleared, Henry said, as he so often did, 'Now we will dance.'

Katharine no longer danced; dancing was for the young and that single, devastating talk with Henry had leeched away the last of her youth. Life went on, day following day, with everyone waiting for the Pope to pontificate, pretending that until the word was given, all was as it had been; but it was not. The strain of waiting that irked Henry's temper and made Anne hysterical had damaged Wolsey, putting fresh lines into his face where hitherto firm flesh now sagged; and around Thomas More's eyes and mouth there were marks not set there by study and the need to issue fair judgment on legal questions. Three of us, she thought, who love Henry . . . and I am in worst case of all, because without him I have nothing. Then she thought: Nonsense, I have Mary; and her face brightened and lifted as she looked down upon the floor where her daughter was taking her place.

Henry had undertaken to see that Mary rode and danced expertly and could make songs as well as play the lute in the ordinary way and in these arts as the more serious subjects she was a credit to her teacher. At the age of eleven she was still shorter than normal, a fact that irked her and for which she tried to make up by holding her head high and by ordering shoes with tall heels; she had inherited her mother's dignity and her father's ability to put dignity away on occasion. This was such an occasion because Henry had given the musicians the signal to play one of the merry tunes which accompanied the dance which the English, with their knack of simplifying French terms, called a 'Brawle.'

He had his reason for that. In the more stately dances done to tunes almost as solemn as church music, and steps performed in formal pattern, ladies and gentlemen danced in pairs and though the pairs mingled, forming foursomes and eightsomes, the partners always came back to one another and at the end exchanged the kiss with which most dances concluded. A Brawle was different: though it had an almost infinite variety of forms, one movement was repeated at intervals, all the men formed a circle on the outer side and skipped in one direction, all the ladies in the inner circle, skipped in the opposite way for exactly twenty steps and stopped; ladies then faced outwards, gentlemen inwards, the ladies curtseyed, the gentlemen bowed and the pair immediately opposite one another were partners for the next movement, three running steps forward, three backwards, hand in hand; then a swinging motion, in which ladies were often lifted from their feet; then the kiss, and off to the next pattern, the square, the circle, or the running under an archway made by one pair holding their hands high. Then the two circles again. In a lucky evening, with a little jostling, Henry might find himself opposite Anne three or four times, hold her hands, hold her waist and kiss her, all without being in the least conspicuous. There was torment in the joy, but that he did not grudge.

In the soft bright light of hundreds of candles the colours of the clothes of the dancers shone and shifted, blended and contrasted. Henry wore yellow slashed over cloth of gold; Mary was wearing bluish green; apart from their colours they were easily distinguishable, he the largest, she the smallest of the dancers. Other people stood out from the mass, too: Elizabeth Conyers, only eighteen but with hair completely white; it was said to have changed colour in a single night – romantically minded ladies whispered that young Digby's betrothal to another woman had caused the change, Elizabeth herself said that it was due to a bout of fever. Maria de Moreto who occasionally showed an unexpected softness towards girls thought to be lovelorn, had once suggested the use of henna to her and gained no thanks; Mistress Conyers said that she considered her white hair becoming. When her cheeks were coloured pink it was. The Lady Anne was another easily picked out on account of her collar. Other ladies had copied the ornament at one time, held to it for a month or so and then abandoned it. The truth was that it was not becoming, except to Anne whose neck was extraordinarily long; to others the ordinary necklace, lying at the base of the throat, and with pendant jewels, drawing the eye downwards, did better service. Tonight Anne wore tawny and of the jewels in the collar the topazes seemed to predominate.

Henry, in the outer circle, stood level with Anne in the inner one and they paired off; she curtseyed, without looking at him, and rose, taking his hand without the smile which was obligatory, no matter how unwelcome the partner might be. She was a girl who smiled very seldom, Katharine had observed; perhaps the unfortunate business with Harry Percy had quenched some source of merriment within her. Henry spoke to her as they took the steps forward and backward, she inclined her head in her graceful way but seemed not to answer. Then they swung around, Anne's feet leaving the floor; Henry always lifted his partners high. They kissed, made a foursome with Margaret Lee and Sir Harry Norris, the four right hands joined in the centre, and then back into the circles. Henry's partner this time at the end of the twenty skipping steps was Jane Seymour, plain and shy, now back at Court.

From time to time both Wolsey and More seated by Katharine spoke to her, obeying the unwritten law that those who did not dance should converse. They spoke and she answered them, without removing her attention from the floor.

The colours of the dancers' clothes merged, separated, blurred; the skipping rings went round; twenty steps and a halt. Now Henry, who was wide, stood opposite his daughter and Anne Boleyn whom the dance had placed next one another. From where Katharine sat it seemed that Henry was slightly more directly opposite his daughter whose face already wore a look of welcome and delight. Then it happened. Henry did not step sideways – the rules of good behaviour in a dance forbade that, but he leaned so that his bow was made to the Lady Anne who was just about to curtsey to Sir Francis Westleton who stood on Henry's right. It was one of the jostling movements which, because he was King and because he occupied more space than most men, had served him well in the past. This evening it did not because the female partner thus subtly slighted happened to be his own daughter who, with a movement so like his own that in any other circumstances it would have been comic, rose from her curtsey with exactly the slant to her left that was necessary, and rose and took her father's hand. Francis Westleton took Anne's and the dance would have gone on had Henry not raised his hand as a signal to the musicians and said, into the sudden silence, 'Enough is enough.'

What Mary said was also clearly audible; she had her grandmother's deep, carrying voice. 'Oh! I wanted to be swung. Nobody swings as you do.'

Henry said, 'Swung you shall be,' and there in the centre of dancers halted by the cessation of the music, he lifted and swung her, more turns than the dance would have demanded. And with a dark and glowering face.

Anne Boleyn, Lady Anne Rochford. Nonsense, ridiculous. She did not lie at the heart of this miserable plot. If Henry wanted her – and it seemed that he did – she was there for the taking, as her sister had been. The King of England had no need to shuffle off his marriage on *her* account, a woman he could never marry; not even a woman of noble family. Quite incredible. There had been a King of England, the fourth Edward, who had married one of his own subjects and thus offended most of the nobles. Henry would never . . . And yet, and yet . . . That unsmiling face, the inclination of the head, the ready acceptance in an equivocal situation, of another man's hand. Nobody quite like her . . . I knew it from the first when I thought her a changeling. There is something about her, something unusual and strange after which Henry yearns – I saw that in his face, in the outstretched hand and the attempt to push Mary aside. But not to *marry*. A passing fancy; nothing to do with the great matter involving two Popes, two crowned Kings, the Prince who was now King of England, the Princess who was now Queen; their one living child, Mary Princess of Wales. Nothing to do. No. Nothing to do . . .

She could have asked Henry a point-blank question, and it was pride, not lack of courage which prevented her. Their relationship had altered since the time when she had been able to speak openly about Elizabeth Taillebois – and even then her remonstrance had been futile. Since then there had been the liaison with Mary Boleyn and that she had ignored entirely, largely because in her heart she was not sure, and wished not to be. And that was before the shattering interview in June since when, it seemed to her, she and Henry had been engaged in an elaborate masquerade, each pretending that nothing had changed. But the masks of amiability and ordinariness with which they appeared in public were not dropped when they chanced to be alone together which happened rarely, but did still happen often enough for such meetings to have become as stylised as a puppet show; an exchange of civilities from which every hint of intimacy had been banished. It was as though they were carrying between them some object of such frailty that a misdirected breath could shatter it forever; yet a thing which, if borne carefully would survive and finally be put down in a place of safety.

It was therefore impossible for her even to mention the Lady Anne either as his latest light-o'-love, or her potential rival. And this time, if there were gossip – as there must be if even half her suspicion was justified – none of it reached her ears. She did notice that sometimes when she entered a room where her ladies were chattering a curious silence would fall and once she asked why. The answer was prompt – They had been arguing and it was well known that Her Grace disliked disputes among her attendants. Even Maria de Moreto was unforthcoming, though Katharine, feeling ashamed of the sidelong approach, once invited her to gossip, saying, 'The Lady Anne tells me that she has discovered a new musician.'

'Oh yes, Your Grace. A fellow called Mark Smeaton, taken from the plough-tail, I understand. He is not well liked.'

'By whom?'

'Those with whom she surrounds herself. As Your Grace must know *she* is not much liked among your ladies; but she makes up for it in her leisure hours; her brother, her cousins – one would think they were glued to her; Sir Francis Weston, Sir Henry Norris, William Brereton, Nan Savile . . .'

Once, when there was hope, when there was security, Maria de Moreto had been frank. Now she had no purpose save to comfort. And it was a comfort based on truth; for when the relatives and the friends went to their beds, there remained Emma Arnett, watchful as a dragon . . . Maria knew the whole situation. She also knew that the Pope must move soon and in the meanwhile the less damage done, the better.

So it was left to the ordinary English people, nameless, faceless, to prove the truth of what a dusty courier had once told the Emperor – uninformed ale-drinkers, nine times out of ten, were right.

It was one of those shining autumn days; Katharine and Mary left Greenwich to go by barge to Richmond; and all along the river banks thronging the steps that joined land to water, they congregated, and they shouted. 'God save the *Queen*.' 'God bless the Princess of Wales.' They also shouted, 'We want no Nan Bullen!' 'No Nan Bullen for us!'

'You heard the cries, Maria?'

The campaign of comfort brought to nothing; how many times had she said: One word in her hearing and I will tear out your eyes!

'Your Grace, they cry against her as a witch.'

A witch; there was no such thing, except in those old tales, told by Joanna in the dying firelight, long ago. Even Torquemada and the Office of the Inquisition, under whose shadow Katharine had been reared, held that there was nothing worse than heresy to be rooted out.

'Maria, you cannot believe that.' I do not. The linking of her name with mine and Mary's has another and for me a more sinister implication; more sinister because I do not believe in witches or their craft.

'I do believe it,' Maria said. 'She bears two marks. The extra finger and the mole on her neck that the collar covers. That is the teat at which the Evil One suckles. The extra finger is the mark of the beast. And then there is the dog. Have you never marked how in company she never names him; she whistles, snaps her fingers and he obeys. But he has a name, one of Satan's. She calls him Urian. And was ever a hair of him singed?'

Katharine had seen the dog's performance several times. A page held a hoop bound about with strips of linen so old, so dry as to be instantly inflammable. The boy held the hoop at arms' length, using tongs and when the flame made a full circle, the Lady Anne would call and snap her fingers or say, 'Come to me!' The dog, a mastiff with some other blood, would run, leap through the fiery circle and emerge – as Maria said – unsinged, and put his head on his mistress' knees. It was, in dull moments, a useful entertainment because afterwards several gentlemen – and a few ladies – would endeavour to prove that their dogs were equally brave and docile. Not one had ever shown itself to be so. But what did that prove, except that the Lady Anne's dog feared the whip more than the fire?

'Maria, how many in the crowd today knew that she was blemished and had a dog obedient beyond the ordinary? They cried against her for another reason, linking her name with mine because they fear she will supplant me . . .'

On me, Maria thought, always the load falls! This time I refuse it! She said firmly, 'And how could that be? His holiness will give an answer favourable to Your Grace and then you will see Mistress Boleyn bundled off back to Hever with no pension and no husband. She is a witch, she has put a spell upon the King – but to one end only; that she should be Queen. Once she sees that is impossible and he sees that he will never have his way with her, it will be over. Like that,' Maria said, clicking her thumb and finger with a sound like castanets.

'I pray so,' Katharine said. 'But even you, Maria, seem uncertain of mind. You say that she is cried against as a witch; and in almost the same breath that she does aim to take my place. Everybody seems better informed than I . . .'

'She *is* a witch. How else . . .Did you ever know *him* to admire a woman with no looks? No bosom. No amiability. Not even young. And of an unyielding disposition. May I say what I think? She had set herself to be Countess of Northumberland and was thwarted. *Then* she took up with the Devil and he, Father of Lies, promised her more. But when did he ever keep a promise? Oh, she may toss her head and walk proudly and guard herself and say the way to her bed lies through St. Paul's. But that will gain her nothing. The Pope will declare for you – and as you heard today, the ordinary people will never accept her.'

The conversation had come back to where it started, the cries from the river bank, from the people jostling on the steps and little jetties, all the way from Greenwich to Richmond.

And I kept in the dark; until that moment when Henry passed over his own daughter and looked . . . and looked with the naked, yearning, hungry gaze which once he turned upon me . . . and even then doubting, until today. Maria knowing so much; every blacksmith, baker, butcher, huckster knowing. It was impossible not to feel shamed. Now she understood why the chatter had ceased as she entered a room and why two people, almost whispering together in a passage would look startled at her approach and begin to talk in voices, overloud, about some trivial matter. Everyone knew and tonight she must face them all, for tonight, to mark the move to Richmond, supper would be eaten in public. She thought of the eyes, sharp with curiosity or soft with pity, the tongues, venomous or wondering, and felt that she could not face them. Unless strength were found from somewhere.

'I wish to be alone for half an hour, Maria,' she said, and as soon as the door was closed she knelt and prayed for courage, for control, for patience, for the power to remain dignified in a supremely undignified situation and finally for victory. Strength flowed in from somewhere; the Pope, Christ's Vicar on earth would decide rightly and she would be vindicated. In that certainty she could find all the courage and patience and control that she needed.

She sat by Henry's side and looked around the hall and thought: All concerned in this business are here. Mary had her own table at which this evening M. du Bellay, the French Ambassador, was seated, together with Lady Salisbury, Reginald Pole and various other ladies and gentlemen. The Spanish Ambassador, Don de Mendoza, sombre in black velvet, was with Wolsey, splendid in scarlet, and they appeared to be in amicable conversation. The ladies-in-waiting and other Court officials sat at a lower table, from which at intervals sounds of merriment drifted. Anne this evening was clad in crimson and below the never discarded collar she wore a parure of rubies. I know now where she gets her finery! But whence comes her power to fascinate? There are women younger and prettier at the table, but she is the focus of attention, Westleton, Carnaby, Wyatt, Norris, even her own brother have eyes for nobody else. And it is always after something she has said that the laughter breaks out, though she never smiles. I must not stare! I will never, if I can help it, give a sign that she is anything more than one of my ladies-in-waiting.

Henry seemed glum; he did not brighten even at the sight of the sucking pig, brought to table with an almost shocking appearance of life, its eyes made of the whites of hard-boiled eggs with circles of pickled walnut in their centres. Did he envy the merriment at the low table? Had he heard of, and been annoyed by, the calls from the river? He himself had made the journey on horseback, perhaps he had been shouted at, too. She wished that she could think of something sprightly and amusing to say, but she had never been apt with verbal quips and she had already said that Richmond looked its best at this season and that they had had fine weather for their move. She was meditating some remark about Mary when Henry gave up the pretence at eating, shifted a little in his chair and said:

'Well, we have heard from Rome.'

Her heart seemed to stop and then moved again, thumping so heavily that the diamond pendant she wore shook and shimmered. The answer was wrong for him, in his present state of infatuation, but right for her, for Mary and for England. She waited, too breathless to speak.

'Clement is sending a special Legate to go into the case thoroughly.'

Not what she had hoped for. The facts were there. The Pope could read; he had the best lawyers in the world to consult. What was there to be gone into?

She managed to say, 'When?'

'Early next year.' Autumn and the Christmas festivities to be lived through; but having faced this evening I can face anything.

'Do you know whom the Legate will be?'

'Cardinal Campeggio.'

'I remember him.' He had been in England twelve years earlier – on another special errand, urging England, as part of Christendom to join Europe in resisting the encroachments of the Turks. Apart from bringing about a treaty between France and England it had come to nothing: the age of positive Crusades was over, but Henry had liked Campeggio who spoke excellent English, and had presented him with an English bishopric – that of Salisbury.

For a second or two she thought, feeling hollow and sick, that the choice was sinister – a man whom Henry had favoured, being sent to decide upon a matter in which only one decision would please the King. But she put that thought resolutely aside; it was unworthy. The Pope would be seeking justice and it was natural that he should send a man who knew the language and the country and was, besides, one of the great jurists of the day.

'He is a good lawyer,' she said.

'What we need is less law and more common sense,' Henry said grumpily.

'And that, alas, cannot be hired, my lord.'

'No,' he said, dragging the word out. The disgruntled look gave way to one almost wistful. 'If only it were you should have a wagon load, first thing tomorrow morning!' Then to her surprise he laughed; not quite the hearty booming laugh of former days; her practised ear caught the sourish undertone as when a man joins in a laugh against himself. But it was laughter, loud enough to attract attention. Several heads lifted or turned. And she smiled, deliberately assuming the look of a woman who has said something amusing and been pleased by its reception.

Let them all puzzle over *that* she thought with a flash of her mother's combative spirit. Here we sit, a King who wishes to put his wife away because in his dangerous middle-age he has met with a woman who rates her virtue too high; and a Queen who refuses to be put away; but who, coming into this hall, uninformed, would guess at our predicament? And that is how it must be, until judgment is given. Early in the new year. Oh God speed Campeggio's journey across Europe, God guide his decision, and God grant that in this waiting time I may do nothing, say no word, cast no look, make no gesture which would make our life together difficult when the verdict falls in my favour.

Henry's thoughts were busy, too. He had put some spite into the remark

which hinted that she lacked common sense and there had been a jeer in
his laughter. But it was like trying to fight a feather pillow. Still, it looked
well. Appearing in public together, talking, even laughing, over their
food, bolstered his claim that nothing but the qualms of conscience had
persuaded him that his marriage was not good. And that was a claim far
from being wholly false; nor was it wholly true. Only very simple minds
were capable of making such judgments. He wanted Anne as he had never
yet wanted a woman; he needed an heir, he doubted the validity of his
marriage – and he was not alone in that. If it had been a sound, lawful
marriage would Clement have hesitated for two whole years and then sent
Campeggio as co-adjutor with Wolsey?

But there were the cries in the streets. Scattered and few, just sufficient
to warn him. Along the river, no doubt, those whose sympathies were with
Katharine and Mary had clustered, yelling vociferously. But on his own
ride a voice had said, 'No Nan Bullen for us,' another had said, 'God bless
the King – and the Queen,' and one had said, 'Kill the witch – and her
dog!' And amongst the loyal shouts of 'God *bless* the King' there had been
others, 'God *save* the King,' with an emphasis which a poet's ear for stress
could hardly miss.

And how, Henry wondered, how by Christ's Wounds, had the secret, so
closely kept, leaked out? Who told the common people that his aim was to
marry, not seduce? Wolsey would be difficult now; paternal speeches –
This I say from concern for Your Grace's good . . . And the Emperor
would undoubtedly take umbrage at the thought of his aunt, a Princess of
Spain being supplanted by one of her own waiting ladies. Still, Wolsey
could be cajoled, and if necessary ordered, and Charles could be ignored;
he had enough on his hands without taking any practical measures in
defence of his aunt. And now that the secret was out life would be easier;
the elaborate subterfuges could be dropped. Also the very fact that she
was being cried against in the streets would give Anne confidence in the
sincerity of his intentions.

Early in the new year. It was now October. January. February. March
at the very latest. Five months. In five months' time . . . And Wolsey's
little homilies could be cut short by orders to get to work, use every
influence, pull every string to expedite Campeggio's arrival. After that
more orders, to see that the right verdict was given.

The year 1527 ran down into the trough of winter. The new year, so
eagerly awaited by everyone, began.

Cardinal Campeggio was to set out for England at some time loosely defined as the spring of 1528. Wolsey wrote to him, expressing his pleasure that they were to work together, and urging him to make haste. He then brought his talent for organisation to bear upon the arrangements for the journey; he had many contacts, many friends in France and could expedite or delay travel as he chose. Good horses and baggage mules stood at the various posting stages, eating their fill; comfortable places, such as Wolsey himself would choose to spend the night in, were chosen, hired or borrowed and kept in readiness. And Campeggio, as Wolsey knew, travelled light; in fact, when Campeggio had come to England earlier, Wolsey had felt so strongly that his paucity of baggage was unbecoming to a Prince of the Church that he had sent twelve empty coffers, covered with scarlet cloth and with gold furnishings, to augment his poor display for his entry into London. Wolsey knew his countrymen; they admired ostentation.

But that was years ago and Clement had another reason for choosing Campeggio in addition to the facts that he knew his law and spoke English. In the interval Campeggio had become very gouty; there were times when he could not hold his horse's reins, or bear to put his feet into the stirrups; worse days when he could not bear the jolting of a litter; and worst of all days when his eyes were affected and he must lie, immobile, in a darkened room. His journey across France would necessarily be slow, and – Clement hoped – never concluded. The rumours had reached Rome and made it clear that all this bother was less a matter of the King of England's conscience than his lust for Anne Boleyn. Clement knew that men's passions could burn out as quickly as beacon fires; so let enough time be wasted on moves that could offend nobody – Clement knew that he could not afford to offend either the Emperor or the King of England – and all might yet be well.

So Campeggio moved, very slowly towards London, where impatience mounted. Wolsey fretted, this business was making an old man of him; although despite the rumours, he still did not believe that, once free to remarry, the King would actually risk the unpopularity that must come from marrying Tom Boleyn's daughter; Henry fretted at the waste of another sweet summer, another year of his life; Anne was frantic, sometimes actually hysterical under the strain, sometimes rebellious, threatening to retire to Hever. Katharine waited with outward placidity – she learned to wait – but she looked forward to the day when the special Papal Legate would arrive and justify her.

But the sweating sickness reached London long before Campeggio did.

The sweating sickness was a disease peculiar to the English. In the Irish Pale where the English settlers lived, in Continental Towns where they went as traders, even on a ship the sweating sickness picked out the English with a deadly precision, sparing their neighbours. That Katharine herself had suffered from it, was in her opinion proof that she had become English by marriage. And unlike some plagues, it made no distinction between those who lived in crowded hovels and those who lived in high, airy houses; the well-fed man was as likely to fall victim as a starving beggar, the man who had a fresh clean shirt every day as the fellow who wore one until it dropped to pieces.

Henry was terrified of it; at the first whisper of the sweating sickness abroad in London, he fled; and since the place he made for was one of Wolsey's manors, he thought it wise not to take Anne with him; it would have been too obvious. Wolsey's various manors, The More, Tittenhanger and others were all well appointed, but small, with no accommodation for ladies . . .

Katharine, sure of the immunity conferred by her earlier experience, remained in Greenwich with a depleted Court, a circumstance she welcomed because it brought a return of close association with Mary, whose household had also dispersed. It was the nearest thing to real family life that she had known since she was young and Isabella had dragged her family hither and thither and they had lodged where they could, sometimes sleeping three to a bed. She sometimes spoke about those days to Mary, who listened intently.

Anne was still resident at Greenwich; still a lady-in-waiting; until the morning when Emma Arnett came in her stead and said:

'My lady is sick – it is the sweating sickness.'

Mary was there then and the moment Emma had gone she said, 'And I hope she dies of it! That would solve all.' The ferocity in her voice was almost frightening.

'I cannot think it right, Mary, to wish death upon a fellow creature. And would her death solve anything? As I see it she is the result rather than the cause of this dispute. The question that is to be settled is not whether the Lady Anne lives or dies, is or is not your father's paramour, but whether Pope Julius' dispensation was good. Whether for nineteen years I have been wife or an unwitting harlot; whether you are heir or not. That is what Cardinal Campeggio is coming to decide and, to my mind, whether *she* lives or dies makes no jot of difference. And she is only twenty – twenty-one – we must not wish her dead.'

'I wish her dead and in Hell,' Mary said. She jumped up from the stool upon which she had been sitting and began to walk up and down. She was twelve years old, small and spare for her age – as the French Ambassador had said, short, almost squat of stature and of complexion pale – but she walked as Henry did, or as Henry might, hampered by skirts, and her russet head shone and her young voice had undertones of her grandmother's gruffness.

'Oh, I know,' she said, 'you and my Lady Salisbury and everybody else have tried to hide the truth from me, fearing to hurt me. At the whisper of bastardy, I am supposed to go and cry in a corner. I do not. I am not meek. Our Lord said the meek should inherit the earth; but was He meek when he took a whip and drove the money lenders from the Temple? Was He meek when he stood before Pilate and refused to answer? Was He meek when He hung on the Cross and said to the dying thief who had given Him His *rightful* title, 'Today shalt thou be with me in Paradise.' The word has been much misunderstood. I am meek in so far as I recognise authority. *I do*. Julius gave you and my father leave to marry. He had the power to do so, and to that power I bow. But I will not be put upon. And if Cardinal Campeggio decides against us, I shall not accept his verdict. Will you?'

She swung round and faced Katharine fiercely.

'Dearest, I have already promised to do so. I said when the matter was first mentioned that I would be guided by the Pope's decision.'

'But will it be *his* decision? Campeggio already has cause for gratitude to my father – he gave him a Bishopric last time he was here; what bribe will he offer this time? We know what is in Wolsey's mind. Will Campeggio be able to withstand him and his cajoleries? Besides, His Holiness is in no position to make a just and impartial judgment. Since the Imperial troops sacked Rome he has been under the Emperor's thumb.'

'That surely is a factor in our favour. Charles is our relative.'

Mary made a wordless sound of repudiation.

'Not even the Pope enjoys bondage. Clement looks to my father and to the King of France to liberate him.' She narrowed her eyes and her likeness to Henry in one of his worse moods was startling. 'If my cousin and the Pope were truly on our side they would have declared themselves at the beginning; not sent a sick old man to waste more time.'

She had evidently heard more about the business than Katharine would have wished; Lady Salisbury had tried to protect her; but of course women talked. And much of what she said was very shrewd, uncomfortably so. If, as Henry had said, he had first drawn the Pope's attention to his qualms of conscience two years ago, it would have been simple enough, then, for Clement to have replied unequivocally – the dispensation was good. Why had he not done so?

Such thoughts were useless, and weakening.

'We must have faith, Mary, and hope and patience. It is not an easy situation; but we must not give way to doubt – or to anger.'

'Anger is a great heartener. I am very angry – on your behalf as well as my own – when I see *her* flaunting and setting such a high price upon her virtue, which is in fact no virtue at all, simply inordinate ambition. How you can bear to have her about you I cannot understand.'

'It was your father's wish.'

'Would you jump into the Thames if that were his wish? I know – Lady Salisbury told me – that you consider that you owe him obedience in all matters not touching your conscience. But suppose – just for a moment suppose,' she halted her pacing and stood just in front of Katharine with her hands behind her back – another of Henry's gestures – 'Campeggio comes and decides against us. What action would your conscience then dictate?'

'Cardinal Campeggio comes as Papal Legate; he will have instructions, perhaps even his orders. I should feel bound to comply. I should do so with great sorrow, but I should comply.'

'I wonder,' Mary said, 'if you realise how the common people feel about all this. We are very popular, you and I. They howl against her in the streets.'

'The common people have no say in great matters.'

'They are the stuff of which armies are made.'

There was such deadly intensity in those words that Katherine's heart jolted. She reached out her hands and took Mary by the shoulder.

'Mary, you must not *think* in such a way. Never, no matter what the circumstances, or what our personal wrongs, must we resort to violence. Sit down and listen to me. I spent my youth in scenes of bloodshed. It was supposed to be a Holy War, a Crusade against the Infidel, and we celebrated our victories and mourned our defeats without much thought to the cost in dead men. The war was necessary and men were expendable. Then, when I was about your age, my sister Isabella lost her husband – he did not die in battle, but of disease – and she came back to Spain. I realised then what the death of a man meant. I had never seen Alfonso of Portugal – but I saw Isabella; and ever after, when I saw a dead man I saw the women who would weep for him. That is something to think upon; not the trumpets and the flags and the brave display. Mary, I speak of what I know. Three years before you were born it fell to me to raise an army against the Scots. Invaders *must* be resisted . . . but always I thought of the dead men and the women whose hearts would break. On no account over this dispute must even one man shed his blood. It would be civil war – the worst of all. And to have men die over what is, after all, a purely domestic matter, the concern of a mere four people, that would be so horrible that it must not be contemplated.'

Mary said, with a cool reasonableness more frightening than anger:

'But you say invaders must be resisted. Is *she* not an invader? You speak of *four* people concerned. Mother, it is the concern of *all*. Julius' ruling can only be one of two things – the inspired dictate of the Vicar of Christ on this earth, or the scribbling of a silly man who wrote what he was asked to write and whose authority can be set aside by another silly old man. Which was it?'

'Mary, you are speaking like a heretic. What have you been reading?'

'Everything that came my way. I am no heretic; but it is better to know your enemy than to blunder about in the dark. I hold Julius' dispensation good. By that I stand. But I also think that this may be the testing time. Just at this minute when Papal authority is questioned, Papal power so much reduced, this which you call the concern of a mere four people could turn the balance. There have been Popes who were renegade, or mad – the Devil is cunning. Clement is weak and hesitant. If Cardinal Campeggio, on the Pope's orders, reverses the dictate of his predecessor . . . what a triumph for those who refuse to admit that the Pope is anything more than Bishop of Rome. I wake in the night,' Mary said, 'and I think upon these things. I dread Cardinal Campeggio's coming. If he gives verdict against us, then Julius was wrong and Papal authority is cut down. If he gives verdict for us, then my father will be angry and there will be schism. In either case, through us, Holy Church will be stricken and that is a thought which I find almost unsupportable, except when I am angry and think the thoughts which you say I must not think.'

It was pitiable; only twelve years old . . .

'Mary, until you are of age you should not concern yourself too much with worldly matters. I am your mother; leave decisions to me. Be confident that whatever happens I shall have a care to our interests, and at the same time do my best for Holy Church. The interests are not incompatible; as you say, this may be the testing time. Let us have faith in God.'

'I do. And I do recognise my duty to you, my mother. And then I think . . . I cannot feel dutiful to him who tries to repudiate me.'

He was her father and until this trouble started she had adored him; handsome, sweet-smelling and merry, tossing her about in his strong arms, what could any little girl want more of her father? And later, praise, for the way she handled her lute, her good memory, the way she rode a horse. His loud voice and hearty laughter, even his bouts of ill-temper appealed to something boisterous in her, something which had sometimes chafed under Katharine's admonitions and instructions and rules about what a little girl must and must not do.

Her recoil, when she learned what he was planning to do, was proportionate to her former esteem. The prospect of not being Queen of England was galling enough; to learn that one's father had set himself to prove one a bastard was humiliating in the extreme; but worst of all was the fact that he was hurting her mother to whom, as she grew older and more sedate, she had become passionately devoted and whom she looked upon almost as a saint.

'I think, Mary, that you must try. He still is your father; he is the same person . . . this is very hard to explain. He has been ill-advised.'

'And led by the nose by a light woman.' Mary, who was one day to love recklessly and without reserve, spoke with savage scorn.

'Not light,' Katharine said. 'Had she been light we should not now be speaking to her. And I think we have had enough gloomy talk. We can do nothing except await Cardinal Campeggio's coming and hope and prepare ourselves to accept what comes with resignation and dignity.'

'I shall not. Whatever he says I shall never look upon you as other than Queen of England, or upon myself as anything but Princess of Wales. If the Pope himself ordered me to do otherwise, I *could* not. And,' she added, 'if I play for you; it will not be any of the songs my father made. I never play them now.'

'Play what you like, darling.'

Henry scurried from place to place, always just one day's journey ahead – or so it seemed – of the sweating sickness. He would leave a place in the morning and by nightfall someone in that place, a resident or somebody of the royal train, left behind to overlook the loading of the last of the baggage, would be smitten.

Anne Boleyn did not die. Henry, when he heard that she was ill, sent his second-best physician to attend her.

Campeggio moved northwestwards, covering on a good day as much as ten miles.

In Spain Dr. Puebla's son, going through his father's papers came upon a Papal brief, more lengthy and explicit than the original dispensation. In particular it omitted the word *forhans*, the Latin for *perhaps*. The dispensation gave permission for Henry and Katharine to marry even if *perhaps* the marriage between Katharine and Arthur had been consummated. The brief lacked the conditional word and Dr. Puebla's son realised the importance of his find.

In England it rained and rained; a disastrous summer murrain – a disease amongst cattle, curiously similar to the sweating sickness amongst men – decimated herds and the blighted, mildewed crops lay sideways in the fields.

So the autumn came; and since no journey can last forever, Cardinal Campeggio who had set out in June on a journey which in midwinter would have taken six weeks and had taken him four months, arrived in England on the first of October and went straight to his bed. And I would to God I could do likewise, Wolsey thought, heaving his ailing, failing bulk up to make the necessary visit of welcome and condolence. He had not fled before the threat of the plague; he had laboured away in London, confident in his belief that the sweating sickness, so eclectic, fastened upon the healthy and the well-born. He was no longer healthy and he was a butcher's son who by using his wits and his phenomenal capacity for work, his talent for intrigue and his gift of ostentation had climbed so high that his enemies called him King of Europe.

But he knew that for him this was the supreme test of his life. Henry had made that painfully clear. By hook or by crook the verdict must be made to go in Henry's favour or the blame would fall upon the most faithful, clever, cunning servant any king ever had.

CHAPTER 14

When, after some days, Campeggio, accompanied by Wolsey, shuffled into Henry's presence, Henry looked him over sharply and was satisfied that the long drawn-out journey had not been a trick to waste time. Inside the soft cloth shoes Campeggio's feet were grossly swollen, his puffy, glazed fingers fumbled stiffly with the papers and even his eyelids were swollen and red . . . A sorry sight, the King thought, quickly averting his eyes. Me too? One day?

He looked at Wolsey and because he saw him almost every day, failed to notice how much he had altered lately, the firm red cheeks mottled and sagging into heavy jowls and pouches under the eyes, the nose sharpened. Wolsey was twenty years older than his master and to Henry his servant's physical endurance, his mental energy and clarity spelt hope. Fifty-four this year, and as good as ever.

Wolsey had had several talks with Campeggio already, and Henry had dropped a hint, no more, that the investigation might be avoided. 'He is very secretive, and says nothing outright – one must remember that he is Italian by birth – but there is something which seems to indicate that he has instructions which do not concern the investigation. He said, quite seriously, Your Grace, that he hoped he would not be obliged to winter in England. It is now October; he knows how long a full trial would take to mount . . .'

Henry's hopes ran high, and now, having greeted them and invited them to be seated, he prepared himself to hear that Clement had found a short cut out of this impasse. Perhaps in an hour he would be free; a bachelor again; able to rush to Anne and say, 'Sweetheart, it is over. We can be married tomorrow, tonight . . .'

He said, 'Well, my lords?'

He was not perturbed when Campeggio began with a dissertation about the sanctity of marriage. The man was a lawyer and lawyers like preambles. And with everything in this speech Henry agreed. Marriage was a sacrament, man and wife one in the sight of God.

He listened, impatience well-concealed, but mounting.

'His Holiness has taken into consideration the tenderness of Your Grace's conscience,' Campeggio said, and paused; a lawyer's pause. Henry leaned forward, a smile already beginning to form.

'He has, therefore, instructed me to tell Your Grace that he is prepared to amend any flaw in the original dispensation, and to extend it, so that your marriage to Queen Katharine is good and valid, whether or not she was formerly the wife of your good brother, and this would allow Your Grace to resume marital relations with a completely clear conscience.'

'Christ's wounds!' Henry said. Precisely what he did *not* want. He sagged back in his chair and for a moment or two he looked almost as old, as worn by life as the two men who confronted him. Then he rallied.

'The offer astonishes me. It admits the possibility of a flaw and at the same time ties me down to acceptance of a flawed dispensation. Julius was either right or wrong. I claim that he was wrong. On that my case rests. This is no answer. Mending up a wrong. You sit there and tell me that if Julius was in error, Clement with a stroke of the pen can make it right and I have leave to take to my bed in good conscience a woman past child-bearing age who has borne me dead children, or children dead before their navels have healed. Can Clement, lifting his pen, remove the curse of Leviticus?'

'It is a matter of law, Your Grace,' Campeggio said. 'And if one gives consideration to Leviticus one should give equal attention to Deuteronomy, where a man is ordered to take his dead brother's wife and raise children in his brother's name. The study of such ancient, Jewish writings leads to confusion – as your case exemplifies. The teaching of the Church, the authority of the Pope are far more reliable guides to any Christian.'

'I am a Christian,' Henry said vehemently. 'Nineteen years ago, acting under the direction of a dispensation which now even Clements admits may have held a flaw, I married within the forbidden degree. The consequences proved me wrong; I searched my conscience. Can Clement's amendment give me back the lost boys, the lost years?'

'His willingness to amend any flaw should be a salve to any pang of conscience,' Campeggio said imperturbably.

Henry looked at Wolsey who had so far said nothing.

'Thomas, what is your view on this? Am I not right?'

'Your Grace repudiates the notion of amendment. It is to be hoped that Cardinal Campeggio did not travel so far, and so painfully, in order to offer a single, so easily rejected suggestion.'

Let Campeggio show his full hand; let Campeggio see what it meant to deal with a man like the King of England.

'There was an alternative suggestion,' Campeggio said, after a short, tense silence. 'His Holiness is fully prepared to absolve the Queen from her earthly marriage, if she retires to a convent and takes vows.'

At that Wolsey looked up and his eyes met Henry's. 'You see! All this running to and fro, all this talk and what result? They now point to the way out which I suggested more than a year ago.'

'There is nothing new there, either,' Henry snapped. 'My lord Cardinal proposed it last year; before he left for France. The Queen repudiated it utterly.'

'Saying that she would await His Holiness's decision in the matter. Is it not possible that Her Grace might regard the suggestion coming now as it does direct from him, as a decision? She has now had ample time for thinking over her position.' And to see how little hope she had. 'Have I permission to see the Queen and lay this proposal before her?'

'If that is the best you can do. You might as well save your breath. I've been married to her for hard on twenty years and never yet seen her change her mind over a principle. She looks on herself as my wife and will do so until I get a plain yes or no to my question, put to Rome three years back. Is my marriage legal or not? It warranted a plain answer. And what do I get? This stale stuff.'

He glared at them. This would be a fine thing to tell Anne; he could just imagine how she would take it; tears, hysterics, or mockery. God's eyes! People applauded when the old dog went through the hoop. He went through it every night.

'Had the answer been so simple, I should not be here,' Campeggio said. All those miles; so much pain.

'Why are you here? This nonsense could have been put on paper. Clement promised me a full investigation.'

'Which I am here to conduct. If needs be. But I was ordered to bring about, if possible, a decent, private settlement. We can talk about the trial when I have seen Her Grace.'

'That word does not please me. Who is on trial? Kate . . . Her Grace and

I are both innocent victims of a Papal error, which Clement could put right with a pen stroke. If he has power to amend the dispensation he has power to annul it.' Impotent anger choked him. Then suspicion flared. Campeggio wanted to see Katharine. Alone with her what might he not say? Clement lived under the Emperor's thumb, and the Emperor was her nephew. The long delay, the sending of this slow-moving devious man to make more delay. Part of a plot against him.

'And another thing,' he said, speaking to Campeggio but bringing his hard, blue, down-bearing stare upon Wolsey. 'You go together. His Holiness yoked you . . . Go when you like. England is a free country. Anyone may talk to whom he wishes. That is all I have to say. I wish you Good day.'

As usual, Wolsey thought, the King had summed the situation in a few words. England was a country where all men were free to obey orders.

'I have nothing to say to Her Grace which I should not wish Cardinal Wolsey to hear. Indeed I hope that he will lend his persuasions to mine to bring about a happy issue, agreeable to all.'

Outside the audience chamber Wolsey, matching his step to Campeggio's shuffle, said:

'That was unfortunate. The Queen neither likes nor trusts me. You would have done better alone.'

'If we could travel by river it would suit me well. A boat jolts less and we might avoid the crowd.'

The crowd had been very vociferous; shouting for the Queen and against Nan Bullen. Campeggio had wondered whether the English had no work to do, no homes or children to tend that at a moment's notice, or no notice at all, they could flock into the streets and shout. He had made only one comment; 'His Grace must know how his people feel.'

'He has no intention of marrying her,' Wolsey said, putting into words his own deep-seated belief. 'And while they are shouting against *her*, they are happy.' And not shouting against you, or me.

They shouted lustily at Westminster steps where the Cardinals embarked and here and there along the river, and at Greenwich. And today every now and then, after the call, 'We want no Nan Bullen,' there was a postcript. 'Nor no Cardinals neither!'

Campeggio said, with tact, or malice, one never knew:

'I seem to share Mistress Boleyn's unpopularity. They mistake my errand if they think I come to break a marriage.'

'It broke years ago,' Wolsey said morosely. His disappointment was almost equal to Henry's. Campeggio, after all, had nothing new to suggest; no easy way out. And the Queen would never yield. A proposition which she would not take from the King, whom she loved, she would not take from Campeggio. Unless that secretive man had, somewhere concealed about him, a definite order from Clement: Get into a convent! Nothing less would move her; and the investigation would go on, taking time. *And unless it ends as he wishes, the bell will toll for me.* Wolsey thought wearily that God in His wisdom had made women, child-bearing animals or playthings – his own woman, Joan Larke had been both, and he still enjoyed the company and was interested in the well-being of his son and daughter, known as his nephew and niece. But the western world had given the creatures a ridiculous importance; dowries, marriage settlements, rights. The Turks had better sense; a man had only to say, 'I divorce you,' three times and it was done.

So they came to Greenwich, where the lower steps, washed by every tide, were clean, those above slimy – 'I beg you be careful, my lord!' and then a few which except in an exceptionally wet spring the water never touched.

'We want no Nan Boleyn!' The crowd greeted them.

You muttonheaded fools, Wolsey thought, *do you think I want her?*

You silly English people, Campeggio thought, *she will be grey-headed and forgotten before His Holiness gives consent; get back to your looms and your counters!*

Katharine was at work with her women, stitching away at an altar cloth, a Christmas gift to the chapel of the Observant Friars, when the two Cardinals, with something of a flurry, were announced. She pushed her needle into the cloth, rose, curtseyed to the two Princes of the Church and led them into the little private room on the far side of the apartment. It was her own sanctum, the place where she wrote her letters, sometimes meditated, sometimes prayed. It was, as regards aspect, on the wrong side of the house, lighted only by a narrow, ancient window that never caught the sun. It had no hearth. Walls and floor were bare and it contained the minimum of furniture. Apart from the table, directly under the window and the chair in which she sat when writing, there was nothing except a bench against one wall and against the other a prie-dieu, and that very stark.

Campeggio, taking the whole place in at a glance, thought: *This should not be too hard; she is halfway to a nunnery already.* For a moment he saw himself, successful in this tricky business, back in Rome before the English winter set in, his task accomplished, taking his ease.

In that same moment Katharine was concerned with a triviality, a matter of precedence. There was the one chair; offer it to either and the other would be offended; and her eye, sharper than Henry's in this respect, saw nothing to choose between them, physically; Cardinal Campeggio was the more obviously disabled, but Cardinal Wolsey did not look well; the high ruddy colour that he usually carried was unequally distributed, separate islands of red and white all over the full-fleshed face; and the lips bluish.

So she seated herself in the chair and asked them to set themselves on the bench, and said to Campeggio:

'You bring me news of the decision that His Holiness has made in my case?' And she waited as avidly as Henry had done.

Campeggio said, 'Your Grace, in this matter a decision is hard to reach. I bring a suggestion . . .'

He did not lecture her on the sanctity of marriage; he made no preamble. He told her, quite frankly and with a bluntness that Wolsey would not have thought him capable of, that the best, the only thing she could do, was to renounce her dubious earthly marriage and become the Bride of Christ. A nun.

Until he said it she had not realised how much she had counted upon his coming; how much she had relied upon the Pope to espouse her cause. All along she had not set her hopes too high, had been careful to say, even to Mary, 'If . . .' and 'Whatever happens . . .' But her inner certainty that she was right had coloured her thinking; she realised now that in her inmost heart she had been certain that when Campeggio arrived he would bring proof that she was right, that His Holiness, in Rome, had sorted all things out and was prepared to stand by her.

People said, slapping words about like coins on a counter, 'my heart sank,' 'my heart stopped,' 'my heart broke' and there was, after all, some groping after truth in such expressions. Campeggio's words went into her ears, her mind absorbed them and lower down, in her chest and stomach there was a drop, a stop, an emptying, as though her whole body was suddenly hollowed out. It needed a deliberate, almost desperate effort for her to gather enough force and breath to say:

'But for me to take such a course . . . apart from the fact that I have no vocation for the religious life . . . would be tantamount to admitting that I was not, never had been, his wife . . . And I was, I *am*. I am his wife. The dispensation was granted; we were legally and properly married; all our children were born in wedlock and this talk of Leviticus is nonsense. Mary is alive; her father's daughter and his heir.'

'That is,' Campeggio said in a very gentle voice, 'one view. Your view, and others share it. But . . .' For the first time since his arrival in England he smiled and even Wolsey, watching with a cynical eye, saw how a smile transfigured the undistinguished face. 'The nub of the matter, Your Grace, is that the King thinks otherwise, is troubled in his conscience. If

you would retire, your honour in no way impugned, your material possessions in no way diminished, there would be no scandal, no investigation,
no outcry. There is a precedent; the saintly Queen of France, Jeanne de
Valois, retired to a convent in order to allow Louis XII to marry again.'

'I am not a saint.'

'You are a woman of great piety,' Campeggio said coaxingly; 'you wear
the Franciscan habit under your fine clothes, do much good work amongst
the poor. You are a faithful and obedient daughter of the Church. Would
it be so great a sacrifice?'

'Does His Holiness order me into a convent?' Behind her clear steady
gaze something flashed.

'Your Grace must know that the taking of the veil is a voluntary act.'

'And one that I shall never commit. I am sorry for your wasted errand,
my lords. I look upon myself as a married woman and shall continue to do
so.' Wolsey had so far said nothing but sat, twisting his great cardinal's
ring upon his finger. Katharine turned to him and said. 'This you will
understand better than one lately come into this country. I have a dozen
reasons, all good, for holding to my position; one is that I have no more
desire to see Mistress Boleyn Queen of England than have the crowds out
there, or you yourself. You are much mistaken, my lord Cardinal, if you
believe, as some do, that once freed of this marriage, the King would not
wed her. He would do it within a week. His will is strong and once his
heart is set . . .' As once it was on me! She thought of how cunningly and
patiently he had waited, avoiding other betrothals and how he had come
to her the moment he was master. She remembered the young green of the
lime-walk; now the yellow and rusty leaves were falling; soon the trees
would be bare. Like life . . .

She felt her throat ache, her eyes sting. In a second she would be crying.
What had Mary said about anger being a great heartener? She said, with
at least a show of anger, addressing Wolsey still.

'I blame you for this trouble. I once ventured to criticise your voluptu-
ous way of life and remarked that it was strange that Christ, who was so
humble, should have a servant who was so proud. From that moment you
marked me down. And you hate my nephew the Emperor because he did
not support you when you hoped to be Pope. So you are trying to end my
marriage. Were I weak enough to be persuaded you would be one of the
first to regret it. I say nothing derogatory to Mistress Boleyn herself, but
she is surrounded by men tainted with heresy, men who read Lutheran
books, smuggled in.'

It was all true, Wolsey reflected grimly; on the other hand he must obey
the King or fall.

'Your Grace is mistaken if you think I bear you malice.' A half-smile twitched his fleshy lips. 'If you ever criticised me, I have forgotten it, I have been much criticised. Perhaps rightly. We are all as God made us, and He made me proud and comfort-loving. But that is neither here nor there. What concerns us is that His Grace is determined to obtain a divorce.'

'Divorce!' she exclaimed, pouncing on the word. 'When he, or you, or anybody else uses that word I am proved right. Where there has been no valid marriage – that is the contention – there can be no divorce.'

They were both startled by the swiftness, shrewdness and truth of that statement; it was out of accord with her appearance and demeanour. It had a lawyer's touch.

When Campeggio next spoke the gentleness and coaxing note had left his voice.

'Whatever word is used, Your Grace, the point remains. His Grace is determined. If necessary the case will come to open trial.'

'That is what I have always wanted. Not secret talks at York House,' she flashed a look at Wolsey, 'or secret conferences in Rome. I want an open trial, where men can study all the evidence and decide.' And see that I am right.

'Do you?' Campeggio said; and again, into two words he put a vast meaning. 'I wonder if Your Grace has *seriously* considered what a trial would involve. The question of whether or not you were virgin on the night of the eleventh of June in the year of Our Lord 1509, will certainly come under close scrutiny. Would that not be offensive to your modesty?'

It would be almost intolerable She no longer blushed easily and prettily, but she felt the heat in her neck and in her cheeks, just below the eyes. She remembered her first wedding night, Arthur's whispered words, and her own little trick which had seemed so clever at the time. Would somebody find and drag into the open an old woman who had made a bed at Baynard's Castle on the morning of November 15th, in the year of Our Lord 1501? Well, that could be countered, if it came to that, by the evidence of whoever made the bed on the morning of the twelfth of June, eight years later. No need for trickery then.

'It will be painful and embarrassing for me,' she said, 'but there is too much at stake for me to shrink. I can say to you, my lords, that my marriage to Arthur, Prince of Wales, was never consummated; so I can say it in open court. And mark this; there are many men, nobles, churchmen, lawyers, still alive, who saw my marriage made, accepted Pope Julius' dispensation as valid, did not question it then, do not question it now. Some of them will sit in that court.'

Not if I can help it, Wolsey thought; but how could the adherents of one side or another be identified? This was not a tourney, where every man displayed his colours. But his mind, that sharp instrument with which he had carved out a place for himself in a world where the poor and the lowly born seldom enjoyed preferment, looked ahead, beyond the trial – whichever way it went. He saw the rift that could never again be closed, the wound that would never heal. For once he was not thinking of himself but of the far future when he and Katharine and Henry and Campeggio and Anne Boleyn would be lying quiet in their graves.

He got up, took three paces across the narrow room and fell on his knees before Katharine.

'Your Grace, I beg you, think again on this matter. More is concerned than you dream of. The world is already riven in two. Half Germany no longer acknowledges the authority of the Pope. The German landknechts sacked Rome and made monks the target for their arrows, nuns the victims of their lust. To bring Pope Julius' dispensation into question in open court, at this most critical moment, will, whatever the verdict, do the Papacy irreparable damage. I implore you to listen to me, to look ahead. This thing could throw a decisive weight into the scales. Ordinary people have no discrimination, they see things as black or white, right or wrong. If this comes to open trial they will say: If Julius had power to dispense why did Clement not stand by that dispensation; and if Julius had no such power why did Clement think a trial necessary? Your Grace, upon the question of a marriage – to you, I grant, a thing of great importance, but in itself a trivial thing – the whole future of the Church may hinge.'

Campeggio thought: Very clever; and what a good actor the man is.

Katharine said, 'My Lord Cardinal, the embarrassment that confronts me begins here, with you on your knees to me. Rise, I beg you. Stand up and consider. In taking my stand, so far from undermining Papal authority, I am upholding it by every means within my power. I believe that Julius' dispensation was good; and when all has been sorted, it will be *seen* to be good. The marriage that the Pope permitted was a true marriage and will continue – until one of us is dead.'

She believed it. She was Isabella's daughter and although she shrank from the thought of physical violence and bloodshed, she was as confident in her cause as Isabella had been in her Crusade against the Moors. Times changed, methods changed; this would be battle fought out on parchment, in argument; but it would be, it must be, a victory of right over wrong.

The sight of a man grown old and heavy with the years who had momentarily cast away his dignity and knelt and been told to rise, his plea not granted, was one upon which she did not care to look. So, as Wolsey scrambled to his feet, she directed her gaze to Campeggio.

'If an open trial is to come about, I shall need legal advice,' she said.

'You will arrange it for me?'

You, Campeggio thought, need no legal advice; you need a clout, two, forehand, backhand each side of the head. You are right, but right in the wrong way, and everything that Wolsey just said is true; Clement himself realises it. And because you are so obstinate, I must winter in England . . .

'No Nan Bullen for us!' the crowd chanted; and the solitary voice added, 'And no Cardinals neither!' This time Campeggio made no comment.

CHAPTER 15

'It was so horrible, Maria. You can have no idea.' Here, back in the safe familiar room she weakened, put her face in her hands and shed a few tears of sheer self-pity. Unfair! Blatantly unjust! 'Not one of *my* legal advisers was there. Nor Cardinal Campeggio. I was completely alone. His Grace once said to me that those who took an impossible stand must stand alone. And it was not merely what I was obliged to do this morning, bad as it was. It is an omen. What happened this morning will happen again . . . My heart, my very mind is shaken.'

'Was the King there?' Maria de Moreto no longer called him *His Grace*. He was lost to grace.

'No. Just the Council. Headed by the Cardinal. And they said that if I did not sign, I should be taken straight to the Tower.'

'Jesu Mary!' Maria said, her face going greenish. 'The Tower? But on what charge?'

'Treason,' Katharine said.

'Treason! Your Grace, Your Grace, I beg you to listen to me. Let him have his way, before worse happens. You are right, everybody knows that, but he is King and will have his way. Ask yourself how many go in by the Traitor's Gate and ever come out. There is nothing here for us and we could be happy and comfortable, elsewhere. I fear the worst to come.'

So do I; I saw this morning how little justice . . . All those hard faces. All the men who give *him* such ill advice.

'Where could I be happy and comfortable, with my daughter made illegitimate and *her* child looked upon as heir.'

'The Emperor would find the Princess a husband. We could all go to Spain and feel the warmth of the sun. He would be glad to see us go. And we should be safe.'

Yesterday Katharine would have derided such talk; today it did not seem ridiculous. But the mention of Mary had strengthened her and reminded her of something.

'That is impossible, Maria; but if you crave to go home and sit in the sun, you have my leave to go – and my blessing.'

'I shall never leave you. Never.'

'It may be forced upon you. Meantime – I promised to dine with the Princess today. I should not wish her to see me distraught. And I have something to do. Maria, go along and make some excuse. Tell her . . . tell her that I am detained. Proffer my apologies. Make light of it.'

Really it would be better if Mary were out of London while all this business was going on. Perhaps even Henry would agree to that.

'And tell Griffith to send Francisco to me.'

Once again Filipez stood before her, not behind her; a reliable ally, not a server; he was older, stiffer and his hair was greyer, but he looked lively and tough.

'I will tell you quickly,' she said. 'Concerning the matter between His Grace and me, there exists a very important document – the brief found amongst Dr. Puebla's papers. The Emperor has it in his keeping. I had a copy, signed and witnessed and gave it, with other papers, to those who in the forthcoming investigation will plead my cause. This morning I was called before the King's privy council and told that a copy was not sufficient; the *original* must be sent. They had a letter, all written, lacking only my signature, ready to be sent requesting the immediate despatch of that document to England. Francisco, upon receipt of that letter, which I signed under duress, the Emperor will speed it on its way; I am sure that it will never arrive. My enemies wish it out of existence. If my letter reaches the Emperor *before* the countermanding request, it will be sent and destroyed somewhere and all that I shall have will be the copy, already suspect. Would you ride again, very fast, and this time without safe-conduct, and tell the Emperor on no account, *on no account* to let that brief out of his hands. I know it is much to ask . . . but whom else can I ask?'

Whom else should Your Grace ask?' Whom but Francisco Filipez, a devoted servant who had a way of getting the most out of a horse.

'I shall be on my way in less than an hour. I think I shall need no safe-conduct this time; they will think of rats leaving a ship about to sink. But, Your Grace, may I say a word . . . as your server? Lately I have been very careful; I have never offered Your Grace a dish, or a cup which has not been tested by myself or by some other person beforehand. I have been aware that . . . some would have found their way smoothed . . . if a dish . . . Your Grace understands me?'

'Poison,' she said, shattered for the second time in one day. She had
never thought of it. In Italy Medicis and Borgias had used it often against
their personal or political enemies, but this was not Italy.

'I will, with Your Grace's permission, choose the man to serve in my
place. And may I ask: Have you, amongst your jewels, a turquoise?
Perhaps not,' he said, as she hesitated. 'It is only a half-precious stone, but
there is an ancient belief that in the presence of poison it changes from
blue to black. If Your Grace would . . . It is unworthy . . .' He began to
wrestle with the ring he wore on his fourth, left-hand finger. It stuck below
the knotted knuckle.

'Francisco, you will pull off your finger.'

'So I would. Every one, if it would serve.' He wrestled with it, remembering how once, on the middle finger of his right hand, it had slipped
easily up and down.

'I will have it cut off,' he said in a fury. 'And I beg you, carry it about
you, pass it over everything you are offered. Until I am back.'

For a day or two after Filipez's departure she lived in trepidation;
turned back at Dover? At Calais? Rouen? She followed him, in her mind,
on his headlong ride; she prayed for his safety. Sometimes, waking in the
night at the hour when hope was at ebb tide, she imagined him waylaid, or
dead.

Then she learned that to fetch home this precious brief, one of her own
chaplains had been chosen – a man named Thomas Abell. He was part of
her household, but she did not know him well, had never noticed him
much. He came and went, performed his duties; a rather close-mouthed,
cold-eyed man.

That Wolsey should have chosen one of her own chaplains, and
Thomas Abell of all men, to bring back the disputed brief, was dreadfully
significant. A letter signed in her own hand, asking for it, a member of her
household sent to fetch it. Charles would be completely deceived – unless
Filipez arrived first; and without a passport, could he? Could he?

Maria de Moreto, speaking sourly, offered a way out of this predicament.

'That worthless cousin of mine, Juan Montoya, has been engaged to
conduct Dr. Abell on his journey,' she said. She had not always thought
him worthless. She had once been in love with him. That fact lent venom
to her voice as she said, 'It will be the first honest job he has done for years;
but Dr. Abell will benefit. Juan has a knowledge of inns . . .'

An idea that might have come direct from Heaven flashed into
Katharine's mind.

'Maria, what kind of man is he – your cousin? One who would carry an
urgent message for me?'

'He is an idle fellow, overfond of women, and of wine. He borrows money and does not repay it,' Maria said. 'But,' she added simply, 'indubitably a man of honour'. Neither she nor Katharine saw anything contradictory in these remarks.

'Could you ask him to come and say goodbye to you; and then smuggle him in to me?'

'I will do that,' Maria said; knowing that to see Juan would give her pain, and that he would certainly borrow every penny she had laid by – about ten shillings.

Montoya came and agreed, enthusiastically, to carry a secret message. He had the born scamp's charm and self-confidence and the ability to induce trustfulness.

'Your Grace may rest easy. *Your* message shall be delivered before Dr. Abell's saddlebags are unpacked. And until that moment thumbscrews would not wring a word from me.'

So now, if Filipez had failed to get through, Montoya, on an official errand, with everything expedited and made easy, would. And he would keep his promise – indubitably a man of honour.

The two oddly assorted men moved through France less speedily than Dr. Abell had expected or would have wished. He would have pressed on, missing meals, missing sleep. But he was in Montoya's hands. Dr. Abell had never before been out of England and spoke only English and Latin. Montoya knew the road and had an almost uncanny ability to make himself understood everywhere: and he would say, 'There is no point in going farther today. The next inn is twenty miles away, and we benefit nobody by sleeping in ditches.' Or he would say, 'I am not satisfied with the horses. I have ordered better ones, but they will not be here until morning.' Such excuses were usually made in places where some response had been made to the lascivious glance which Montoya directed at any woman under thirty and not positively ugly.

Dr. Abell's patience wore thin; and then as they moved south and the food grew worse, his digestion began to trouble him. Even Wolsey's long arm could not make crossing the Pyrénées other than a test of endurance. Montoya seemed to thrive on the smoked raw ham, the barley bread and the sour local wines which – having given it fair trial – Dr. Abell said was no better than horse piss.

One afternoon they halted to eat and change horses at a lonely little tavern kept by a surly old man and his daughter, a buxom girl with what Dr. Abell had come to recognise as *that* way of walking. The ham was even more raw-seeming than usual and the crumb or two of bread which Abell forced down seemed to lodge in his chest and glow like hot coals.

'Come along,' he said, after watching Montoya eat and drink his fill. 'The horses are the worst I have yet seen. We shall have our work cut out to get to Roncevalles tonight, even if we start at once.'

'And who wants to get to Roncevalles?'

'I do,' Abell said crisply. 'And so should you. You were sent to accompany me, not to delay me. These long overnight stops have already wasted much valuable time.'

Montoya, making no move, took another gulp of the unpalatable wine and said, 'I am not delaying you. There is only one road to Roncevalles: you will not lose your way. And tomorrow morning, on a horse that has had a bellyful and a day's rest from the plough, I shall overtake you easily.'

Had he known only a little Spanish, Dr. Abell would have left immediately. As it was there began to grow in him the dangerous cold anger of his kind.

'You were engaged to conduct me,' he said. 'Your attitude is no more nor less than blackmail. And do not think that I fail to see through you. I know that the horses we rode today are by regulations bound to remain here, and that the ones provided are poor, very poor . . .' Dr. Abell entertained a certain amount of feeling for horses. 'But that is simply an excuse. You wish to spend the night here because you have cast a lecherous eye on that flaunting girl.'

'I still have the use of my eyes, thank God,' Montoya said, drinking again. He focused them, a little owlishly on his companion. '*And* my ears,' he said. 'Blackmail is an ugly word, not to be used between gentlemen . . . Not that you could be expected to understand that.'

Dr. Abell did not even realise that he had been insulted. He came of sound yeoman stock, people who said, faced with any cause for special elation, 'I am so happy, I would not thank the King to be my cousin!' With such a background – and a degree gained by hard study – Thomas Abell was immune from any sneer Montoya could throw.

'If the word offends you, cease the practice,' he said. 'Unless we make better speed than we have done I shall report upon your behaviour in such a way that you will never be employed in any capacity again.'

'Oh, I live by my wits,' Montoya said, retorting to this reference to his occasional employment as courier, interpreter, go-between. 'I drink when I can and whore with any wench who is willing. But I have never yet betrayed a lady whose bread and salt I have eaten!'

His tone and his look made an accusation of the last words; an accusation so unfounded, so completely irrelevant that the innocent Dr. Abell could only say:

'I think you are drunk now.'

Montoya had drunk just the amount which, in ordinary circumstances, would have made him cheerful good company, but the little squabble had tipped his mood.

'I am sober enough to see you for what you are,' he said. 'One of *her* household, sent to do *her* grave damage and unable to do it fast enough. Blackmail is an ugly word, but there is a worse one. Traitor!' Montoya laughed. 'And if the word offends you, cease the practice,' he said. 'God in Heaven, man! Can you not see that you are being *used*? Her Grace, under threat of being sent to the Tower, signed a request for that brief to be sent to England. *You*, one of her chaplains, are sent to fetch it home. A very pretty arrangement. And the moment you hand it over Wolsey will put it in the fire. But,' he said, the wine fumes mounting, 'you will not do it. That I swear on the Cross.' He put a rather fumbling hand on the haft of the knife at his belt. It was, like sword hilts, made in the form of a cross.

Dr. Abell made a gesture, not matching, but reciprocal in its fashion. He reached out and took the jug of wine and emptied it on the floor. He had asked for water, and water had been brought, in a coarse earthenware jug and he had taken a few sips, to cool the furnace in his chest and no more, because the water here was almost as unpalatable as the wine. But it was cool. Deliberately he lifted the jug and poured it over Montoya's head.

'Now,' he said, as Montoya gasped and spluttered, 'let us go. It is plain to me we are on the same errand and haste is imperative.'

'The same errand . . . you mean the same side?'

'I am for Her Grace. I believed that the brief, in the original form, would help her cause. You have undeceived me and I thank you. But if we dally more the Cardinal will give us up for lost and may send another messenger . . .'

After that they made much better speed and were more at one until the moment when they stood in the anteroom, waiting to be received by the Emperor – 'an emissary from England and his interpreter.' And at this last moment Juan Montoya suffered a return of doubt and suspicion. Abell, so typically English, could have deceived him. He put his hand to his knife again and said, 'Ask for that brief to be sent and you get this, straight to the heart.'

'And how could I ask,' Abell said, 'except through you?'

'In Latin,' Montoya said. 'One word in Latin and you are a dead man.'

'I am for Her Grace,' Abell said again. 'And if I say a word to wrong or hurt her, cut my throat.'

The Emperor had received the request which Katharine had been compelled to sign and was awaiting Dr. Abell's arrival. Now, most confusingly, the doctor said that on no account was the original brief to be handed over. A new, exact, properly attested copy was to be made, if the Emperor so pleased. The man, Dr. Abell, one of Katharine's own chaplains, made this request, in English; his attendant, a Spaniard, translated, but he seemed wary and watchful. Charles thought: All this is in direct contradiction to what she *wrote*; and neither man is completely at ease. Why not? Some conflict of interest? Some English trick?

He said, 'At this hour, on a working day, I take my belated dinner, here at this table. I am ready for it now.' He lifted the silver bell from the clutter of papers on the table and rang it in the way that alerted, not the pages with the pappy, well-chopped meat, but four stout guards.

'Remove him,' the Emperor said, indicating Montoya. 'Handle him gently; he has given no offence. I will speak with him later.'

Within the gentle but purposeful grip of the guards, Montoya said loudly, 'Beware what you say! My knife is ready.'

'Speak in Latin,' the Emperor said, as soon as they were alone. Dr. Abell said, in Latin, precisely what he had said in English; adding, 'I did not understand the situation when I set out. My companion enlightened me along the road.'

'And is he to be trusted? Could the enlightenment have been planned in order to make you say what you were not sent to say?'

'I think not, Your Imperial Highness,' Dr. Abell said after a moment's thought. 'No. He was somewhat drunk at the time, and afterwards regretted allowing his errand to be known to me.'

'And what was his errand?'

'To forestall me: or by some other means prevent the brief from being sent.'

'And it is your honest opinion that it should not be sent?'

'I am sure – now that I have thought it over.'

Dr. Abell was led from the presence and Montoya admitted. His story matched; and the details – being sent for by his cousin, the Queen's lady-in-waiting, and commissioned by the Queen herself – were convincing.

'You appear to be of one mind,' Charles said. 'Why is there distrust between you?'

'I was ready to kill him if he broke into Latin and argued the other way,' Montoya said simply. 'He is English. But he seems to be honest.'

The honest Englishman sat in his lodging, waiting for the brief to be copied, and began to jot down a few arguments that had occurred to him concerning the legality of the marriage. Conviction grew as he pondered and worked; and on the return journey, every night he took out the copy of the brief and studied it. It seemed to him to be flawless; and he could see why the Queen had been anxious for the original not to fall into the hands of her enemies. It was God's Providence which had given him a drunkard and a lecher for guide. And that was a strange thought, leading to some even stranger. Had Juan Montoya been destined from birth to be bibulous and lecherous in order that on one particular moment of time . . . in a dirty little Pyrenean tavern . . .?

All the way home Dr. Abell was very tolerant of Montoya's peccadillos, supplied him with money – Montoya being penniless again – and when they reached the region where the wine was drinkable, sometimes took a glass or two with him in good fellowship. On the whole however, his attention was on the problem of the marriage and he began to plan a book. It took some time to write, and before it was published it had become an offence in England to give Katharine the title of Queen.

Francisco Filipez had said: Until I am back. He was back in a fortnight with a grubby bandage on his head and his right arm splinted to a piece of a broom handle.

'I apologise for appearing before Your Grace in this state,' he said, 'but I knew you would be anxious. I failed.'

'Are you much hurt, Francisco?'

'No. A cracked head and a broken arm. I was set on, at Abbeville.'

'By whom?'

'I never saw. They came behind me.' There were moments when even the most wary man must turn to a wall for a moment. 'When I came to my senses I was on a boat bound for Dover. And I thank God, Your Grace, that I had no papers about me. Nevertheless, my errand was guessed at. I was not robbed. I was sent back to England, admitted at Dover without question. I think it was intended that I should be living proof that no messenger you send will get through.' He looked at her miserably.

'I sent another, Francisco, in case you were intercepted. My second messenger travelled with every safeguard the Cardinal could provide. Nothing like so swift as you are,' she smiled at him, 'but he will arrive. So you need not worry. You must go to bed and I will send Dr. de La Sa to attend you.'

'Your Grace, I need no physician. A night in my own bed will restore me.' He had failed; he had two major injuries and a dozen smaller ones, he needed no purgings or bleedings to add to his miseries.

'Your ring served me well, Francisco. It stayed blue all the time.'

There was no lady like her; so brave; so kind. Filipez made a choking noise in his throat. 'If the other man, for any reason, should fail, I will go again, as soon as my arm is mended. I will go in disguise.'

'I hope there will be no need,' she said. She did not think it necessary to say to this discouraged man that it would then be too late. By the time he could ride again, the Emperor would have listened to Dr. Abell and to Juan Montoya and decided one way or the other.

But Filipez's return, in such a state, was an indication of the viciousness of her enemies. She felt weak and isolated; aware that somebody – and still she thought Wolsey chiefly – was determined to be rid of her. However, she had spent enough of her youth on the perimeter of battlefields to have learned that minor defeats could be preludes to victories, so long as one did not allow oneself to be demoralised by them. That was the real nub of the matter; not to lose courage, or hope, or faith in God.

On the whole, as the days ran by and the date of the court of investigation, which everybody now called the trial – so wrong, since the word postulated some criminal action – drew nearer, Katharine fared rather better than the others who were concerned. Henry was anxious and pressed hard upon Wolsey who, arranging everything, gathering witnesses, compiling statements, some most contradictory, still felt that Campeggio had some typically Italian trick hidden in his sleeve: Anne, facing the moment that would decide her whole future, was frequently hysterical and always nervous; Mary, her future equally in balance, and her heart concerned, sometimes wept, sometimes raged, throwing books, needlework, her lute away, riding horses to exhaustion.

Spring, in England in the year 1529, came in with its usual heady promise; daffodils nodding in the grass, bluebells, the cuckoo's call, and the lime trees translucent green. What happened? Where did the magic go? I loved him; he loved me. And now even the consummation has been reduced to words upon paper – some of them, used in any other context, positively óbscene.

Those appointed to advise her and to speak for her in court, came and went. They had been carefully chosen so that the watching world might be assured that there had been no flaw in justice and that the Queen had been properly represented. There was Warham, Archbishop of Canterbury, growing old, not in good health and plainly regretting the whole business; he inspired little confidence, John Fisher, Bishop of Rochester, was plainly on her side and was not afraid to show it. She had also Tunstall, Bishop of Durham, a leading member of her own favourite order, the Observant Friars, and her own confessor, born a Spaniard to whom, in happier days Henry had given the Bishopric of Llandaff. Nobody should say afterwards, when the King had won his case, that the trial had not been scrupulously fair. There was even an attempt to give an international touch with the appointment of two Flemish lawyers to help her, but everything, even access to the relevant documents, was made so difficult for them that they cut short their stay in London and went home.

Campeggio came and took from her a statement, under the most solemn oath, that she had gone virgin to Henry's bed. When she had made it, he said, 'Naturally *I* believe Your Grace but . . . there is evidence to the contrary.' He looked at her and then away again.

'Bedmakers?'

With ill-concealed distaste he moved his hand. 'That, of course. But conflicting. Of more importance are the words spoken by the Prince of Wales on the morning following the nuptials.'

Two children, playing a game of make-believe, conspiring to deceive their elders! The little idyll, so soon over, and now dragged out into the pitiless scrutiny of the law.

'His Grace knows the truth, my lord Cardinal. A statement should be asked of him.'

'It has been. He merely repeats that you were his brother's wife.' There seemed to her to be something of warning in Campeggio's voice and in his eyes, now again bearing upon her.

'And that is true,' she said, ignoring the warning. 'Nobody denies that the Prince of Wales and I were legally married. I deny that the marriage was consummated; and this His Grace could confirm. But in fact this court should not be concerned with that. All that is in question is the validity of the dispensation which made my second marriage legal.' Campeggio said nothing. 'Is that not so?'

He thought of all that was involved in that so simple-sounding question, and sighed. If only she had been less clear-headed, more easily frightened or shamed, cajoled, coaxed, persuaded. . . .

Then, in June, with the court already in session, John Fisher came and said, in his blunt, forthright way:

'Your Grace, I have come to say something which you may not welcome, but which my thought and my feeling obliges me to say. It is this: You will not get justice at the Court now sitting at Blackfriars, and you should repudiate its jurisdiction. *At once.*'

He had always been her staunchest supporter; always certain that when everything was brought out into the light of day, the verdict would be for her.

She said, 'You must explain to me . . . why . . . and how can it be done. Be seated, please. You do not look well.'

'I should be dead,' he said. His old rough-hewn face lost for a moment its nobility and solemnity and produced a wry smile, not much different from a boy's grin. 'But for my Meg, I should be dead. But that is neither here nor there – except as evidence of what I say.'

'Meg is your hound.'

'She *was*.' He was grave again. 'This is of no importance, Your Grace, though I was fond of her and she of me, and she was sadly spoiled. Last night she sat by me, avid as usual. I took two cuts at my meat. I was in ill-humour. I was wrong, I suppose, but I had little appetite. I threw the meat at her and said: Here, take the whole. She did, and was stiff and dead in less than five minutes; and my two mouthfuls left me considerably indisposed.'

'I am truly sorry,' Katharine said.

'I am sorry too. Poor Meg. But had she been less importunate . . . Your Grace, somebody wishes me dead because I am the loudest voiced of your supporters. And if someone is prepared to poison my meat to stop my tongue, how have others been dealt with? You must discount this court. You ask how it can be done. On four counts. Your nationality; a place hostile; the possibility of prejudice in the judges; and, most important of all, the illegality of the whole procedure; a case *sub judice* at Rome cannot be tried elsewhere.'

'That is law?'

'As it has been understood for the last thousand years.'

'And how do I go about it?'

'You are due to appear on the eighteenth of this month. If you agree I will tomorrow make formal application for you to appear and enter a plea, on the fifteenth. And in good faith, Your Grace, I can assure you that your rejection of this court will be welcomed by Cardinal Campeggio.'

'Because it will mean more delay?'

Just a trifle too sharp. Even Fisher, completely convinced that her cause was sound and good, prepared to sacrifice his career and if necessary to give his life, felt that momentary repellence, the feeling – quite unreasonable, as he instantly admitted – that no woman should be so clear-thinking, so concise, so ruthless even to herself, even in handling words.

He said, 'I do not think that Cardinal Campeggio wishes delay of itself. I have reason to believe that he feels as I do that a more equable judgment might be reached in Rome. Things move slowly there, but there is experience, and impartiality. The advice I have just given is the best I can offer Your Grace.'

'I thank you for it. And I will take it.'

When Henry heard of this move he thought, as Katharine had done – that it was another time-wasting device and thought – as Fisher had done – that a trial in Rome was less likely to give the verdict he wanted. He said to Wolsey, 'Whether she acknowledges the court or not it *is* a court, legally constituted; and it must remain in session. If she refuses to appear before it, she can be declared contumacious, and be tried in her absence. I want an answer. And you know what answer I want.' The dangerous, reddish glare took possession of his eyes again. 'I can tell you this, Thomas. If you allow Campeggio to shuffle this back to Rome, my case is lost. *And so are you!*'

So the court solemnly debated its own legality and satisfied on that score continued to sit through a spell of unusually warm weather. The Queen was not expected to occupy the place reserved for her.

CHAPTER 16

'Tighter,' Katharine said. 'Much tighter.'

Concepcion strained at the rigid, iron-stiffened stays. Maria de Moreto watched with disapproval and finally said, 'Your Grace, if it is tighter you will not be able to breathe. And it will be hot in that place.'

'The new dress is cut to a smaller waist,' Katharine said.

It was all so futile and so pitiable, Maria thought. The whole project was absurd and quite out of keeping with the Queen's character; she was not given to hasty decisions or to sudden changes of mind. One day to go and deny that the court at Blackfriars had any jurisdiction over her; and three days later to be preparing to appear before it. What good could that do? Maria looked at the new dress, royal purple in colour, its low square neckline encrusted with gold thread and pearls; the new headdress of gold tissue with a band of pearls at the front; the new shoes with high heels. All this and the false pink and white of cosmetics, the newly brightened hair; wasted on a roomful of clerics and men known to be on the King's side.

Lady Salisbury who had slipped in to attend this robing, in order to give proof of her sympathy and fidelity, felt the same, but she said, 'It is a very beautiful dress, Your Grace. And I think it will fit without further tugging.' Concepcion gladly ceased her exertions and tied the cords.

'And what was the King's response to my request?' Katharine asked. Lady Salisbury had not intended to mention that abortive plea at this moment.

'He did not favour the suggestion. He said that if the Princess were old enough to take interest in the proceedings – and to gossip – she was old enough to understand and prepare herself for her change of status.' Katharine had asked Lady Salisbury to suggest that it would be better for Mary to go to the country while the trial was at this critical stage.

'Shield her so far as you can.'

'I always have,' Lady Salisbury said. 'But it is not easy. She is mature for her years; and nowadays very suspicious. A conversation abruptly ended, even a euphemism employed and she is alert at once.'

'I know,' Katharine said. 'Let us comfort ourselves that this will soon be over.'

Nobody said anything but Katharine was aware of being the only person in the room who retained any optimism at all. But then, she was the only one who knew what she planned to do.

In the great hall at Blackfriars, borrowed for the occasion, Henry sat highest, under a canopy; at a lower level sat the two Cardinals, fully robed and wearing their wide tasselled hats. A little lower still was Katharine's place with the chair draped in gold tissue, and the canopy of royal status. The King's counsellors sat on one side of the floor, the Queen's on the other, at tables covered with tapestry and laden with papers. All around, less comfortably accommodated, sat the nobles of England.

Wolsey felt ill with anxiety and sleeplessness. The road from Ipswich had led steadily uphill and had had its stony as well as its flowery places. To have come so far, and done so much, and now at the age of fifty-four to have his whole career jeopardised, and in such a fashion made nonsense of it all. The very nature of the case offended his fastidiousness; toothless old crones claiming to remember the condition of beds twenty, twenty-eight years ago; doddering old men boasting that at Prince Arthur's age they had been fully potent, had begotten children. The question of whether a woman could be twice deflowered and whether the sheet at Baynard's Castle could be evidence directly favourable to the King's cause. It was disgusting.

'If she keeps her threat and does not appear . . .' he said softly to Campeggio, and looked again at the vacant place. Surely now, with the decision within hours of being made, Campeggio would offer some clue of what was in his mind. He did not. He said with maddening calm, 'We shall see.'

Wolsey thought angrily: Yes, you may be placid. Whatever happens you can pack up and go to Rome; I have to stay here, with a maddened bull of a man who is in a witch's thrall. If things go badly, if there is even more delay, I am finished.

There was a stir as Katharine, attended by her gentleman usher, walked in and took her place. At fifteen Henry VII had thought her well-grown and she had been too tall for Arthur; at eighteen a trifle too tall for Henry, but she was not actually tall. She moved however with dignity; her gown and headdress and jewels had been chosen to convey an impression of grandeur, and from a distance, anyway, the cosmetics detracted from her age. The Duke of Norfolk thought: Forty-four this year; that niece of mine will not wear so well; nothing ages a woman like tantrums.

The herald cried, 'Henry, King of England, come into the court,' and Henry replied in a loud clear voice, 'Here, my lords.' At the back of his mind there stirred the thought that it was wrong that he, King of England, should have been driven to the point of laying his cause and pleading his case before his inferior, as though he had wittingly done wrong, instead of having been wronged and then denied justice. But the thought was flooded out by his confident hope that this would be the end. This sweet summer would not go to join the other wasted ones.

The herald cried again, 'Katharine, Queen of England, come into the court.'

She said nothing, but stood up and, moving slowly, through the silence and the following eyes, went to where Henry sat. She knelt at his feet, drew a steadying breath against the racing of her heart and the merciless grip of the stays and began to speak as though he and she were alone in a room together. Yet every word, spoken in the voice that Henry had once said was like black velvet, carried to the farthest end of the great hall.

'Sire,' she began, 'I beseech you for all the love that hath been between us, let me have justice and right, take on me some pity and compassion, for I am a poor woman, and a stranger born out of your dominion. I have here no assured friend. I flee to you, as to the head of justice within this realm . . .'

Henry was completely appalled, both by this unorthodox behaviour, so unexpected, so unsuitable in a court of law; and by her appearance. That mockery of youth! The grease which formed the base of the pink, the white, the blue, had melted a little in the heat of the crowded room on a burning June day and the colours had blurred. And yet, and yet . . . there was just enough of illusion left to rouse the ghost of the pretty Princess whom he had admired enviously at St. Paul's and claimed under the Greenwich limes. And there was also the sharp, shattering realisation of the damage the years did. Me too? One day! Anne also? It was not a situation where a shilling and an order would bring release. But after that one glance he looked away, fixing his hard blue stare on the wall opposite, at a window where, against a heat-whitened sky, some green boughs hung. He tightened his hands on the arms of his chair and assumed the tense attitude of a man bearing physical agony without outcry. She went on and on. She told him how she had striven to love his friends, how she had borne his children. 'This twenty years or more I have been your true wife . . .'

Then she looked at him. She knew him well; every mood, every response.

She had made this last gamble because she had believed that appealed to as the final arbiter – that would touch his pride, and reminded of a love, once free-flowing, now silted up – that would touch his sentiment, she might even at this last moment, move him.

But she had miscalculated.

She saw that and was, not quite consciously, glad of the iron-braced stays. They supported her while she said the last, most cogent thing, so difficult, so almost impossible to say. But she said it:

'And I take God to be my witness, I was a true maid, without touch of man you had me first. Whether that is true or not I put to your conscience.'

He knew; he knew it was true; he was the only person in the world . . . and he had a conscience, he must admit . . .

He did not. He stared ahead, immobile as a figure in stone.

She said, 'If you will not, to God I commit my cause.' Then she stood up and walked and walked, not to her place but towards the door. There she was glad of Griffith's arm. The herald called her back, but she seemed not to hear. Griffith said, 'Madam, you are called again,' and she said, in that low but penetrating voice, 'This is no court of justice for me. Let us go.'

'And now,' Campeggio said to Wolsey, 'we must listen, I suppose, to His Grace's declaration that if she were adjudged by law to be his lawful wife nothing would be more acceptable to him; and were the marriage deemed good he would choose her above all other women.' He was quoting from one of Henry's earlier statements and his voice had a sarcastic edge.

'That display of feminine guile,' Wolsey said, 'was irrelevant and, as law runs, meaningless. She has proved nothing, except that she is contumacious and must be declared so.'

'With that I fully agree,' Campeggio said. Now, Wolsey thought, now, surely he must give some indication of the conclusion he has reached, the verdict he favours. Campeggio presently did so. 'Our best course, now,' he said, 'is to conclude this business and advoke the case to the court at Rome.'

Wolsey's heart, no longer reliable, began to stammer in its beat. He managed to say, 'His Grace will be much displeased.'

'There are other considerations,' Campeggio reminded him, quite gently. Wolsey knew then that this was what Campeggio had been told to do, should his efforts to bring about a reconciliation fail. But to level that accusation would be useless.

Henry had no such reticence. In a rage which made all his other outbursts look like fits of childish peevishness, he sent for them both and stormed in a way that shook even Campeggio's calm. If Clement, if the Emperor, if Campeggio, if Wolsey thought he was to be put off in this way they were much mistaken. 'Seven months to get here,' he said, halting in his stamping up and down and placing himself foursquare before Campeggio, 'eight months to set up the court! Advoked to Rome where it has been four years already! You hobble home, my lord Cardinal, and tell your master that if he cannot decide, I can. I am not married. I am free, you hear me? Free to marry when and whom I wish.'

'Bigamously,' Campeggio said.

'Then ask Clement to permit me to commit bigamy! Maybe he can give an answer to that!' He then turned upon Wolsey and accused him of ingratitude, lack of zeal, conspiring against him . . . This tirade Campeggio interrupted, 'Your Grace if you would permit me a word . . .'

'More blockhead's talk. Thousands, millions of words, spoken and written and no sense in any one of them.'

'It has occurred to me that the Queen will be equally disappointed by our failure to reach a verdict.'

'God's name! So she should be. I hope she is.'

'She can hardly have failed to see – by Your Grace's demeanour – that she is repudiated. She might at this moment be prepared to concede if Your Grace would make a concession. Throughout I have gathered the impression that she is less concerned for herself than for her daughter. If it were put to her, in good faith, that the Princess Mary's rights would be recognised after those of the child, or children born of any subsequent marriage, she might be prepared to admit that her own marriage was invalid.'

And if she would, Campeggio's first mission would be accomplished.

'If that is the best you can think of! Go and try.'

Campeggio had underrated Katharine's resilience. The closure of the Blackfriar's court, the advoking of the case to Rome had heartened, not discouraged her. She had always trusted that her vindication would come from Rome. Henry's behaviour in the courtroom had hurt her so deeply that a self-defensive process had begun in her mind even before she was back in Greenwich. It had seemed heartless and she could not, would not, must not believe that. She was now well on the way to convincing herself that he had not looked at her because he dared not, and had not answered her because he could not deny the truth of what she had said.

When the Cardinals arrived she was sewing with her women and rose to greet them with a skein of white silk hanging round her neck. Wolsey asked for a talk in privacy and she led them to the stark little room where eight months earlier he, on his knees, had said things which were to haunt her all her life. Campeggio explained the King's offer while Wolsey stood by, his eyes, the shrewdest in Europe, looking like those of a dog begging one merciful word. She had a feeling that Campeggio, though more composed, was begging too.

Her answer was ready. 'If my daughter's rights were dubious, my lords, this would be a generous offer. But they are not; her rights are indisputable – and no subject for bargaining. I see how you are placed, and, believe me, I am sorry for you. You have your masters to please. I am answerable only to God, and to my conscience.'

Wolsey's brain, battered but still lively, produced a cogent argument.

'And to your daughter, Madam. Have you ever asked yourself what her rights would be should you die before the verdict is given. Or if the decision went against you? Correctly worded, signed and sealed this agreement could safeguard her in the event of such contingency.'

Very subtle, Campeggio thought with a flash of admiration.

'Such matters I must leave in the hands of God,' Katharine said.

On the way out Campeggio said, 'Sailors bring home birds which learn a few words and repeat them tiresomely. Her Grace is much the same.'

Wolsey said nothing; he was brooding over what the King had said. One sentence stood out: 'You fail very seldom, my Lord Chancellor, and you would not have failed this time *had your heart been in it.*'

CHAPTER 17

There followed a time that was like a long pause in a chess game.

Remembering the blind, avoiding stare in the Court at Blackfriars, Katharine was prepared for Henry wishing never to look upon her again; yet in that late summer and early autumn she accompanied him on his progresses and was with him at Grafton when Campeggio came, accompanied by Wolsey, to take formal leave before escaping to avoid yet another English winter. At Grafton Henry's uncertainty of what next to do was made plain. He seemed to be on the point of taking Wolsey back into favour, put his arm around his shoulders and talked to him for a long time, in a window embrasure, but in the sight of everyone. Then, next day, he refused to speak to him. Anne Boleyn's doing?

To Katharine Henry behaved with a stately civility which deceived some observers to the point where bets were laid and taken. The Blackfriars Court, inconclusive as it was, had shown the King that his case was poor, so he was making it up, and any day now Nan Bullen would get her marching orders. Katharine interpreted Henry's behaviour as being the same as her own – let nothing be done or said which would make life together intolerable once the Pope had pontificated.

Even Mary's removal from Court did not seem to her a punitive measure aimed against herself. She had suggested that Mary would be better away from it all, before the Court held its first session. Henry, she thought, was acting belatedly on that suggestion.

Mary was more suspicious. 'And why am I to be sent away this time?'

'Because moving about with the Court interrupts your education. Because Hunsdon is your own manor and should be occupied. Because country air is better for you.'

'Shall I be back for the Christmas revels?' Mary eyed her mother with a piercing curiosity. 'You will keep Christmas with him, as usual?'

'Dear child, I am his wife. Where else should I keep Christmas but beside him?'

'With *her*, just around the corner. I often wonder how you can bear it. Mother, do you never long to scratch her eyes out?'

'Would that benefit us? I am convinced that for you – as for me, Mary – to be uncivil to her would be to give her undue importance.'

Mary said impulsively, 'I wish I were more like you,' knowing the wish vain. She did not realise that it had taken two people to make her and that, within her, two natures would always conflict. She simply knew that she admired her mother and wished to be like her and could, somehow, never manage it.

'Before Christmas,' Katharine said, 'the answer may come and all will be as it was before.'

So they took leave of one another; neither thinking that it might be forever.

Just before Christmas Katharine suggested that Mary should come home. Henry said, 'She is better where she is. *But if you wish to go to her, you have my permission.*'

It was the most forthright thing that had been said for months and the implication was ominous. He wanted her away. The Roman courts had reopened in October, but the question of whether she was or was not Queen of England, Henry's wife, had not yet been brought up; and to make one backward step, even so ordinary and human a move as to go to keep Christmas at Hunsdon with Mary, would be to open a breach in the defence.

She hated war and would never voluntarily have anything to do with it, but she still thought in the terms of the war that had been the background for her impressionable childhood years. Yield an inch over any debatable ground, retreat one step down the ladder of the escalade, and defeat was certain. Hold out a siege long enough and relief came.

She said, 'I have no wish to go to Hunsdon – though it seems long since I saw Mary. I shall keep Christmas as usual.'

Parrying every stroke, Henry thought with unwilling admiration. And the situation must be painful. For since everyone, even Clement knew of his intention to marry Anne so soon as he was free – and in any case if they dallied much longer – he had taken no pains to conceal his movements. Anne now had a fine handsome house, next door to what had been Wolsey's residence, York House. And York House Henry had 'borrowed' so that on these winter evenings he had only a few steps to take in order to be with Anne. To be nagged and scolded; to be charmed. Wolsey no longer needed York House, or Hampton Court or any of his manors. Stripped of secular office, he had gone to York and was attending to his clerical duties, living modestly and piously, the world put away. Strictly speaking York House, becoming transformed into the Palace of Whitehall, was the property of the diocese of York, but it was convenient for Henry's purpose, and nobody had protested. The borrowing of it had been his first exercise in the confiscation of church property and if he thought about it now and then, convinced him that the Church owned so much that it could hardly keep check on its possessions.

'Keep it as usual,' he said. 'I trust it will be happy. It will be your last with me. Kate, you must understand . . . I loved you . . . I defied all advice. I admit it . . . but we had our good years, though the marriage was cursed . . . dozens of learned doctors concur with me now. It will go against you and then I shall be obliged to pity you, as I did at Blackfriars. Kate, we enjoyed an illicit love affair. Call it that, let it go, a song well sung . . . But over. Could not the last note be tunable?'

This was the first time that he had appealed to her in this way. All his former stands had been taken upon the basis of law . . . Papal dispensation, Cardinal's conferring, hard argument. This was more difficult to resist – but it must be resisted. And she was encouraged by current gossip – now faithfully repeated by Maria – that the Lady Anne, disgusted by the result of Blackfriars, angry with Henry, angry with the whole world, was on the point of giving up and returning to Hever. It seemed to Katharine that Henry, making an appeal to sentiment, was trying one last desperate measure.

Victory in a siege went to the side that could hold out longest.

Then came the business of the cramp rings.

Night cramp, like toothache, was a common affliction and there were many charms and superstitions concerned with its prevention. There was a belief that cramp could be avoided by wearing a silver ring that had been consecrated by a special ritual in which a Queen of England had played her part. It was akin to the King's touching for the cure of scrofula. Year after year Katharine had watched the silver rings put into a basin and blessed in the names of Abraham, Isaac and Jacob and then signed with the Cross. She had joined in the prayer which asked that the rings might restore contracted nerves. Then she had taken them and rubbed them between her palms, put them back into the basin and seen the Holy Water poured upon them. Such rings were much coveted, worn with pride and regarded as heirlooms.

She was deeply shocked when she learned that this year Anne had sent cramp rings to be distributed to all the men who were in Rome waiting to represent the King when the cause came forward.

'But they will be worthless,' she said to Maria. 'It is the virtue of the Holy Oil with which the Queen is anointed at her coronation which confers the curse. Besides, what priest could be found to perform the ceremony for *her*?'

'Some renegade.'

The truth was that while the common people still howled against Nan Bullen, and her imminent withdrawal was talked of in taverns, those closer to the centre of things saw that Anne's power over the King was increasing. They quarrelled frequently and rancorously, but every quarrel was followed by a reconciliation, marked by some gift or privilege. Weatherwise people followed the King, and at Suffolk House, Anne now kept unofficial Court.

'I wonder at His Grace agreeing to a procedure so irregular,' Katharine said.

He had not done it willingly. It was a concession to mend a quarrel in which Anne had accused him, hysterically, of being insincere and half-hearted. If he meant one half of what he said, Katharine would not still be at Court, housed and treated like a Queen. That was one of her recurrent grievances and she refused to see Henry's point of view – that to deny Katharine the outward show of Queenship would seem to be forestalling Clement's decision and thus prejudice his case.

Katharine never mentioned the cramp rings to Henry; except that the recipients would still wake, agonised in the night, the matter had no importance. Anne could wear the Queen's crown and still not be Queen. And to refer to the encroachment would be to bring up the subject which, since his sentimental appeal, had by mutual consent, not been mentioned.

When it next was it was broached by Henry himself. They were seated side by side watching an old morality play in which Virtues and Vices and the figures representing Good and Evil contested so noisily, shouting accusations and counter accusations and striking blows at one another with staves and clubs and blown-up pigs' bladders, that under cover of the din a private conversation was possible.

'I heard today from Rome. Things are moving at last. We are to be called before the judges of the Holy See.'

Thank God. A neutral court. No Wolsey there.

'I cannot attend,' he went on before she could say anything. 'I foresaw this. My advisers assure me that there is no precedent. No King of England can be called before a foreign court of justice.'

She thought: He knows his case is weak; he fears humiliation. She said, 'If that is the rule you must abide by it, I suppose. In many ways the English have always been a people apart.'

Abstinence hit Gluttony over the head with a dried codfish, hard and solid as wood and Gluttony retaliated by throwing a string of sausages, steaming hot.

A people apart, Katharine thought. And it was due to geography. To their island position. When the Roman Empire broke up they had not been overrun by Huns, Goths, Visigoths – they had enjoyed the sunset period with Arthur and his knights. When they were overrun it had been by Angles, Jutes, Saxons, looking for land to till. They had become English. Then, as conquerors, the Normans had come and been so thoroughly absorbed that except for a few names and some words, all twisted, their very language had been lost. England absorbed all, made its own rules and produced a people who could call a most ferocious civil war by a pretty name – the Wars of the Roses. And could end it with a flowery symbol, the Tudor rose, half white, half red. Certainly, a people apart.

'I must also forbid you to attend,' Henry said.

On the floor of the hall Avarice bent over his money bag and Charity gave alms to the poor.

'On what grounds?'

'As my subject.'

She said slowly, 'Am I? If I am your wife, then I am your subject, and glad to be. But if, as you contend, I am not your wife, then I am a Spaniard still; and if called to Rome, must go.'

Charity hit Avarice over the head with the bowl and the money bag dropped, spilling pebbles, grass, rubbish.

'That would be a good argument,' Henry said, 'except that you were Arthur's wife and thus made English enough to take the sweating sickness.'

'I was never Arthur's wife – as you well know.'

Now on the floor, Lust, immodestly attired, wrestled with Chastity.

'We will not argue upon that point,' Henry said. 'Nor about attendance at any foreign court. I have, as you know, been at Waltham and there I met a man who seemed to me to have the right sow by the ear. He made a very sensible suggestion – that this matter could best be decided by canvassing a consensus of opinion from all Universities.'

'French and German as well?' she asked, as Chastity, all in white, eluded Lust's embrace.

'All Universities. Would you accept their ruling?'

'How could I? A Pope made our marriage legal. Only a Pope can undo it. And I wonder at you! The King of England must not be called before a foreign court, but is willing to accept the decision of foreign Universities.'

'Let us not be hasty,' Henry said. 'This fellow – Thomas Cranmer is his name – is something out of the ordinary.' Having said that, he stopped, halted by the fact that for once his well-trained and exercised royal memory for faces had failed him and he had no idea what the man looked like. A negative man, neither young nor old, good-looking nor ugly, bold or retiring. The little that the King had learned about him so far, gave no clue to his real character; born of a respectable family he had married an innkeeper's daughter and for that been suspended from the Cambridge College of which he was a Fellow. She died before the suspension was final, and he had resumed his Fellowship, taken orders and become a tutor in divinity. Again, neither one thing nor the other. And yet this unremarkable man had made a suggestion which no one had offered before, and, brought into Henry's presence to expound, had, though showing some signs of nervousness, spoken concisely and firmly. And he had said one thing which Henry, so orthodox, had first found shocking and then so promising that the mind reeled under the impact. Perhaps that was why he could not remember the face or stature of the man who had said, 'It would then be a matter for the ordinary ecclesiastical courts; not for the Pope.' What made Thomas Cranmer something out of the ordinary was that he had *vision*. He saw over, or around, the problem which others – including Henry himself – looked upon as a blank wall. 'If the general consensus of opinion in *all* established Universities agrees that a man cannot marry his brother's wife – and that much, surely, Your Grace, all will agree; then your marriage is null and void.'

'But that,' Henry said, 'is what I have said. All along. From the first.'

'But never, so far, in a court composed of ordinary English clergy, not under the Papal thumb.' And that was true. Wolsey, Campeggio . . . servants of that dilatory, time-wasting, shilly-shallying fellow in Rome. . .

To Katharine, as the symbol of Evil, all in black, threw a little ball that burst into flames and stank of sulphur at Good who held up a crucifix, Henry said:

'He is one of the few who can see farther than the end of his nose. The best canonists, the best lawyers, the best minds centre about the Universities.'

She said with that shrewdness which seemed so out of keeping: 'Do they? Are Wolsey, Warham, More *still* at Oxford, centring about the source from which they wish not to be weaned? And is yours not a good mind?'

It was unlikely that Henry would weigh her words against those of this new, visionary adviser, but she felt forced to voice her doubts. French Universities were French – to her, automatically suspect; German Universities were Lutheran; Italian Universities would no doubt wish to return an answer in line with the Pope's opinion, but who knew what that was? If only Clement would decide and waste no more time in shuffling expedients. If only she could understand why a *simple* question – Was Julius' dispensation good? – could not be answered by a simple yes, or no. Was it because there was some aspect or complication of which she was not aware?

With the final triumph of Virtue over Vice, the entertainment ended and the performers lined up to be applauded. Henry kept his hands gripped on the table's edge, but Katharine clapped – it was not their fault, good souls, that their performance should have happened to coincide with a momentous conversation. Henry looked sideways at her without turning his head and there was something dangerous, something like a goaded desperation in the glance.

'You are,' he said, quite softly, 'the most damned obstinate woman God ever made. But we cannot go on in this way. I cannot accept Clement's latest proposal and you will not accept Cranmer's . . .'

'*Cannot*,' she corrected. 'Only the Pope's verdict can decide.'

'The Universities can give their opinion; and if they decide that we were never legally married, an ordinary English ecclesiastical court can release me. *I shall declare the Pope a heretic and marry whom I like!*'

He spoke with emphasis, but without raising his voice and that set the threat in a class apart; very different from anything he had ever said in a moment of rage. It called up a prospect so appalling that it was like feeling the preliminary tremor of an earthquake. She felt her face go stiff and put up her hands, pressing them against her cheeks, staring at him over her fingertips with eyes gone wide and dark with dismay.

'You see, you cannot win,' Henry said, still softly but with venom. Then with an abrupt change to an almost coaxing tone, he added, 'But it is not too late. Give in gracefully and you shall never regret it.'

Do *not*, he thought, and you will see some changes which you will not relish. Among other things which the featureless man of vision had said, was that it would be wise for the King and the lady who called herself Queen, to cease all appearance of cohabitation. A break between their households should be made. Welcome as such a change would have been to Henry, he was not prepared to make it until some firmer ground was under his feet. He wished to avoid seeming to persecute Katharine.

'Think about it,' he said.

She managed to say, 'I think of little else these days.'

She thought about it endlessly, through the routine-patterned days, and often in the night, too. She no longer slept well. She often woke with the panic feeling that she was about to suffocate, and that feeling mastered, the inside of her head would seem to expand, become a vast, empty space, as large as the hall at Westminster, ringing with ominous phrases. She heard again Wolsey's old voice saying: More is concerned than you dream of. The world is riven. And Mary's young voice saying: Schism. To those, tonight would be added Henry's wild statement about declaring the Pope a heretic. She had only one answer to them all – I have no voice. I honour and am ruled by the decision of one Pope and wait, with what patience I can muster, for another to confirm it. What else can I do? To any faithful daughter of the Church, Papal authority must be absolute – if only because, in the end there must be some unchallengeable authority, otherwise all would be chaos. She faced, increasingly as time went on, the possibility that when Clement pontificated, it might be against her – the lengthening delay sometimes undermined her confidence. In that case she would give in gracefully; accept the verdict, the fact that through some technicality, her marriage was void, her one living child a bastard. But not until . . . not until. Clement could not defer decision forever; canvassing the Universities would take time. God send there would be no need for Henry to keep that terrible threat. God grant that whichever way Clement decides, we may both accept it. . .

An hour or two of this and she would think: Such fretting shows a lack of faith. God knows the answer. Thousands upon thousands pray: Thy will be done, on earth as it is in Heaven; and His will will be done . . . Upon that thought, she would sleep again.

The Emperor's Ambassador, Don de Mendoza, had found the whole situation more than he could deal with and had asked to be recalled. Charles' choice of a successor for him was significant both to Henry and to Katharine.

To begin with he was not even a Spaniard; he was Savoyard, born in Annecy. He was not of noble birth; he came from an impoverished, middle-class family; the son of an attorney who had died young, leaving a widow and several children. He had made his way by use of his brains; he was a lawyer, said to be a good one. And he had spent some years in

Geneva where new ideas flourished. In the end Don de Mendoza had sided so openly with Katharine that he had been placed under house-arrest; Messire Eustache Chapuys had been chosen, Henry and Katharine felt, because he was unlikely to repeat his predecessor's error.

In Henry's mind this opinion was confirmed at the first interview. Chapuys had a scholar's face, thin, ascetic, with cold grey eyes and a thin-lipped mouth. It was impossible to imagine him being moved by enthusiasm for any cause except, perhaps, the proper application of some legal principle. Logic, not emotion, would be his fulcrum. And if his appearance was reassuring, his manner to the King was even more so; in his rather remote way he seemed to be making an effort to be agreeable, and to skirt skilfully around any subject of a controversial nature. Even when Henry said, 'I consider, Messire Chapuys, that your master has dealt shabbily with me,' Chapuys said, 'Never knowingly, Your Grace. The Emperor respects and admires you more than any other monarch in the world. This is not mere diplomatic talk. I have heard him say so, in various connections, many times.'

'Nevertheless he obstructed me. Even over so small a matter as the sending on of that brief.'

'But, Your Grace, that was a precaution. He was afraid to allow the original out of his hands. I have seen it, and the copy; they are exact in every detail.'

'Water under the bridge now,' Henry said, not too easily appeased. 'The Legantine Court wrung what they could out of the copy. The fact remains that I was denied what I asked for. However, if your master is truly well-disposed towards me, he can do me a service now.'

'I am so certain of his mind that I can answer for him. He will do it willingly.'

'Then he can use his influence on the Pope to have the place of trial shifted. I cannot go to Rome. *Ne extra Angliam litigare congantur.*'

'Your Grace wishes for another trial in England?' Chapuys, who had studied the case most thoroughly, put a slight stress on *another*.

'No. But I could attend a court in France. In the interest of peace in Christendom, I have not pressed my claim, but I am King of France. There I should be in my own realm.'

Chapuys' eyes remained as clear and as cold as the waters of the lake beside which he had been born, but his mind moved rapidly. That moss-grown old claim had been used for three hundred years as an excuse for English invasions. In theory no Christian king was supposed to attack another, except in defence of his own rights. The English kings who had made use of it had all been touched with megalomania.

'It is a solution that no one else has thought of, Your Grace. And well worth consideration.'

He had already considered and rejected it. A French court, a French Cardinal in the chair, the whole climate anti-Papist, anti-Imperialist. Henry would get what was now widely, but wrongly, called his divorce there, and ever after be grateful to King Francis and to France. Quite disastrous!

'I thought Cambrai,' Henry said.

'Ah yes. And the Lady Katharine would accept the venue?'

It was the first time she had been mentioned directly and Henry noticed, almost avidly, that Chapuys did not say *Her Grace* or *the Queen*.

'I have not yet mentioned the matter to her. There has been no time.'

He had, in fact, only just thought of it himself, prodded on by one of Anne's hysterical outbursts. How long, she had demanded, would the canvassing of the Universities take? A year at the very least; any man who claimed to be scholar could argue six months about nothing. Given something to argue about they would argue until they were dead, until Henry was dead, until she was dead! And meantime she occupied this invidious position and Katharine was still housed and treated like a queen. It was an intolerable situation and unless he did something to end it soon, she would. She would go back to Hever. That was the threat which always cut so sharply and so deeply that there were times when under it he felt a wild impulse to say: Go! And good riddance! That impulse, fleeting as it was, always frightened him it was so akin to that of a suicide who cast life away because life had not given him what he wanted. He always restrained it and soothed her as best he could, with gifts, with promises, with honied words.

Leaving her he had thought again about Cranmer's suggestions. Anne was opposed to the waiting for a consensus of scholarly opinion, Katharine said she could accept no decision but Clement's. And there was something else to be considered. If he followed Cranmer's plan it would inevitably lead to the setting up of the authority of a simple English ecclesiastic court in direct defiance of the Pope. It was all very well, coming straight from Waltham to say to Katharine: I will declare the Pope a heretic, but once one realised the full implication and saw, as he did, that a blow against one form of authority was a blow against all authority . . . that if the Pope could be defied, so might a king be, and bishops, lords of manors, mayors in towns . . . there was no end to it.

So he had thought instead of the swift, decisive court in Cambrai.

To Chapuys he said, 'It would come better from you, Messire, than from me. She no longer understands me. She is most noble and honourable, and I swear to you, as I have sworn to others, that were things otherwise, there is no woman in the world whom I would prefer before her. But she is a woman and women have fancies; they can be perverse and very stubborn.'

And for that, Chapuys thought, God be thanked. Had my mother not been the most *stubborn* creature in creation – donkeys excepted – I should not be here. In his coldly amicable voice he said:

'Your Grace wishes me to suggest a court at Cambrai?'

'Yes. As soon as possible. She is at Greenwich.'

Chapuys went to Greenwich a man committed to nothing except his master's service. Charles had instructed him to use his best endeavours to bring about, if possible, even at this late hour, a reconciliation between the King and Queen of England whose matrimonial dispute had assumed absurd proportions. Every time-wasting device had been employed. The King of England's passion for the waiting lady must soon burn itself out – he was forty; his wife forty-five; full time that they settled down. They had a daughter, about fourteen. Charles had a three-year-old son; there was a difference admittedly; but when Philip was fourteen, Mary Queen of England would be only twenty-five, greater disparities in age had, in the interests of political or territorial interests, been compounded in the past.

Chapuys was not surprised to find that Katharine was opposed to the suggestion of a court at Cambrai; and it was not difficult for him – a seasoned diplomat – to make a few remarks which sounded as though he was using persuasion upon her, but were in fact calculated to strengthen her opposition. 'It would,' he said, 'be much the *quickest* way, Your Grace.'

'I am in no hurry to be the subject of a wrong decision,' she said. He felt that his point had been taken. 'I appealed to Rome and the only verdict acceptable to me will come from Rome.'

'The delay must be very tedious.'

'Perhaps less so to me than to others concerned. I sometimes think, Messire Chapuys and may God forgive me if the suspicion is unwarranted – that everything is being deliberately delayed in the hope that His Grace's infatuation may die down of its own accord. That is a fatuous hope and underestimates both His Grace and Mistress Boleyn, as much as the hope that long waiting will change my mind underestimates me. You would serve us *all* if you conveyed this fact to the level where decisions are made. If His Holiness pontificates in my favour and says that my marriage is good, it will be a great relief to me and also, I think, perhaps to His Grace, when the anger has died. He has been unfortunate – and only I who love him can see this . . . I know,' she said, clasping her hands together and hammering them upon the air, 'I know what is said, and believed of him. It so happens that his doubts about our marriage, our having no son, were fomented by evil counsellors and coincided with the fancy he had conceived – as many men do – for a younger woman. The timing was bad. And the woman . . . Messire Chapuys, it ill becomes one woman to wish another less virtuous, but had she been less virtuous, less of a bargainer, it would all be over now and we should have been spared much suffering. I do not know, Messire Chapuys, why I say such things to you, except that I hope you will convey to your master, my nephew, the certainty that more time wasted will be wasted indeed and that a firm directive from Rome would be to the benefit of us all.'

'And if,' the Spanish Ambassador said, 'it should go against you, Your Grace?'

'I should grieve for my daughter. For myself, I should accept it, putting as they say, a hard heart against a hard sorrow.'

Chapuys knew then. In another place, in another tongue, the only woman he had ever cared for or respected, had used that phrase many times. And once the likeness between her and the Queen of England was recognised . . . Dignity in humiliating circumstances, clear thinking, straight speaking, tolerance just on the wry side, and at the heart of it all a rocklike resistance. Like his mother!

His father had died leaving nothing but a house. To the widow friends and advisers had come, meaning well. Sell the house, they said; buy a modest property; Eustache and the next boy, they said are big enough now to take service, in some merchant's house . . . She had listened with the very same manner as Katharine had listened, to his proposal of the court at Cambrai. She had then gone her own way. The clear, rather chilly air of Annecy was reckoned to be good for people with faulty lungs, and she had turned her house into a place where such could lodge, squeezing her own family into the minimum of space and cooking, cooking, the good simple food that did as much as the air. Her first-born, Eustache, should never be a menial, he must continue at school, proceed to University, become, like his father an attorney. The younger boys, if they showed a gleam of promise, should have similar opportunities; and her daughters should be brought up – no matter at what sacrifice – to be marriageable within the class they would have occupied had their father lived. It had been a hard and bitter struggle, worse than poverty because poverty could always show its sores and find dogs to lick them. But Eustache, her first-born, taken into confidence too young – to whom else could she talk frankly? – had never seen her lose composure, dignity or faith. The pallid, languid lung-sufferers would die, what was owing would be disputed; the flour would be weevilly, the onions rot in the ground, the best milking goat slip its tether: and she would say, We must put a hard heart against a hard sorrow. And she would press on, undismayed by the fact that everything in the world was against her – except Eustache, the dependable little boy always ready to shoulder any task, even those beyond his capacity.

Eustache, the man, the Imperial Ambassador, came away from Greenwich deeply committed.

It was, however, the goodwill of the King that the Ambassador appeared anxious to gain. He made a point of never seeking private interviews with the Queen and in public exchanged only the few remarks demanded by custom and by courtesy. But he kept a sharp ear for gossip, however trivial and would shamelessly eavesdrop on occasion. Now and then, even in a crowded room, he would slip into the formal conversation a warning word. One evening he said, speaking in a low voice, but with no glancing to left or right or leaning forward or any other sign that he was speaking of anything but the weather or the quality of the entertainment just ended:

'Your refusal of Cambrai is likely to have unpleasant repercussions.'

'I trust God will give me the necessary fortitude.'

There had been times when the clean, polished rooms at Annecy had stood empty; when food was scarce and shoes outgrown. His mother had never failed in fortitude.

'The Lady is bringing pressure to bear. She wishes you away from Court.'

'I am grateful to you, Messire,' she said, with the amiable look, the gracious inclination of the head with which she might have received some flattering, ambassadorial words. She was aware of the bystander. Not hovering, as Wolsey had hovered. Henry's new man, Thomas Cromwell, who had been Wolsey's servant and who, the moment his master fell from favour, had ridden post-haste to take his place with the King, lacked the physical dignity, the urbane manner of Wolsey. He did not hover, he approached and stood, his stance a little awkward, his intention of interrupting the conversation plain. Finesse, the art which his old master had perfected was no longer needed; Katharine's days as Queen, even in appearance, were numbered. Tomorrow, or the day after, she would be informed . . .

Informed already she was prepared for the deputation which called upon her to demand that she should accept, and appear at, the Court in Cambrai. Cromwell, more brutally direct in spheres where retaliation was unlikely than Wolsey had ever been, had chosen the men who were to form the deputation. The Duke of Norfolk, Anne's uncle; the Earl of Wiltshire, Anne's father; the Duke of Suffolk who, ever since the King had spared his head and taken him back into favour, had been a willing pliant tool.

Knowing what the repercussions were likely to be, she said to them what she had said to Chapuys: For her the only acceptable verdict must come from Rome. And when they had gone she turned back into the apartments – to the rooms where, on a June evening long ago Henry's love had installed her, his forethought kindled fires – and began to make preparations for her removal.

It was a dismal task. This is mine, this is state property; this I brought from Spain; this has been given me since. A severance of bone from bone.

'And the jewels?' Maria de Moreto asked. They had been, for years, her special care and responsibility.

Katharine hesitated for a moment. Then she said:

'They are the jewels of the Queen of England; and until the Pope says I am not, I am Queen of England. They belong with me, wherever I go.'

When the order came, very promptly, to remove herself and her personal belongings, out of London and to The More, a manor which had once been Wolsey's, near to Harrow Hill, she took her clothes, the silver and the linen that she had brought from Spain, and the jewels of the Queen of England.

She did not look upon her banishment from Court as final. It was part of the waiting time; and the order for it had been given in part to punish her for not agreeing to go to Cambrai, in part to pacify Anne for the delay which the putting into practice of Cranmer's schemes must involve. The move had something to recommend it; the last period of waiting would be spent in private, away from watchful eyes, pitying or scornful, away from gossip, away from the scarcely veiled insolence of Anne and her friends; but it was also away from Henry and although for a long time now their appearances together had seemed to be a cruel mockery of a former happy relationship, she found herself missing the almost daily meetings. Sitting or standing beside him, on public occasions, she had been aware of constraint, the constant wonder as to his mood, what he would say and in what tone; but there had been many occasions, twice, thrice a week, when anonymous among her ladies, she could sit and watch him and admire, and slip away from this troubled present into memories of the happier past. He still jousted with skill and vigour, and though 'Sir Loyal Heart' had been replaced by the cryptic, 'Decline I Dare Not,' she still liked to see him win. It was the same in the tennis court, where, stripping off his doublet, he revealed one of the fine linen shirts that she had sewn for him. Had Anne ever made him a shirt? She never saw him as a middle-aged man, a little heavier, a little slower, redder in the face, shorter of breath. For her his image was fixed and immutable, and with no danger of a surly, chilling, or merely formal word to spoil the illusion, she could still watch him with love. There would be no more of that.

She accepted the irony of The More as her place of residence. One of Wolsey's properties. *De mortius nil nisi bonum*, but long before Wolsey, in a dark November had halted, and died at Leicester Abbey on his way back from York to trial in London, she had forgiven him. Like everybody else, she believed that Wolsey had died of a broken heart, surviving by only a few months the withdrawal of Henry's favour. Wolsey had so stoically concealed his ills, his ominous symptoms, that this belief was current. Sometimes Katharine thought seriously about this – the King turned his face from Wolsey and Wolsey died; he has now turned his face from me and I am not dead, have no intention of dying. Am I less loving than the butcher's son? Put that thought aside. I am not yet forty-six; Wolsey was fifty-five; he had no hope. I have. Clement will issue his verdict and I shall be reinstated.

She held this conviction so firmly that at Christmas 1531, the first of her banishment, two visitors from Venice, having been entertained first at Court and then, by their own wish moving on to The More, declared that in the latter place the food was better and the diversions merrier.

Only those close to her, and, closest of all, Maria de Moreto, saw that at The More Katharine did not flourish. She grew paler, more susceptible to cold and to little ills. She never lost faith or hope or confidence or even good humour, but there was a difference. Maria de Moreto who had herself survived love's loss, remembered her own lessening of gusto and resilience, her own settling down into resignation. Chapuys, still allowed to visit and more punctilious now, wrote to his master, amongst many other things, 'The Queen has aged much in a few months.'

CHAPTER 18

It was life in a void. She was allowed visitors – anyone except Mary. Every time that she considered this restriction it would seem to be an act of spite on Henry's part. But that was so sickening a thought that she could not accept it; such malice was incompatible with the Henry she knew. She would remind herself that years ago she had felt in the same way about Mary's being sent to Ludlow, but Mary's stay there had been good for her, good for the Welsh. One must not cherish destructive suspicions. It was better, surely better, at this point, for Mary, with her passionate nature, to live quietly, to continue her studies and not to be too closely involved in a situation which must – and soon – be resolved.

Other visitors made the twelve-mile journey from the centre of London to The More; but in their manner, in their words, what was said, and what was not said, Katharine detected an unwelcome sympathy, a kind of finality, as though she were stricken with some fatal disease that could only end in death. Nobody had any real news to impart and everybody was just a little too eager to remark upon the amenities of The More, which, like every other place upon which Wolsey had laid a hand, was comfortable, handsome, well-appointed. Doomed to death, but on a good bed, under a soft blanket.

To this general behaviour there were two welcome exceptions. The Countess of Willoughby who had been Maria de Salinas came and did not adopt the death-bedside manner. Far from it. She had no eye for the pleasant view, no praise for the painted ceilings. 'You will not be here long,' she said cheerfully. 'His Holiness must decide soon, if only to forestall this ridiculous scheme of putting so much authority into the hands of the English church.'

'That is still spoken of?'

'Constantly, Your Grace. The Archbishop of Canterbury is much opposed to it. But he is old, and ailing. And if things are allowed to drift until Cranmer is appointed . . .'

'Cranmer?'

'He is said to be earmarked for the honour. May I ask what sounds like an impertinent question?'

'I have known you in many moods, Maria, but never impertinent.'

'Have you written to the Pope and to the Emperor, urging a decision soon?'

'Many times. I have written with my own hand: and Messire Chapuys almost always includes some plea for a speedy settlement in his communications.'

'I think,' the Countess said, 'that it would be wise to write again. The King himself blows hot and cold on this matter. He can see where the putting of so grave a decision into an English church court might lead. But when Warham dies and Cranmer succeeds him . . .' She finished the sentence with an eloquent movement of her hands. Then she added, 'When promotion results from the putting forward of an idea, that idea will be put forward. And a sheep in wolf's clothing is a notoriously dangerous animal.'

'Cranmer?' Katharine said again.

'Cranmer,' the Countess said. 'He even looks like a sheep. But in return for the mitre he would act like a wolf and carry the King with him.'

'I will write yet again,' Katharine said. 'Maria, you go back to London?'

'On my way home. For one night only.'

'Will you take, or send a message to Messire Chapuys for me? Tell him that I should be glad to see him at the earliest possible moment convenient to him.'

'Most gladly,' the Countess said.

Seeing Katharine, even paler and much preoccupied, writing, writing, Maria de Moreto said, 'Is it something that *she* said to worry Your Grace?'

'The other Maria? Oh no. It is something I must do before Messire Chapuy's next visit.'

'And that will not be yet. He was here only five days ago.'

Chapuys had carefully spaced out his visits, frequent enough not to let the Queen feel that she was neglected, not frequent enough to merit Henry's disapproval. On his visits he never admired the view, the wall hangings or the special scented rushes on the floor – the very same rushes as had been spread, as a tribute to the occasion, on the floor at Baynard's Castle all those years ago. Wolsey had ordered that all his residences should be supplied with them and since nobody had ever cancelled the order and since Suffolk people were slow to change, the rushes were still cut and despatched to all the places which had once belonged to the great Cardinal. The bill was mounting . . .

Chapuys never mentioned the comfort, indeed the luxury, in which she was housed; he never told her that she looked well. He reported what he thought was relevant and withheld what he thought might disturb, and always managed somehow to convey his belief that her cause was right and that her sojourn at The More would not be long. She had found his visits very heartening.

Chapuys was well aware that Thomas Cromwell who had taken over many of Thomas Wolsey's functions – but not all, and certainly not Wolsey's place in the King's heart – had taken on and even elaborated the Cardinal's spy system, and riding out to The More for the second time within a week, he knew that he should be ready with some excuse that could be offered, not extracted. Katharine handed him that excuse; two letters, folded but not sealed; one to the Emperor, one to the Pope.

'To be despatched in all haste, Messire. That is why I troubled you. My own impatience for a settlement, great as it is, is as nothing beside the need for some positive action before the see of Canterbury changes hands.'

He wondered, on the fringe of his mind, who had told her that Warham was ailing, Cranmer almost certain to follow him. He himself had refrained from mentioning such matters. But he was not surprised that she knew. The King might say that if he thought that his cap knew his mind he would throw it on the fire, but there were those about him who, unlike the cap, had eyes, ears, tongues. They might not know his mind, but they could observe his attitudes.

'They shall be sent,' Chapuys said, taking the two letters, 'and if I can arrange it, make better speed than usual.'

'Once,' she said, 'but before your time, Messire, I sent not a letter, but a message which reached Valladolid, from London in fourteen days.'

Impossible. And quite impossible to believe, Chapuys thought. And again he was reminded of his mother. Women, looking back to circumstances happier than their present ones, tended to exaggerate; his mother had often said, 'And when your father was alive we had meat every day, sometimes twice.'

'I cannot promise such swift delivery, Your Grace,' he said. But he looked at the unsealed letters and had a thought, just a little thought. 'I will do what I can,' he said.

He went straight to Henry and said, 'Your Grace I was last week at The More on a routine visit – my master being interested in his aunt's health and well-being. Today I was there again. Summoned to take charge of these letters. I ask Your Grace's permission to send them on.'

Henry eyed the two packets, unsealed, addressed in Katharine's unmistakable hand, bold, flourishing, rather unfeminine. He had a faint sickish feeling, remembering how that writing had come to him, with faithful regularity, almost twenty years ago, when he was in France, at war; the news of Flodden . . .

He said, more petulantly than he had ever yet spoken to Chapuys, 'Send them on, Messire, send them on. Do not flap them at me. I am not in the habit of reading letters addressed to other persons.'

'I have read them both,' Chapuys said. 'They are harmless. Both urge the desirability of a speedy decision. Both refer to Your Grace in terms of respect and affection.'

And that, Henry thought, is the very devil of it. The woman I no longer care for, *in that way*, the woman who failed me, regards me with respect and affection; the one I crave for, who might bear my son . . . No, even to himself would not admit it. Anne was prudish, cautious, she would not admit that she loved him . . . but he was sure that if only she could be sure, that once their union was sanctioned, once he was made free of her bed, the fires of passion, so long banked, would blaze into an unimaginable glory.

'I agree with the need for haste,' he said, 'I reciprocate the respect and affection. Despatch the letters, Messire. But do not hope for a speedy answer. Clement's indecisiveness is hereditary. His father could never make up his mind to marry his mother and give the boy a name.'

Chapuys was old enough, schooled enough not to wince, but he was shocked by this irreverence. It was true that Clement was illegitimate, but it was not a fact that a faithful son of the Church would mention in *that* tone of voice. More than anything yet – more than the calling of the newly assembled Parliament, the Reform Parliament, more than the intention to appoint Cranmer, such a remark showed what was in the King's mind. Unless the Pope decided soon the English church would be lost to Rome. Perhaps it was already too late. . . .

Chapuys said dispassionately, 'Delay is always exasperating. Your Grace, it would speed communication to some degree if my post-bag were not delayed at Dover.'

'Has it ever been?' Henry's surprise was genuine. Neither Wolsey who had instituted the spy system, nor Cromwell who had inherited it, had felt it necessary to inform their master of every squalid little trick they practised.

'I can think of no other reason for some tardiness, Sire.'

'I shall personally give orders that in future your bag is to be taken straight from the horse to the ship readiest to sail.'

'I shall be grateful,' Chapuys said, giving no sign of jubilation. In future he would be able to express himself freely, to issue definite warnings instead of conveying hints. He had no doubt that Henry would honour his promise. The King of England – especially where his marriage tangle was concerned – was capable of acting the humbug; though even there he probably deceived himself as well as others: but he was not the man to deal in petty lies or shabby tricks. Indeed, Chapuys reflected, this whole sorry business was the result of a kind of clumsy candour on his part. There were many men in positions of power, known to Chapuys, who would never have breathed a word about the doubt as to the legality of the marriage. An unwanted wife was easily got rid of. One had only to impregnate a pair of gloves with arsenic, exclaim over the resultant rash and offer ointment containing the same poison. Death was then certain, suspicion unlikely. The vanity of women led them to try almost any concoction, however vile, in order to whiten and soften their hands. The dead woman, poor lady, had tried something which produced unhealed sores; and presently the widower married again.

Compared with what he might have done, Henry's actions had been honest and straightforward; and in Chapuys' eyes it was greatly in his favour that in a material sense he had not dealt harshly with Katharine; she was comfortably housed, properly attended, surrounded by her personal belongings, still wearing the sapphires, the rubies, diamonds and pearls of the Queen of England. Many an autocrat, opposed as Henry had been, would have brought some physical pressure to bear on a helpless woman who had so obstructed and defied him.

With his lawyer's habit of looking at every aspect, Chapuys considered the possibility that Henry was anxious not to do, or even to say, anything that would leave unexpungeable bitterness should Clement declare the marriage good, and order Henry back to his wife. This was still possible. Until the break was made, the King of England was a Catholic; it was within the Pope's power to order him to send Mistress Boleyn from Court. But time was running out. 'The Lady is all powerful here,' Chapuys wrote; Pope and Emperor would know what that meant, Lutheranism, thinly disguised. 'The Queen,' Chapuys wrote, 'is the most virtuous woman I have ever known, and the highest hearted.' He urged, with increasing insistence as the year 1532 added week to week, the necessity of a decision before the situation had deteriorated beyond repair.

In May, Sir Thomas More, who had become Chancellor of England after Wolsey's fall, resigned from his office. He pleaded failing health and even Henry, accepting the resignation most unwillingly, could not be blind to the fact that little more than two years in office had taken the flesh from More's bones, lined his face, greyed his hair, made his step heavier. They had not enriched him; he had never taken a bribe, and of the vast sums he had handled not a penny had stuck to his fingers. Henry was concerned for him and knowing that More would never accept an outright gift, moved, secretly and tactfully, so that More was voted by a Convocation of Clergy, a gift of £5000. More said, 'Throw it into the Thames,' a thing he had said of lesser bribes, and went into private life to live on £100 a year, and that none too certain. 'My poor women folk,' he said, 'must learn to perform the miracle of the five loaves and two fishes. Thousands of other women have.'

Every day some women who had failed to perform such miracles, and men who had no woman to do it for them, gathered about the kitchen door at The More. The good Queen was known to be charitable. The stream of visitors might dwindle, but the beggars came, together with pedlars, hoping to find, in a household of ladies, customers for needles, thread and other feminine gear. And there were entertainers, contortionists, men with dancing dogs and bears, minstrels, strolling players, mixed with the beggars with nothing to offer but their rags and their sores.

Among them were many who, in any age, in any form of society, would have been paupers, but there were others, good workmen now unemployed because the land they had tilled had been turned into sheep-runs. One man could tend the sheep that grazed on land that would have needed twenty to plough and sow and reap. Years earlier More had written, in his fantasy *Utopia*, against the enclosure of ploughland for sheep. 'Your sheep that were wont to be so meek and tame, and so small eaters, now as I hear say, be become so great devourers and so wild, that eat up and swallow down the very men themselves.' Katharine had read the book, and though More had, about this and other subjects, an exaggerated, poetic way of putting things, there was enough truth in it for her to give orders that so long as there was food in the house nobody was to be sent away unfed.

So in the yard there was always some coming and going. It was beneath Maria de Moreto's dignity to go down and listen and gossip, but Francisco Filipez was usually about, and he would pass on to Maria what he had heard, leaving her to be the best judge of what was, or was not, suitable for the Queen's ears. On a sunburnt August day there was news, highly unsuitable, but necessary to relay.

'The Archbishop of Canterbury died,' Maria said.

'God rest him,' Katharine said. He had been no friend to her, weak, yielding man, accepting the appointment as one of *her* advisers before Blackfriars, but conniving with Wolsey, wishful to bring about a decision favourable to the King. Dead now and gone to his judgment. God rest him.

'There was more to it,' Maria de Moreto said, half-turning away, picking up some lace, just washed and ironed by Concepcion, a girl who needed strict supervision. It was a horrible thing to be obliged to say. But if I do not say it, Maria thought, somebody else surely will and maybe with malice. 'It is said that with him dead and Cranmer sure of the office, *she* gave in and took the King to her bed.' So tactfully as to seem sly, Maria looked up from the lace, saw Katharine's face and quickly looked away again – as she had looked away when, as a child, she had been taken to see an unrepentant heretic burned in Toledo.

Feeling the searing flame of jealousy, momentarily consumed by it, Katharine wondered at herself: tried to reason. Henry had slept with Elizabeth Taillebois, and with Mary Boleyn. But that had been different; they had received the falling crumbs from a rich table; they had not been wooed, or waited for. Anne had been wooed, Anne had been waited for and when the consummation came . . . Oh God, God! Deliver me from carnal thoughts . . .

She said, 'And who, in our yard, was so well-informed?'

'A button-vendor,' Maria said. 'He has a cousin, a server at Hampton Court. *They* were there, to watch some entertainment on the river. They left together; the King went to her apartment and did not leave until morning. And that has never happened before.' Maria put down the lace, with which no fault could be found and put her hands to her face. She did not cry easily; tears were an appeal for help and she had learned, long ago, that when no help was available tears were useless and merely made your head ache. But now a few scalding drops squeezed their way out and fell over her hands. She shed them partly from sympathy, partly from rage at the injustice of life.

Katharine did not weep at all. Once the fury of jealousy had passed she tried to think coolly over what this news meant and what it implied. Anne had held Henry all this time by saying 'No'; to have yielded now must indicate that she was either very sure of herself, or very desperate. Which? And having gained the thing he craved would Henry become more, or less, infatuated? She considered the possibility of their coupling producing a child; a son. Another bastard, she told herself firmly; no different from the Duke of Richmond. I am Henry's wife and Queen of England – until the Pope says otherwise. And Mary is heir.

An answer to her speculation as to the effect of the yielding upon Henry, came quite soon – again through backdoor gossip. The King was going to give Nan Bullen a rank of her own, something no woman had ever had before. She was going to be a Duke or some other thing, very grand. It was going to be a great occasion with free food and wine in the London streets. Maria de Moreto, reporting this, said:

'Did I not say from the first that she was a witch?'

Katharine, with the wry humour which was sometimes her last stand-by, said, 'If so, she must be very powerful, Maria. To become a Duke she must change her sex; and then where would they be?' But the news – even garbled as it was – was a blow to the small, secret hope that she had cherished; which was that once between the sheets Henry might have found Anne no different, nothing special, just another woman in a bed. That he planned to ennoble her suggested that she had lost no ground by yielding; and it held a darker implication – that he seriously intended to marry her and was providing against the accusation that he had married a commoner. And that would be bigamy; a graver sin than mere adultery.

If those about her knew when this ceremony took place they did not mention it; but she knew; there were several days when the beggars, the dancing dogs and bears and their masters deserted the courtyard at The More and went to the richer pastures of the city streets. Eagerly as Katharine had awaited Chapuys' visits, she had never been more impatient than during that September. He came, disheartened because he had no news for her and because he saw, as clearly as anyone what the recent ceremony might imply, and because here he was, lively, active and committed but chained down to the service of a master with feet of lead. If the Emperor had only moved the Pope would have moved too. The wish to be powerful, in order to help and the realisation of his impotence, took Eustache Chapuys back over the years to when he was eight years old, longing to be a man, to earn, to provide and able only to gather driftwood. He intended not to talk about the ceremony at Windsor, but Katharine herself began to question him about it almost as soon as he was in her presence. Woman enough to ask, 'And how did she look?'

'Not beautiful – though there were some who said so, of course. Not beautiful; but impressive.'

'I can imagine it. As though she were honouring the occasion, rather than being honoured by it.'

'Exactly so, Your Grace.'

'And what is her rank now? One hears such foolish things. I was told that she was to be a Duke.'

'That I never heard. Marquis, yes; the title has been mentioned since no woman has ever before been created a peer in her own right. But the patent read Marchioness of Pembroke. And there was one interesting omission which has caused some speculation. Ordinarily such a patent of nobility, providing for the title to be passed on to the heir, says *legally begotten*. In this instance the words were omitted. I have thought about that omission . . . and it seems to me just possible that the King is providing, beforehand, for the birth of another illegitimate child.'

'I had thought that the ennoblement could be a prelude to marriage. But the omission is certainly significant,' Katharine said thoughtfully.

'His Grace must know that any form of marriage he goes through in the present circumstances would be bigamous.' He paused for a second and then put into words something he had never actually said before. 'Your Grace knows that in this matter I am wholly on your side. Your cause is just and I would stop at nothing to prosper it. Yet there are times when even I feel sorry for the King. Seven years ago he asked a simple question, and still awaits an answer. And at the moment his position is exceptionally difficult.'

'How so, Messire?'

'He is about to make a visit to France and he has been informed that even if he takes the Marchioness of Pembroke with him, she will not be received or acknowledged in any way. He was obliged to inform her of this and she felt much insulted. Her reception of the snub is, of course, hearsay, but my sources of information are usually reliable.'

'So much unhappiness! And it could all have been avoided had the King only resigned himself and accepted his daughter as his heir.'

True, up to a point, Chapuys reflected, but an over-simplification. The Concubine – as he now called Anne in his mind and in his letters – plainly has some extraordinary hold over the King. The cynics who had said that once she abandoned virtue she would be abandoned, had plainly been wrong and in London bets were in favour of a marriage as soon as she proved herself capable of child-bearing. Even Clement, while still hesitating to declare that Henry was lawfully married to Katharine, had

openly said that should he marry Anne Boleyn he would be excommunicated. What a muddle!

Before the end of September the Duke of Norfolk and Suffolk came to
The More with a request which showed Katharine how far Henry was
prepared to go in the effort to soothe Anne's injured feelings. They had
come, they said, by the King's order, to take away the Queen's jewels.

Considering what she had already lost, Henry's love and companionship, her place at Court, the society of her daughter, the removal of a few
coloured stones, however valuable and pretty, might seem a trivial thing;
but she had always taken a pleasure – almost sensuous – in jewels, and
these ornaments held symbolism. They had always belonged to and been
worn by the woman who was Queen of England and by nobody else. And
Henry himself had poured them into her lap in those first days of love. She
did not intend to part with them without a struggle and taking advantage
of the fact that the Dukes carried no written order, she sent them
empty-handed away.

Next day Henry's own Groom of the Stole, Sir Henry Norris, brought a
written order signed by the King. He was one of the young men who
cherished a romantic passion for Anne and managed to blurt out that the
Marchioness of Pembroke had not asked for the jewels; she had never
asked anything of the King, except marriage. But there were, Katharine
knew, other ways of demanding than reaching out a hand and saying,
'Give me.' She could imagine Anne saying bitterly, 'So, if I go with you to
France, I go as a camp follower,' and Henry saying, 'No. You go wearing
the Queen's jewels.'

So the lovely sparkling trinkets were taken away and she was left with
the gold collar she had brought from Spain and her wedding ring. Looking
down on *that*, she thought with a certain tartness: This is the only Queen's
jewel of any real value and it is mine until . . . Oh, God, move Clement to
decide soon . . .

Chapuys wrote to his master that if things were allowed to drift further,
only war could prevent schism. And the drift went on.

CHAPTER 19

News that Mary was ill, simply ill of no recognisable sickness, brought dismay and concern, but no surprise. She had always tried to think of Mary, at Hatfield, at Beaulieu, as removed from the main, turbulent stream, sheltered by Lady Salisbury, busy with her books. But Mary's outburst at Greenwich could not be forgotten. Mary was not one to be easily sheltered or to take refuge in self-deception.

The one thing above all others which girls facing the onset of womanhood needed was a centre of security; and that Mary lacked entirely. Her father had failed her; her mother was separated from her; her status was in the balance; she was either Princess of Wales and heir to England or an illegitimate child, ineligible for marriage, lucky to be provided with the necessities of life. Katharine, considering these things, could look back and see how fortunate she and her sisters had been, at one stage in their youth. They had known what the future held and they had not foreseen upheaval or disaster; disaster had come, but at least not until they were full grown.

When she wrote to Mary she wrote cheerfully, urging patience and trust in God; and Mary's replies had been loving, cheerful, and completely unrevealing. She had never mentioned the situation in which she and her mother found themselves, or her health, except to say that it was good. Now she was ill.

Chapuys, bringing the news, hastened on to say, 'But the King sent his own physician – Dr. Bartelot. And he is a brave man. He said that the Princess ailed nothing that he had a cure for. She was in low spirits and suffering from the separation from Your Grace, her mother. For this information the King gave him twenty pounds. And volunteered an excuse for the separation. He said that to allow you to be together would increase the hardness of heart towards him.'

'There he is mistaken. The one thing I have always urged upon Mary is obedience. I have myself set an example. Save in the one matter, which is one of conscience, I have never been other than subservient to his will . . .'
She thought for a moment and, as always, the better aspect of Henry came uppermost. 'He sent his own doctor . . .'

Chapuys, whose own attitude had hardened lately, said:

'Is that to be wondered at? The Princess Mary at this moment is the only legal heir he has. Talk in London is rife, and wild. The Concubine is now with child – that I can say with certainty. With less certainty I can say that there is talk of a marriage, last month, in January. This I cannot, with all my resources, verify. Who performed it and where, I know no more than you. But I do know that the new Archbishop of Canterbury is proposing to gather some kind of court together and to declare the marriage legal – even retrospectively.'

'Is that possible?'

'Anything, in these days, is possible. Your Grace, may I speak with a frankness that may, to you sound brutal?'

'You have always been frank with me, Messire Chapuys. Brutal never. But I am listening.'

'To what I am about to say, I have given most serious consideration. The present situation, as we have just seen, has had an ill effect on the Princess' health, and it would be idle to pretend that the separation and your mode of life here have done anything to improve your own. And things are likely to worsen.' He looked around the handsome, well-furnished apartment, and then back at Katharine's carefully controlled face. 'I know that the King is utterly determined to have this child born in wedlock, or at least in such semblance of it as will be acceptable to the English. To this end the new Archbishop of Canterbury proposes to set up a court in some out-of-the-way place – Dunstable has been mentioned; and there, with all speed, your marriage will be declared null and void. This will have a very unfavourable effect upon your position. I fear that you will suffer much humiliation, possibly even some discomfort.' He paused deliberately.

She said equably, 'I have been humiliated already. And I spent my early years in circumstances where comfort was the last consideration. I must accept what comes, having no alternative.'

'But, Madam, you have.' He leaned a little forward and his cool eyes glittered. 'I have gone through the formality of resigning my post. I have begun to pack. I have bespoken passage for myself *and my household* on a German ship, sailing from Tilbury on Maundy Thursday. No questions will be asked as to the identity of those who embark with me. The Princess will be at Hatfield, you will be here. A long, hasty ride for you both, but not, I think, beyond your powers.'

'You are proposing that my daughter and I should run away?'

'Escape,' Chapuys corrected. 'While there is time. Once on the Continent, you can appeal in person, to the Emperor, to the Pope. The fact that you have been driven, by intolerable circumstances, to seek refuge will shock them both into a proper realisation of the seriousness of what is going on here. Your Grace has written, I have written; I can only conclude that in the press of multitudinous concerns neither of them has properly estimated the danger. I am certain that your appearance and that of the Princess, as refugees at the Imperial Court will lead to immediate action to reinstate you. It is a desperate resort, but the only one left to us now.'

She said, 'Allow me to think for a moment.' She closed her eyes and placed one hand over them. God, God, help me to think clearly, to decide rightly . . . This man is my friend, he is well-informed, experienced, cool-headed, should I be guided by what he says?

It was a long moment. Then she opened her eyes and folded her hands in her usual posture.

'You mean well, Messire, and for your care for me I thank you from my heart. But to such extreme action I see no end but war. I could only be reinstated by armed force. The last thing I desire. This is not a matter to be decided by who can put the most men into some battlefield. It is a legal business, to be settled by lawyers.'

'It *was*,' Chapuys said harshly. 'It is beyond that now. Your case is about to be decided by a procedure absolutely outside the law as we understand the word; outside the Church that we recognise – a court of English ecclesiastics owing no allegiance to Rome will take its directions from Cranmer whose only law is the King's wish. And this court you will be called upon to attend. It will be argued that for your own convenience you should move to Ampthill, a place within easy reach of Dunstable.'

Ampthill was her own manor; she had once offered the stewardship to Francisco Filipez. The man appointed, when Francisco refused, had said the house was too ruinous for occupation, and that was years ago.

She said, 'If I am ordered to Ampthill, I shall go. I shall not attend Archbishop Cranmer's court. A case still *sub judicia* at Rome cannot be tried at Dunstable, or anywhere else in the world.'

Admirable; immensely courageous, but utterly foolhardy. He said as earnestly as he had ever spoken in his life, 'Madam, I do *beg* you to consider. For five years you have obstructed the King – he has been – I will not say magnanimous, but cautious. He has sustained himself with the hope that Clement's final decision might free him. He knows now that by this secret marriage and the setting up of a court to justify it, he has put himself into a position where no favourable verdict for him can ever be given. And the Concubine, never at any time gentle, and now about to bear, perhaps, a prince, will take vengeance on you. It would surprise me very little if the word *contumacious*, applied to you at Blackfriars, very shortly became *traitorous*.'

To that she said nothing and he went on. 'Even I shall not be allowed to visit you freely. Ambassadors do not wait upon private ladies. Your Grace, unless you set sail on Maundy Thursday, I foresee nothing for you but hardship and misery.'

'For a time,' she said. 'Until the Pope decides. And you, Messire Chapuys, I shall always regard as my especial friend; and although I cannot avail myself of what you offer, I shall always be grateful for it.'

'You reject the plan entirely?'

'I must.'

Inconsequently he felt as Campeggio had felt, a strong desire to hit her. A good plan, cunningly made, backed by reason, expediency, good sense, brought to nothing.

'I do hope,' Katharine said, 'that in your next post, Messire, you find no such difficult problems.'

He said bleakly, 'My resignation was a blind. I shall stay in England now until I am recalled. And that will not be soon. My master may not heed my letters, but he knows my worth. I shall see this thing out. And since you cannot find it in your heart to avail yourself of the escape I offered, there is one more thing that I should mention. Had you been prepared to come away, I should not have bothered you with it. As it is: Has anyone ever, at any time, suggested that you should have contact with a nun of St. Sepulchre's, in Canterbury?'

The abrupt change of subject confused her for a moment.

'Elizabeth Barton. The holy nun of Kent?'

'That is the woman. Did Your Grace ever receive her, write to her?'

'No. She once – this was when I was still in London – sent a message, offering to use her prophetic vision on my behalf . . . There was something, just something Messire Chapuys that made me feel that for all her talk of conversing with angels and being able to locate lost property, she was fraudulent; or at least, if not fraudulent, more inspired by devils than by angels. I refused to see her, or to communicate with her.'

'Thank God for that,' Chapuys said. 'Sir Thomas More and Fisher of Rochester were not so careful. Her visions, her prophecies and ecstasies attracted them – among others. And she, poor silly woman, will be used, when the time comes. Cromwell seldom misses a trick. Unless I am very wrong in my reckoning she will be arraigned as a witch, and those who have consorted with her will be, with her, condemned. Her latest pronouncement was that if the King marries in your lifetime, he will die, within seven months. That – and the consorting with a woman who said such a thing – could easily be regarded as treason, of another sort. I am glad that you avoided that trap.'

'Sir Thomas More,' she said, 'could talk himself out of a foxhole and have all the bystanders laughing as he did it. Bishop Fisher's integrity is graved on his face. As for the King . . . No. That I will not believe. She cannot know. God alone decides the hour of our death . . .'

Chapuys had been right about Dunstable, right about Ampthill. In May 1533, May always in England thought to be the merry month, the beginning of summer, but this year cold and wet, more dismal than any, even old men, remembered, she was ordered to remove to Ampthill.

It was a part of England that she had never seen before; rather as though England were showing another face, flat, sparsely populated, infinitely dreary under the grey skies and the rain; only the oaks, standing solid and putting forth as oaks always did in spring, the reddish-ochre hues of autumn, redeemed the bleak landscape and the decaying house from complete desolation. Dunstable was about twelve miles away in distance; the court about five days distant in time.

But hard on her heels, so close behind her that they arrived before she had arranged herself, her household and her belongings, came the Dukes of Norfolk and Suffolk, bringing as Norfolk said gruffly, her last chance to behave reasonably. 'His Grace calls upon you, Madam, as his *subject*, to obey him and renounce the title of Queen. If you will be amenable, he will deal with you and your daughter more generously than you could expect.'

It was a last-minute attempt to avoid the coming together of the Dunstable court and it showed that in his heart Henry was not sure of the legality of what he was about to do. He might brag and bluster and threaten, but he had no real desire to make the breach with Rome.

'His Grace already knows my answer, my lords.'

Inwardly Norfolk groaned; he had known it was useless; a man might as well talk to a stone. But he was a pious, orthodox Catholic and viewed with dismay the changes about to take place. It was useless for the King to argue that no fundamental changes would be made, that the English Church, with himself as its head would hold the same beliefs, follow the same ritual. When one said, 'I believe in the Holy Catholic Church,' it meant the one, indivisible Church of Rome; not some half-baked, mongrel affair devised by Cranmer.

Norfolk, having a little trouble with his own conscience, looked at Katharine with distaste and thought: All because I persuaded her to take that flibbertigibbet niece of mine into her household. All because two stubborn, stupid women want to be called Queen. Devil take them both.

Suffolk said, 'Disobedience to such a direct order can be regarded as treason. It could take you to the block.'

Her eyes narrowed a little and the corners of her mouth lifted. 'From you, my lord, such a warning must come from the heart.' He had been near the block himself, actually in the Tower, for marrying Henry's sister.

'Times have changed since then,' Suffolk said, answering the half smile and the thought, not the words.

And that was all too true. There had been a time when Henry's rage died of its own violence, the stamping and the shouting acted as a purge.

'If you are still set,' Norfolk said; 'you must take the consequences. You will henceforth be known as the Princess Dowager. Your income will be cut by three-quarters; your household reduced. And you will be held in custody. Lord Mountjoy, who has served as your Chamberlain, will in future be your custodian and govern everything.'

This was what Chapuys had foreseen when he urged escape while there was still time.

She said, with infuriating placidity, 'Fortunately my needs nowadays are small. But I would assure you, and my husband, the King, that if I am reduced to begging in the streets, I shall do so as *Queen of England* – until the Pope says otherwise.'

Suffolk seemed about to say something, but Norfolk pulled his sleeve and said, 'Let be. Enough time has been wasted.'

Katharine said, 'This is desolate country; food for men and bait for horses is hard to come by. Allow me to offer you hospitality while I am still in a position to do so. We will not speak of things likely to ruin digestion.'

Norfolk thought: That niece of mine, Tom Boleyn's daughter will never attain queenliness if she wears the crown for fifty years. Suffolk, who had married a Royal princess, thought sourly: It is something they are born with!

To Lord Mountjoy, uncomfortable in his new role, Katharine said, 'I trust, my lord, that to me you will be as good a custodian as you have been Chamberlain. I am afraid that upon you will fall the task of making ends meet. Despite some practice at the art, I was never good at it.' Her acceptance of the new situation made him more uncomfortable than ever. He had no intention of acting as gaoler to a lady already deeply wronged. Making ends meet was another matter; sometimes in the past he had wondered whether she could even count. He would stay long enough to get her affairs in order then resign.

With the minimum of fuss and publicity, Cranmer opened his court in Dunstable, the little market town where another Henry – first of the name – had founded an Augustinian Priory and built a palace. The Priory still stood, the palace had fallen to ruin, and all about Dunstable the wind, blowing from the Chiltern slopes, tugged at the growing corn and lengthened and strengthened the straw, making it desirable for thatchers. In that quiet place the verdict was given. The King of England had never been, could not have been, married to the wife of his deceased brother. Therefore his marriage in the previous January – he being a bachelor and Anne Boleyn a spinster, was sound and legal. The offspring of this marriage would be legitimate.

'So here we are,' Maria de Moreto said grimly. She looked around the dilapidated place which, even in its best days, had been intended more for defence than for comfort. Beyond the windows the countryside lay flat under the rain; indoors in addition to the pervading damp there were places where the moisture leaked in. 'With Your Grace's rheumatism growing worse every day and everybody sneezing and coughing.' It seemed to her that life had made a full circle, she was back where she started, living in penury and discomfort; but it was worse in this detestable, sunless climate.

'We are no worse off than before,' Katharine said, meaning that the court's decision had altered nothing. 'And Lord Mountjoy has promised me that he will urge a move to some healthier place.'

Maria did not doubt his goodwill but she felt that if a move were made it would be to some worse place.

Certainly Ampthill was not healthy. When Katharine stepped out of bed on to a pin which had lodged between the floorboards, the trivial little puncture did not heal; a circle of swollen, purplish flesh surrounded a green-lipped, festering hole; and she was in bed, in considerable pain when Lord Mountjoy, obeying instructions direct from London, came to tell her that she must recognise the Dunstable court's verdict. For the first time he addressed her as Your Royal Highness, and Katharine raised her hand. Since his change of function he had been very tactful, therefore she now spoke to him gently:

'My lord, I am Queen of England, and this is my bedchamber. Those who enter it and wish to have speech with me, must address me correctly.'

He said plaintively, 'It makes things very difficult, for everyone. An order direct from the King is not lightly to be disobeyed.'

She would not look at him or give any sign of hearing what he said. She stared at the wall. Her foot throbbed.

'My position is untenable . . .' he said. 'His Grace has ordered me . . .' Finally in a desperate bid for her attention, by way of curiosity, he said, 'And there is news from London . . .'

She thought, as she always did: Mary! The Pope? But she had said that she would not listen to anyone who denied her her title, and she continued to ignore him. Mountjoy, who shared the affection felt for her by most people who came into close contact with her, who admired and pitied her, felt a flicker of exasperation. It was all so futile. She had put up a splendid fight, and been beaten, being one against many and with no ally of any worth. Continued resistance now would only injure her further, whereas a grain of amenability . . . Well, perhaps, when she heard the news, she would realise. With this in mind, he said, 'Your Grace . . .'

'I hear you,' Katharine said.

'Queen Anne was crowned on June the first . . .' Not – the purely feminine thought would intrude – all in virginal white, with pearls, wearing the Orient crown.

'To deny her title is now treason.'

'I do so deny it, my lord. In Christendom a man cannot have two wives, or a country two queens. His Holiness has not yet refuted my claim to be wife and Queen.'

'Your Grace,' having said it once, he could say it again, 'if I may say so, this is an unreasonable stand, and can only do you damage. May I tell you something – it is not something I was ordered to say, but it is a little straw showing how the wind blows. Gossip, but it should not be underrated. The lady whom I am compelled to call Queen Anne, for her progress from the Tower of London to her Coronation, chose to use your barge. She had your arms and insignia burned off and her own painted on . . .'

'Natural enough. Compared with a husband, a crown, a barge is negligible.'

'But His Grace was *enraged*. He said she had no right. He said that the arms were yours, as a Princess of Spain, and though a properly consti-tuted English court could, and did, deny that you were Queen of England, that you were Princess of Spain nobody could deny . . . There was a quarrel of some ferocity. Your Grace, does this not indicate to you that His Grace retains respect, affection . . . things which in the future could be put to good purpose? I am a simple man, neither cleric, lawyer or politician, but it is clear to me that with the modicum of acceptance, you could vastly better your situation.'

'But I have known that all along.' The slightly self-mocking smile which made those who saw it think how pretty she must have been when she was young, lightened her face. 'His Grace told me years ago that if I would say I was not his wife, he would treat me as his sister. But I am his wife. And you, my lord, are temporarily in Satan's guise, offering comfort in return for sacrifice of conscience, And to you I say: Get thee behind me, Satan.'

'I was endeavouring,' Lord Mountjoy said, 'to make it plain that His Grace is not ill-disposed towards you. What I fear is that if you continue intransigent, you may winter here.'

'And that is a matter of no importance.'

Exasperated again, he said, 'But there is another way of looking at it. It is now an offence, a capital offence, to apply to any court outside England.'

She shifted the burning, throbbing foot into the temporary solace of another, cooler area of the bed and said, 'That can hardly apply to me, unless every act – like a bigamous marriage – is to be made retrospective. My appeal to Rome was made years ago.'

Yes, Mountjoy thought; and it was never answered, it never will be.

And from here onwards things will worsen for her. And I will have no part in it. I will do her, if I can, one last service, to get her moved from here . . .

He went about it cunningly, or so he thought. No appeal, no mention of the house falling to ruin or the rain seeping in. Reporting in person to Henry his failure to persuade Katharine to meekness, he said, 'Your Grace, Ampthill is the Princess Dowager's own property; and there is an old country saying that every cock crows loudest on his own dunghill. A move might be advisable.'

Any move, Mountjoy thought, could only be beneficial; and when he learned that Katharine was to be moved to Buckden, to a palace belonging to the Bishop of Lincoln, he felt that he had done her at least one good service.

CHAPTER 20

The move, like everything else that was done in miserable summer, was made in pouring rain. Northeastwards the diminished company plodded through the mire. It was July and the hay, which should have been safely gathered a month since, stood in the meadows still, mouldering and rotting side by side with the fields of barley, wheat, oats and rye, beaten flat and unripening, with harvest only four weeks away.

So they came to the place to which she had been ordered; Buckden, in Huntingdonshire, one of the properties which since ancient times had belonged to the Bishops of Lincoln. It was half fortress, half dwelling place; and passing through the outer gateway, across the moat, under the archway of the inner gatehouse and across the courtyard to the Tower, Katharine, and all those with her, thought that this was a vast improvement upon Ampthill. Solid red brick walls, giving out even on this desolate afternoon a warm glow. Completely deceptive. The rooms assigned to her – called the King's Lodgings – and which King of England, she wondered, had ever lodged there – were as damp as those at Ampthill. The Tower stood with its feet in the moat and the bricks had absorbed the moisture, so that even in the hall, six feet or more above water level, the plaster peeled from the sweating walls and the hangings, some of them old and beautiful, were so rotted that they were unsubstantial as a spider's web. In the room above, her bedchamber, within a week there was mould on her shoes and everything taken out from the heavy clothes chests, leather covered, cedar lined, had a clammy feeling and a mouldy smell. The pains in her fingers and wrists and knees grew worse and the stairs tried her sorely; they came up, very steep and sharp, in a spiral inside one of the round turrets at one corner of the building, and there was no handrail, merely a groove in the sweating wall. Francisco Filipez, helped by the local blacksmith, drove iron stanchions into the wall and slung a rope by which she could haul herself up or steady herself down. On such a stairway no human arm or shoulder could avail, the stairs were too narrow and too cramped. Everybody who mounted or descended them must go alone. Often, on evenings, summer evenings that should have been so warm and kind, as she went down to the chapel, or to the hall, and then came up again to bed, she saw a kind of symbolism in those stairs; the loneliness – and the mute support of the slung rope which faithful hands had rigged.

Outside Buckden, all over England, people facing a ruinous harvest and a winter when bread would be scarce and dear, said that nothing had prospered since the good old Queen was put away. And in London, wherever Anne went, the crowds were silent, sullen and hostile. Henry could not make them cheer; nor could he bear to see Anne fret over the coldness of her reception by the common people and the withdrawal of all the old nobility from Court, on this or that feeble excuse. One day he said to her, 'Sweetheart, I shall order the Princess of Wales to come and join your attendants. That will bring the rest flocking back.'

Anne said ungratefully, 'And who *is* the Princess of Wales?'

'That,' he said, 'was a slip of the tongue . . . My daughter, the Lady Mary.'

Katharine, at Buckden, heard that Mary had been recalled to Court and received the news with mixed feelings. She retained sufficient faith in Henry's paternal fondness to feel that it would be good for Mary to be where he could see her and talk to her rather than be shut away and forgotten. Mary had done nothing to offend him so far, and would, Katharine hoped, be discreet. But, at the same time, being at Court, obliged at every turn to yield precedence to the usurper, would be an ordeal for Mary, so young and so proud. In many ways Mary's position was worse than her own, she had lived more than half a lifetime and known great happiness; she could afford to await Clement's verdict. Mary was seventeen, an age when girls' thoughts turned to marriage and motherhood – and what suitable match could be made for a young woman in her invidious position? Sometimes, when Katharine's thoughts took this trend, she thought of Reginald Pole, with his good looks, his great gifts and his Plantagenet blood. He had been one of those despatched by Henry to canvass the opinions of the Universities of Europe and was still abroad, in Bologna. He had not married; nor had he taken priest's orders.

Katharine knew that Mary was very fond of him, and he would be a suitable husband for her whichever way fortune went. However, from Buckden's semi-imprisonment, she could do nothing except write Mary heartening letters which always included the injunction to obey her father in all things except those respecting conscience.

She also wrote to Chapuys, requesting him to ask for her removal to some other house, less damp and cold; to winter in Buckden, she told him, would impair her health and that of her faithful servants. But although Chapuys went about the business of getting her moved before winter, and used all his diplomatic skill, she was still there in December of 1533 when the Duke of Suffolk came on another special errand, this time ominously accompanied by a posse of armed men.

In September Anne had borne her child – a girl. Henry refused to be daunted; the baby was alive and well, she would have a brother next year. The child was named Elizabeth, after his mother, and given as stately a christening as though she were the prince Henry had hoped for. She was to have, from the first, her own household at Hatfield, and Mary was to be one of her attendants. Mary, stripped down, seeing the honours that had once been hers showered on the harlot's child, was torn in her mind. The baby was innocent of all wrong, and very attractive, especially to a girl who should have been having a child of her own; but to call her *Princess* was to deny her own legitimacy and to make nonsense of Katharine's long, lonely fight; so she said, 'I will call her sister and no more.'

Henry was touchy; marriage to Anne had not conferred the joy he had expected. No hidden fires had burned. That slender, lithe body, for whose possession he waited so long and given so much, was, once between the sheets, no different from any other.

However, she had cost him so dear that even in his darkest moments he could not bring himself to admit that he had made a bad bargain. He had defied the Pope; he had made himself Head of the Church of England, all in order to put Kate away and marry Anne, who must, must surely, next year, give him the son he needed. He had set his course and must go on. His complaisant Parliament had passed the Act of Succession and everyone of any importance, down to the most petty official, must swear to observe it, to recognise Anne as Queen and Elizabeth as Princess.

Katharine and all her servants must swear. And it was the Duke of Suffolk who was commissioned to force the oath upon them; he set out saying that he would sooner break a leg than go on such an errand.

Arrived at Buckden, he installed himself in the Great Chamber which lay between the Tower and the Chapel, sat himself down with his back to the fire and decided to begin on the servants, feeling that it might give him some advantage if, when he came face to face with her, he could tell her that if she resisted she would be alone.

Her confessor, Llandaff, set the pattern. He could rightly claim to be a Spaniard by birth and therefore unconcerned with oaths of allegiance to anyone other than the Emperor.

'Stand aside,' Suffolk said.

The next chaplain was Thomas Abell, who refused point blank.

'I thought that my views were made clear in my book. I hold that England has only one Queen, and that Queen Katharine.'

'Stand aside. No; on the other side.'

Her doctor was a Spaniard though he spoke perfect English. He had come, he said, to serve, first the Princess of Wales and then the Queen of England and he could not regard anyone else as Queen.

Maria de Moreto, her English perfected years ago, pretended not to understand a word; with Spanish gestures and a fluent flow of Spanish she defeated him entirely. Even when he said, 'Stand aside,' waving her to where the other Spaniards stood, it needed the doctor to take her by the arm and pull her into position.

So it went on. Stupid people. A kitchen maid, 'Sorry, my lord, but if I swore to this, Her Grace'd never forgive me. And when my hand was scalded . . .'

A fluttering little woman, a sempstress, or a laundress. 'No, my lord, I don't think I could. I've worked for Her Grace for twenty years. To me she is Queen. I'm sorry to be so disobliging.'

He ended with two groups, the Spaniards for whom there was some excuse on one side, the English for whom there was none, on the other. Only three people and they all officials appointed by the Bishop of Lincoln to have a care for his property during the occupation, took the oath. And it was long past dinner time. The short December day was beginning to darken.

'Take the lot to the gateway and lodge them in the alms room.' He could no longer bother to distinguish sheep from goats. Let them all cool their heels. 'Go across there,' he said, indicating the place where Katharine lodged, 'and bring the Princess Dowager here to me.'

While he waited he went nearer the fire, warming his back and determining to take a high hand with Katharine from the first moment. Women lived too long, that was the trouble; they should die with the bloom of youth still on them and before they learned to be headstrong. He scowled as he remembered his last encounter with a woman over forty and set in her ways. Arrogant, unyielding old bitch. But the Dowager Countess of Willoughby had to be deferred to, the Princess Dowager was in no position to dictate.

Henry's sister, Mary, who had married him for love and whom he had neglected and left alone in a remote manor in Suffolk, had died in June, setting him free to marry for the fourth time. His choice had fallen upon the Countess' daughter, just fifteen, pretty, well-dowered. Her abominable old mother, after raising a number of objections, one absurd – that at forty-nine he was too old – had at last mentioned a most astonishing condition as the price of her consent. Worsted by her and still smarting, Suffolk was prepared to deal harshly with another female who had lived too long.

His messenger came back alone. 'My lord, the Queen . . . I ask pardon . . . The Princess Dowager says that she is prepared to receive you.'

The distance between the main hall and the Tower was not great, but across the flat plain of Huntingdonshire the wind blew keenly. Under its bite, and the feeling that he had been summoned like a lackey, Suffolk's mood hardened still more.

In the hall of the Tower it was not much warmer and Katharine, huddled into some woollen wrapping, her face pinched and bleached, looked smaller than he remembered and far from formidable.

'I am here,' he began without ceremony and speaking in a loud, hectoring way, 'to administer to you the oath that all must take or be reckoned traitors. Raise your right hand and say . . .'

She could still, when necessary, speak with authority.

'Stop, my lord. Someone should have informed you. I hold no conversation with those who do not approach and address me correctly.'

'I am not here for conversation. I have already arrested your household and if you refuse the oath I shall arrest you, and take you to London with no more regard for your comfort than that of any other traitor. You have been dealt with very leniently but this state of things cannot continue. Now you have been warned . . .'

She stood still and gave him one hard defiant look, a mute answer. And then she turned her back and looked out of the window. From it she could see the end of the chapel and beyond it the flat countryside. Sleet was falling now – and if Suffolk kept his threat to drag her to London as a common traitor, she might very well die.

'Take your time to think it over, ' Suffolk shouted. 'You have had five years – but take your time!'

When he saw that she was deliberately ignoring him, red rage exploded, colouring even the whites of his eyes. He began to shout abuse at her, using coarse terms that made her understand how sheltered her life had actually been. And she was sure that Suffolk was exceeding his mandate: Henry had never visualised, and would never countenance this. She almost wished that she had not, by her own resolution, cut herself off

from talk with this upstart. She could have turned and with a few words
silenced and reduced him. As it was she thought: I must avoid being
taken; give him time to come to his senses and remember that though the
King does not regard me as his Queen any longer, he still remembers that
I am a daughter of Spain and Princess of Wales. The man is railing at me
as though I were a fishwife who had given bad measure. And she thought:
He is ungrateful too; I pleaded for him when he was in danger of death for
marrying Mary . . . But that is neither here nor there. I must get away
before, having shouted himself out, he lays his hands, or calls for some
minion to lay hands on me. Such an affront I do not think I could survive.

'. . . and the King would thank me,' Suffolk said, 'for ridding him of an
obstinate, contumacious bitch.'

To her left, only a few paces away, was the door that opened upon the
spiral stairs. A strong, heavy door which she had never yet opened for
herself – now that she came to think about it she realised that she had
never opened any door . . . But I think I could . . . She took the few swift
necessary steps, hauled at the door, felt its weight, thought – I am done –
pulled again; slipped through and safe on the far side shot the bolts home.
Suffolk heard them screech and beat on the door, yelling and cursing, but
the four inch slab of solid oak, heavily nailed, had been designed to resist
sterner assaults. It would take a battering ram. Or fire.

'I'll smoke you out, you vixen.'

Katharine stood at the foot of the spiralling stairs, trembling and
breathless and aware of pain; not the familiar, accepted pain in her knees
and fingers and neck, a new one, and worse, in the left side of her chest.
She attributed it to the strain of opening and slamming the door. She drew
some careful, steadying breaths and then climbed the stairs to her bedroom where silence lay heavy.

For the first time in all her life she was entirely alone. Always before
someone had been within call. Now Suffolk had arrested her whole
household. She would never see them again. That was a thought to bring
tears. She cried a little and then sought her usual refuge – faith in God. She
knelt down and prayed for her servants, that they might be spared hurt,
or, if they must suffer, be given strength to sustain them in their ordeals.
For herself she asked courage to face whatever might happen next and
that her faith might not fail, that, whatever the evidence to the contrary,
she should continue to believe that God had not deserted her. And as
usual, she prayed that the Pope might be guided to pontificate in her
favour. Despite everything, she was still convinced that once this happened, Henry would see his error, do penance for his sins and resume life
with her to whom he was lawfully wedded.

In the hall below the sergeant who had charge of Suffolk's small force, hurried in, 'My lord, come and look!' Some urgency in his manner prevented Suffolk from asking what was to be seen. They hurried to the outer gateway and climbed some stairs. Suffolk went to an aperture in the wall and looked down into the village street.

A crowd of men, work people by their clothes, stood staring at the gateway. They stood silent and still and the only sign that they had come to do anything more than gaze, was the fact that every man carried a weapon of some kind; an axe, a sickle, a hammer; three or four had bows and arrows. The threat was plain; and they already outnumbered the force which Suffolk had judged sufficient to intimidate and if need be, arrest, a few recalcitrant servants.

Suffolk leaned from the opening and shouted:

'Good people. I am the Duke of Suffolk; here on the King's errand.'

Not a hat was doffed; not an expression changed. They stared. Suffolk was a man of courage and knew that more dangerous crowds than this had been dispersed by words and a show of confidence.

'I call on you to disperse. In the King's name.'

Nobody moved: but one man cleared his throat and said:

'Sir, that b'ain't for you to say. You b'ain't our magistrate.'

'Who is?'

They moved then, shuffling, heads together in muttered consultation, murmurous as bees. The spokesman said:

'*Could* be Mr. Alington. Some think different. Who'd you reckon, Bill?'

The names of several local gentry came out in a confused spate; Gostwick, Tanfield, Hynde, Malory, Mordaunt. And there were comments, 'Been dead a year you fool!' 'He winter in Huntingdon.'

Suffolk recognised with fury the age-old peasant trick.

'Anyway,' their leader said in a consoling way, 'we don't need none. We b'ain't doing nothing. Just looking.'

Two men, better dressed, strolled up; one carried a fowling piece, the other a musket.

Then, from around the bend in the road, came the rattle of hoofs. Relief on its way. There were three riders, a gentleman and two servants. They reined in abruptly. Suffolk shouted. The gentleman took no notice, but bending over the man with the fowling piece, exchanged a few words; turned his horse and rode quickly away followed by his men.

'Who was that? You there, with the fowling piece. The name of that gentleman?'

The man removed his cap.

'My lord, how should I know? He asked was this the London road. I directed him.' There was a little subdued laughter.

It was one of those who had authority and had refrained from using it. And Suffolk knew why. The country's sympathy lay with *her* and unrest was rife. People were glad enough not to have to pay dues to Rome any longer but all the other changes were resented and further changes were feared. In such an atmosphere a few blows struck in a remote village might precipitate a crisis. Blows must not be struck here.

'What are you waiting for?' he roared at them. 'Nothing is happening here. I have come to ask some questions and carry back the answers. Go to your homes.'

'We're just watching,' the spokesman said.

Suffolk climbed down and went to the alms room in which the pensioners were huddled.

'Send out the physician and the waiting woman, Maria what ever her name is.'

He spoke sternly to Dr. de La Sa. 'Your mistress has done a foolish thing. She has locked herself in the turret of the Tower and will not listen to me. You are to go in and make her see reason. If she does not open up she will starve. Persuade her to come out and your own offence shall be overlooked.'

'For her own good I must persuade her,' Dr. de La Sa said, not seeing exactly how it could be done.

Maria broke into a flow of Spanish.

The doctor said, 'Women are always concerned with the unimportant. She is concerned that the kitchen fire, left untended, will be out.'

'She may look to it. Tell her to be quick.'

Maria was quick. The three crossed the courtyard and went towards the Tower. Dr. de La Sa gave evidence of his wish to be helpful.

'It would be better, my lord, to call from here so that the Queen may look out and see for herself. Also, this way she has more chance of hearing.' So, in full view of her window, they stopped and called that they had permission to visit her and Katharine called back that if the Duke returned to the far side of the courtyard, she would come down and admit them. Even so she was cautious, asking them again from behind the barred door if they were alone and then opening it so little that they had difficulty in squeezing through.

'He released you?' she asked breathlessly.

'We were sent to persuade you to submit, Your Grace. And I speak now as your physician. The Duke spoke of allowing you to starve and, as you know, I have always held even a fast detrimental to your health. Would it not be possible for you to take the oath, with spiritual reservations, as is permissible under duress.'

'My daughter would not know that it was with spiritual reservations that I had sworn away her birthright.'

'I thought you would say so,' Maria said and began pulling from inside her clothing the bread, the wedge of cheese that she had snatched up. Dr. de La Sa looked at her with displeasure. It would merely prolong the misery; and the Queen needed no encouragement to be headstrong.

'At best enough for four meagre meals. What will you do for water, for candles?'

'He will leave when he sees that I am not to be shaken.'

'I fear not, Madam. And I fear discomfort and privation for you.'

'Go down, Dr. de La Sa and tell my lord of Suffolk that I shall remain here until he withdraws, unless taken by force.'

He looked indecisive and unhappy. But there was nothing he could do here.

'I shall stay with you,' Maria said.

'If I thought it likely to be a long siege, I should order you to go. But you must stay.'

Suffolk had gone again to the place of temporary imprisonment and ordered out cooks and servers. The larders and buttery were pitiably ill-stocked; his men were hungry. Tomorrow he would have to send out a raiding party, who would, he knew, find very little. Peasants were skilled in the hiding of provender if there was a soldier within ten miles. The wives of those oafs – who were still watching – would by this time be driving livestock into the woods, pushing food up chimneys or under strawstacks.

When Dr. de La Sa brought him Katharine's message, he groaned inwardly. He could take a battering ram to the door or light a fire against it; but he knew that any unusual noise, flames, smoke, a female scream would change those who watched into something dangerous. And when the door was down, what then? Who could, with impunity, lay hands on her, even to drag her to safety? Searching for an answer to such a question one must take the King into account and there had been so far no sign that he would take any rough handling as other than an assault upon royal dignity. He had once or twice reminded people that though Katharine was not Queen of England she was the daughter of Spain. And when a fawning courtier, thinking to please, had spoken of her in a derogatory way, the King had snarled, 'You should wish yourself so chaste a wife!'

Dr. de La Sa said, 'Her Grace has provisions for ten days and a spirit of the utmost hardihood.'

Outside, though the people behind the faces had changed perhaps, the faces had not; bovine, impassive, and growing in number more rather than less, the peasants, curse them! watched. His own men wanted to be home for Christmas, and so did he – the laxity which the season permitted was delightful for a man who, if past his first youth, was still handsome. And if this solemn Spanish doctor said that in her tower Katharine had provisions for ten days, it meant that she could hold out for twenty; in times of famine, in besieged cities, or boats cast adrift, women survived.

In the morning he said, 'Sack the place. To every man what he can carry. We leave in an hour.'

Most of Katharine's personal possessions were in the great chests which she had brought from Spain and which could not be carried up the spiral stairs. Suffolk's men took most of her clothes, all her household linen, the silver and plate which, banished from Greenwich she had felt right to take with her. They ripped the old, beautiful tapestries from the walls, and got little good by that, for they were so rotted by damp that they split, ragged and useless, except as wrappings for other things, the kitchen utensils, pots and pans, spithooks.

Suffolk loosed, into the ruined house, all Katharine's Spaniards. Dr. de La Sa and a comparatively humble fellow, Francisco Filipez, in saying that this had nothing to do with them, that only the Emperor had claim to their allegiance, had struck a note that Suffolk, angry as he was, recognised. But Abell, another chaplain named Baker, and a half dozen other people, born English, were bundled on to the spare horses.

The watchers watched. Did they never, Suffolk wondered, need to sleep or eat or even blink?

'I shall know her,' the man with the fowling piece said, 'I was that day in Buckingham and saw her plain.'

So they watched. She was not taken or Master Falconer would have given the prearranged sign. But her gear was taken. Poor lady, left without so much as a change of linen, or a spithook.

They waited, in case it should be a trick; but the train took the London road and pursued it.

Katharine waited too and then came down to the ruined house. She had withstood the brief siege and the enemy had retreated; in the stripped hall she stood, victorious in principle but on the practical level upon which life must be maintained, defeated. Nothing to eat; nothing in which food could be cooked. And the only bed that offered any comfort, her own.

Disheartenment and despair were not far away. Even Maria de Moreto looked grim and Dr. de La Sa said reproachfully, 'How long can Your Grace live in such conditions?' The others, with one exception, looked at her helplessly. Only Filipez said, 'We must go out and beg or borrow.'

There was no need. All that day those who had watched and then scattered came drifting back, bringing offerings, half a sack of flour, a flitch of bacon, a peck of dried peas, a couple of fowls tied together by the feet. There were also some touching attempts to replace the goods that had been filched; a silver spoon and a glass of Venetian make that had come home in some soldier's pack after Agincourt and been kept as too precious for ordinary use; a spit which a young blacksmith had made in his second apprentice year and which his proud mother had hung on the wall, her old one being still serviceable. There was an iron pot, too large for a couple whose children had all left home, and a wide pewter dish that had been cherished in memory of the grandmother who had bequeathed it.

When she realized what was afoot, Katharine insisted on going out, receiving each gift and thanking each donor. She did so in considerable style, wearing the second best dress of those that remained to her because they had been in her bedroom and her gold collar. It might seem absurd to stand thus arrayed in order to accept two goose eggs from an old woman clad in homespun, but her instinct was sure; these offerings were being made to the Queen of England and as Queen she should receive them.

Nobody could replace the wall hangings which, frail as they were, had excluded the worst of the draughts; and when, just before Christmas there was a heavy snowfall, snow drifted in through some of the cracks and lay for a time unmelted on the floor. But, as Katharine said, 'The Christ Child was worse housed.'

CHAPTER 21

In the ill-equipped household with its diminished staff, something of formality had had to be sacrificed, but Francisco Filipez had never yet come into any room where Katharine was wearing no doublet and with his shirt sleeves rolled up as he did on a bright May morning of 1534. He rushed in, halted and stood still, staring at her, his jaw jerking. He was under the stress of some emotion which rendered him speechless.

She imagined that what she had been expecting, ever since December, had come about; for it had been a shocking year for those who opposed the King. More and Fisher were in the Tower with many others; the Nun of Kent had been barbarously executed; religious houses whose heads refused to acknowledge Anne as Queen and Henry as Head of the Church, were being closed. It seemed to Katharine that she was unlikely to escape, and that what Filipez could not bring himself to say was that men had arrived to take her to the Tower.

'Try to tell me, Francisco,' she said gently. 'I can bear it, whatever it is.'

He fought the rigor of his jaw and said, in a voice so breathless as to be almost inaudible,

'The Pope . . . he has declared . . . in your favour.' He began to cry.

She reached about like a blind woman and found a chair, one of those that Suffolk's men had smashed and Francisco had mended.

She had known all along that this would be the answer, yet now that it had come she was dumbfounded and dizzied. She had so often imagined this triumphant moment, what she would say and do: and now she could only sit and stare and think: Thank God. Five years. Pray God it is not too late.

Presently she asked, 'Who told you?'

'The fishmonger. The news was in Huntingdon. The Bishops are on their way. He rose early and travelled fast.' Bishops rode as befitted their age and dignity; the fishmonger's load was perishable.

'What Bishops? Francisco, use your sleeve . . .'

He did so, but the tears came faster than he could wipe them. When had he last wept? So long ago that he could not remember.

'I beg Your Grace to forgive me. So long a time, and then the fishmonger . . . and I to be the one . . .' Something like a laugh coincided with a sob.

I feel like that myself, Katharine thought. I could laugh and cry and pray and sing and dance all at once. She sat calmly and repeated her question.

'Of York and Durham. And the flags are out in Huntingdon.'

'It was right that you should be the one to tell me. You carried my first appeal. Come, kneel with me and let us thank God.'

God forgive me the moments when I almost despaired, the fears I harboured, the tears I shed, the anxiety of the sleepless nights. Unto Thee, oh God be all glory, honour and praise . . .

When she rose from her knees she was herself again; and busy. An Archbishop and a Bishop bringing news of such moment must be properly received. And she must make ready to return to London; thank God again that it was fair weather, daylight long and the roads good. She would be back in London; she would see Henry . . .

That thought stopped her breath. She had long ago put away the memory of his repudiation of her in the hall at Blackfriars; the petty persecutions of the succeeding years she had excused and forgiven almost as soon as she suffered them. That was not Henry. He had been ill-advised first by Wolsey, then by Cromwell, he had been infatuated by Anne and angered, as a child would be, at not getting his own way. She would not have admitted that she herself suffered an infatuation deeper and more lasting than any Henry could ever know; she simply loved him with the love that could forgive seventy times seven; and she had managed to convince herself that the only thing that stood between her and her husband was his conscience. Now set at rest; so that life could be resumed; the more easily because bigamy had not brought forth a prince.

She would wear the dress that she had worn at Blackfriars and never since, the garment of her humiliation; now the garb of triumph and vindication, the royal colour. The jewels she had worn on that occasion had been snatched from her and given to Anne; but she had the collar which was her mother's parting gift; and she had her wedding ring. Nobody had ever thought of demanding that – perhaps because they knew that to gain possession they would have to hack her finger off.

Buckden for an hour and a half was in a happy tumult; all those who had stayed faithful kissed her hand and some wept; and they said that of course they had known it all along, right must prevail. Good faithful friends, how they should be rewarded! And within a week she would see, not only Henry, but Mary, who had been staunchest of all.

Lee, Archbishop of York and Tunstall, Bishop of Durham, coming into the hall where the best that Buckden could offer was spread, found their task made easier by being confronted not with the ailing, broken-down old woman of popular report, but by one who looked younger and more vigorous than she had done just on four years earlier at Blackfriars. The Spanish Ambassador was always saying that the flat, damp country was ruining her health, and even Suffolk, to soften the report of his failure, had said that she looked ill and would not last long. In fact, as she welcomed them, there was colour in her face, and a light in her eyes and she moved lissomely.

Of the two, Tunstall felt the worse about the business because he had been one of those assigned to her defence in 1529 and had seen the validity of her case. But he was no hero, he did not wish to be a martyr and in such upset times, with everything moving so swiftly and so inexorably what could a man do when forced to choose between his bishopric and the Tower?

Katharine was not surprised that as she greeted them, both men looked sheepish; many people would in the next few days. It was not easy to admit that one had been in the wrong. She would be very gracious to all – even to Anne . . . She greeted the two men very graciously indeed:

'My lords, I bid you welcome. I understand that you have news for me.'

Get it over and done with, Lee thought.

'Madam, the Bishop of Rome has declared in your favour, but his word no longer carries any weight in England. Therefore we, Edward of York, now call upon you, the Princess Dowager, to take the oath of allegiance to our lord the King as Head of the Church of England, and to acknowledge the validity of his marriage to Queen Anne and the legitimacy of the Princess Elizabeth.'

Everything, the grave clerical faces, the bare wall, the window from which the light streamed in to fall upon the set table, receded, darkening and reeling. Mary, Mother of God! She fell into the dark, spiralling down. Dying, unconfessed . . . God, to you I commit my spirit, have pity, have pity . . .

The everlasting hands of the Almighty caught and held her and there she was, not dead; she was lying on one of the leather covered chests which were too big to be carried upstairs. The nails which made a decorative pattern around its rim and formed the letters *KR*, her mark, Katharine Regina, felt like stones beneath her, and under her nose Maria was waving stinking smouldering feathers.

What a plight to find oneself in.

She pushed the feathers away and struggled into a sitting position, 'That will do, Maria. Help me to my chair.'

'A momentary weakness, my lords,' she said of a spell of unconsciousness that had lasted ten minutes. 'You have more to say?'

They had both, in those ten minutes, entertained thoughts of fantasy, riding at all speed to London with the news that she was dead.

'A warning, Madam, that the penalty for refusing is death and that you are not immune.'

'If you have a commission to execute such a penalty upon me, I am ready. I claim only the ancient right, to die in the sight of the people.'

Traitors, or those accused of treachery, had this one right; their bodies might be mangled, their property confiscated, but they must die in public, their last words heard by all who could get within hearing distance.

'We have no such commission. We were told to inform you, and to warn you,' Lee said.

Tunstall broke in, speaking hurriedly. 'Madam, before Blackfriars, I was assigned to advise you. I do most gravely advise you now. The decision of the Bishop of Rome has hardened His Grace's determination. Where formerly there were words and arguments, there will be bloodshed . . .'

Afterwards, looking back, she realised that this had been the real parting of the ways, the moment of truth. Give in now and there would be the long, easy downward slither into heresy. She remembered again Wolsey on his knees – saying more was concerned than she dreamed of; the world already riven. But to give in now would be fatal; a halfway stand was worse than no stand at all because it implied recantation.

'Then my blood must be shed,' she said. 'His Holiness the Pope – that newfangled term, Bishop of Rome sits awkwardly on your tongues and upon your hearts, I doubt – His Holiness has proclaimed my case good, my marriage legal, my daughter legitimate. And by that I will abide.'

The Archbishop and the Bishop went back to Huntingdon where now almost every house was decorated with a flag, a streamer of new woven linen or a green bough.

London, too, had shown signs of rejoicing, Henry noted grimly; but people were mistaken if they thought that Clement's decision would influence things. He was angered by it and felt that he had been unfairly dealt with. That he was also thoroughly misunderstood was proved by something that the Spanish Ambassador had said, or rather by the way he spoke and looked. The conversation purported to be about Katharine's place of residence, but there were undertones.

'If there is any impairment in health, premature demise or other misfortune,' Chapuys said, 'the deepest suspicions would be aroused.' He felt that he would now be justified in referring to Katharine as Queen, but he avoided doing so; there was no purpose in annoying the King who was very easily provoked nowadays.

'Great God in Glory! What do you think I am? A poisoner of helpless women? I resent that, Messire. I resent it very hotly.'

'Your Grace, how could you place such an interpretation upon words that held no such intention? I was urging a removal from Buckden, which for some people seems not to be a healthy place. Nothing more I assure you.'

'She shall be moved as soon as I find a suitable residence.'

'My master will be relieved,' Chapuys said detachedly. 'May I – since Your Grace has made mention of the matter – say one more word, well meant?'

'We have always spoken openly so far as I know.'

'Sir, Henry II did not desire the death of St. Thomas à Becket. As the story goes he said, 'Will nobody rid me of this turbulent priest?' Your Grace might well make a similar remark, substituting *troublesome woman*. And there would be those ready to do what they believed, wrongly, to be your will.'

'That,' Henry said, 'is not a thought to keep you awake at night, Messire. Have you ever heard me say a word against her? Has anyone? She is the most damned stubborn, obstinate woman God ever made. But that is her only fault . . .'

And was that a fault, he asked himself, indulging in a momentary feeling of self-distrust. Clement had pronounced the marriage good and in the eyes of half the world at least Kate had been not obstinate or stubborn, but *right*.

Chapuys thought: This should never have happened to him. He is one of those who flourish best in sunshine; healthy, gifted, handsome, he was not prepared for anything to go wrong for him. Given a son all would have been well with him, with Queen Katharine, with England. It was all a great pity, one of God's mysteries.

But Eustache Chapuys had done his best which was all a man could do. He went home to write to Katharine, advising her, despite what Henry said, to be very careful of what she ate and drank; for now, he suspected, the Lutherans would be busy; they looked to Anne, they would want her, before the next child was born, to be Queen beyond any question. Clement's verdict might well have been Katharine's death sentence But not, of that Chapuys was sure, by any connivance of the King.

Henry went straight to Cromwell's office.

'The Princess Dowager must be moved. The Spanish Ambassador has been at me again. Buckden is not healthy. If she dies of ague or malaria it would look ill. Get your map.'

Turning towards the open shelves where the maps lay, neatly rolled into cylinders, Cromwell said:

'A move is advisable for other reasons, Your Grace. Buckden is too accessible – as my lord of Suffolk discovered.'

He found the map, unrolled it and weighted it flat with a book at each corner.

'Not more than half a day's journey away,' Henry said. 'Long processions tend to invite demonstrations.'

Cromwell had been about to make that very statement. He moved a thick finger in a circle, the radius half a day's ride from Buckden.

'There is Kimbolton, Your Grace.' The map was a new one, marked with little secret signs; prominence given to any place capable of being held in the event of trouble. On it Kimbolton was marked as more important than many a sprawling, open town.

'Before the late wars,' Cromwell said, 'it was a manor. It was fortified during the troubles. It is remote. It is now a castle, with . . .' he peered at the signs, 'a moat and a drawbridge.'

'How near is the moat to the dwelling? I am tired of complaints about dampness.'

'It stands on a mound, Your Grace. To the south I should say,' he made a rapid calculation, 'between thirty and forty feet. Away from the moat, that is, and well above it. To the east the same. North and west at least double that distance.'

'It sounds . . . suitable.'

It was also final; The More, Ampthill, Buckden, all temporary, places where – he hoped – she would come to her senses, and the moment she did he would have installed her at Greenwich the place she loved and which he no longer could endure. Now, supported by that weakling, that vacillating, dilatory Clement who did everything too late and then wrong, she would never give in. In consigning her to Kimbolton he felt that he was putting her into her tomb. The thought was enough to hurt a little, still; and in response to the hurt anger flared, directed, paradoxically, at Katharine who had made difficult what should have been so easy.

'She is to have no communication with anyone,' he said sternly. 'And those in charge are not to be likely to sympathise, or even listen to complaints. You understand?'

Cromwell pondered for a moment. 'May I suggest Sir Edmund Bedingfield as Steward, and Sir Edward Chamberlayne, perhaps as Chamberlain?'

'Well chosen,' Henry said. Both were known King's men; they were unlikely, even within the fastnesses of a lonely castle to call her anything but Princess Dowager. They were also decent men, equally unlikely to treat her harshly.

So that was dealt with. Henry and Cromwell went on to talk about the dissolution of the religious houses which still regarded the Pope as the ultimate authority. For Cromwell this was a profitable business; he was frequently approached by Abbots who felt their establishments to be in danger, and offered a bribe in return for leniency, or delay. He would accumulate a fortune. He was less spendthrift than Wolsey, architects, builders and painters did not find a patron in *him*. He had seen what happened to his old master. When Thomas Cromwell grew old, or fell from favour, he would have something to fall back upon, money soundly invested in the City of London, or with merchants in Germany and the Netherlands.

The move to Kimbolton was made in late May, in cold driving rain, for after opening with promise this summer showed signs of being as inclement as the previous one. And everyone knew why. Before the Pope had decided, there had been an element of doubt in the business, the faintest shadow of excuse for the King's behaviour; now there was none at all. Katharine was Queen and the majority of the people genuinely believed that there would be no good times, no good harvests until she was restored.

Despite the weather a menacing crowd gathered again by the gate at Buckden. Suspicion was allayed, even some hope engendered, when they learned that she was on her way to Kimbolton. That was a grand place, a fit residence, even for a Queen. Few of them had actually seen it, but they knew about it; it dominated the countryside and, to a degree, their thoughts.

It was not, like Buckden, in the heart of a village. It stood, as Cromwell had said, on a mound, completely isolated from the few humble houses that seemed to crouch in its shadow.

The moat, much wider than that at Buckden, had the dull gleam of pewter. The drawbridge was lowered with a crank and a creak, and as they rode in the hoofbeats sounded hollow and doomful. She had a sharp feeling of prescience: For me that bridge will be lowered only once more, when I go to my burying. I have not been sent here for the sake of my health, but to be out of sight and out of mind.

She was still unwilling, or unable to think ill of Henry. This was the doing of Anne, and her friends. She remembered wryly how on that dazzling morning of promise, when she expected the Bishops to bring her recall to London and the throne, she had determined to be gracious to Anne – to propose that she should have The More – a place which she herself wished never to see again – and an adequate pension; and how, presently she would treat the young Elizabeth exactly as she had treated the Duke of Richmond.

I was born to suffer disappointment.

No, I was born to bear what God sees fit to ask of me. And bear it I will, with God's help.

She was strong again as they arrived in the large inner courtyard and the bustle of moving in began. She had less baggage now. Once she had needed twelve great chests to carry her clothes and her personal belongings; now two sufficed.

The rooms assigned her were to the north and west, and the accommodation was better than any she had had since she left The More. There was a sizeable room with a wide hearth and opening from it at one end a small one, which she intended to make her own private retreat, at the other two, medium-sized ones. The Chapel, surprisingly beautiful, was close by, backing on to the small room; and the stairs, part of the old manor house around which the fortifications had been built like a shell, were of wood, with shallow steps and a stout handrail.

It was as well that at first sight she should be contented with the rooms assigned her; for within a few minutes of arrival she had confined herself to them for so long as she was in Kimbolton.

Sir Edmund and Sir Edward came to welcome her officially, to express hopes that she was satisfied with her accommodation and to inform her that supper would be served shortly in the great hall across the courtyard. Civil and courteous; but they addressed her as Your Royal Highness and she said:

'Sirs, I am Queen of England. If you cannot bring yourselves to address me correctly, I can neither talk nor eat with you.'

'Madam, we are sworn . . .'

'And so am I. In this part of the house I am Queen, and those who enter it acknowledge me. No other arrangement is possible.'

It was as though the moat had been diverted and now lay, impassable between the two households.

Both the knights had been prepared to deal justly with her. In the great hall across the courtyard the table was set, her place at the head of it – she was Dowager Princess of Wales, the widow of that pale, fair-haired boy long dead. And, as Henry had thought, in Cromwell's meticulously neat little office, these men were likely to be just. But the snub rankled.

Sir Edmund said, 'Madam, this will be awkward. There is no kitchen on this side.'

'Then, unless I and those who acknowledge me are to starve, food must be sent to us.'

It will be sent over, Sir Edmund thought furiously, but it will not be to your taste! He thought sourly of the preparations made, the orders given, the pains he had taken for the proper treatment of the Princess of Wales. What came across the courtyard for the woman who insisted that she was Queen of England, would be the worst of every dish; those who refused the first cut must be satisfied with the scrag end, and lukewarm at that.

She could have reigned in a minor way, wearing her purple dress and her jewelled collar; she was the daughter of Isabella of Castile and Ferdinand of Aragon; she was the widow of a Prince of Wales. From a wide area, people adjudged by Sir Edmund and Sir Edward to be 'safe' would have been very glad to come and visit and stare and grovel. She was allowed no visitors, but no such embargo applied to the two knights. As it was she lived in a gaol of her own making, in an isolation of her own choosing; and as the year tipped downhill into autumn, in increasing discomfort, for fuel as well as food came from the other side of the courtyard, and the logs brought over were mainly green, giving more smoke than heat.

The single link between the two households, apart from a few careless pages, was Franciso Filipez who was drawn to the stable yard and stood about there, at first quietly and then throwing out a few laconic words which showed that he was knowledgeable about horses, and then lending a hand, giving advice, until he was part of the scene. If he had cause to refer to his mistress he invariably gave her her title, and this caused no offence. He was a Spaniard, he was old. He was also half-crippled with rheumatism but astonishingly spry, therefore admirable, and he was friendly, the only one 'from across the way' who was. Nobody in the larger establishment envied anyone in Katharine's or, given the option, would have joined it, but simply because it was so rigidly exclusive it exerted a certain charm and Filipez, coming out of it – with a civil word and a grin, seemed to be conferring a favour. He had tales to tell, too, of campaigns in Granada when he was young and although some of them must be taken with a grain of salt, his listeners thought, they helped to while away a wet afternoon. In yet another rain-drenched summer in England it was not unpleasant to sit in the shelter of stable or smithy and hear an old Spaniard speak of droughts in Spain when trees as tall as those on Kimbolton Hill died for lack of water, and rivers wider and deeper than the Ouse ran dry. In return he was made free of any story current in the yard, mainly kitchen door stuff, what a page had overheard between Sir Edmund and Sir Edward last night at table; what was being said at the little ale house on the London road. It was none of it momentous, but to Katharine who would not speak to anyone who would not give her her proper title, nor set foot in any place where she was not acknowledged, Filipez's little gatherings provided human interest, a breath from the outer world.

CHAPTER 22

In the outer world a great deal was going on and Chapuys was in the thick of it. He had many visitors, some coming boldly in open daylight, some secretly by night. They all said the same thing. He could with truth and confidence write to his master, the Emperor, that England was on the verge of revolt; that the Pope's declaration in Katharine's favour had brought many waverers to her side; that though in and around London the new ways were being reluctantly accepted, the North and East were for Katharine and the Pope. Now, if ever, Chapuys urged, was the time for action; if the Concubine bore a son, fickle public opinion would veer. All that was needed was firm and positive leadership. The old nobility, some of whom had taken the oath from expediency, were willing to rise, so were the peasants; of the merchant class Chapuys was doubtful, but if the Emperor would only forbid all trade between Flanders and England, *because* of the way the Queen had been treated, even the London counting-houses would take notice.

Occasionally, usually when he was undressing before going to bed, Chapuys would mentally step back and take a look at himself. *Eustache Chapuys what are you about? What has happened to you?* Men entrusted with ambassadorial duties were supposed to act with impartiality and, unless given orders to the contrary, to promote goodwill between countries. He was unable to plead either youth or inexperience in his own defence, yet here he was behaving like a novice Knight instead of a seasoned diplomat.

Such moments of self-examination never lasted long; he had only to think of Katharine wronged for so many years and now since Clement's verdict, wronged more than ever, and the crusading spirit was lively again. Increasingly, throughout that summer he spent time and energy and cunning and money which he could ill spare, in testing public opinion and making contacts. He could not lessen his allowances to his family, he was the only one of his mother's children to have made any sort of headway in the world, so he entered a period of self-denial and it was often not from policy alone that he dined or supped wherever Henry was keeping Court.

He saw clearly that the pivot of all his plotting was the Queen herself. In the days when he was allowed access to her he had suggested flight, and later resistance. She had replied that she would never do anything that would lead to war. She had also said, with that smile which so changed her appearance, 'Imagine my position if I resorted to force and then had the decision given against me.' Being vindicated might well have changed her point of view; Henry's ignoring of the Papal verdict might have dis-illusioned her at last. But Chapuys had no means of knowing. He had requested permission to go to Kimbolton and been refused, civilly but firmly, not once or twice but several times.

In September he asked and was given private audience with Henry, and after greeting him said:

'Your Grace, I am in need of advice in a very difficult position.'

'Tell me your trouble,' Henry said. He liked giving advice.

'I fear that my master will be displeased with me. Your Grace, if a relative of your own were incarcerated in some foreign fortress and your Ambassador there *appeared* to do nothing, would you not incline to the opinion that he was idle, or puerile?'

Henry saw the point. 'Would you like a certificate to witness that you have made a number of applications for leave to visit the Princess Dowager?'

'That would be better than nothing. An actual visit would be better still. As Your Grace knows I have been careful to maintain neutrality in this matter, but I think the Emperor is justified in wishing to hear, through me, that she is well-housed, in good health, and perhaps – even – resigned.'

'She is well-housed; she is in good health. Resigned she will never be. We know that, Messire. And I cannot allow a visit. I said that she should have no visitors and I cannot make exceptions, even for you.'

It was the answer Chapuys had expected, and he had come prepared.

'Then I wonder . . . It is much to ask, I know . . . but if Your Grace would connive with me a little. Permit me to make a gesture. Allow me to set out from London, openly, even with some ostentation. Then when I am near Kimbolton, halt me with an order to proceed no farther, giving as your reason that such a visit might disturb the lady's peace of mind, or that my noisy suite had caused a breach of the peace in your realm.'

'An extraordinary suggestion. It is, Messire, that by appearing negligent you risk recall?'

'That, amongst other things.'

And Chapuys might well be replaced by someone far less personally aggreeable, more meddlesome, critical and biased.

'Very well; to strengthen your position we will indulge in this piece of mummery. But – you will not get nearer than five miles to Kimbolton.'

'Five miles from the place Your Grace's messenger will overtake and halt me. My gratitude is unbounded.'

So he went about London, saying that he was going to Kimbolton to visit – and if he never said 'The Queen' he also never said 'The Princess Dowager.' He invited a number of people to go with him. There were Spanish merchants in London who could well afford to fit out their servants with fine new liveries, to buy good horses and great silk flags embroidered with the arms of Spain. With his own money he hired trumpeters and drummers.

Cromwell said, 'Your Grace, this is open defiance. The man must be mad.'

'Rest easy and see what is to be seen,' Henry said.

'I see it now, Sire,' Cromwell said. He thought he did. He believed that Henry was tired of Anne, so unpopular as Queen, so unsatisfactory as a wife – a daughter and a miscarriage – a difficult and demanding disposition. The King was going to allow a reconciliation with Katharine to appear to be *forced* upon him. Very clever indeed! Devious himself, Cromwell admired deviousness in others; and what could be more devious than this?

September was unseasonably warm, just as June, July and August had been unseasonably wet. A cool, windy month would have served the harvest better; as it was the sunshine caused the flattened ears of corn to start sprouting; there would be little to gather in but straw. An unlikely season, part of, symbolic of, the troubled times. But there was hope; the Spanish Ambassador was on his way to Kimbolton to bring the good old Queen back to London; so people thought, as they gathered on every village green, at every crossroads, to see the gay cavalcade go by, the flags hanging limp in the hot air, the music calling, calling . . . A pity it had been left to the Spaniards to do, a pity it had been left so late, but better this than nothing; better late than never.

Chapuys, who amongst other motives had planned this as a test of opinion, was delighted by the response. Spaniards were not well-liked, even in country places where no Spaniard had ever been seen, but it was astonishing how many geese, fattening for Michaelmas, were killed untimely, mute offerings, and how many voices, once they were out of London, shouted for Katharine and how many men oddly armed, came up and said, 'If you need any help . . .' and how many owners of manors and yeomen found themselves able, even in such bad times, to offer shelter and food for man and horse.

Chapuys had his own cynicism; many of these people felt the threat to the monasteries as a threat to themselves; monks were, on the whole, lenient landlords; as for the gentry, every possible closure would affect them too. Younger brothers, second sons, sisters and daughters for whom for various reasons marriage had not been possible, had taken to the religious life, permanently provided for. At least half of the enthusiasm and goodwill could be attributed to self-interest in one way or the other, but even self-interest could be used; and the other half was formidable, men and women, even children, on their knees, weeping 'God bless the Pope!' 'God bless the Queen!'

In his assessment of popular feeling he had been right. And after St. Neot's, drawing near to his five-mile limit, the flood of gifts became almost embarrassing, ranging from bunches of flowers from cottage gardens to a silk dress: 'So that Her Grace may make a good appearance . . .'

Out of St. Neot's and nearing Kimbolton, Chapuys began to cherish hope and fear, so evenly balanced as to be almost insupportable. He had tricked Henry; had Henry tricked him? Was he, after all, to be allowed his visit? Or were he and those with him moving towards a trap? Of the conversation with the King there was no record, save in their minds; he was openly defying the order, no visitors to Kimbolton; he had acted as no Ambassador should, and if tonight he found himself lodged in a dungeon under the castle, taken prisoner by a force pre warned, whom could he blame but himself, and what defence could he make? Worst thought of all, what, as a discredited Ambassador, could he do for that poor lady?

The scheme which he had concocted with such care seemed suddenly worthless. Locked up for open defiance of the King. He would be worthless, too. He sweated more heavily than even the heat of the day warranted.

But the King had kept his word. Precisely five miles from Kimbolton, when Chapuys was considering calling a halt, the messenger arrived.

Messire Chapuys was not to go one step farther along the road to Kimbolton.

'Then I must stay here,' Chapuys said imperturbably. 'But news travels faster than men, and the poor lady there may already have heard of our coming. I will send a man on to inform her.'

'There is no need. I shall carry the word myself,' the man said and spurred on.

That was a setback. Chapuys' somewhat shaky little scheme had depended upon getting one of his men, armed with this valid excuse, if not into Katharine's presence, at least into the castle, where, under the pretext of speaking nothing but Spanish, he was bound to be brought face to face with one of the Queen's household.

Now he must plan anew.

'We will rest here for a while,' he said. There were trees by the roadside, limes still green, chestnuts beginning to turn colour. Into the shade the cavalcade moved and dismounted.

Sir Edmund, at Kimbolton asked, 'How many?'

'Sixty at least.'

'Armed?'

'Not openly; but the Spanish are tricky.'

'And they did not turn back?'

'No. The Spanish Ambassador said that he would stay there. I looked back once. They were dismounting.'

Sir Edmund gnawed the inside of his cheek. Sixty men could not take Kimbolton, but they could raise the countryside. It needed only a spark now.

He went across to the other side, where an indifferent dinner had just been eaten and cleared away and said to Filipez, 'Where is your mistress?' Filipez indicated the little room.

When the door opened and revealed Sir Edmund, who said, 'Your Highness,' and bowed, Katharine, holding to her rule, ignored him; but the pain in her chest leaped. It must be something of grave importance to bring him here. Mary?

'I must ask you to listen, Madam. The Spanish Ambassador with a considerable force is now within five miles of this place. A message from His Grace halted them there, but they did not turn back. A message from you might deter them.'

It was all very confusing. Messire Chapuys knew that he was forbidden to visit her. Why had he come? Why had he not been halted sooner? And what was a considerable force? She looked at Sir Edmund and saw that he was suffering some agitation. She broke her own rule.

'Do you think, Sir Edmund, that a message from the Princess Dowager would be effective where one from His Grace was not?'

'They look on you as otherwise.' And there were times, in the dark of the night, wakened by cramp, when he had some curious thoughts himself. Two Popes had been concerned, one in the making, one in the confirmation of her marriage; and even in her present miserable circumstances she behaved as Queen. Such thoughts, highly unsuitable to one the King trusted, did nothing to endear Katharine to her gaoler during the daylight hours.

'Send and say that there is no purpose in their delay,' he said. Get them out of the district. If trouble threatened, let it not be near Kimbolton. 'Send that fellow of yours who is so good a horseman.'

'Fetch him to me,' she said. 'And I should wish you to overhear the message I entrust to him.'

It was of the utmost correctitude. 'Please tell the Spanish Ambassador that I am sorry he has come so far for nothing; but that in obeying the King's order to withdraw he will be pleasing me. I think it might be permissible for you to enquire after the health of the Princess Mary.'

Chapuys was entirely unprepared to see one of Katharine's own people. He had been so busy planning his next move. At the sight of Filipez, so obviously at home on a horse, he leaped to the next objective. He hardly listened to the message which was meaningless, anyway.

'Tell me, he said urgently, 'is there any person that you know of, in this district, allowed access to the Castle, and friendly to Her Grace?' One of his purposes in this seemingly fruitless journey was to establish some secret contact. It might have taken days, it might have failed altogether. As it was it was settled in a minute.

'Only one,' Filipez said. 'And she has no access to the Castle. She is faithful; I know because whenever I go there . . .'

'*You* go? Where? How often?'

'I get out when there is a horse to be tried out. The place is a little tavern; about a mile that way.' He nodded in the direction from which Chapuys had come '*The Goat and Compasses*'

'I will try . . .' Chapuys said. 'Tell Her Grace that I will try to arrange that she has news, regularly. You must get out as often . . .'

'I shall not get out again if I delay now,' Filipez said.

'Tell Her Grace to be of good heart . . .'

Filipez nodded and disappeared in a cloud of dust.

Chapuys after a second said to himself: You blundering fool! You could have given *him* the letter. The truth was that this entirely unexpected, God-sent chance of possible operations in the future, had driven this day's doing out of his mind.

So back to plan two.

He had been concocting it ever since his offer to send a man with a civil message had been forestalled.

He said to his fool, 'You understand me. Fail in this and you are no longer my jester.'

To the eight picked men, all young, he said:

'You understand me. Your object is to entertain and draw attention from the fool. You must look as harmless as you are. Ride without hats and in your shirts. If ordered to retire, do so, a little way, but continue to make a show.'

The Spanish Ambassador, the banners, trumpets and bugles had been turned back; but it was just permissible that eight high-spirited young men should go on a sunny afternoon, out of curiosity, to see the place where the woman who was a Princess of Spain was held, and to offer, by a show of Spanish horsemanship, an hour of entertainment in what must be a life of superlative dullness.

'You did not even ask, Francisco. The one thing I most longed to know.'

'Your Grace, there was no time. *They* know how long it takes to ride five miles and back. I was neither trying a sick horse nor schooling a young one. And Messire Chapuys talked of other things. Of sending news through Jennie Turnbull.'

'The kind, very kind woman who sends the food?'

'That woman, Your Grace.'

The little tavern was nothing to look at but it had resources. To the rear a duckpond and a dovecote, a row of beehives, pigs in a sty, two cows, a productive garden and an orchard. Filipez always rode in that direction and he never came back without some token of goodwill from the landlady for the poor lady shut up in Kimbolton for no fault of her own. Jennie Turnbull, like most married women, was wholeheartedly in sympathy with Katharine.

Whether her sympathy was deep enough to lead her to engage in surreptitious handling of messages, Filipez was not sure; it was a service of rather different order from the sending of what Jennie called something a bit tasty for the poor lady's table.

The eight young Spaniards – one with a clown perched behind him – arrived. The drawbridge was up, and they looked harmless enough, but Sir Edmund went out and shouted to them to go away. One called back that they had only come to show off their horsemanship, while their elders rested, could they not have permission to do so? Life, even for the gaolers, was dull in Kimbolton and soon Sir Edmund was watching as eagerly as the rest of its inmates, as the Spanish trained horses showed their tricks. Then one of the young men took the lute that was slung on his back and sang, a Spanish song. A voice from the battlements congratulated him, in Spanish. He said to the clown, 'There is your mark.' Then he sang again, Spanish words to an English tune, one of Henry's own. It was an eerie experience to hear, 'Pastance with good company I love and shall until I die,' rendered, the tune faultless, as 'The Princess waits upon the babe and keeps her dignity; When at a doorway she yields place, each time she says: It is my father's will that I obey.'

Katharine said, 'Men's voices carry better. Dr. de La Sa, ask is she well? Are her spirits cheerful?'

Across the moat question and answer. Somebody called, in Spanish, 'Watch the clown!'

Nobody not particularly instructed to do so would bother to watch the clown, who, in truth was not very good except at turning somersaults, which he did so near to the moat's edge that he seemed likely to fall in – and serve him right. When the horses, having rested, drew away a little and resumed their display, most eyes watched them; and the clown fell into the moat and struggled, throwing off his motley coat, letting go his stick with the bells, one shoe, then another. Then, with a deadly accuracy, for he had no wish to end his days competing with dancing bears in Cheapside, he aimed the little casket. Maria de Moreto caught it and pushed it, wet and dripping green slime as it was, into her bodice.

In English and in Spanish he shouted for help, he was drowning. He was happy to realise that nobody was paying him any attention at all.

'Poor man, he is drowning,' Katharine said.

'He swims like a carp,' Maria said. It was true. He struggled out and with an oriental gesture, put his hands to his brow and bowed.

Chapuys and the main party rode back to the little tavern, and with a brusque, 'Wait here for me,' he dismounted and entered alone. He asked for ale which Jennie Turnbull served, her temper already ruffled. Why had only one of the fine gentlemen come in? Why did that one ask for ale? She had hoped, watching the party rein in that all would enter and demand wine, of which she had a small store, though it was seldom called for.

'Would the other gentlemen not like something to drink?'

'Probably,' Chapuys said haughtily, 'but it would be unfitting for them to drink with *me*. You could not know that my good woman. I am the Spanish Ambassador.'

There were a few people – all local gentry – entitled to address her thus, from a foreigner the term was offensive; and the idea that nobody was good enough to drink with him angered her. Chapuys knew the English well; they were as riddled with class-consciousness as any people on earth, but they did not like it to be mentioned. He completed his task of enraging her by drinking her ale without a word of praise, and with an expression of faint distaste.

'If it's not to your taste there's wine to be had.'

'This sad drink is more suited to my mood,' he said. 'I am disappointed in my errand. I had hoped to see the prisoner at Kimbolton, but was turned away.'

The woman's neck reddened, a sure sign.

'She's got a name, you know. And if you're scared to call her by it there's no need to say *prisoner* . . . as though she'd done something bad. The bad's been done *to* her.' She had not been angry in quite this way since she found her husband in the hay with the serving wench. She turned and began to flounce away. There were times, Chapuys noted, when a starched petticoat or apron or whatever it was could rustle and crackle like the stiffest silk.

'That is a matter of opinion,' Chapuys said.

'Oh, is it?' Jennie said, turning again. 'No wonder you couldn't get in. She won't speak or look at anybody that can't give her her name. And I don't blame her. When I married Tom Turnbull I took his name and anybody that couldn't call me Jennie Turnbull after that I wouldn't talk to neither.' Often enough, when she thought of Katharine, Jennie equated her case with her own. If, when that young slut had her claws on him, Tom could have got rid of his rightful wife just by saying so, he was fool enough to have done it. Pity the poor Queen couldn't have snatched up a pitchfork and clouted Nan Bullen with the handle and broke her nose so no man'd ever want to look at her again. That was what Jennie had done to her rival; and given Tom one for good measure.

'You misjudge me,' Chapuys said. 'It is because I am prepared to give her her rightful title that I am not permitted to see her.'

That needed thinking over; Jennie did not move in circles where attitudes changed from one minute to the next; in and around *The Goat and Compasses* you knew what a man would say minutes before he said it.

'You mean you're on her side?'

'I am. And so, I think, are you.'

That could be a trick. Foreigners were full of tricks. And this one, coming in here and first making her angry so she let her tongue loose, and now changing his tune. And all those men outside, waiting. Arrest? More unlikely things were said to have happened. The red faded from her neck, and even from her face.

'And how do you make that out? All I said was she'd got a name and liked to be called by it, like any woman would. And I said that under my own roof. And nobody heard but you. It'll be your word against mine.'

'I rather think,' Chapuys said, 'that in you I have found what I was looking for. I am not allowed to see Her Grace or to communicate with her. I understand that one of her friends comes here from time to time.' He waited; the woman said nothing. 'If I found a way of sending a verbal message, or even a letter here, would you be willing to pass it on?' He looked outside the window. 'Perhaps inside a duck or a dove. Fresh food is hard to come by in winter; and nine women out of ten in England would wish to send the Queen a tasty morsel, if it were within their power to do so.'

He then made his first mistake; he opened his pouch.

'I'm not taking your money,' she said. 'And I'm making no promises.'

He would not have been surer of her had she sworn on the Cross.

'Any messenger I send,' he said, 'will carry one of these buttons about him. And now, let my company come in. They are mainly Spaniards and will choose wine, thereby depriving themselves of the best ale in England.'

In Kimbolton Katharine and Maria forced open the casket which was locked, but had no key and Katharine read the letter which had taken Chapuys a long time to write since every word must be set down with double intent – to enlighten and confuse. He praised the English virtue of sympathising with the oppressed; he said that it was embarrassing for him to have no real news of her because wherever he went the first question everybody asked was how was her health; of mind and body; and had there been any change of late? The Princess Mary was in good health and good heart so far as he knew. Then there followed a passage of peevishness; in all his life Chapuys had never known people so boastful as the English; one could understand the Lords Darcy and Dacre, far to the North, with the border in their keeping, saying boastful things about their power, but surely it was a national mania for grandeur that made a tannery owner count his retainers! He said that he hoped to have some real news of her before he sent his next letter to the Emperor who was greatly concerned about her. And so, and on . . . It was a letter which, falling into the wrong hands, would have done Chapuys little harm, and Katharine none at all.

Out of deliberate obfuscation the message rung clearly, and was answered, in her mind, even as she read it; there was no need for her to think about it even. She would never encourage war. But what of Mary? Were seductive whispers about Darcy and Dacre and armed tanyard workers reaching her? Were there people, meaning well, who would perhaps suggest to Mary now that it was her duty to head any kind of rising that would set her mother free? She must, somehow, communicate with Mary. But how?

Then she noticed in Chapuy's letter the strange assumption that it would be answered. Yet he knew her circumstances.

She sent for Filipez.

'Can you get out tomorrow, or next day? One of my letters is very important.'

'I can always lame a horse,' Filipez said.

In the morning it was Sir Edmund's favourite mount which limped and was restive. It was at best an ill-tempered animal and pain had not improved it. Filipez's offer to try it out was gladly accepted.

Once he was well out of sight of the Castle, Filipez dismounted and pried out the bean that was the cause of the trouble and the horse ran smoothly and swiftly to *The Goat and Compasses*, where, watching his moment, he took two letters from inside his doublet and offered them to Jennie who said:

'Letters are useless to me; I can't read.'

'May I leave them with you, Madam?' What she had liked about him from the first was his mannerliness. Francisco would have been surprised to know how often, lying on the fat featherbed, beside her snoring Tom, she thought, even dreamed of him; not as he was now, old and growing decrepit, but as he had been once, when she also had been very different.

'What people leave here is their business,' she said. 'A man once left a goat. I fed it for a fortnight before it was called for.'

'You have a heart of gold, as I have said before.'

'I've got sense enough to know that if these are left to lay about they'll get dirty. I'll put them in my lockfast place.' That repository of sweet things gone sour; the first fairing Tom had ever brought her, a curl from a dead child's head, a corn-dolly made by another child who had lived longer but not long enough; her grandmother's charm against toothache, a chicken's wishbone, broken and put together in the form of a crooked cross. It had not worked, despite the connection between chickens and teeth – a chicken having none – and the old woman's muttered incantations. Every time Jennie Turnbull opened her lockfast place to add a coin, sometimes two, to the hoard which Tom knew nothing about, she wondered why she kept such a lot of old, sad things.

Francisco had hardly gone when a pedlar came in. He was a poor one; the kind who if he earned two pence in a day, spent three. She knew his kind. And today he was plainly short of money; she could have anything that he carried in return for a mug of ale. He carried nothing that she needed or fancied and she told him so, bluntly.

'I have some learning, mistress. I could write a letter, or read one.' He stood humbly, cap in hand, as so many had stood; too many of them thought that taverns could give ale away. But in his ragged greasy hat, a silver button shone.

That was quick work, she thought, not realising that in Anecy, if you were the eldest and wished to help your overburdened mother . . . if you were a student at Turin, with your own work to do and the work of other, luckier, lazier young men to help with, in order to eat, you learned to be quick. And the habit stayed.

She went, for the second time in less than an hour, to the haunted lockfast place; she took the two letters, and a mug of ale and placed them before the pedlar, saying no word.

He was a quick worker too. She turned the pig meat that was to be ham in its bath of brine and honey and came out. The man and the letters had gone. The mug was drained and beside it lay a knot of red ribbon and a length of lace, wound about a spool. Twenty years earlier, eager to attract Tom Turnbull's attention, she would, God forgive her! – have given her soul for such trimmings. As it was she picked them up quickly and added them to her collection of sorry little things, best forgotten.

But Chapuys had made contact with Katharine. He proceeded to find a way of communicating secretly with Mary.

CHAPTER 23

When Chapuys received Katharine's letter he was agonised. He had imagined that the months in Kimbolton would have induced a different state of mind. She must realise how things were trending and that her passive attitude could not be maintained forever. He wrote to his master: 'She is so scrupulous and has such great respect for the King that she would consider herself damned without remission if she took any way tending to war.' But even as he wrote he considered the scruples excessive and the respect misplaced; and he could think such things without any diminution of respect.

The letter to the Princess had been addressed to her, but sent to him so that he might find means of delivering it and as he stared at it, he faced one of the major temptations of his life. He could guess its tone. Expediency, common sense, wordly wisdom, even his loyalty to Katharine herself, urged that the letter should be destroyed and Mary left to make her own decisions. Mary, torn between her understanding for the need of immediate action and her mother's urge towards inaction, could only take refuge in delay, and delay would be fatal to the cause.

Twice he carried the letter to Mary towards the fire, and each time he held his hand. The Queen had trusted him and if he – even in her own interest – betrayed that trust, he would rank with the others who, in large matters or small, had betrayed her in the past. So he sent on the letter by Lady Jane Rochford, the wife of George Boleyn who was one of the Concubine's ladies, her sister-in-law and deadliest enemy.

Chapuys' experience had taught him that apart from a few exceptional cases, hatred, malice and grudge-bearing were fully as powerful and slightly more reliable than love and devotion. The pedlar who had so soon appeared at the *Goat and Compasses* was actually a respectable young wool-buyer who had hoped to marry one of Katharine's English maids, taken from Buckden by Suffolk. So long as his resentment lasted – that is until he fell in love anew – he could be trusted to use his legs and his wits in order to do the King an injury and therefore the Queen a service. My enemy's enemy is my friend, was a sound and workable principle upon which Chapuys relied.

Jane Rochford's motive for hating Anne Chapuys had never fathomed; but she did hate her so much that when, shortly after the birth of Elizabeth scandal about Anne had been circulating, her accusation was most disgusting of all; she said that her marriage was ruined because of her husband's unnatural passion for his sister. It had not been said openly and what Chapuys called 'the filth campaign' had been withdrawn; but a woman who would say that about Anne would be the friend of the Queen and of the Princess.

Jane Rochford was useful because she had access to Mary. Anne went to visit her daughter and her ladies went with her.

Mary, reading her mother's letter, was dismayed. 'Dear daughter, I urge and command you, stay still and do nothing, remain in obedience to your father in all things save those of conscience. To those who advise otherwise, be deaf. Of violence no good ever came, or will; patience and time sort all things. It is by tribulation in this world that we reach happiness in the next . . .'

It was the letter of an ageing woman, resigned, to a young one, unresigned. It was the letter of a woman, never very politically astute, and now shut away behind walls, to a girl who, faced by insecurity too early, tended to confuse, and always would, politics with personalities, and who for some time now had lived, if not at the very centre of events, on the immediate periphery. Mary's world, except for one small space, was occupied by people good or bad, by notions right or wrong. Black, white, friend, enemy. The exception was the child Elizabeth, too young and too enchanting to be dismissed from or included within any narrow category.

Mary spent a good deal of time in the ordinary, eventless days, in trying to make Elizabeth walk. She was a sharp, knowing little thing, with an astonishing vocabulary and a will of her own, but so many people were anxious for the honour of carrying her – and thus taking precedence of all, when the cry came, 'Make way for the Princess Elizabeth' – that she was extremely lazy. And what would happen to her, Mary wondered, when the time came when nobody craved the honour of carrying her?

That time could come by two roads. A rising in England which would restore Katharine to the throne and Mary to the position this child now occupied: or Father, tiring of the Concubine – there was a good deal of talk about this – might put her away, and in that case as Mary put it to herself – we shall both be in the same case. Either way it was advisable that Elizabeth should learn to walk well and strongly, against the day when there would be no eager arms.

So she would set Elizabeth against some solid object, take some steps backwards and squat on her heels, 'Liz, come to me. Come to Mary. Come!'

'Mary carry!'

'No. Liz come to Mary.'

Eventually Liz would totter forward and fall into Mary's welcoming arms saying, 'Here I am!'

'Here you are. Safe and sound.' Then Mary would repeat the process. Nobody else could persuade Elizabeth to take more than two steps. And because her father whom she had loved could no longer be regarded even with respect, and her mother whom she loved was immured in Kimbolton, and Reginald Pole whom she could have loved was still on the continent, Mary loved Elizabeth.

No sign of that love showed on the days when Anne came to visit her daughter. Most often then the Lady Mary was absent, keeping to her room with a cough, a cold in the head, a stiff neck, a headache, a pain between the shoulders. The little ailments were genuine enough; it was by the grace of God, she thought, that they coincided with the visits of the usurper. When, in a sunless January, they came all together, for apparently no cause at all, and continued, accompanied by high fever and moments of delirium, she took to her bed willing to die rather than face again the torture of indecision, the knowing that every message which Chapuys sent her urged one course of action, the one she longed to take, while Katharine said, 'be still,' 'be deaf'.

She had borne for months the conflict of loyalties. Was Fisher to die, and More and Abell and more than two score others while she sat with folded hands? With the whole of the North, and the East, ready to rise and the Emperor willing – so Chapuys said – to come to the aid of any party that declared for the Pope and the Queen. It needed only the word which Katharine, at Kimbolton, was unwilling to give, but which Mary could, and perhaps should.

She saw, quite clearly, where one duty lay, the stemming of heresy; but there again, all was confused. Father had dipped a toe into Lutheran waters, just long enough to justify his defiance of the Pope and to take, with English connivance, permission to make this bigamous marriage. Then he had retreated and taken up the untenable double position of Head of the Church in England *and* Defender of the Faith. Even he could not long hold the balance between the old and the new. And if Anne gave England the needed prince, the slide into heresy would be certain.

Her indisposition offered a respite; she was now unable to do anything but to stay still; too sick to ride northwards and rouse Darcy and Dacre; too weak to be responsible for anything. So she lay in bed sometimes thinking that perhaps this was God's will being made plain to her, and at other times thinking that it was a test of her resolution; sometimes, blessedly, not thinking at all, back at Ludlow, back at Greenwich, or here, at Hatfield, teaching Elizabeth to walk.

Chapuys was assiduous in his enquiries and expressions of sympathy whenever he came into the presence of the King.

'I sent my own physician, Dr. Butts, who reports that he can find nothing that would account for the trouble. But she is ill; and I am worried.'

He was worried; he still had no son.

'I wonder,' Chapuys said, 'whether Your Grace would consider calling upon Dr. de La Sa?' He said it gently, almost humbly, but the memory of another conversation hung heavily between them.

'If he can be spared and if his presence would give any reassurance,' Henry said, answering the implication rather than the words, 'we will send for him.'

Chapuys' message to Katharine went by devious ways; the King's order was carried direct, so the first Katharine heard of Mary's illness was a message from Sir Edmund requesting that Dr. de La Sa should leave at once to attend upon the Lady Mary. January days were short; the courier anxious to reach Huntingdon before dark. There was not even time to send a letter, 'Give her my love, my dearest love. Tell her to banish troublesome thoughts and think only of recovering her health. And Dr. de La Sa, let me know. I must know. Inform the Spanish Ambassador . . .'

There followed an endless time. Chapuys' letter came at last, but it was the one he had written before Dr. de La Sa was sent for, so it told nothing new and it contained an ominous sentence. 'Illness can be of mind as well as of body; indecision can destroy and forced inaction can drive men mad.' For her own sake Katharine must be prodded and made to understand – as Chapuys was sure she did not – that Mary's position was worse than her own.

Katharine felt the prod and moved in a direction opposite to the one Chapuys had planned.

'I must write a letter,' she said to Maria, and went into the small, cold, north-facing little room. It was a letter which must go openly and fast.

Filipez had brought back from his outing, as well as Chapuys' delayed letter, one of Jennie's goodwill offerings, a tender little pullet which Maria was about to cook over the fire in the big outer room. She had no spit, a string, hung from a nail served. A youth of privation had made her resourceful and lately she had plied every poverty-inspired trick, things she had thought to be done with forever when she embarked at Corunna, one of the ladies of the Princess of Wales. Presumably Concepcion and Manuella had known poverty, too, but of a different brand, a brainless acceptance of circumstance. Maria did not accept, she combated; she had even solved the business of getting a fairly bright fire. One day, when the daily allowance of logs, most of them damp and green, was delivered, she raised a great fuss because no fuel had come. A second lot, after some commotion, was sent over, and all that day while half the double allowance smouldered and smoked, the other half stood on end, drying out, turned every now and again. Next day, and ever after, the fire was considerably brighter.

The pullet was done to a turn when Katharine came out, a letter in her hand.

'I am going across to the other side. I shall not be long.'

Startled – for never once had the Queen set foot in the part of the house where she was not acknowledged – but practical, too, Maria tied a knot in the string so that the fowl would stay warm but cook no more, and said, 'It is a cold night, Your Grace. We shall need our shawls.'

'It would be better that I go alone.'

'You cannot go *there* unattended.'

'Those who ask favours must go humbly, Maria.'

Those who asked favours were often repulsed and she wanted no witness to her humiliation.

So she went humbly, her head wrapped in a square of grey woollen cloth. A thin cold sleet was falling.

The humiliation, through a boy's mistake, came early.

In the great hall of the other house supper was over and the trestle-tables were being cleared; hounds were crunching bones. Some of the boys, laughing and shouting as they made preparations for the night, had never even seen her, but one recognised her, ceased dousing the candles, came towards her and bowed.

'I wish to see Sir Edmund or Sir Edward. Either would do.'

'They are this way.' He ran ahead to the door of the little room, similar to her own sanctum, to which the knights had withdrawn. He opened the door with a flourish and said:

'Sir, the Queen!'

He was a local boy and sometimes slipped home to his family where Katharine was regarded as Queen, and once, when he had referred to the Princess Dowager, his mother had said, 'Up at the castle you must do as others do. But not here, James. Not here.'

She stood in the doorway, a small shawled figure. She had, both knights remembered, rebuffed every well-meant overture.

'Come here, boy,' Sir Edmund said. '*Who* is at the door?'

'Sir, the Princess Dowager.'

'To help you to remember . . .' Sir Edmund reached out and clouted the boy, a buffet on either side of the head. The eager young face creased, the bright eyes began to water.

She had a weakening thought: Does it matter so much how I am named? Poor little boy! Had I borne such a one none of this would have come about.

By this time Sir Edmund and Sir Edward too were on their feet, bowing, saying 'Your Royal Highness,' and offering her the chair nearest the fire.

'Thank you; I will not sit. I need not detain you long. I have come to ask a favour. I know that I am allowed no communication, but my daughter, the Princess, is ill, as you know. And I have written to the Spanish Ambassador asking him to ask His Grace to allow her to come here, where I can tend her. Will you despatch the letter?'

Both remembered the snubs which had rankled.

'We have our orders,' Sir Edmund said.

'I beg you, disregard them. My daughter is ill, she needs a mother's care. If you will forward this letter I will take the onus upon me. Say that I begged you and that you, out of pity, disregarded orders. Or say that as Queen I ordered you . . . Either way, any way . . .'

'If Your Royal Highness will leave the letter with us, we will deliberate,' Sir Edmund said.

'And inform you, shortly,' Sir Edmund said.

'I thank you,' she said, and went away.

'And what do we do with this?' Sir Edmund asked.

'Open it.' It was typical of her arrogance that it should be sealed. Anyone with the slightest sense of what was proper would have offered the letter open, inviting them to read what they were asked to despatch. 'It may well contain something other than what she said; the Lady Mary's illness might offer just the needed excuse to slip a letter out.'

It contained exactly what Katharine had said.

'And do we send it on?'

'I *think* so. The cat may not have taken its last jump. Even the King veers. Sending all this way for that doctor fellow,' Sir Edward said thoughtfully.

'Everybody veers. Even the new Pope; one minute promising to look into the business again as though he questioned Clement's ruling; and the next minute making Fisher a Cardinal – and he in the Tower for holding to what Clement said – even before it was said. Things have never been in such a muddle. *And* you heard what the boy called her. A slip of the tongue, but it shows how they think. The country is riddled with it. We'll send the letter.'

Chapuys hurried straight to Henry, took the letter from his pouch and offered it. Henry recoiled, recognising the writing at a glance.

'I ordered her,' he said angrily, 'not to write to me.'

'The letter was sent to me, Your Grace; I thought it wise to bring it to you.'

'Read it.' He had no wish to touch it; those regular letters when he had been away in France! The very news of Flodden had been written in this hand!

'The answer to that is no!' he said angrily. 'Of all the impossible things to ask. My daughter's place is either at my Court or with her sister. And there is this to consider; separately they are wilful and headstrong beyond bearing; together they would be worse. And there is another thing too, Messire Chapuys.' The bright blue eyes narrowed and looked dangerous. 'I have heard rumour of a plot to steal my daughter out of my kingdom. This might be the first step.'

'Indeed? No such rumour has reached me. But naturally Your Grace has sources inaccessible to me.' He looked innocent and between them was the fund of carefully fostered goodwill; and there was no evidence against him, but Henry's suspicion was no longer dependent on evidence; it was rapidly becoming self-sustaining.

'Kimbolton,' he said, the stare bearing down, 'would be just the jumping-off place.'

'Would it? Your Grace may remember that I have never seen it.'

A reminder that he had been implicitly obedient.

'I have, so far, been lenient,' Henry said warningly. 'I am astounded at my own leniency. But those who work against me, or oppose me will learn . . .' His mind's focus shifted, as it did so often, to Thomas More, in prison. He had valued More beyond price; so much so that when, offered the Chancellorship after Wolsey's fall, More had demurred and said, 'But, my lord, you know that I am against you in this great matter,' he had said, 'Thomas, I promise you freedom of conscience.'

The distasteful truth was that freedom of conscience was a thing that could only be allowed when things went well.

'. . . they will learn. Leo may send Fisher his Cardinal's hat, but there'll be no head to wear it!'

And yet, if they would only give in, how good he was prepared to be to them. More with any office he cared to name: Fisher back in his Bishopric; Mary given some resounding title – if he could make Anne a Marchioness in her own right, he could make his daughter a Duchess; Katharine, completely free, properly and even regally attended, could have Greenwich.

If they would give in.

'I do not think,' Chapuys said, 'that I, in any regard, have opposed Your Grace. My impartiality has become a byword and prevents me, perhaps, from hearing things of interest.'

'Your impartiality is such, Messire, that people hesitate to say to you, It is a fine day, lest you should make some qualifying remark.' If only you knew some of the things that are said to me!

'Thank you, Your Grace,' Chapuys said, as though replying to a compliment. 'I trust I shall not be thought partial if I remind you that there is now no physician at Kimbolton. In case of illness or accident . . .'

'The fellow can return . . .' No, that would not look well, to remove the Spaniard as soon as Mary showed signs of improvement. '. . . to Kimbolton, if a house can be found, not too near, suitable for my daughter until she is fully well. They can share a doctor, but have no other communication.'

Both the women whom Chapuys wished to influence within a short distance of one another and a physician making daily visits!

Concealing his jubilation, the Ambassador said:

'Both ladies will find that hard, Sire.'

Let them! Why should he be the only one to suffer. They had defied him, and by defying him driven him out on to a lonely, uphill road; and his situation was made worse by the fact that occasionally he could only admire their steadfastness. When Mary refused the oath and sycophants said, 'Were she my daughter . . .' and mentioned what they would do, he said nastily, 'You are unlikely to sire such a daughter!' And in his own Privy Council, issuing a warning about conspiracy, he said, 'The Lady

Katharine is a proud, stubborn woman of very high courage. She could easily take the field, muster a great army and wage against me a war as fierce as any her mother Isabella ever waged in Spain.'

It was a possibility which he had considered and dismissed as improbable, though it did no harm to keep the Council alive to the danger. Katharine would never rebel against him because – Jesu, what irony! – she still considered him her husband, and her duty submission to his will. And anyone else who tried open rebellion would come up against something that would jar their teeth – his personal popularity, so far unshaken. People might grumble and mutter and receive Anne in silence, but he had only to ride out of any palace gate or appear on the river to be greeted with enthusiasm. People who utterly deplored his actions were susceptible to something, a gift almost, as eclectic as water-dowsing. He did not give it much thought, it was something he had been born with and would carry until he died, gross and with death's corruption already upon him. As he had said to Katharine long ago. 'They are only people.' He thought about it so little that he never realised that therein lay the secret. Elizabeth, taking her first steps, had inherited it; Mary, moving to a house more than twenty miles from Kimbolton and hoping every day that the rule about not seeing her mother might be relaxed, had not. And Henry, counting on his popularity wherever he made contact with people, overlooked the far north and the west; the thousands of people who had never seen him or come into contact with anyone who had seen, spoken to, or brushed shoulders with anyone who had.

Chapuys knew better, taking a wider view.

CHAPTER 24

Dr. de La Sa failed, as Dr. Butts had failed, to find any physical reason for Mary's ill health; the head cold had cleared by the time he reached Hatfield, the cough lingered and would not disappear, he thought, until the weather grew warmer. She continued to complain of pain in the head, in the shoulders, and she still suffered short spells of something that was neither genuine swooning nor fever delirium. Whenever she recovered from one of these the pains vanished for a little time; if she slept well under the influence of one of his sedative potions she had no pain for an hour or two after waking, and once when Elizabeth was brought in to see her – at her own insistence, 'I want Mary! Where is Mary? – Dr. de La Sa, coming in to say that he thought the visit had lasted long enough, found his patient out of bed, playing some game which demanded more exertion than he would have believed her capable of making.

From this he deduced that misery of mind lay at the root of the trouble. Released, by sleep or unconsciousness or distraction, from the melancholy of her thoughts, she was better; and alas, he knew of no cure for melancholy. Yet, unwittingly, he supplied one.

They talked, naturally, a good deal about Katharine and Dr. de La Sa described the routine of life at Kimbolton. He was a man who had enjoyed, and still missed, the comforts of life and without fully realising what he was doing, he allowed to slip into his account mention of the privation which Katharine and those with her had lately endured. The indifferent food, the inferior fuel, a shortage of linen. 'In fact,' he said one day, when the talk had taken this turn, 'I hope that when Your Highness is sufficiently recovered to dispense with my services, the King will receive me for a moment. Then I pray God to give me courage to say what I believe – that another year in such conditions will gravely damage the Queen's health.' The moment he had said it he regretted it; the worried expression which made the Princess look so much older than her nineteen years, formed itself there, under his watching eye. He said hurriedly, 'I shall plead for a removal to some more comfortable place. And if my ministrations have improved Your Highness's condition, His Grace may be grateful enough to listen to me.'

'My condition is greatly improved,' Mary said.

He had solved the problem for her, reducing the whole muddled matter to something plain and clear, the simple duty of a daughter to save her mother from intolerable and detrimental conditions.

Mary was now so embittered towards her father that she knew that Dr. de La Sa would waste his breath in pleading – it would suit Father only too well if Mother died. He could then go through a mockery of remarriage to the Concubine and the next child – Anne was said to be pregnant again – would be legitimate by any standard.

The sending of Dr. Butts, the calling of Dr. de La Sa from Kimbolton, had not deceived Mary at all. She knew her value to her father, the man with one son, illegitimate, and two daughters, one regarded, if Chapuys was to be believed, by three quarters of the country as his legal offspring, and a woman grown; the other regarded by a quarter of the people as his heir, a mere toddler who, since Mary had taken sanctuary from the world in illness, had almost ceased to toddle.

This was the moment; she had been right to wait. Mother had been right in saying that patience and time sorted all things. God has His own way of doing things; He chose His time and His tools.

'I am quite restored today,' she said. The torturing indecision was over. She knew what she had to do.

And then, as though by a miracle, came the order that as soon as the Lady Mary was well enough to travel she was to go to a house, near enough to Kimbolton to allow her to share a physician with her mother, the Dowager Princess.

'I shall be able to ride tomorrow,' Mary said. Every omen seemed propitious; she would be in touch with her mother; in or around Kimbolton Chapuys had his secret contacts; Huntingdonshire was nearer the North than Hatfield. All things work together for good for those who love God.

'Now,' Henry said, bringing the down-bearing stare to focus upon de La Sa, 'understand this. You are the Princess Dowager's personal physician, I thought it wrong to deprive her of your services; you have done something to restore the Lady Mary's health – and for that I give you thanks. But in coming and going between them you are *not* to act as messenger. Enquiries about health may be answered; nothing more.'

'Any order that Your Grace gives me shall be observed to the letter,' de La Sa said. 'But if I might venture to remind Your Grace, the present conditions in Kimbolton are not conducive to health.'

'*You* look well enough.'

'I am a man,' de La Sa said. 'And I am kept busy. Even in so small a household . . . and the other side of the house, having no physician of its own, calls upon me from time to time. So I have other things to concern me. For the lady it is different, Your Grace. The bleak conditions, the poor food, the . . . the . . .' he spread his hands in an un-English gesture, 'the general atmosphere is unfavourable to health. I do not think she will survive another winter there.'

'She has the remedy in her own hands, Dr. de La Sa. A few words and she could be back at Greenwich. Or Richmond. She could have Hampton Court if she chose.'

He was no longer wholly comfortable anywhere. Greenwich was peculiarly Katharine's place; there was the lime avenue down which he had walked to meet and claim her, the room where Mary had been born. In Richmond there was the room where an old man had used his last breath to gasp out a few warning words; and the room in which a most precious child had died. Whitehall and Hampton Court had been Wolsey's and memories hung heavy in both places. What he needed, Henry realised, staring at the Spanish doctor's earnest face, was a brand-new palace. And he knew where. The idea came to him in a flash, as in earlier days his songs and their tunes had come. A manor named Cuddington, on the Kingston road; near enough to the City of London to be accessible, far enough removed to be healthy. He visualised it, not unlike the fairy-tale palace of the Field of the Cloth of Gold. (Wolsey again!)

'She could live where she chose,' he said, his inner eye entranced by towers rearing into the sky, such a palace as had never yet been built; and he would call it nonsuch. My Palace of Nonsuch.

De La Sa refrained from making the obvious retort and simply said, 'As her doctor, Your Grace, I wish she could be ordered elsewhere.'

'That needs thinking over,' Henry said, dismissing it from his mind.

The house which had been chosen as a temporary residence for Mary was nearly twenty miles from Kimbolton. To Dr. de La Sa the journey seemed endless – he made it in different directions each alternate day and the spring weather was cold that year – but to Katharine and Mary it seemed so short a distance that the proximity was cruel. The promise which the doctor had made to the King he tried to observe, stretching health to include looks. 'The Princess appears to have shed five years,' he could say, with truth and without feeling that he was breaking his word. He could say, 'The change of air has greatly benefited her.' And since Mary now seemed fully recovered, lively and strong, he felt that she could bear to hear that her mother suffered a good deal of pain from the rheumatism which the winter had exacerbated, partly from some puzzling cause. 'High in the chest, Your Highness, and sometimes it strikes into her arm.' He demonstrated on his own body the site of the mysterious pain – mysterious because, so far as he could tell, neither heart nor lungs seemed affected.

'Will you tell her that I hope she will be better soon? That I *know* she will be better.' Dr. de La Sa would carry only messages concerned with health. 'I gave my word, Your Highness, hoping thereby to lend weight to my plea that the Queen should be removed from Kimbolton.'

'She will be removed; and shortly,' Mary said, 'I know, Dr. de La Sa, that you are allowed only to speak of my health to her and of her health to me, but this is a word concerning health. Tell her, from me, to be of good cheer and to cherish herself. Better days are coming.'

It was incredible, de La Sa thought to himself, comparing in his mind's eye this upright, sturdy, lively girl with the miserable creature to whom he had been called at Hatfield. And he felt at liberty to deliver the message; it concerned health; good cheer and self-care were healthful measures; and the better days, the summer days must come.

Katharine never knew how nearly she missed liberation or by how narrow a margin civil war had been averted. On a comparatively mild day Francisco Filipez rode out and came back with three eggs, a pot of honey and some news. 'It is only gossip, Your Grace, but they are saying that the

Princess is to be more closely watched, and recalled to London very soon because the King has heard a whisper of a plot against him. A rising, Madam, led by the Princess and the Spanish Ambassador. And it is true that four men, spies by the look of them, Jennie said, stopped at her place to drink ale and asked direction to the place where the Princess is.'

Let it happen, had been his first thought. Singlehanded he would deal with Sir Edmund and Sir Edward, and glad to. And there were several others, within the walls of Kimbolton who could be counted upon to take the Queen's side or remain neutral.

Everything suddenly fell into place; Mary's sudden improvement in health; 'a different person,' de La Sa had said. The messages about better days on the way; the doctor's assurances that she would not spend another winter in Kimbolton; and from Chapuys, of late, nothing. The focus of his attention had shifted. To Mary?

He could not persuade me, she thought, he found Mary more malleable. And it must not be!

She said, 'Francisco, tomorrow you must make some excuse to ride again. I have a most urgent letter to despatch.'

She sat down and wrote to Chapuys so forcibly that the quill spluttered. 'I have heard that His Grace has some suspicion of her surety, but I cannot think that he has so little confidence in me. I am determined to die in this kingdom and I offer my own person as surety for my daughter to the end that if any such thing be attempted, the King, my lord, may do justice upon me as the most traitorous woman ever born.'

She sent for poor Dr. de La Sa and spoke to him so sternly that it seemed another transformation in a patient had taken place.

'What do you know of the plot in which my daughter appears to be involved?'

'Nothing Your Grace. What plot?' His innocence was manifest.

'I believe you. But think back. Her recovery was sudden. What happened on that day? Was she visited? Try to remember.'

'So far as I can recall, Your Grace . . . I gave her, perhaps incautiously, yes, I thought after, it was incautious, some account, moderated because of her condition, of the way in which you were housed and treated. And I said that I hoped that when her condition had improved His Grace would be sufficiently grateful to receive me and give some heed to my plea that you should be removed from here. She then said that her condition was improved; and from that moment she has never looked back. She became, as I have told you, a different person altogether.'

'Then I regard you as responsible for all that has happened since.'

'Responsible for what, Your Grace? I am sorry. I fail to follow . . .'

'You told her that the food was poor? The fire, despite Maria's trick, insufficient, bed linen scarce; and that another winter in Kimbolton would be the end of me? True or not?'

'Your Grace, I mentioned hardships. The advisability of a change of residence . . . The Princess appeared to be concerned but not unduly distressed. And as I said, she immediately announced that she was better. I thought at the time she said so in order to expedite my interview with His Grace; but she *was* better and has remained so.'

He was completely puzzled.

'As I thought,' Katharine said still looking at him with disfavour. 'You must now undo the harm you did – unwittingly, I grant you, but grave harm which must be undone.'

'But, Madam, what harm? How can I undo something that I am ignorant of having done?'

'You must break the promise that you made to His Grace and carry a letter for me to my daughter. And be ready to ride with it within ten minutes.' He had only just arrived back in Kimbolton. 'Moreover, to-morrow morning you must rise early and come back to me bringing the assurance that the Princess has understood and is prepared to obey my order.'

'Perhaps Your Grace will permit me to say that this is precisely the kind of communication which I undertook not to assist in.'

'You were to concern yourself with health only. I know. Health is concerned – I shall neither sleep nor eat until I am reassured. The health, indeed the lives, of thousands of people are in danger. Do you wish to see civil war in England, Dr. de La Sa?'

He gaped at her.

'Madam, are you feeling quite well?'

'Quite well, thank you. You can occupy yourself while you wait by making a copy of this letter,' she tapped the one she had written to Chapuys. 'And in a legible hand, please.'

Never, in all the long time he had served her had he seen her like this. Then, when he had glanced through what he was to copy, he felt again that she was suffering from some disturbance of the mind. He said, almost timidly:

'Your Grace . . . Are you fully aware of what this means? The situation is not clear to me, but what is clear is that such a statement might involve grave risk to yourself.'

'It was intended to,' Katharine said, without looking up.

De La Sa wrote with unaccustomed slowness and clarity, rounding each letter like a child. He still could not see in what respect he had offended.

'Make the best speed you can,' Katharine said, handing him both letters, folded together. He had never heard her speak so curtly to the youngest page and he did not realise that the manner was deliberately assumed in order to frighten him into an act of disobedience.

Mary looked stunned when she read the letter and the enclosure and then burst into a passion of weeping more violent than Dr. de La Sa had ever seen, even in a house from which Death had snatched an only child, or a breadwinner. Most women sat down in order to weep; Mary walked up and down, wringing her hands together and drawing harsh noisy breaths that sounded more like the death rattle in the throat of a strong man than the sobs of a woman. Dr. de La Sa, weary – he had ridden forty miles that day – and under some emotional stress himself, was flustered.

'Your Highness; sit down; try to be calm. You will undo all the good . . . you will bring on a headache . . .'

'This ruins all,' she said hoarsely, and continued to walk and wring her hands while the tears – not copious, the doctor observed, but slow and difficult – squeezed themselves out and ran down her face which was as pale now as when she lay in bed at Hatfield.

'You must,' he said, 'Your Highness *must* strive for calm. You will be ill again . . . I beg you, sit down . . . Take a little wine . . .'

'Leave me be. I have to make up my mind.' She locked her fingers together and beat on the air with them as though hammering something.

Then, abruptly, she was calm. She sat in a chair and brushed the last tears away with the tips of her fingers.

'So!' she said. 'It is over. I cannot, even her own cause, sacrifice her. There she sits, a prisoner, helpless and without hope. She is ill-housed, ill-fed, ageing, ailing – and she is the most powerful woman in this world, Dr. de La Sa, the most powerful woman in the world.'

As she said it she shuddered, a spasm that rattled from her teeth to her heels on the floor.

'A little wine now?' Dr. de La Sa suggested again. Wine heartened and soothed; given enough of it a man could bear the amputation of a limb by a barber surgeon with no more noise and complaint than a man with no wine in him would make at the removal of a splinter or the lancing of a boil.

'Yes. This bitter pill needs something to wash it down; and you have made a double journey. Pour for us both; I should not wish to be seen in this state . . .' She brushed away two more slow running tears.

In this house whose owners were uncertain of their role – host and hostess? unofficial gaolers? – a natural good-heartedness had tipped the balance and Mary had been served with the best. The wine which the doctor poured – his hand a little less steady than usual – was both heartening and soothing.

Mary said, 'I am well now. I need you no more. I shall return forthwith to Hatfield or any other place to which the King orders me.' All over, the trumpets, the banners, the release of Katharine, Queen of England, the triumphant ride into London, the restoration of Papal authority. Finished, done with. God's will.

'It is a wise decision,' de La Sa said – not knowing what it concerned. 'Being so near, and not allowed to meet, has imposed strain upon you both.' He was still in the dark; he had, he realised, become involved with something outside his sphere; the Queen's strange manner towards him; his own breach of faith; the Princess's behaviour. From his confusion and exhaustion and the effect of a full glass of good wine after more than a year of abstinence, he took refuge in his profession and the Hippocrean oath: 'The regimen I adopt shall be for the benefit of my patients according to my ability and judgment and not for their hurt. Whatsoever house I enter I will go there for the benefit of the sick.'

He said, 'Your Highness, wherever you go, and whatever happens, I advise calm and contentment of mind. Upon such basis all health depends. The Queen, your mother, has survived trials that could have destroyed her had she has not maintained a quiet mind, willing to wait upon events.'

'And never one event brought her good. I could, I would have saved her. But faced with this . . .' she tapped the papers which she had flung down in the paroxysm of anger and frustration, 'I am helpless. A hobbled horse. She waits in Kimbolton for death to release her. For what do *I* wait with this quiet contented mind?'

Bit by bit, helped by the wine, he saw the situation in which he had played his unwitting part, like Justice, blindfold, in the morality plays.

He thought quickly; the King was not his patient; the Princess was.

'I can no more look into the future than any other man – except as a doctor. And this I can say: Men who in their forties grow fat and continue to eat as though they were still young and are of a choleric disposition, seldom make old bones.'

Mary said, 'Oh,' and put her hand to her face.

'Your Highness, that is an observation, not a prognosis.'

'But my mother might, despite all, outlive him?'

'It is possible; even likely. With an untroubled mind . . .' He realised his duty to his other patient, and in turn tapped the papers. 'This kind of thing is not good for Her Grace.'

'There will be no more of it,' Mary said. 'Tell her that from me. I yield to her will as to the will of God. Tell her I shall not stir, that remembering she is my surety I shall walk most warily and wait. Go now, Dr. de La Sa and give her this assurance.' She added with the good common sense that the doctor recognised as a sign of mental health, 'It is almost dusk; but every horse knows the way to his own stable.'

Sixty miles in a day!

CHAPTER 25

In April Fisher, More, Abell and others taken from Buckden, and a number of Carthusian monks, forty-five people in all, were executed. Fisher took with him to the block all immediate hope of Paul III's making – as he had considered doing – any compromise with Henry. The political situation had seemed to warrant a review of the whole dispute and Paul had thought about making an offer to recognise Henry's present marriage in return for the restitution of Papal authority in England. That was now impossible. Fisher was a Cardinal, a man of learning and of exemplary life and his sole offence was that he had believed in Julius' dispensation, which Clement had confirmed; the olive branch could not readily be extended to the man who had killed him. Also, word came seeping through that the Carthusians, while awaiting trial, had been villainously treated, so shackled that they could neither sit nor lie down and practically starved. The papers for Henry's excommunication were drawn up; but not signed.

More went to death almost gaily; at the scaffold he said, 'I pray you, master Lieutenant, see me safe up, and as for my coming down, let me shift for myself.' All London mourned him. He had been an honest lawyer, insusceptible to bribery. He took with him the last vestige of Henry's youth. Henry had loved him like a brother, enjoyed his company, revelled in his wit. In allowing him to die Henry had again violated his own nature and he was less resilient now. He refused to admit any sense of guilt or of wrongdoing and took refuge in a vast corrosive self-pity. He was right; those against him were wrong and they would regret it.

Even in the streets of his beloved London he seemed, for a moment, to have lost that personal popularity which meant so much to him. Immediately after the executions he rode out and faced, for the first time in his life, a crowd whose cheers were thin and faint-hearted. He reined in his horse and said in a loud, carrying voice, 'I did not know that so many of you were dumb. You have my sympathy.'

'You,' was the magic word; it was addressed directly to every man, every woman in the crowd, with the mocking I-know-you, you-know-me grin. Had he shown discomfiture at the silence, or merely ignored it, it would have lasted and there would have been other, longer silences. But he had challenged them, and they responded. There he sat, solid, confident, handsome, their King. They proceeded to show him that they were not dumb. It was a gift, like being able to walk a tightrope, this ability to establish intimate contact with people whose names he would never know, whose opinions and feelings he was prepared to disregard if they conflicted with his own. Such moments provided the exact counter-balance to those of self-pity during which he would think: Forty-four this year, and still no son; love for Kate dead, passion for Anne soured into something worse than indifference; the damned heretics battering on the gate that only he, good Catholic, kept barred; and the Pope threatening to excommunicate him. Lonely, too; one daughter a mere prattler, the other a surly, defiant young woman who by rights should be in the Tower.

And Katharine was to blame for it all.

He could no longer bear to be reminded of her existence. When Chapuys began to speak of the advisability of her removal from Kimbolton before another winter set in, Henry said, 'Speak of something else, Messire, or withdraw.' When Cromwell said, 'I have another communication from Sir Edmund Bedingfield . . .' Henry said, 'Forget it.' He did not wish to hear that the allowance was inadequate, in the face of rising prices, or, presently, that it was not paid at all.

Chapuys had recovered from the failure of what he now thought of as the Winter Plot which had come to nothing because a woman who could not order herself a proper dinner or a supply of new bed linen, had issued an order which her daughter had obeyed. He was eagerly awaiting the day when Henry should be excommunicated. Excommunication was a curse and it cancelled out all bonds of allegiance. Those who, in January, might have stood by the King or wavered, could turn against an excommunicated man with clear consciences. The Queen would feel differently, too; a staunch upholder of Papal authority would be bound to take the ban very seriously.

But sentence must be executed before the Concubine quickened again. So just as Chapuys had urged Clement to give his verdict before Henry took matters into his own hands, so now he urged Paul to sign and seal the sentence of damnation before it was too late.

Clement had adopted time-wasting measures in the hope that Henry's infatuation for Anne would wear itself out; Paul delayed from making the final breach in the hope that Katharine would die. In Rome the shock and horror of Fisher's execution had begun to die down. With Katharine dead the way might yet be open to some kind of bargain with the man who held the balance of power between France and Spain.

Paul's delaying tactics made Chapuys anti-Papist for several minutes. It was a letter explaining that the papers of excommunication could not be risked, signed and delivered because the aggrieved person – Katharine – had not made a formal application for such action to be taken. If she would write to Rome, requesting the King's excommunication, matters could proceed.

Chapuys saw through that all too clearly. The Pope and his officials believed that Katharine, shut away and denied all communication with the outer world, was incapable of making such a demand. And that was where they made a mistake; reckoning without Francisco Filipez and Jennie Turnbull and ten or eleven other people who formed the secret network. Most of all reckoning without Chapuys, the son of a stubborn woman who had once fallen down the cellar stairs of the Annecy house and put her knee out of joint. She had never laid up for a day. She sat in a chair, the injured leg, with the knee hideously swollen, stretched out on a board nailed to the chair seat, and propelled by the sound leg had hitched herself about the kitchen and cooked for her family and a houseful of guests. Eustache and the younger ones could go to market, fetch water, sweep floors and empty slops, but they could not cook. So she did it, though the pain was so great that when it was necessary to move from the chair, she fainted. This quality of doggedness she had transmitted to her son and it was the thing which he recognised in Katharine.

When Katharine received from Filipez's hand the letter from Chapuys telling her what she must do, she was as much distressed as she had ever been in her life. She was in poor health; the April executions had shattered her; she felt directly responsible and lost – never to fully regain it – that absolute certainty of being *right*. She had so firmly repudiated the idea that any blood should be shed over a purely domestic matter; and now blood had been shed, the most innocent blood, the blood of best and the most faithful. Fasting, she had prayed for the souls of the dead; in the Chapel the Bishop of Llandaff had said Masses for their souls. They were martyrs, he said, reminding her that the blood of martyrs was the seed of the Church. She listened, but could not be wholly comforted. And the pain in her chest came more often, more sharply, sometimes leading to nausea which she tried to conceal from Maria who took such pains over the food.

And now this. This momentous and terrible decision.

It seemed such a horrible thing to do. To ask that Henry should be cut off from every sacrament, cursed, severed from God; in worse case than any animal which, never having known the communion of souls, did not know the lack.

The Henry she remembered was the man so meticulous about his religious observances, making his confessions, doing his penance; 'Six Masses and on a hunting day!'

Could she do this to him? She had failed to give him a son, she had lost his love, by holding to what she thought right she had driven him to defy the Pope who also thought she was right. She had loved him, loved him still, and had been his ruin.

And now she must decide upon this.

She looked at the word *aggrieved*. The aggrieved person. The word was inapt; it held implications of a desire to retaliate. She had been wronged but she had never for one moment felt any desire to be avenged. Never a day, from that terrible one at Greenwich, eight years, eight dragging years ago, when she would not have been ready to go back, with no recrimination, no reserve, to be his wife again.

Thinking was useless; she must pray about this. She went into the Chapel and knelt, said the ritual prayers and laid the whole problem at the feet of God, of Mary, the Mother of God, and of Christ Jesus their Son who had died for the sins of the world.

She prayed for help and for guidance. From time to time she realised that she was no longer praying, but thinking in her limited, human way.

Mary's rights had to be considered and protected.

The Concubine may yet bear a son. She reads Lutheran books and on one occasion, at least, begged for leniency for a man who had smuggled such books in. No child of hers – when Henry is dead – would bring England back to Rome, thus denying its own legitimacy. When Henry dies, unless Mary becomes Queen immediately, England will go headlong into heresy. If I write this letter will Henry realise . . .

The thoughts, the questions went round and round in her mind like an old horse turning a mill wheel. From time to time she realised that she was not praying, but trying to reason, and pulled herself up sharply. God help and direct me. Mary, Mother of God, pity me – not meant for such great matters . . .

Time passed.

Maria de Moreto, hovering in the narrow place between the door of the Chapel and that of the large room, was relieved to see Dr. de La Sa come in from the third door which opened on the courtyard where he had been taking his afternoon's exercise.

'Her Grace has been in there,' she said, looking towards the Chapel door, 'for three hours. I have looked in four times. She might be turned to stone for all the notice she took.'

'The letter Filipez brought her this morning disturbed her. I could see that. I am seriously considering asking Sir Edmund to forbid these rides of his. Whether he brings back a letter or mere gossip, she is always disturbed.'

'You do that, Dr. de La Sa,' Maria said, speaking between her teeth, her eyes narrowed, the very image of her formidable old father, 'and you will have no blanket on your bed and no pillow. And I will use every book you have to stoke the fire.'

Taken aback, he said, 'I meant no harm. It was her welfare I had in mind. Every time Francisco goes out . . .'

'He brings something to eat,' Maria said fiercely. 'Something *fit* to eat. The smell of autumn is in the air already. How can she go through the winter on such fare as we are given?'

How could any of them, de La Sa wondered. The coarsest, darkest barley bread, pease porridge, a kind of stew, mainly cabbage with little shreds of meat: and even this poor fare none too plentiful.

'I have done what was possible,' he said, with hurt dignity. 'I went across to the other side and made my protest.'

'You might as well have spat in the moat,' Maria said, still angered. 'Now, get in there and persuade her to come out – for her health's sake.'

Dr. de La Sa tiptoed in, bowed to the altar and then, stooping above Katharine, said softly, 'Your Grace! I think you should come with me now. It is cold in here. We are concerned for you.'

On the hottest day of summer the Chapel was chilly, its thick wall to the north never catching the sun, the southern one shaded by the buildings on the other side.

She ignored him as she had ignored Maria, and for a moment he thought that she might be dead. The immediate result of death was a flaccidity; people keeled over, collapsed into a huddled heap; but with her elbows propped, her head in her hands and her knees already bent, the Queen might have passed that stage. Rigor mortis? The timing was unpredictable; surrounding temperature, the bodily build. The Chapel was cold, and she had wasted since April.

He reached out and touched her hand. Cold as stone, cold as clay. He withdrew his hand and thought a dispassionate doctor's thought: Perhaps, for her, just as well, before the pain which he could neither diagnose nor cure, passed the point where the laudanum brought no relief – or the apothecary in Huntingdon ceased to give credit.

He was about to investigate more closely when Katharine moved, lifting her head, dropping her hands and attempting to rise. He helped her up.

'I have been trying to pray,' she said. 'But my thoughts went round and round.'

'Your Grace is exhausted, and chilled.'

'It is something I have never felt before. As though God were no longer there. Only my own thoughts, turning in emptiness. Is it possible . . . No, the notion is too fantastic.' Yet she considered it. Suppose that far away in Rome the Pope had not waited for her request but had signed the papers and excommunicated Henry, and the sentence had fallen upon her, too. Husband and wife were one; no couple had ever been more truly one than she and Henry in the golden days.

'Without God life would be unbearable,' she said.

It seemed to be a thing for her confessor to deal with; so de La Sa sent for him. Maria de Moreto fussed about with the little shawl and found a place in the larger room where the westering sun was still warm.

'What troubles you?' Llandaff asked gently, yet with a certain authority.

'Something to be decided. And I cannot. I cannot even pray about it. For the first time in my life, *I could not pray*. I was alone.'

Maria and de La Sa made to withdraw, leaving her with her confessor. But Katharine said, 'Stay. It is too great for me alone; and God gave me no answer. *You* must help me.'

It took only a few minutes to explain what had been going round and round in her head for three hours. The three looked at one another in silence. Then the doctor said irritably:

'The Spanish Ambassador shows little sense and no consideration. You were better in every way when you had no communication with the world. I should advise you to ignore the request and do nothing at all. A letter whose delivery depends upon the schooling of a baulky horse might never have reached you.'

'But it did,' Katharine said.

Llandaff also brushed the main question aside. 'The feeling that God has withdrawn is a test of faith. Many saints have experienced it. And Our Lord on the Cross cried that God had forsaken Him.'

'Have *you* ever felt it?'

'I have never attained sufficient virtue. Only the strongest spirits are called upon to pass through the dark night of the soul. It will pass . . .'

Only Maria had been thinking about the original problem. She hated the King; she wished him to be punished in this world and throughout eternity. Hell was too good for him!

But it would never do to say so. It must be put cunningly. Her ability to make the most of very little, to whip up an omelette from one egg and half a cupful of water must now be employed on a different level.

She said, 'I think your prayers for guidance *were* answered, Madam. In the feeling that God was lost to you. So the King must feel when he is excommunicated. And it will bring him to his senses. For eight years he has been in error, and for the last two living in a state of sin; and nothing so far, nothing, has ever been done, or said to bring home to him the perilous state of his soul. This well might.'

She saw, and so did the others, the bewilderment and hurt lift and vanish. Katharine made one protest,

'It might also lead to bloodshed.'

'Blood has already been shed,' Llandaff said. 'More's, Fisher's, and the rest. And unless this headlong course is arrested, more blood will flow.'

'Not in battle,' de La Sa said, contributing his mite, anxious only for the matter to be settled and his patient's mind at rest. 'For who would fight for an excommunicated man?'

She had her answer. Conveyed by human voices, but direct from God who chose His instruments.

Writing the formal demand for Henry's excommunication she felt like a mother, chastising a child for its own good; my dear one, my darling, I slap you to teach you that fire is not a thing to play with . . .

When she had written she went back to the Chapel and prayed that the curse might be the instrument of Henry's salvation. And this time God was there; in a physical sense at the altar in the wafer and the wine which were His flesh and blood; and in the space which had been dark and empty, a terrifying void; now occupied again by all the unspeakable glory . . .

The days shortened; the weather worsened; the waiting time dragged itself out. Nothing happened.

'That request which cost me so dear to write,' Katharine said to Maria, 'might have been dropped down the well for all the good it did. I sometimes think I shall die as I lived, waiting.'

'Your Grace, do not speak of dying.' How could I bear to go on living? And what will happen to me? To us all?

CHAPTER 26

'I fear, Your Grace, that I must insist,' Chapuys said. So soon as he had mentioned Dr. de La Sa's name the King's face had darkened and he had made a dismissing gesture with his hand. 'It is the last time I shall be obliged to trouble you, on this subject . . . but now I must, and immediately. Five minutes will suffice.'

'If you tell me the gist of the letter and do not read it word by word. It is still Christmas, Messire Chapuys, Christmas, and out there they await me.'

'The gist of the letter, Your Grace,' Chapuys said, pushing the rejected missive back into his sleeve, 'is that the Princess Dowager is dying and has expressed a deathbed wish to see me and her daughter.'

'Dying?' The word jolted, though he had known her to be ailing, been warned that another winter in Kimbolton would kill her.

'So her doctor says. And sorry as I am to disturb the festivities, I must ask Your Grace's permission to go to Kimbolton and to take the Lady Mary with me.'

Kate dying. He had pushed her away, out of sight, out of mind, refused to listen to any plea on her behalf. Let her suffer, he thought without any very clear idea of what she was suffering because he had never in his lifetime sat down at a table that was not well spread or slept in an ill-furnished bed. When he thought of her he thought of a stubborn, proud woman who had kept him and Anne apart through several good breeding years and ruined their whole relationship by the uncertainty and the distrust and suspicion which even bedding together could not wipe out. It was a long time now since Katharine had seemed anything to him except an obstacle and nuisance. Now, for a second the past revived, and with it the knowledge that she was only fifty, this very month. Me too? One day.

He said defensively, 'She was never a strong woman.'

For once Chapuys forgot to be mindful of his tongue. He said with asperity, 'Her circumstances of late have not been conducive to good health!' What was he saying? Provoke Henry now and he would not obtain the necessary permission. He added quickly, 'She has, I understand, voluntarily confined herself to a few rooms and refused what company was available.'

'All her troubles have been of her own making. Except her poor health. Her experiences in childbed prove that she was never strong.'

'She has been very unfortunate,' Chapuys agreed. It seemed to him that the byword about fortune favouring the brave was without truth; those who bore one trouble bravely had others heaped upon them.

'You may go to her when you like,' Henry said, with the magnanimous air of one conferring a great favour. Katharine's death would be timely, he thought, recovering from the jolt. Anne was pregnant. That news had been the best of Christmas gifts. It must be a boy this time; and if Katharine died the boy would not be born to a man with two wives. If Anne gave him a son he would send her into dignified retirement, possibly at The More; give her whatever in the way of worldly goods she cared to ask for, and never see her again. If she bore another girl he would take more drastic steps to be rid of her . . . He had recovered some of his old buoyancy; the year was ending, the sentence of excommunication had not fallen upon him, and if by the end of the coming summer he was the father of a prince all England, all the world would see that he had been right.

Chapuys, prepared to take a prompt leave, was thinking much the same thing. But if he could reach Kimbolton before Katharine breathed her last, and could get her and Mary into one room together, there was still a chance. People often had moments of enlightenment on their deathbeds, looked back over their lives and saw where they had made mistakes. And in any case Katharine's promise – or threat – to hold herself as surety for Mary, would have no more validity now.

Henry was also thinking of deathbed scenes. He remembered that room at Richmond, smelling of death on a sweet April afternoon; the gasped-out warning which he had disregarded. Mary was more dutiful. Whatever Katharine said to her at such a moment would be held sacred. And what might Katharine not say?

'*You* may go, Messire; but I cannot entertain the thought of the Lady Mary travelling so far in such weather, and – if she ever reached Kimbolton – witnessing a distressing scene. She is not a strong woman, either.'

'Your Grace, it is a deathbed request. The Lady Mary is a good horsewoman, and I promise to see that she is not overtired. Or, if you thought it wise, she could travel in a litter.'

A litter would delay them; a litter until they were out of London, perhaps.

'Messire, I have expressed my opinion.'

There was nothing more to be said, except, 'Has Your Grace any message you wish me to convey?'

Idiot? One kind word now, and something of a kindly nature was plainly expected – and back it would come, borne on the wind to Anne who must not, must *not*, be upset in any way, by anything, from now until July. August?

'Tell her I commend her to God.'

Hatred of him flared in Chapuys' unemotional mind.

I shall ask to be recalled. I will *not* remain in a position where I must be

civil to the brute. If she dies without giving her daughter permission to
lead a rising against him, there is nothing more for me to do here and I
cannot force myself any longer to say things to her murderer. And I will
not take another diplomatic post. The Emperor will give me a pension,
which I will turn over to the family, and I will retire, perhaps to Louvain
and spend the rest of my days in quiet study. I have had enough of this.'

Then Henry said the words which were to twist Chapuys' life in another
direction. 'And, Messire Chapuys, when it is . . . over; I commission you to
break the news to my daughter. She is at odds with me at the moment and
there is none about her who would do it . . . kindly.'

What a mass of contradictions the man was!

'I will do that, Your Grace. And now, if you have no further instructions . . .'

Both men, as they parted, looked past Katharine's death and misread
every sign. Henry looked ahead and saw the birth of a prince reconciling
even the most stubborn Papists to the new régime. Chapuys saw himself
cloistered from this troublesome, disappointing world, with only fellow
scholars and books for company.

And before a month was out Henry was to be unhorsed in the tiltyard at
Greenwich, lie unconscious and get up with a wound in the leg which was
never to heal: Anne, told by her stupid uncle, Norfolk, that the King was
dead, was to miscarry. And Chapuys, going to tell Mary of her mother's
death, was to transfer to that tough, tender, passionate, controlled young
woman all that he had felt for Katharine, and was to stay on in England
for the next ten years, watching her interests and furthering her cause.

All unknowing Henry went to join the Christmas revels and Chapuys
crossed the courtyard where a thin sleet was falling, to collect his pass for
Kimbolton from the office where the Duke of Suffolk presided.

Suffolk remembered Buckden. Handing the pass to the Ambassador, he
said cheerfully, 'When she is dead, Messire, there will be no barrier
between my master, the King and your master, the Emperor.' Suffolk had
reason to feel and speak cheerfully; Katharine's death would solve for him
a very troublesome problem. He had recently married again, and his
mother-in-law, a truly fearsome old woman, before allowing him to marry
her daughter had extracted from him a promise, the thought of the need to
keep it enough to make him sweat in the night, even lying beside his bride.
He would be free now.

Chapuys thought: You are hateful, too: it is a living woman you thus
dismiss as though saying that when the mist clears the day will be fine.

He said politely, 'It will not be an enviable journey. North of Bedford is
a harsh country, as your lordship knows!'

In another December, north of Bedford, in Buckden, Suffolk, hero of the battlefield and the tiltyard, victor of many a bedchamber, had been defeated, outmanoeuvred by a headstrong woman and a group of peasants. It had been the joke of London for a month and any mention of it could still make him writhe.

The wind blew from the northeast, the sleet fell down, the mud splashed up. Chapuys could stay nowhere long enough to have his clothes properly dried out and brushed; mud layer caked upon mud layer until they were as stiff as armour, and in the morning just as cold. And because he was travelling at speed he could not turn aside to rest for the night in any comfortable manor, but must hold to the road and lodge at inns where in such weather, with the Twelve Days of Christmas still being kept, chance travellers were not expected or welcomed.

He reached Kimbolton late in the afternoon of the second day in the year 1536. The place looked dead. He had brought two men with him, for even on such an urgent, hasty errand a man of his rank could not travel unaccompanied, and it took the full force of their united voices to provoke any stir of life. When, from the inner side of the leaden moat, the shouts were answered, 'Who are you? What do you want?' Chapuys had reached the point of recklessness that enabled him to answer, 'The Emperor's Ambassador, come with the King's permission to wait upon the Queen.'

'It will be,' Katharine said in the weak voice, so unlike her own, 'my last public appearance. Prop me high. My collar, where is it? And the headdress I wore . . . at Blackfriars? Maria, this shawl is cosy, but it is peasant wear. The skirt of my purple gown; drape it over me, bedgown and all.' The Spanish Ambassador was going to be correctly received: she had already sent Llandaff to command the presence of Sir Edmund and Sir Edward, and Manuella to search for, if necessary borrow, some extra candles.

Filipez conducted Chapuys to a comfortless room and hurried away to fetch water, saying simply, 'It will not be hot, sir. Since Her Grace has kept to her bed the only fire has been in her chamber.'

Chapuys had known that there was a lack of comfort, but he had not visualised a shortage of fuel. Gloomily he washed in water so cold that it seemed to burn, and changed his muddied riding clothes for others, much creased. There was no glass in the room, so he tidied his hair and beard by sense of touch alone and waited, growing more chilled every moment, until Filipez returned to say formally, 'Sir, the Queen is ready to receive you,' Filipez had discarded the nameless garment, a kind of knitted shroud, which Jennie had made for him after he had confided to her that he felt the cold in the Castle more than the lack of palatable food, and had dressed himself in the rose and white tunic and hose designed for wear in places which, if high and draughty, had heaped hearths and the heat of many bodies to warm them.

At the door of the room where Katharine lay he announced the Spanish Ambassador in proper fashion and then slipped to take his place with Maria, Llandaff, de La Sa, Concepcion and Manuella, on the right-hand side of the bed. The two knights stood on the left. The Queen of England was receiving the Emperor's Ambassador with all the style and formality that could be mounted at a few minutes' notice and with such slender resources.

Between the low bow at the door and the dropping to his knees beside the bed, Chapuys noticed all that there was to see. A macabre scene; the Queen so bleached and emaciated, propped up upon pillows frayed, mended, frayed again; the hangings of the bed were faded and tattered; some of the candles mustered on a table at the foot of the bed were not candles at all, they were rushdips, the lights of the poor. Chapuys had made thousands of them in his time, in Annecy, a thousand years ago.

He seemed to notice nothing; to walk straight towards her. He knelt; she extended her hand.

'Messire Chapuys, you have come. I thank you for coming. I feared that I might be left to die, like a beast in a field.'

'Your Grace, you must not speak of dying. The King and the whole country are anxious for your recovery. The Princess is not with me, but that is because His Grace was averse to the idea of her travelling so far in such foul weather.'

For a long time he had dealt in half-truths; never the lie that could be nailed down, but now he was reckless. She shall die happy, if I can contrive it, he thought.

'I have many messages to convey to Your Grace. The King is concerned for your health and well-being . . .' The lies rattled out; a move to a more comfortable place; an increased allowance, more company. On the right-hand side of the bed the waiting woman who looked as if she had been crying for a week, choked and put her hand to her face; on the left-hand side the two knights shuffled their feet. And midway between them, propped in bed, Katharine's ravaged face wore a look of incredulity and of understanding. Chapuys had time to think: That is their strength, these honest ones; they never attempt to deceive and they can tell the false from the true in others. But he was sorry that she had not believed and been cheered by his lies.

She asked a few questions of general interest and then said:

'I would like a few words with you, Messire Chapuys. I will not keep you long. You must be very weary.'

When the others had gone she said, 'Tell me about my daughter. How is she?'

'I have not seen the Princess for a long time. But I have reports, from a reliable source, with fair regularity. Her health continues good, her spirits variable, but that is understandable.'

'I have messages for her; but they can wait.' She slipped down against the pillows and the headdress tilted. She lifted her hand to remove it and drop it on the floor beside the bed, and the movement allowed Chapuys to catch a glimpse of the shawl under the purple silk that she wore as a cape. His heart burned and his stomach knotted: Poor, foolish woman, had she only listened to reason, taken up arms, allowed Mary to take up arms . . . too late now. She was dying in less comfort than any merchant's wife. The hearth in the room was wide, but the fire was small and dull.

'I understand,' she said, 'that the Concubine is with child.'

Who had been foolish, or brutal enough to report that? In fact, Katharine had heard Maria telling Llandaff in the outer room; Maria was crying as she spoke and the words carried.

'That has been said before,' Chapuys said cautiously. 'And with little truth. It was said in September. Nothing came of it. I sometimes think that the tale is put about to retain the King's interest.'

'There are times when I pity her,' Katharine said, knowing what the loss of Henry's interest meant. 'Tell me truly, did he send me any message at all?'

'Yes. He said: Tell her, I commend her to God.'

It had been a grudging message and it was grudgingly repeated; but her sunken eyes brightened.

'What better message could he send?'

'Time was very short. I was anxious to set out and the King was awaited elsewhere.'

'I think I could sleep now. I have not slept well of late. Your coming has brought me great comfort. You have always been my truest friend . . . This is a disordered household and I apologise for it; but if you would send Maria to me – and tell Filipez to look after you well . . .'

He thought: Sleep, poor weary soul, and God grant the last merciful gift, a drifting sleep into death, out of the world that has been so cruel.

Chapuys, Llandaff, de La Sa and Maria sat down to supper and Filipez served them with a dish of doves, freshly cooked and sent across from the other side of the house wrapped in woollen so that it was hot.

Maria de Moreto, her face swollen and in places almost transparent from weeping, said wildly:

'Have I not said, time upon time, that they could have done better by us had they willed? These doves did not fly in on the wind. They are from the dovecot in the garden. And while she *could* eat did she ever see one? She did not. And now that she cannot even sip broth . . .'

She turned away from the offered dish and bent her head over her hands, crying again. 'God will punish him,' she said; and everyone knew whom she meant.

The three very different men, the diplomat, the priest and the doctor, looked at her with a curiously similar expression of misery, distaste and resentment. They were all distressed, but they were also hungry and they had the male ability to dissociate emotional state from physical need. Maria's outburst had ruined appetite and they ate almost guiltily.

Afterwards Chapuys talked with Dr. de La Sa.

'There is no symptom of any mortal disease that I can recognise,' the doctor said. 'For the pain, once sporadic, lately constant, I cannot account at all. Nor indeed for the nausea. And she is certainly not being poisoned.' It was necessary to say this, for within a few days he, like the others, would be looking for new employment; and who would want a doctor whose last patient had died of poison? 'As a rule, we all eat the same food – and very poor. And even when Filipez smuggles in some little offering from a kind woman whom he visits and Maria de Moreto cooks it, she is most careful and invariably eats herself, first. She has never been even mildly indisposed. I am positive, sir, that there is no question of poison. I think . . .'

'Yes?' Chapuys said.

'I think it began with her removal to The More. She has never been quite the same. It was an uprooting and neither Buckden nor this place – as I have said before – were suitable residences. And there is more to it . . .' Dr. de La Sa became for a moment heroic; for when he was unemployed the favour and patronage of the Spanish Ambassador would be his best hope. 'Your communications have disturbed her . . . I have observed the effect. Only once has Her Grace taken me into her confidence in this regard and that was over the question of whether she should or should not make the request for the King to be excommunicated . . . That decision, which I think she should never have been called upon to make, did her great damage . . .'

'It was for her own good. Everything I have done, Dr. de La Sa, has been for her good, from my wish to see her vindicated and reinstated.'

'And everything *I* have done . . . though as a doctor *my* concern has been with her physical welfare. You may not have noticed, sir, but even when you were formally received, I did not wear my doctor's robe. I sold it, and other things, all I had of value, to help to pay the apothecary's dues. It did not suffice and his reckoning against us is heavy now. If she lives the week out even the doses that deaden pain . . .'

'I will guarantee,' Chapuys said. 'If she can be kept alive . . .' The Emperor's resources were infinite. Let go the great wide issues, politics, religion, military alliances and concentrate on fuel for the fire, linen for the bed and an apothecary's bill . . . It was many years since his mind had been called upon to operate at such a level, but his experience of penury in youth was useful now. 'I will give you a warrant, Dr. de La Sa. And for Sir Edmund also . . . And believe me, if necessary I will go to the Emperor, to the Pope and explain how ill she has been used. I had no idea. Nobody has any idea . . .'

He slept badly on the thin hard mattress in the unheated room, broke his fast on a bit of dark barley bread and a cup of the sourest ale he had ever tasted. Sir Edmund and Sir Edward had heard his promise to Katharine of better conditions pending and they had sent across the courtyard a better, an edible supper dish. Then, over their own, they had discussed the situation and decided it would be inexpedient to send Chapuys away under a false impression.

'If we feed him well it will deny the truth of the letters and the petitions,' Sir Edmund said sensibly. 'We said, and it was true, that we were in sore straits. He will stay until she recovers, or dies and in either case let him know what it is to live without means. How say you?'

'I say wait. If his promises have any worth, supplies will be ordered and the payment for them guaranteed. Boy, I will have some more ham.'

Katharine had slept better than usual and Maria coaxed her to take a little broth; but soon afterwards, while Concepcion was about to wipe her face and hands with a dampened cloth and Maria stood by with the comb ready, pain and nausea returned.

'The worst yet,' she said feebly; and Maria who had dared to hope a little, began to cry once more.

It was drawing on to midday, but hardly light, the sky was so low and dark, before Chapuys was admitted to her room, with Maria whispering at the door, 'Do not tire her. Agree to whatever she says.'

He greeted her and said he was glad that she was better – meaning better than she had been earlier in the morning.

'I am dying, Messire Chapuys, and I know it. I do not grieve. I hope no one else will. I know that we must bear what we are called upon to bear, but the pain is fierce . . . However the drops are beginning to take effect. What is necessary for writing is on that table. I must make my will – though I have little to leave but debts.'

A married woman could not make a will without her husband's consent, Chapuys remembered; but, as law in England now ran, she was not married; she was the widowed Princess of Wales. And that brought him straightway into difficulty.

He said, 'We will begin in the usual way – In the name of God, Amen. The other formalities we will leave to be put in later.' That dispensed with the writing of 'I, Katharine, Queen of England,' which would invalidate the document, and with 'I, Katharine, Dowager Princess of Wales,' which must inevitably offend her. 'If you would just tell me your wishes . . .'

'I want Mary, my daughter, to have my gold collar, my prie-dieu, and my books.' Most of her books had been wantonly destroyed by the looters at Buckden. 'And my furs. They are somewhat worn, but while the Concubine rules she will get no better . . .' So little to bequeath, really; less than any yeoman's wife would leave. That extortionate dowry, half never paid, but what had been paid was substantial; the revenues due to her if she were, as Henry claimed, Arthur's widow; all gone. 'No, my friend, make an exception of my sable cloak, that to Maria de Moreto, with the rest of my clothes. And all else that is mine to be equally divided between Concepcion and Manuella.' Nothing, not even a memento to Llandaff, de La Sa and Filipez. 'Write down that I commend my servants to His Grace and beg that they be given pensions and that he will discharge my debts and bury me with some respect. If not as Queen, the title he bestowed on me and then denied, then as one who regarded herself as his wife, and was always faithful, and chaste. Do I go too fast?'

'I have it all here,' Chapuys said, forcing the words through the iron stranglehold in his throat. 'Now, if you could sign . . .'

She signed, and, handing back the pen, said, 'So that is done with. I thank you.' She lay limp against the pillows and closed her eyes. In the silence the green logs, still damp despite Maria's management, hissed a little.

Then Katharine opened her eyes and in a voice of more vigour and less certitude said, 'My message for Mary. More important than my poor leavings . . . And more difficult. I should have written, but it needed thought and I put if off until, as you see, it is as much as I can do to sign my name. So, first give her my love, my dearest love. You know, Messire Chapuys, it was for Mary's sake that I took my stand. Had my marriage been truly childless I should have agreed to be put away, though still regarding myself as lawfully married.' She stopped and brooded. 'As you know, I eschewed violence and urged her to. I believed, I still believe that God would recognise her rights. So tell her, from me to be patient, and steadfast, and to obey her father to the limit of conscience, as she has done hereto. But say this also . . .' Something flashed in the dull eyes and changed the ravaged face. 'If when *he* is dead any child of the Concubine's, male or female, makes a bid for the throne . . . and if there is no possible alternative, then she will go into battle with my blessing . . .' She looked back over a lifetime of failure and knew that she had failed again, too weak now to pass on to Mary what she knew about waging war, things no woman brought up as Mary had been, could possibly know. The value of surprise, of doing the unexpected, apparently impossible thing, the importance of a strong rear, the worth of personal leadership and a sharing of hardship. It was too late, now. She must lie still and gather strength in order to issue her last order to Chapuys.

Chapuys looked ahead and foresaw a pretty tangle. The London he had left had been sibilant with whispers. If Anne bore a prince it might be her son who would one day challenge the Princess Mary's rights. Another girl would seal her fate. It could very well not be her child at all who would push Mary aside . . . But such speculation was no subject for deathbed talk.

'And now, my friend, I want you to leave at once. Now, as soon as your horses are ready. When Mary hears of my death I wish her to have someone she can trust close at hand. I want her to have my message before some ill-advised person can use my death to provoke her into ill-advised action. It will snow later, but if you leave now you may just be ahead of it – moving southwards.'

The suggestion distressed him. He had intended to use his influence to gain her more comfort. He hated the idea of riding away and leaving her, dying in this demoralised household. Maria de Moreto had broken down with the thoroughness of which only strong-minded women were capable, the girls were poor helpless creatures, and though both the doctor and the priest would do their duty in this room, they were men, so accustomed to discomfort that they hardly noticed the cold or the fact that the bed itself needed fresh linen.

'If that is your wish,' he said. 'Though I am reluctant to leave you.'

'It is the last thing you can do for me. For all you have done and for all you have tried to do, I thank you from my heart . . . Let us have no long leavetaking. I wish you Godspeed. I pray God guard and bless you to the end of your days.'

He could not speak at all. He could only kneel again and kiss her hand, with reverence and love.

CHAPTER 27

By the time that he was in his cheerless room Chapuys was practical again. Pulling on his riding clothes and boots – still insufficiently dried, and stiff with cold – Chapuys was thinking: If I could wish one wish it would be for some good sensible woman to come and be with her till the last. Somebody not too grief-stricken; but kind. He must snatch a minute, before he left to speak to Sir Edmund.

Over the courtyard the sky sagged, purplish, and the wind which yesterday had driven the sleet in his face had dropped, giving way to an unnatural hush, sure sign that the snowfall would not long be delayed.

Sir Edmund and Sir Edward, alerted by the bustle, saw that his horses were being made ready. The Spanish Ambassador, after the shortest possible visit, was leaving. He had brought no money, issued no definite order; his promises of yesterday afternoon were mere empty words. They were glad that they had not provided him with a good breakfast, and sorry about the dish of doves.

'A woman of that kind,' Sir Edmund said, when Chapuys had made his request, 'would be impossible to provide. The Princess Dowager would not welcome the ministrations of anyone who will not call her Queen, and anyone who *would* cannot be admitted to Kimbolton – as you must see, Messire.'

'She needs other things too, bed linen, fuel, delicate food. It is in my mind, sirs, that neglect has played no small part in her decline.'

'Not ours,' Sir Edmund said firmly and with some justification. 'You, of all men, should know. The allowance was never enough and for the last six months it has not been paid at all. *We* have not been paid. But for the fact that we had some small means of our own . . .'

'I know, I know,' Chapuys said placatingly. 'I left London hurriedly, with only just enough money for my journey. But I do assure you, sirs, that my master, the Emperor, will be responsible, will pay all debts, re-imburse any expenditure – if the King fails. As I think he will not. He, no more than I, realised the true state of affairs. But he will know, so soon as I am back in London.'

'What is that?' Sir Edmund asked, cocking his head.

It was a voice; the loud, confident, carrying voice of an Englishwoman of rank, accustomed to issuing orders in spacious places and to having those orders obeyed.

'Fetch your master, fool. Don't stand there arguing with me.'

The two knights and Chapuys ran to the archway from which the moat and the drawbridge were visible. The men who were preparing to lower it for Chapuys' exit, stood staring across the moat's width, at a woman on the farther side. She held a horse by the bridle.

Chapuys recognised her and turned so dizzy that he almost fell down. An answer to prayer, and he had not even prayed; he had simply thought that if he could wish one wish . . . And there she stood, the Dowager Countess of Willoughby, who had once been Maria de Salinas. One of the secret friends . . .

Sir Edmund went forward a few paces and before he could speak the voice bellowed,

'Are you in charge here? Order that bridge let down and let me in.'

'I can admit no one who does not carry a pass.'

'I have no pass. I have a lame horse. Am I to be benighted? In the snow?'

Chapuys said, 'It is the Countess of Willoughby. Her daughter recently married the Duke of Suffolk.' He then turned away, back to the courtyard where his servants and the horses waited.

'Lower away,' Sir Edmund said. The moment the moat was spanned, the Countess was on the bridge, her voluminous skirts bunched in one hand, the other tugging at the limping horse. Chapuys, waiting on the inner side to allow her passage, gave her the mere, formal salutation that any well-bred man would give a lady in such circumstances. He bowed from the saddle, doffed his cap; but when she was dead level with him, he said, 'Thank God you are here!' Then, followed by his servants, he clattered across and took the road to London, just one hour ahead of the snow.

Filipez, as usual, had come out to see what was afoot. The Countess's dark eyes, undimmed by the years, saw him. She left the horse, tremulous and with broken knees where he stood, and said to Filipez 'Take me to her.'

Maria de Moreto sat by Katharine's bed with a bowl of broth growing cool between her hands. She had said, 'Just a sip, to please me,' and Katharine had said, 'I would do anything to please you, Maria. But it sickened me this morning and the very smell of it sickens me now.' So there they were, quiet and waiting, when Filipez opened the door and said, 'Your Grace, the Countess of Willoughby.'

The other Maria; the fortunate one. Maria de Salinas over whose dowry the Queen had taken such trouble – all wasted, for the Englishman was so infatuated that he would have taken the girl in her shift. And off she'd gone to a great house, two great houses, in the country, coming back to Court now and then, Lady Willoughby, more English than any native. She had sent gifts and messages at New Year and on the Queen's name day. Until trouble came. She had made one visit to The More. After that nothing.

'You!' Maria de Moreto said in a voice that held everything, the old jealousy, the envy, the accusation of faithlessness. 'Her Grace is asleep.' She made a silencing gesture.

Katharine was not asleep; she had closed her eyes to avoid any more pestering with the broth. Dr. de La Sa's latest dose of drops had dulled the sharpest edge of the pain and she had lain neither sleeping nor waking, drifting, the Alhambra and Joanna, Ludlow and Arthur, Henry and Greenwich all one, all muddled. When, with a great effort, she opened her eyes and saw Maria de Salinas – the other Maria, the high-spirited one, she was no more real, for a moment, than the phantoms. But she was real; here in the room, the daylight dying, no candles yet, we must be sparing with candles; and a poor sulky fire. I was on my way . . . now I am called back. There is something different, an outdoor smell . . .

'It was good of you to come, Maria. I am glad to see you.' Even though your coming pulled me back. 'How did you get in?'

'I shouted,' Maria de Salinas said simply. She had learned, so long ago, that if you shouted loudly enough and in the right tone of voice you got what you wanted; so that the ease with which she gained entry had not surprised her. 'I should have been here earlier, but my horse fell. I walked the last six miles.'

'Can you stay?'

'I shall stay until Your Grace is better.'

Dimly, aware of being dragged back, farther and farther into the pain, the need to think, Katharine remembered the old enmity between the two Marias.

'That will be good,' she said. 'My other Maria has watched tirelessly and is worn out. You can relieve her.'

'I need no relief. Or at least . . . it would relieve me if Your Grace would take just a spoonful . . .'

The Countess looked into the bowl and then into Maria de Moreto's face and her expression was eloquent: Is this the best that you can tempt her with?

'Could you take a little manchet bread, sopped in wine?'

'Maria, explain,' Katharine said.

'Her Grace has seen no wine for more than a year. As for manchet bread, we have forgotten what it looks like. While you, uncaring, full-fleshed, not a wrinkle, not a grey hair, nothing but the sagging jowls to show that you are of our age, you have fed full every day! *We* have shared her hardships and her exile.'

The Countess's sharp eye had taken it all in; the shabby bed, the poor fire, the other Maria's air of hopelessness and defeat. It was plain to her that there was some more shouting to be done.

She said, 'If Your Grace will excuse me for a moment . . .'

'And a fine pair of rogues you are,' she said to the knights. 'Guzzling and stuffing your own bellies while the poor Queen dies of neglect. Your fire halfway up the chimney and hers worse than a tinker's. You will rue this. I will make it my business to see that you are properly punished.'

For the second time in an hour they tried to explain.

'So!' she shouted. 'What are you drinking? Well water? I need wine for her.'

They admitted that they had a little, a very little wine; and she was welcome to it. But when she mentioned manchet bread they said, truthfully, that there was not a crumb of it left in Kimbolton.

'Get somebody to make a batch then. And the linen on her bed is a disgrace.'

'She brought very little,' Sir Edward said, not without spite. 'Most of her stuff was looted from Buckden.' And who was responsible for that? The man who was now this termagant's son-in-law. 'And I would inform your ladyship that Sir Edmund and I have made repeated requests . . .'

'Words on paper. Filed away and forgotten. Did either of you think of going to London and *asking*? Well, I am asking now. I want fresh linen and some logs that will burn, and bread made of flour sieved three times and mixed with milk. And do not tell me that you have no milk. I heard a cow. Are you keeping it for a pet?'

It was not until she had gone, carrying the jug of wine snatched from their own table that they remembered that she had no right here at all.

'You should have come sooner, my Lady Willoughby,' Maria said in a soft, very vicious voice.

'So it seems. And so I should, had I known half. It was not until I was at Bedford to attend a wedding that I heard that she was sick, not likely to live long. Even so I had no idea that she was living in such discomfort and squalor.'

The words cut Maria de Moreto who had tried so hard and managed so well on so little.

'Things have changed since you last saw her – at The More, was it not? Three years ago.'

The Countess was not prepared to explain to the other Maria what lay behind this seeming neglect and indifference. When the Queen rallied – as she must, now that things were taken in hand – she would explain to *her*, and she would understand that some causes were best served in secret. She said:

'You know full well that after The More visitors were not allowed. But you should have known that if *I* had been informed of how things were here I should have sent such a plentitude of what was needed that even when those vultures over there had eaten their fill, *she* would have had enough. Why did you never think to let me know?'

'How could I? *I* have shared her imprisonment.'

'People go in and out every day,' the Countess said scornfully. 'Any woman with a tongue in her head can find some man to carry a message for her, if she has a mind to.'

'And why,' Maria de Moreto asked, 'should I think of appealing to you? *You* who married your daughter to the lout who robbed us at Buckden?'

That bolt found its mark and the fact that it was fired in ignorance did not lessen the blow. Perhaps the poor Queen had also looked upon what had been a shrewdly diplomatic move as a sign of disloyalty. Yet there had been no shadow of reproach in her greeting.

'What he did at Buckden cannot be blamed on me; and he is already sorry for it. He will be sorrier still, that I promise you,' Lady Willoughby said. 'Now what you need is a sound night's sleep. Go to your bed and leave watching to me.'

'I have one mistress here and it is not you. I shall watch as I have done.'

'As you wish. I see no sense in it.'

It was an echo of the past when they had bickered continuously and energetically, mostly about trivialities. Both looked back for a moment and thought, mistakenly, that the sun had always shone then and the future had seemed long, full of promise. What the future had brought to them was very different and had worked superficial changes on them both, but in a way, obscure and perverse, the discovery that something, even an enmity, had survived intact, rejuvenated them.

Katharine, under the influence of Dr. de La Sa's soothing drops, slept in fresh linen. Each Maria took a chair, one on each side of the bright fire. Presently Maria de Moreto's tired mind accepted the lessening of responsibility, communicated the fact that another person shared it to her will, and from her will the message passed to her exhausted body. She slumped in her chair, slipping downwards and forwards until her head sagged against the chair's unaccommodating back and her body seemed about to slip over the edge of the seat.

Maria Willoughby rose to her feet and moving softly, put a stool under the other Maria's legs, waited, and then, assured that Maria de Moreto had fallen into a sleep from which she would not easily be awakened, folded a shawl and wadded it between her head and the back of the chair. Nothing but her sense of good management activated her and when

Maria de Moreto, made more comfortable, sinking deeper into the restorative sleep, began to snore, she thought: Yes, I remember; you always slept like a pig! She mended the fire and sat down again.

Katharine woke to pain. The syrup, in doses large enough to induce sleep brought dreams too, very strange dreams, quite unlike those in ordinary sleep which, however unlikely and fantastic, had some relationship to this world and could be described. Each time as the pain lessened and she drifted into sleep and crossed the boundary of the other world her last conscious thought was that she was dying, very easily and with a sense of happy anticipation. Wakened by pain she thought, *still here and still in misery*, and then lay, adjusting herself to this world again.

Tonight the adjustment took longer than usual because when she opened her eyes the room seemed so bright, the bed felt different, and she could not see Maria. Only the pain was familiar and for a moment she knew real panic; *not here and still in pain*; was pain to be her companion through all eternity? Then her confused mind cleared and she saw that the unusual quality of the light was due to the fact that the fire burned brightly and that a real candle had replaced the dim rushlight; that Maria de Moreto was asleep in a chair and the other Maria sat bolt upright on the other side of the hearth. She said softly, 'Maria.'

'I am here, Your Grace. Maria de Salinas.'

'I know. I think God sent you. To do me a service I could not ask of anyone else around me.'

'And small wonder; handless, spiritless lot, letting things drift into such a state. God sent me to save you. You are just my age, fifty, nothing! Look at me! I dragged a lame horse six miles – and, at the end of a long ride, I ground Sir Edward and Sir Edmund into the dust where they belong. I have strength, I have power, I will save you yet. . . .'

'Could you prop me a little,' Katharine asked. 'Sometimes a change of position eases my pain.'

This Maria's arms, in the tight sleeves of her riding habit, were strong and well-padded, lifting effortlessly.

'Is that better, Your Grace?'

'Yes. Yes, thank you.'

'Wine helps,' Maria de Salinas said. 'I had an abscess once, in my breast. Wine deadened the worst pain. Will Your Grace take a sip or two?'

'Dear girl, we have no wine here.'

'We have now. You took a little. And kept it down.' That had been a triumph and it had encouraged the Countess. Tomorrow, if she knew her way about, there would be a bowl of good veal broth. Wherever there was a cow in milk there was a calf not far away. Of course the gluttonous scoundrels on the other side might have eaten it, in which case they could

send out into the countryside to find another. Inch by inch, with a sip of
wine, a spoonful of good broth, a slice of manchet bread, a slice of boiled
fowl, with comfort and cossetting and with *hope*, she would drag
Katharine back from the brink of the grave. Only fifty, she thought again,
just my age and ailing nothing that anyone can put a name to . . . but I
have always eaten well!

Katharine took the wine. There was a slight, too slight to be acknowledged, link between this bright, warm world in the heart of the night and
the world into which she slipped away when the dose worked. The quality
of the light, Maria de Salinas, suddenly back and moving about so
cautiously, not to wake the other Maria. And the wine running down,
easing the pain a little. Once she had seen a man, dead drunk, have his
arm cut off . . . This was a halfway world, not completely real, not
completely fantasy, a stopping place on the road to death. She must make
the best use of it.

'Come and sit near me, Maria. There is so much to say . . .'

'I have something of importance to say to Your Grace,' Lady Willoughby said earnestly.

'About my daughter? Do you see her?'

'No. Of late I have avoided London, and the Court. It is about that that I
wish to speak. She . . .' she jerked her head at the sleeping Maria, 'considers
me disloyal because I allowed my daughter Catharine, to marry the Duke
of Suffolk; and because I have not embroiled myself by asking permission to
visit. Visits have not been allowed and to ask would be to draw attention to
myself. Some causes are best served in the dark.'

'Until I was known to be dying no visitors, not even the Emperor's
Ambassador was allowed to see me. That you should be here now is
miraculous. You must not mind Maria; hardship has soured her. And if
your Catharine wished to marry the Duke . . .' Maria de Salinas' own
marriage had been a love match, she would probably have sympathy with
her daughter's choice.

'She wanted to be a Duchess,' the Countess said cryptically. 'And,
being so young, she was flattered by the attentions of so experienced a
womaniser. But she did not *love* him and that gave strength to my hand. I
talked to her very straightly.' Maria's voice rose a little as she remembered that straight talk and its result. Katharine made a warning sound
and looked at the sleeper. In an incongruous whisper the tale went on. 'I
said to her, "Do you wish, in ten years' time to be put away as his second
wife was, or to live in loneliness and neglect as his third did – and she once
a Queen?" The child said, "No," of course. "Then," I said, "you must
establish supremacy over him *now*; what is lightly come by is lightly
regarded and what is lightly regarded is easily discarded." She is a dutiful

girl, well brought up and she heeds me. She asked what she must do, and I told her: "You must say to him," I said, "and hold to it, that you will not marry him unless he agrees to your mother's condition." And that she did. Perhaps it will surprise Your Grace to know what that condition was. It was,' – the voice hardened again – 'that when the time came for the people to rise in your cause, against the King, my lord of Suffolk would not take arms against you. That promise I extracted from one of the King's closest friends and one of his best soldiers! I have not been idle!'

And Suffolk had dared to call *her* a traitor! What a muddled, corrupt, horrible, world! Who would not be glad to be done with it?

'There must be no rising, Maria. I repudiated that idea years ago. I have instructed Mary to repudiate it when I am dead.'

'There is no other way to right the ills of this country, Your Grace. You have been locked away so long you have no knowledge of what is going on in the world. Things go from bad to worse.'

'Civil war would not improve them.'

'There would be no civil war. A rising, to restore you and bring back the old ways. Who would fight for him and his trollop? Do you realise what force you can command? In various places, discreetly prepared, I alone have two hundred men ready to ride at short notice. Well armed, too. There are hundreds like me. A word from you would be enough . . .'

'Maria, I am sure you mean well. You and all the others. But I have had this out with my conscience . . . I may have been wrong. But it is too late now. For my errors, as for my sins, I must soon answer to God.'

'Not yet,' the Countess said, again trying to put force into a whisper. 'Not yet. With a little care and comfort and proper feeding, you will be restored and if . . .' with some reluctance she turned away from the dream of riding at the head of her two hundred men under the banners of Spain and the Wounds of Christ, 'if Your Grace is truly averse to taking up arms, I will still get you out of here. My son-in-law shall himself beg for your removal. Catharine and I have him well-bridled now.'

Katharine turned her head away from this Maria's persuasions as she had turned away from the other Maria's broth.

'I tire easily, my dear. And there is something yet to do. Maria, did you love your lord?'

'So much that when he died the sun went out for me.' Even to her own ears the statement sounded somewhat extreme; but she thought: Yes, that is how I felt, at the time; but the years pass and there was always so much to see to.

'Then *you* will understand, as *she* could not. As no man could. That is why I think God sent you. To write a letter for me . . . I delayed . . . every day thinking that tomorrow I should be better. This extreme weakness took me unawares. But before I die . . . a letter to *my* lord. Maria, all my friends look upon him as an enemy. He was, he *is*, my husband, in the sight of God: and in my heart.'

Maria de Salinas had certainly loved the English lord who had been willing to marry her without a dowry, who had given her wealth, title and status, and being by nature kind and peaceable, had accepted her competent, mild bullying role. But by Christ's Holy Wounds, had he ever so much as looked at another woman, he would have had something to reckon with; she would have spat in his face, torn out his beard, hit him over the head, cut his clothes to shreds, set fire to his house. He would have learned that Spanish blood running hot in love, could be equally hot in hatred.

Thinking these things, actually far less understanding of Katharine's attitude than poor, withered Maria de Moreto with her unrequited love for her worthless cousin who when she had a little money had borrowed it shamelessly and when she was penurious had never offered her a penny, Maria Willoughby went to the side table and came back with all that was necessary for the writing of a letter.

She tried the quill experimentally on her thumb, and as she suspected, it shared the general decrepitude of the household; it splayed out like a goat's foot.

'Begin then,' Katharine said. 'My most dear lord, King and husband . . .' The Countess thought: A fine lord, repudiating the lady he had chosen, an admirable King who had denied his subject a just trial, a splendid husband who had made a bigamous marriage. But she wrote and as Katharine paused said, 'Yes, I have that. My hand is fast, if not elegant.'

The temporary relief of the wine was weakening, the amnesty wasted by Maria's talk, the pain drove in its fangs and tore and gnawed. But God was good; He had spared her until this letter was written.

She said, 'The hour of my death now drawing on, the tender love I owe you, my case being such, forceth me to commend myself to you and to put you in remembrance with a few words of the health and safeguard of your soul . . .' She had done with his body, except in memory, she was still concerned for his soul.

'Do I go too fast, Maria?'

'No,' Lady Willoughby said, scowling at the sputtering, flat-footed quill. 'I have it.'

'. . . which you ought to prefer before all worldly matters and before the care and pampering of your body, for the which you have cast me into many calamities and yourself into many troubles.'

She paused again and Lady Willoughby thought: No truer word was ever spoken. She seems to be so saintly, so remote, but she knows the urgencies of the flesh and to what, unreined, they lead. *His* body and its hungers must be to blame for everything that has happened in the last nine years and if even a half of what I hear, remote from London as I am nowadays, it is through his body that he will be punished. He is a man who would sooner have faced an armed rising than the hint of physical lack which the word 'cuckold' implies. No woman, the Countess thought, curling her lip into a sneer, ever went out to buy a slice of bacon when a whole flitch hung from her own kitchen beam. Anne was said to have five lovers – her own brother one of them.

Katharine said, 'For my part, I forgive you everything, and wish to devoutly pray God that He will pardon you also . . .' She paused once more and said, 'Maria, that is true. From the first he was misguided . . . Sometimes I think this, running the whole thing through my mind, misguided in marrying me, lawful though our marriage was and made by the dispensation granted by the Pope; and made in love . . . as it was, Maria. He loved me . . . once. But I can see that for a King who needs an heir . . .' This was difficult to put exactly, even to Maria, even in the middle of the night. 'There are family trends, a colouring of eye, of hair, of disposition . . . And Maria, strange as this sounds, it is not in opposition, but in accord with the will of God who made everything after its kind, the blackbird black, the wren brown. In *my* family girls live, boys die. My mother was Queen in her own right; and my sister. And so, God willing, will my daughter be. So I am sorry for Henry and find it easy to forgive him. He wanted a son; he should have passed me over and married some Princess with two or three thriving brothers.'

Unable to make the one retort that occurred to her: Nonsense! the Countess was silent.

Katharine said, almost apologetically, 'It is such thoughts; and the knowledge that he has always been ill-advised that makes it impossible for me to be angry with him. Now, to continue . . . For the rest I commend unto you our daughter, Mary beseeching you to be a good father unto her. I entreat you also, on behalf of my maids, to give them marriage portions.'

Maria Willoughby wrote, lifted her head and looked at the other Maria and wondered derisively just how large a marriage portion would be needed to bribe a man to marry her. And the serving wenches were little younger.

'For all my other servants I solicit the wages due to them, and a year more, lest they be unprovided for.'

Even so, the Countess reflected, the future was not very bright for them. She might herself find a place for Filipez with his knowledge of horses. The chaplain and the doctor she considered not worth their salt to have let things get into such a state.

'Maria, there is only one thing to add. Write – and lastly, I make this vow, that mine eyes desire you above all things.'

That was the sentence which nobody could be expected to understand, except a woman who had known love.

The Countess wrote that extraordinary sentence, of which her mind disapproved and then blinked her eyes several times. She was *not* weeping. It was the strain of writing with a bad pen, by the light of a single candle and the fluctuating gleam from the fire that was affecting her eyes.

A log burned through and fell inwards. Maria de Moreto, half roused by the noise, stirred and muttered. Katharine signed to the Countess to push the letter and all concerned with its writings under the bed. 'Her feelings would be hurt.' They waited, rather like children almost caught in some forbidden activity. Maria settled to sleep again. Somewhere a cock crowed, greeting the false dawn.

'I will sign it now.'

Dipping the pen, the Countess said, 'It is the worst I ever handled.'

'It will serve,' Katharine said, taking it with fingers limp as wilting candles. She wrote *Katharine*, and then when Maria would have removed letter and pen, shook her head and with a last gesture in support of the belief she still held, added, *The Queene*.

'You will see to its safe delivery?'

'When needs be,' the Countess said in a voice that sounded as though her throat was stuffed with flannel.

'Thank you, Maria. It was on my mind. I shall rest now.'

Die, perhaps, the last duty done, the last effort made. But the pain was lively, gnawing away and though she tried to think of it as a friend, loosening the last bonds of flesh that held her to this finished life, presently she was driven to ask had Dr. de La Sa left drops. He had, but so few, so meanly measured out that the Countess thought that here was another thing she must speak about and organise tomorrow.

The dose was insufficient to ensure Katharine's entry into that indescribable other world, but it deadened the sharpest edge of the pain so that she lay in comparative comfort, with scenes from the past drifting through her mind, muddled in time and mixed in nature. The Midwife at Richmond held a child by the heels and said, Thanks be to God a boy! In Granada Isabella spoke of the world's betrayal. At Windsor Joanna cried that Philip was her disease. At Buckden a door slammed and the pain started.

It had snowed during the night, a heavy fall and she was glad that she had sent Chapuys away when she did; he might reach London ahead of it.

Maria de Moreto woke and declared that she had not slept at all; she had merely closed her eyes to rest them. Lady Willoughby, having splashed cold water on her face, resumed her organisation of the household. There was the business of the comb. The Countess took it up and Maria said, 'Give that to me, my Lady Willoughby. I always dress her hair these days.'

'Go get to your breakfast. Nobody can do anything properly on an empty stomach!'

'Some of us have learned to ignore our stomachs.'

Silly jealous girls. She saw them so; two lustrous-eyed, nubile young creatures who had sailed with her from Corunna. Always bickering.

'Give me the comb,' she said. 'I can make shift to dress my hair myself.'

'Now look what you have done,' the Countess said angrily.

'Look what *you* have done,' Maria retorted. Using her right hand only because to move her left arm provoked the pain, Katharine combed her hair. 'I would you were better friends,' she said.

But at some point in that timeless day she was roused again by a sibilant exchange.

'Let me offer it? I have fed her, spoonful by spoonful, this last week,' Maria de Moreto said.

'And a fine job you made of it,' said the other Maria who had organised that crowing cock into the stewpot, with onions and oatmeal and some dried herbs wrested from the store room on the other side of the courtyard. 'Take it then. But try not to cry into it. It is salted already!'

'I weep because I love her and she is dying.'

'Not if I can prevent it.'

Katharine said, 'If you persist in this squabbling, you will both go back to Spain, forthwith. And with no dowries and word of recommendation.' She had made this threat several times in the past. She added, 'And whatever it is, it will only sicken me. In my condition.' Pregnant again; God in Thy infinite mercy a boy this time . . .'

With the clouds which had shed their load sailing away in a brisk wind the day brightened and the sun, peering out with the January promise, shone on every whitened surface. Katharine said, 'A bright moon.' It linked with other times of cold, clear light. Moonlight on the minarets of Moorish cities, on the fairytale palace of the Val d'Or, on Windsor's solid walls and oaks, on the Thames, near Thomas More's garden steps at Chelsea.

'I spend a great deal of time with the dead,' she said petulantly, returning to full consciousness and to the two Maria's, urging a sip of this, a sip of that, 'to please me, Your Grace'.

*

'For the love of Christ,' Lady Willoughby said as Dr. de La Sa measured out the two doses, one to be taken immediately, the other held in reserve for later in the night, 'give her *enough* this time!' Behind her bold front and the bustling she was now as despairing as the other Maria. Unless food could be taken, and kept down there could be no hope. That the end should be without pain was all she could ask.

The doctor looked at her coldly. She was a great lady now, and she had improved conditions for them all; but he was a physician and not to be dictated to in his own sphere.

'A larger dose would defeat its own object, my lady.'

'In what way?'

'It would cause vomiting and that would increase the pain.'

'How can you know, never having tried?'

'By rule; and by experience,' he said with a certainty he did not feel. He could not even be sure that the apothecary, unpaid and resentful, had sent of his best.

'She suffers,' the Countess said fiercely. 'She writhes in pain. A woman of less courage would be screaming.'

'I know,' he said dolefully. 'But this is the maximum dose that can be given in safety.'

'Safety!' she spat the word at him and flounced away. He thought of the many ways apothecaries knew of adulterating drugs, and then, since she was not watching, added a careful couple of drops to each dose.

Exasperated by this defeat at the end of a long day of defeats, Lady Willoughby turned upon Maria de Moreto and said:

'Go to your bed. You do no good sitting in a chair, snoring!'

Maria said, 'You are the one who needs sleep. Running about all day like a hen with its head off!' But, settling down to watch, she avoided the chair and sat on a stool near the foot of the bed. Lady Willoughby, not to be outdone, pulled up another stool on the opposite side.

Katharine slept, granted swifter entry than usual to that world where nothing was recognisable and all senses were one, music something to be tasted, fragrance a thing to be held between the hands, colour a sound in the ear. The apothecary in Huntingdon, though he could not go on forever supplying drugs without payment, was honest in those he did supply and divorced from her pain, Katharine moved about in the opium-created world.

At the foot of the bed one Maria and then the other abandoned the bolt-upright position, put elbows on to the bed, heads on propped chins, weakened, sagged forward, slept. The candle guttered and presently the fire sank down, unmended; a mere heap of ash but still capable of sending a warm, rosy glow on to the opposite wall.

When Katharine woke it was not to pain. No pain at all. It had gnawed itself free and set her free too. Dear God, I thank you; all my life I have valued dignity and I did so fear that if the pain went on, increasing as it has of late, I might cry out. As I never did . . . miscarriages, dead children, living children, I bit upon my thumb; and through this later agony, longer and with no hopeful end, I bit upon my thumb. And I am blessed that now, too weak to lift my arm – a marked decline, this morning, or was it yesterday? I combed my hair – I am blessed that now there is no need to bring my thumb to my mouth.

The pain is dead, and I am dying . . . She said, 'Maria!' and there was no answer. But one of them would have stayed. One had never left her; the other had come back. Neither would have left her to die alone. She gathered what strength was left to her and said, 'Maria!' Two sleep-heavy heads lifted, two sleep-blurred voices said:

'I am here, Your Grace.'

Katharine said, 'I am about to die. My confessor . . . please . . .'

'I know my way,' Maria de Moreto said. She snatched up the candle and blundered away. The Countess of Willoughby, left standing by the bed and with no light except the rosy, diffused glow from the fire, reckoned that she could make her way to the table where the meagre second dose stood.

'And if it is not sufficient,' she said, making her way to it, 'I will have him out of bed, by his ears!'

'I have no need of it, Maria. The pain is gone.'

The Countess swung round. 'Gone? Is it true? Then you are better. You will live. I knew . . . I said . . .' She found Katharine's flaccid hands and held them in her own. Hold on to me; hold on; I am strong. Even now, some strength must flow . . .

Maria de Moreto roused Llandaff roughly, taking him by the shoulder and saying, 'Wake up. Get up. She is dying. And asking for you.'

'The end?' He knew that she was dying. Dr. de La Sa had said so when he wrote to the Spanish Ambassador. But the doctor had also said that Katharine would suffer a long, slow decline; and death had seemed still at a distance when she received Messire Chapuys: and Lady Willoughby, coming in from the outer world, bringing a fresh eye to bear, had said with assurance that with good nursing and good food the Queen would recover . . . live for years. Now this.

'I will come,' he said. Maria looked about for a candle to light from the one she had. She failed to find one. Did he go to bed in the dark? She set hers down and went out and stood in the pitch dark while he dressed, which did not take long since in this cold room, in this poor bed he slept in all but his outer clothes.

'I must go to the Chapel,' he said. There was only the one candle. Without its light she could not fumble her way back to the Queen's room, nor could he, without it, go downstairs to the Chapel. So she followed him and again stood in the dark, waiting by the window of the corridor. She was unfit to enter the Chapel because her soul was in a state of rebellion against God who, in the last years, had assumed, little by little, a terrible resemblance to the heartless, unreasonable old man who had been her father; the images were now inseparable. A parallel transformation had overtaken the Blessed Virgin, no longer a willing advocate, a useful go-between, but like her mother a pretty, spiritless, powerless appendage. And now that the Queen was about to die deprivation would be total, loneliness complete.

She stared into the blackness of the courtyard and it was no darker than the future she faced, alone and without hope, heresy, or worse, in her heart. She saw no symbolism in the light which appeared suddenly and made a slow, bobbing course around the open space. It was only the old watchman making his midnight round.

Even in this isolated place where time meant little, it must still be measured by various means; Sir Edmund's mechanical device, the sun dial, the marked candles and the sandglass. This ancient man sat in his tiny lodge from dark till dawn, turning the glass about and making notches on a stick; at midnight he emerged to see that all was well in byre and stable, that no seemingly dead fire had flared.

When Llandaff emerged she took the candle from him and said:

'Now, listen to me! It is only midnight. I know the canonical hours. But she is *dying*. God will forgive you . . .' The words emerged smoothly from long habit, but remembering her father she thought: When did *he* ever forgive anybody? She hurried on, 'Or if not, on me be the blame. I will do penance for the rest of my days, never eat meat, or even fish again, sleep on the floor. But for her, the last Sacrament, even at midnight . . .'

Llandaff looked at this Maria much as the doctor had looked at the other and said, 'You may safely leave the decision to me.' Once inside Katharine's room, however, being a meticulous man, he felt it his duty to inform her of the hour.

'I thought it was morning,' she said. She was now too weak to point or even move her head; but straight in front of her eyes, behind her chaplain's form was the rosy glow on the wall, the first sign of the dawn. She had watched it many times.

'Your Grace, that is only the reflection of the fire,' he said gently. She thought: Yes, the fire is mended later now, and burns more clearly; I was deceived.

'Then I will wait.'

'I will put forward the hour,' he offered.

'No. I can wait.' She thought, without self-pity, with a wry, secret amusement: That is the one thing that life has taught me: to wait. Waiting to come to England, waiting for Arthur to grow older, waiting for my future to be decided upon, waiting to be pregnant, waiting to give birth, waiting for the Pope to give verdict. I can *wait*.

'You can pray with me,' she said. 'And the girls can rest.'

They protested; they needed no rest. She gathered energy to say, with gentle authority, 'Do as I say. Leave me with my confessor.' Lady Willoughby mended the fire, Maria lighted a fresh candle and they went out together.

They did not go far, only into the little anteroom just beyond the door. It had no hearth and was very chilly. The chest which held Katharine's shabby furs stood along one wall, there was a table, a bench and a stool. It had formerly been kept very neat, the table bearing only Katharine's jug and ewer, soap and towel. Now, as an annexe to the sick room, it seemed cluttered. A pile of fresh linen lay on the top of the chest and the table held the evidence of Maria Willoughby's activities and failures; the bread, not real manchet, but white enough; the bowl of chicken broth, so good that as it cooled it had set into a firm jelly, a syllabub in a stemmed glass, a sage poultice, so hopefully tried but quite ineffective, a jug of wine.

Maria de Moreto saw only the smooth, fresh linen; she thought: There will be no bed-making tomorrow! From some still undepleted source, fresh tears gushed. She set the candle down on the table, so near the edge that it was in danger of tilting over, sat down on the bench and wept. Lady Willoughby moved the candle into safety and looked about at what the table held; one clean wine cup. She tipped the syllabub into the bowl of broth and then poured wine for them both. She pushed the cup nearer to Maria de Moreto's bowed head and said, 'Drink that. It will fortify you.'

Maria said ungratefully, in a tear-sodden voice, 'Drink it yourself!' She wished to be alone in her misery. Still without raising her head she said, 'My room is there. Have my bed and be welcome.' The offer reeked of hostility – '*you* can sleep!'

The Countess lifted the syllabub glass and drank deeply. The cream which had been the basis of the syllabub had left traces which affected the flavour, not unpleasantly, Sir Edmund's wine being somewhat harsh.

She said roughly, 'You think that I do not know how you feel. I know it all. You wish to die and you imagine that by refusing food, drink and sleep, you will bring death upon yourself. Be assured by me, *it never works that way*. I know. I have buried a husband.'

Not worth answering. *She* would, at this moment, choose to remind me that she had a husband. And surely his life must have been so wretched that he was glad to die. In any case, what is it to me, who, when the Queen dies, will have lost everything, even God and the Virgin. Because if God were just, or merciful, He would not allow *her*, so brave, so faithful, to die defeated.

'When my husband died . . .' Lady Willoughby began.

'God in Glory,' the other Maria said, 'I am well aware that you married and I did not. Is this a time to remind me? What is it to me? Go busy yourself elsewhere!'

'I pined,' the Countess said. 'I refused to eat or drink. I was determined to die, too. But I did not. One day I half swooned and my daughter, my Catharine, a loving child, still young, poured wine and offered it – to make me better she said . . . I drank it, to please her. And it restored me. For the next two years, whenever misery threatened to take the upper hand, I drank; and I survived. I can therefore commend wine to you. Drink and feel better . . .'

Maria de Moreto did not even look up. Lady Willoughby, somewhat astonished at herself, tried another tack.

'And is Her Grace to go to her burying with only one of the ladies she brought from Spain in attendance?'

Maria de Moreto's head came up. 'You mean you will not follow her?'

'I shall. You will not, unless you are able to walk. And you will not be able to walk unless you pull yourself together . . . And there is another thing that we should speak of, but I will not, until you have calmed yourself . . . and drunk your wine.'

Maria de Moreto lifted the cup and in a defiant gesture, drained it. Wine might have comforted the frivolous, heartless Maria de Salinas against the loss of a mere husband; it would not comfort Maria de Moreto against the loss of the Queen who had been everything, husband, child, friend . . . I will show her, she thought, how false and hollow her refuge from grief was.

But it was a long time since she had tasted wine; she had not eaten properly, or slept. She drained the cup, set it down, and waited for a sensation she had never known before to subside. When it did not she thought angrily: So much for her remedies! I feel worse rather than better. She was, however, no longer crying.

'What was this other thing?' she asked.

'I wondered whether you had considered what is to become of you, after . . .'

Trust her, always the tactless one, to mention such a matter at such a moment.

'I have brothers and sisters in Spain.'

'And you wish to go to them?' the Countess asked relentlessly.

As a penniless dependant? An ageing spinster aunt, grand aunt to children she had never seen? She saw in clearest detail what her life would be; endlessly put upon, earning her keep by helping with the very young, the very old, the sick, acting as a buffer between the servants and those they served, and despite all these services, regarded as an object of charity. A prospect to appal. Yet, but for the curious almost lightheaded feeling induced by the wine, her pride was such that she would have said, Yes, and they will be happy to have me! As it was she said:

'No. I have lived in England so long, my family seem strangers to me now.' She thought: And what am I about, talking of myself and my future when she, who has been my family all these years lies dying? And what am I about, opening my heart to *her*? She made a sound, half-sob, half-hiccup. 'But there is no reason for you to be concerned for me. I shall manage.'

The Countess was also a managing woman. Life had treated them differently, but they were made of the same stuff. Their enmity was rooted in their similarity.

The syllabub glass had been emptied four times, but Lady Willoughby was accustomed to better wine than this and knew what she was doing.

'You could come home with me,' she said.

'You are *inviting* me?'

'So I thought,' the Countess said drily. She knew she was doing a crazy thing: high and wide as her house was there would not be room enough for them both under one roof; they would provoke one another twenty times a day. Even had they been amiably disposed to one another the situation, with one dispensing, the other accepting charity, would be fraught with difficulties. But she was a woman who, once having conceived an idea, did not easily relinquish it. 'With my daughter married,' she said, 'I am often lonely; and shall be more so as the years mount.' I am making, she told herself, a fine rod for my own back; when we quarrel, as we must, she will turn upon me and say: You begged me to come.

Maria de Moreto looked across the cluttered table and saw this old enemy as altogether more vulnerable than a sister or sister-in-law forced to be charitable. *Lonely*. Maria de Salinas, disarming herself in a single word. When the day came, as come it must, and the battle between them was resumed, she could always say: You begged me to come to you; you said you were lonely!

She said, rather cautiously, 'If you wish my company . . .'

'I do,' the Countess said recklessly. 'And I think it would please *her* to know . . .' now, mind your tongue, Maria de Salinas! Put it prettily. '. . . that we were company and comfort to one another.'

Maria de Moreto, momentarily lost to God, had grace enough left to think: In her place I should not have put it so well; nor would I have admitted to loneliness. Under all the bustle and bluster, she is gentler than I! But even as she thought it the other Maria wiped that impression away. She said, 'Francisco Filipez, I can find a place for him. The doctor's manner I dislike – and to take as chaplain one known to be of the old opinion would be unwise. The village priest, who has his ear to the ground, serves me well enough. And the maids are slovens.'

Slovens! Under *my* supervision! It would not be seemly to wrangle here, on the threshold of the death chamber, but across the table two pairs of eyes threw their challenge. You accuse me of allowing slovenliness? Slovens I said, and slovens I mean. There and then began the wrangling which was to continue until one of them died. And both lived to be old, for friction produced its own energy and interest; and when one ailed, the other nursed her assiduously, eager to prove her own superiority.

Dawn came at last, with no rosy glow upon the wall, a slow, sullen lifting of darkness as another January day broke. Llandaff administered the Sacrament for the last time. 'This is My body . . .' Lutherans might deny the miracle of trans-substantiation, but for those who believed the words had the validity of their first utterance.

Then on her eyes, the touch of the blessed oil. 'By this holy anointing and with His most loving mercy, may the Lord forgive you whatever wrong you have done by the use of your sight. Amen.' Ears, nose, mouth, hands and feet. And even as the solemn ritual was performed, she drifted again into the past, not this time with the dead, but with Henry; she had loved him lawfully, but perhaps overmuch. Her hands had been so eager to caress him, her feet had danced to his measure; her nose had been greedy for the smell of him – leather, clean linen, horseflesh, the sweat of desire, the scent of love's culmination; her ears had been attuned to every tone of his voice and her mouth, under his kisses forgetful even of God. As for her eyes . . . Llandaff moved on to the Viaticum: 'May the angels lead thee to Paradise. At thy coming may the martyrs receive thee.' She lay so supine that she seemed already dead, but still clenched in a body, fifty years old, wasted with disease, and knew that of all the wonders that Heaven might offer what she most desired was the sight of Henry, young and eager, coming towards her under the green leaves at Greenwich. For a moment it seemed to be so and the people who stood by the bed considered the transfiguration of her face as a sign of her passing. But even for death she must wait; held back by a troubling sense of something left undone, unsaid. It took some time to find and longer still for her to muster strength for the words.

'Maria . . . de Salinas.'

'I am here, Your Grace.'

'Care for them all.'

'I will. I will. I promise.'

'All,' Katharine said, and although her voice was too weak to be insistent, the Countess understood.

'She shall be as my sister. I have her hand in mine now.'

She reached out and took the hand of the other Maria in case, as sometimes happened, the dying eyes should open for a last look upon the world. It was a wasted gesture. Katharine's eyes remained closed as she thought: All done now. I can go.

As she plunged into the abyss she had such a feeling of liberation that the fall was no more than a bird's swooping flight, a seagull's flashing curve, over Dover, Tilbury, Corunna . . .